ACE RUN

By: Ian Anthony

To A
Fellow Sci-Fi
Fan,
My Cousin
Aidan
Read and Enjoy!

APT, Toronto 2003

Best Wishes,
August 2008

First Paperback Edition, Bookbooters Press October 2001
First Hardback Edition, Bookbooters Press August 2002
First Paperback Edition by APT, August 2003

Cover art concept by Ian Anthony Prepared by Blair MacKinnon
Visit the author at: http://www.secretbookcase.com

Printed in Victoria, Canada

A cataloguing record for this book that includes the U.S. Library of Congress Classification number, the Library of Congress Call number and the Dewey Decimal cataloguing code is available from the National Library of Canada. The complete cataloguing record can be obtained from the National Library's online database at: www.nlc-bnc.ca/amicus/index-e.html
ISBN: 1-4120-1378-X

TRAFFORD

This book was published *on-demand* in cooperation with Trafford Publishing. On-demand publishing is a unique process and service of making a book available for retail sale to the public taking advantage of on-demand manufacturing and Internet marketing. **On-demand publishing** includes promotions, retail sales, manufacturing, order fulfilment, accounting and collecting royalties on behalf of the author.

Suite 6E, 2333 Government St., Victoria, B.C. V8T 4P4, CANADA
Phone 250-383-6864 Toll-free 1-888-232-4444 (Canada & US)
Fax 250-383-6804 E-mail sales@trafford.com
Web site www.trafford.com TRAFFORD PUBLISHING IS A DIVISION OF TRAFFORD HOLDINGS LTD.
Trafford Catalogue #03-1756 www.trafford.com/robots/03-1756.html

10 9 8 7 6 5 4 3 2 1

IAN ANTHONY

"COME WHAT MAY"

DEDICATED TO:

ALL MY
FAMILY AND FRIENDS
EVERYWHERE

Table of Contents

Submitted for your Reading Enjoyment . . .

♠ ♦ Ace Run ♥ ♣

a tale of anticipation, disaster and piracy in the outerworld frontier

A Novel By

Ian A. Anthony

CHAPTER ONE
Birth and Baptism

As with most things, it begins as a dream. A fantastic business dream which becomes an exquisite project taking form as a proud ship. The project inspires many noble thoughts of aspiration, grandeur, and full-fledged excellence. Yet, in the midst of this also spawns a diabolical idea that hatches as a fiendish plot, lurking in the villainous side of human ingenuity, hiding on the periphery, watching, waiting.

"She's ready." Those were good words to hear a few days ago when said by Chief Builder Thoms after the last circuit was fused, the last weld was laid, and the final strokes of paintbrushes complete a fresh coat of color. These bring an end to those all-important finishing touches, making her done, along with the distinction of being brand new. Today, Saturday the fifteenth of March in an era when humankind has long mastered the challenges posed by venturing beyond their own home-world, the new starship will shed the dark confines of her metallic womb and see the light of day. She is a mystery to all except the ones transforming the mental image into a solid object, and those privy to this top-secret knowledge dared not send word of it, by voice or print, beyond the company walls as the Top Secret status came down from the top-brass itself.

There is not complete silence, though. Couldn't be, after all, at least *some* attention is needed. Publicity comes by speculative advertisements, vague press releases and gauged interviews – all official, each a product of marketing genius. They appear within the mainstream SolNet, the primary computer interlink service around the world and between the Earth and her colonies. And yes, the other media venues are remembered as well. These 'teasers' raise more curiosity than provide answers, which is exactly what they are supposed to do, and are extremely successful in stirring interest.

Especially in one person. He sits in the dark, quiet, fingers steepled, contemplating. Like a fan obsessed with a celebrity, he has gathered every advertisement and article and recorded every commercial and story relating to it. He knows everything an outsider can know about this topic, his "pet project". He is, by far, an expert - and a devious one at that. But to look at him you would not think he was crazed or fixated or even particularly sly because there is no three-days growth of beard or unruly hair or bugged-out eyes with a faraway gaze - he is clean, groomed, dressed casually and is calm. He goes to his den and from a desk drawer takes a large silver pistol fixed with a telescopic sight. In this single, simple act he goes from man to gunman. He releases the ammunition clip from the handle, checks it, then slams it home once again. He is ready, and now a slightly sinister grin appears. "Bring it on," he whispers.

"... and when you do it, do it well." Laughter, cheers and applause erupt, then slowly subside. In a place far removed from the gunman, in a lavishly appointed room with a salon feel, well-dressed people have gathered in celebration. Damien Enkel has just finished his 'Welcome Remarks', which were laced with the quips and puns he is readily known for among both friends and business associates. He looked good up there in front of the small crowd, his crown of thick white hair combed back from his high forehead, light blue eyes looking attentive yet cheery from his tanned face with its kingly features. The new dark blue suit was bought especially for the occasion, and makes a smart fit over his square shoulders yet falls well over his sturdy and tall form - just how he likes it. He radiated confidence and ease, speaking evenly with good tone at a good pace. Enkel has a certain strength of being, and is one of those individuals who seem in a way to justify the family name, which in his case, means 'angel'.

Wearing a bright smile, he weaves his way through the group, picking up a cocktail from the tray of a passing waiter as he returns to his wife, Anne. She looks at him with pride, her eyes holding a certain shine, her smile wide, her heart skipping a beat for him. A quick kiss-on-the-cheek from her and a whispered "Well done." receives a nod as he takes a sip.

The dreamship everyone is about to see today is his own brainchild, a product of his boundless ambition. Enkel is a proud American of Finnish heritage, being well schooled in the exceptional traditions of Scandinavian style shipbuilding. He is a self-made man of substance, the president and chief executive officer of a massive company bearing an embellishment of his surname: The Archangel Line. He is the supreme lord of this corporation, and as seen, his very form alludes to power.

The Line is a principal contender in a business that has survived the ages; neither economic strife, market trends, nor even war has ever checked its prosperity. This is the travel industry, that which offers "escape"... forays out of the monotony of day-to-day existence and dashes into a near mythical world of relaxation, experience, and adventure. The Archangel Line provides exquisite tourist comfort within its fleet of ultra-luxurious ocean, air and astral liners. The revelation today of the new ship is the culmination of two years and five hundred million dollars worth of steadfast work by designers and engineers striving to meet the project mandate on the directive penned by their fearless leader: "Surpass All."

The new vessel will stand as the flagship of the Interplanetary Division. She promises to usher in a new standard of luxury in space travel, to redefine the essence of extraterrestrial cruises to the resorts and communities within the biocols on the Moon and Mars. Since the beginnings of regular solar journeying and the building of stable and actually attractive and comfortable artificial locales, there has been steady improvement in the scope and speed of passenger ships with a near-perfect safety record. Her first moments in the outside world for this celestial craft will be markedly special. Preparations have been meticulous, and with good reason, for the eyes of many will be focused on the event as the public is eager to behold this newest creation. Like a beautiful, nubile young Debutante taking her fist tentative steps toward an introduction to society, the ship holds the potential to dazzle and enthrall her suitors.

Attempts at previews have been made. The guises come in one of three forms; news reporters hungry to break the story, corporate spies conducting business espionage, or curious thrill-chasing Solins (the moniker of logged-in SolNet users). All try to see the ship before the proper unveiling, only to find their ingenious and creative efforts met by three separate provo tiers where each apparatus holds its own triple-checks against breech. The rigid protective measures will not be relaxed until the moment the dream is revealed.

"Didn't bother me one bit," says the gunman-Fan as he thinks about being unimpeded by the security net. He had not even bothered to try and sneak a glimpse. The company is feeding him all the information he needs, slowly but surely. Like a subtle predator, he bides his time. Good things come to those who wait, as they say. The age-old maxim holds true well enough regardless if those waiting are good or bad, he observes dryly while cocking a whimsical smile. He strides aimlessly through his apartment, his mind alive with thoughts and facts and questions. He spins his pistol absently on the forefinger of his right hand as he moves. No one bothers or even challenges him because he resides on his own in this spacious, tastefully decorated cubicle within a stately building resting just on the fringe of the downtown core. Not because he is anti-social, but the very nature of his business, this industry of the forbidden, requires a 'lone wolf'.

He is the mastermind behind the treacherous plan that makes a target of the dream. An encrypted, unmarked, pentigital diskette stores scanned clippings, downloads of SolNet information, real-time videos of the televised segments, and his typed thoughts about possible plans. The disk possesses a safety-feature where if someone attempts to access files without the correct password, it will automatically erase all information. The raw data is, like all information for potential "scores", kept in a double-locked strongbox hidden behind a panel in a hollowed section of the door to his den closet. The material comprises the clippings themselves, a videodiskette labeled with an Alpha symbol, plus detailed sheets of scribbled notes written in code. The strongbox is rigged so if tampered with by an outsider, an interior acid compound will spray out and decimate the contents in an instant. In his television program guide, today's listing announcing the ceremony is circled thrice in red. He will be watching, studying, taping. If his gambit proves correct, this can be very, very lucrative for him. He checks his wristwatch. An hour left before showtime. He is anxious.

Everyone is anxious. The spectators are anxious for the event to begin, but those doing the presentation are anxious for it to end, as the pressure in making it happen perfectly - completely perfectly - is almost unbearable. No one is so eager to see the event be over and done with as Darcy Phillips, vice president of the Archangel Public Relations Department. He is in the executive box of the specially built grandstand with Mr. Enkel and the other company chieftains. His chuckles and clapping for the 'Welcome' fade, and he shakes his head in wonderment at the savvy and style of his employer as he turns to look outside. This brief moment of humor for Phillips disappears in an instant as he intently watches the last minute preps far below in a section of the maze of concrete and steel which is the shipyard. Although everything is prepared to the approved specifications, he scans the area keenly, even after having surveyed it time and time again since his arrival some two hours earlier - - there is always room for flaw. "Can't leave anything to chance..." he mutters, and gives voice to the knowledge that his standing in the executive circle hangs in the balance.

From his vantagepoint, at the far right end of the right bay window, he can see the entire yard unhampered. "Look at that, it still awes me every time I see it." To his left, a fifth of a mile from him, is the mammoth hangar where the dream silently lies. The hangar itself is an imposing sight. The windowless black steel building is seven stories tall, five hundred feet wide, and one thousand one hundred feet long and has been specially built to house the dream machine it encloses. The front of the building consists solely of the hangar doors, which run from ground level directly to the roof. Attached to the gargantuan black doors are two golden letters, an "H" and a "W" representing Harrison Wulfe Shipbuilders Incorporated, as those who constructed the vessel are not about to let the event occur in their shipyard without obtaining some worthy, and free, promotion.

Phillips tears his gaze away from the hangar and studies the area which directly concerns him: the runway. The black tarmac from the hangar doors to his end of the grandstand is spotless. Brightly colored flags and streamers form a wide lane and are perfectly in place, adorning the area and fluttering in the breeze. Broadcast cameras are stationed at key points along the ground and atop high turrets, ready for the dual telecast and netcast so not a single minute will be missed by those who cannot watch first-hand.

"Looks good," he says to himself, and a small smile curls around his lips. The runway is ready for its esteemed guest. A glance up reveals a bright yellow sun and a crystal blue sky dotted with the occasional pure white cloud - - a beautiful southern California afternoon. The weather appears sympathetic with Phillips' cause; this pleases him, perhaps God is on his side. Satisfied with the outside, he gazes around the box. The fifty people here seem to be enjoying themselves; plenty of smiles, talk punctuated with laughter, the champagne is flowing, and the hors d'oeuvres are rapidly disappearing. The catering staff is doing an excellent job at keeping serving trays replenished and ensuring no guests are at want. He smiles, another aspect is going well.

The executives are huddled in groups of three or four, quietly conversing. They represent the upper echelon of both the Archangel Line and Harrison Wulfe Incorporated, and are typical business people one can find in any corporation – the ones who stay in shape mixed with others content to mask their broadening waistlines. We have some men whose hairlines are beginning to recede, and women with bright smiles and fresh perms who project a professional air. They are all suited, polished, and proper, remembering that this is a company function as they mingle with their escorts in various parts of the spacious and luxurious room. These companions include the inevitable trophy brides and buffed toy-boys, but for the most part are mates inspired by genuine love. Phillips can imagine all the feigned interest occurring in at least some of these animated conversations conducted by office politicos. The executives contrast the other group in the room, that being the staff officers selected to command the ship.

The officers are relaxed and chatting amicably with the guests, looking authoritative in their dress uniforms, which are white with gold piping. Phillips studies each in turn. First are the bridge officers. "It is quite an honor to be given her, certainly," says Captain John Arges in his conversation with a smile, he being the quintessential master of a vessel; presenting an air of authority without even trying, being tall and sturdy with strong features and dark hair which is graying at the temples. Arges holds the distinction of being Commodore of the Line, meaning he is the finest captain in the firm. His reputation of being a congenial, efficient, fair-minded, well-spoken gentleman is solid among colleagues, crew and passengers.

"You couldn't ask for a better day," comments First Officer Peter Rish to another person; close in height to Arges, he is slender with angular features, whose brown hair is just beginning to thin, providing a high forehead and markedly intellectual look.

"I haven't seen her myself for quite some time, so I am looking forward to it as well," says Second Officer Alyssa Rayburn, who is as friendly as she is attractive, which makes her extremely personable. She is a brunette of average height with a pleasant figure.

"Best ship ever, bar none," remarks Third Officer Mitchell Hearst. He least resembles an Officer. Lanky, with excess bulk settling at his midriff and below, he possesses dull eyes, a narrow chin, and a weak face with a terribly pale complexion. He brushes a loose strand of hair from his face; his brown hair is at the maximum length permitted by the company, and is always oily from styling spray which fails to keep it in place. However, he knows his job and does it extremely well, which makes him valuable.

Next come the operations officers. "We rolled out the red carpet, and stocked up on the bells and whistles!" Light laughter follows on this cheery voice, and Staff Captain Jennifer Syranos gives one of her fabulously bright smiles. She is a lively brunette with a round face and distinctive Mediterranean looks.

"Plenty of surprises in store," says Purser Fritz Mueller - a former Detective who has the build of a linebacker and the hard face of a drill sergeant; his black hair is kept in a crewcut which is routinely trimmed.

"Can hardly wait to get her into the sky, I can tell you…" remarks Chief Engineer Tac Holden, a stocky man with a broad face and dark, wavy hair.

"State of the art systems, sophisticated controls," Cybernetics Officer Krystal DeMornay comments. She is Rubenesque with red-blonde hair and sea-green eyes.

"You are the one which guides them, correct?" asks a man as he approaches an officer.

"Yes, that would be me," answers Astrogator Christian Miasaki, who looks every bit the chartsman with his slim build and blunt, intellectual features.

"And when they want to talk, they go through me," offers Communications Officer Roberta Escoto with a chuckle. She is petite with a round face framed by dark curls of thick hair. Doctor Julius Washington rounds out this officer corps. He is a tall black American whose soft eyes and jovial face convey a warm and comforting look inspiring trust in many a patient.

"Quite a motley assortment…" Phillips thinks to himself while comparing the executives and officers. It is times like this when he appreciates his devotion to exercise and his full head of dark hair. While observing the crowd, he notices no one is looking in his direction. He turns again to the window and skillfully removes a silk handkerchief from the breastpocket of his suitcoat. He quickly cups it in his left hand, hooking his forefinger into a small hood naturally formed at the corner of the handkerchief. He then slyly runs his forefinger over his forehead, just above the eyebrow, then studies the silk. It is dry. Good, no showing of the tension occurring inside. A display of apprehension - such as perspiration - would discredit him in the eyes of his fellow executives and knock him down some rungs on the company ladder he had so feverishly climbed. He deftly returns the silken square to its pocket and takes a long drink of ice water, just to be safe.

Phillips takes a palm-sized, paper-thin bronze rectangular device from the inside pocket of his jacket – an infokeeper. He switches it on and the viewer alights. His fingers move over the screen as sensors respond to his commands, and soon it appears: The Checklist. He quickly scans it while taking his personaföne from his coat pocket. It is time to confer with his team. "Dial Peter," he says while looking toward the hangar, and hears the autodial tones sounding.

"Hello, Peter here," comes the quick response.

"I trust everything is ready there?"

"Yessir. Everything is perfect."

"Excellent. Carry on. It's almost time."

"Yes, Mr. Phillips. Thank you. Peter out."

Phillips likewise speaks his other associates, and all reports are favorable. He makes some notations, then returns the infokeeper and microphone to his jacket, and waits.

The Fan waits as well. Soon, he will have the answer to the question posed when first learning about the ship - - the question at the root of all criminal intent - - Will it be worth it? He absently paces in this living room, pensive, arms folded across his chest. He snatches the remote control from the coffee table and takes aim at the large television set. There is a click from the remote control. The blank screen suddenly fills with the vibrant color and ecstatic action of a commercial. Soon…

Three soft chimes sound simultaneously over the speakers in the executive box, the media box (directly below) and the grandstand itself, which today plays host to three hundred specially invited guests of the Line. All fall silent. The deep, pleasant voice of Gerald Eston, today's master of ceremonies, reverberates through the structure. "Ladies and Gentlemen, our christening will commence in five minutes . . . five minutes until our event begins." Phillips looks at Eston. Perched upon his platform the man stands; a well-cut tuxedo on his tall and slender form, impeccably styled hair, perfect teeth encased within a perpetual smile . . . a typical emcee, a 'mr. game-show host', Phillips thinks.

Eston looks out from his platform. "All these people," he quietly mutters while looking at the crowd. The platform itself is at the right end of the grandstand, elevated to rest at the half-way point of its height (including the boxes). He also spies the lens of a broadcast camera fixed beneath the Media Box, and trained on the platform to catch all the action. "An unobstructed view, fantastic," he says…if anyone had heard it, they would have wondered if his comment referred to an unobstructed view of the ship, or of himself – could go either way in the case of Mr. Vanity. He looks around. At the left front corner, a metal rod extends seven feet up; at its top is a housing which holds a 1989 magnum of Dom Perignon champagne. A gold cord hangs lazily from the base of the housing, and another line tied to the bottle-neck droops across the width of the platform where it connects to the top of an eight-foot rod stretching up from the back-left corner. The platform also has a microphone stand in its center, and a small table holding a bottle of champagne and two glasses stands at the back-right corner. "Everything I need for the ceremony," he says with a hint of satisfaction.

"Here we go…" Philllips whispers, then takes a deep breath.

The executives, officers and guests make their way to one of the three bay windows in the Box on hearing Eston's announcement. Damien Enkel, the man himself, takes a place in the middle of the center window - fitting that the prime location would go to him. His wife, Anne, a flaxen-haired grand dame society matron, takes a place at his left. Mr. H. Conrad Wulfe IV, the President of Harrison Wulfe Incorporated and the great-grandson of the esteemed founder of the firm, takes a position at Enkel's right side with his wife, Donna. Enkel scans the crowd of faces trying to stand near him and sees Phillips standing at the right window. "Darcy," he calls. Phillips snaps his head in the direction of the voice. Enkel raises his hand and motions for Phillips to join him.

Phillips nods and smiles, then immediately begins to make his way to The Man. The invitation is certainly important, as evidenced by the jealous stares of the others, but a small part of him is unsure if he wants to be next to Enkel as the event occurs. If everything goes as planned, it will be the best place to receive the man's praise, but, if the ceremony is not a success, the last place on Earth he will want to be is near Enkel and his wrath. He knows cannot refuse the invitation anyway, so, with a knowing smile he calmly eases his way along, silently praying for good fortune.

Seeing Phillips approach, Enkel again searches the group with his eyes. Ah, there he is, Captain Arges. Arges, who is much more at ease on the bridge of a ship than at an affair such as this, is with the officers and their escorts at the left window. "Captain, if you please," Enkel says with a smile as he waves him over.

Arges grits his teeth. "It will be over soon enough," he quietly tells himself. He manages a smile and takes the hand of his attractive wife Trish, then walks toward his employer. Phillips and the Arges reach the Enkels and Wulfes at the same time; everyone exchanges pleasantries and handshakes. They then turn their attention outside, as do those who surround them.

The hour strikes three and Eston pipes up again. "Ladies and Gentlemen, the Archangel Line proudly welcomes you to the christening of its newest spaceliner!" He extends his right arm toward the hangar, all eyes turn left: it is about to happen!! The spectators and broadcast audience watch with great anticipation and bated breath . . . eagerly awaiting the unwrapping of this, their newest toy.

Alarms at the hangar sound, signaling that the doors are about to open. The videographers train their cameras at the doors; around the world and at the Lunar and Mars biocols people intently stare at their receivers as there is little else worth watching this Saturday afternoon. Laserlight images of the Archangel crest dance in the air. Slowly, the doors of Hangar Thirteen begin to part. They roll back from the middle along a roofline track, stopping when reaching the edge of the doorframe. The interior of the hangar is as dark as night. All eyes strain to see inside. Something moves - - this is it!!! Wait, no, - just a little yellow guide truck with its amber roof-lights flashing. The truck moves along the center of the runway. The audiences grow more excited as they are on the verge of seeing the great marvel which the Line has been teasing them about for the past month.

Phillips' insides tense; Arges checks his wristwatch. Another truck appears. This one is larger, black, and has more importance as it is the primary towtruck whose lines are attached to the forward wheel strut. The truck pulls, as do those stationed at the midship and aft struts. Inside, the wheels of the spacecraft strain . . . it is almost as though the dream resists delivery. Inertia battles torque. The trucks increase their pull toward forward motion. Finally, the wheels relent. One strained revolution; progress! After two more laborious turns, the wheels slowly begin to roll more freely, and the trucks are able to lessen their pull. The dream begins to nose its way outside.

"Look! Look!" The bow breaks free of the dark prison. It possesses a noble beauty whose gently sloping form glides back from the forepoint and conveys spaceage style. The sunshine graces its white exterior. The spectators rise to their feet and crane their necks to better see the ship. The videographers extend their lenses to obtain the best view possible. The bow clears the hangar and the remainder of this ship follows. Where the audiences expect to see the tail they are surprised to find this is only what appears to be midship. The craft continues to exit the hangar and some wonder if it will ever end. The liner moves along the grandstand and the spectators can now see the grand ship better, though they must shade their eyes from the reflected brightness of the sun on the white . . . the ship seems to have a glow all its own. The massive tailfin finally appears at the doorway. It is flanked at its base by two immense delta wings, beneath and behind which, jutting from the hull, are cowls housing the stern thrusters. Phillips relaxes slightly and takes a glass of champagne from the tray of a passing waiter. Toasts and celebration will soon be in order.

There she stands. She is truly a glorious sight and to look at her is to marvel at her greatness. She has an utterly magnificent profile: one thousand feet long, a breadth equivalent to a five-lane highway, one hundred and thirty-five feet tall from the base of the struts to the top of the tailfin, and seven decks built for passenger pleasure. Her titanium hull runs an average of a foot deep, and high-tempered steel beams form her frame. Anti-gravity discs immersed in quicksilver within the ribs of the fuselage will aid in providing lift for the heavy vessel, and an eight-inch thick white ceramic coating provides an atmospheric heatshield at the lower bow and over the keel.

The aerodynamic grace of her bow, fashioned after a dolphin head, with the smooth curvature of her fuselage, the sweeping style of her wings and the handsomeness of her cowls make her appear more a sculpture than a ship. Her heavenly whiteness is broken by a solid line of bright silver airelons embedded along the middle of the hull, the etching of her name in pristine black on the sides of her bow, the coverless windows of the Forward Observation Lounge and the bridge viewport, and the majestic corporate seal of the Line, mounted on the sides of the tailfin. Again comes her name, emblazoned in black and tattooed across her broad stern, beneath which, in smaller letters, is written her birthplace, "Los Angeles, California". Below that is a painted rendition of the red, white and blue of the starred and striped flag belonging to the United States of America.

"There she is! Look at her!" Enkel says with pride.

"She's divine. Ravishing," his wife answers as he hugs her closely and kisses her lightly on the cheek. He releases her from his grasp and clasps hands heartily with Wulfe. "We did it, Harry!"

"That we did Damien," Wulfe replies with a broad smile.

The Man then turns to Arges, who has become more at ease with the sight of his new commission, and takes his hand in a firm grip. "Good to see finally her out, isn't it?"

"Yes, it's…. yes it is good, Sir, very good," says the captain with a smile.

"Be even better when we see her up above," Enkel comments with a wink.

As Enkel moves on, Arges turns to the window looks in awe at the proud ship. He beams and after a moment turns to Trish, who looks up to him and smiles widely with a genuine look of pride. "There she is…" he whispers to her.

"Magnificent!" she replies. "Better than I expected!" She gives a quick kiss to his cheek, then wipes away the trace of lipstick. Arges smiles, and again looks back to his ship.

Enkel next shakes hands with Phillips "Well we got her out, so far so good." These words win a nod from the p.r. man as Arges embraces his wife. While the others applaud, cheer, and congratulate Enkel, Wulfe, and Arges, Phillips sips his champagne and mouths a whispered prayer for continued good fortune for the other two segments of the ceremony.

As the excitement and adulation in the Executive Box subsides, one of Wulfe's senior aids approaches and passes him a black leather folder bearing the HW Shipbuilders corporate seal in gold in its center. Wulfe gladly accepts it, and as the aid fades back into the crowd, he raises his left hand, silencing the still murmuring group. "Well, Damien, this is what we've been waiting for..." he says with a broad smile while taking a gold pen from his suitjacket and opening the folder. Inside is an official-looking document on which are many paragraphs in small type, and a smaller pink card; the bill of sale and vessel registration.

Yesterday at three o'clock in the afternoon, amidst a phalanx of lawyers, financiers, accountants and bank officers all linked by compuconference, five hundred million dollars was electronically transferred from the Archangel corporate account at the Royal Bank into the Harrison Wulfe holdings at J.P. Morgan House. This meant the right and title to the ship had effectively passed from her builders to her owner-operators. This next act will complete the transaction.

While steadying the folder in his left hand, Wulfe signs the bottom of the sheet, dates it, and does likewise to the card. He turns the folder toward Enkel, offering the documents for signature, which is given with flowing and bold strokes. Wulfe reclaims the folder, glances at its enclosures, then closes the cover. He reaches into his coat pocket and produces a small black velvet case. Wulfe opens this and displays to the room what it holds: a large, bright, gold key fastened by a gold keyring to a tag bearing the Harrison Wulfe crest. In short, the ignition key. There are 'oooohs' from the crowd, then he speaks. "Mr. Enkel, I am pleased to say you are now the proud new owner of Harrison Wulfe Hull Number J-2 NCC1314. Treat her well." Wulfe smiles broadly as he passes the folder and key to Enkel and shakes his hand. A camera flashes from one of Phillips' photographers as Enkel accepts the items, and the moment is recorded for posterity.

Enkel is positively beaming. "That I will, old boy, that I will!" The men pose for a few more photographs as applause again erupt.

"This is amazing!"

"Incredible!"

Comments like these join others made by reporters in the media box, where pandemonium broke loose once the full ship appeared. Fingers dart across keyboards, cameras flash, and commentators speak with tense voices, barely able to blurt words as they spring to mind. This excellent coverage assures that the public is kept abreast of everything that happens at the shipyard. SolNet becomes alive with opinions about the ship as message-boards and e-mails fly between Solins (the moniker of logged-in SolNet users): **<Wow, Check that out!> <I bet their server rocks!> <Come on, get on with the interiors!> <You've *got* to see this!☺> <Where can I download a pic?!> <Damn I wish I was There! *In* person!>**

Most appreciate the coverage, but one distinct group wishes the reports are not so thorough. From their offices high atop the skylines of Los Angeles, New York, Toronto and London, the principal competitors of the Archangel Line watch the proceedings on television. They stare in awe and shock, blankly regarding what surely spells out a problem for them in the space-travel industry. The owners collectively feel ill, and their "loyal" executives quietly wonder if they can join the Archangel Line. This is murder!!! How in the hell are they supposed to compete with that monstrosity? Stomachs begin to turn.

As the rivals fear, the public, and especially the wealthied, are taking a keen interest in the new ship. Such style! Such grace! If this is the exterior, imagine what lies behind those ivory walls... If they only knew the half of it. The spectators and broadcast audience will have to wait for their tours later in the hour.

Click. "POWwwwwwwwwwwww......" The sound slowly fades from his mouth. The Fan keeps the gaze of his squinted right eye fixed on the flickering television image of the supership, contained compactly within the crosshairs of the round sniper-scope of his pistol. In a swift move he brings the gunbarrel to his lips, and blows away an imaginary puff of smoke. There had been a click when the hammer fell, but no gunshot, because the ammo clip was empty, as he knew from checking earlier. A wicked smile forms. What a prize this is. His hunch was right! He thinks of the great treasures the ship will carry on her maiden voyage . . . vast wealth in the cargo hold and Purser's Safe, not to mention the riches of the First Class passengers. Wheels are set in motion. Ideas spark to life. As with most things, it begins as a dream. Eyes glued to the screen, he picks up the end-table vidcom and dials a travel agency, setting it so he can be only heard and not seen. What a prize, indeed.

The vidcoms and SolNet sites of travel agencies around the world and at the BioCols are jammed with activity. Each caller and visitor wants a reservation on the new ship. The agents love the business of course, but hate the hectic pace. Having anticipated the surge in interest, the Line made reservations available precisely at three o'clock as per Phillips' orders. Accommodation is possible in all classes, save for half of the Royale suites set aside for those spectators who desire passage on the liner. As reservation capability becomes possible, brochures about basic information on the ship (travel rates, scheduling and tour routes) are delivered to the agencies while the same facts are made available on the Archangel website and the general vacation databases within SolNet.

"There we go, all done for you sir," she says as she finishes processing the request. He notes the agent who has taken his call has been very pleasant. "As a helpful reminder, please bring identification with you when you come in to pick up his ticket, and we will hold your reservation until the close of business Friday."

"Thank you," he says. Payment will definitely be made, he thinks, in cold, hard, untraceable cash. "You have been very accommodating."

"My pleasure. I hope you have a pleasant trip, and thank you for using Go-Travel. Goodbye!"

"Goodbye."

After booking passage for himself and a fictitious and as yet unknown wife, both under an assumed name, he leaves the television and strides into his den with man-on-a-mission intensity. Setting his gun down as he seats himself behind the desk, he rolls his shoulders back and quickly slips a Relayor over the middle finger of his right hand. This is common hardware, a small silver piece which goes from the fingertip to the second knuckle and remotely sends commands for cursor control, among other things, from its bottom tab to either a stationary circular pad or the vidscreen, whichever the user finds easiest. His, of course, has been specially treated against tracking so he can do his cyber-deeds without fear of being monitored.

With a flick he activates the computer, then enters SolNet using a false identicode. With pen and paper in hand and his Relayor as a hunting dog, he is set. "Come to Daddy," he whispers. The wait is not long as within seconds there is a screen filled with multiple sources for information on the ship. His eyes play over flashy text which summons his attention, and he smiles with each click of his finger as data and images spill forward to feed his inquisitive mind. Wait. His eyebrows come together, and this smile drops as he tenses the muscles of his athletic body, then runs a hand through his sandy brown hair. It will take a considerable amount of effort to accomplish this task. However, it can be done, and well, particularly with his evil genius set to work on it. His thirty-five years of life have taught him many things. Russell Hans Maddox, a proven and self-proclaimed 'thief extraordionnaire' begins jotting notes as his devious mind plans to relieve the ship and her passengers of their valuables.

Oblivious to the terrors hatching within the criminal mind of Maddox, the Archangel Line continues its christening ceremony. After letting the spectators indulge in dismay and fascination, Eston expertly regains control. "Ladies and Gentlemen," his voice bellows with authority yet delicacy, causing the stupefied audience to reluctantly redirect its attention to him, "Cindy Dahl Salter, this year's Miss California, will now christen the ship." The spectators seat themselves and applause begin as Cindy rises from the VIP Box and sashays up the steps to the platform and the waiting Eston. The statuesque woman is pure eye-candy with cascading, spiraling silken blonde curls, bright blue eyes, perky nose, perfectly full red lips and red-sequined dress which flatters her full, round bust and clings to her shapely hips.

On reaching Eston, she turns toward the grandstand and flashes a bright smile. "Hello Gerry," she says, her smile unwavering.

"We're glad to have you with us, Cindy," Eston answers with a nod and a grin.

"It's my pleasure to be here with you all today! And what a great day it is. Cheers to California weather!" There is some light laughter from the crowd, then her right hand reaches up and clasps the gold cord above her. With a sweet yet seductive voice she speaks. "It is with great pleasure that the Archangel Line makes its newest ship available for cruise service. With a warm heart, I do christen thee *Emprasoria.* May you know a long and happy life." Miss California then turns her prize-winning face to the bow, pulls her right hand down, and releases the Dom Perignon. Aided by its guideline, the bottle swings gracefully through the air and crashes spectacularly against the letters of the ship's name to the roaring cheers of the spectators. The name "***Emprasoria***" is as special as the ship itself. Using the letters from the paradises of ancient mythology; Olympus, Elysium, Asgard, Yaru and Heaven, the Line formed a word incorporating size, speed, flight and luxury - - all in ten characters to appease the numerologist in The Man.

Cindy brushes away the champagne spray which lightly sprinkled her face and hair. Eston uncorks the champagne on the platform table and pours a glass that he hands to the lady, who graciously accepts. He quickly fills a glass for himself and turns to the spectators. Eston and Cindy Salter raise their glasses as they say "To the *Emprasoria*!" They each enthusiastically take a sip as the spectators cheer.

"Well, there she is, all officially named," Eston comments following his drink. "What do you think of her, Cindy?"

"Let's just say I'm glad this beauty won't be in this year's pageant..." Cindy jokes while rolling her eyes in an exaggerated way.

Eston chuckles, and again there is laughter from the audience. "No, no competition for you there."

"Honestly though," Cindy continues, "this is a fantastic ship. I mean, just look at her." She pauses and looks toward the white vessel, then turns back toward Eston and the spectators. "Could you imagine riding through the skies on something this sleek? Travelling with her would be an honor."

Eston looks to the ship, then back to Cindy. "I agree. They really went all out, didn't they?" Cindy nods her agreement. "Thank you for your help, Cindy," Eston continues.

"Thank you too, Gerry." She gives him a quick kiss to the cheek, then waves broadly to the spectators. The applause rise again, and still wearing her bright smile, she descends the steps from the platform; hand still waving, and hips in full swing.

Congratulations are again exchanged in the executive box in the form of praise, handshakes, or blackslaps, and Phillips relaxes a bit more, as phase two has been flawlessly executed. If the remainder goes to plan as successfully as the beginnings have, he should be up for some sort of commendation. Arges becomes more relaxed in the knowledge that after a little while longer all this parading will be finished.

Eston pauses while Cindy seats herself, then continues by pitching the product. "Ladies and Gentlemen, the *Emprasoria* is truly an exquisite vessel. She's the largest ship ever built for cruising, and can accommodate an astounding *three* thousand *five* hundred guests. The *Emprasoria* has been built with passenger service in mind. Every effort has been made to assure your voyage will be a relaxing and pleasurable experience. En route to your destination, you are free to enjoy any of the extensive recreation services available. The design engineers of the Archangel Line have striven to assure that all passenger needs are provided for, and exceeded, and to make boredom an unknown concept once you step aboard the *Emprasoria*."

"But, saying it is one thing....after all, why take my word for it," Eston says without pause as he imperceptibly touches a button on the table; two escalators begin to extend diagonally up from the base of the grandstand - - the spectators hold their collective breath - - "when you can see it for yourselves!" At this time, the platforms of the escalators connect far above with junctions beneath the forward and aft hatches of the ship's B deck. Once the linking secures, the forward hatch slides open to reveal three pretty tourguides beckoning the audience up. Eston continues, "The Archangel Line is pleased to provide an escorted tour of the Royale Class and Entertainment Decks. As you visit the ship, feel free to ask questions of your guide."

The extremely eager spectators begin making their way to the forward escalator, each wanting to be the first to see inside. Spying the movement, Eston hastily concludes. "The Archangel Line thanks you for attending the christening, and sincerely hopes you take advantage of the luxury and splendor of the *Emprasoria* on your next vacation." The spectators applaud as they prepare to board the magnificent liner.

"You too will be given a tour, after our spectators have finished," an Archangel media assistant informs the anxious and inquisitive news reporters.

"That's good to know," comments one from the crowd. The others chuckle, then use this spare time to review their text about the christening, prepare questions for the tour guides, or to simply stare at the mammoth creation. The telecast and netcast begin a special documentary program about Damien Enkel and the Archangel Line in the interim period before the camera crew tour. In the executive box, Enkel turns toward his guests, and raises his hand to gently quiet those who are talking. "Just a reminder everyone, we're having a Christening Ball at eight o'clock tonight in the Grand Ballroom of the Ambassador Palace Hotel in Beverly Hills, for ourselves, our spectators and other special friends, and we want to see you all there..." Chatterings of approval come from the crowd. "Captain," Enkel quietly says to Arges as he raises his eyebrows, "I'm sure we will see you there..." Enkel knows well of his Commodore's dislike of pageantry, and Arges understands the implied order. He is not thrilled with the prospect of enduring more celebrating, but with all the sincerity he can muster, he lies to his superior.

"I am looking forward to it, Sir." A discreet smile follows.

"As am I," says Trish Arges, with genuine enthusiasm and a bright smile.

"Great, great," says The Man with a broad smile. He turns to Phillips. "Of course, we'll see you there too, Darcy."

"Definitely," Phillips answers with a nod. Phillips will surely be there to receive all the compliments for a job well done - - or so he hopes. At this point, phase three can still cause him trouble. He puts this notion to the back of his mind while talking with others, but every now and then he eyes the ship, and is pleased not to hear calls for his assistance coming through his earphone or infokeeper. As the Archangels, the Wulfes, the executives and officers continue to socialize and one by one begin to leave, he stays behind, and eventually positions himself at the left window, looking outward. He remains there, hands resting on the windowsill, staring intently at the aft hatch. After what seems an eternity, the hatch opens. He quickly brings a pair of small binoculars to his face and instantly focuses on this hatch as the first tour group disembarks.

He can clearly see these people appear pleased, and many even wear broad smiles. Phillips breathes a sigh of relief and visibly eases as he lowers the binoculars. Finally, he can relax to his heart's content. Phase three has clearly happened without problems. His countless hours of preparation which have culminated in this grand ceremony will reward him now. He is one of the last to leave the grandstand, and goes away as an extremely happy man. As he strides to his silver Jaguar, he raises his personafône to his face while twirling his keyring on his forefinger. "Christine," he says, and hears the tones of the autodial rapidly sounding. An answer comes on the second ring – "Hello?"

"Went great, sweetie," he says, the smile clear in his voice.

"Excellent!" she replies enthusiastically.

"Everything was perfect, the Boss went away pleased."

"Fabulous – I knew it would go well for you."

"Thanks. I'm on my way home now. The Ball tonight should be good too."

"I'm looking forward to it – I have a new dress to show you Mister...." Christine blows a kiss into the phone, and Phillips grins widely.

"Right back-atcha. See you in a bit."

"Drive safe. Bye."

"Bye." He slides behind the wheel then adjusts the rearview mirror. The engine roars to life and he speeds away from the shipyard to prepare for the upcoming soirée – perfect end to a perfect day. He relishes the thought of the celebration, eagerly anticipating the compliments he is sure he will receive.

Russell Maddox is on the road as well. He is in his red sport coupe, racing down the highway. Resting on the black leather passenger seat is a locked black leather attaché containing general non-descript papers, files, notes, and a concealed interior compartment holding the diskette pertaining to the *Emprasoria*. He is on his way to an impromptu meeting with one of the men he has selected to be a partner on this job. His mind concentrates on the various issues involved with the task. He has scarcely twenty days to finalize plans and prepare. Much to do. The soft leather of his driving glove closes around the gearshift, the clutch is punched down, and he slides in to high gear as he presses harder on the accelerator pedal. The engine revs and the car leaps forward in response to newfound power. Much to do.

CHAPTER TWO
Glories Behind Ivory Walls

There was a rumbling. Inside, when the ship rolled out - the motion of the strut-wheels bring quaking which can be felt throughout the vessel. The sensation encourages excitement tinged with mild trepidation already present in the crew aboard. “It’s happening!” is actually voiced, or said by specific looks of anticipation. Frenzied last-minute shouts between personnel are heard as the ship moves in a final push toward exact readiness. When the ship comes to a rest the high-strung feelings are heightened further because this only means that the exhibition is just minutes away! On-board televisions and monitors are tuned to the christening broadcast so those inside can witness the event. The ones at the starboard bow hear a muffled ‘pop’ from the outside when the champagne bottle bursts on the hull.

“Excellent!”

“Yahooooo!”

These and other cheers and shouts of joy burst from the crew to celebrate that their liner had just now become official. The guest service associates (GSA’s) tense when they hear the escalators connect to the outer wall, because unlike the others in different parts of the ship, they will be the ones interacting with the spectators. However, there is plenty for the behind-the-scenes crew to do, and from the bridge, Second Engineer Christopher Corté clicks on a communicator. “Engineering, this is Second Engineer Corté. I want a complete check of the ground transport system to assure the wheels and struts are in exceptional condition after their first movement – I want to confirm that the rumbles are nothing more than harmless noise. Also, a rudimentary inspection of the rest of the ship, and done in a highly discreet way which does not interfere with the tours."

"Yes, Mr. Corté, right away sir," comes a quick reply. "Discretion assured."

With the entire command staff absent, which is almost impossibly rare, he has in effect becoming the Acting Commanding Officer. So for the time being, the *Emprasoria* is all his and he wants to make sure she is handed back to her masters in prime condition. He straightens the sleeves of his tan duty uniform shirt and self-consciously rubs the back of his neck with his hand, feeling the bristles from the fresh haircut of yesterday. Corté sits calmly at the command platform, with all computer, communicator, video, and telephone lines open, ready for anything.

As the GSAs take a deep breath, and the once-over begins, the forward hatch slides open.

"Hello?"

"Tell me you saw it."

"Yeah, still watching right now," speaks the male voice on the other end. "Looks good,"

"Glad you agree," Maddox says into his telephone. Still at his desk, he is looking at his computer monitor, clicking away. "It's a go."

"I figured as much. You know, they've got some really good coverage on this show."

"Yeah, they do. The netsite has a lot too. I'm just waiting for the camera tour to start, hopefully it will be as informative," Maddox continues; secretly he knows he would die for an in-person guided tour, to say nothing of being with the crew during their inspection. "I already made a ticket reservation – you should do the same."

"Will do."

"Make it for two, by the way – two in a room I mean."

"A bunkmate on this trip? Ok."

"Don't worry, you'll get along with her. And, if you don't it, will only be a few weeks anyway." A pause. "I want a meeting – in person."

"When?"

"Right after they do the tour. I'm craving to see what they're hiding under those clean whitewashed walls."

"Ok, there'll be a cold beer waiting for you."

"Great. See you in a while then."

"Ok, bye."

They hang up. Maddox cracks the wrap on a pack of cigarillos, pops one, and lights up. He only smokes when on a job. A cloud of gray smoke fills the air above him, then he smiles, and clicks on the infoheader that leads him to the maiden voyage tour route information. His eyes play over the graphics and words there. "What do we have here?" His smile widens. "A chance for a double-down? Yesssss….."

"Yes! Yes look at it!" From the bottom of the escalator, the spectators look up in sheer awe at the gigantic vessel which rises above them.

"It's almost surreal, reaching so high into the air like that," comments another.

"Larger than life!"

"Utterly massive – almost beyond comprehension."

Two by two they step aboard the escalator and ascend to the ship, quickly climbing up into the sky and to a smiling, pretty hostess who awaits. She wears an original and exclusive Archangel haute couture design 'flying-colors' uniform ensemble of a cropped indigo jacket, subdued copper-colored silk blouse with burnt orange trim and matching neck-scarf, electric blue skirt with sheer stockings, and cobalt shoes with fleur de lis accents in bronze. A stylized Archangel logo is embroidered in ivory on the left breastpocket.

As the first guests approach, she unhooks a red velvet cord which spans the hatchway.

"Welcome aboard the *Emprasoria.* We are glad to have you with us." This statement, along with a wide smile, is how guests are greeted as they board.

"Behind the velvet cord, just like through the looking glass," says a man, then he looks down to his feet, at the small ship gangway platform which is joined to the escalator and boasts a bright red covering, "and look, they really rolled out the red carpet for us!" Nods and handshakes are exchanged between the guests and the hostess, then with an outstretched arm, she directs visitors across a corridor to an ornate archway where smiling tour guides in the same striking uniforms await. Bethany Parris will take the first group through, and once ten have gathered, she leads the way into a spacious and decorative room. A turn to the right brings them to the elevator bay which houses three lifts.

She faces them and smiles, teeth white and perfect between red lips, but her guests barely notice as they look wide-eyed at their locale. "Good day, my name is Bethany, and I'll be escorting you on your tour." They turn their gaze to her and give polite nods and smiles in reply. "How is everyone today?"

Various comments of "Fine." and "Well." come from the small group.

"Did you enjoy the christening?"

"Yes, very nice," says one.

"Exciting!" proclaims another.

Other similar remarks concur that the event was a positive one for the spectators. Bethany nods. "Excellent. I'm pleased to hear you enjoyed it so well. Shall we begin our tour?" Enthusiastic nods make the answer. "I didn't think there would be any hesitation…." chuckles come from the group.

"We are in the Halo Lounge on the B deck. Above us is the flight deck, which has the bridge and officer's quarters. Below is the Royale class accommodation deck, which is just above the ship's two entertainment decks. Please follow me as we begin our walking tour of the *Emprasoria.*" Bethany pauses though, when she sees a man warily raise a digicam and the look on his face says he wants to ask something, but is reluctant. Anticipating the question, Bethany smiles again and nods. "Please feel free to take any photographs or video during our walk. As well, we will provide you with a complimentary show-disc featuring highlights of the ship's construction and the key passenger areas." Other cameras appear from handbags and jackets, and with the touch of a button by Bethany, the guilded bronze doors of the middle lift immediately open and she ushers her group inside. With a whisper the doors close and soft chamber music plays from hidden speakers as a news readout appears on a square screen above the doorway and they are whisked down.

"The *Emprasoria* is pleased to be the first starship equipped with twin Mercury V15 engines which are of a bold, revolutionary new design for space travel," Bethany continues as the elevator moves. "The Mercurys have been specifically designed for the *Emprasoria* by Archangel technicians. These combined with our four thrusters ensure a speedy voyage for you. Our ventilation tanks are stocked with high-grade Alpine Breeze oxygen, and all water onboard is supplied by Diamond Springs. Our twenty-four hour kitchen serves the finest of foods prepared by Juliard Renaissance Cordon Bleu chefs, while our bars provide the best liqueurs and wines available. We also have an onboard winery which produces our own brand, *Emprasoria* Beauentente." The Line wishes to ensure the guests know all the specialty features the ship offers.

The chamber music fades as a soft tone sounds and from the speaker a female voice says "Welcome to the Royale deck." Then doors part to reveal an elegant hallway. The carpeting is deep crimson, and the walls are soft beige around dark wooden doors boasting crystal doorknobs and ornate Greco frames. The ceiling is a plain white with evenly- spaced glass dome light fixtures. At the far end of the corridor is a set of two large, stylish, sweeping staircases, connecting the Royale class to the Halo lounge. On the wall behind these, centered between, is a rectangular oil painting of a forest landscape.

"We shall now view a model stateroom at Royale, suites specially designed for you with luxury in mind," says smiling Bethany as the group steps into the corridor. Upon entering a suite which has been perfectly arranged for the tour, the guests gather in the middle of the sitting room. "This rectangular room itself is the size of entire staterooms found in first class on other liners." The guests' eyes roam the lavishly appointed room and they marvel at the elegance they see. "The décor includes stylish wooden Chippendale and Boulle furniture inlaid with copper, brass, ivory and tortoise-shell ornaments atop plush carpeting, an intriguing yet pleasing three-dimensional spectrascape painting, an antique longcase timepiece with a truly ornate moonroller clockface boasting roman numerals, and a miniature crystal chandelier. You can see it is laid out in accommodating feng shui design. Our complete home-entertainment system is equipped with EntQuest, a special amusement offering where any music album, film, television program – including made-for-tv-movies, and videogame from any era can be called up and enjoyed on demand. There is also a fashionable computer console, and a fully stocked refreshment bar," says Bethany. These all attest to the claim of "luxury in mind".

"This tassled pull-cord," she remarks while going to the gold velvet cord which spirals down from the ceiling in a back corner, "summons stewards immediately for you. Or, touching this switch on the cord instantly brings an on-board V.I.P. to your service. Yes, our Virtual Interactive Pass-assisters go a step beyond. Let me show you." She pressses the small tab woven into the gold threads of the cord, then a flash of white light appears, and forms into two distinct shapes. A half-second later, pentigital-quality high resolution hologram images have filled out into a male and a female, each as attractive a person as one would see on a newscast, and wearing a smart Archangel uniform.

"Hello, I'm Evie!" says the smiling woman.

"And I'm Evan," states her smiling male counterpart. "We're your V.I.P.'s for the Emprasoria! We're here to answer questions you may have about the ship, to guide you to a specific area, to page another guest for you, or help you request an entertainment or specialty service."

"We are always here for you," chirps Evie, "any time, day or night! And it's so easy to reach us! We can be reached through your in-suite compuface, through the pull-cord, through your suite phone or even over your personafône!"

"So remember," continues Evan, "we're always here for you. Enjoy your day."

"Thanks, Evie and Evan," says Bethany. The two V.I.P.'s look over to her, then smile and wave as Bethany clicks the pull-cord button and they disappear. "Evie and Evan will be reference-programmed to identify each guest in a particular suite, and address each person by name. You may interact with the both of them, or if you have a particular preference for just one, than that one will be the one tailored for your suite. The V.I.P.'s can and will appear anywhere in the ship to assist you. When visiting the Emprasoria's SolNet site, you'll be happy to see that Evie and Evan appear as page-guides there. We are happy to provide Evie and Evan to assist you, but otherwise, the Archangel line is pleased to offer the classic style of the personal touch with catering compliments of a fully human serving staff. The only automatons are within the engine room or cargo hold."

"My, they looked almost real!" comments a woman.

"Only the best for passengers of the Emprasoria," answers Bethany.

Bethany goes on to briefly yet thoroughly explains everything the sitting room offers. Of the more interesting features, "We have optional use of this wall-panel which permits the joining of suites for passengers traveling in groups. Our internal communications network is equipped with all personafône homeband frequencies as well as recharge adapters for all models, so you may bring your mobile phone with you, or feel free to use our in-ship system. We also provide limitless access to SolNet." She pauses as her guests look around.

"And now, we shall see the verandah," Bethany says while walking to the wall of stained-glass dividers, which run the length of the room on its far side. She opens the sliding door in its center, and invites her group to follow. The verandah is relatively narrow, though is wide enough for people to walk around easily. The wall opposite the dividers is white behind a clear glass cover which goes from floor to ceiling. The ceiling, right and left walls are also plain white. The verandah has track lighting, potted plants, four white rattan lawn chairs, and two small, white circular tables.

Bethany gracefully stands to the right of the door in front of a small, rectangular video screen embedded in the wall, under which is palm-sized silver panel holding two black buttons. Her group forms a semi-circle around her. "These control the viewport," she says while indicating the two buttons with a long and polished fingernail. These have 'OPEN' and 'CLOSE' printed on them in small white letters. "Pressing this will raise the viewport cover, and likewise, this one lowers it. If you tire of looking at space, but wish to spend time in the verandah and do not want to look at a bare wall, Archangel has provided for you." She gently touches the middle of the video screen, which comes on to show four tiny nature images, one in every corner. "Each of these offers a pleasant scene for you. When the cover is down, you have the option of enjoying one of four views: meadow, woodland, beachcoast, or cloudflight, or blending them together. The sound and lighting systems compliment the scene. Let me demonstrate." With a tap to the top-left image, the view expands in a blink to fill the mini-screen as the meadow program instantaneously begins.

The lighting in the verandah dims and Bethany directs her guests to the viewport with a motion of her hand. From the middle of the blank surface a dot of white light appears. The dot expands, coloring as it does, until it encompasses the area. The stark white of the cover screen is replaced with a colorful meadow scene. The sun shines down on a field of green grass, with trees lining the picturesque edges. Birds fly across the bright sky dotted with billowing, drifting clouds, and rabbits scamper in the foliage. From the speakers come the sounds of bird chirps, rustling grass and blowing wind, in sequence with what is shown. The vents provide the pleasant scents of a meadow and cause a breeze when one can be seen swaying the grass and leaves. Though the lights are lowered, their thermal intensity has increased to cause the feeling of sunshine. It is difficult to remember you are in fact in the stateroom of a ship rather than the rural pleasantness of an empty field.

After believing the scene has made its effect, Bethany touches the screen, which now has *'Finish'* printed on it in small letters. Slowly, the scenic system brings its audience back to reality. The edges of the screen begin to close in to the middle, the sounds fade, and the scent and breeze effects lower as the lights brighten. A minute later and the scene returns to its original dot-form, then disappears altogether. The amplifiers are silenced, and the vents begin injecting pure air at a steady pace as the lights resume normal illumination. The dazzled guests collectively look to their guide.

"I've never experienced a manufactured vista as thorough as this before," remarks one in the group, and the others nod agreement.

Bethany smiles. "Our illusiary system is unique to the *Emprasoria.* The ship possesses state-of-the-art recreational facilities to keep her passengers entertained." No one chooses to question her statement.

Bethany exits the verandah and her group reluctantly leaves the room which makes such incredible scenery. She continues by displaying the lavish bedchamber, where a four-post, king-size, elliptical Slumberking bed dominates the room, complete with gold babysoft silk and satin sheets, four thick matching decorative pillows, and a thick, ornate royal blue comforter. The other stylish furniture is offset well by recessed lighting. There are two square viewports with floor-length drapes, as the verandah does not extend here, and a luxurious, private ensuite lavatory with gold-plated fixtures and a marble jacuzzi bath.

"We shall now see our dining salon, the White Feather," says Bethany as she escorts her group from the bedroom through the sitting room into the corridor and leads them to its far end. They approach the staircases, and pass through the opening between the sweeping steps. "This seems odd…" a man whispers to his wife and the others seem confused as well because there is nothing behind but a mahogany wall on which hangs that spectacular painting of countryland. Bethany takes them to the left, to a barely perceptible side panel. With a slight push, it opens inward, then she pauses and turns to her guests. "This is not the ordinary way to enter the Salon," she says with a smile, "but rather through the main entrance in the Halo." Her hand glides up, indicating the deck where they began. "However, we shall use it for our tour." She passes through the unexpected portal, with the guests following.

"Oh, my, look at this….." remarks a woman with a gasp as she enters.

"Spectacular," says another as the door closes.

A few moments later and the tour group emerges from the extraordinary salon, wide-eyed with wonder from the room. "Quite nice, wouldn't you say?" Bethany remarks with a sly smile as they walk to the elevators.

"Quite nice? Dear, it was trés fantab," comments a woman.

"That staircase makes for a perfect entrance by a socialite in an evening gown, wouldn't you say?" asks Bethany.

"My, yes...." remarks a woman whose gaze hints that her imagination is working well.

"I can hardly wait to dive into a porterhouse steak in there!" jokes a man.

"And be sure we'll have it ready for you just the way you like it," Bethany chimes.

Descending a floor brings them to Escapade, the first of the entertainment decks. "This is our forward observation lounge," says Bethany as they enter the room, "An excellent place to relax as the sky flies by." At the back wall, between the entryways, is a small bar. A spacious window stretches across the front of the room and into the walls, and the lounge is furnished with sofas, easy chairs, and small oak endtables on Persian rugs over a hardwood floor. At the forefront, at centerpoint facing the window, is a stunning figurehead.

"Her name is 'In Excelsis'," Bethany says as they walk over. "She is a six-foot art deco statuary formed from polished copper." The guests see that the statue's left hand points high and forward from her outstretched arm, drawing the eyes of her spectators to the course the vessel is flying. In fact, her entire form is leaned in the direction of the point, giving the illusion of perpetual movement; she is a conveyance of fluid motion. Her head is thrown back, her long metallic hair cascading behind, blowing in an imaginary wind. Her chin juts out with pride, and her bust is thrust forward from her taut body. She is garbed in a pleated white metal robe which flows around her figure. Her feet are together in ballerina tiptoe on the top of a three-tiered circular black mahogany base which supports the statue. Her right arm extends back from her torso, and resting in the hand is a smooth maple flagpole. It is topped with a large crystal hewn in a diamond cut, and ends in a sharp point. The pole is held on a sixty-degree angle. On the pole are two brass rings.

Following tradition dating from the earliest maritime history, they are to hold the state flag of the ship's destination. Currently, the flag belonging to the Utopia Planitia colony of Mars drapes majestically down from the pole. The flag has a near regal bearing with its border of fringed gold thread, blood-red backdrop, and centered black circle which houses the colonial Coat of Arms in white and is crowned with three yellow stars in semi-circle and decorated below with a yellow oakleaf garland.

In the hallway again, Bethany continues. "This is our speedwalk, built to make moving within our ship easier," she says while stepping on to a black rubber track that runs down the center of the carpeted hallway and functions like a conveyor belt. "We also offer courtesy carts to help with inter-ship travels," Bethany says while indicating a small fleet of compact four-seat vehicles, of the hovercraft variety no less, resting at recharge stations.

Bethany touches a small red button on a squat round post next to the speedwalk, and the track moves forward at a comfortable pace. They tour the deck from bow to stern, and first visit the stately library which has tiers of books ranging from fine literature to texts on a variety of popular subjects as well as a vast collection of film and music discs. Bethany next shows other specialty area such as the Parisian Bistro, and the Caesarea Pool, which brings the elegance of ancient Rome to the twenty-first century with its ornate pillars, ivory figures, colorful tile mosaics, miniature pine trees, cascading fountains and steaming hot-tubs which, atop a deep red carpeting, surround the bright blue water of the Olympic-sized pool. There is a small bar at Casearea in the form of a grotto, Friendship Cove, and next door is Samedi Beach, a large and open tanning salon with genuine white Caribbean sand, also having a volleyball court and a boardwalk.

"One of the more interesting aspects of this deck is MagnaStar," says Bethany as they approach mid-ship. There, in the center of the hallway, is a magnificent sculpture. "This is a masterpiece of the mysterious art of alchemy. You can see it is formed like a small mountain, made of light browned mettle, with a pointed peak and a large base. Melded into it and displayed in an intriguing fashion are pieces of alabaster, jade, baltic amber, crystal, gypsum, quartz, enamel, fire opals, water opals, fiberglass, ebony, ivory, porcelain, silk, nickel, gold lamé, black leather, foxfur, lost dutchman gold, twenty-four carat gold, an uncut diamond, black-earth, wood, a bare, lit electric wire, and white dove feathers. In the middle is a clear glass globe. This houses the core of MagnaStar. Raging magma and liquid Mercury swirl within two separate spheres. Surrounding these are dazzling stalagmites and stalactites of Chernobylite and clear glass pipes each funneling human blood, fuel oil, and golden champagne around and through the core." The overall presentation is exceptional.

Following MagnaStar, they see the Arctica ice skating rink which features artificial snowfalls and a crisp winter temperature around its large ovular and circular icerinks. Then the rifle range, having skeet shooting and stationary targets and a wide selection of firearms, and the Green Acres nine hole golf course and driving range.

Going up a floor by the aft elevators brings them to a stylish vestibule. "This section of the flight deck has been modified into a nightclub," Bethany says while walking them through glassed French doors boasting intricate carvings into a chic and expansive room. "Plenty of window space for spectacular views." The upper part of the walls are clear glass, and there are mirrors and multilevel glass and chrome platforms throughout, a polished wood floor, three bars, and assorted tables and booths. At the back of the room, in the middle, is a large and solid red triangular architectural amenity decorated with flashing lights, and having a stellar sculpture on its rounded front. The ceiling combines curved and flat glass panels such as one would find in the viewing car of a train, and when looking up, you can clearly see the tailfin of the ship standing tall and mighty above.

By some sort of illusion, it appears as though the triangle wall is one piece with the tailfin, but that couldn't be poss— "I know I should be impartial," Bethany comments, "but to be honest, this is one of my favorite parts of the ship." She has a genuine smile as she strolls over to a claw-footed stainless steel pole resembling a vintage street light with a bowl lamp at its top flanked by two small porcelain birds, and delicately rests her hand on its side. "This club was built to make the best of an aspect of the ship which can offer breathtaking views," she continues, almost dreamily, "imagine what it will be like once we are up in the stars…." Bethany pauses. "We are in Finesse, at the top of the ship. And yes, that really is the ship's tailfin you see there at the far end of the club." A man from the group ventures over and actually touches the triangle, then raps it with his knuckle – to find it is solid metal. He looks up, and his eyes can follow the edge straight through the glass ceiling and out to the sky.

"Quite impressive," he mutters.

Bethany enjoys the room as her group breathes it in; she checks her watch and after they stay as long as they possibly can, she leads them back to the elevators.

They travel down and arrive at Camaraderie, the other area devoted to pleasure. The first stop on this stern-to-bow tour is the Equestria Riding Range. "Our main attractions on this deck include Sk8 & Scale, which has an inline skating track on its floor, lined with inclined, irregular, cratered and cliffed walls in redstone stucco for those would-be mountaineers who have are burning desire for climbing or rappelling. Then is the ZeroZone Spatial Pool, a circular vault where, once in space, gravity can be withdrawn - or 'zeroed' - for passengers to float, fly and play in the air."

Down the way, at the end of Primrose Lane, is the Langshott Parkette, named for the famed English country garden. It is a grassy arboretum featuring an exquisite garden of flowers and tropical plants, a gazebo, and a Monet-style pond complete with a curved footbridge, as well as the vineyard which provides red and white grapes for the winery. Harp music plays continually from speakers formed in the shape of rocks to provide pleasant acoustics. There is a pleasing grove of trees in the Palm Court, whimsical fountains, exotic birds in guilded cages and a large aquarium filled with brilliantly colored fishes. Here hangs a magnificent tapestry. Called "Lakefield", this is a grand millieux of fabric art taking form in hand-sewn embroidery, crushed pearl, metallic thread stitchery, silverkid, dupioni, silk-screening, fabric painting, fiber braids, rose silk, needlepoint and appliqué all woven together in majestic brilliants on layered tableaux to show sunset on a woodland lake.

"Here is En Vogue Avenue," Bethany says as they walk into a stylish plaza. "A variety of specialty shoppes and boutiques for you to browse and find the perfect gifts, and there's even a coffee house to relax in." After her group does some window-shopping, they move on. "Here we see the Windsor Arms, an authentic English pub, and there is the Tuijana Cantina. Club Ritz is here for your enjoyment, and for gaming there is the Arcade, and Casino Royale. Last but not least, the Cosmos Showlounge which has a stage for musicals or band performances, as well as a spacious and illuminated ballroom dance-floor with Enliven effects".

After Camaraderie, they return to the Halo lounge. "Well, that was our trip," Bethany says, smiling again.

"So fantastic," a woman remarks. "There's something for your eye everywhere you look!"

"Staggers the imagination!" comments a man.

"Thank you, we are glad you like it," Bethany replies. "Do you have any questions?"

"Yes," pipes up one man quickly, "how can I book a trip?"

"We have Archangel Tours associates with us here today to help you, or feel free to make a reservation through our website, or if you prefer, by your travel agent. Our maiden voyage is scheduled for Saturday, April 5 to Mars."

"Are we able to dine in our suites if we prefer?" asks another guest.

"Yes, by all means, we can cater to your suite. The White Feather itself serves breakfast, luncheon, dinner, and late supper. Passengers may also reserve the forward observation lounge or Club Ritz for private parties." Bethany notes that several in the group perk up on hearing this.

"Do you do both summer and winter cruising?" inquires a third.

"Yes, sir – we pride ourselves on being an annual operation to meet the varied vacation needs of our passengers."

"This ship has everything one could dream of," begins a man, "and is certainly sturdy. How can something this heavy manage air and space travel?"

"A very good question," Bethany says with a smile. "We have specially designed antigravity disks in the frame, with several inside each cross-beam and in the support ribs of the hull. These are contained in a special solution, and with the touch of a switch from the bridge, the solution warms and the disks activate, allowing the ship to have lighter-than-air capability." The man who raised the question nods with satisfaction at the answer. "As well, we have a line of airelons on each side of the ship which work in conjunction with the delta wings at the stern to assist with flight maneuverability."

"Those verandahs are excellent – is each one more or less the same?" asks another person.

"Yes, each verandah is identical in terms of the scenic system and layout."

There is silence for a moment. "Are there any other questions?" Her guests remain quiet. "Going once…." she jokes, "twice, three times…"

A man speaks. "Bethany, I think you've done a great job at our tour, and you've given us all we need to know – and more." She blushes self-consciously and bats her eyes for a second, then quickly regains her composure. "Well, I try…." Light laughter comes from the group.

She pauses a moment. "Thank you for joining me today on this tour of our great new ship," says Bethany with her now well-known smile. "We know she is the empress of the air, and hope she will come to be queen of your travelspirit as well. Our Liner has been built with you in mind, with the desire to not only be your choice of travel, but an interactive entertainment experience as well. So, on your next vacation, indulge your desire for elegance, experience, and essence, and let the *Emprasoria* be your personal chariot among the stars. Thank you."

There are applause, and the guests are now free to enjoy the ornate design of this spectacular room. The Halo boasts plush red wall to wall carpeting and oak-paneled walls. A gold brocade lines the juncture between the walls and the white patterned ceiling. The middle of the ceiling is dominated by a massive, glittering gold and crystal chandelier. Torch-shaped light fixtures, held aloft by cherub statues, protrude from the walls at key points. A large etching of the Archangel Line corporate seal decorates the wall above the bronze doors of elevator bay. Beneath this, written in gothic script within a ribbon design, is the Latin motto of the ship, "SIC AD ASTRA OMINA OPTIMUS" which in English translates as "Thus To The Stars With Every Excellence". On the wall opposite is a large Roman-numeralled clockface on a circle of mother-of-pearl held upright on either side by two angelic figurines. This timepiece is above the heavy oak doors to the dining salon and is flanked by the grand staircase which sweeps elegantly down to the Royale deck.

In the center of the lounge, as in all Halo receiving rooms of the Line, stands the Archangel Statue. The ivory figure is eight feet-six inches tall on its pedestal and is a perfectly proportioned male angel with rippling muscles and prestigious wings folded down his long back. A strong chin, pristine nose, and perfectly molded eyes form the sculpted glory that is his head. A gold band encircles his stone locks of curled hair, and in the center of this band, at the forehead, is a glorious white diamond star. The right arm hangs at the side of the figure, while the left extends out, his forefinger pointing ever forward, which are the words inscribed on the brass plaque bolted to the square pedestal: 'EVER FORWARD'.

The guests enjoy a Tour Reception where the festive atmosphere of the ship is showcased. Classical music played by the *Emprasoria* band blends with tinkling glasses and excited chatter. Avid discussions abound about the ship among the partygoers. The tour guides are available to answer questions, as are at least a dozen incarnations of the V.I.P.'s Evie and Evan, being attentive in their holographic manner. Waiters bearing trays of champagne cocktails, good-sized pieces of angelfood cake, and hors d'oeurves assure that guests are well satisfied, and flowing, cooled, floral-scented air from the vents provide pleasant breezes to chase away any but the best of sensations. It is like living in one of those fantastic LeRoy Neiman paintings, where the colors jump out at you bold as life itself, and a kaleidoscope party awaits.

The *Emprasoria* stands as a monumental achievement. Everywhere aboard ship is evidence of meticulous and painstaking labor conducted by talented and enterprising architects, designers, decorators, builders, metalworkers, carpenters, sculptors, painters, and every other type of artisan, each steadfastly devoted to expertise within his or her chosen craft. Their gifted hands formed, honed, and styled the masterpiece vessel from a hundred million shapeless pieces. She is a tribute to the creativity of the human spirit.

Eventually, the party moves its way along from an energetic high to an easy twilight. As the guests begin to leave, they are given a genuine "Thank you for joining us!" and presented with a midnight blue Archangel canvas travel bag which holds the promised show-disc as well as other novelty items, all with the Archangel logo. The exit hatch and return escalator are outside the arch at the far end of the lounge, where guests must pass a line of six desks. Each of these has a computer manned by an Archangel Tours travel agent dressed in a stylish soft blue uniform, who with a cheery sentiment is more than pleased to reserve staterooms for the upcoming maiden voyage – or the 'ace run' as goes the jargon in Archangel. All the suites Phillips had set aside are taken, demonstrating that his Phase Three went well, thanks to the crew coterie.

Following the guest visitation, the media is escorted through the ship. ("Took them long enough," Maddox mutters from his den.) Archangel media representatives accompany the tour guides to field any unusual questions which may appear from journalists hungry for sensational stories. The newspeople and camera crews are given the same tour as the guests, as well as being shown the bridge and engine room, where the flashing consoles and mammoth motors satisfy (or, more correctly, intensify) the intrigue of those watching who are technically-minded.

The Continental and Tourist staterooms are not shown; the audiences are left to speculate as to how these sections look - - however, if the Royale class suites are like this, how much different can the other cabins be? Well, actually, the Continental accommodations, located beneath the Camaraderie deck, are less stylish than those of the Royale class as they have smaller sitting rooms and no verandahs. The Tourist cabins are a far cry from the Royale in that they have no sitting rooms, rather two chairs and a table included with the bedroom furniture, and no jacuzzi. Even so, the Continental and Tourist cabins on the *Emprasoria* are larger and more fashionable than those offered on other astral liners, and all passengers are permitted to enjoy the recreation facilities on the entertainment decks.

To help assure favorable coverage, the media people are also treated to a reception in the Halo, and presented with gift-bags. Rodney McPherrin, renowned travel reporter whose vacation prose is featured in 'The Compass and Current' syndicated column appearing in McCartney Publications' infosites, newspapers and Travelog magazine, captures the nature of the ship best in this quote: *"The Emprasoria is perfection personified and quite astonishing in every respect. A deity could scarcely form a more exquisite vessel."*

The Archangel executives are extremely pleased on learning of the guest reservations from the ship, and equally excited when the extensive bookings of the travel agencies are tallied at the close of business. The 'exquisite vessel' remark is icing on an already incredible cake, a publicity statement which makes Phillips beam. As had been hoped, the project is beginning to handsomely reward the coffers of the Line.

Before he had hit the road for his meeting, the fan Maddox had done plenty of media monitoring. While recording the televised tour on disc, he divided his attention between watching the preening for the reporters and continuing in virtual tours himself from the Archangel netsite, and the one devoted to the *Emprasoria* itself by using both his primary computer and his laptop. "Window dressing," he huffs, a bit of frustration evident under his breath. "Well, at least the coverage is pretty good." On his monitor, he looks at deckplans and views of the various public areas of the ship. This and the tv views give some important indicators, they do not tell him what he particularly needs to know. Not that he expected them to really – have to do some major first-hand reconnoitering in person. There are plenty of open-ends. One fact is for sure: this is a big, fancy bird, and big birds attract big prey, which is exactly what he wants.... He smiles and takes a long haul on another half-smoked cigarillo. Maddox packs his laptop and notes into a black attaché, then leaves, grabbing his jacket on the way out.

When the last reporter left the ship and the aft hatch closed, the GSA's breathe a sigh of relief and visibly relax. It had all gone so well! Everything was beyond perfect – the owners should be pleased.

"Very good," Corté says from his office, satisfied with the reports he had been given about the inspection – "Shipshape, all the way through," He writes an analytical master copy comprising all the findings, including his own observations, and keeps a version for himself which he stores with the original reports. He then sits back and with the click of a button sent an e-file complete with timecode video references to Chief Engineer Holden, Captain Arges, Builder Thoms, and Purser Mueller. From the bridge, he supervises the roll back into the hangar. Once the ship is safely berthed and the doors to the hangar are secured, he makes a brief log entry then releases the bridge staff and stands alone for a moment at the now docile controls. He releases a breath; all done, ready to be handed back she is. He smiles to himself, it had been good – he could get used to being in command. He loosens his necktie and undoes the buttons at his collar and cuffs as he walks away, then pauses and turns, gives a last look, and leaves the bridge, shutting off the lights as he goes.

With the ship docked, the crew make their way to Club Ritz for a well-deserved party. Once everyone is at the Ritz, a cruise entertainment supervisor stands at the stage and raises her hands to quiet the animated crowd. "Shhhh, shhhh," she begins. After a hush falls, she continues. "We did great today!" and she thrusts her fist into the air and a roaring cheer from the crowd follows. When the din dies down, she speaks again. "Our ship is named, our guests had a great time, everything went perfectly. We should all be proud. Let's give a great thank-you to Chris Corté! He watched it all for us! Come on up, Chris!" Corté slowly goes to the stage and steps up quickly, gives a brief wave and raises a bottle of beer in salute as the crew applaud, then quickly returns to the group. "Fantastic. Well, ladies and gentlemen, we have a special message for you…."

With that, she steps aside and the large screen behind her clicks on, to reveal Captain Arges in his dress uniform, coming live from the christening ball, standing next to a scale model of the *Emprasoria*. A respectful, attentive silence comes; all eyes look to him. "Hello, friends. I've heard what excellent work you did with our guest tours, and I want to personally congratulate you on a job well done. Our first trip is fast approaching, and I look forward to working with each of you on our new vessel. We've started on a great note, and will only go 'up' from here." He pauses, "Pun fully intended," There is laughter from the crowd. "Enjoy yourselves, and have a good night." The televised image ends, and the screen darkens as the supervisor steps up again.

"You heard him everybody! Let's all have a BLAST! Captain's orders!" Loud music blares from the speakers to cheers as confetti falls and the party begins. Bethany loosens her scarf, runs her fingers through her hair, and begins to sway, then to dance.

If the remainder of the life of the *Emprasoria* is as pleasant and profitable as her first moments in the outside world have been, then good times are to be expected. Good times, to be sure.

CHAPTER THREE
Premiere

Yes, the celebration – fun-filled revelry inspired by the christening and tour went on well into the night. The music played, the wine flowed. Dazzle met sizzle; effect happened. Then, the afterglow of the good time; the unwinding, then 'instant recall' of the highlights: the who-wore-what, the "Wow, that was amazing!", the inevitable kiss'n'tell, but before long, there is work to be done – and the travel world is no exception. 'Carefree entertainment', 'enjoyment', and 'recreation' may be important buzzwords that illustrate their catchphrases, but a high degree of effort goes behind that sensation of relaxation.

Captain Arges stands on the bridge in his duty uniform, and checks his watch. "Just after nine. Monday morning rush-hour should be ending, which means we won't distract any frustrated motorists jamming the freeway near the shipyard." Just then, an alarm sounds and the large doors to the home of the *Emprasoria* slide open once again. Arges looks out from the main viewport, and smiles at the sunny day; good way to start. Two attendants stand beneath the bright morning sun, hosing down the tarmac in front of the hangar, freeing it of dust and any straggling decorations left after the christening. They look to the doors and shade their eyes, being able to see the edge of the rounded bow just inside.

Arges turns and walks back to the command chair. "Prep for rollout."

"Rollout prep," First Officer Rish repeats. The command is passed along and soon reports appear on the screens, and internal communications show the ship is ready to move. "Set for motion," Rish informs the captain.

"Very well. Miss Martingale, please take us out."

"Yes, sir," comes a solid response from the pilot at the helm. She flips some switches and puts her hands steady on the u-shaped wheel, then looks outward. "Running lights active. Brakes released and wheel-stops removed. Radar shows area ahead all clear. Commencing hangar departure." An ensign makes an entry into the ship's log and the *Emprasoria* moves forward. Even through the filtered viewport glass, the bridge becomes awash with bright sunlight as the shadow of their enclosure recedes. The two attendants move to the side together, and well away from the advancing spacecraft. "Man, will you look at that," whispers one to the other, smiling and impressed. "Sure is nice," comes a reply with a toothy grin.

The ship is about one-third free from its hangar when a dull green sedan with government license plates drives along the street outside the fence of the shipyard, moving parallel with the emerging vessel, and approaching the main driveway. Two men and a woman ride in the car, dressed plainly and looking official – the woman has her dark hair slicked back into a tight bun. They turn and look for a moment at the ship, then face forward as the car pulls ahead of the slower moving behemoth and soon they turn left off into a gated lane.

A few minutes later, the *Emprasoria* is clear, coming to a stop just as the green sedan pulls up to the bow and parks to the left. The three step from their vehicle; their dress and mode of transportation convey an overwhelming sense of 'bland'. "Here we go," mutters Captain Arges as he watches them from the bridge window. Arges reaches for a microphone and sets it so he can be heard through the every speaker aboard. "Everyone, this is the captain speaking. We are about to begin the Inspection. I want top-notch all the way along. Go beyond your best. Captain out." He switches the communicator off and turns to Martingale. "Lower the forward ramp please," he says while moving to exit the room.

"Yes, sir," she replies as Rish allows the captain to pass him, then quietly follows. Far below, an angled stepway lowers from the keel to the ground.

The three visitors walk to the vessel, each with a compuboard in hand, looking wholly unimpressed, remaining silent. Arges and Rish step down from the stairway ramp and greet them. "Hello, I'm John

Arges, captain of the *Emprasoria*. Welcome," he says, smiling, with an outstretched hand.

"I'm Lewir," remarks the man who takes Arges' hand. "That's Mirsah," he says, indicating the other man, who nods, "and Bantree." The woman nods as well.

"This is my first officer, Mr. Rish," Arges says as a round of handshakes follow. "We are prepared. I'm sure you will find everything in order."

There is silence for a moment. "That's for us to decide," Lewir snaps. "Us and us alone."

Arges nods slowly. "Of course, by all means." He steps to the side. "This way to the ship." The three walk to the ramp with Arges and Rish following. Arges visibly rolls his eyes, and Rish nods knowingly to him.

Eight hours later, the liner completes a detailed, thorough, and rigorous atmospheric timing trial and strenuous operational readiness testing overseen by the three stern-faced and emotionless inspectors, who incidentally do not intimidate Captain Arges or the crew in the slightest. The ship passes all her tests with flying colors. Having met this bureaucratic qualification, the *Emprasoria* is granted her license certifying her as Spaceworthy from the Los Angeles Bureau of the United States Space Authority. This stamped and signed credential means she is ready to go directly into service. Arges and Rish escort the government reps off the vessel, and the green sedan meanders away. Arges and Rish watch them go, then the captain turns to his next-in-command. He smiles, "We did well. Got the paper on the first try." He shakes hands with Rish.

"Yes, John. Exceptional I would say."

"Probably the best damn ship they've seen in a while, though they'd never show it." Rish nods in agreement and they walk back to the ramp. Arges contemplates the report he will send to the Line and to H&W, and the congratulatory message for the crew.

"Yeah! That is excellent!" Darcy Phillips shouts when he reads the announcement on his computer. He leans back in his chair, confident in knowing a very important piece of information. He spins around to his desk and is about to grab the phone when he sees his assistant already standing in the doorway – on hearing the enthusiastic yell, she guessed that her services would be needed soon. "Ruthy! The Emp got her Pass on the first try!"

"Fantastic!" she replies with a big smile.

"So," Darcy continues, slipping into a serious mode, "we now know how to date the invitations." He pauses a moment. "We let the scheduling secretaries of the 'specials' know a year ago that we'd be having something important planned in late March, and to keep this timeframe as open as possible, so the invites now won't come as a surprise. Let's get them out tomorrow for a Friday launch." Darcy reaches over and grabs his infokeeper. "The twenty-first." He looks up to her. "Got it?"

"Our printers will have the date in thirty seconds. The rest of the card is approved, right?"

"Right. All we needed was the date – we're good to go."

Ruth nods and returns to her desk and is on the telephone before she sits down. Phillips jots an e-mail to Staff Captain Syranos to confirm the plans for the twenty-first.

The Premiere will be a specially orchestrated, golden opportunity promote the new ship. Key journalists from the most popular print, broadcast and electronic global news media, as well as writers for travel and technical magazines, executives from senior travel agencies and representatives of the World Tourist Organization, find invitations printed on goldleaf cardstock bearing the Archangel crest in their morning mail. The Archangel board of directors and all of the Line's class A stockholders are invited as well. All invitations are accepted that afternoon. Over the next few days, the *Emprasoria* is made ready to embark on a round-the-world voyage with her full crew and passenger-list of special, select guests.

At 12:45 that Friday, the *Emprasoria* makes her final flight preparations at the shipyard. The Archangel executives and their spouses socialize in the Halo lounge as this occurs. Darcy Phillips is there too, a bit more relaxed than he was at the christening as this is Staff Captain Syranos' affair. However, as he exchanges wit with the others, he keeps his keen eyes alert and his perked ears attentive for issues which may need diplomacy or expertise.

Outside the hangar, H&W staff have gathered to watch the great ship depart. The shipyard gates are surrounded by family of the crew and general well-wishers to see the ship off. The lenses of still and video cameras glimmer within the crowd. With the security veil now lifted, people are free to take as many photos of the ship as they please, and many take full advantage of this privilege – including Russell Maddox.

He has already seen the security camera at the gate that is watching the group, and the lone television camera which likewise pans across the gathering. He has spotted them from behind the tinted lenses of his sunglasses. A dark wig with flecks of gray covers the top of his head, and the glue holding a neatly trimmed salt-and-pepper beard is itchy on his face. The last thing he needs is the chance of being identified after-the-fact from a random photograph. He cups his hands to his mouth and blasts a hot breath into them; even with the sun shining brightly, there's a bit of a chill in the air. His digicam hangs from a strap at his neck, ready to go. A noise catches his and everyone's attention, and they look left.

Alarms sound at 12:55, then the hangar doors open. Minutes later, the ship is outside. "There she is!" A cheering roar wells up from the HW staffers, who wave their hands and caps in the air. The gate crowd joins in this yell and the tv-man swings his camera around to catch the scene. Maddox can now clearly see the call-letters written in black beneath a sunburst logo; WKLA - he memorizes this as he brings his own vidcorder to his sunglassed eyes. A welling "Ooooooooohh!" is heard from an admiring crowd; Maddox catches his breath as well – to see the vessel on video or in photographs is one thing, to study the blueprints gives an idea of scope, but, to actually see her plain-as-day is something entirely different….massive, remarkable, breathtaking…

The ship pauses once outside, almost as though she is gathering herself after waking from a nap. Then, she moves. She taxis down the runway, gaining speed and picking up momentum while racing forward. The wheels spin, propelled by giant engines. With the aid of the antigravity discs immersed within electrified quicksilver in the beams and ribs of the frame, the bow rises, followed by the rest of the ship in response to the angle of the wing flaps and the hull airelons. She is gracefully airborne. To the joyous roar and wide eyes of her audience, she soars toward the horizon, to the city proper. Maddox keeps his camera trained on her until the tail disappears from sight.

At the L.A. International Airport, a large group waits in the Archangel departures lounge, each with their prized invitation. The shareholders calmly chat. The agency people are calm, yet eager to see the new ship; the reporters there are simply restless - but reporters are usually restless anyway, wanting to get on with the facts and get their stories filed. Nathan Lang finds an empty place next to a pillar by a window and pulls his infokeeper from his overcoat and apprehensively double-checks the powercell indicator – it is strong, ready for impromptu notes; he smiles the slips it back into the pocket. "All set, Nate?"

Lang turns to see his friend and fellow journalist Bob Pacco. "Right and ready," Nathan replies while offering his hand. "Got you on this too, do they Bob?"

Pacco shows his invitation. "Couldn't resist a free ride." He chortles during the handshake. "Were you at the christening?"

"Had to pass on that one – how about you?"

"Negative. They sent a new girl from our group. She did a bang-up job."

Lang nods appreciatively. "Yeah, I was just getting back from a new hotel in Baja. Deksi from our paper covered it." Lane next looks out over the crowd, recognizing a few faces from the industry, yet seeing a lot of new people too. "Well, look who's here...." he murmurs. Pacco turns and looks as Rodney McPherrin walks into the waiting area. Wearing one of his well-known Hawaiian shirts and tan leisure pants, he looks well rested and ready to travel. Some of the agency reps greet him as he enters, and he chats avidly while finishing his soda. Suddenly, there is an audible "Ooooohhh" from the group – the second today for this particular ship – and everyone is looking outside. Lang and Pacco turn to the window and their eyes widen.

In the distance, a massive white vessel is seen coming in – a leviathan of the air, a modern age pterodactyl. This is the first time that the *Emprasoria* has been flying for the public to see, and she makes quite the visual - utter amazement for the travelers, pilots, and airport workers. Others in the airspace heed respectfully to this mistress as the air traffic controllers allow the substantial signal on their radar screens a wide approach. "Damn will you look at the size of that bird!" says the tower control supervisor as he studies the ship through binoculars. Moments later, with minimal wind disruption, she touches down gracefully. With eyes gazing on her, she taxis smoothly to the terminal.

Excited guests gather at the boarding corridor, turning their attention from the ship just outside the window to the closed blue door with its stylish white "A", and back again. Two smiling hostesses at the registration desk do their best to keep them relaxed. Finally, the deskphone rings and is answered before the first chime ends. A conversation of rushed whispers, then one hostess smiles and nods to her compatriot. She sets the phone down, tosses her hair back and raises a microphone to her face. "Ladies and gentlemen, the Archangel Line is pleased to announce that those with invitations for the premiere of the *Emprasoria* are now invited to visit the reception desk for boarding." The blue door opens. While anxious to enplane, the guests know that clamor will cause delay, so they form a line and calmly wait. McPherrin and the entourage of reporters particularly 'hold their cool'. The ticket-invitations are quickly scanned (always check for imitations!), then the guests go aboard as luggage is stowed and the *Emprasoria* is skyward once again.

"Will you look at this place!" Lang says quietly while staring at the lavish surroundings.

"Mucho gusto, amigo," Pacco replies in an equally subdued voice – there is no indication anywhere about silence, but the ambiance almost dictates quiet, like a museum or a holy place. However, you can hear conversation and music in the background. Lang switches on his infokeeper and begins typing rapidly with one hand as a mini electro-pad appears in Pacco's palm and he begins jotting notes, both tuning out the party.

A woman approaches. "Hello there," she says cheerily, nodding to each one. They look up, initially annoyed at being disturbed, but then smile at her. "My name is Bethany, and I'm one of the cruise entertainment hostesses."

"Nathan Lang," Lang says while passing her one of his business cards.

"Bob Pacco," Pacco remarks while doing the same.
They notice that others in Archangel uniforms or people in business suits with Archangel lapel pins are making the rounds among the crowd who moments earlier were in the waiting area - Pacco catches sight of Enkel himself, shaking hands with someone. "Mr. Lang, Mr. Pacco," Bethany continues after taking their cards, "we are glad to see you here. How do you like the ship so far?" There is a burst of laughter, and Lang and Pacco look over to see McPherrin holding court within a small circle of people.

"She's very fine," Lang answers a half-second later he turns back to her. Pacco nods while looking at the stunning décor.

"Excellent. Well we hope you find the rest of your stay as pleasurable. Feel free to ask for me if I can be of any help to you." They nod politely, and with a return nod she excuses herself and approaches another person. At that moment, a waiter with a silver tray of drinks appears.

"Gentlemen, wine or a martini?" he asks. Pacco helps himself to a martini as Lang takes a glass of white wine. They both give their thanks and the waiter nods, then moves on into the crowd.

"Wow, they know how to do things well here," Pacco says after a sip.

"Sure seem to," Lang agrees. "Wonder what else they have in store...."

Staff Captain Syranos steps to a microphone near the center of the room; the Archangel Statue looms behind her. She clinks her wineglass with a silver tuning fork, causing a hush to fall over the crowd and the music to fade. "On behalf of the Archangel Line, allow me to welcome you to our Premiere," she says. "I'm your staff captain, Jennifer Syranos, and we are very glad to have each of you joining us. Our eight-day itinerary for this grand tour allows the *Emprasoria* to call on every natural wonder and manmade landmark the world has to offer, including each cultural attraction on the UNESCO World Heritage List, and the vessel will be cruising low enough to clearly see scenery. Relax and enjoy – we'll take care of the rest... Cheers to the *Emprasoria*!" A "Cheers!" echo comes from the group as the music begins again.

"This promises to be the ultimate in highstyle sightseeing," Enkel comments to his wife. As well, he knows the excursion will permit both the officers and crew to accustom themselves to the nuances and particulars of the new vessel, in not too bad a way.

The course is set, the wheel turned, the trim leveled and the wingflaps fixed, then the *Emprasoria* journeys out over the Pacific. Since the ship will be traveling in the terrestrial atmosphere, she will not be utilizing the interplanetary Mercury V-15 engines, but instead the Orbitaire motor drive system. The Orbitaire is less powerful, and therefore slower, but perfectly suited for global flight on either Earth or Mars. The California coastline quickly disappears behind the tailfin and the sea below becomes a blue-green carpet beneath the keel as the ship gracefully soars to her cruising altitude. She races on like a woman in a rush for a date, and her first destination is a special one.

In the normal course of day-to-day Archangel operations, the promotions department does not interact with the fleet travel routes division, but months earlier, they conferred about a special occasion for this very day. Preparations were made, notifications sent. A reminder would be needed, so closer to the time, the comm officers on two ships are advised that an important message will be coming about location-scheduling near mid-March. Beginning on the tenth, the comms practically jump each time incoming message alerts sound. Finally, the communiqué they are waiting for comes by both e-mail and fax early Tuesday:

03/18/2088
PRIORITY MESSAGE FROM LINE HEADQUARTERS: -=(DJE1)=-

ATTENTION OFFICER STAFF:
You are hereby requested and required to have your course heading to 35 degrees North bearing 125 degrees West, Northbound, arrival time set: 13:00 Hours 30 Minutes, Pacific Time, Friday, March 21, 2088. Specifics to follow. Your cooperation is appreciated. Gratitude in advance. Smooth voyage to you.

Best Regards,
D. J. Enkel
President and Chief Executive Officer
Archangel Line Incorporated

These orders go to the bridge of the *Aquinan*, and in the cockpit of the *Corona*, the flagships of the marine and aerial fleets. When the messages are presented to the captains, they personally pass them to the navigators with statements which are identical and whose tone indicates importance, "Make sure we are there." To stress the point yet further, the signature at the bottom of the sheet is shown. The navigators nod gravely and reference the 'specifics' that state what speed to travel, and in the case of the *Corona*, what altitude to fly, then make the necessary computations, triple-checking to assure accuracy.

The *Aquinan* is an immense and elegant three-funneled triplescrew cruise steamship. She is a bright white and her tapered superstructure stands five decks high from her sleek hull, whose clipper bow slices along the surface of the deep blue sea. Clouds of light gray stream from the smokestacks. The flag of Canada, her destination, flies high from her foremast, fixed just below a smaller company flag, and that of the United States drapes from the staff at her stern. All billow regally in the breeze created by the motion of the vessel. Her name is painted in black on the sides of her bow, and the sun reflects from the many windows which jewel the liner.

The *Corona* is a majestic and massive jet airplane. She too is white. Her bullet-shaped nose commands respect and conveys a sense of speed as the forepoint of the long and wide fuselage. Two great wings grow from the midpoint of the craft and each hold two massive, round turbothrust jet engines. Her tail bears the company crest, and her name adorns her nosecone in black. She soars through the wide blue yonder with the magnificence of an eagle. Captain Reyes of the *Aquinan* and Captain Clarke of the *Corona* both acknowledge receipt of the request with Headquarters, though neither knows of the other's obtaining of the order. The fact that it was sent from Mr. Enkel indicates particular importance. They personally pass the sheets to their respective navigators for course planning.

Near to 1:25, the *Corona* approaches the destination as specified by her new flight plan. As they fly above the waves of the Pacific, First Officer Murdock peers through the cockpit windshield at a ship below. It is a cruiseship. He believes he recognizes it. "Jim," he says to Captain Clarke in the pilot seat next to him, "is that the *Aquinan* down there?"

Clarke looks down. "Sure is. I'll contact them." The *Corona* is flying the same path as the *Aquinan* is sailing, coming on the vessel from behind. The radio speaker on the bridge of the *Aquinan* crackles. "S.S. *Aquinan*, greetings from the *Corona*. This is Captain Clarke speaking. Looks as though our paths cross today."

Captain Reyes raises the microphone to his lips. "Hello there Jim. Jonas Reyes here. Our scanners had spotted you. What brings you out our way?"

"Your guess is as good as mine. We had a surprise message yester--" Clarke stops in mid-sentence as his radar suddenly blares. The sky around has been empty save for them until now. "What the devil is that?" he asks Murdock.

"I don't know, but it sure is big!" The mystery craft flies behind them, and approaches fast. The radar on the *Aquinan* detects the same object. It is practically 1:30.

"Greetings *Corona* and *Aquinan*, this is John Arges of the *Emprasoria* on our premiere," state the radios. The captains are about to answer when the radars sound again. A helicopter is flying in low from the coast, and paralleling their course.

There they are, a triumvirate of excellence. The flagships of the three components of the Archangel Line, gathered together. The *Aquinan* sailing, the *Corona* flying above and just behind, the

Emprasoria above and just behind the *Corona.* An amazing and beautiful spectacle wrapped in a bright and clear spring day.

The helicopter pulls alongside the great scene, but remains at a fair distance, and close to the water. Its side panel opens, and out leans a photographer with a camera at his eye. Click; the moment is recorded on film for posterity. Other photos follow rapidly as a safety measure. A videographer joins in and records the event on motionpicture. Utterly beautiful. With this task done, the panel slides shut, and the helicopter veers away, heading back to the coast for some rush film developing. The three Captains exchange pleasantries for a few moments, then the vessels break formation and the Aquinan continues to Vancouver as the Corona makes way for Seattle, and the *Emprasoria* begins her Premiere.

Follow the rolling waves of the Pacific as they lull their watery way to San Francisco Bay…tour California…tear through the air to the fantastic circus atmosphere of Las Vegas as gamblers wager in the oasis-city that never sleeps. As you can imagine, the fantastic ship blends well with the amusement architecture that defines this city. "And you thought Veg was good, look at that!" comments a woman from the street below.

"Outta this world," replies her husband, then takes a drink. Afterward, enthralling beauty…the Grand Canyon, the Petrified Forest, and the Painted Desert. At Dallas, reverently pause over Kilby Shrine, a site honoring Jack Kilby and his invention of the integrated circuit, which paved the way for the microprocessor that launched the computer age.

As twilight falls, the ship graces the orange-and-purple sky above the hub of Cajun mystique and allure, New Orleans. They make a low and slow cruise above the French Quarter like some sort of dazzling float in an airborne parade. The ship's band plays jazz echoing the music hitting the breeze from Bourbon Street. "Ho-yeah, look at this!" Lang jokes to Pacco while entering the dining salon with other equally bedazzled guests. The salon is decked out in Orleanesque culture with riverboat accoutrements, fun spirals, and servers dressed snappily in 1890's period outfits – so begins the first party of the Premiere.

"These fellows sure know how to do it," Pacco remarks. They find their seats and he reads a menu. "We're going to be treated tonight….listen to this, Frank. Crawdad soup, then a choice of shrimp creole, catfish, gumbo, jambalaya, red beans and rice, or chili, with a dessert of assorted crepe suzettes!"

"I said it once and I'll say it again; '*ho-yeah*'!" Lang jokingly makes an exaggerated point of loosening his belt a notch, then takes his white napkin and rests it across his lap as he takes a drink of his Singapore Sling. "All set." Nods and chuckles come from Pacco, then he takes a hearty drink of apricot wine.

After their down-home good dinner, the well-satisfied guests amble over to the Cosmos. The lounge is laid out in fine Mardi Gras fashion; white, pink and lime-green streamers, large multi-colored plastic doubloon coins, decorative bead necklaces, sparklers, and super-sized novelty masks make a perfect setting for a fabulous party. The quintessential joie de vie of *La Nouvelle Orléans* permeates the ship where a fantastic night is enjoyed. After lazily criss-crossing the city for hours as her patrons play, the ship lands at the Louisiana Airport as the passengers drop off to sleep in their crisp-sheeted beds.

Out in the darkness, Maddox is awake. In that sparsely lit den of his, he rubs his tired eyes after having spent hours meticulously studying the video he had made and cross-checking the footage which was on the evening news. Quite a ship, this one is - he smiles. A long yawn follows, then a drink of soda. He presently looks back at his computer screen, which is fixed on the *Emprasoria* website. "The premiere..." he absently whispers to himself, "their acquainting run." He runs his hand over a stubbled chin, and scratches lightly at his left cheek which is still a bit itchy from the beard glue.

"Press opportunity. Let's see if they list who's on." Clicking of the keyboard. "McPherrin, sure...." He scans over the other names, then backs out of the site and goes into SolNet search mode. A few taps for well-worded queries, then a few moments while hits and metatag information are retrieved. He reads through somewhat blurred eyes and spots a possibility. A few more searches brings him to a Travel Journalist Guild...member contact information....primary email communication through the particular media site, and ah yes, a secondary email address....any journalist worth their salt needs a more clandestine addy away from the peering eyes of editors. He writes a very carefully worded email, then posts it anonymously to the more obscure account. MESSAGE SENT. He sits up and after a few keystrokes leaves SolNet. He clicks off his computer and goes to his bedroom, where he falls with a heavy thud on the bed, wondering what sort of reply he will get tomorrow...

By mid-morning, as most guests gingerly nurse hangovers and make half-hearted 'never again!' promises to themselves, McPherrin files his first article, including lively photos from the party. Lang and Pacco ignore their headaches and let their imaginative prose flow and file theirs. Over the bayou to its aquatic neighbor, the vast birdsfoot ebb of the Mississippi Delta...a dip through the swampy mist of the Everglades...over the Florida Keys for a jaunt to fiesta splendor in Havana...amble through the sunkissed Bahamas.

They glide back to the Florida coastline. In the distance stand the tall and empty launch scaffolds of the Cape Canaveral Historic Park. Arges is on the bridge, standing at the viewport and looking through his binoculars at the skeletal structures. "Just think Peter, that's where it all began," he says while lowering his binocs and turning to Rish. "A birthplace that's what it is." He smiles as Rish nods.

"Truly impressive, sir."

"And with that equipment they had to use back then....astounding," Arges continues as he shakes his head ruefully and again raises the binoculars to his face and looks at the naked links of steel which stretch into the air.

"Pilot Hared," Arges says as the *Emprasoria* draws nearer, without lowering his gaze.

"Yes, sir?" she asks.

"I want us to mark the occasion by paying tribute to our countrymen who pioneered astronautical travel." He turns and looks down to her. "I believe a round-salute would be fitting." His eyes go to Rish, who nods his agreement, then the eyes return to the pilot.

"Excellent, sir." Hared answers.

Moments later, the ship circles in a show of respect over the Cape, in a maneuver that is recognized and appreciated from the ground. "Look at that there," says the curator, who is on the lawn with a group of tourguides to watch the *Emprasoria* fly overhead. "Incredible. That is the future of space travel."

With esteem properly shown, the ship flies on and turns at Norfolk for a flightline to the District of Columbia. An exterior mast extends from the roof of the bridge and the flag of the United States is hoisted. As the ship's band plays 'The Star Spangled Banner', the massive white vessel with its bright flag soars up the Potomac. While launching red, white and blue fireworks, she flies over the Lincoln Memorial, then respectfully passes the White House at a safe distance. They cruise above the Washington Monument before easing over the Capital Dome. Publicity photographers and photojournalists capture some exceptional moments. The ship lands at Dulles Areospaceport, and is directed to a secluded area.

That evening, Damien Enkel and Captain Arges host a gala dinner-dance honoring the President and First Lady. A motorcade of limousines and black escort vehicles pull up to the massive white ship, which is lit up against the night sky. Secret service guards are already aboard, having coordinated with Purser Mueller and inspected the vessel. Enkel heads the receiving line at the boarding ramp, with Captain Arges and his officers in their dress uniforms, ready to greet the Presidential party. The ship's band is behind them. As the procession stops, and agents open the doors to the luxury cars, Captain Arges nods quickly to the expectant band conductor. The notes of 'Hail To The Chief' fill the air.

The President steps from his limousine, smiling, wearing a tuxedo. His wife follows, looking elegant in her wine-colored evening gown. He offers his arm, and together they approach. "Damien, good to see you again," the President says once reaching Enkel.

"The pleasure is all ours, Mr. President Thank you for taking the time to visit us." As the two shake hands, ship photographer Michael Priest immortalizes the moment.

"Glad we could make it." The President looks up, craning his neck to see as much as he can of the *Emprasoria*. "Damien, this is fantastic!" Enkel nods politely. "I mean, it's one thing to see images, put in person it's a whole different experience!"

"Yes, we tried to do our best."

"The sheer magnitude of scale!" the President effuses while still craning his neck, and now arches his back.
"Damien, always a pleasure," remarks the First Lady while he delicately takes her hand.

"Thank you, Sandi. Looking lovely, as usual." She nods her thanks. Priest's camera continues its work.

"President and Mrs. Cartright, may I introduce Captain John Arges, master of the vessel," says Enkel as he rests his hand on the captain's shoulder. Arges removes his had, nods and shakes hands with them both. "We are honored; Sir, Madam."

The First Couple and some select politicos make their way through the receiving line and are provided a ship tour by Enkel, Arges and Syranos. The Washington guests are suitably dazzled by the grand vessel and its ultra-posh amenities. There is a cocktail party in the Halo lounge, where the passengers wait. The room is decorated with several flags along with red, white and blue streamers and balloons, as well as a large portrait of George Washington. The band again plays 'Hail To The Chief' as the President exits the elevator.

"That was exquisite!" the President remarks as he finishes his meal, which happened to boast his and the First Lady's favorite dishes.

"My compliments to your chef, Damien," Sandi Cartright continues.

"Thank you," Enkel replies. Following dessert, he rises from his chair at the head table and moves to a podium. The President turns in his chair while his aide-de-camp discreetly passes him a small plaque. "Ladies and Gentlemen, we hope you enjoyed your tour and dinner tonight," Enkel begins, and applause and cheers occur from the diners. "We are very pleased to make the Capital one of our first port-of-calls on our Premiere. Thank you for having us to your city, for your warm reception, and for joining us here tonight." He pauses. "I understand the President would like to say a few words. Sir?" Enkel steps aside as the President rises from his chair and walks to the podium; those in the salon respectfully rise from their chairs, and once he has reached the microphone, sit again.

"Thank you, Mr. Enkel. I am sure everyone will agree with me when I say what a truly exceptional ship you have here!" Applause and cheers are enthusiastically repeated. "She's a great tribute to your vision, and our nation." President Cartright lifts the plaque he was given, and turns it to face the crowd. "I am pleased to present you and the ship with a tribute citation. Allow me to read it; 'Presented to Damien Enkel and The Archangel Line: In honor of your new and exceptional spaceliner, ***The Emprasoria***, the United States of America wishes you and the vessel every success among the stars.'" The President looks out to the room. "Please accept this with our best intent." A beaming Enkel accepts the plaque from the President as even louder applause come from the crowd.

"Thank you, Sir," Enkel says, then waves Captain Arges over to see the gift. Enkel pauses a moment, then looks to his guests. "A wise man once said:" he pauses for effect as they wait for him to continue, "The party's just begun…let's all have some fun."

Laughter and clapping follows, then to the lively music of the ship's band, dancing and enjoyment follow well into the evening – under the watchful eyes of ship security personnel and the secret service. Captain Arges shares a dance with the First Lady while Staff Captain Syranos dances with the President. Almost too soon the festivities come to a close and the limos pull away, then the ship closes down for the evening. As the city slumbers, the *Emprasoria* is given a thorough check-through from stem to stern by Chief Engineer Holden and his technicians. Adjustments and fine-tuning are made here and there to assure a good running order, but overall, she shines.

As the passengers have breakfast, an Evie hologram appears in the Staff Captain's office. "Good morning, Jennifer. A couriered package has arrived for you. Should it be sent up?"

"Yes, thank you Evie," Jennifer responds, then Evie vanishes. Soon after, a knock comes to the door, and a steward hands over the parcel. Secluded in her office, she sets the heavy, plain brown envelope with the Archangel crest on her desk. "Hope it looks good," she says to herself as she gingerly opens it. Inside is a thick stack of freshly-printed photographs wrapped in tissue paper. She carefully removes the paper. "Ohhh..." She sees a brilliant eight by ten-inch photo of the *Emprasoria*, *Corona*, and *Aquinan* together. The words 'Three Sisters', written in gold script, adorn the top-center of the photo, and the full-color crest of the Line embosses the lower right corner. "Beautiful," she whispers.

Setting one aside for herself, Jennifer tucks the others away, save for one extra. At the bridge, she finds Captain Arges. Surprisingly, Darcy Phillips is with him. She playfully puts the photo behind her back as she approaches them with a 'Guess what I've got?' smirk. "Gentlemen, the photo." With that, she brings her hand around.

"Oh, nnnnice," says Captain Arges, who smiles with pride as he accepts the picture.

"This is great!" echoes Phillips while looking over Arges' shoulder. He looks over to her expectantly "How many do you have?"

"A stack – off hand, three hundred or more."

"Perfect," Phillips turns his attention back to the photo. "Wow, they really did a good job with this. The Aquinan looks good enough to eat." He looks at Syranos again. "Can you have five or so sent to my cabin?"

Syranos nods. "Already on their way."

Arges hands his back to her. "Could you get this framed and returned to me? And another one, to be placed on the bridge?"

"Yessir, right away Sir," she replies.

"Oh, has Mr. Enkel seen this yet?" Arges asks.

"Not so far as I know, though if his assistant saw it she may have emailed it to him."

Arges pauses a moment. "Have a third one framed, post-haste, and sent to me for Mr. Enkel." He looks at both of them. "I would like to present it to him."

Syranos and Phillips nod, understanding. "Yes, sir," Syranos says, then leaves as Arges and Phillips resume their conversation.

Syranos is not the only one being given photos. A good supply of images are regularly sent to a dummy email account held by Maddox, courtesy of a journalist on the Premiere who he rightly guessed would not be adverse to some under-the-table cash in exchange for innocuous photographs of random areas within the vessel. The person on the other end is rather generous with compu-payments, thinks McPherrin one day as he provides the photos. A rich enthusiast, and probably a flake, drooling over the new ship. Little does McPherrin know that Maddox is studying – the details in the background, the general layout, what-fits-where, that sort of thing; all pieces to a puzzle, all clues to an answer. "Good stuff coming through," Maddox says. "Not *exactly* what I need, but sufficient for the moment." He knows that making specific requests could possibly create a tip-off.

Lang and Pacco are finishing their eggs benedict when they notice from the scene passing by the large windows of the dining salon that they are leaving Dulles. "Should be a good day to take a bite out of the Big Apple," Lang remarks.

"Yes, very clear outside," Pacco says after a drink of freshly squeezed orange juice.

"How are your stories coming?" Lang warily inquires.

"Well, thanks," Pacco answers with an equal degree of caution. "Yours?"

"Moving along – my editor is happy, which means I'm happy." They both chuckle.

"These guys are gonna clean up with publicity," Pacco remarks.

"And they deserve every good word they get."

Maddox of course is monitoring every word, good or bad, written about the ship.

Up from Dulles, to Atlantic City, Coney Island…turn at New York Bay…Lady Liberty, sentinel to a great city. The massive towers of the World and Planetary Trade Center stretch high while the still impressive Empire State Building dominates the cityscape; lavish Broadway stretches to the action of Times Square. There is the stylish cathedral to commerce, the Woolworth Building, and the quintessential art deco architecture dream of the Chrysler Building... Rockefeller Center with its golden Atlas statue....the Flatiron Building, New York's angled dowager queen...the defined elegance of the Plaza Hotel, and the twin-spired and inspired St. Patrick's Cathedral...also, the United Nations Headquarters, the League of Astral Colonies Complex, and Central Park.

People stop, and stare. "Look at that!" From the observation rooms at the World and Planetary Trade Centre and the Empire State Building, and the countless windows of the buildings which form the skyline, tourists and office-workers gaze. Brunchers in the Rainbow Room and Tavern-on-the-Green look up from their tables as motorists and pedestrians teeming on the city streets gape upward. Not since the Hindenberg visited in 1937 or the Concorde raced overhead in 1976 has the city been so astounded by a vessel in its airspace. Many more photos are taken, and the *Emprasoria* launches colored fireworks.

One of Maddox's operatives, an unknown face in the crowd, watches as well. A woman with a short-and-sassy haircut, sunglasses, and grey overcoat, gets a numerous photos, including some excellent close-ups of the complete underside of the vessel.

She lands at JFK. That evening, she is lit up with lamps aglow spectacularly through her unshaded windows, beckoning guests forward. The Halo lounge and dining salon host an exciting party attended by the brightest and best that New York City offers. Celebrities, socialites, gadabouts, performing artists, businesspeople, politicians, models...they relax and mingle in an open and funfilled atmosphere defined by freeflowing drinks and festive music (a few revelers find their way into some of the Royale suites for amusement of a more intimate nature). Causing even more of a thrill, dandy articles and exciting photographs appear in the society columns of the city newspapers and newsnet sites the next day. "*WASN'T THAT A PARTY!*" screams a headline on New York Newsday.

As the pleasure cruise sways through its early throes, Maddox is hard at work. After an all-night drive, he wakes up mid-morning in a motel room, still clothed and lying on a bed that was not turned down. Groggy, and with a stale taste in his mouth, he reaches over and checks his watch with a squinting eye – he can still make it. An hour later, his car pulls up to a truck stop alongside a lone highway, beneath a hot desert sun. Maddox sees his appointment is already waiting for him, leaning up against a blue two-door which has seen better days. In chinos and a denim shirt with the sleeves rolled partway up the forearm to reveal tattoos, he waits with his arms crossed and a half-chewed toothpick sticking part way out of his mouth. The gray cowboy hat is worn low on his forehead; strings of slick black hair appear from under it, and the sunglasses covering his eyes complete the picture.

Maddox steps from his car, smiling, feeling better after the shower, shave and breakfast allowed him to return to his 'regular style'. "Enrique, amigo!" he says jovially while pulling on a sportcoat and walking over.

The man-of-few-words Mexitalian nods. "Russ," he answers, looking straight ahead and twirling the toothpick to the other side of his mouth. "What brings this meeting?"

Maddox slaps his arm over Enrique's shoulders. "I have a lead on an operation. Top-drawer, sure fire, high take – a sweetheart deal."

Enrique looks into Maddox's face and can see pure enthusiasm. He cracks a wide smile. "You always know the words I like to hear….." he says with a laugh.

Maddox laughs as well. "We can grab a beer and talk. I have info in the car to show you."

"Let's get on it."

They walk into the restaurant. By the end of the afternoon, Maddox has recruited his third partner for his task. Three down, two to go.

"Well, it's time for us to be off," Damien Enkel says in the Halo that same morning, and his troop of Archangel executives politely nod. "As everyone knows, there's still work to be done back at the office." This early departure is noticed by the Board members and the shareholders, who appreciate the Archangel businessmen's dedication to their professional lives. Enkel momentarily leaves his group to visit the bridge. Those on duty tense and subconsciously come to attention when he enters. "It's alright, it's alright. It's only me, after all…." Enkel jokes with a pleasant smile and dismissive wave of his hand; he is appreciative of the show of respect, but would prefer their focusing on their assigned tasks. The staff resumes work, but remains slightly rigid, being aware of his presence.

Arges rises from his chair. "Mr. Enkel, I was just about to head down and see you off."

"Quite alright, John," Enkel says while offering his hand. "I wanted to get another look at the bridge anyway." As they shake hands,

Enkel tightens his grip slightly and moves closer to Arges. With an intense look in his eye, he speaks in a hushed tone. "You and the crew are doing an excellent job – everyone is liking the ship, keep it up; keep our VIPs happy."

Arges nods. "You can count on us, Sir."

"Always knew I could," Enkel replies, then ends the handshake and slaps Arges on his arm. Enkel steps back and looks at the bridge for a moment, impressed with its cleanliness and order. "Good job everyone," he says, and the staff turn to him. "The *Emprasoria* is doing well on her training run. I look forward to keep seeing great reports on her. See you all back home in a few days." Enkel turns to leave, then stops himself. "And, oh, John, thank you again for that framed photograph of the three vessels together. Looks great."

Arges nods. "My pleasure, Sir. Glad you like it."
Arges escorts Enkel to the Halo, where the other executives wait. Further compliments, good-byes and handshakes are exchanged between the head office entourage and the captain, then he returns to the bridge as they leave for Los Angeles on a charter flight.

The ship continues her trek…over the St. Lawrence Seaway into Canada, making their first international crossing…banking west, pass Montreal and the Laurentien Mountains… in the waters below, the large schooner and icon of Canadian pride Blue Nose 5 travels at full sail to the Atlantic. At Ottawa, they launch colored fireworks above the astute Freedom Tower and over the downtown core. They will make this same tribute when calling on any capital city. From there to the lake-and-forest beauty of Algonquin Park, then to Toronto with its fluted gray disc-topped C.N. Tower, which is one of the tallest free-standing structures in the world, and the high rising Maple Place….then the misty waters of Niagara Falls….over the Great Lakes, to Chicago with its large-scale monoliths… cruise up the shoreline to Lake Superior, with its churning waters and white-caps. "Glad we're not down in that," Rish comments as he looks at the tumult through his binoculars.

"Looks as though the last of those winter gales are ending brutally," Arges replies while looking at a monitor on the command platform. "I concur – good to be up here."

After the wonders of the Midwest…soar over the Rockies and Victoria Glacier….Western fare that night; buffalo burgers, venison…mesquite flavoring all around…cactus ale….a Winter Wonderland party at the Arcitca rink following. As the party begins,

Captain Arges looks out from the bridge viewport. "The auroras sure are out tonight, aren't they?"

"Yes, very much so," Second Officer Rayburn answers. The vessel is bathed in iridescent, luminous color and surrounded by the vibrant rainbow beams of the aurora borealis, known popularly as the 'northern lights'.

Arges raises his communicator. "Michael, this is Captain Arges, are you ready?"

"Yes, sir," says Priest as he steps into the captain's launch wearing a heavy blue parka and having three cameras hanging around his neck. "Heading out now, Sir."

"Shall we go?" asks a yeoman at the controls.

"Yes, quickly please," Priest answers hastily as he sits, not wanting to miss the lit spectacle. A small white shuttle drops from the forward keel and lands on snow-encrusted tundra. Priest pulls the parka-hood over his head, "I won't be long." He takes a deep breath and steps out. The chill wind whips him as he walks. He looks up and smiles – there she is, surrounded by the amazingly vivid borealis, looking superimposed and almost surreal. He clicks off a number of photos, capturing a moment of beauty ten times over. Satisfied, he trots back to the shuttle and welcomes its warmth from the bitter cold. "Let's go back," Priest says with a gasp. "Take her in slow, for some shots on approach."

"That I can do." The launch lifts off and returns to its mother craft; even through the viewport, Priest is able to take more excellent photos.

"Here we are, at the North Pole," Arges says the next morning as they round the perpetual winter wonder of the Arcitc Circle. In the bridge, he shades his eyes with his hand, even behind the polarized, tinted glass of the viewport. The sun is strong here, especially today since there are just a few clouds out – almost a blinding brightness on the ivory snowflakes and sapphire sea. "Very odd up here at the top of the world," Arges continues, "you have this strange sensation, and can almost feel the planet spinning beneath you."

"It is quite a phenomena," Rish agrees.

"Let's do a radio-check with Alpha on our way south," Arges orders as he walks back to his chair. The ship soon nears the principal interplanetary harbor of Spaceport Alpha, where several varieties of spacecraft are seen launching into the sky, or landing from it.

"Spaceport Alpha has noted us, Sir, and is getting a clear signal," advises Suarez.

"Very good. Let them know our status checks are well and good."

"Yes, Sir. And, Captain, they also wish us a good trip," the comm officer continues.

Arges looks up and smiles. "Very nice of them. Please pass along our thanks."

Across Greenland....over iceberg-laden waters before finding clear ocean and a fast-moving jetstream...to the Caribbean Sea. They appear over the massive ocean liner *Explorer of the Seven Seas* which currently is the largest vessel on the waters. As Captain Arges confers with Officer Rayburn on the bridge, a fax is given to him. Arges pauses and reads the note on *Explorer* letterhead:

"FROM THE LARGEST ON THE SEA TO THE LARGEST IN THE SKY, GREETINGS TO THE *EMPRASORIA*! PAYING OUR RESPECTS TO YOU FROM Exo7sea."

Best Regards,
Captain Roland Nysetyr
p.s. You look great up there!

Arges smiles. "Well, will you look at this!" he says while passing the sheet to his second officer. She reads it while he takes a piece of *Emprasoria* letterhead and clicks his pen open. ***"Always good to acquaint ourselves with like-minded sisters. Our pleasure to share airspace with such a noble seaship. You and the Aquinan bring grand style to the waves – you'll have to do a cruise regatta with the Aquinan some time and together show the others how it's done." Best to you as well – Cap't John Arges.*** Arges summons the yeoman back as Rayburn returns the fax to him. "Quite nice," she remarks, smiling.

"One for the log, that is for sure," Arges answers while carefully setting the note in his folder. As the yeoman arrives, he quickly lets Rayburn review the letter, and she nods.

"Always good to mention our fellow company-people." She smiles and returns the letter, and the captain hands it off to the yeoman to send to Captain Nysetyr.

As the *Explorer* is sent the message, the Latin America Sojourn begins. Through the vibrant West Indies....enter the mainland at Veracruz.....enjoy a 'Buenas Nochas' luncheon of tamales and the like with margaritas, daiquiris, and meil wine. Candied delicacies are displayed within bright pinyattas, split on desert carts...the musicians play Latino tunes in the costume of a Mariachi band....journey across land where nature mixes with famed ruins and technological marvels...Teotihuacán, the Mayan Palace, the Bridge of the Americas, and AtPac Canal! From the Galapagos to the gigantic statues of Easter Island, and the majestic Andes...follow the winding Inca Trail to the sacred mountaintop city of Machu Piccu with its fabled geo-energy flows and renowned Hitching post of the Sun. Angel Falls....the Amazon Rainforest....the spectacular Iguassu Falls...River Plate.

Then, the festive-heaven of Rio de Janeiro. Yes, the Cosmos is transformed into a giant and exciting Copacabana Palace – ready for a Rio Carnival. There is salsa and samba dancing, and conga lines, with flash and glam in overdrive as the ship cruises slowly along the beaches, then back along downtown. "We musta done somethin' right to deserve all this!" Pacco shouts to Lang from within the din of blaring music and excited partygoers.

"Enjoy, amigo, enjoy!" Lang shouts back, then is pulled into a dance by a lithe woman.

"Will you look at that..." Rish says ominously while looking out from the bridge at mid-morning the next day. Ahead is the treacherous rolling dark waters of Drake Passage beneath a low, gray cloud cover and the jagged, steep, knife-blade terrain islands around Tierra Del Fuego, as well as the Oceanus Isthmus.

"Looks a bit rough, doesn't it?" mentions Rayburn with a cautionary tone.

"That is for sure. Glad we are touching down for a while." Yes, before reaching this nightmarish scene, they land smoothly at Magellan Airfield. Magellan is the closest airport to Cape Horn, the southernmost point of the continent.

"Bridge calling Engineering Control," Arges states authoritatively.

"Tac here, John," Chief Engineer Holden replies quickly, having expected the call.

"How are things there, Tac?"

"All I need is some fruit punch and I'm in paradise," he replies with a chuckle.

"That good, is it?" Arges chuckles as well.

"You heard it here first."

"Excellent. Well, time to put your money where your mouth is, as they say. Let's give the E a once-over; a full technical inspection commencing on the hour,"

"Yes, John. Confirmed. Full tech exam beginning at the top of the hour. Once the results are in, they'll be sent right to you."

"Thanks Tac. Let's see if you can earn the drink."

As lunch plates are cleared, Holden calls the bridge. "John, we're in perfect order."

"Excellent news, Tac," Arges replies enthusiastically.

"Thank you. I'd like to come up and show the results to you, if you're not busy?"

"Certainly. Say, in forty minutes?"

Holden checks his watch; by that time, they should be airborne again. "See you then."

A knock comes to Holden's door, and he looks up; "Come in?" The door quietly opens to reveal a burgundy jacketed steward holding a tray with a glass on it filled with pinkish liquid. He enters, smiling as he approaches the desk.

"Mr. Holden, Captain Arges requested that this be delivered to you," the steward says while laying out a white napkin on the blotter in front of the chief engineer. The steward carefully sets the glass itself in the middle of the napkin, then raises his tray and takes a step back. "Is there anything else, Mr. Holden?"

Holden smiles to himself, looking down, trying to stifle a chuckle. "No," he manages, then pauses and looks up. "No, no, that will be just fine thank you."

"Very good, Sir," the steward replies, then exits the office, closing the door behind him.

Holden looks at the report, then at the glass. He eases his chair back and lifts the glass to his lips. A quick drink, a sweet taste, let its flavor linger… "Aaahhhhhhh," he says in a long, relaxed breath while looking at the glass. "Nothing like paradise."

"Looks like we have a clean bill-of-health," Arges advises Rish from the chair.

"That's reassuring," Rish comments. "It also means no delays, at this stage anyway."

Arges nods and turns to the pilot. "Please contact the tower, we're ready to continue."

"Yes, sir," he replies. Mackee looks through the window; the skies and waters look better, but are still foreboding. As Arges and Rish confer over some notes, Mackee speaks. "Captain, they would like us to launch from Runway 4."

"Very good," Arges replies without looking up, "let's go then."

They taxi to the assigned runway, and are given an "All clear" from the tower. Her engines build to a powerful whine and she races down the tarmac then tips her wingflaps to the air. No sooner have they left when a high and strong wind whips up, carrying a banshee scream as it zips with rabid ferocity across the cloud-laden sky. The angry and gusting zephyr wildly twists and turns before clobbering with a heavyweight slap into the side of the still ascending *Emprasoria*. The ship shudders, suddenly caught in the tempest.

"What in the hell?" the shocked Mackee mutters as he fights for control of the vibrating steering wheel. Alarms blare and warning lights flash through the bridge. Arges and Rish look up in a start as the ship quakes again and is visibly forced to the left, then a packet of wind clobbers into the bow and pushes the ship back.

"A williwa!" Rish shouts as he bounds to the pilot.

Mackee has one hand clutching the wheel, the other on the accelerator lever, holding it steady to keep the engines from stalling. "We're still powering up - - need more strength!" Mackee says through clenched teeth as he watches the ship be blown off course. "Past the point of no return, can't go back…." He keeps pressure on the lever. He clicks on the afterburners and the engines are given an extra 'push'. The wind continues its assault, unrelenting against the moving vessel caught in its draft. The *Emprasoria* resists, pressing in its upward thrust, struggling against the squall. "Come on! Come on!" Mackee mouths as he puts the flaps fully down to help raise the bow.

"Throw on the parajets!" the captain barks. "Give us positive thrust!" Rish and Mackee do exactly this, flipping switches and allowing minute thrusters to appear along the mid-section of the craft. The parajets at the bow are angled down while others near midship are pointed back to aid in the lift and all these begin to spew pressurized exhaust into the air. "Rise, damn you rise!" Arges whispers.

The bow finally picks up and the *Emprasoria* rockets forward, bursting from the pocket of whirling atmosphere. The windstorm is left to toss the streaming exhaust of their wake as the ship settles at her cruising altitude. Mackee takes a deep breath and sits back. He looks over at Rish and says nothing, his face doing all the talking for him. Rish pats the pilot's shoulder. "Good job, Mr. Mackee, good job."

"Thank you, Sir," Mackee answers, and as Rish turns to the captain, Mackee notices his shirt feels damp; he looks down to see crescent stains beneath his arms, and a line of moisture runing down the middle. He takes a deep breath to calm his still racing heart, and rolls up his sleeves to help cool his perspiring body; it will be a while before he can change.

Holden appears on a vidscreen, his face shows concern. "John, what just happened?"

"A williwa," Arges spits. "One of those goddamned blows that crop up out of nowhere – and run rampant here at the Horn."

"Captain," Suarez interrupts, "Magellan Field wants to know if we are alright, Sir."

"Tell them we are fine and got through the storm ok." She nods and he returns to his conversation with Holden. "Tac, before you come up here with the Inspection Report, can you oversee a diagnostic in light of what we just went through?"

"Already begun, John. From what I can see, our new bird got through it without any damage. All primary systems are online and unfazed. Just a bit of a shake up, that's all. As soon as the diagnostic is complete, I'll ring you and come up."

"Very well. Thank you." The communication ends and Arges calls Staff Captain Syranos. "Jennifer, we just went through a williwa but we're ok. Could you get on the horn and reassure our passengers that it was a random storm and we are fine? Also, update the Virtual Interactive Pass-assists to provide the same information if they are queried."

"Yes, John. I'll prepare something suitable and announce it momentarily."

"Thank you." He clicks off the communicator. "Pilot, continue," he says.

The ship jets off the tip of the Americas…over icy waters surrounding Antarctica...after the South Pole, Africa. "Cape of Good Hope coming up," Rish remarks. "Looks as though a storm is brewing," he says to Arges while looking at clouds through his binoculars.

Arges looks up and sees a mass of gray clouds looming over the area. "That's why she's known as Cabo Tormentoso – the Cape of Storms, as they say. Maybe we'll get a chance to see the Flying Dutchman," he jokes.

Rish turns to Arges. "Ah yes, the perfect entryway for good Captain van der Decken. Do you think our passengers would like a chance to glimpse that phantom ship glowing in red as she tries to round the Cape?" This is said with a healthy dose of tongue-in-cheek humor.

"I'm sure some of them would jump at the chance. But as for us, we'll give the masts and spars of that doomed brig a wide berth. Can I get a weather report please?"

"Yes, sir," replies an ensign as she quickly checks. "A downpour for part of an hour, with cloud cover expected to break afterward."

"Pilot," orders Arges, "take us above the storm. After it lets up, we'll lower for the tour."

After the Cape is bathed in rain, the clouds separate, and Table Mountain glistens spectacularly in the sun. Their airborne safari involves Paarl Rock, the Zambezi River, and the breathtaking Victoria Falls – the largest curtain of falling water in the world. Then Madagascar, crest Mount Kilimanjaro, across the Serengeti Plain, glide over Lake Victoria, on to the Congo Jungle, known in bygone eras as 'deepest, darkest Africa'…then span the sand ocean of the Sahara. The Nile brings them into mystical Egypt. Where asps slither in congress with the cobra, they soar in the realm of Ra and see the Ramesses II Temple, then cast their shadow over the the Mortuary Temple of Hatshepsut and the Colossi of Memnon. Ahead is the Valley of the Kings at Luxor, the perpetual glory of Karnac, and the step pyramid of Saqquara, first of its kind in the world. Above the ruins of Memphis they move on to the three pyramids at Giza, with their Sphinx sentinel.

Then, Petra, where red sandstone cliffs have been crafted into temples, monuments, tombs and buildings….over the salt laden Dead Sea to Masada, and Jerusalem with the golden Dome of the Rock….then to the Mediterranean Sea. The glitzy beaches of the Riviera…. Monte Carlo, Cannes….then the magnificent Costa del Sol beaches…the Castillas and casas of Spain…..the Rock of Gibraltar, then views of Tangiers, the Casbah, and Casablanca….over the Atlas Mountains, on to the fabled and enigmatic city of Timbuktu. Move round Cape Verde…the Canary Islands, then the Azores.

A Celtic Caleigh brings Ireland…the Isle of Man…the Scottish Highlands….the Northern Isles of Arran….the rolling hills of Great Britain. Through Lake District…crest Scafell Pike….see the land of Robin Hood at Sherwood Forest….on to Mount Snowdon, Oxford, and the River Thames. "Welcome to London," Captain Arges comments as they enter the airspace of the city which for an era was the center of an Empire on which the Sun never set. They are escorted by three dark blue RAF Spitfire jets. The *Emprasoria* lands with much attention along with exceptional British decorum and hospitality at Heathrow. A sleek black limousine awaits them. Once they have rolled to a stop, the chauffeur exits and steps to the rear door. He nods as the occupant, neatly dressed in a three-piece gray suit, emerges – Charles Fitzhume, the United States Ambassador to England. "I'd heard this was large, but Mick, look at this!"

"Seems like quite the vessel, Sir."

Following Fitzhume is his aide, Cheri Dellaporte, who carries an compuboard. "Oh my!"

The stairway ramp lowers. Arges, Rish and Syranos exit; Arges extends his hand as he walks over. "Mr. Fitzhume," he begins, recognizing the man from photographs, "it is a pleasure to meet you, Sir. I am Captain John Arges."

A firm handshake follows. "And you as well. You were quite the buzz in the D.C. I must say, I heard about the ship from quite a few of my cronies there."

"Thank you," says Arges, then the others exchange introductions and handshakes.

"I take it you are ready for this evening?" Fitzhume asks Arges.

"Yes, ready for your inspection, Sir. Come aboard, please." Arges steps to the side and motions for Fitzhume and Dellaporte to proceed up the ramp, which they do.

The Halo is decorated with American Flags, Union Jacks, and the Royal Crest. "This really does like quite good, John," Fitzhume remarks, then takes a sip of wine.

"Thank you, Mr. Ambassador. We're pleased to know it meets your requirements."

The two look out over the large group. With formality, and following protocol to the letter, courtesans, titled members of the aristocracy, and key government people assemble, along with a detachment of Royal Marines in dress uniform. The guests and passengers mingle well, then suddenly, a trumpet blares. A hush falls, and everyone looks to the main door. A courtier in red clears his throat then speaks crisply: "My Lords, my Ladies, all within the sound of my voice, His Royal Highness, King Richard."

The King strides into the room with Queen Kathryn on his arm, followed by the Prince of Wales, Prince James, and Her Grace, Princess Stephanie. The ship's band regales the room with 'God Save The King' and 'Rule Britannia!'. Fitzhume stands at the front of the room. "Ah, Charles, a pleasure to see you," says the King with a friendly smile.

"Thank you, your Highness," Fitzhume bows quickly. "May I present the officers of the ship…" The Royals are introduced, with Priest taking photographs. High tea is served during a city flight. A dinner of Beef Wellington follows, and a ballroom dance. When the *Emprasoria* lands at Heathrow after midnight, the Royals and their guests are brimming.

"Quite splendid," King Richard comments. "I dare say we have a new angel in the sky."

Following the encounter with royalty is another inspection, and after minor touch-ups, the ship again wins a verdict of 'excellent'. "Look at this," Darcy Phillips says the next day when the ship garners a story on the front page of The Times. "Astounding!" As he reads and the others have breakfast, they fly over the White Cliffs and cross the Channel.

"Fit for a king," says a voice in America. His eyebrows had raised when he spies the story on The Times newssite. Maddox routinely checks SolNet for updates about the ship and her journey, and attentively watches live action video streams, then studies still photos. "Live it up, flyboys," he mutters. He continues to be supplied with images from his contact as well, and is building quite an impressive, and completely clandestine, file on the ship.

Enter Europa with a soar…over the champagne region…through the Ardennes, the Netherlands; the 'vunderbar' of Scandanavia, the lavish Yekaterinsky Palace in Russia. Cross the Carpathians…through the goth lands of Transylvania and Bohemia. The Quardriga statue at Berlin greets them, then comes Cologne Cathedral, and the Rhine River. Scenes from the pages of a Grimm Fairy Tale in the form of mountaintop castles in Westphalia and Bavaria; the Black Forest and the blue Danube…then round to the Eiffel Tower….up the Champs Elyées….the Arc de Triumph…the 'jewel of Europe', the Notre Dame Cathedral, on to the grandiose Palace of Versailles….a "Bon Appetit" dinner of French cuisine and Bordeaux wines offered by servers in mime whiteface and striped shirts as the ship hovers over the Versailles gardens….a Soirée afterward…Oui, the Soirée – done in the grand style of Marie Antoinette and held in Finesse, which has been remarkably transformed to resemble the Hall of Mirrors. Powdered wigs and handheld masks are available; candelabras light the room, and a harpsichord played by a pianist dressed as the Phantom of the Opera complete the fantasy.

Tomorrow, across the Alps and over the Matterhorn...the elegance of the St. Moritz and the sublime beauty of Lake Geneva...over the Rubicon...the Leaning Tower...captivating Florence, beautifully aquatic Venice with the Rivoli, Doces Palace, and gondolas... spectacular countryside vistas.....Vesuvius....after the Tiber River, into Rome with the classiest of classical architecture; the Coliseum, the aqueducts, the Golden House of Nero...a substantial lunch of pastas and gelattos tempt the pallots. An afternoon tour of Mount Olympus and the Parthenon. The night brings a banquet of lamb, feta cheeses, souvlakis and uozo, and a Greek Myth party – with togas!

The next day brings a magic carpet ride over the wonders of Arabia; Sheba...Istanbul...the Great Silk Road...Frankincense Trail...Mount Elbrus...Dubai...the Taj Mahal. Tonight, couscous, and the Cosmos is decorated in a style from Tales of the Arabian Nights..... Persian rugs, Pasha tents, leather pillows, a palm-treed oasis, and glass-bowled water pipes aplenty – Sinbad, Alladin, and Ali Babba would find it welcoming. A stage show of belly dancers and snake charmers add the extra touch. At sunrise, become a flying 'Orient Express' to tour amazing Asia...the Ganges River...the Shangri-La land of Nepal...the Great Wall of China...the Gobi Desert. Crest Everest, and Mount Fuji...visit Forbidden City, Shanghai, Hong Kong, Singapore, and see the brightness of Siliconiaz, a massive multi-level glass community – the first in the world devoted solely to compu-technology. Then, a 'Konnichiwa, Ni Hao!' party; paper lanterns, dragon decorations, arrangements in bamboo, origami creations, and dazzling mini-fireworks along with Asian delicacies. There is a kabuki enactment, a Taiko drum performance, and Samoan torch dancing.

A day of touring the easy pleasantness of the South Pacific...then the last night of the Premiere...'Farewell' is the theme of the evening...a good party while floating above the spectacular colors of the Coral Reef...a sumptuous feast of international delicacies...in the Cosmos and Finesse, large screens display three-dimensional imagery from all the fantastic locales they called upon. Between images flashes a word for 'Good Bye' in each language.

Afterward, the guests saunter back to their cabins, including Lang and Pacco. Lang stops and looks around the hallway. "Think of all the excitement that will happen within these walls. I mean, really think about it. All the thrills so far, and she hasn't even been outside the planet yet!" He pauses. "The creation and Premiere are just the start."

"Astounding, actually," Pacco replies. "See you tomorrow, Nate."

"Another day in paradise, amigo."

That day brings the Hawaiian Islands....pass over Kilauea, where scalding lava erupts continually in fiery orange and yellow fountains....ride the winds to Oahu...at Honolulu, photo ops, posed with grass-skirted hula girls wearing floral leis...a bright sky overhead. And now, the last leg of the journey. Across the Pacific, to set down at Los Angeles. She has circumnavigated the globe. There is a pleasant musical tone, then Captain Arges appears on the monitors. "Ladies and gentlemen, we are home. History has been made with our inaugural flight. History for us, and hopefully history for you as well. We saw exciting locales and sites; we celebrated and entertained. Our ship proved herself well in overland flights and oceanic travels. We operated with total merit, and exceptional precision. We were honored to have you aboard, and glad to share our vessel with you. Take away fond memories, and we look forward to seeing you again. All the best." The screens cut to the Archangel crest and the passengers applaud loudly.

The dazzled guests reluctantly leave the fabulous, dreamy-magical ship. The sheer magnificence astounded them, as did the amazing Premiere. The reporters are pleased with their interviews, as all the officers were available for query and comment. The travel agency execs are suitably impressed with the design and amenities, and recommendations are assured. As well, the *Emprasoria* is bestowed a Five Diamond rating by the World Tourist Association in everything from service to food to performance. "Look at these!" Damien Enkel says while smiling over the emails from the Archangel board members, stating how well the crew and ship performed. Enkel's shareholders also go away confident that their investment dollars have been well spent. As the guests depart, each is given a bright smile and hearty handshake from Captain Arges and Staff Captain Syranos, then she presents a stylish souvenir infokit, including a Three Sisters portrait.

Nathan Lang walks out of the exit tunnel. "Well, that was rough." He yawns and laughs.

"One of the hazards of our chosen profession my friend," Pacco jokes while nudging his friend, "wining and dining, living in fancy rooms, parties and fun, seeing great sites."

Lang laughs, then spies his wife waiting for him; Pacco spots his wife too. "Well, Bob, it was great travelling with you." He offers his hand, which Pacco takes in a firm grip.

"Me too, buddy. See you in the papers." With that, they separate.

When only the crew remain aboard, a boatswain whistle sounds over the speakers. "Hello, this is Captain Arges again. You all did an excellent job. The guests are very impressed, and went away with good thoughts. If we keep up this standard, our ace run will go as smoothly, or even better. Our fine new ship has gotten a remarkable workout, and performed superbly all the way along. Tonight, have a good sleep – we all deserve it. Thank you." The *Emprasoria* basks in the bright lights of the airport. Then, home again. At H&W, she touches down and taxis directly to her hangar. She 'tucks in' as the staff fondly say, and the colossal doors close as dusk falls on Saturday.

"Welcome back," says Maddox from the darkness of his den. At his desk, he watches from his computer. "I've been waiting for you. Yes, waiting and working. I've got my team assembled, five of the best, and we've got all the stuff we need. We are ready for you." He lights another cigarillo and puffs away, feeling very confident about the upcoming task. A fiendish laugh follows. Had anyone been there to hear it, they would have been chilled to the bone.

CHAPTER FOUR
Bon Voyage?

Over the next two days, the *Emprasoria* is tested and replenished. Engineers and technicians inspect the minutest details of the engines and flight systems, of the computers and life-support. Her crew, now generally acquainted with every element of the ship, check her five times over in every aspect from stem to stern. She is re-stocked with the staples which are necessity, and the extras which are luxury. Every step is taken to ensure that the *Emprasoria* will be more than ready for her ace run, all under the watchful and paternal eye of Captain Arges.

The captain personally reads every report on the vessel, making notes and often sending inquiries to the person generating the commentary. He schedules several walking tours daily, and he sees each part of the ship three times, and in most cases four, so he can know every single inch as well as his own back yard. He also does random quizzes of the Evie and Evan V.I.P. holograms, and is satisfied that they know their buisness too. Arges has moved in and settled himself aboard ship, as have his officers and most of the supervisors. Some of the crew return home in the evenings, but a good many opt to stay in their quarters on the liner.

***

Tuesday night finds the captain alone on the bridge. The numerous consoles and switches are dark and silent, and the place has an almost serene calm about it. He is dressed casually, in khakis with a blue pullover sweatshirt bearing the Archangel crest over its left breastpocket, strolling with a cup of tea in hand. Rish walks on to the bridge, and stops himself – "Oh, pardon me…" he stammers; not wanting to intrude, he turns and is about to leave when Arges stops him.

"It's alright, Peter." He then waves him in.

Rish nods self-consciously and continues into the room. He is also dressed casually, in jeans and a running jacket. "Thanks, John. I wanted to come up here too, for another look," he says while walking toward Arges.

"This will be the last time this area will be so quiet for quite a while."

"Yes, I can imagine," Rish says while looking around the room.

"Almost hard to believe in less than twelve hours it will be a nerve-center, running the whole show." Arges takes a sip of his tea.

"True enough." Rish looks down and slides his hand along a control panel. "Dormant, like a sleeping giant." He shifts and props himself against the edge of a desk, crosses his arms over his chest and looks straight at Arges. "I believe we're ready."

Arges nods as he lowers the cup from his lips. "I agree. Ready as we'll ever be."

Rish is relieved at hearing those words, though does not show it. He knows Arges can be a hard taskmaster; a fair one, true, but he can at times be overly stringent – comes with the territory of being a captain. That would be the one thing the first officer was hoping to avoid: rousing the crew in a last minute scurry for ultra-perfection, adding stress to an already tense situation. Rish looks out the viewport to the lit skyline against the darkened sky, then lets his eyes drift up to the stars which the clear night offers. "I can hardly wait."

"Me too. Quite a day ahead."

"That is for sure," Rish says. He straightens himself. "I think its time for me to turn in," he says with a smile, "I want to be as ready as this ship is tomorrow."

Arges nods. "See you in the morning, bright and early." Rish gives a quick, light-hearted salute and Arges replies by raising his cup in a 'cheers' gesture, then the first officer walks off the bridge.

Captain Arges stays a while longer, finishing his tea and looking over the bridge. He spies the framed Three Sisters triumvirate ship photograph hanging on the left wall, and smiles at it. When he feels ready, and notes the tea is taking its toll, he turns and leaves the room through the starboard entrance, locking the door behind him as he goes. He walks down the vacant passageway to the captain's quarters and enters the suite; yes, that tea has given him some much-needed relaxation. The door closes, and all is quiet on the flight deck for the eve of the ace run.

On Wednesday afternoon, she again slowly taxis out from her hangar. Her second departure does not receive near as much attention as the first, but there are some on-hand to witness it. She powers-up and rockets down the runway, lifting off and letting the shipyard disappear in her wake. The vessel travels a more direct route this time, diagonally jetting across North America for Spaceport Alpha. Fortunately, the spaceport can accommodate the superliner. Had the vessel been a mere five feet longer, the Line would have had to build an extension on to the Port especially for the ship, at considerable expense.

The Alpha is a technical marvel itself. It stands out as a massive black rectangle in the midst of the icy whiteness of the arctic circle at Cape Morris Jesup, the northernmost landmass of the world, a peninsula jetting from Greenland into the Arctic Sea. One- hundred furnaces in the basement keep the interior at a warm and functional seventy degrees Fahrenheit. Each of the fifty port-stalls have ten ground attendants to care for the freighters and liners during their stays, and twenty flight controllers man the control tower day and night. The C.T. is situated in the center of the Spaceport, a small and squat dome structure atop a strong and tall cylinder.

The Port-stalls are lined with thick cement walls to prevent adjacent launches or landings from interfering with one another. Steel doors in each wall allow attendants or equipment to move from one stall to another. When a vessel docks, the twin-paneled roof of a stall opens upward, remaining that way until the operation is completed, at which time they close and effectively seal out the polar winds. The only drawback to the facility is that it can only handle vehicles with horizontal docking thrusters, those able to launch or land straight up or straight down. Conventional aircraft cannot use the Spaceport and runways do not exist.

Each stall has two elevators connecting to a subterranean tunnel which links the Port to a square, black complex nicknamed 'Alpha Minor'. Alpha Minor provides accommodation for the spaceport staff and the crews of the various ships which are docked for two or more days, has storage facilities for assorted supplies, and acts as a reception area for passengers waiting to board cruiseships. Ten small docks at the far end of this building are used by inter-Earth shuttlecraft for the delivery of supplies and passengers.

"Welcome to Spaceport Alpha," says a voice over the bridge speakers as the vessel nears.

"Thank you. This is Second Officer Rayburn," replies the Officer.

"Good afternoon. Controller Kriesen here. Did you have a good flight up to us?"

"Yes, it went well thank you."

"Great, glad to hear it. We'll have you in Dock 29."

"Confirmed – Dock 29."

So, Dock 29 will be home to the majestic vessel for the next two days as she makes final voyage preparations. The *Emprasoria* lines herself above Dock 29 and gently lands. Once the ceiling doors close, the ship is welcomed by a team of awe-struck port attendants.

Leslie Grey, the port commander herself, and a group of uniformed port officials make a special trip to the control tower to witness the docking. This is a rare privilege for a ship. "Well, look at this will you…" says Commander Grey, a tall, slim woman with short and styled straight red hair, wearing a crisp, blue port uniform.

"Quite a marvel," comments the Port Authority Superintendent, Hasen Dupree.

Similar statements are made by the other officials, and whispers can be heard among the tower operators.

Once the *Emprasoria* is berthed, Commander Grey and her party make their way to the Ready Room of the glass personnel tower at Dock 29, and wait there for a few moments before the forward hatch on B deck opens with a vacuumed-gasp. Captain Arges, First Officer Rish, and Staff Captain Syranos are on the other side, smiling, ready to give the Commander and her party a tour.

"Hello Leslie!" Arges says warmly.

"Nice to have you back with us, John," she replies. "Quite a bird you have here."

"Like her, do you?"

"From what I've seen so far, she'll give the other ships a run for their money."

"Come aboard, let me show you around," Arges says, and steps back from the hatchway.

Captain Arges introduces Rish and Syranos, then Commander Grey does likewise for those accompanying her. As the Alpha guests are given a tour and treated to dinner, the crew of the *Emprasoria* disembarks and moves in to Alpha Minor to take full advantage of the pre-launch period to relax and socialize before what will be, for them, quite far from any vacation.

The sunny dawn of Saturday April 5 is met with excitement by people the world over. Not everyone, mind you, but only those privileged enough to have passage tickets for the *Emprasoria*. Today is The Day!!! Embarkation Day!!! At three o'clock that afternoon the "flying palace" will whisk them to the stars.

The officers and crew are likewise thrilled with the premise of the ace run. Immediately after their breakfast, the ship is given another once-over to assure perfection in all respects – that everything that should be polished is shining brilliantly, and anything that has a part to play, regardless of how small, is beyond ready. Bethany Parris works with her fellow cruise entertainment staffers in assuring that the various amusements are prepped for passengers. She checks her watch and smiles; only eight hours to go and they are on their way. She feels really lucky, as she has been one of the ones assigned to the forward observation lounge during the launch – a 'totally fine' vantage-point to witness the lift off.

At ten-thirty in the morning, without any fanfare or excitement, a suited courier carrying a black briefcase handcuffed to his right wrist and escorted by three armed but plainclothed guards arrive at the spaceport. With alert eyes they walk briskly and directly to Dock 29. Purser Mueller is waiting there to meet them, with Security Lieutenant Davidovich, and two ship security officers. Mueller nods curtly as they approach, and the nod is returned by the courier with an equal amount of brevity.

"Mr. Papadakis?" Mueller asks.

"Yes, Purser Mueller," the courier replies and offers an identicard with his left hand, which Mueller takes, reads, and compares the photo with the man then shows the card to Davidovich who nods his agreement.

"Very good," Mueller continues as he returns the card. He glances at his writstwatch. "Right on time too, excellent. Let's go." With that he leads Papadakis and his guards to the ship with Davidovich and the officers following.

The visitors are quietly ushered aboard the *Emprasoria* through the entry hatch on B deck. The quick nods and brief greetings are not out of a lack of friendliness, but just the preferred method of security-types while on duty. The group makes its way down the corridor to the ship's lobby. Mueller winces slightly, and his right leg moves in a mild limp; his old street-wound acting up again. Once at the lobby they go to a five-foot tall marble pillar in the middle of the room. Atop this rectangular stand is a royal blue, velvet, headless bust in the shape of a human female neck and shoulders. The courier lifts his briefcase and sets it squarely in the palm of his outstretched left hand. One of the guards clamps his burly hands around the case and steadies it as the courier releases himself from the handcuff and works the combination on the latches.

Click, click say the locks as they spring open and the courier lifts the top of the briefcase. Inside is a small parcel wrapped in plain brown paper, and some forms. The courier puts on white cotton gloves and gingerly removes the package, then begins to carefully unwrap it as the guard closes the briefcase. With the paper away, a slim mahogany box is revealed. It is embossed with the Harry Winston and Sons Jewelers emblem. The courier again enters a combination in a tiny lock at the front of the box, and there is a minute click. The courier moves toward the pillar and takes a quick glance at those around him. Then, focusing his attention on the item in his hands, he slowly opens the box.

Inside, resting on sheer black satin, lies the Hope Diamond. There are muted gasps at the revelation. The magnificent blue jewel shimmers in the bright lights of the lobby. This most splendid of the splendid was formed and discovered in nature's glorious garden, India. Once a prize of Louis the Sixteenth, the famed Sun King of Medieval France, the Diamond resided in Versailles and was gazed upon lovingly by Marie Antoinette. Now, as it has been since 1958, it is in the possession of the Harry Winston Family. Long a guest of the Hall of Gems at the Museum of Natural History within the Smithsonian Institution, Washington, D.C., the Winston Family is generously allowing the Diamond to be displayed at the Utopia Planitia Grand Museum. In a publicity coup, Darcy Phillips managed to arrange to have the *Emprasoria* be the shipping agent for this priceless piece of jewelry.

The Hope Diamond weighs forty-five karats and is worth some five hundred trillion dollars. The brilliant blue gem is set in a pendant surrounded by magnificent white diamonds grandly suspended by a glimmering platinum chain. The courier gingerly removes the necklace and pendant from the box, and carefully sets it around the neckline of the bust. He closes the eagleclaw clasp securely, then circles the pedestal. He makes some minor adjustments here and there, scopes the scene through squinted eyes, then finally nods with a smile to Purser

Mueller, who turns to his security officers. "Gentlemen," he says, "we're ready."

The two men go to a thick, rectangular glass box resting near the far side of the pillar.

They carefully lift the box, whose bottom-end is open, from the floor. They heave it up and, with Lieutenant Davidovich guiding them, align it with the top of the pedestal, and carefully set it down, perfectly in place. Mueller now circles the pedestal, checking for any gaps. There are none. He next turns toward the Purser's office, which is fronted by a massive blonde-wood reception desk that spans the width of the Lobby at the back of the room. On duty are three security staff. "Miss Conway," Mueller calls out, and she raises her head toward him as do her two colleagues, "please activate the Pedestal Security."

"Yessir," she quickly replies with a nod as she enters a code into the console at the desk. Four silver triangles rise from the corners of the pedestal into the base of the glass box and firmly merge the two together. Seconds later, the bust begins to slowly rotate within its enclosure. Light spectacularly glints off of the Diamond and its necklace.

A slight hum begins to emit from the pedestal, and a security camera positioned in the ceiling directly above the display, looking down on it, begins to rotate behind its black plexiglass bowl-like shell. The purser turns to the courier, wearing a broad grin. "There we are, safe and secure. All ready for her trip."

The courier gives a sharp nod. "Right enough," he responds, genuinely impressed and smiling. Now, more relaxed, he takes a look around the ornate lobby as he removes his gloves. "Quite a ship you have here."

"Yes, she's a beauty. We're proud of her," Mueller replies. Papadakis retrieves his briefcase from the guard and opens it again. He removes the form, in triplicate. "Now, Mr. Mueller, if you could sign this release and receipt," he says, still wearing a smile as he offers the papers and a pen to the Purser. Mueller signs and dates the topsheet, as does the courier, who then tears away the middle copy and hands it to Mueller. The other copies are returned to the briefcase, which is locked-shut. "Very good. Well, we wish you a fine voyage," the courier remarks.

"Many thanks," Mueller replies in kind, and the group leaves the lobby, then the delivery team exits the ship. The most luxurious liner in the world now holds the most precious jewel in the world.

At noon, shuttles begin arriving at Alpha Minor with passengers and cargo for the *Emprasoria*. One of these, a Suncoast Airlines flight, has a person intent on using the cruise as a 'working trip'. He stubs out a cigarillo into the sand of an ashtray as he steps into the boarding corridor – it will be his last for a while. The man in question is Kurt Kendall. The former Russell Maddox, renamed as Kendall (and with all the forged identification to prove it). Thanks to a colorspray treatment, he now has dark hair speckled with hints of grey. There is also a light goatee. He is dressed in a suit, and wears padding at his midriff to hide the true state of his physique. On boarding the flight in Seattle, he nonchalantly takes an aisle seat near the middle of the cabin, and gives a pleasant smile to the couple already seated alongside him. He fastens his seatbelt, then sits back and relaxes. He checks his wristwatch. Soon. Soon, they will be going, and he will be on the beginning of executing a masterplan which can net him hundreds of thousands . . . perhaps more.

Although at a glance he appears comfortable and without a care in the world, his mind is in fact brimming with anticipation and excitement. He leans forward and takes a newsmagazine from the sleeve in the back of the seat ahead of him, and as he calmly flips through the pages, he reviews the steps and details of his carefully organized heist. He stops at an article which seems to catch his attention. His eyes play over the words, though his thoughts are elsewhere. True enough, there are factors which are completely out of his control, and this he detests. However, he has devised contingency arrangements for just such occasions, but, there is always that "unseen" element of the unexpected. He stops. No sense in worrying about the unknown. Whatever happens, happens, and you deal with it logically then, and not a moment earlier. He relaxes, and concentrates on those aspects he can control. He turns the page in his magazine.

Resting in the luggage compartment is a burgundy leather suitcase which does not attract any more attention than any one of the countless other bags. This particular piece, however, holds special significance to Maddox. He had watched from the window of the passenger lounge with keen and steely eyes as it was carted out from a freightshed on a tiered wagon by an automated baggage-handler then passed onto the packagetrack and finally loaded on. Thus he knows it is safe.

Four other members of Maddox's team will be arriving at Alpha on later flights from San Diego, Denver, Chicago and Atlanta. The fifth will be joining them from the Lunar colony. Certain special parcels accompany these dark-haired, bearded men who are using aliases and are of similar height and build. The average sized, ordinary-enough brunettes who accompany them each also have important packages. Maddox keenly split his counterparts and equipment so if there is a stop, the mission itself will not suffer, as no single person or suitcase is integral to the task. Any one can be replaced easily; extremely easily.

Passengers are permitted to board the *Emprasoria* at 1:30. Members of the Cruise Entertainment Staff are stationed within Alpha Minor, the tunnel, and Port 29 to guide passengers to the vessel, and inside the ship, multiple Evie and Evan holograms are ready to assist. Bethany Parris smiles as she sees those who will be her guests on the voyage move along, and witnesses first hand their enthusiasm. Anticipation and excitement builds for each passenger as he or she draws nearer to the liner with every passing step. So close!!! We're almost there! Hearts race as they step aboard an elevator to the Port, they exit and rapidly walk down an enclosed passageway and . . . My God! There she is! Gasped breath becomes caught in the throat at the sight of her, and most pause as they look. Towering above them. So massive, and so spectacular.

The effect is the same for the christening spectators who have seen her before, as well as those who only glimpsed televised, SolNet, or still photographs. The passengers move more gradually now, their pace slowed by sheer awe as they move toward the passenger entrance. Here, their tickets are checked and stamped, then they are directed to glass elevators which take them from ground-level to the entry hatches on B, E, or F decks. As the passengers board, the port attendants work efficiently with the *Emprasoria* cargo personnel to ensure that the proper luggage and freight reaches the ship. In all, the boarding goes quite smoothly. The Royale passengers are treated to a wine and cheese party in the Halo, while the Continental and Tourist travelers find complimentary fruit baskets bearing bottles of wine in their staterooms. The *Emprasoria* Beauentente wine is well received.

As is to be expected, the Royale Class Passenger List reads like a veritable 'Who's Who' of society's rich and famous. The List was virtually scoured once it was printed and mailed to the Royale passengers, and made available on SolNet. This 'A-List' of sorts was reviewed closely by people who want to be 'in the know' about who will be on this grandest of trips (and who won't be) and, what sort of social or business connections could possibly be made. As the band plays cheerful tunes in the Halo lounge, they mingle.

The tall yet stout communication magnate Edwin S. Roggin III is traveling with his beautiful wife Lauraleigh, who holds a doctorate in infrastructure logistics. "Come on, shouldn't they be *going* already?" an exasperated Edwin remarks to no one in particular after checking his watch.

Lauraleigh rolls her eyes, but he does not see it. "Edwin, you're on vacation. Let someone else worry about it. The ship will go once they are ready. Relax," she says while resting a comforting hand on her nearly-always-time-constrained husband. She passes him a drink which he reluctantly takes.

Alexis Zolnick, a Shakespearean actress, playwright and expert in literary aesthetics, is with her husband, J.D. Zolnick, a barrel-chested and burly Wall Street raider of the finest kind who made a fortune through the stock market. They are travelling with J.D.'s lifelong friend, the world-renowned journalist and publisher Jack McCartney and his wife, a leading war correspondent, Diana. Alexis and Diana have known each other for many years too.

"We're quite glad you two could make it," J.D. says to the McCartneys.

"I know it was touch-and-go there for a bit, given the news climate and all," says Alexis.

"Well," replies Diana, "we thought about that too, but the people back at the office will just have to fend for themselves for a while." She laughs, as do the others. "But seriously, they can always reach us if they need to, and rest assured we'll be online to them at the slightest suggestion of anything of importance."

"I agree," says Zolnick. "We have a big deal going through too, and I double-checked the communications capability of this ship beforehand – top notch all the way, so there won't be any problems," Zolnick looks around the opulent room, and the crowd of passengers. "Sure am glad I own some stock in these guys."

"By the way, Diana, have you read the new Zandissi work?" Alexis inquires.

"I have been meaning to, but have not yet had the time. Have you?"

"Yes, astounding. I bought the theatre rights to it, and hope to develop it in time for the launch of the fall season."

"That already guarantees a winning performance!"

Alexis smiles appreciatively. "Thank you. Actually, I brought the book with me on the cruise, if you would be interested in taking a look at it?"

"Great! Maybe I could look at it tomorrow?"

"Count on it."

"Good, very good," says Calvin Gregg as he reads a message on his infokeeper. A bar-code scan on a piece of freight below in the cargo hold informs him that a very important parcel has been loaded and registered. He smiles, and slips the infokeeper into his pocket.

"What's got your eye, dear?" his wife, Genvievve asks – she has a certain stylish manner of annunciating, a tonal quality which is positively enthralling.

"The package is aboard," he whispers.

"Ah, nice, that must be good to know." She raises her glass of champagne in a quiet toast.

He clinks his glass with hers, and they both share a smile as they take a sip. Gregg, a son of Highland heritage, is the extremely successful polished but rugged President of Gregg Firearms. Genvievve, a walking definition of elegance, is a finance lawyer with a penchant for photography.

A couple pass them, and Gregg pauses in recognition. It is him! "Tyler! You ol' dog!" he says while reaching out and tapping his friend's arm.

"Cal! Great to see you!" Adam Tyler replies, and they shake hands heartily – and in the hallowed manner known by all of Beta Theta Pi – Cal and Adam are fraternity brothers of university days. Tyler is a tall and red-haired chairman of the leading retail website chain on SolNet. "I had no idea you would be on this trip!"

"A surprise for us both."

"Cal, you remember Christina...." Tyler says.

"Of course, great to see you again." Gregg kisses her once lightly on the cheek.

"Christina, darling, a pleasure," Genvievve greets her.

"And you as well, Genvi. No pressing cases these days?"

"Well, I'll plead the fifth on that...." They both laugh. "How do you like the décor here?"

"Stunning." Christina says this having the eye and distinction of being both an architect and interior decorator.

"My, my, look at our new playground," says Rave DiMedici, a son from one of the most wealthy families in the history of mankind, who opted for the maiden voyage over his own opulent astral-yacht as a means to reach his luxurious villa in the Utopia Resort. He, with long dark hair reaching down to the shoulders of a fine suit and silk shirt, escorts his entrancing companion, la blonde, Octavia Vickers – a well known painter in her own right.

"And play we will, Rave; play we will," she whispers.

"Should be good for some fun," says a man with a whimsical smile as his tongue shifts a half-chewed candystick to the corner of his mouth. His eyebrows rise for a moment from behind dark lenses of sunglasses as he looks around the room approvingly. The rock n' roll star Peter Bull steps into the lounge, and has more than a few looks sent his way. The six-foot, sinuinely fit lead guitarist of the supergroup 'The Blythe Heathens' exudes a god-like presence as he strides through the room. He looks like a rogue gentleman with his mane of thick black curls and his stylishly cut white three-piece suit. The miniature white velvet cape which hangs from his shoulders and the white cowboy boots covering his feet complete the outfit. Bull is instantly approached by some adoring female fans, much to the chagrin of his supremely gorgeous girlfriend, a lawyer with a penchant for the wild side, Myrie. Although she is very secure in their relationship and knows Peter does not have a wandering eye, she still does give 'the extras' a clearly intoned *he's mine – back off* look which quells anything beyond a certain music-appreciation interest.

There stands His Royal Highness Tsarevich Alexsander Romanoff, looking resplendent in his dark blue uniform. The row of medals on the left side of his chest attest to the action he has seen on the high seas as a Lieutenant in the Imperial Russian Navy. "For my initial voyage up there, this is definitely the way to go," he comments to a smiling and attractive woman who is quite taken with his uniform.

"Another notch for American ingenuity and style," says United States' Congresswoman Sharon Jackson, a blonde with glowing west coast vitality whose spirit radiates from within, with confidence in abundance, explains in part why she is the youngest person to hold the position in that nation's history.

The distinguished Japanese industrialist Xian Ng is aboard with his wife, an urban designer, Karisu. Tabbi Kahen, a transportation route engineer, is with her husband, Israeli diplomat and Hebrew philosopher Daniel Benshabbot. Dr. Stephen Radsky adjusts his round eyeglasses, which always seem to slip down the bridge of his narrow nose at the worst possible time. His ground-breaking treatments established him as a legend within the psychiatric community, is traveling abroad to give a series of lectures on psychoanalysis.

Other notables include Deborah Barrett, the chief executive officer of Barrett Enterprises, is with her husband, Weston Parkes. Ms. Barrett has been given the trip by the multi-billion dollar corporation she directs as a reward for her recent securing of a highly profitable acquisition. Another is World Bank president James P. Kennedy and his wife Caressa. Also, the Indian beauty and super-model Adele, who is on the April cover of ***STYLE!*** magazine, believes the voyage will be an excellent opportunity to remain out of the public eye for a time. This idea may sound good, but it isn't exactly working presently as a mild stir is being caused because she is locked in an intense conversation with the vivaciously eccentric stylegod/king of fashion Kyle Kleen. "KK, I *so* would like to launch your summer session!" she is overheard saying.

"Babifia, ta ta! It would be a tragedy to even think of not having you along."

And so they go, chattering along those lines.

The Man and the Grande Dame, the Enkels, are also in attendance. Damien is in high spirits over how the guests are enjoying themselves. Cudos are coming in by the dozens, and Anne is positively beaming over the compliments. In a moment of calm, Damien whispers to her, "Looks like we really do have a winner."

"Was there ever any doubt, dear?"

Damien shakes his head "no", then checks his watch. "I can hardly wait until we can get her up and going."

"I'm sure if you really wanted to, you could made a call, they could start earlier…I would suppose our guests would not mind, they probably would like it…."

Damien thinks for a moment, and takes a drink of his wine, then purses his lips. "Well, you are right that I could pull some strings, or hell, even get behind the wheel up there myself" – he chuckles –"but, sometimes the anticipation is as exciting as the deed itself." His arm finds its way around her hip and he gives her a quick hug.

"Point well taken. And, well said, Mr. Enkel."

He smiles warmly. "Thank you."

They turn from their brief interlude as another gushing person approaches them. "I just love the color scheme in here…."

These and all the other Royale class guests enjoy themselves. Captain Arges is also among the crowd, though he would prefer to be on the bridge. His well-hidden lack of enthusiasm is more than compensated for by the vivacious Staff Captain Syranos, who is genuinely savoring every minute.

Maddox passes through the entry-hatch and slowly walks to the lounge archway. "Welcome aboard, Sir." is the immediate greeting he receives, as does everyone else, from a smiling cruise directress. He nods and smiles back to her. She may as well have welcomed a wolf into a field of sheep. He takes a drink from a passing waiter and mingles with those who will be his victims. He appears no different from any of the other passengers who are innocently enjoying themselves. Appearances, however, can be deceiving. Innocence is the farthest thing from his criminal mind as his eyes silently study his prey. The Halo is a room filled with obviously expensive hairstyles, sparkling jewelry, glamorous dresses, and tailored suits. These are the signs of wealth. The scent of money hangs in the air like a sweet perfume. He is almost drooling with desire. A small smile curls across his lips. A smile inspired by newfound wealth.

Another passenger is observing the crowd, but for an entirely different reason. The black suit he wears hangs well on his slim, six-foot frame. His pressed white Dior shirt and silk blue patterned tie, with a small, round, gold tietack, show him to be a man of refinement. He has well-styled medium-length brown hair and small sideburns on an otherwise clean-shaven face which has a strong look about the chin. At this moment, the thirty-three year old Darian Dade is sizing up the romantic prospects for the voyage. He strides through the crowd, drink in hand, and sees a number a stunningly beautiful women. He is quick to note that a good number of these same women glance in his direction more than once. This should be a *very* interesting voyage, Dade things as he sips his cocktail.

At 2:35, chimes are heard over the public address system, followed by the voice of Officer Rish, who says, "Good afternoon. Any guests of passengers are requested to leave the *Emprasoria* as soon as possible. The ship will be launching shortly. Thank you." With that, the few guests who are aboard begin saying their final farewells. Bethany Parris subconsciously bites her lip in anticipation – an anticipation felt by the entire crew – soon the ace run will begin!

Upon hearing the announcement, Captain Arges eagerly looks to his watch. He smiles. At last! He politely excuses himself from Enkel and the small circle of people who surround him. "I guess it's that time. Duty calls, you know," Arges says, smiling.

"By all means, John," The Man replies. "Jennifer here can keep us entertained." The Staff Captain smiles as Enkel continues. "Let's get this show on the road!" With that, he lightly slaps Arges on the back of his right shoulder. There is chuckling as the Captain nods, then moves away from the group and strides to the front of the room, and exits through a door to the right of the elevator bay marked AUTHORIZED PERSONNEL ONLY on a copper plaque. Behind this is the avionics room, which houses flight and astrogation instruments, and two stairways which lead up to the flight deck.

Darcy Phillips also perks up when he hears Rish's statement. He leaves the small group he is socializing with and walks over to a steward. "Hello, I'm Darcy Phillips."

"Sir," replies the burgundy-coated man, straightening himself on recognition of the name.

"In the Purser's Office you will find a microphone on a tall stand and two thin black vidscreens. Please bring them here and set up the mike in front of the statue, with the vidscreens on either side of it. Get help if you need it."

"Right away, Sir," the steward states, then nods sharply and walks toward the door. Phillips scans the crowd and quickly spots the ship photographer, Michael Priest, taking candid photos of the reception. He trots over to him and whispers in his ear. Priest nods and makes his way to the statue. Phillips straightens his jacket and smoothes his hair, then approaches the Enkel's group. "Hello," he says with a crisp nod and a smile as he arrives.

"Ah, Darcy" Enkel says.

"Sir, if you, Mrs. Enkel, and Staff Captain Syranos will make your way to the statue please . . ."

The three excuse themselves, and head toward the statue, with Phillips following.

Moments after leaving the lounge, Arges strides into the bridge through its starboard door. He smiles as he enters his environment and his eyes roam the nerve-center of the ship. Across the front of the room, and stretching somewhat into its sidewalls, is the main viewport. Along this window is the central control board, which consists of an impressive array of consoles. The board is alive with vidscreens, flashing lights, dials, gauges, and monitors. Every inch of space is occupied with some sort of button, switch, function selector, lever or keyboard which controls the vital functions of the ship. These backlit elements are all set within shiny thick black bakelite, and at key points along its breadth are five stationary, black, square and squat swivel chairs for technicians assigned to pilot and otherwise operate the craft.

Three feet behind the board, in the center of the room, is the command platform. This is an upraised ledge which chiefly supports the command chair. The front of the platform has a solid, dark blue, sectioned, white-lit faceplate that is curved upward, and slopes from the deck of the bridge itself boasting the Archangel crest in its center. Surrounding the chair are five large monitors which can display views from the external cameras, or in an instant switch to a computer readout. The chair is currently occupied by Rish, who is consulting a clipboard. The black leather chair conveys power. It is elevated, sizable but squat, straight-backed and square with a contoured seat. For all intents and purposes, it is a throne. Embedded into the armrests are multicolored buttons to easily relay orders to any part of the ship. A compact five-inch rectangular microphone rests in a slot in the left armrest. This is used for vocal communication within or outside the ship. Behind the chair is the Astrocon cartography table, and behind that a white wall which holds the two entryways and contains various monitors and switches, as does the wall-space between the doors and the viewport.

For a few moments, the ten members of the bridge staff do not notice the presence of the captain, as each is thoroughly involved with specific tasks. An ensign looks up from a starboard wall monitor and sees the captain. His face becomes flushed in surprise and he quickly snaps to attention as he blurts, "Attention on Deck! Captain on the bridge!" Rish rises from the chair and stands to its left as the staff immediately stop what they are doing and stand at attention.

The captain strides across the room and steps up to the platform, then seats himself in the chair. "As you were," he states. The staff resume their activities. "Mr. Rish," the captain continues as he takes the electroboard from the hands of his first officer, "I believe the time has come to get our ace run underway."

"I couldn't agree more, Sir," Rish answers with a smile.

Arges opens the cover of the clipboard and sees the standard Prelaunch Checklist.

"How are things going in the lounge? Is everything ok?" Rish asks.

"Yes, our excellent staff captain has everything well under control," Arges replies. He smiles absently as he reviews the list. He has great respect for Jennifer Syranos. As staff captain, she acts as the social arm of their officer corps, representing the command staff at most passenger functions (this role alone makes her gold to Arges) as well as overseeing the cruise directors, the entertainment agenda, and related activities. Arges looks up and nods to Rish.

The first officer addresses the pilot, who is seated at his station at the middle of the Board. "Mr. Koehler, the key please."

"Yes, Sir," comes the answer as the pilot removes a gold key - the very key given to Enkel by Wulfe - from a small drawer in the Board and inserts it into a small keyhole beneath the ship's wheel. He turns it clockwise three hundred and sixty degrees, and in so doing links the main bridge controls to the avionics and engine systems. A red light just ahead of the wheel brightens, and remains lit. "Link secure, Sir," Koehler reports.

"Thank you," Rish responds with a nod, and Arges makes a notation.

Rish next goes to the intercom microphone at the left of the board, next to the communication center. He enters a code on the numerical button panel at the base of the microphone stand. A three-toned boatswain's whistle is heard over the operations intercom. As the whistle ends, Rish speaks. "Engage all pre-launch checks. Calibrate all systems." He then enters another code, accessing him to the general intercom. Chimes are heard, and Rish again advises any visitors to exit the ship within the next five minutes.

Reports from throughout the ship are sent to the bridge vidscreens. System lights click green on the consoles. "All systems check as operational Sir. No problems encountered," Rish reports to the captain.

"Primary computer system likewise online, all operational programs running with all relays and redundant safeties ready, Sir," Cybernetics Officer DeMornay says.

"Very good," Arges remarks as he makes appropriate notations on the checklist. He turns to his left and looks at Escoto, who is seated at the communications center. "Roberta, would you please contact the control tower?"

"Aye, Sir," she replies, and a moment later a tone sounds at her station. "Connected, Sir,"

"Alpha Tower," A voice sates over the bridge speakers. "This is Controller Adams. How may I help you?"

Arges removes the microphone from the armrest of the chair, activates it, and speaks. "This is Captain Arges of the *Emprasoria*, Dock 29. Our checks here show all systems are functional. Confirm, please."

"Roger, Captain Arges. One moment please, Sir." Using a cable connection with one of the ship's external outlets, the Tower is able to run a complete systems check. One by one, green lights light at the station manned by Adams. After a few moments, the Controller reports back. "Captain Arges, our checks read as positive across the board. All systems are green and go."

"Thank you, Mr. Adams. *Emprasoria* out," Arges says as he switches the microphone off and returns it to the armrest.

"Copy, Sir. Call us when you are ready to leave. Alpha Tower out." There is a short burst of static as the channel is closed.

The captain makes some further notations and turns to the yeoman at a console on his right. "Yeoman, please make the following entry in the Log. '05 April 2088. 14:45 hours. Onboard systems check shows All Normal. Confirmed by Alpha control tower 14:47 hours, Controller Adams directing. Primary launch permission granted 14:57 hours by Adams." This data is quickly entered into the main computer memory cell of the vessel.

Arges turns to Rish. "Peter, please confirm that all hatches are closed and sealed." Rish moves to the center of the Board, consults a vidscreen, and presses some buttons. The entryway hatches slide shut and lock, as does one of the cargo bay doors which was still open. Any visitors are now passengers, regardless of what they desire.

"Verified, all hatches secured," says the first officer. "We're sealed tighter than a coffin." Arges makes more notations and instructs the Yeoman to make the appropriate Log entries.

"Please release any ground umbilicals," Arges orders Rish. Some tubes and cables fall to the tarmac as they are cut free from their outlets on the hull of the ship. There is a "popping" sound as the outlet openings seal shut.

"Done, Sir," Rish dutifully responds.

"Please instruct Tac to energize the main turbines and prep the engines for primary ignition sequence," Arges states without looking up from the Checklist.

"Orders being relayed, Sir."

Far below, in the deepest recesses of the ship, Chief Engineer Holden admires the technical beauty of his engine room. He stands in front of two massive, yellow cylindrical structures which stretch out along the floor before him. These enclose the engines that will drive the ship to the stars. Even in their dormant state, the Mercury V-15s are very impressive. Each is ten feet all, six feet wide, and fifteen feet long. The aft thrusters grow out through the stern bulkhead behind the motors, and other pipes emanating from the bottom run beneath the grated flooring to route exhaust to the base thrusters when necessary. Pipes reaching down from the ceiling are attached to the tops of the engines. These feed the motors their life-giving fuel. The engines possess a special Tsiolkovsky-Goddard action/reaction drive system propelled by a nutomydien energy source. He reaches out his left hand and lightly pats the cold steel, his wedding-ring making an ever so slight clink as he marvels at the power which will soon be bottled within those walls. "I can hardly wait to get these puppies up and running…" he whispers.

The pungent aroma of fuel, oil, and grease, mixed together, permeates the room but it smells good to the machinists who work there; it is the welcome scent of their environment. Their nostrils fill with this byproduct of impending motion, and their spirits are enlivened.

"Chief Engineer Holden, could you go to the E.O.C. please?" The voice summoning him distracts him from the engines and he looks first to the smiling hologram Evan, who spoke them, then up to the E.O.C. - - the Engineering Operations Center, which is a rectangular office attached to the ceiling and located within a latticework of catwalks. Through its large three windows, Holden can see crewmembers hurriedly working. "Mr. Corté asked me to locate you," Evan continues – then his image blurs and skips slightly for a second, given that transmissions of any kind are somewhat disrupted in the engine room.

Holden turns back to Evan. "Right away, thank you." With that, the hologram nods and disappears. Holden checks his watch, then smiles. Soon, things will be underway. He pats the engine again, then makes his way to the middle of the wall across from the engines, passing other hurried staff as he goes. He steps aboard the elevator and is soon inside the E.O.C. This office has vidscreens, monitors, gauges, alarms and switches on all its walls. Along the windows is the Control Board, which at this moment is manned by Second Engineer Christopher Corté and an ensign. Six others occupy the E.O.C., performing assorted tasks.

The E.O.C. controls the entire engineering section of the ship, and can act as a Secondary Bridge if the need should arise. Engineering runs from stern to midship. This includes the Engine Room itself, the power plant with its Strickfaden Elektra-werks turbine generator array and quad of Sunvolt batteries, the Climacirculation room, which holds the air conditioners, furnaces, air filters, and air distribution system. Next comes the Cohesion Compartment with the boilers, condensers, radiators and evaporators, then the Aquox Vestibule holding the two water and oxygen tanks. Then come the five fuel supply cells, the fuel refinery, and the Compucenter which protects the main computer, cybernetics core, and central processing unit which together in this information shrine regulate all shipboard automation and keep the mechanized operations of the vessel functioning on a precise schedule. Lastly, flanking outside midship at the 300 and 800 foot markers respectively, are two Ballast Chambers, which house the pillar-like Gravitationers, then the gyrostabilizers and cabin pressure regulators.

Thus Engineering bears the dual responsibility of providing a mighty, efficient propulsion drive and maintaining a comfortable life-sustaining ecosystem.

Like the storage facilities in the cargo hold, each of the eight rooms are situated in bulkhead fashion and separated by thick steel walls in order that a problem originating in one area can easily be contained and not spread to adjacent sections. Each wall has port and starboard doorways, but in the event of a difficulty, the doors automatically swing shut.

The floor of Engineering consists of grated metal panels, beneath which are the pipes that feed the base-thruster network. These compact Von Braun hydrogen booster rockets launch the vessel from terra-firma, or, when in retro-fire mode, provide a cushioned landing. They are inlaid deep within the strong keel which forms the tempered backbone of the *Emprasoria.* They are topped with dolomite firewall buffers. This, the strongest stone on Earth, reflects the searing heat produced by the base thrusters and keeps technicians or other crew completely safe from what otherwise would instantly turn them to smoldering ash.

Upon entering the E.O.C., Holden goes to the command board and sees the bridge orders on the primary communications vidscreen. Corté turns and sees him. "Hello, Mr. Holden," he says with a smile.

"Good day, Chris. Looks like they're ready to go," he replies. "On the verge of starting our ace run."

"Yes, quite exciting," Corté responds. "This will be my first for one of these."

The ensign rises from his chair at the Board, freeing it for Holden. The chief nods thanks, and seats himself. "Really? Well I'm sure you'll enjoy it."

Holden adjusts the board's microphone arm and brings the device to his face. He reads the orders over the loudspeaker, and his white jumpsuited technicians scurry about the engine room to perform vital tasks. The turbines hum loudly as they feed more power to the ship, as up until this moment they released only enough energy to let the vessel function at a minimal level (lights, main computer, etc.). The Mercury V-15s come to life as they are invigorated with power. Their fuel injection systems are likewise activated, and Corté reads aloud what he sees while monitoring the vidscreen reports with a steely gaze, as the engines slip from one mode to another within a minute: "Pre-Staged." "Staged." "Ignition Stand-By." He turns to Holden and nods.

"Engines holding on Stand By, Sir. We're ready to go on your command," Holden informs Captain Arges over the radio.

"Excellent, Tac," Arges answers. "Please energize the Gravitationers." and the engineer does just that. Arges turns to his right and sees Second Officer Rayburn reading a gauge. "Alyssa, please monitor the gravitometers as we lift off."

"Yes, Captain," she says as she takes a seat on Arges' far right. The Gravitationer pillars provide an artificial gravity field for the ship by means of a rotating axis that creates centrifugal force. As the vessel rises and distances itself from the Earth, the Gravitationers increase their magnetic field strength in direct proportion to the weakening planetary pull, so when the Liner enters outer space, its inhabitants can note no discernible difference. After a moment, Holden's voice is heard on the bridge speakers. "Gravitationers are ready to compensate for extraterrestrial gravity reduction."

"Very good," the captain says. "Peter, please activate the running lights and transponder." Rish flips two switches up and punches a button, then nods as video relays show the external lights of green for port, red for starboard, and white for top brighten, and the homing beacon activates. Arges turns to Escoto, and asks her to again contact the Tower. The radio crackles and Controller Pascal identifies himself. "*Emprasoria* requesting launch clearance, Dock 29," remarks the captain.

"Roger that *Emprasoria*," Pascal replies, then pauses for a moment. "Ceiling doors will be opening shortly." The Controller notes a small freighter is landing at Dock 30. However, flight maneuvers routinely occur alongside one another.

Warning alarms sound at Dock 29, alerting any attendants that the area will soon be flooded with freezing cold wind. "CEILING DOORS WILL OPEN IN ONE MINUTE," a mechanized yet pleasant female voice warns over the stall's speakers. "THIRTY SECONDS," it states after the appropriate time passes. Shortly after that announcement, the doors swiftly part, providing an exit to outer space. "*Emprasoria*, the doors are open. You are cleared for launch. Have a good flight."

"Thank you, Mr. Pascal. We'll see you again in a few weeks. *Emprasoria* out," the captain replies, then calls the E.O.C. "Tac, please ready the VonBrauns."

"Yessir," Holden replies. He presses a series of buttons which first open the panels in the keel of the ship which cover the Von Braun rocket housings, then gently extend the rockets down and prepare them for firing. "Von Brauns exited and primed, Sir," Holden reports. Arges is pleased. The voyage will begin at his command. He pauses for a moment to indulge in the exuberance of the outset of the 'Ace Run' of the new flagship. The time is 2:55, and Rish quietly advises Syranos on her communicator that they are ready to go up in the bridge.

She nods to the band, who eases their song to a close. "Good day All!" Jennifer Syranos says with the bubbling enthusiasm of a cheerleader. She is speaking into the microphone set up in the lounge, standing just ahead of the Enkels, with the statue looming behind their tiny group and two large blank vidscreens on either side of them looking like two black, flat wings. Her voice is heard throughout the ship. "My name is Jennifer Syranos, and I am your Staff Captain for the maiden voyage of the *Emprasoria*!" Her audience in the lounge applauds. "We're ready to begin our flight, and to do the honor of getting us on our way is Mrs. Anne Enkel." Further applause follow as Syranos steps away from the microphone and the Grand Dame moves up to it. Phillips, who is observing from the left, nods to Priest, who has been waiting for the signal and raises his camera to his eye as he takes position.

"Captain, can you hear me?" Mrs. Enkel asks into the microphone with a clipped Vasser tone as she looks quizzically to the lounge ceiling.

"Yes Mrs. Enkel, loud and clear," comes a distended yet cheerful voice. Arges immediately cuts his microphone from the lounge speakers following the statement.

"Take her up!" the Lady says with enthusiasm. A flash bulb pops, and the event is recorded for posterity. The lounge clock rings with Westminster chimes and sounds the hour, then the band strikes up again, playing an instrumental version of the classic song '*Fly Me To The Moon*'.

It is precisely three o'clock, West Greenland Time. Arges sits up in the command chair. "Ladies and Gentlemen," he says to his bridge staff, "let us begin." With that, he presses a light blue button on the right armrest. The ship's whistle bellows; high-A, middle-C and high-E are heard through the dock and the vessel. A thrill of excitement is felt at the sound; it is the signal of departure. The captain presses the switch marked "FRAME ANTI-V-GRAV". The quicksilver within the beams and ribs of the frame becomes jolted with electricity. The antigravity disks which it soaks come up from being flat on the bottom of the pipes, and begin to dance and enact their weight-lessening abilities.

Arges presses the orange 'ENGINE FIRE' button. The message rips from the bridge to the EOC and is instantly conveyed to the waiting Holden. "It's go time!" the engineer shouts with exuberance as he eagerly clicks switches that permit the brand-new engines to run through their ignition sequence. At first there is only a faint sound, a mild rumble. Then, the Mercurys roar to life and begin to pulsate with their newfound power. "Yes babies, go to it," Holden whispers. A feeling of pride and accomplishment, unique to people of the mechanical trade, swells in the hearts of Holden and his engineers as they witness the ignition and feel its effect. "The bird is hot!" Holden shouts to no one in particular. The sound of the active motors and the mild vibration caused by their motion are carried through the *Emprasoria*, bringing smiles to the bridge staff, crew and passengers alike.

In the bridge, Rish reads the countdown as displayed on a vidscreen. "This is a real count. Ten. Nine. Eight. Seven. Six. Five. Four. Three. Two. One. We have ignition." Thirty thousand pounds of hydrogen-fuelled thrust are quickly routed to each of the several exhaust cones which dot the underside of the vessel. Flames spew from these cones and slam into the cement floor of the dock with tremendous force. An ear-splitting clamor, like one-thousand crashes of thunder merged into a single moment, envelops the stall. Clouds of pure white exhaust flow up and around the ship before being drawn down into the massive floor fan, which began to spin beneath its grating when the ceiling doors opened.

The ship begins to rise. "Landing struts have separated from the docksite, levitation has begun," Third Officer Hearst dutifully reports. Slowly, the *Emprasoria* climbs to the awaiting sky. Tremors from the engines increase; they are not violent, but strangely pleasant and reassuring. The excitement of the moment builds. Along the ship, once vacant viewports become occupied by eager faces watching the ship leave the dock. On-board televisions and computer monitors likewise display the launch via the ship's external cameras, and in the lounge, the large vidscreens flanking the statue show the scene. Bethany Parris watches excitedly from the forward observation lounge, which is crowded with people. She has to stand on tiptoe and peer over shoulders, but is able to see through the window. "We have cleared the upper doors and are now entering the Troposphere," Rish advises. Keybird is aloft – the ace run has begun.

In Dock 30, the interstellar freighter *Albany*, which is less than a third the size of the *Emprasoria*, has just landed. Its two pilots, the only inhabitants of the craft, have shut down the engines and are taking a moment to relax in their cockpit as they wait for the ceiling doors to close and the dock to thermalize. They are ragtag merchants with three-days growth of stubble on their faces, long hair tied-back into greased ponytails, and wear outfits which serve more to function than answer to style. The co-pilot spins open the cap of a bottle of red Kentucky bourbon to toast the landing as the pilot, Tyrekka, reclined in his chair and with his booted feet propped up on the control panel, pops a candy into his mouth. "'Nother smooth one, aye Jonsey?" he says, praising his docking. Jones nods enthusiastically. The dock doors are half closed just as the exhaust displacement of the launching *Emprasoria* thrusts in to the still exposed area. The doors immediately jerk upright, and whirling wind is forced down toward the unsuspecting freighter.

Near hurricane-force exhaust swirls under the *Albany* and begins to jostle the craft. The ship bounces once. "What the hell?" says the shocked pilot as his jaws clamp around his cigarette and he swings his feet off of the panel. Alarms begin to wail and warning lights flash within the cockpit. The controllers in the tower are equally puzzled with what is occurring in Port 30. "*Albany*, this is Controller Ahmed. We thought you had docked. Explain what just happened, please?"

The pilot Tyrekka spits out his candy. "You tell us man!" he shouts excitedly into the headset he has just slapped on his skull. "Our engines our down! *We* didn't do that!"

Oblivious to what is happening in Dock 30, the *Emprasoria* continues her ascent, ever increasing her thrust. The exhaust and surrounding air grow steadily in their ferocity. The swirling winds bounce the *Albany* roughly twice more, and then what is already terrible suddenly becomes worse: the ship rises off the floor and does not return. It is drawn uncontrollably up toward the open ceiling doors.

"We've got a fucking serious problem here!" Tyrekka yells in a panic as he desperately tries to re-start the cooling engines. The freighter suddenly bursts wildly out of the dock, colliding sharply with the right door as it goes. Now the *Albany* is exposed to the full force of the launch displacement. It is swept farther up, spinning savagely, moving quickly toward the bottom of the *Emprasoria*.

"*Location Alert! Location Alert!*" the speakers on the bridge bark an warning from the computer. "*Deviate course immediately! Object fast approaching on port!*" A proximity alarm sounds its tone in trios, and a confused Arges looks to Rish for an answer. The first officer races to a monitor and reads aloud what he sees: "Small vessel rising toward us off the port bow! Vessel seems to have minimal or no self-control! Impact with us soon!" His voice changes to a questioning tone. "The vessel isn't showing heat output . . ." he turns to the captain, puzzled. "its engines appear off-line." Arges leans forward in the chair, his mind racing for an explanation; What the devil is this idiot doing? Why doesn't he get away from us? How can he fly without power? Arges' eyes open wide in shock in sudden realization.

"Alpha Tower calling Sir! They say we have a launch problem!" yells Escoto.

"Computer suggests immediate evasive!" DeMornay shouts louder than she wishes.

Arges grabs his microphone from the armrest to try and save the situation. "Engineering!" he barks. "Cut power! *Stop the launch*! Have us hover and nothing more!" Holden immediately and unquestioningly complies. "Helm!" Arges shouts. "Hard a-port! Fire starboard parajets at full!" The pilot jerks the wheel hard to the right while also punching buttons on the Board. The ship veers sharply to its right as the engines slow their combustion processes and the thrust is instantly reduced to a fraction of what it had been. The careening *Albany* slams into open space that just seconds before had been occupied by the *Emprasoria* just as the disrupted air eases its torment.

There is a barely perceptible nudge felt through the ship, and the ascension has clearly been halted, as felt by the lack of upward motion and shown by the stationary scene on the viewers. In the Halo lounge, a combined look of anger, uncertainty and tension crosses the eyes of Damien Enkel. However, he maintains his poker-face *'everything's fine'* smile for his guests, though not without stealing a glance to Phillips – who has seen that look before. Phillips in turn looks to Syranos, who is watching the monitor in dismay. She turns and catches his look then immediately reaches for her communicator to call the bridge. The few Evie and Evan holograms who are in the room continue to smile pleasantly to the guests. At a whisper from the Conductor, the band pauses in *'Fly Me'* and changes to the soothing *'Moon River'*.

Maddox tenses slightly, though like Enkel he gives no indication that anything is wrong. He swallows hard and looks about the room, his half empty glass of wine in hand – untoward thoughts scream in his mind: What's going on – are they going to have to cancel the trip? Have they stopped the liftoff because they caught on to something? He brings his wine to his lips and takes a drink as his eyes fix on one of the large monitors, while also noting the location of the nearest exit.

The *Albany* takes a plunge toward the Spaceport. The pilot's eyes bug out and he bites his lip in tension – a trickle of blood forms at his bottom lip and his face is a mess of pouring sweat. "Come on....come on you bitch...," he wheezes as he jerks back on the steering column and slams every possible button he can think of for an emergency re-start. The roof of the spaceport races up to them as the freighter falls heavily. Jones stares, open-mouthed, transfixed and paralyzed with fear. "Come on! Come on!" Tyrekka shouts. A cough is heard – from the engines. The pilot punches more buttons and slams the dashboard in agonized frustration while his feet do a dance on the pedals below. The cough repeats, then becomes a rumble as the engines take hold. Tyrekka puts all his strength into a massive jerk of the wheel and a pull of the wingflaps and is able to pull the vessel out of its dive at the last second.

"Goddamn, goddamn it..." he manages between labored breaths. He eases back into his seat, shaking from nerves as he rockets away from the area. "Damn that was so close....too damn close." He wipes the sweat from his brow with his shirtsleeve and looks over to Jones, who has regained himself and looks back. "Good flying," he manages, then looks down at the bottle of bourbon to find it half empty, with the top half of Kentucky's best splattered over his clothes.

"Gimme that," Tyrekka says while snatching the bottle. He brings it to his lips and takes a long swig, then passes the bottle back and Jones does the same.

"Alpha, what in the fuck was that shit!" Tyrekka shouts into his headset as he circles the Port. The pilot looks with angry eyes at the massive liner which by this time has maneuvered herself back into position. He eases the *Albany* to a slow stop and hovers at the far end of the spaceport, between Docks 1 and 2 to put a wide expanse between himself and the cruiser. "Alpha! What the fuck was that!" he yells again.

"*Albany*, this is Spaceport Alpha. Please maintain your location," comes the response.

"We're not planning on goin' anywhere," the pilot responds curtly, then shuts off his microphone while still burning a hated gaze at the smooth white hull of the supership.

The same instructions come to Escoto from the control tower. "Roger that, Alpha. Holding position," she answers.

"Good god that was close," Arges says while running his palm over his face.

"Their coming at us was a one-in-a-million fluke, Sir," Rish responds. "It was handled expertly, if I may say so," Rish continues, and Arges nods his thanks to his first officer.

"We have Jennifer asking what is going on," says Escoto. "Tell her we had an incident but everything is ok now and we're waiting for instructions from the Spaceport, but expect to be under way soon. Have her advise Mr. Enkel I will have a report for him soon," Arges answers. "Also, contact engineering. I want them to run a thorough diagnostic and damage check from stem to stern."

"Yes, Sir."

"And, everyone," the captain continues; those on the bridge turn to him, "excellent work. We now know what pure might our vessel holds when she wants to get up and go." They nod solemnly in respect of that fact.

"Roberta, can you find out if everything is alright with the other ship? Let them know we are able to provide assistance if needed."

"Yes, Sir. I will check for you."

The controllers attempt to sort things through. The control tower is practically a madhouse of flashing lights and blaring alarms, and officer-of-the-day Port Supervisor Innoche is trying to maintain a sense of order. "Ok," he begins, and little attention is paid to him by the frenzied staff. "Okay!" This time, the controllers quiet and turn toward their Mexican supervisor. "Thank you," he says with a mock nod. "So, we had an upset because of that big bird out there," his forefinger stabs the air as he points toward the *Emprasoria*. "It's all over now. Let's find out where we stand." Soon he learns that the ceiling mechanism to Port 30 has been ruptured due to its forced opening, so these doors will not be closing anytime soon. All other aspects of the Alpha are unharmed, and both the vessels in question seem fully functional, and no personal injury is reported. "Good. Now we know what condition we are in." By this time, a good number of the lights have blinked off and the sirens have quieted. "First, let's get the minnow stowed," Innoche orders.

"*Albany*, this is Controller Pitaski. We appreciate that you held position for us. Please proceed to Dock 37 and land."

"No way," Tyrekka barks. "Still seems to close to the big boy over there."

There is a pause. "We understand your concerns, *Albany*. Be assured that you will be safe and the other ship will not be moving until you are safe and your stall secured."

This time, Tyrekka pauses. "You are sure?"

"Yes, quite sure. You will see the other ship has not moved, and will not until we give it a go-ahead."

"Alright," Tyrekka replies, reluctance clear in his tone. "But will we take the lengthwise route around the spaceport. We want to keep as far away from the other one as we can."

"Understood *Albany*. Thank you for your cooperation." Minutes later, the *Albany* reaches Dock 37, and there the freighter safely lands and the ceiling doors are secured.

Those on the bridge of the *Emprasoria* witness the *Albany* move slowly along and set itself inside a dock. Escoto turns to the captain. "Sir, Alpha reports there are two people aboard the other vessel. They are not injured, and the freighter itself - the *Albany* - has not been damaged."

"That's a relief," says Arges, then ponders a moment. "Yeoman, come here please." The yeoman reports to Arges, who is jotting a note. "I want you to get a case of the Beauentente wine and a carton of frozen babyback spare ribs and report to my Launch," he says while passing the note to the man. "Have other crewmembers help you if need be."

"Yes, sir," replies the yeoman, who then leaves the bridge. Yeoman Clancy walks down the stairway from the flight deck. Seems like an odd request to him, but the captain knows what he is doing. Knowing he cannot disturb any of his fellow crew in the Halo lounge, he heads directly to the Escapade deck. He walks into the forward observation lounge and lightly taps the shoulder of the first uniformed person he sees. "Excuse me, are you busy?" he asks.

Bethany Parris turns to see a man in a yeoman's uniform. "Hi, I'm not occupied right at this moment," she replies, then her voice scales down to a whisper. "What happened with the launch?"

"I'll explain later," he answers in an equally quiet tone. "Captain's got me on a special project – can you help? It's an easy job."

"Sure," Bethany answers.

"Great – thanks." The yeoman smiles. "Richard Clancy," he says while offering his hand.

"Bethany Parris" she answers during the handshake.

"Ok, for now, we have to go down to the pantry," Clancy says, and she looks at him oddly. "I know, it sounds strange, I'll explain on the way." They leave the lounge and go to fill the captain's request.

Spaceport Alpha had never experienced the launch of a ship the size of the *Emprasoria* before, and was therefore unprepared for the severe displacement caused by its liftoff. The Port Authority enters the following regulation into the Launch Protocol section of its Standard Operating Procedure Guide later that same day:

> When the Archangel Line vessel *Emprasoria* - - or any ship her size equipped with Mercury V15's - - launches, all dock doors in the immediate vicinity must be closed and secured and any airborne vessels be well clear due to excessive atmospheric displacement caused by the thrust exhaust of the Mercury V-15's.

Arges enters a similar requirement into his ship's Prelaunch Checklist. He then pens a note to Captain Tyrekka of the *Albany*, which he hastily dispatches to the compartment of the Captain's Launch, and the rapid but thorough diagnostic of the ship systems as ordered by Arges brings a clean bill of health, and no damage resulted from the mishap.

The speaker on the command platform of *Emprasoria* sounds. "Hello Captain Arges, this is Port Supervisor Innoche."

"Good afternoon, Sir."

"Good afternoon. We are going to put all traffic into a port-wide holding pattern for you and lock down the Dock. This should take roughly fifteen minutes. We'll keep you advised."

"Thank you," responds the captain. "I understand the other ship and its crew are alright?"

"Yes, they are all fine," answers Innoche. "How is your vessel?"

"Undamaged, thank you. The other ship - they went into Dock 37, is that right?"

"Yes, that is correct – they have safely landed there."

"Excellent. I am dispatching a shuttle with an envoy to the Receiving Area of Dock 37 with a good will gesture."

"I see. Is your envoy ready?"

"Yes. Believe me, we are as anxious to get things going as you are."

"Very well," Innoche says. "Please have it occur as quickly as possible."

"We'll be prepared to go by the time your holding requirements are concluded."

"Perfect. Alpha out."

Captain Arges calls down to the Captain's Launch shuttle in the keel of the mighty liner. He speaks to Yeoman Clancy. "Yeoman, are you ready to go?"

"Yessir. And I have Miss Parris from Cruise Entertainment with me."

"Very good. I want you to go to the receiving area of Dock 37 and drop off the two boxes for the captain of the freighter *Albany*. Tyrekka is his name. Did you find the envelope?"

"Yessir, I have it right here with the packages. We will head out immediately."

"Thank you. You have fifteen minutes."

"Understood, Sir."

Clancy and Bethany fly down in the small white shuttlecraft and quickly dock at the berth 37. They each carry a package and walk toward Tyrekka and Jones, who are standing outside their freighter with their backs turned, talking to two Port Attendants. Clancy swallows nervously. "Captain?" he calls out as they approach.

Tyrekka turns. Bethany pauses and takes a quick gasp, and her eyes widen appreciatively. "Yes, this is my ship, the *Albany*," Tyrekka says; he has a baritone voice which resounds well in her ears, and she smiles. As for him, he takes subtle note of her reaction.

"I am the captain's aid from the *Emprasoria*," Clancy begins; Tyrekka and Jones both sneer initially – Clancy continues quickly and offers the case of wine. "We sincerely regret the incident, and are thankful there was no damage. We hope you will accept these as a gesture of good will." Clancy rests the case at Tyrekka's feet, then takes the carton of spare ribs from Bethany and sets this alongside the wine.

Tyrekka and Jones look down and read the labels. "Wine? Meat?" Tyrekka inquires as he looks to Jones, then at the emissaries from the cruise ship.

"And, a letter," Clancy says while pulling the envelope from inside his uniform jacket.

"I see," says Tyrekka while taking the envelope. There is a moment of tension as again Tyrekka looks to the two boxes silently. He looks up at Clancy and Bethany, then smiles widely. "It was a close call. We all learned from it. The gesture is appreciated." He offers his hand, which Clancy takes. "Pass my thanks to your captain."

"That we will, Sir. Oh, pardon me, I am Yeoman Clancy, and this is Ms. Parris of Cruise Entertainment."

"Captain Tyrekka, Copilot Jones," Tyrekka says. Handshakes are exchanged. "The pleasure is all mine," he continues with a sly grin while taking Bethany's hand; she smiles a bit wider than she would have liked, and bats her eyes without realizing it.

"Thank you, and please enjoy these gifts," Clancy says. With that, he and Bethany turn and walk back to the captain's launch. She sneaks a look over her shoulder and notices Tyrekka's eyes linger on her. She smiles again, then faces forward.

"Class act," Tyrekka says, and kneels and hoists up the carton of spare ribs. He raises his eyebrows. "Looks like we eat well this week, Jonsey."

Fifteen minutes pass as the Spaceport advises incoming vessels about being in temporary stasis, and closes its ceiling doors - with the exception, of course, of Dock 30. Just as captain's launch returns, the speakers on the bridge sound again. "*Emprasoria*, this is Supervisor Innoche again. We have cordoned off the area for you. The Port itself is secure. You are granted permission to ascend."

"Thank you, Mr. Innoche, and thanks to your staff."

"We all learned for the better. Have a good trip."

"Let us continue," Arges states to his crew, and he again takes his place in the command chair. The noise and rumble of the engines strengthen as the *Emprasoria* increases her thrust and resumes her launch.

"Ah, on our way once again," Enkel says smoothly with a smile. "Very nice." Passengers watch from windows and monitors, and Bethany is again in the observation lounge, this time watching with fingers crossed. The band which has now gone from '*Moon River*' to an instrumental version of '*Fly Like an Eagle*', goes back to '*Fly Me to the Moon*'. The Evies and Evans never once broke their hologram smiles, because for them, nothing had changed. Maddox breathes a subdued sigh of relief on seeing the image on the vidscreen move again, and move down – showing they were going up; he smiles to himself. Though the bridge staff is stressed from the near catastrophic incident, they nonetheless remain at their stations and do their duties, each silently praying for safety and good luck.

Eyes glued to a monitor, Rish keeps the captain abreast of the ascension status. "Ship is traveling through Troposphere. Mach speed attained. Now in Stratosphere. Mesosphere."

Rayburn keeps a close eye on the gravitometers. "Gravitationers are compensating for loss of terrestrial pull. Internal gravity field reads as normal," she reports.

"Operational programs running at best," DeMornay remarks.

"Passing through Thermosphere," Rish continues. "Trim is good." Holden increases thrust so that the ship will reach an optimum escape velocity. Blackness above the cloudy blue is clearly seen. "Entering Exosphere," Rish notes, then turns to the captain. "Suborbital flight complete. We are now clear of the atmosphere. The launch itself took eight minutes. Time is 1500 hours, 47 minutes." Log entries are made.

The bridge staff relaxes after the ship successfully reaches the vast expanse of outer space. In the distance, they see the endless starfield that is the Milky Way; millions of tiny white dots suspended in extraterrestrial darkness. There are the planets of their own solar system, and the gray Moon seems so close . . . just barely beyond the viewport. Closer still are various mechanical satellites floating in Earth-space, including news units which film their launch. On their right is the Galaxia Hotel lazily rotating in orbit, and from the hotel's Dennis Tito Lounge, named in honor of the worlds' first space tourist, people look with wonder at the bold new ship. To the left of Galaxia is the massive triple-sectioned Earth connector SolNet satellite. Beyond that is the UNINAS international space station, and farther still, surrounding all, is the ring of Distant Early Warning (DEW) watchers which provide alerts about incoming meteors or harmful anomalies.

"Tac, please shut down our base thrusters," Arges orders, and the flames emitting from these cones simultaneously wink out.

Controllers at Spaceport Alpha and UNINAS both call the ship. "Our GPS satellites track you as having safely exited the atmosphere. Confirm your situation please."

"All is well. Ship is safe and sturdy. Trim good. Ready to go forward," Escoto replies.

Just as Arges is about to give another order, a steward enters the bridge and approaches him with an envelope on a small silver tray. Arges opens this, and inside, written on the sheet of *Emprasoria*-crested paper are the following words:

"I expect us to reach our final destination in the

best time possible."
- D. Enkel

Arges reads the note and with a grim look passes it to Rish. "Have this posted on the control board, please," he says to his first officer, who reads it and gravely looks at Arges, then immediately tapes it where it can be easily seen by the pilot. Arges turns to Miasaki who is seated at the Astrocon, an array which provides cartography displays, gyrocompass reports and sextant readouts, and ship perception. Above this chart-table is the VeLoc screen which reads the speed and checks the course position of the vessel on a forty-minute mark, and next to that, the commutator, which shows the angle of the ship respective to the Earth. The chartsman is intently studying a three-dimensional map of the solar system on his vidscreen. "Mr. Miasaki, the coordinates please."

Miasaki clicks a button, and the display changes to a grid, again in three dimensions, where each line holds its own number, and clearly maps the space between the Earth, the Moon, and Mars. With another press, his pre-determined course appears and is superimposed as a bright red track across the projection. He raises his head and turns toward the Captain. "Trajectory 7-0, 0-5-0, 6-9-9-3, Sir."

"Bearing 7-0, 0-5-0, 6-9-9-3," Rish repeats. "Copy, Mr. Koehler."

"Course 7-0, 0-5-0, 6-9-9-3. laid in, Sir. D.E.W. ring reports all safe forward and surrounding for planetary egress."

"Confirmed," Miaskai agrees.

"Peter, please extend the airelons," Arges says from the chair.

"Yessir," Rish answers, then presses some buttons. Hyrdaulic gears neatly unfold the multitude of silver airelons from the sides of the hull. "Extended and ready, sir."

"Very good. Thank you." Arges next radios the E.O.C. "Tac, we're clear. Please activate the aft thrusters. Let's spread our wings. Full speed ahead. Steady as she goes."

"Exactly what I wanted to hear," Holden mutters with a smile, his eyes locked on the engines. "Yessir. All ahead full," the chief engineer says into the microphone, then excitedly pushes a heavy lever forward and lets the Mercurys go full force.

Immediately, power is routed to the stern, and the plasma-based propulsion motors rather than the hydrogen lift-rockets take control and the tailcones begin to spew fire. Holden watches with wide eyes as a speed intensity gauge climbs higher and higher. One bar-marker light is passed, then another….one-fifth power, one-quarter…..one-third….half power…..three quarters! They approach the red zone, and still the meter climbs. The vessel moves forward into the cold blackness of space, slipping its moorings from the invisible tug of the Earth gravity field and moving onward. The *Emprasoria* thus begins her ace run.

CHAPTER FIVE
The Stopover

Captain Arges sits for a few moments, making notes. "Peter, how is our speed?"

Rish consults a display screen and looks back to the captain. "Have achieved top speed and holding, Sir. Travelling at an average of one-fifty thousand kilometers, or point zero-zero one astronomical units, per hour."

Arges makes some mental calculations. "In that case, we should likely arrive at the Lunar Base in the neighborhood of three hours, give or take, wouldn't you say?"

"I believe that is a fair estimate," Rish replies with a nod.

Arges ponders outloud; "We were originally going to move at three-quarters power, but at this rate," he smiles, "that means we should make up for our lost time and arrive on schedule."

Rish nods. "Yes, Sir, that is correct – barring anything unforeseen."

"True enough." Arges turns to Escoto. "Roberta, could you advise Spaceport Beta that we will arrive on time, and if anything changes, we will advise."

"Yessir," she replies, then tunes her transmitter to the correct setting and begins typing.

Arges jots more notes and closes his folder, then pauses and looks up, out through the viewport at the extraterrestrial space in which they soar. Up here, it's different, and he is always glad to arrive. No matter how many times he has crested the atmosphere, there is always a certain sentiment that greets him, like an old friend. All this great splendor, and such wide-open expanse, limitless and exciting…..enchanting every time. It really gives a lot to ponder. Arges clicks the platform's middle monitor to provide a rear view as shown by the aft camera. There she is, Earth. Beautiful, turquoise and lime beneath the veil of swirling and light white clouds – perfect and round, like a swirled marble on a sheet of black velvet. Whenever he sees 'Old Bluey' from space, it somehow always brings everything into perspective for him.

After a minute, the captain rises from the command chair. "Mr. Rish, you have the con," he says as he steps from the platform and exits the bridge.

"Aye Sir," Rish replies as he slips into the seat.

A minute later and the captain is in his office. He is sitting at his oak desk, looking at the telephone. He slowly picks up his handset, hesitating at what he must do, but also knowing it is unavoidable. He dials Enkle's personafône. There is a first ring, then part of a second.

"Hello, Damien speaking."

"Mr. Enkel, are you able to talk?"

"Just a moment John." There is a pause, and Arges can hear the rustling of fabric, as though Enkel is holding his telephone against his suit jacket as he is walking. "Ok, go ahead. What in the hell happened?"

Arges gives a quick run-through of the occurrence. Enkel is initially infuriated that something should mar the prestige of the launch, until he learned the facts, then takes pride in the fact that <u>his</u> masterpiece had enough power to rip another ship from the ground. "Thank you for the call, John."

"Always good to speak with you, Damien. I'll email you a report within the hour."

"Thank you. So, we'll see you at dinner tonight?"

"Looking forward to it."

"See you then. Goodbye."

"Goodbye." Arges hangs up. It had not gone as badly as he anticipated. This done, he types a report, including the facts as presented by Holden, then emails it to Enkel, Syranos, and Phillips; the latter two being pleased as well - - pleased that a potential public relations disaster had been avoided.

With the email on its way, the captain retires to his cabin. A silver tray with a teapot and two cups is already there, waiting for him. He pauses, and looks up. How excellent... he thinks to himself. Our ace run for this fine new ship. Incredible. He sits at his desk, and begins to study readouts on his computer, then a knock comes to the door. Mildly irritated at having his thoughts interrupted, he speaks. "Yes?"

"It's me, John. Julius."

"Come in . . ."

Dr. Washington steps in. Smiling, Arges rises and greets him, shaking his hand firmly. "Good to see you, friend." Arges indicates the vacant chair next to his own as he again seats himself. "Care for some Morocco blend?" Arges asks.

"You know I could never turn that down," replies the doctor as he sits, unbuttoning his uniform jacket as he does so. "Well, here we are, on the first trip."

"Yes, I was just thinking the same thing. It's always a special feeling to give a new one the first stretch of her legs." Arges smiles broadly while passing the Doctor his cup.

"Thank you. You know, I envy you sometimes, John. All the power, the command . . ."

"The responsibilities, the schedules, the demands," Arges concludes, mildly chuckling. He takes a drink of his tea. "Only joking, of course. All in all, I love every minute of it."

"As I have known in the many years we have been friends."

"Thank you. But your 'hitch isn't so bad either, doctor."

"Aside from all the airsick passengers and imagined maladies." Now it is Washington's turn to laugh.

"There we go," Arges comments, joining in the laughter. The two relax and reminisce as the ship moves on.

Half an hour into the voyage, a tone is heard over the public address system, and those near any active monitors or televisions see Staff Captain Syranos smiling from the screen, and ready to make an announcement. "Ladies and Gentlemen, passengers of the *Emprasoria*, our maiden voyage has begun!" She says with an enthusiastic yet pleasant voice, then pauses a moment. "We hope you are enjoying yourselves. Our new ship has reached its cruising altitude, and is traveling onward perfectly." Another gentle pause. "You may have noticed a mild launch delay due to a slight traffic issue at the Spaceport." Her cheery explanation does not waver in its tone. "Rest assured, everything is well and we are keeping to our schedule. Our first visit will be to Spaceport Beta, and we expect to arrive by six o'clock. Thank you, and if there is anything we may do to make your voyage more pleasurable, remember we are always here to assist, and are only a touch away. Best wishes to you, and thank you for making the *Emprasoria* your carrier to the stars!"

After studying the wealth of the Royale class passengers, Maddox leaves the reception to see for himself if the B deck layout he has studied is identical to the actual ship itself. He exits the lounge through the back of the room, passing the grand staircase as he goes. Soon, he rounds a corner and enters an alcove. To his left, at the rear of the ship, is the medical complex and an elevator bay. Maddox walks through an open archway and enters an ornately styled lobby. On his right is the passenger communication center which permits passengers to send or receive ship-to-shore messages. The office is open twenty-four hours a day, and staffed by three of the eight communication technicians. Five cubicles offer privacy for passengers making personal interchanges. To his left is the photo studio, where the ship's photographer develops photos about life aboard the vessel. Embedded in each wall between the offices and the back of the room are three VacaBank (*the* Vacation Bank) automated teller machines which accept every bank- or major credit card and provide cash on command.

Maddox looks straight ahead and sees the 'treasure chest'. Across the back of the lobby is the Purser's Office. The massive desk spans the width of the room, and is manned all hours of day or night by three receptionists. On the far left of the oak wall behind the desk is a double-bolted black steel door. Maddox imagines what riches lie behind that door. In that room is the ship's vault and the safes which hold currency for the bank machines and the casino. The door opens for a moment, and his heart jumps at even a hint of access. This vanishes instantly when a uniformed security officer steps out. Yes, Officers stand between him and the "loot", one of many obstacles, but that just provides more excitement. Maddox smiles a wolfish grin. Soon . . . soon . . .

He takes another glance around the lobby. He spies something unexpected. What's this? Some sort of attraction in the middle of the room; other passengers are gathering around it. Maddox is curious. He walks toward what appears to be a rather small marble pillar with a clear glass top. As he nears, he can see something moving inside the glass enclosure. A blue bust, slowly spinning. Closer still, just as the bust turns to face him . . .

He stops dead in his tracks. His eyes grow large as saucers and his jaw drops in shock. THE HOPE DIAMOND! Realizing the image he must be presenting, he quickly coughs and runs his hand over his mouth and rapidly composes himself as he resumes his walk toward the display. He joins the small crowd around the pillar and watches with admiration and desire as the gleaming blue gem makes its revolving journey within its little glass domain. It captivates him. The incalculable value contained within that pendant . . . not to mention the sheer allure of the challenge in acquiring it.

Maddox reluctantly moves his eyes away from the Diamond and quickly surveys the surrounding area. First, he can easily see there is a clear line-of-sight from the Purser's Office to the pedestal. Not a good thing. He glances upward and spies a black plexiglass bowl fixed into the ceiling, not to hard to guess it holds a vidcam which looks directly down at the display. Another sore point. Then, the glass itself, which appears to be at least an inch thick and is certainly wired to an alarm system. A third element to contend with, but these merely make "the game" interesting.

Maddox backs away from the display, turns, and exits the lobby. Everything is exactly as the layouts say, and now, the Diamond. He is a very happy man indeed. Upon entering his suite, Maddox sees the burgundy bag with his luggage in the middle of the room. His smile grows, then he closes the door and goes to it. He kneels and unlocks the zipper, then partially opens the bag and inserts his forefinger. After a moment of probing, he finds the spot he is looking for and pushes the button on the small boxlike unit attached to the top of the interior and deactivates the scrambler which let him smuggle the special contents through the security checkpoints of the Los Angeles airport.

He completely opens the bag and takes from it a holstered .338 caliber Smith and Wesson handgun. He removes the long gunmetal blue pistol from its black leather holster and cradles the weapon in the palm of his right hand. It feels good there. He spins the revolver on his forefinger and catches the wooden handle in his palm, tightly clenching it. It feels very good. The smile widens and his eyes radiate with excitement. A knock comes to the door. Irritated, he thrusts the holster and gun back into the bag, hastily zips it closed, and tosses it into the luggage pile. "Yes?" he says as he stands and turns toward the door.

"It's me," replies a voice from the other side.

Maddox recognizes it and walks over. He opens the door, and takes a step back – there is a person looking almost identical to him standing there. Same height and build, same hair and eye color, a moustache though instead of a goatee. Maddox of course had been the one to think up the similar disguises, but to see a near twin of him standing there did give him pause for a second. Maddox steps to the side and Alex Parker, the senior member of his team and the one who

Maddox had first visited after seeing the christening on television, walks into the room. They nod hello, and Maddox quickly closes the door.

"Good to see you," Maddox says, and they shake hands.

"You as well. Everything ok?" Parker asks.

"Yeah, fine. You?"

"No problems. Ruby's down in our cabin, and she's ok. The others made it on too, I saw them personally."

"Great, glad to hear that," Maddox says with a smile and nod. Parker pauses a moment. "Hard to believe we're actually here, and that it's starting…."

"I had been thinking the same thing earlier. Yes, things are rolling that is for sure. No turning back, as they say."

"True enough. That launch thing was a bit of a scare."

Maddox rolls his eyes. "No kidding. I thought they might have to call the whole thing off at first, or the jig was up."

"Well, they recovered – and we're safe and sound." Parker pauses. "This disguise stuff takes a bit of getting used to though." Parker then runs his hand through his colored salt-and-pepper hair, and over his moustache.

"Yeah I know, but on the other hand, our real hair is just a spray away. I don't like it much either, but if we ever need a quick-change, you'll thank your lucky stars you have it." He pauses a moment. "Hiding in plain sight does have an intrigue to it." He winks.

"That it does. I just need to get comfortable with the look, that's all. Hey, mind if I?" Parker asks, indicating the bar. Maddox waves his permission. Parker goes over and pours himself a drink. "I think everything'll go fine."

"We'll see," Maddox responds, a bit irately. "But keep on your toes until the job's done." He hates it when his partners in crime expect an easy job. This tends to breed sloppiness, which can spell failure. Maddox always wants his cohorts alert and wary.

Parker nods appreciatively to the warning and sits down in an easy chair as he takes a drink of his rum and cola. He looks around the suite releases a long, slow breath in a whistle. "Boy, you guys have it made up here. Swanky."

"Yeah, it's all right," Maddox replies offhandedly. He sits himself on the edge of the coffee table, and looks at his partner in crime then smiles widely. "I made a discovery." Parker looks up, raises his eyebrows in curiosity. "The Hope Diamond is aboard."

Parker's face drops in shock. His mouth falls open, and the glass begins to slip from his hand before he quickly recovers and tightens his grip. "The Hope?" he says in bewilderment. He whistles again, longly, and one can see a spark in his eye. He grins wickedly. "What a surprise. I take it we will be modifying our agenda . . ."

"Goddamn right," Maddox replies with a chuckle. "The ace plan which became a double-down is now a triple crown."

Parker laughs. "Excellent. Hey, where are they keeping it?"

"It's in a display in the lobby, on a pillar inside a glass case."

"The lobby . . ." Parker's voice fades in thought.

Maddox sees where his partner is going and voices the conclusion. "Yes, a high traffic area, well secured, maybe thirty feet from the Purser's Office. It will be tough." Parker shakes his head, bemused.

Maddox sits back and looks at the floor as he thinks. His last comment was an understatement. It will be <u>very</u> tough. Practically impossible. The most obvious way will be to somehow replace the real gem with a fake, how can he get a counterfeit Hope Diamond out in the middle of space? If only he had known earlier, but obviously the Smithsonian and the Archangel Line had kept things quiet to prevent people like him from making plans. Well, it will be an interesting mind teaser to acquire the Diamond. Once he has safely returned to Earth with the jewel, he knows it will be easy to fence within a syndicate of 'no questions' collectors in the Orient.

But that will come later. He sits up and retrieves his precious bag, then begins rummaging through it. He sets each item on the coffee table as he withdraws it; his gun, its holster, a small, rectangular silver case, another handgun, a sheathed hunting knife, a small laptop computer, a medium-sized battery, a watch, and a roll of electrical tape. Lastly he takes a short, thin white cord. Parker sees this has a standard plastic connector tab on one end, yet where the other end should have a matching interface, a narrow silver needle with a sharp point protrudes in what appears to be a homemade modification.

With knife, computer, watch, cable, and tape in hand, Maddox goes to the sofa. He lifts one end with his free hand, and heaves it aside. He kneels at the now exposed area and rests his tools on the floor. He unsheathes his knife. His eyes and forefinger follow an imaginary sightline along the floor; calculating, estimating. Yes, this should be it, right about here . . . he plunges the long blade into the plush carpeting. It enters smoothly. He cuts a large rectangular hole and removes the patch to reveal a section of the beige plastic floor. The floor itself consists of several long rectangular panels. Maddox jams his knife into the seam of two panels at a corner. His muscles tense and a strained look comes over his face as he pushes down on the handle. The seam begins to split. He pushes harder and pries the corner loose with a loud crack. The other three corners get the same as Parker watches. Maddox sets his somewhat damaged knife down and lifts the panel to sees exactly what he expects.

Parker peers over his leader's shoulder. He sees a row of seven multi-colored cables. The white cable in the center is thicker than the others. Maddox reaches over and grabs the watch, then reads the time. He smiles; it is almost ready. Maddox had activated the watch and set its time at noon six hours before the ship had been christened. This is the time that the main computer would have first come on-line. Every four hours from that moment, the CPU would conduct a diagnostic local area system network check lasting under five minutes. The next scheduled check will be occurring in about the next two minutes. Maddox primes the alarm on the watch.

Using his knife again, he slips the blade under the white middle cable, raises it, and leaves it propped up. Beep beep! The watch-alarm sounds; he knows time is of the essence now. With his free hand, Maddox quickly grabs his special cable, holding the needle-tip between his thumb and forefinger. With the precision of a surgeon he pierces through the thick rubber insulation and into the wire itself. He grits his teeth in tension, but his hand remains steady. He carefully inspects the junction and makes sure the needle has not gone all the way through, then seals this crude union within a cone of electrical tape. Next, he connects the terminal end of the cable into the laptop. The process takes under a minute to complete.

Maddox attaches the computer power cord to the battery then flips the laptop cover open. The laptop has already been synchronized to the *Emprasoria*'s application program. He looks at his watch and pauses as he does a mental countdown as the seconds tick past. At an exact moment, he takes a deep breath which he holds in suspense as his forefinger slides the power switch to the 'ON' position. There is an instantaneous boot-up and the screen fills with a status report on the *Emprasoria*. Maddox releases the breath and smiles. Success! He has tapped into the main computer! This, of course, puts him in a decidedly advantageous position given his task. Beep beeeeeep says the watch, then it falls silent.

A technician on the bridge notices a mild interference on a vidscreen as Maddox performs his handiwork. He notes it occurs during a sweep, and tiny glitches are common during those times. He ignores the problem when it quickly corrects itself and does not make any record of the disturbance, or inform anyone of it. The *Emprasoria*'s mainframe network tracks passenger use of the in-suite and lobby computer consoles and monitors SolNet downloads with sophisticated virus filters. However, Maddox did not try to log-in or break into the network, and his relatively simple 'tapping' acts as solely an information reader of the system does not trigger any alarms. As well, since the infolink is only being shunted through his laptop, and is not interfered with, it will not register as a problem during routine system checks. Only a detailed check-and-cross-check would detect a parasite such as his, and he would be aware of that happening before it occurs. His spying of the central processing unit should pass undetected.

An impressed Parker returns to his seat. "Good work, boss!" Maddox lies the laptop out flat, tosses the knife, tape and watch toward his bag, then moves the sofa back into place. This piece of furniture effectively hides his invasion into the ship's onboard control system.

"Wasn't bad, eh?" Maddox says. "So now we are voyeurs. WE can know what they know anytime." He sits back in the sofa and runs a hand through his hair as he lets out a long sigh.

"Check with the others in a few hours, one at a time," Maddox instructs Parker. "Make sure they're ok, and that they have all their gear. Remind them never to be seen together in public outside of their assigned couples. No visits to each other. No calls to one another either. Anything they have questions about, they go through me."

"Gotcha," Parker says as he rises from his chair. He returns his empty glass to the bar and strides to the door. "I'll see you later," he remarks as he leaves.

"Yeah, later," Maddox quietly calls after the form exiting his room.

Now in solitude, he has time to ponder and relax. His high-stakes caper has now become a colossal heist, a 'big score' that will go down in history. It might even rank as a "Crime of the Century". Just like the Newton Brothers' Rondout Train robbery, Tony Pino and The Brinks Job, Bruce Reynolds' legendary Great Train Robbery, the burglary of the American Museum of Natural History by Jack 'Murf the Surf' Murphy, Albert Spaggiari's Nice raid, Jimmy 'The Gent' Burke's Lufthansa-JFK heist, the Martin Cahill art-raid on Russborough House, or Jenniveve Patricks' embezzlement of Worldwide Insurance. All 'Robin Hoods' of the post-modern era, antiheroes revered, awed, admired with an odd fascination by a curiously adoring public. And, if all goes well, he too can enter this rogues gallery of criminal infamy, albeit under an alias. His bit of dirty business does allure, that is for sure. A long sigh. The Hope Diamond of all things! Like grabbing the Mona Lisa or a Shakespeare manuscript! Utterly amazing. Smiling, Maddox stretches out on the sofa and lets himself drift to sleep.

After the Reception ends, Dade goes to his stateroom as well. He is wearing a smile, firm in the belief that the cruise holds a lot of promise - - enough to fulfill his high expectations. Dade is that rare breed of man who pursues happiness to its highest degree, and lets nothing stand in his way in his quest for a good time. His extended hours of steadfast work over the years, combined with wise and lucrative investments, have placed him in a highly comfortable situation. So he can take time here and there to experience a long, illustrious exercise in leisure . . . parties, vacations, exciting times . . . the social scene is key among Dade's priorities. Like F. Scott Fitzgerald and Errol Flynn before him, he lives tempestuously during "off" times and holds no regrets. Not that Dade is an unruly carouser, rather, he has the exquisite quality of mixing a wild desire for amusement with an air of refined dignity, much the same way that gin and vermouth are beautifully blended in the perfect martini.

Once inside his room, Dade unpacks his luggage and gets settled. He tosses his empty suitcases into the closet, save for one. He opens the false-bottom of this bag and turns off a scrambler unit, then removes a small silver pistol and two ammunition clips from the custom made form-crafted case. He loads the gun and tosses it and the spare clip into the top dresser drawer. One can never be too careful, you know. The suitcase joins the others in the closet, and he leaves. He makes his way to the forward observation lounge for a drink and some companionship. Both come easily.

With the astral engines operating at their maximum level, the ship enters the vicinity of the Moon three hours after departing Earth. During that period, at four o'clock, she completes her first quadric-hour status check with Spaceport Alpha.

"*Emprasoria* calling Spaceport Alpha, come in Alpha."

"Controller Riggs at Spaceport Alpha, go ahead *Emprasoria.*"

"Hello Mr. Riggs, we're filing our initial q-h check."

"Roger that. Proceed."

She clicks some keys and the following information appears on a readout. 'A.L. *Emprasoria.* Captain J.S. Arges. USA/CA/LA, Hull S/N: J-2 NCC-1314. Location: Quadrant 1. En route to Moon/Spaceport Beta. Condition Excellent.' Next follows a thorough list of system reports.

"Confirmed, *Emprasoria*, we have it. Thank you."

"You as well. *Emprasoria* out."

As the *Emprasoria* approaches the moon, she decelerates. Since Spaceport Beta, that being the port at the lunar north pole, has no dock large enough to accommodate a ship the size of the *Emprasoria*, the vessel will orbit the moon for the duration of her stay there. Shuttles from ports across the lunar surface will ferry additional passengers, their luggage, and cargo from the biosphere regions to the hovering liner.

As the first shuttle approaches the vessel from the stern, its pilot radios the bridge. "*Emprasoria*," she says, "this is the shuttlecraft Southampton. My passengers request that I be permitted to circle your ship in order to fully see it."

Escoto asks Rish, then responds. "Roger, Southampton. One pass before docking."

"Affirmative. One pass. Thank you." The pilot and passengers become excited as they hear the message - - a close look at the new ship will be a special and unexpected treat.

The pilot guides the shuttle up from the underside and slowly moves closely along the starboard hull of the vessel. The Southampton passengers can easily see the *Emprasoria* guests at their windows, raising drink-filled glasses in silent toasts to the shuttlecraft. The tiny ship next moves across the bow and then back to the tailfin along the port side. The size and grandeur of the *Emprasoria* is breathtaking - - she is so, so beautiful. The shuttle rounds the aft exhaust cones and its pilot sees the docking brackets hanging from the keel, awaiting the arrival of the Southampton.

In order for the *Emprasoria* to take on passengers or supplies in situations like this, the midship cargo bay had been especially designed to accommodate small shuttlecraft. When necessary, the bottom doors of this bay open downward. Then, four brackets, two front and two back, are lowered on tracks inlaid in the doors. The shuttle then secures itself via magnetic clamps within the assembly, which raises the craft into the ship. After the doors have closed, the bay re-pressurizes and crewmembers enter to assist passengers, remove cargo, and otherwise attend to the shuttle. The average turnaround time for a visiting ship is ten minutes. This feature is unique to the *Emprasoria*, and makes things extremely convenient for interspace deliveries.

When the other shuttles see the first of their member circling the *Emprasoria*, each of them desire the same privilege. The bridge agrees, and each craft takes the same route around the ship in turn. Bethany Parris and other members of the cruise entertainment staff are stationed in the bay to direct passengers to the elevators, and two are in each of the two lifts to guide people to the proper decks. Lunar passengers either join the reception with their Earthling predecessors, or are given a fruit basket and wine, depending on their booking.

At moonbase Mount Caramel, there is a slight delay. The line to board a shuttle is moving along well when a well dressed brunette approaches the registration desk. Smiling, she passes her ticket to an equally smiley hostess, who takes it, reads it, and looks up. "Hello Ms. Marlow, welcome to Archangel," she says. The passenger nods and the hostess scans the card's barcode. A few seconds pass, then a mild look of concern comes over the hostess' face after reading her monitor, then she runs the ticket again over the scanning device and is given the same information. She scans it a third time, and still not satisfied, reaches for her telephone.

"Is anything wrong?" Miss Marlow asks; a look of annoyance flashes across her deep brown eyes.

The hostess looks at her, smile wide and lipstick bright. "Just a glitch, I'm sure."

Both the passenger and hostess can sense the irritation in the line of people behind them. "Just a moment please," the hostess says, then turns slightly away from the passenger and speaks into the telephone. "Hi Bob, this is Josie down at the Archangel check-in…." A security man looks in the direction of the reception desk. The passenger turns to the man behind her and shrugs in a 'beats me what's going on' way, and he nods sympathetically, while silently praying he does not have to go through the same delay once it is his turn at the desk. As she turns back to the desk, she has noticed the attention of the security officer.

The hostess hangs up the telephone and faces the waiting passenger. "I apologize Ms. Marlow, if you could;" the passenger tenses, then the hostess rolls her eyes in embarrassment. "I mean, I am very sorry for the delay." She turns back to her computer and scanner. "Ok, we'll try this one more time...." With the passenger watching her eagle-eyed, she runs the ticket over the scanner and.....a smile comes to the hostess' face and she brightens. "All ready!" she says and passes the ticket over. "Thank you for your patience and understanding." Brenda Marlow nods as she takes the ticket. "Quite alright. These things happen. Life with these *modern* conveniences...."

"Thank you, and have a pleasant flight!"

Brenda nods, then walks off. She adjusts the brown leather purse on her shoulder as she walks up the boarding ramp with a firm hold on her boarding pass. She takes a window seat, and sits back as her fellow passengers enter the shuttle. Soon, the door to the craft is being sealed shut and the flight attendant is activating the Safety Awareness video, then they are off. They fly, with her seeing the gray cratered moonscape she knows so well below, and the surrounding darkness...then...ahead....a great white vessel; the *Emprasoria*.

Brenda likes the quick fly-by of the ship, this is quite the piece, but she does not completely relax until the shuttle has docked and she has stepped into the liner. Her ticket is verified again, this time without any calls to 'Bob', and she is welcomed aboard. "Hello there, how was your flight to us?" asks a woman in a blue cruise uniform.

"Went alright thank you," Brenda answers.

"Glad to hear it. My name is Bethany, and I with cruise entertainment. Do you know how to find your suite?"

"Yes, thank you, I took a look at the deck map beforehand. The elevators are this way?" Brenda asks, indicating a corridor with a tilt of her head.

"Yes, just ahead on your left," Bethany answers.

"Thank you."

"If I or anyone may be of help, please call on us." Bethany smiles.

"Seems like quite the palace from the outside."

"Icing on the cake, as they say," says Bethany. "It's all here for you to enjoy!"

"Thank you, I'll see you later." Brenda nods and begins to make her way to the elevators.

"Oh, Miss?" Bethany comments, and Brenda pauses.

"Yes?"

"I couldn't help noticing your perfume, it is very nice."

Brenda smiles with that easy smile someone gets when complimented. "Thank you. It's Parisienne Peaud by Chanel."

"Is it new?"

"Yes, actually I was lucky and got an advance bottle – the real launch should be in a few weeks or so."

"Ah, I see. Well, it is very pleasant."

"Thanks again." Brenda moves on, and Bethany makes a mental note of the perfume name, then turns her attention to the next passenger in line.

Along the way, Brenda Marlow brushes her way past a few smiling V.I.P. holograms, then finds her suite easily and opens the door. She enters and looks around as the door closes; it seems a bit dark in there.

"I like you better as a blonde."

She jumps, startled, then relaxes and slumps against the wall on recognizing the voice. She puts her hand to her chest and Angelique Yusacre, alias 'Brenda', takes a deep breath. "Boy, you know how to put a fright in someone!"

Maddox laughs in the shadows.

"Anybody ever tell you how to greet a person?"

The chuckles continue. "Yeah, sure, but surprise has its value." He clicks on the lamp next to the easy chair where he sits and now has a better view of her. She stands from the wall and sets her brown bag down. She looks great; slender and svelte, a round bustline with the slightest hint of yummy cleavage, pouty lips, dazzling eyes; as good as the last time he laid eyes on her, which was some while ago.

"Ahhhh, the goatee… looks sexy," she remarks with a grin.

He runs his fingers over the false whiskers. "I've been getting used to it."

"What's with the grey in the hair though?"

Maddox shrugs. "Just another diversion." He takes a small silver tube canister from his pocket and sprays his hair with colorspray remover. A minute later he runs his fingers through his natural color. "Better?" he asks.

"Much."

"Thank you. Did you have any trouble getting in?" He takes a drink of soda water.

"Bit of a stall at the boarding gate, but nothing bad – just a scan glitch." The comment gets a nod from Maddox, then she turns away from him and looks at the suite. "Very nice," she says admiringly.

"Yes, they know how to dress it up well," he replies.

She turns back to him. "So, quite a party you have planned...."

Maddox nods. "Glad you could join us."

"Thanks for the invite." She takes a step toward him and smiles coyly. "So, blonde is it?" Maddox nods again. She slips her hand into her bag and removes a small, narrow silver canister identical to the one Maddox had moments earlier. She sets it to reverse, then brings it to the back of her neck and holds down the button. There is a suction-hiss as she runs the canister over her head, allowing it to pull the artificial colorant out. In an instant, and she is natural once again. She shakes her silky blonde hair free; the curled tips tumble down around her face as she drops the can to the floor. Now it is his turn to smile admiringly. He takes another drink of the clear, bubbly soda. "Gentlemen prefer blondes."

"Gentlemen, rogues, or even scoundrels as the case may be."

"Good comeback."

"Plenty more where that came from."

"That so?" she asks. He nods. "So, mister smooth talker, if I were to ask if we were on schedule, what sort of sly reply would that bring?"

"Dead on."

"Good to hear."

"I have a another surprise for you, too."

"Better to hear," she says with a grin.

"We have an extra item to go after." She looks at him, the question evident in her eyes. "There's a trinket in the lobby. The Hope Diamond is aboard."

She takes a step back. "The Hope...." she whispers, then becomes lost in thought. After a moment, she looks up at him with a mischievous twinkle in her eye. "Diamonds are a girl's best friend, natch." She smiles.

Maddox grins in retort. "I thought you would see it that way." He takes another drink of soda and rises from the chair. "So glad my Number One made it on during the Moonstop, as planned. Last, but not least." He winks. "Want to go check it out?"

"Sure. Let me unwind for a minute, freshen up, that sort of thing."

"Ok, no real hurry. By the way, that's a nice perfume you're sporting."

"Thanks, it's new – I've been getting compliments on it all day." She retrieves her bag, and heads toward the bedroom, then stops and turns to him. "Oh, Russ…" He gives her a look that slices the air and silently raises his forefinger, catching her in mid-phrase. She takes a breath, and begins again. "Pardon me. I mean, Kurt, how are the others?"

"They are all fine."

"Good," she answers, then turns and continues into the room.

A short while later, Maddox and his chief female partner appear in the corridor at their suite, their hair looking brown again thanks to the insta-color spray. They make the necessary observations of the lunar Royale arrivals, as does the Lothario-like Dade. Then Maddox and Yusacre visit the lobby, where her eyes reflect the glimmer of the Diamond.

All in all, the *Emprasoria* remains at the moon for one hour. During this time, some photographs are taken of her, and the news satellites are able to obtain excellent footage. The lunar ferrying proceeds well, and after the last shuttle exits the docking brackets, Rish takes the microphone. "Beta, this is First Officer Rish of the *Emprasoria* calling."

"Hello Mr. Rish, this is Controller Jarr, go ahead."

"The last ferry has departed us and is returning to the lunar surface. We are ready to break our hover and continue on."

"Understood Sir. Can you give us a system reading before departing?"

"I'll have it relayed to you now."

"Thank you." Down at the spaceport, Jarr studies a readout which appears on his monitor. "I am in receipt of your systems checks. Your vessel is top-notch."

"Excellent, that's the way we like it."

"Please feel free to exit, there is no traffic inbound or outbound in your vicinity. Have a good flight. Beta out."

"Thank you, Controller Jarr. We will proceed momentarily. *Emprasoria* out."

Rish changes his communicator to another channel. "Captain, Beta gives us a clean bill of health. We're ready to go anytime."

"Thank you Peter. Looks like we made good time on the ferrying. Let's continue."

"Very good, sir." From the command chair, Rish issues the necessary orders, and the ship pulls away from her lunar orbit and begins the voyage to her final destination: Mars.

From his suite, the musician Peter Bull looks out through the large window of his verandah, his gaze fixed on the moon as the ship departs. "I wonder what Waters and Gilmour would have thought of this…." he says absently.

"Sorry, what?" Myrie says. She relaxing in the sitting room as he spoke; she gets up from the sofa and joins him in the verandah. She rests her hand on his back and he turns his head to her.

"I was saying I wonder what Roger Waters and David Gilmour would have though of this, to actually see first-hand the dark side of the moon." He turns back to the shadowed part of the gray orb. "That was one of Pink Floyd's top albums, and I was just thinking what those guys would have thought if they could have looked at what inspired the album."

Myrie wraps her arms around his waist and rests her head on his shoulder. "Makes you think, that's for sure."

"Yeah." Bull pauses, and turns to her again. "You know, in the spirit of the occasion, I think I'll play that album."

"Sounds good," she says with a smile. "Shall I call-up 'The Wizard of Oz' on the tv?"

Bull smiles widely. "Sure, why not? That synchronicity is wild."

Within ten minutes, Myrie has ordered the film to their television through cine-quest, and a steward has delivered to their door the compact-disc Bull requested from the ship's library. With two glasses of wine and the bottle chilling in a pail nearby, and a bowl of flavored popcorn, the two snuggle on the sofa. "Ready?" Bull asks.

"Ready!" Myrie replies, then kisses him quickly on the cheek and settles down into the soft cushions of the sofa. Bull smiles and hits the film-play button on the remote control, then poises his finger above the stereo buttons on the remcon. Leo the MGM lion makes his third roar, then Bull mutes the television audio and drops his finger on the music-play button and the opening credits begin to roll to the heartbeats and ticking of *Speak to Me.*

"Buckle in for a wild ride, babe."

As the two enjoy their film and music experience, those on the bridge prepare to extend the ship's sight. "Please activate the long range radar," Rish orders. Up until this point, they have been using short range because this is the most effective between Earth and moon.

The pilot presses a button as he directs his gaze to the Board, then looks quizzically at a monitor. He presses the button again, then a third time. He turns to the first officer. "The long range radar does not seem to be operating, Sir."

"What?" says a bewildered Rish as he walks from the command platform to the console. He joins the pilot in looking at the radar vidscreen. The short range radar operates perfectly. They can see a graphic top-down display of the *Emprasoria* with four white rings encircling it. However, when they attempt to switch over to long range, the screen fills with static. "This system was operational before," Rish remarks in a frustrated tone as he repeatedly presses the LONG RANGE button. "Well, it's not now," he finally says, admitting defeat. "Krystal, can I see you here please?" Rish asks over his shoulder. A moment later and the Cybernetics Officer is by his side. "We can't seem to get the long range radar on-line."

A puzzled look comes over her face as DeMornay looks at the vidscreen. She extends a red cord from a tapered silver compulink gauntlet worn on her left forearm and connects this to an outlet on the command board and soon a readout appears on a small screen embedded within the bright silver of the armband. She studies the display, making entries and sending queries by pushing small buttons adjacent to the mobile viewer using her right hand. After a moment, she looks up at Rish. "Not a problem with the screen up here," she says. "My first guess is that it's not getting a signal feed to display."

"No feed..." Rish echoes. "you're sure?" She nods her reply. Rish turns his back to the main viewport. "Please remain in short range until further orders."

"Aye, Sir," answers the pilot while switching back.

Rish returns to the chair with DeMornay following. "Looks like we have our first malfunction – our cherry's been broken," he jokes with a chuckle. She laughs, then as they reach the chair he takes the microphone from the armrest and calls the E.O.C. "Engineering, this is Officer Rish."

"Yes, Mr. Rish. Chris Corté here."

"Hello, Chris. We've encountered a problem with the long range radar. It refuses to operate. Krystal reports everything on this end is fine, and it appears as though there's a problem with the signal origin. Please investigate and advise us."

"We'll see to it right away."

"Thank you. Bridge out."

Rish and DeMornay exchange nods and the yeoman makes entries into the log. Rish crosses his arms across his chest and stares out the viewport, contemplating his predicament. The maximum area the short range radar can monitor is ten miles around the ship, whereas long range can scan a seven mile radius. It can be dangerous running at full speed outside the Earth-Moon corridor with on only short range. Rish considers slowing the vessel down, until he spies the note he posted on the Board. It stares back at him ominously. 'I EXPECT US TO REACH OUR FINAL DESTINATION IN THE BEST TIME POSSIBLE.' He cocks an eyebrow and this scrap of paper makes the decision for him. "Put the short range on its maximum scan. Steady as she goes, Mr. Koehler." The ship plows on into the night.

As the passengers enjoy themselves in the early hours of the cruise, and the intercom tone on the bridge sounds.

"Bridge, E.O.C. calling. Engineer Holden here."

"Tac, this is Alyssa," Second Officer Rayburn replies into the chair microphone, having relieved Rish after his watch. "Go ahead."

"Hello, Alyssa. I'm afraid I don't have good news. We discovered the problem with the long range radar – the signal repeaters blew because of a short circuit during the attempted activation."

"I see. How long will it take to repair them?" Rayburn inquires.

"That's another problem. They are burned beyond repair, and we don't seem to have any spare long range repeaters aboard - - we're supposed to, but don't. The pieces in the L-R repeater drawer were actually extra S-R ones. We checked the S-R drawer, and they were all S-R as well. So, we have a wealth of short range, and none of L-R. We'll either have to wait until we reach Mars, or requisition some from the Archangel warehouse in California and wait for them to be delivered to Beta."

Rayburn considers the situation. Of course, the rules of safety dictate that they return to the moon, wait for the delivery, then make repairs. However, to do that will use hours of valuable time, and likely anger Mr. Enkel. "Christian," Rayburn begins, checking with the astrogator, "what sort of route do we have ahead?"

"The path I have chosen is direct and quite clear," Miasaki answers. "No obstructions; no need to divert around satellites or spacestations. It is the most efficient and quickest way there. We should be on 'the straight and narrow' as they say for the whole voyage."

"I see." She nods. "Thank you." She then summons Cybernetics Officer DeMornay. "Krystal, do you see any issues with putting the short range radar on a max-scan for the voyage?"

DeMornay pauses. "Well, none that I can reasonably expect. They should not affect any programs or computer systems; it will of course run through a lot of S-R repeaters. I could also put a highly-sensitive thermal check on the wiring and relays down there to let us know the minute that there is even a hint of an overheating."

Rayburn nods again. "Thank you." She again thinks about the situation; given the choice of running at minimal risk, or facing the legendary wrath of the Man, she decides to acquire the repeaters at Mars. She radios Rish's quarters. "Peter, I need to talk with you about something…" then, she briefs him on the situation and consults him.

"I agree with your decision," he says finally.

"Thank you," she answers, then ends their call and contacts Holden. "Tac, we will continue on to Mars. Once there, please requisition twenty L-R repeaters from our supply depot. As for now, we will set the S-R radar on maximum scan and use them to their limit. See if you can repair the wiring and perhaps bypass the burned areas and somehow activate the system."

"We've already rewired the damaged section of the system, Alyssa. I'll have my team experiment and see what we can do. We'll try our very best and give all we can."

"Thank you, Tac."

"My pleasure. And, also, mild electrostatic singeing has started in the byproduct damper of the fourth fuel cell. No danger though, it's contained and under control. We're watching it."

"Very well, Tac. Keep us informed. Bridge out." Rayburn switches the intercom off. "Pilot, please set the short range radar to its maximum range. Tight fix."

Buttons are pressed, adjustments made. "Yes Ma'am. Max range set. Sharp watch."

The second officer turns to the yeoman. "Please make the necessary log entries."

The ship moves onward. She is nearsighted and suffers from mild heartburn, but is otherwise in exceptionally fine condition.

CHAPTER SIX
Days of Splendor, Nights of Magic

"My my my, look at all this fun!" Lauraleigh Roggin says while reading the *Tour Itinerary* booklet. She admires the leather covers, the heavy stock on which it is printed, the exciting and bright photos, as well as the gold cord which serves as a binding. She is sitting on the edge of her bed, and kicks her shoes free from her stockinged feet. "Sweetheart, the Captain's Ball is tonight!"

Edwin is at the desk in their sitting room, logging in to SolNet. He does not hear her at first, being intent on trying to access his corporate website to download his email files. "What's taking so long! Come on!" he says in a rough but quiet tone.

"Edwin, did you hear me?" she calls from the room. "They're starting off by having a gala this evening."

"Very nice," Edwin replies absently, clearly having not heard a word of what she said. Lauraleigh appears at the doorway and spies him sitting in front of the computer. Annoyed at first, a playful grin appears and she tiptoes into the room. She creeps up to him, he not noticing nor sensing a single motion. She comes closer and closer, and he remains fixed on the readout. "These guys are failures at ultra-speed downloads," he mutters to himself.

Suddenly, she pounces. From behind, she wraps her arms around him in a big bear hug, pinning him to his chair. He jumps, startled, and turns his head to his right. He relaxes an instant later. "Yeah, yeah, ok you got me," he says with a chuckle.

She kisses his ear with a loud smack. "I want you to listen to me, mister…" she says, then takes his earlobe between her teeth and gently nibbles.

"Yes dear, I'm listening;" his smile widens.

Her tongue joins in, toying with the lobe between soft nips, then she pulls back, and opens the Itinerary booklet which she carried in her left hand, holding it so both she and her husband can see it. She rests her head on his shoulder and begins talking softly as she reads. "Tonight they are holding a formal dinner dance in the White Feather dining salon, hosted by the captain."

"Excellent," Edwin replies as his eyes play over the words. "I can hardly wait." She playfully jabs him in the ribs, causing an 'umph!' from him, and he recoils with an equal level of candor.

"Funny, funny Edwin. We're going to go, and once you get there, you know you'll enjoy yourself, just like always."

"True. Yes, you are right, I complain, but once it gets started I like it." He tries to turn toward her but she keeps him pinned in the chair as she flips through the other pages of the booklet. "They've got all kinds of exciting things to do. And you, Sir, are going to take some time to relax and enjoy yourself." He takes a breath to protest when she darts her finger forward and switches off the computer.

"*Bayyyyybbbbeeeeeee!*" he complains. "It was just about done downloading. Come on, I just want to check my email."

"No can do." She hugs him tighter and kisses his cheek. "No work, no kids, nothing but you, me, and this amazing ship to play in."

"I never could say no to you, sweetie," Edwin answers, relinquishing when he knows he cannot possibly win. He gives her a quick kiss on the lips. "It does sound entertaining, actually."

"That's the spirit!" She tightens her hold on him quickly for a hug, then releases him. Lauraleigh turns and is about to go back to the bedroom when Edwin slyly slips his arm across the front of her hips and pulls her into his lap. "What do we have here?" she says with a smile while putting her arms around his neck.

"Just showing how I like you." He grins. "This vacation will be great, and I am glad to be here with you." He begins to nuzzle her neck, and she bunches and giggles.

"Well, looks like we're fully underway," Damien Enkel says, beaming with pride. He makes this statement in front of the large and angled front windows of his palatial suite, at the forefront of the Royale deck, a massive sanctus sanctorum beneath the forward observation lounge fittingly named "Celesticus". It is the largest stateroom on the vessel, where he can live like a King – and his wife like a Queen. "Clear on through until Gamma."

"That is good to know," Anne replies while walking to him. She slips her arm around the back of his waist and rests her head on his shoulder, then looks out to enjoy the view. "It will be smooth sailing I am sure, dear."

"With that vote of confidence, I am sure we will go beyond well." He smiles and kisses her gently.

"Good afternoon everyone, this is Staff Captain Syranos," the friendly female voice says over the public address system – from his room and the embrace, Edwin looks up, annoyed. "We are beginning our flight to Mars, and as required by Interspace Travel regulations, we will be holding a lifecraft drill in five minutes." Syranos anticipates the groaning coming from the various passenger areas, even though she cannot hear them from her office. "When the tone sounds, please report quickly to your assigned lifecraft station on B deck. Our crew will be pleased to assist you, and answer any questions. The entire drill will be done as quickly as possible. We thank you for your understanding."

Bethany Parris and the other crew perk up on hearing the announcement. She double-checks her role on her infokeeper as she makes her way to her lifecraft duty area. "Hope it goes smooth," she whispers to herself. This single task, the safety drill, should be the only distraction from the passengers' pleasured lifestyle. Taking less then half an hour overall, it is relatively easy, yet tends to be the activity which brings the most complaints from the passengers.

"At least they get this nuisance out of the way early," Cal Gregg comments.

"They all have to do it, all the ships," his wife answers. "Just one of those things."

"True."

"Once it's over, there's nothing ahead but pure, unadulterated pleasure."

"Sounds good." He gives her a wink. Cal then presses a button on his personafône and says, "V.I.P." Instantly, the Evie and Evan holograms appear. Cal looks approvingly at the female pass-assister and grins slightly.

"Hello, Mr. Gregg," Evan says.

"How may we help you?" Evie asks.

"The way to our lifecraft?" inquires Gregg.

"The best way is to take an elevator up to B deck, then down a starboard corridor to number 45," Evie offers. "Let me send a path diagram to your personafône screen."

Gregg looks down a moment later to see a route mapped out for him. "Thank you," he says with a smile.

"Our pleasure!" Evie says cheerfully, then the two disappear.

"Mmmm, if only to live in a cyberworld," Gregg comments, and his thoughts drift.

"Our chance to see the lifecraft, perfect," Maddox says, eyes raised, after hearing Syranos. He looks to Angelique. "Holed away in those compartments, they can be hard to get at."

"I can imagine," Angelique replies.

Precisely five minutes after Syarnos had ended her announcement, a tone begins to sound through the ship. It repeats in doubles, and is a relatively placid 'bong' sound rather than a blaring siren or some squawking klaxon. '*Attention, attention. Please report to the lifecraft deck*,' says a calm, computerized female voice over the speakers. The message is then repeated in cycles of three. Evacuation maps in each stateroom and every public area showing the directions to the lifecraft stations brighten, being backlit. Evies and Evans appear in the corridors to direct people and answer questions. Rish clicks on a stopwatch and begins counting the seconds as he walks from the bridge to B deck.

Stewards and stewardesses walk the hallways in the hotel area while security officers and cruise entertainment staffers make themselves available in the entertainment decks and at the lifecraft stations. Passengers appear from their rooms and mill in the passageways, then file up to B deck in an orderly fashion, where lifecraft shuttles line the corridors. Soon the corridors surrounding the lifecrafts are lined with people. Once it has been determined that each passenger has arrived at a lifecraft station, the tone and automated announcement ends, and Rish clicks off his stopwatch. He lifts and inter-ship phone and dials the Command Platform. "Arges," the captain says after the second ring.

"Peter here, John."

"Yes, how did the drill go?"

"Very well. Twenty minutes, twenty-seven seconds."

"Quite acceptable."

"Thank you, I agree. I will have a report ready for yourself and the Purser within the hour."

"Excellent."

A forward compartment is opened for passengers to see the interior of a lifecraft, and a simulated launch of this craft is done as well for passengers to acquaint themselves with the mini-vehicles. Maddox and his team pay particular attention to both actions.

"Thank you, everyone," Syranos says over the speakers after the compartment is re-sealed. "Our safety drill has been completed with great success! Enjoy the rest of the afternoon, and we will see you at dinner!" The passengers disperse from the B deck, to return to their cabins or explore the ship.

In the early evening, Captain Arges stands in front of his mirror, putting the final touches on his black bow tie. Once finished, he steps back for a full view. He gives a tug to his dress uniform jacket, and smoothes its lapels. "All set," he says, then walks into the sitting room of his Quarters. He checks the time on his wristwatch while picking up his officer's cap. While he does not enjoy the blatant 'schmoozing' when there is work to be done, he does have a particular preference for the Captain's Ball; there is good food, it is relaxed, and a good chance to acquaint himself with the passengers.

Arges puts on his cap and leaves his cabin, locking the door behind him. Minutes later he is on the bridge. "Everything ok?" he asks while entering.

"Yes, fine sir," Second Officer Rayburn says while rising from the command chair, she looks at him approvingly for a moment. Arges looks around the room. "Good to hear. Well, I'll be down in the Royale if you need me. Have a good night."

"Thank you, and you as well John," she says. Arges nods, then turns on his heel and leaves. After waiting a minute, Rayburn turns to Escoto at the communications center, jokingly fanning her face while the communications officer mouths 'wow' in response. "He always looks so good in the dress whites."

"That's for sure, Alyssa," Escoto replies. "Very good looking." She turns back to her console as Rayburn seats herself, each entertaining private thoughts.

Continuing unawares, Arges soon arrives in the Halo lounge where he finds Rish, Hearst, Syranos, Varsten and Washington already there, likewise in their dress uniforms. The room is empty save for them. "Gentlemen, Lady," Arges says with a nod as he greets them. They nod in return. "Any sign of the Boss?" he asks.

"None as yet, John," Rish replies. "He and the Mrs. should be along shortly I expect."

"Very good." No sooner has Arges said this when the elevator gives a ping and Damien Enkel enters the room with his wife on his arm. "Mr. Enkel, very good to see you."

"You as well, John." Handshakes are exchanged.

"Looking very lovely this evening, Madam," Arges says to Anne.

"One could say the same of you, Captain."

Arges nods. "Well, it looks as though we are all ready here."

"All we need are the guests," Ann jokes, and everyone laughs.

A waiter approaches their group and nods. "Would anyone care for a beverage?" he asks. Drink orders are placed, and he returns moments later with a silver tray bearing the requested cocktails. The captain, first officer, staff captain and Enkels form a receiving line in front of the center elevator. Two stewards set up two red velvet ropes between black plastic poles form an elegant way to guide people from the right and left elevators to the receiving line.

In due course, and given that people tend to shy away from being 'the first' to arrive at an event, the elevators begin reaching the Halo lounge filled with passengers in formal attire. Before long, the lounge is full, yet does not seem crowded as the large chamber can easily accommodate them. The cocktail hour is soon in full-swing as the ship's band plays lively songs. The drinks, hors d'oeuvres and chatter flow freely, and serve only to enhance the good spirit held within the room.

"This is pleasant," Edwin says to Lauraleigh as he passes her a glass of white wine.

"Very," she answers while accepting the drink and giving him a quick kiss on the cheek as thanks.

"You look very nice tonight, dear," Edwin observes with a genuine smile.

"I believe that is the third time you've mentioned it – must be the truth." She winks.

"Three times?" he answers with a mock expression of disbelief. "Well, expect to hear it plenty more before the night is over." His turn to wink, then he puts his arm around her.

"Not exactly the ol' frat house, is it Adam?" Cal Gregg remarks to Adam Tyler as he greets his friend.

Tyler looks around the room. "Needs more kegs, less suits. More rock posters, less light. And less furniture too while we're at it," Tyler jokes.

Purser Varsten and Doctor Washington are enjoying a talk as the Tsarevich Romanoff enters the room from the middle elevator. He is in his Russian naval dress uniform, complete with ceremonial dagger in a sheath on the large white braided belt worn on the outside of his jacket. "This fellow gives us a run for our money," Varsten remarks, and Washington turns to look at Romanoff, who has also captured the attention of almost everyone else in the room, especially the ladies.

"We'll have to get the Line's designers in touch with the Russian Navy, I guess," Washington replies.

"Salutations, babe," the rock star Peter Bull says to Myrie while clinking her wine glass with his own, then resting his hand on the small of her back.

"And to you as well, Petey," Myrie replies with a whimsical grin.

From the inside pocket of his dark blue crushed velvet jacket he brings a long, black plastic tube-like candystick holder. He puts the holder in his mouth, then quick-slaps a small silver box against his leg and brings a gold liquifilled-candystick to the tip of the holder. He inhales, and a moment later releases a perfect circle of yellow mist. Myrie laughs quietly, then her nose krinkles. She takes two more quick whiffs, seemingly recognizing a particular aroma, then looks at him. "Pete.....is that?"

He looks at her and smirks. "Just a hint, to brighten things up a bit." He offers her the holder. She takes it and likewise enjoys a long draw. Smiling, she hands it back.

"Only my boyfriend would bring hash to a high-brow event." She rolls her eyes and giggles slightly, then takes a drink.

"Somebody's got to put the 'high' in high-brow," he says, and she chortles as the effect of the sweet grains makes its way along.

"Ever been on a job before that requires you to dress to the nines and hob-nob with champagne?" Maddox whispers to Angelique.

"I would have to say that this is my first," she replies with a hint of sarcasm.

"Enjoy every minute of it – I am," Maddox answers, then takes a drink.

"Agreed; agreed in spades." She smiles and looks at some of the gowns in the room.

Maddox catches her eye-glance observations. He too looks about, then comes back to her. "They've got nothing on you, you are a knock-out."

Her eyes steal back to him. "Flattery is it, Kurt?"

Maddox is pleased that she now uses his alias continuously – there was just that one slip-up at first. "In spades." He answers with a wink, then leans in close to her ear, and whispers "We just have to do something about that darn hair-coloring, is all."

"Down, boy."

He chuckles, and she takes another drink then lets her eyes browse the outfits again.

Darian Dade is enjoying himself. He walks through the room, and as he sips his Long Island Iced Tea, his favorite drink, he notices her.

She walks into the lounge. There is an inherent confidence in how she carries herself - - a look which radiates positivity. She smiles her way through the receiving line and comes by the attention of many men as she enters; she is the type that makes testosterone boil. The stunning red velvet and satin gown she wears flatters her slim yet marvelously shaped figure. She possesses a near goddess-like beauty. Her eyes are two sparkling blue-grey jewels, and her red lips hold a glamour unto themselves. High cheekbones, square jawline, and perky nose completes the picture. Her gorgeous auburn hair frames her pretty face as it flows thickly down in long, loose spirals around her soft shoulders. She is the desire of every man and the envy of every woman - - a diamond in a world full of glass. Is she real, or a vision? Oh, she is real all right, a dream in human form. In a word, she is, Amazing.

She stands for a moment and studies the room, then goes to the bar specially set-up at the left, carrying her gold eveningbag gently in her hand. Dade becomes captivated by the bewitching creature - - the way in which she walks does not help ease his enchantment. He has to meet her. Dade takes a drink of his long island, then strides over to her. She is waiting for her drink, with her back to the room, as he comes up beside her. He leans against the bar and indicates to the bartender to bring another l.i. She does not notice him at first, but he quickly rectifies the situation.

"Hello," Dade says. He is not one for cheap opening lines.

She turns and looks at him. Approval is shown as her eyes sparkle and her face livens; the ends of her lips turn up into a tiny grin, then she smiles brightly, showing perfect white teeth. "Hi," she answers back; she has a soft, sweet voice.

He smiles. "Looks like it'll be quite a party."

She turns her head ever so slightly and her eyes lazily sweep the room - - then her gaze returns to Dade. "Sure seems like it." Another smile. Her drink arrives, and she goes to open her evening bag when Dade suavely interjects.

"Put that on my tab," he smoothly tells the bartender, who nods.

"No, no, I can't . . ." she protests.

"I'd like to." Another smile.

"My, such a gentleman."

"It's my pleasure." His own drink arrives, and he extends his hand to her. "I guess I should introduce myself. I'm Darian Dade."

"Adrianna Hartwell," she replies while taking his hand. Using the charm which comes so naturally to him, Dade raises her hand to his face, and his lips lightly touch her soft skin. Her smile widens, and a tiny grin curls across his lips.

"So, tell me more about you...." Dade begins

"What would you like to know?" She replies as she casually leans against the bar. A coy smile follows.

"Anything you want to tell me." A wink.

She giggles flirtatiously, then their conversation moves along at a good pace. They enjoy each other's company, and things are going well. She finds Dade to be a sophisticated gentleman, and he discovers that she has a wonderfully energetic personality - - she is as beautiful inside as she is out. He also learns she is an interior decorator, operating her own business in Miami.

The two find they have much in common; they both have an appreciation for the finer things in life, such as traveling. They share similar taste in films and music, and have a common knowledge of a variety of subjects. As they talk and laugh, Dade notices he is the target of a number of jealous stares from men who also wish to speak to the lovely Ms. Hartwell. They circle around the area like vultures. Dade ignores them, as does she.

The band ends the song they are playing, then a serving call chime is heard as the clock strikes seven and lights flicker twice. Captain Arges takes his pen, and raps it against his half-empty wineglass, causing a shrill plinking, and the crowd hushes for him.

"Ladies and Gentlemen, if we could make our way to the tables please, we are ready for the dinner..." Arges looks to the back of the room and nods, and two uniformed porters pull open the two large oak doors of the Epciure Gourmet dining salon.

Edwin and Lauraleigh Roggin happen to be closest to the doors, and as people gather behind them, the two make their way through the portal. "Oh, my, look at this!" Lauraleigh comments with a gasp, and pauses in awe at the upper landing of the room.

The salon is based in white. It stands a full two decks in height, and has a great vaulted ceiling which draws the eyes of patrons upward. The focal point of the ceiling is a massive wrought iron and stained glass dome. Vibrant rouges, violets, ambers, blushes, oranges, jades, blues and grays radiate from the backlit structure to bathe the area in breathtaking rainbow artistry. Surrounding the dome are two spectacular fresco scenes depicting winged angels flying across a bright skyscape. A railed balcony lines the upper perimeter of the room, whose length is supported on each side by three massive white pillars.

The side-walls each hold four long, leaded-glass, rectangular windows which top in a peak as one would find in a cathedral. The far wall boasts a spectacular bas-relief carved in polished granite showing the sun god Apollo with his fiery chariot and racing steeds soaring across the starry heavens. At the front of the hall is a multi-level staircase. As one would enter from the salon's main entrance of two large oak doors, they would come first upon the balcony. Two sets of steps join each side of the balcony level a small platform, and then a grander stairway leads down to the main dining room.

The salon is furnished with a multitude of large, circular tables adorned with flowing white tablecloths which stretch to the floor and are dressed with complete settings of painted china dinnerware, crystal glassware, silver cutlery, and exquisite napery to serve ten. Five-point golden candelabras and tropical floral arrangements form the centerpieces. The surrounding chairs are rounded, backed in white velvet, and black framed. All this is on a deep mauve carpeting. White-gloved, liveried waiters and waitresses stand at teach table, each holding an empty tray and ready to serve.

"Edwin, look!" she says while clutching his arm.

"Yes, I see it dear, astounding…"

Lauraleigh takes a tentative step forward, and enters the dining wonderland. Edwin follows, and the other guests come in themselves, each experiencing the site of the room in its full effect.

"I guess it's that time," Dade had said with a smile when the lights had flickered.

"Guess so," she replied brightly.

They leave the bar, and stroll over to the seating plan perched on an easel next to the salon doors. The chart is a map of the circular tables, stating who will be dining with whom. Identical thoughts race through both the minds of Adrianna and Dade minds, a similar hope that they will be together. Dade's eyes fall on his table list . . . he quickly reads the other seven names . . . and . . .no such luck. She is not there. Adrianna becomes similarly disappointed when she realizes Dade has not been seated at her table. To make matters worse, their tables are not even remotely near one another. They turn and look at each other, and can each see the mild disappointment in the other's eyes, but there is not a single thing they can do to change the situation. Fate has dealt a hand, and they have lost.

"That's a shame," Dade says.

"Yes, isn't it though," she replies.

"Would you save a dance for me later?" he asks with a gleam in his eye.

She brightens on hearing the invitation. "I'd love that," she says with an enthusiasm which causes Dade's spirit to soar.

"Until later, then." He takes hold of her hand, and gives it a light squeeze.

Now her spirit takes flight, and she nods to him. They reluctantly separate and slowly walk to their tables. Each is riding a euphoric 'high' inspired by the tremendously exhilarating time spent together. They feel as though they are on top of the world, sharing that certain special feeling felt when a new "interest" is brought into one's life.

Once all the guests are seated, the band ensconces itself in the balcony of the dining salon to play classical selections. The band begins a tune, then eases the song it is playing into a premature finale as Captain Arges rises from his chair at the head table, which fronts the Apollo bas relief. "Ladies and Gentlemen," Arges says, causing everyone to direct their attention to him, "it is my distinct pleasure to welcome you to the Captain's Ball." The guests applaud his introduction while Arges raises his glass of champagne from the table and lifts it in high in the air. "Please join me in a toast to the *Emprasoria*, the greatest ship in the galaxy!"

Spontaneous chairs of "Hear, Hear!" "Bravo!" "Brilliant!" and "Well done!" erupt in support of the captain's toast as everyone rises and takes a sip of their drinks.

Mr. Enkel, who is to the left of Arges, remains standing as the others seat themselves. "Friends," he says while spreading his arms wide, "it is our pleasure to host this event for you this evening. Please enjoy yourselves to the fullest."

There are applause as he sits. Waiters then quickly and attentively serve the appetizer of cream of mushroom soup, followed by Julienne salad, and finally the main course of breaded veal cutlets in hollandaise.

At the tables, diners ease themselves through the first awkward moments of making new acquaintances. Luckily, the drinks served during the cocktail hour and dinner make the experience easier than it otherwise might have been, for the spirits make the guests more open and amicable. In due course, the dessert trays make their appearances at the tables, where guests make choices of a number of delectable treats. When it appears as though everyone has finished, or near finished, the Conductor Fitzroy motions his baton and the band moves from soft classical music into up-tempo dance songs in an effort to entice people to the dancefloor created in the center of the room. The tantalizing notes seductively slip into the ears of the guests, and before long, a number of people succumb to the temptation. The polished wood surface soon becomes filled with couples dancing to lively tunes.

This is the moment Dade and Adrianna have been waiting for all evening. They certainly had enjoyed the company of their dinner companions, but deep inside, each had a subtle desire to be with the other. The problem now is to locate each other within the crowd. Dade is quick to begin the search. He rises from his chair, excuses himself, and walks into the crowd lining the dancefloor. Within minutes, he has spotted her. She looks dazzling - - an unbelievable beauty surrounded by festive people. The sight of her makes him swell with pride. He straightens himself, gives a quick tug to his tuxedo jacket to make it fit snugly against his frame, and runs a hand through his hair to smooth it. Now, feeling ready, he approaches her.

Dade quickly moves into and through the forest of people which stand between him and the object of his desire. He moves swiftly and stealthily, much like a panther moving on its prey. Despite the fact she is facing in his direction, she does not notice him at first. When he emerges from the crowd and stands in front of her, she brightens and flashes a smile. He takes her hand in his, and as if on cue, the band plays the final notes of its current song and immediately launches into the opening chords of another. "Care to dance?" he asks.

"Love to!" she answers.

Dade turns on his heel and leads her to the dancefloor. He brings Adrianna deep into the crowd of swaying bodies, then spins around and softly pulls her into his arms. Dade is a smooth dancer, and she melts into his strong lead. They look perfect together as they move to the song.

During their first dance, both Dade and Adrianna keep calm, as neither has the desire to move too fast. They whisper, and flirt lightheartedly. As the next song begins, Dade slowly pulls her to closer to him, and she does not resist. He lowers his head slightly and presses his cheek to hers. The skin is warm to the touch. Her perfume wafts up around him, and he is soon lost in the seductive scent; she in turn inhales the robust musk of his cologne and falls victim to the rapturous aroma.

As their second dance grows into the third, she pulls her face away from his and looks deeply into his eyes. He cannot break away from her intense gaze. Her eyes speak to him, and his answer. Dade slowly leans forward and brings his lips to hers. The kiss. Soft and tender. Their hearts race and their souls stir. Fireworks ignited by supercharged passion explode within their minds. Their interaction together is phenomenally exciting, and this is just the beginning . . .

Darian Dade and Adrianna Hartwell are not alone in their pursuit of 'l'amour'. The air of the Royale is alive with romance. Guests become caught up in the amorous feel – in this musical, dimly-lit setting seemingly designed by Cupid himself. Single men and women seek each other out and flirt shamelessly - - and often successfully - - while married or involved couples rekindle lost fires.

The officers are enjoying themselves. Captain Arges is relaxed and in good spirits. The captain and other officers enjoy three drinks, then contentedly remain with soda. They make visits to the dancefloor, and converse with many of the guests, but are careful to restrain themselves in keeping with the strict policy of the Line regarding 'limited social contact' between ship personnel and passengers.

Third Officer Hearst is stretching the social contact regulation to its limit. As he similarly ignores the hair-length policy, he brushes aside the rule which he believes unfairly limits his prospects for social advancement. Since this is the first opportunity he has to mix with the rich and famous passengers, he wishes to make the most of it.

Hearst introduces himself countless times as the evening progresses. He blatantly worships accomplished men like Edwin Roggin, Calvin Gregg and J.D. Zolnick, and all but kneels at their feet upon meeting them. In the process of trying to make connections which he believes can help him socially and financially, Hearst in effect does himself more hard than good as he endlessly clamors on about how 'great' these people are. Roggin, Gregg, and Zolnick have experienced ass-kissing lapdogs like him all too many times before. They clearly see through the façade Hearst is creating, and are wholly unimpressed by the fat and awkward man. Hearst's harsh treatment of the serving staff - - ordering them about as though they are subhuman slaves - - does nothing to earn him respect in the eyes of those whom he wishes to impress.

The attention of the third officer is not limited to the men of the Royale class. He is more than willing to use a woman to improve his status. As a significant other or a husband to an important woman, he can enter the lifestyle of his dream. Hearst presents himself to many women throughout the evening. He attempts to be charming as he converses with the ladies, and is failing miserably. He brings numerous women to the dancefloor in an effort to acquaint himself at a personal level with the Royale women. Here again he thwarts his efforts at gaining favor, as he is by no means an accomplished dancer. He stumbles around the dancefloor without any sense of rhythm. His cumbersome feet, which seem to move without direction, land on his partner's shoes more than once during the songs. His heartfelt apologies do nothing to ease the throbbing pain in the delicate toes he tramples.

Once their respective dances end, the women excuse themselves from Hearst before he may ask for a second and quickly exit the dancefloor. Once away, they hastily find more suitable male companions in the crowd. They do this to avoid any further tortuous moments with the Third Officer. Hearst spends the remainder of the evening continuing his hero-worship and attempts at finding a princess in a vain effort to locate that one person who can rescue him from his perceived 'common' life.

When the last notes of the last song are played at two o'clock a.m., and the brightness of the chandeliers is raised to signal that the Ball has come to its close, the guests regretfully leave the salon. A truly spectacular time has been had by the evening's end.

Dade and Adrianna have been together for the entire soirée. The time has come. He looks at her and smiles. She is so utterly beautiful. He hears the wolf howl inside his mind; the tigercat is poised to strike. She sees the wanton desire in his eyes. Hunger. The first of many signs which precede lust. The look thrills her to her very core and stimulation fires.

"Shall we go?" he whispers into her ear.

"Yesssssssssss......" she coos with a smile.

The fifth pulse begins. It is the bloodrush of arousing passion.

The two make their way along with the other guests. Some passengers invite small groups of their newfound friends back to the sitting rooms of their suites, where small parties continue until people stop out of sheer exhaustion. Others, like Dade and Adrianna, participate in events of an entirely different sort . . . those couples lucky enough to have been seduced by the romantic aspects of the evening indulge the beckoning.

He unlocks the door of his suite, opens it, and ushers her inside. The door closes. The room is dark. He leaves it that way. The shadows cast by the deep amber nightlight serve only to enhance the aura of the moment. Dade gathers her in his arms and kisses her. Deeply. They quickly find themselves in the bedchamber. Kissing and caressing in the darkness.

She gently eases back from him, and with her eyes locked on his, smiles playfully. She raises her hands to her head; with a quick tousle, her auburn silk cascades, and she has let her hair down for him.... She puts her hands into her hair, ruffling it on both sides, teasing it to give it more body while shaking her head from side to side at the same moment.

She stops, and looks back at him. Her grin radiates a mixture of playfulness and seduction. He stares at her, wide-eyed. She moves to him once again. She traces his lips with her finger, while licking her own lips provocatively. Her eyes meet his, and she touches the sides of his face, pulling him toward her. "Oooohhhhh baby…" he says, and they kiss once again. The threshold of intimacy. Reclined on soft sheets, skin released from clothing shed, bodies intertwine.

He nibbles her earlobe. Feels her scented hair upon his face. Kisses along her jawline. Next, to the lips. She offers her neck. Kiss, nibble, lick. He makes a home of her cleavage. More touches. Gentle rubs. Kiss away the sweet sweat as it appears. Their worlds begin to swirl. Intensity on an upward swing. He can hear magic in her sighs. She wraps her legs around his waist. Universes merge. Locked together in carnal bliss. She arches her back and his strong arms close round her tightly. His name escapes the bonds of her glossed lips in a hushed gasp. Time and time again. A chorus of more breathy utterances inspired by unbridled passion in its purest form. Their spirits experience metaphysical excess and skirt the edge of nirvana via supercharged coitus. Heighten. Heighten! Climax. His mind tastes fire. Her dazzled eyes see stars. The mortals achieve the pleasure of the gods.

They lie together, embracing, languishing in the moment. They partake in the ultimate sport again, hour upon hour, through the night, until drifting into a peaceful slumber. She lies along his left, her head resting on his chest, his arms 'round her. Cupid smiles.

Maddox and Angelique return to their stateroom, he escorting her on his arm, both nodding pleasantly to the other couples they meet in the corridor. "That was enjoyable," he says with a genuine smile as they enter their suite, and he closes the door behind them.

"Yes, very nice," she answers while walking to the bedroom. He loosens his bow tie and undoes the top two buttons of his shirt as he walks to the sofa. "You know," he begins while leaning down and reaching for the laptop computer, "it's putting together the deal that really gets me jazzed. Finding the right people and bringing them together, selling the idea, the background planning, then closing the deal. There's something about all that which I find fascinating." He pauses a moment as he finds the thin device, brings it forward and shifts himself around. "Don't get me wrong, the score will be good, and the task is thrilling, but the art of the deal has its own allure." He sits and sets the laptop on his lap.

"You're a motivated person, Kurt," she says from the bedroom – at present, she is in front of the mirror at the dressing table and removing her earrings. "You have a knack for and sorting through things, and convincing." She pauses. "A networker and a problemsolver, all rolled into one. I'm just glad I'm on your side."

"Functionality to profit, whatever that profit happens to be. That's the name of the game," he says absently while opening the lid of the computer, which still slyly observes the compu-operations activity of the ship. His eyes quickly scan what appears on the thin screen. He senses her entering the room, her presence preceded by the scent of her perfume which suddenly makes itself known, but does not look up. Angelique walks over and props herself on the plush arm of the sofa as next to him he reads. "Find anything interesting?" she asks.

"Nothing out of the ordinary. Straight routine."

He turns and looks up at her. She has removed the colorspray again, and her blonde hair is hanging loose at her shoulders. The red silk robe she wears fits her well; its lapels crossed tantalizingly at her chest, and the garment itself ending tantalizingly at her upper thighs. Her green eyes, now natural and free from the brown contact lenses, are focused on the screen of the laptop, processing the information there. "You're right," she says while turning to him, "run-of-the-mill material."

"Yes," he says, then snaps the laptop shut and gently sets it on the floor, and with a swift move of his heel, slides it to its place beneath the sofa. He leans back to allow the deep cushion to provide comfort.

She begins to rise, yet he hooks his fore and middle finger into the back of the satiny belt which binds her robe, and gives a slight tug, pulling her back to her perch on the sofa arm. She looks over her shoulder at him and says nothing, but smiles. Maddox rests his hand on her back, and feels the gentle material beneath his fingers. He begins to rub her back in soft circles.

"That feels nice," she says softly while turning her head forward again.

"Good. It's meant to."

"Mmmmmmmmmm," she mutters while closing her eyes; the eyeshadow looks good. "Mr. Kendall, should we really be doing this?", whimsy clearly evident in her tone.

"Well, this excursion we are on does allow us to mix business with *some* pleasure."

She opens her eyes and turns to him. "Yes it does, but, wouldn't it be the slightest bit compromising?"

"A paramour as well as a 'fait accompli'? Nothing compromising about that."

"It could be distracting though."

"Yes," he concedes. "But on the other hand, the odd diversions are ok, will keep us from being stressed over the job."

"I like how you think."

"Well, you did say I was a problemsolver." He winks.

"That I did." She slips from the sofa arm into his lap and wraps her arms around his neck as he puts his arms around her. Maddox kisses her deeply.

He pulls back. "Did you notice the jacuzzi bath?"

"I sure did. Looks quite nice."

Maddox nods. "This is a brand new ship, with brand new accoutrements. How much are you willing to bet that that particular piece of equipment is un-christened?"

"Marinate while we fornicate?"

He playfully slaps her firm posterior once through the robe. "That's the ticket, water baby."

She laughs and swats his shoulder, then he nuzzles her neck.

"Ok, aqua-man. I'm game. I'll be a mermaid."

With that he rises, still holding her in his arms, and as they kiss he walks sturdily to the bedroom, and to the bathing chamber within.

The ship's guests are the only ones free to enjoy such superior amusement. The officers do not attend any passenger parties (most by polite choice, Hearst because he was not invited), and certainly do not partake in any pleasures of the flesh. Unlike their carefree charges, the officers are expected to be alert and ready for work the next day.

Captain Arges makes a point of checking-in with the bridge as he walks to his quarters. "How is everything, Alyssa?" he asks as he enters.

"We're running perfectly," she reports with a smile from the command chair.

The news pleases Arges. "Excellent," he replies, a broad smile upon his face as well. "The Ball went quite well, looked like the passengers had fun. The Man and the Grand Dame certainly enjoyed themselves."

"Good to hear."

"Well, thank you Alyssa. Have a nice night," he taps the brim of his cap with his fingers.

"Thank you. You as well, Sir."

Arges strides down the port corridor to his cabin. Setting his cap down on his desk and undoing his uniform jacket, he sits at the desk and activates his computer. He makes some notes in his trip file, then writes an email to his wife back home on Earth. Arges smiles on reading a message to him from his son, and replies quickly to the boy at boarding school. Having finished, he switches off the computer and stands, stretching his arms wide into the air and walking to his bedroom. Minutes later, he is in bed and fast asleep, as are most of the others on the ship.

Hearst lies awake in bed. His mind is alive with recollections of what had transpired that evening. His behavior had been 'par unending and time seems at a standstill. We are at play in an nending day, and dance through an endless night. It's like living in an musing anecdote, or thriving in a dreamy smile. Mystical. Fresh. An arly taste of how many see heaven. It's easy adapting to life here. We an o.d. on a permabuzz of joy. Every second is here to be savored like sweet candy. It's recess, it's spring break, it's a carnival funhouse, a backstage pass to your favorite band, an illicit drink at an afterhours club...all wrapped into one sweet bundle. Livin' large, livin' the life of Riley, Gatsby's pleasure, in like Flynn, fandango, posh panache, in the pink, whatever you want to call it, this is it." Dade pauses. "So endeth my prospero monologue, my dear."

Adrianna giggles. "An expert summation, if I do say so myself, Mr. Dade."

Dade does a mock bow. "Why thank you."

Even though the entire ship is awash in being busy almost constantly, the *Emprasoria* still manages to convey a sense of "relaxation". Events are pre-arranged in order that there are never any lines of waiting people and no over-crowded areas; there is no stress at all. Staff Captain Syranos and her cruise entertainment staff are miracle workers in this respect. The presence of the many elevators, the speedwalk tracks and the chauffeured courtesy cart hovercraft even make going from one end of the ship to the other an easy pleasure. Passengers quickly find it is easy to adapt to life here on the *Emprasoria*. This is what a vacation is meant to be, calm and enjoyable. The Archangel Line has outdone itself, and very well at that.

One element which particularly impresses the passengers is how accommodating, friendly and efficient the crew is toward them. The cruise entertainment and serving staffs speak the King's English with Oxford precision, and are collectively fluent in the linguistics of the world. They articulate with precise accents the European languages and the key dialects of Indo-Asiatic, Arabic and Afric speech, as well as having five who are versed in the intricacies of Sign Language. The overall effect makes communication for passengers occur with extreme ease and clarity. Also, the seven muscle-toned fitness training instructors gladly set exercise routines which are not time-consuming nor difficult, but accomplish a great deal. The clerks in En Vogue Avenue are extremely courteous and helpful, as are the attendants in the specialty areas of the ship, such as the riding range and arcade.

excelanté' . . . yes, the *Emprasoria* cruise will be his ticket to the good life . . . he is sure of it! These are his last thoughts as he falls into a dreamy sleep.

Bright and early the next morning, Damien Enkel arrives on the bridge to find Captain Arges, First Officer Rish and Staff Captain Syranos waiting for him. "Good morning everyone," he says with a smile.

"Good morning, sir," comes the reply in three.

"Quite the time last night, wouldn't you say?"

"Yes, quite enjoyable," Arges says. "Looked as though the guests enjoyed themselves."

"That is true," agrees Enkel. "I will be interested to see Priest's photos." He looks around the bridge. "Looks as though everything is fine up here."

"Oh yes, Damien. Ship-shape, as they say," remarks the proud captain.

"Well, shall we begin?" Enkel asks.

"Yes, we are ready if you are."

"Very good. Let's go then." With that, the first morning walking tour of the cruise begins. He surveys the surroundings with an eagle eye, but everything meets his high and impeccable standards. An hour later, the four are back at the bridge. "Excellent, excellent," Enkel beams. "Not a single flaw."

"Thank you, Sir," Arges nods.

"Well, I'd better get back to the room and take the missus out to breakfast. I'll see you three here again tomorrow, if not before." This is said as Enkel intends to make a tour of the ship with the three each morning in the early stages of the voyage, then intermittently afterward.

"Very good, Sir. Have a pleasant day." Arges smiles and escorts Enkel away from the bridge.

And so, the first full day of the voyage begins. The social scene moves quickly within the white hull of the *Emprasoria*. One of the finer qualities about the *Emprasoria* is that she offers so <u>much</u> for her passengers. Premiums abound; there is always some sort of performance or event scheduled - - a person would be hard pressed to find him- or herself bored. There is something for everyone in this man-made paradise, whether listening to the ship's band play the music of Beethoven, or a rigorous exercise session, or a shopping spree. There is a high level of accommodation and recognition; all sorts of tastes are catered to - - there are no 'unusual' preferences or 'bizarre' requests, and in this respect, the passengers have a high comfort level and are made to feel as though they are 'at home'.

The *Emprasoria* guests fit themselves into a very exciting, yet relaxing routine. During the evenings, they attend assorted social events well into the early morning hours, then sleep until late in the morning, spend the day doing as they please, then repeat the cycle as the dusk hours fall on the ship. Friendships blossom when, out of simple circumstance, people encounter each other several times over the course of a day or an evening! If anything, life aboard the ship has a danger of being <u>too</u> luxurious for her passengers. To avoid the perhaps unpleasant affects of this, the Line provides for her passengers, at no cost, supplies of Peplyn capsules for energy boosts, Dietrim tablets to maintain their waistlines, and Babysleep pills to aid in peaceful and dreamy slumber.

The White Feather salon serves sumptuous breakfasts, luncheons and dinners. Each multi-course meal is accompanied with a menu offering a multitude of sumptuous cuisine. As at the Captain's Ball, the soft 'serving call' chimes sound to announce a meal sitting, which lasts an hour. If, however, a passenger becomes hungry when the salons are closed, food may be ordered from cabin stewards, who quickly provide a tray bearing whatever delicacy is requested. The White Feather attempts to convey a familiar feeling for the mealtimes. During breakfast and luncheon, the window covers remain closed, and their scenic systems display vistas appropriate for the hour, such as a sunrise dawn over a meadow for the morning, and a mid-day sight for the afternoon. The covers are opened when dinner is served so patrons may dine with the stars.

The *Emprasoria* accommodates passengers who wish to be informed about current events. Just because one is in the middle of an interplanetary voyage does not mean he or she should be isolated from the happenings of the day. The Transastral Times news service provides the answer by means of a newspaper, and an electronic infosite.

The masthead of this daily is impressive, and identical for both the paper and the infosite. To the left is a round and robust portrayal of Mother Earth. Clothed in a lengthy toga gown, her dark hair is piled high in a bouffant, and her fertility is represented by two babies resting at her sandaled feet. She stands with her right arm resting demurely against her side, her left extending outward, the dainty palm facing up, its fingers stretching. Her noble head is turned in the same direction . . . toward the Archangel Crest, which dominates the center of the design,

its base being decorated in garlands. On the right is an i
representation of the war-god Mars. He is adorned in ful
armor; his broad right hand and muscular forearm likewis
toward the crest as his strong and square-jawed face looks
arm rests against a tall and foreboding spear which stands
side. Three five-pointed stars occupy the space between th
the crest. Beneath the design is the name of the paper writt
black calligraphy.

Stories from the three major wire services on the E
Moon and Mars are relayed to the ship's communication cen
the course of the day and evening. Photographs and graphics
transmitted. Midnight is the deadline when a communication
technician reviews the submissions and selects which stories
included in the next day's edition. When there is enough mate
the seven sheets, including the space reserved for television lis
select advertisements, the technician routes the layout to the mi
printing press, and ninety minutes later there are enough copies
every person aboard ship. As well, an electronic version appear
elevator viewers and is available on the en-suite vidscreens, with
updates every four hours.

"This is 'The Perfection'. We can go where imagination
us. We can unleash possibility, we have that power. We have a 'd
you please' atmosphere here. From the minute we stepped aboard
grand ship, we were given a license to overindulge, a pass to live to
extreme. And lots are using that rare privilege to its highest potenti
believe me. When we are hungry, food is brought to us, whatever w
want, and we nosh on the best. When we thirst, the drink flows. Al
served on warmed plates and in chilled glasses no less. Clean, pure
cool, scented air surrounds us, piped in silently. We can sleep anyti
we want, or not at all. We do what we please, when we please, acti
when the mood strikes. Desire is the order of the day aboard this sh
every day. Whatever we want, we get – it's all at our beck and call
The pursuit of hedonism, through and through. Or, it can be whate
you want it to be. Flourish in it, splash in it, live the spoils of it. A
there's the timeless quality. Timeless and spaceless. We exist in a
totally enclosed environment. Time, what is time for us? Out here
there's no movement of the sun or rising of the moon. There's noth
but clocks to mark the passage of time, and they're avoided easily
enough. Time flies when you're having fun they say, well here the

A highly visible aspect of the crew is the ship's band. The conductor of this orchestra is Maestro Reginald Fitzroy, the white-haired, slim and always tuxedoed previous director of the London Philharmonic. In their smart uniforms of soft blue with gold piping is a highly talented ensemble. The group consists of three on violin, a five-piece horn section, one on flute, clarinet, piccolo, oboe, lute, harp and bass respectively, a percussionist with a full drum kit, a guitarist, and Reynold Fische, a brilliant pianist whose fingers dance on the ivories with a skill like no other. They play classical music as well as current tunes, and are well versed in swing, jazz, r&b and fusion. Theirs is the music of Heaven, whose sound make ears tingle and the heart stir . . . not from volume, mind you, but from sheer beauty of tone.

In the early days of the voyage, those passengers on their first interplanetary voyage find it difficult to live with a continually black sky. However they quickly learn to rely on what the clocks read, which for simplicity remain set on Pacific time, to determine such things as mealtimes and bedtimes. As Dade noted though, time is not much of a concern on the *Emprasoria*. During the waking hours, passengers do not hesitate in taking full advantage of all the extensive recreational facilities the *Emprasoria* offers. Days are whiled away in the luxurious and leisurely pursuit of pleasure. Happy passengers use their ensuite computers and SolNet to send pictures and 'Wish you were here!' recountings to friends and relatives back home. Hours are spent within the specialty rooms on the entertainment decks where individual enjoyment runs unchecked.

For the athletically sensed, there is everything. The gymnasium is quite busy, both its swimming pool and exercise room which has every type of fitness machine available. All seven separate sections of the aerobics studio, the racquet ball court and tennis court are likewise all well used. The children aboard find the day nursery to be a colorful wonderland of toys and games, overseen by two attentive governesses and five au peres. For those who prefer just to bask, the turkish bath, beauty salon, sauna, Swedish spa and solarium are favored attractions. The ZeroZone spatial pool is a 'hit', as the officers and crew expected; all the passengers – children and adults alike – love the weightless play the vault offers. The Cinerama Theatre has a massive curved screen and surro-sound stereo system to display a variety of first-run films and a royal blue ceiling with simulated twinkling stars.

As the voyage proceeds, some passengers become affiliated with specific recreations.

Congresswoman Jackson, with her in-bred west coast love of water, visits the Caesarea Pool once daily for some vigorous swimming, and suns herself in the Samedi Beach tanning salon daily to maintain her California glow. She also spends part of her day riding at the Equestria, which provides grand Andalusian horses and fine ponies, as she has a deep fondness for horseback riding.

Each morning at six o'clock finds Xian Ng and his lovely wife practicing the art of Tai Chi in the natural splendor of the Langshott Park. Dressed in white robes, they conduct this ancient Oriental ritual undisturbed, which ends with them feeling well and relaxed for the coming day. Early in the voyage, Tabbi Kahen approaches Karisu Ng, who is wearing a red kimono decorated with goldleaf. "Konnichiwa" says Tabbi with a respectful half-bow at the waist, her hands brought together in front of her chest.

"Konnichiwa," replies Karisu, who smiles and returns the bow.

"I too am Geisha, having studied your ways and practices many years ago."

"Very nice!" Karisu comments, being pleased and rather surprised to find a kindred spirit aboard the spaceliner.

"'Perach-chan' is the name I chose as Geisha. Perach is blossom in Hebrew. I am Israeli."

"How delightful!" She then turns her voice to a whisper "My husband's nickname for me is Cherry Blossom!"
The two laugh, then discuss aspects of the Geisha lifeculture.

Dr. Radsky, who given his practice of and interest in psychology, is by nature a perpetual researcher. He also enjoys leisure reading. So, it was natural for him to visit the ship's library on the first day of the voyage. When he walks in, his jaw drops.

A spectacular mural on the far wall depicts a scene from ancient mythology and honors the patron saints of artistry. In the sunlit courtyard of a piazza is the Roman deity Minerva reclined on a low, long, red couch, her hair piled in an auburn bouffant and wearing a white aegis tunic while gold necklaces adorn her neck. A lyre rests in her right hand and a golden goblet brimming with red wine is held in her left. Her high-crested helmet rests on the ground next to the couch, and her breastplate, shield and spear are next to her against a tree, with her totem owl perched on the breastplate. In the foreground, a stream comes from a park. Riding a white swan in the rippling water is the Hindu goddess Sarasvati. Flowing midnight hair falls from a golden headdress to surround her caramel skin, and she wears a white sari with a red sash trimmed in patterns of gold. Using her four-arms, she cradles the sacred Vedic book of knowledge in one hand, holds a lotus in another, while the other two hands play a sitar. An ibis bird is flying in the upper right corner, representing the Egyptian god Thoth. They are amidst a host of tiny, frolicking nymphs and muses who each represent one of the fine arts and sport either stems of purple grapes or poppies while being on hand to attend to their lady's whims and wants. The women stare out from the painting, their look to entice an indulgence of one of their noble pastimes. On a brass plaque across the bottom of the frame is written: ***"There is so Much to Learn That None of Us have Time to Learn It All..."***

"This is amazing!" he mutters. He then looks around and sees the tiers and tiers of volume upon volume of books and discs. "My god, I've hit the mother lode!" he says, in a whisper. He eagerly takes a step forward, anxious to acquaint and indulge himself with this capsule of knowledge and entertainment. The Tsarevich Romanoff and the philospher-diplomat Daniel Benshabbot, both men of letters, also enjoy browsing the titles and reading at least part of the afternoon.

The Tsarevich Romanoff makes a point of seeking out Chief Engineer Holden. "Hello, you are the Chief Engineer, correct?"

"Yes, Tac Holden," Holden says while offering his hand.

"A pleasure to meet you. Alexai Romanoff," Romanoff answers during the handshake. "I have been meaning to speak with you," he begins. "This cruise is very excellent."

"Thank you, always glad to hear that, we hope to have our passengers enjoy themselves."

"You and the others have done very well at that," Romanoff smiles. "I must admit that while I am more at home on a ship charging through the sea, this spaceship has inspired an interest in me for astral travel." Holden nods on hearing this. "Could you provide me with some information, about how space vessels function, that sort of material?" Romanoff is toying with the idea to undertake to be a Cosmonaut, and serve Mother Russia in the great beyond.

"I will be happy to, sir. I can have a book sent to you, and I can provide you with a number of data infosources as well. Which suite would you be in?"

"C-15," the Tsarevich answers.

Holden notes this in his infokeeper. "Very good. I will see to it this afternoon, or tomorrow morning if you prefer."

"No hurry," Romanoff says with the brush of his hand. "Whenever is most convenient for you to find the time. I do appreciate it though." Romanoff pauses. "Are you terribly busy at present?"

"Never to busy for one of our guests."

"Thank you. Could you be so kind as to brief me about interspatial propulsion?"

Holden gives a hearty grin. "I always like to talk shop, Mr. Romanoff. Well, it all starts with the most unusual of things…." Romanoff listens attentively, and the two continue this conversation for the next hour. This developed friendship eventually leads to Romanoff being treated to a rare passenger privilege of a tour of the engine room.

Lauraleigh Roggin returns with Edwin to their suite after dinner one evening. She goes to the verandah, and leans against the heavy glass of the window, and looks outside. "You know, this ship has everything, but there's just one special element missing."

"What's that?" Edwin asks while walking into the verandah.

"A sunset," she says longingly, still looking outward. She sighs. "Out here, the sun is always up, bright at a continual level, and then there's the polkadotted black and white of the outer space." Lauraleigh turns her face to Edwin for a moment. "I mean, it's beautiful in its own way, sure, but a sunset gives off such pleasance." She turns to look outward again and her eyes glaze as if she is having a daydream.

Edwin pauses and thinks for a moment. Then he steps over to the silver control panel, and with her back still to him, begins running his hand over the touch-screen and making some requests by fingertip. Satisfied, he turns to the large window, crosses his arms over his chest, and waits.

Lauraleigh jumps, startled, a half-second later when the viewport cover begins to close. "Wha?" she says as she turns to him, and sees a familiar smile and glint in his eye. She returns the smile. "What are you up to?" she says with a wink.

"Wait and see," Edwin replies, and with a motion of his hand, bids her to look forward. She turns to see the cover has closed and the scenic system is active. The Cloudflight is merging with the Meadowland, layer-on-layer, in settings that are a bit unusual for them. Colors flash and blend; violets, pinks, bronze appear in a fantastic spectral skyscape with a meadow below, which has a half-sun image lowering on its horizon.

"It's amazing!" Lauraleigh utters, her eyes wide at the array before her.

Edwin walks up behind her and slips his hands around her waist; his chest subconsciously puffs outward with the pride of someone who can provide for his woman and give her what she wants. "Not exactly the real thing, but a good substitute," he whispers while nuzzling her ear.

"Thank you sweetheart!" Her hand reaches up and strokes the back of his head gently. "I love it!"

"Good, I am glad." He holds her closer and she turns and kisses him. They cuddle there a while longer, as the scene runs its course.

"What a menagerie," says Rave DeMedici after touring the zoo in the arboretum with Octavia. DeMedici has a fondness for all creatures of the world, and a great knowledge of them, holding a Masters Degree in Natural Sciences from the University of Calcutta. He has his own game reserve in a forest in England, and freely donates to Preservation Societies both on the Earth and Mars. He visits the wildlife daily, sketching their varied likenesses in his drawing pad with colored charcoal, and develops a friendship with the curator, Zookeeper Byron Devinski.

DeMedici is also fascinated by the sculpture MagnaStar. "Utterly astounding!" he says to Octavia while they enjoy raspberry scones and herbal tea in the coffee shop.

"Quite exquisite, Rave," she replies, likewise sharing his interest in nature.

"And that Langshott Parkette!" He shakes his head in wonder and takes a drink of tea. "Enticing."

"That it was, dear. The harp music was splendid as well," she says, and Rave nods in agreement. He and Octavia can also be found at times in the Arctica, speedskating to their heart's content along the inner wall of the ice rink.

Cal Gregg and Edwin Roggin visit the rifle range at least once daily. Gregg, being a professional in the firearms trade, is very impressed with the variety of pistols and rifles available. Roggin is an amateur enthusiast, and likewise pleased with the stock. Both are notoriously good shots, and are pleased with the condition of the pieces.

One day, while reloading his rifle, Roggin pauses and watches Gregg line-up a shot. Greg fires, hitting his target square on. "You've got quite an eye there," Roggin observes.

Gregg lowers his rifle and turns to Roggin. "Thank you," he replies with a nod. "I've noticed you aren't so bad yourself."

Roggin nods back. He then extends his hand. "Edwin Roggin."

"Cal Gregg" comes the reply during the handshake.

"You know," Roggin continues, "healthy competition is a good thing."

Gregg raises his eyebrows. "I tend to agree," he remarks, hearing the implied suggestion.

"We could ask the Rangemaster to set up some interesting target variations for us. . ."

"That we could. In the interest of sportsmanship."

"Good enough."

The men shake hands again, then Roggin hails the Rangemaster. An impromptu match soon begins. The two soon begin competing with one another daily. Each provides the other with formidable competition. Other passengers begin wagering on Roggin or Gregg, and enthusiastically watch the intense matches between them.

Other 'healthy competition' occurs as well. At one point, the Equestria holds court to a Polo match. The Tsarevich Romanoff heads one team, while Rave DeMedici leads another. The match is riveting and exhilarating. Romanoff, being a European Royal, has played the game since his teens, and is able to lead his team to victory, thought it is a close winning at that.

Darian Dade is one who can be found in the Casino Royale at some point during the evening. Dade derives a certain wicked pleasure from the thrill of playing 'the devil's sport'. He visits the casino in full evening dress, and, with Long Island in hand and cigarette burning, entertains himself with games of blackjack or poker. More than one of his fellow players falls victim to his steely face which betrays neither confidence nor fear. After indulging himself for a time, Dade exits the casino and joins Adrianna, often with several gold-colored plastic *Emprasoria* gambling chips the pocket of his tuxedo jacket.

Dade also drops by The Cards and Billiards room for some wagering and play, bit of a different spirit her though, as the studded leather chairs, heavy tables and high style dictates decorum.

Most passengers largely forget their business responsibilities in favor of the relaxing atmosphere of the ship. Most, but not all. When Lauraleigh isn't looking, Edwin Roggin sneakily obtains reports about his communications empire and its stock, and manages to do this at least twice a day. Jack and Diana McCartney keep abreast of all Earth, Lunar and Martian happenings by checking with the World newspaper offices three times a day, while Jack files his exclusive stories about vacation life on the maiden voyage. J.D. Zolnick contacts his New York office twice a day from the Passenger Communication Centre. Three days into the voyage, his personal pager unexpectedly sounds and calls him away from the drink he is enjoying with McCartney in the Forward Observation Lounge. He returns moments later, a broad smile curling around his thick cigar.

"What're you so happy about, Zol?" McCartney asks as his friend sits down.

"That was the office calling for my final approval on a deal we've been working on," Zolnick says as he removes his cigar and takes a drink of scotch. His smile returns. "I just made ten million."

McCartney's eyebrows rise. "Damn good," he says in admiration.

"Goddamn great!" Zolnick says with a loud chuckle.

"I think that calls for another drink," McCartney says with a smile. With that, he hails a waiter and orders more liquor. The two toast Zolnick's success that entire afternoon.

Xian Ng checks for status updates from his executive assistant numerous times during the day. He directs his corporation with the rigidity of a Samurai. He devotes three hours of his day to reviewing portfolios and reports. Karisu takes pride in the strong work ethic of her husband, yet, she also wishes to enjoy herself. She spends delightful time with Tabbi Kahen, discussing aspects of Japanese and Israeli culture over herbal tea.

Peter Bull is also at work. With him is his ever-present guitar, as well as a custom-made amplifier (or, 'boomer' as he calls it) with a built-in compact disc device which records any sound that is sent through it. Bull strums his tunes and sings through his headset microphone as the disc spins. He is experimenting with music for the Blythe Heathens' new album; some are cover versions of hits by other bands, but most is original material. The walls of the Royale suites are thick enough to cushion Bull's playing so his rehearsals do not disturb his fellow passengers.

One evening, Bull joins the *Emprasoria* Band for an impromptu song performance on the Cosmos Showlounge stage. They were pleased to share their space with such an accomplished musical talent.

Another night, Bull and Myrie take a table at Club Ritz. Bull presses a small light blue touch-screen monitor at the table and after a minute calls up the disk jockey's playlist. He looks over and nudges Myrie's arm. "Babe, check it out, they're going to spin 'Exphoria' tonight!" Exphoria is a classic Heathens tune, and one which Bull helped write.

"That's fantastic!" Myrie says enthusiastically and kisses him on the cheek. "This ship knows class, everywhere you look." Bull nods to the compliment and takes her hand in his, then brings it to his lips and gives a kiss.

"Back in a sec, honey," Bull says, then stands and kisses her forehead and strides to the disk jockey booth on the far side of the room where he has a quick chat with the energetic fellow there. Enthusiastic nods occur between these lovers of music, then Bull returns to Myrie, whispers to her, and exits the Club, only to return to his table five minutes later with his guitar and amp. Bull, Myrie and the others drink and dance, enjoying the evening for all it holds.

When the time is right, the dj sends a message to the monitor at Bull and Myrie's table, just before he is ready to cue up the song. As the current song ends, Bull rises from the table with his music maker and its boomer. "Check this out, babe," he says, then runs his fingers beneath her chin and gives her a long kiss. She watches as Bull walks out to the dancefloor, positions himself with his legs spread and body taut, then straps on his guitar.

The current song ends and the voice of the dj comes to the speakers. "Laaaiiidieeesss and gentlemeeeeennnn! We have a fandango treat for you tonight!" Silence falls at the Ritz. "Our next tune is Exphoria, and bringin' you some livvvvvvvvve riffs tonight is none other than the wizmeister himself, the one, the only," the vocal effect turns into a deep bass sound, "Peeeeeter Bull!"

The spotlights of the stage spin and focus on Bull, bathing him in white light against the darkened room. Myrie takes a gasp and begins applauding loudly, joining with the claps and shouts from those within the packed club. Bull looks up to the ceiling, puts his fingers on the strings while raising his playing hand and pauses for effect. In a whipcrack he rips into the opening cords of Exphoria. He plays live with the prerecorded sound of his bandmates – his guitar mastery reverberating through the entire club – to the crazed thrill of the audience.

Bull cuts through the rhythms and pitches of the song, and does an astounding solo. Three minutes later, Exphoria ends, with Bull sweating like a madman on the stage and breathing heavy. The spotlights click off, and Bull slips his guitar from his shoulders to the cheers of the crowd. "Fuckin wild," he blurts, then takes a step backward, momentarily feeling off kilter, but he regains himself. The dj comes back on the speaker again as Bull makes his way back to Myrie, getting backslaps of gratitude from the audience. "Ladies and Gentlemen, that was Peter Bull on guitar!" Shouts and applause again erupt as Bull throws himself into a chair and takes a long drink of his rum and cola to quench himself.

Myrie throws her arms around her gasping man. "Pete! That was *amazing*!" she squeals. Bull throws a cocky smile and looks over to her.

"Thanks, babe, it was a blast." He takes another long drink, then reaches for a cigarette. He takes a moment to look down at his amplifier, and pats the top of it, then looks back at Myrie. "Boomer got it all, babe," he says, meaning the impromptu music mastery had been perfectly recorded on his speaker disc.

Bull spends his days 'on the songs', eating, drinking, making energetic love to Myrie, enjoying marijuana-laced candysticks, or going out . . . his life here is not that much different than back at his palatial Palm Springs manse, but he is pleased to be part of this 'phenom'. At one point he turns to Myrie, who is naked and languishing beneath the sheets, her head resting at the footboard, reading a magazine. He has on an open bathrobe and silk boxer shorts, sitting with his chair leaned back on two legs, with the guitar laid casually across his lap. "You know, babe, I'm really happy with the work I'm doing. I bet the bandmates will dig the tracks."

"What's not to like?" she says while flipping the page of her magazine. "I've heard it, it's terrific."

Bull strums the guitar and looks out the window at the stars flying by; "Off I go/to a never-neverland/Here you know/lightshow paradise at hand."

Zolnick and Bull are not alone in their good fortune. From the outset of the voyage, the boutiques and shops of En Vogue Avenue enjoy constant business. The passengers aboard this ship do more than browse - - - they buy! A steady stream of customers pass through the mall daily, providing handsome profits for the store owners.

The two fashion houses sell many evening gowns, party dresses, and accessories to the wives, daughters and women of the Royale Class, while the men's clothier accommodates their male counterparts. The two jewelry stores do extremely well, as does the art gallery. The *Emprasoria* Gift Shop sells a large amount of photographs and postcards showing the ship in flight, in addition to the other souvenirs it offers, such as coffee mugs, golf- and tee-shirts, caps, and the like. The three other gift emporiums, which offer more unique items such as antiques, glassware, and novelty products, record large amounts of sales as well.

All eighteen VacaBank machines in En Vogue (three front, three middle and three back, on each side) are used frequently.

This activity within En Vogue does not escape the attention of Maddox and his partners. "I originally didn't expect the mall to be as profitable as it is being," Maddox says somewhat ruefully to Angelique on Tuesday afternoon. "I had only included the jewelry stores and the art gallery on the team's hit list. Our plans are going to be adjusted." She nods.

"We should go check out En Vogue," Maddox says to Angelique. "I want to scope it out more closely."

"Fine by me, I like how they have it set up down there," Angelique responds.

So the two pay a special visit to En Vogue Avenue. As they window-shop and browse, they 'case' the area. Four small, rotating video cameras, one facing each direction, are suspended from a circular rigging around a large, round, decorated ventilation cover in the ceiling. As well, square electronic sensors guard each side of the shop's doors. He finds the stores have average security measures. Nothing he hasn't seen before, nothing he can't bypass with little difficulty.

Maddox enters Nicholby's, a jewelry shop, as yet another stop on his 'tour'. He notices the door give a chime as he steps inside, and he comes upon a standard yet stylish showroom. Well-lit, the inside perimeter is lined with display cases, all brimming with glittering gold and sparkling with jewels fashioned in rings, bracelets, necklaces, earrings, broaches and watches. This is an impressive collection. Maddox maintains a calm demeanor, but smiles inside: soon, to be his! Maddox strolls about, takes casual glances at some pieces, then turns to leave when something catches his eye.

'MAJESTIC GEMS OF THE WORLD' a sign boldly proclaims over a display. Set on black velvet within a glass box are twenty-one replicas of the most beautiful and most famous gems known to man. A tiny italicized inscription beneath each stone identifies it. Prominently centered is the large and glorious Cullinan Star of Africa diamond whose authentic counterpart adorns the top of the Royal Scepter of England. Circled around this are the amazing diamonds of Koh-i-noor, the Jubilee, the Regent, the Shah, the Florentine, the Great Mogul, the Star of the South, the Polar Star, the Sancy, the Pasha of Egypt, and the Light of the Desert. Then come the Star of India sapphire, the Delong Star ruby, the Midnight Star sapphire, the Rosser-Reeves Star ruby, the Victoria-Transvaal diamond, the Star of Bombay sapphire, the Star of Asia sapphire, the Maharam cat's eye. Last but not least, Maddox's eyes fall on the Hope Diamond, within its ringlet of white diamonds no less. A quick breath becomes caught in his throat.

"Caught your attention?"

Maddox steps back, startled, and turns toward a smiling well-dressed gentleman. A sales clerk. 'Richard' as given by the nametag pinned to his lapel. "Quite a scene, isn't it?"

"Yes, astounding," Maddox replies as he recovers from the unexpected intrusion. He smiles.

"All reproductions, of course," Richard comments as he takes a step toward the display and rests his hands on its glassed sides. "Excellent work, though. Flawless in every respect." He turns back to Maddox. "Could you imagine if we had the real ones?" He chuckles. "It would be tighter than Fort Knox in here!"

"Yes, I can imagine," Maddox responds.

"Was there anything you would like to see, Sir?" Richard prods, itching to make this guest a customer.

"Just looking for now," Maddox answers.

Still maintaining his smile, Richard continues. "Well, if you come across something, I will be pleased to help . . ."

"Thank you, I will," Maddox answers. He smiles, nods, then exits the store.

There is something I want, Richard, Maddox thinks as he strides through En Vogue, but I doubt if you can help me with it. Maddox recalls his earlier question: Where can he find a counterfeit Hope Diamond out in the middle of space? The answer: Nicholby's. Maddox smiles slyly. Well, this is great . . .

As Maddox and Angelique stroll about the ship during the daytime hours, seemingly carefree, they are actually working. They keenly observe the routines of the crew – stalking their prey. Movements and patterns are studied, absorbing the labor habits on everything from the captain's morning walking tour with the first officer and pretty staff captain down to the retinue of the maintenance staff. Maddox overlooks nothing. One must know his adversary if he intends to beat him . . .

In an early stage of the ongoing reconnaissance mission, Maddox manages to acquire a steward's passcard. There were a few people in the passageway, some walking, some standing, all busy with themselves. The white pushcart is there alone. The unsuspecting steward is presumably inside the adjacent stateroom, whose door is ajar. The card was only set aside for a brief moment - just long enough for Maddox to spy this prize. He slowly walk past, and, with eyes forward and face calm, wrap his hand around the thin card, cushioning it in the soft flesh of his palm, then slip it into his pants pocket. He is down the corridor and around the corner when the steward returns, and, baffled, begins the search for his missing card. Maddox's job has just become remarkably easier.

Three trips are made by Maddox to the rifle range over the course of nine days, each visit lasting no more than twenty minutes. His presence appears to be an interest in the marksmanship skills of his fellow passengers, and he happens to observe two of the shooting matches between Gregg and Roggin, and is impressed with their abilities. Too bad I can't have them on my team, he thinks to himself. In actual fact, his visits are an excuse to study the types and number of firearms in the range . . . and if they use live cartridges. They don't; only dummy slugs. The pieces are of your basic sporting variety; single-shot rifles and shotguns, six-round pistols and revolvers – twenty of each. Maddox notes that operational protocols for the use and storage of the guns are strictly controlled.

The firearm and shooting area is contained within a bulletproof vault, and the shooting area is kept separate from the corridor access door by means of an access-controlled waiting room. Attendants remove the firearm of choice from the case, carefully instruct the shooter on firing, then load it, and pass it to the shooter, with the trigger safety switch on. Sensors in the vault and corridor doorframes ensure that the weapons are kept <u>inside</u> the range. As well, there are two Security guards present during all operating hours of the range. Still, a test is needed. Maddox calls DeSantis on his personafône. "Hello?"

"I have a special job for you."

"Name it."

Within an hour, DeSantis arrives. He nods politely to people, and walks in to the shooting vault. Maddox is sitting in the glassed-in viewer gallery of the range. DeSantis heads toward the firearm attendant booth, and as he moves, passes a smiling person just leaving the desk with a small Colt pistol. DeSantis accidentally walks into the person, and knocks him toward the shooting range door, and the person loses his balance and careens into the doorway. *'**ALERT, ALERT**'* says a computerized voice. Alarms blare. Red lights flash. A woman on the verge of firing finds her shotgun has had its trigger-lock automatically sprung and she cannot shoot. Steel doors instantly slam closed in both the vault and the range waiting room, sealing the areas, as a slated metal grid drops down over the attendant booth as the two Security guards jump to the entryway.

The stumbled man looks up, somewhat shaken. "What the hell?" he says, angered.

"Pardon me, sorry...." DeSantis offers.

"What happened here?" a security officer inquires.

"My fault, wasn't looking where I was going, a mishap," says DeSantis, showing evidence of clear embarrassment.

"Just a simple accident, no problem," the stumbler comments. "I am alright." He looks around. "What's with the lockdown? Holy cow, it's like Fort Knox!"

"Sorry, Sir," the security officer says. "The firearms are implanted with special sensors to assure they cannot be removed from the range." Seeing things are quite fine, the officer nods to his partner, who turns and lifts his radio to his lips.

"Security Station, this is Kirsalis at the rifle range. False alarm here, just a passersby accident. Please reset the system."

"Will do Kirsalis," comes the answer.

A moment later, and the steel doors are unlocked, and the alarm bleats cut as the flashing lights wink out. Maddox and the others in the viewing gallery sit back in their seats, as the startled passengers in the range calm themselves. "Interesting," Maddox mutters. DeSantis continues to the firearm attendant and takes some quick shooting practice, only for the sake of appearances.

Over the course of his 'observations', Maddox pays particular attention to the security staff. They alone stand as the only real barrier to the successful completion of the mission. He has already acutely studied the alarm system and video surveillance on the vessel. By modifying his earlier, and close-to-fact, assumptions he has devised a feasible plan to work around them.

One afternoon he returns to his stateroom and sits in an easychair, drink in hand. Angelique is off enjoying a spa treatment, and Maddox softly chuckles to himself after analyzing the procedures of the ship's guards. "Their idea of security is child's play," he says. Well, he thinks, their policing is solid, in fact quite adequate to effectively handle the odd incident by basically law-abiding tourists, but, when put up against professional criminals, they fall far short of the requirements, and in his opinion, stand no chance. A second chuckle. This will be so eas-- Maddox stops himself. He cuts the thought off. Underestimating the guards can be fatal to his mission. He will not allow overconfidence to mire his performance. He forces himself to view them as formidable opponents. His mood changes. The smile disappears. Stern face. His fingers grasp the glass so tightly that it shatters in his hand. There will be no more laughter.

Maddox knows sound leadership is vital to the success of any operation. He checks with each member of his team once a day. They are likewise surveying the standard operating procedures of the crew, and he compares notes with them. He also ensures they are bright and alert, keeping fit at the gym on their assigned shifts (never in pairs and not exercising at noticeable levels of tension), that they are keeping their fingerprints filed down with emery boards. He makes sure they are not "socializing" excessively, and, most of all, that they are mastering the fine art of being inconspicuous - - no "shipboard flings", no heavy tipping of the crew, no odd habits, no excesses . . . nothing to make them stand out in anyone's memory. Just another face in the crowd. Ordinary Joe's and Jenn's, John and Jane Does on vacation. What can be more normal?

Maddox is pleased with his conspirators. He has formed a fine unit. Alex Dimitri Parker is his second-in-command, and a supremely capable lieutenant. Angelique Yusacre, Enrique DeSatnis, Ruby Kobryn, and Salma Jensen form the rest of the team. They are 'tough as nails' fighters who consider themselves a breed apart from the average person, and operate with the cold-blooded efficiency of a Waffen SS commando squad. They have no distractions due to outside personal agendas or warped political motives. They have been hand-picked by Maddox. He has worked with them before, and each has some degree of military experience. They currently are alter-egos of themselves; sporting alias names and identification, and living a masquerade.

Colorspray masks their natural hair, and tinted contact lenses make uniform brown eyes. For the men, dark hair in a medium-length style with a side-part. Artificial brown goatees, moustaches or beards, light on the face and applied with glue, further change their features and distort noticeable differences in their jawlines. A small pock-mark scar by Parker's left ear is discreetly covered by theatrical makeup, as is a tattoo which decorates DeSantis' left forearm. And now, the ladies; brunettes one in all, styled similarly with curls.

Canisters of colorspray remover as well as other coloring agents are carried at all times by each of the team, as are extra colored lens-sigthers. On everyone, mild padding provides the same build . . . stout, with slight paunches typically found on average middle-aged people, a look that speaks 'harmless' in volumes. The padding is formed from a Culver body-armor mesh, so while altering their forms, it protects them as well. Elevator shoes raise those who are slightly shorter to within a half-inch of Maddox's six-foot standard.

They are chameleons . . . and duplicates of one. Nearly identical to the casual glance by passersby. Operating in disguise which can be dropped at the hint of trouble within three scant seconds, leaving the real or another contrived appearance to emerge and fade into anonymity while a search is made for another, who for all intents and purposes no longer exists.

Maddox smiles – they are acting perfectly; following his orders and keeping to the plan. DeSantis and Jensen, the two relegated to Tourist class, are not even complaining. Excellent. The team will reward him well, yes they will. Damn excellent! One element concerns him, though. He is sitting at the laptop, studying ship readouts, tension on his face. "Everything ok?" Angelique asks warily.

"The time-distance ratio has me bugged," he replies without looking up from the screen, "they sure are cruising fast." He clicks a few keys, then looks at her. "If we keep going at this rate, we may arrive at Mars ahead of schedule, odd as that may sound."

"I am sure the officers and crew have it all figured out," Angelique says.

"Yes, true." His gaze returns to the monitor and he clicks some more keys. "I think I'll modify the schedule to have stuff go down on the last night of the voyage, whatever that happens to be, rather than the twentieth specifically."

Angelique nods. "That sounds reasonable."

"The basic plan remains the same, just the date is up-in-the-air." He pauses and types some more. "I'll let the others know." He then looks up at her and smiles. "That other part of the plan is ready, and I've set an auto-timer to release it."

"Do tell?"

"They have top-notch entertainment programs on this ride. Well, some of them are going to rattle the cage a bit when our deal goes down. It's kind of like two parts of the same whole, the entertainment gizmos and the sensor-function drives, that were separated at birth and never supposed to meet, yet two hearts will beat as one. They will mix, merge, congeal. They will work as a unit, and at my behest. Exhilarating. Almost god-like control over it, the fantasy world that I create. A funhouse with plenty of smoke and mirrors... easy for the functioners to become misled in, lost in, wander through...like some sort of bad halucination. Then I'll welcome them to my nightmare, a taste of practical magic, and they won't know what hit 'em." He smiles wickedly.

"Delicious." She winks at him. He motions her over, and she walks to him with swaying hips and sits on his lap. He buries his hand in her hair and brings her face to his, and presses her lips against his, strongly and deeply. He holds her closer and she gasps beneath the kiss, and it is again proven that power –power in the real world or in an imagined one of cyber-puppets and avatar pixel stages– really is the ultimate aphrodisiac.

The voyage continues with the innocent not knowing a hint of the charade occurring in their midst. Who has time to worry about something so outlandish as 'trouble' when aboard the *Emprasoria*? As the grand voyage continues, the passengers are treated to special events nightly. Concerts by the band, musical performances by the *Emprasoria*'s Starflyte dancing troupe, or screenings of newly released films are prevalent. The slim, wavy-haired comedian Gregg Luvv of the hit television sit-com "LUVV" holds an entirely new, always hilarious, stand-up routine every evening for one hour in the forward observation lounge. The doors of Club Ritz open nightly at nine o'clock sharp, and provide disk-jockeyed music, free flowing alcohol, and an electric atmosphere for its patrons well into the early morning hours.

On the second evening, there is a special theme party in the Cosmos Showlounge. Titled "The Ongoing Ballet of Space". Each constellation is displayed by means of special lighting and an exposition of clouds formed by dry ice. The Sun, in all its majestic glory, is showcased by means of special footage, and the nine planets of the Solar System are presented. Then come the phases of the Moon. As well, a supernova is represented along with a quasar, a nebula and Andromeda. This is all done with dance representation, to background music of "The Planets" by Handel.

In the wake of the success of the Captain's Ball, the Cosmos, Ritz, and Forward Observation Lounge quickly become reserved for gala private parties. Edwin and Lauraleigh Roggin host a formal dinner-dance for the Enkels, and Cal and Genvievve Gregg hold another in celebration of the new era of luxury in spaceflight. Other parties abound, and the cruise entertainment staff is very attentive in making the necessary arrangements. Parties are scheduled around ship events in order that Royale class passengers can attend any function they desire without being forced to make arduous decisions about what event will be missed in favor of another.

Maddox and his team socialize as well. If they were reclusive and deliberately avoiding their fellow passengers, they would draw unwanted attention to themselves, not to mention becoming restless and agitated from being 'penned up' in their staterooms. However, the couples are never seen in public with another of the group. Having almost identical persons be observed together would be bound to arouse suspicion. There are some inevitable sightings though, where someone would see one of them, then see another somewhere else, in an entirely different outfit in a short space of time. However, the people answered their own confusion when this occurs. 'But wait, wasn't he . . . no, I must be seeing things. Couldn't be.' Thus, simple logic and a strong desire to avoid embarrassment aids Maddox and his team to no end.

"Looks like things are going well," Parker says to DeSantis one day during a clandestine check-up meeting.

"Very well," DeSantis answers. "I'm getting eager for the job."

"You and me both." Parker pauses. "By the way, how do you like Maddox as a leader?"

The Mexitalian looks over at Parker. "Strong, fair, doesn't put unfair restrictions on us," he answers warily. "Good to work with, just like that mission I did with him before."

Parker smiles. "I agree one-hundred percent. He's a great guy, has a good head on his shoulders and an eye for detail."

A smiling, attractive woman happens to walk by. "Speaking of having an eye for detail..." DeSantis whispers.

Parker turns and watches her as she passes them. "Nice, nice." He turns back to DeSantis. "That's one thing I find really testing about this whole deal. The women. Lots of honies on board – stunners – and all we can do is talk with them, and not much of that either."

"I hear you," DeSantis says. "We're like, what do they say? The metaphorical 'kids in the candy store', where all the sweets are out of touch?"

"Yeah. Even if it weren't for laying low and keeping incognito, we still have to play the 'married' game – even less of a chance of a shipboard fling."

"How do you like the woman you were partnered with?" DeSantis asks.

"We get along well enough. You?"

"Great, better than I expected. Maybe Russ should go into the matchmaking business."

Parker chuckles. "Yeah, be sure to suggest that to him."

"Ah, no, thanks just the same," DeSantis says while laughing himself.

Anyway, it is still incredibly frustrating for them. They are like wild horses chomping at the bit, restraining themselves to the utmost, desiring to be free. However, they know they must maintain control, and keep focused on the mission. It is not worth jeopardizing the Score. There is plenty of time for fun later. Parker reminds himself of this constantly, as he has seen one who has sparked something in him. A woman named "Adrianna" . . .

Another person is being sociable. Third Officer Hearst is an almost ever-present figure among the Royale class, much to the annoyance of everyone. The overweight longhaired nuisance spends every minute of his off-duty hours in the company of those whom he desperately wishes to be accepted by . . . into their exclusive circle. The Royale class passengers avoid Hearst whenever possible, and endure him whenever it is not. They loathe him, but, nonetheless are polite and cordial to him, as their sense of taste and style prevents them from doing anything less.

Enkel quickly becomes aware of the issue. Soon after, the ship's Quartermaster finds a message waiting at his desk. He reads it, frowns, then notes the signature at the bottom. He gives it a second glance. The duty roster thereafter is changed in order that Hearst is scheduled at his station when the Royale clientele are up and about. Hearst complains, as the Q.M. knew he would, but all he can do is shrug and apologize as "that is the way it is". Hearst is angry, and cut off from his chance at improvement - just as he is making headway! But he can do nothing about it, so he broods.

Exciting times proceed during the cruise, creating happy faces enjoying the pleasure of the moment. Michael Priest makes a detailed photographic record of all the amusement. For a thrill for some passengers, some of these pictures even appear in The Transastral Times! How extraordinary! Also, he makes them available to passengers as postcards for sending through SolNet. There is not a single event he misses . . . smiles everywhere, spirit radiates through the celluloid. "The execs and marketing group should both be pleased with these," he remarks to himself in his darkroom, as he knows the photos convey the bright, exhilarating atmosphere of the ship.

But there is one thing, though. In some of the shots, someone has his or her head turned away, or the face obstructed by something – usually because of standing in an obscure place, or raising some reading material at the worst possible second. For a moment, Priest thought he noticed a discernible glare of hatred flashed from a mystery man one time – directed right at him. Later, he is unsure it occurred at all when he recalls the incident. Priest enters the darkroom of his studio and clicks on the overhead light. The room becomes bathed in red. He raises a magnifying glass to his eye and leans over the developing trays as he sets about the touch-up work to strip the unsightly oddities from the negatives. Just what he needs, some folks who are camera-shy. He shakes his head in frustration.

"Edwin, I want us to go to this event tonight in the atrium," Lauraleigh Roggin says as she reads her itinerary book from her bed on Friday morning. Friday happens to mark the mid-point of the voyage.

Edwin, still half asleep, rolls over in her direction. "What is it?" he murmurs.

"They don't exactly say..." she continues, her eyebrows narrowing in bewilderment. "Some sort of surprise for the passengers. They bill it as an 'extra-special' event. Starts at nine."

"Ok, that sounds like fun sweetie." With his eyes still closed, Edwin slips his arm across her stomach and shifts his body closer to her. "We can see what all the secrecy is about. I am sure, whatever it is, it will be good." Edwin slyly reaches his hand up and takes the booklet from Lauraleigh's hands, closes it, and lightly tosses it off the bed as he moves still closer to her. His arm returns to its place, and he hugs her closely. "We can worry about how the day goes later. Cuddle time now, sweetie." She laughs and scoots under the covers, turning on her side toward him.

Up on the bridge, Captain Arges walks into the room with a cup of coffee in hand, having just finished his breakfast and the walking tour. Rish follows him, likewise carrying a cup, and the two walk up to the command platform. "Good morning, Mitchell," Arges says.

"Good morning, Sir," Third Officer Hearst replies while vacating the chair for the captain. "Peter," he continues with a nod, garnering a nod for himself from Rish.

Arges takes the seat. "Report, Mitchell," the captain says while setting his cup in a holder on the Platform and taking a look at the central vidscreen.

"Ship performing to requirements, Sir. Running at good speed, electrostatic fire still burning, but being contained. Radar functioning well."

"Very good," Arges replies while looking over some readouts and punching some buttons. "So we have reached the mid-point of our ace run." He turns and looks at Rish. "I would say we are doing rather well, wouldn't you?"

"Yes, sir. Exceptionally well."

"Have we made any contact with Gamma yet?" Arges asks.

"Yes, sir," Hearst answers. "We did a quadri with them once we entered their region."

"Very good," Arges comments, then looks up, and talks over his shoulder to the Astrocon. "Christian, I take it we'll be passing by Centralis today?"

"Yes, Captain," Astrogator Miasaki answers quickly. "We will be moving past her in the early afternoon, with her on our port side."

"Very good," Arges turns to Rish. "I always enjoy seeing that marvel."

"She is quite something to see," Rish agrees.

Centralis is the primary communications relay satellite between Earth and Mars. It orbits at a point where the gravity of the two planets are balanced, and outside the influence of either the Earth or Martian gravity fields. Centralis is silver in color, being lengthly and large, with a narrow thorax. Its upper section is cone-like with a flat top, and behind the plexiglass shell which forms the middle is a circle of radio telescope dishes facing outward. Intricate strings of pulsating light form a crisscrossing grid above the dish housing. The bottom section provides a solid base as it is thick and rounded, resembling a large puck, with an array of flashing lights, and beneath this is a rod tipped with a large bronze circle. Beacons at the top and bottom of Centralis flash rhytmatically to alert cosmic traffic of its presence.

Centralis is a super-powered communications conduit, and operated exclusively by the Solar Parliament, a body comprised of Earth, Lunar and Martian representatives. It is the single-most important piece of telecommunications equipment between Earth and her neighboring planet, and as such is vital linchpin, born from a need for rapid and stable communications as Earth expanded beyond her planetary limits. Every piece of electronically based interaction, including SolNet activity, between the planets and the Lunar colony, and all interplanetary ships in between, pass through Centralis at some point. Centralis is a matrix and nexus, all in one.

Arges accesses current information on Centralis from a vidscreen on the platform. "Roberta," he says as he reads, "we'll do a standard comm check with Centralis as we move by her."

"Yessir," the communications officer answers from her station.

The captain next calls the communicator of DeMornay from his Chair. "Hello Krystal."

"Good morning, John."

"As a reminder, did you know we will be going past Centralis today?"

"Yes, I noted it in my schedule the other day. This afternoon, isn't it?"

"Correct. So we'll see you up on the bridge after lunch then?"

"Looking forward to it."

"Thank you. We'll see you then."

"Have a good morning. Goodbye."

"Goodbye." Arges turns to Rish. "Feel free to advise anyone else about us seeing the satellite, if they are interested."

"Will do," Rish answers with a smart nod. "I know I'll be on hand for it."

Arges sits up in the command chair and busies himself with some routine business of the cruise. He expects to have good news for Mr. Enkel at dinner tonight.

The ship moves along. Later, as Edwin and Lauraleigh finish their lunch, Edwin pauses in thought. "Is today the half-way point of the trip?"

"I believe so," Lauraleigh answers.

Edwin waves over a waitress. "Yes, Sir?" she asks.

"Is it correct that we are half way to Spaceport Gamma?"

"Yes, that is correct. Your suite vidscreen can give you updates on our progress, or there are ship location maps in the Halo lounge and Purser's Lobby for your benefit, Sir."

"Thank you," Edwin replies.

"My pleasure, Sir. Have a pleasant afternoon," she replies, and as the waitress leaves, Edwin turns to Lauraleigh. "Would you mind if I check that map she mentioned in the lounge quickly?"

"Not at all," she answers, and they rise from their chairs.

A minute later and the two are in the Royale lobby, going to the location map on the left wall. The black electronic map is framed in gold and shows a white, flashing, animated profile drawing of the *Emprasoria* in relation to where she is in the Earth - Mars corridor. Edwin lets his eyes wander over the three-dimensional map itself. At the left end is the blue-green Earth, where tiny representations of North and South America look up at him. Next in line is the crater-dotted Moon with its biocol domes being plainly evident. On the right end of the chart is the red orb Mars and its domes, and two small moons.

Edwin looks it over closely. "Exactly what I thought. We should be going past Centralis soon." He turns to Lauraleigh. "I know you don't like much of the hardware stuff, but care to join me in the front observation room for a glimpse of the satellite?"

Lauraleigh slips her arm into his. Edwin is right, her personal interest in the behind-the-scenes workings of technology is limited, but she sees his enthusiasm. "That sounds good to me, Edwin," she says while pulling him away from the map.

They walk along hastily to the forward observation lounge, which is relatively empty. Edwin leads her to the front windows, to the left of the Excelsis figurehead. Edwin squints and peers forward.

"I believe that's it," he says, pointing with his left hand to a fair-sized speck which rests not too far distant.

Lauraleigh looks in the same direction. "That looks like a man-made satellite." Edwin remains at the window, watching intently as the object grows in size as the ship draws nearer. "Dear, don't strain your eyes," Lauraleigh warns.

"I'm ok." There is silence for a moment as his attention is fixed. "Yes, that definitely has to be it!" He turns to Lauraleigh. "This will be great!" She smiles, and he again turns outward. "Looks like it'll be on the left as we go by, and fairly close too!" he says, noting that the satellite is veering slightly to the left of them as they get closer.

Edwin and Lauraleigh take a place at the portside windows, standing. The outline of Centralis can clearly be seen against the starry backdrop of space. Edwin tightens his grip on Lauraleigh's hand slightly, out of sheer excitement. "Here she comes!"

Thirty seconds later, and Centralis is there. Looking mighty as it spins on its own axis, clean and bright, its operating lights flashing strongly. Edwin Roggin, the stalwart telecommunications magnate, reverts to the wide-eyed wonder of a child as he stares transfixed at the massive transceiver junction. He believes he can almost hear the whirred and hasty sounds of the trillion to-and-fro conversation emissions being processed that particular moment.

Edwin turns to Lauraleigh. "Look at that!" He points to the satellite. "That is where the signals from Roggin Broadcasting pass through every minute of every day to our stations on Mars."

She nods appreciatively. "It really is quite something."

Edwin looks outside again, pressing his face to the window as Centralis falls back, soon being left behind in its stationary manner in the wake of the racing *Emprasoria*. He continues to stare at the device until it is nothing more than the speck it was just moments ago. "That was an unexpected treat," he says while turning to Lauraleigh.

"I'm glad you had the chance to see it."

Edwin looks around the still largely empty lounge. "Care for a drink?" he asks, indicating two easy chairs and a table.

"Sounds divine," Lauraleigh answers and kisses him lightly on the cheek. They seat themselves, and a half-second later a waiter is on hand for their order.

"Well, that was certainly exciting," comments Captain Arges on the bridge. He lowers his binoculars from his face, and is standing at the room's port viewport.

"Yes, quite," concurs DeMornay.

"An exceptional piece of hardware," Rish observes.

"Roberta, how did our comm check go?" Arges asks.

The communications officer turns from her station. "Clear as a bell."

"That's what I like to hear."

Meanwhile, the entertainment staff toils for much of the afternoon in the closed-off atrium of the arboretum in lavish preparation. "This should be very good," Staff Captain Syranos remarks while nodding, approving of what she sees being done.

Bethany Parris approaches her. "Jennifer?"

"Bethany, hi, how are you?" Sryanos answers with a smile.

"Great, thank you. Is it true that this is the first time a performance like this has been held on a cruise ship?"

"That's the case alright. The first time on *any* cruise ship – sea or astral."

"Incredible!" Bethany says with a bright smile.

"It should be a thrill for our passengers, and us," Jennifer comments. "Do you know your role alright?"

"Oh yes, I've been looking forward to this since we left!"

"That's great to hear."

"Well, I want to double check a few things. Have a good afternoon." And with that, Bethany excuses herself.

"Thanks, and good to see you, Bethany. See you again tonight as well."

At eight forty-five that evening, Edwin, Lauraleigh, and other passengers begin to gather within Langshott Parkette and seat themselves on the specially arranged chairs. The back section of the atrium is darkened, adding to the mystery of what the event actually is, as if you recall, the passengers were not told exactly.

The clocks chime nine bells, and a spotlight glows and shines down on the solitary form of Staff Captain Syranos, who is standing in behind a microphone. A hush falls over the crowd. Syranos smiles widely. "Ladies and Gentlemen, it is my distinct pleasure to welcome you to our grand mid-flight presentation, Fantasia!" She steps to the side, and the spotlight winks out. It is so quiet you can hear a pin drop.

Then, a drumbeat begins. Quaint, it is. Bowl-lights on the floor brighten softly, and the audience can see dim silhouettes of Fitzroy and the *Emprasoria* band ahead of them. The drumbeat grows stronger, and is joined by the horn section. Minutes later, the strings begin to sound and, last but not least, Fische and his grand piano blend in with the tune. And this is only the beginning . . . The song continues in its intensity, and colored lights click on behind the band. These are joined in quick succession by spouting geysers from the fountains, and the light dances on the spraying water. Laserlights then come alive, playing against this backdrop and forming a plethora of delightful kaleidoscopic imagery in the air. Next, the Starflyte dancers appear, in bright red, yellow, gold, blue and green bodysuits carrying matching streamers which flow from their hands. They frolic and parade gracefully; pirouetting, leaping, and dancing, moving and merging, making their bodies living art like acrobatic contortioners. All this is perfectly synchronized to the medley of classical music set to an impressive contatta. At certain crescendos, an array of bold fireworks is launched. They explode in all variety of color and style near the ceiling. This grand wonderment of music, water, light and fire lasts ninety minutes. Then, all too soon, Fitzroy snaps his baton down, and in an instant the music stops, the lights darken, the fountains quell, and the dancers disappear.

There is a roar of applause from the audience, and they rise to their feet in an ovation. Minutes later, when the clapping does fade, the spotlight clicks on, and again shines down on the Staff Captain. She smiles, widely. "Thank you," she says. Then the lights come up and the passengers see the band, the dancers and the technicians standing before them. The troupe gives a collective bow, and the applause erupt again as the Atrium darkens for the last time. The dazzled audience make their way to one of the nightclubs, and everywhere is animated conversation and praise for "Fantasia".

"That was amazing!" Lauraleigh says to Edwin as they rise from their seats.

"Spectacular," her husband agrees.

"What did you think of it, babe?" Peter Bull asks Myrie.

"A close second to a Heathens stage-show," she answers with a hug and a wink. Bull smiles and nods a thanks to her compliment of his band's theatrics.

"A fantastic and original interpretation of the nature of the Cosmos," Rave DeMedici remarks to Octavia. "A space opera, through and through."

"Could not have said it better myself," la blonde agrees.

"Really great! Never seen anything like that before!" says Damien Enkel heartily as he claps with strength from his reserved seat at front-and-center.

"They know how to keep us entertained," Angelique says.

"Keep 'em happy, keep 'em smiling....the crux of the travel industry," Maddox replies.

"It was a tremendous showing, certainly," Anne agrees.

"I want to go find Jennifer and tell her what a great performance it was!" With that, Enkel walks quickly to the stage area to find the staff captain as some ladies crowd around Anne to discuss Fantasia.

Three special sporting events send extra excitement through the ship. Saturday April 12 marks the opening of the Major League Baseball season! The large screen television and the smaller corner sets in Club Ritz are tuned in to the game. The Club provides hotdogs, roasted peanuts in bags, draft beer in plastic cups, and even turns up its heat a bit to aid in that 'stadium' feel. Programs, specially ordered from the Baseball Association, are given to the fans as they arrive at the Club.

"Who is playing?" Congresswoman Jackson asks a waiter as she enters the Ritz.

"It's the New York Yankees against the Toronto Blue Jays!" he answers enthusiastically. "On a sunny day at Yankee Stadium."

"Great!" Jackson says as she accepts a program from him, then finds a seat near the front of the room. She is in pony tail, t-shirt and bluejeans – playing the role of the 'all-American girl' for the baseball game. The televisions click on as the pre-game show begins, and the screens show a capacity-crowd at the stadium as the camera pans around the field.

"This is very clear picture, wouldn't you say?" says a male voice from beside her.

Jackson turns to see Tsarevich Alexai Romanoff, wearing a dark golf-shirt and tan khaki pants. "Yes, it is," she answers with an encouraging smile.

"Permit me to introduce myself," he says while offering his hand. "Alexai Romanoff." He intentionally leaves off his title during introductions in situations like this, as he has found in the past that some people become awkward with the 'royal' aspect.

"Sharon Jackson," she answers as she shakes his hand. "Pleased to meet you." She pauses and looks at him a moment. "It's Tsarevich Romanoff, isn't it?" she whispers.

"Guilty as charged," Romanoff says, smiling, his hand raised in mock surrender.

"I have seen your photo before, specifically at the Russian Embassy. I sit on the Congress in the United States."

"Ah, very nice." Romanoff sits back and opens his program, looks at it then turns back to her. "Could you help me with this game? I am rather new to it."

"Yes, Alexai. I would be happy to."

The two watch the rest of the pre-game as others arrive to crowd the club. Soon, the game itself begins. The national anthems are played and the Americans in the room rise and place their hands over their hearts, then President Cartright throws in the first ball to the cheers of the thrilled crowd. Jackson's heart flutters at the sight of her President. "Baterrrrr up!" yells the umpire. The pitching, hitting and base-running unfold, with Jackson providing information to the Russian Prince. Some hours later, the Yankees are victorious over the Jays, 5 to 4 in the bottom of the ninth. An exciting game which is the perfect way to usher in America's national pastime for 2088.

Days later, the Ritz televisions play host to one of the early qualifying runs for the Kentucky Derby direct from Churchill Downs. The Club is again willed with enthusiasts, and his time, Mint Julips are served and the air is scented with magnolia to keep in theme. The starting pistol fires - the gate drops - and they're off!!! The race is thrilling, with three lead horses running neck-and-neck through the final lap, but in the end, it is Sunshine's Glory, a strong and magnificent mustang, a stallion sired in the noble line of the all-time champion Secretariat, and ridden by expert jockey Will Cobbler, who crosses the finish-line first and trots around the Winner's Circle. Small wads of bills are discreetly passed among the betters in the Club, and everyone enjoyed watching the 'run around the track'.

Also comes the season opener of Voltoss. This combines hai lai, lacrosse, ice hockey, rugby and roller derby, is new to the sporting world – only entering its third season. It is a high-impact sport, with few rules, less equipment, and a method of goal-scoring requiring an intense degree of temperance and skill. The Ritz televisions display all the knuckle-crunching excitement, and likewise offer game programs for those who attend. The Phoenix Saints go up against the Yucatan Scorpions, and after three hours of clobbering, tackling, pitching and weaving, the battered and bruised Saints claim the winning ball.

Congresswoman Jackson attends the other two sport events too; a summer dress for the race, and a casual outfit for the other. Her spirit soars on seeing the horses and her adrenaline flows during the Voltoss. She cheers with the rest each time the Yankees score, holds her breath in suspense as the hoofs pound the dirt, then winces at the bone-crushing impacts of Voltoss. She relays letters of congratulation to the Yankees, Jockey Cobbler, and the Saints. The horseracing prompts a visit the Equestria from her for a long, invigorating ride.

Dade and Adrianna attend the sport screenings as well. She wears Dade's blue Yankees baseball cap to the game. He has had it since his woebegone university days; it has a certain 'lived in' feel about it - not tattered, but comfortable. "I like that on you," he says, "you look cute in it." However, to the smitten Darian Dade she looks quite good in just about anything. Sometimes he finds himself just looking at her, for no particular reason. She caught him, once or twice. "What, silly?" she asks with a playful swat on his arm.

He simply smiles. "Just appreciating," is his answer, which scores for him a large smile.

At one point, Dade decides to be playful with her. While she visits his suite, he leads her by her hand into the verandah. He has a certain mischievous spark in his eye, and she smiles back at him coyly. "What are you up t-" she begins.

He stops her by raising his forefinger to his lips. "Shhhhhhhhhhhhhhh." He closes the glass door, then takes her in his arms and kisses her. As their embrace ends, he leans over and punches the Scenic System. The cloudflight program begins to activate. Dade looks back at her as the lights dim and a skyscape appears on the vidscreen. "Ever makelove among the clouds?" he asks.

"Bad boy," she replies coquettishly, then smiles and kisses his finger. They then join the 'mile high club' in a manner never really quite done before.

Dade and Adrianna are seen together at the numerous other social functions, as are others who boarded single, but have since developed a 'certain something' with another. Both new and existing couples stroll hand-in-hand through the Arboretum and window-shop through En Vogue together, or relax placidly in the Forward Observation Lounge or dance the night away at Club Ritz. Subtle hints of affection are in evidence; little whispers, stolen kisses, shared moments. Spring fever mixes with the vacation feel aboard the *Emprasoria*.

Like the passengers whom they serve, care for, and chauffeur through the stars, the officers and crew enjoy a pleasant voyage as well. The ship is operating at peak performance, and although there has been the odd fault, there have been no major issues. A rare privilege for a new ship indeed. The log acclaims the unbridled excellence by recording the status reports, efficiency ratings, supply consumption, energy output, speed achieved, and miles traveled – success in all aspects. The crew is very proud of their ship, and treat her with tender loving care. They even bestow a nickname: 'The Lady E'. The officers allow this term of endearment to unofficially stand. The pride the crew takes in their work and the vessel is seen by the passengers and it extends to them, adding a certain extra-special feeling, an icing on the cake if you will.

"This ace run is really topping the charts!" Damien Enkel says to his wife, beaming with pride in their suite.

"Yes, this is true Damien," she replies with equal enthusiasm.

"Have you seen the faces of the passengers? They are thrilled! It's like they're in another world, on cloud nine or in seventh heaven! Some of the notes that Jennifer and John have been getting, or what Darcy has been hearing, the words people use to describe, they effuse…everyone is so greatly impressed, it's just fantastic! Not to mention what people have said to us in person!"

She walks over and embraces him. "It is good. Flawless, perfect. We did good work, you and I."

Enkel returns the hug. He is the Lord of this spaceborne castle, and conducts Himself in accordance with this fact. He smiles, often – his employees at all levels are pleased with that. The *Emprasoria*…..his prize, his brainchild, is serving him well in every way possible. He basks in the glory she, his ship, provides.

And so it goes. To say life aboard the *Emprasoria* is glamorous is a great understatement; it is a magnificence. With each passing day, the vessel draws nearer to her destination of Mars. The passengers wish with all their hearts that this is not true, but it is. All too soon, they will be docking at Spaceport Gamma, and their extraordinary journey will have come to an end.

CHAPTER SEVEN
The Centralis Episode

ALERT ALERT ALERT

CENTRALIS SATELLITE STATION RUDIMENTARY CONDITION

PRIMARY ONBARD REDUNDANT SYSTEM:	**OFFLINE**
SECONDARY O.R. SYSTEM:	**OFFLINE**
TERTIARY O.R. SYSTEM:	**OFFLINE**
QUATERNARY O.R. SYSTEM:	**OFFLINE**
PENTIARY O.R. SYSTEM:	**OFFLINE**

FAILSAFE COMPROMISED / MIRROR DRIVES DISABLED

IMMEDIATE ATTENTION REQUIRED

"Holy shit, All the backups are down!" yells a technician in the communications section of Spaceport Gamma.

"What?" blurts his supervisor. "Randell, what are you talking about?"

The tech jerks his chair around from his monitor to the main console in the middle of the room. "Centralis! All the backups just failed!"

"That's not poss" the supervisor says with utter disbelief as she types with one hand on the keyboard next to her, that of the maincom status board. Information spills back in a millisecond: it is TRUE! Her eyes widen in sheer terror; "What the hell!" she says as her mouth falls open in shock.

"It's totally vulnerable!" Randell shouts as he spins his seat back into place. He rapidly types commands – by this time, others in the area have begun their own checks of the satellite.

"I need verification!" the supervisor yells as she enters more commands and reaches for the telephone.

"Is this a drill?" someone asks.

"I hope to God so," Randell whispers as he types furiously, and sweat is beginning to show along his forehead and moist blotches appear on his uniform shirt. He makes a silent prayer to Vishnu for guidance and strength.

"Getting the same readings over here!" comes a yell.

"Got it here too!" exclaims another.

"Initiating recovery attempt," Randell states while typing commands. "Sending restart."

"Network ops, this is Supervisor Janet Maki in Comm1 of Gamma," says the supervisor hurriedly but with forced calm into her telephone, the handset being shoved between her bent neck and shoulder as she uses each hand to type on two different keyboards. "I need confirmation on some readings we are getting here."

Another message appears on Randell's screen: **While talking to Centralis/Safebase-sub REQUEST TO SATELLITE UNACCEPTED AT DESTINATION. DELIVERY PORT UNFOUND. RECEPIENT ADDRESS HAD FATAL ERROR, USER UNRECOGNIZED/UNKNOWN. Please direct further questions regarding this message to your origin-point administrator.**

"It's cordoned off to incoming commands!" Randell shouts. "We're locked out! Got to get some kind of remote override going!"

"How in the hell could this have happened?" Randell asks himself, thinking aloud. "If the logic logs have been wiped....if the controller cards are shorted..." He stops himself, not wanting to panic over these vile thoughts.

"Ops says these readouts are the real deal!" Maki calls from her desk.

<Simon Says: <<Are you scared yet?>>

The eyebrows of Randell come together in tension as he blinks, then re-reads the message which suddenly appeared on his screen, over top of the system warning.

<Simon says: <<Are you scared yet?>> The message has appeared again, just beneath the original.

"We've got to think about a recovery, people!" continues Maki. "We still have the alternate back up system working down here. Ops is implementing a special containment protocol as an extra safety measure to keep it solid, but we need to discover what happened upstairs and get a plan to counter the incident then restore all five of the onboard safeties. Give me ideas, people!"

Randell stares, transfixed at his monitor, saying nothing and remaining motionless.

`<Simon says: <<I said, are you scared yet?>>`

"Janet," Randell says, it being a hoarse whisper. He clears his throat and swallows. "Janet, I've got something here for you to look at."

"Patch it through Randell!" Maki shouts back at him. With a few keystrokes, it is done. The same look of bewilderment comes over her face. "What is this?" she asks as she looks over to him.

"Don't know, it just came in." He pauses and looks at her. "What should I do?" The image changes on his screen, drawing his attention back. **`<Simon says: <<If you don't feel like talking, I can leave.>>`**

Randell makes a hasty decision and types a response to the anonymous moniker. **`<We are here. Sorry for the delay.>`** "Janet, I had to answer. I'm going to tag you blind on the exchange."

"Go ahead," she answers. "Everyone else, I want to work on solutions. Get creative."

`<Simon says: <<I hate delays. But anyway, are you a bit shaken up? All of a sudden, not an ordinary day, is it.>>`

Randell's telephone rings. He jumps in his chair, startled, unsure about who might be on the other end of the line.

"It's me, Randell," Maki says from her desk. "Pick up."

"Janet?" he answers.

"Yes. I want us to be able to have direct contact, without the others hearing."

"Ok."

"Switch over to your headset and plug-in."

Randell does as she asks, putting on the headphones and placing the microphone at his lips, then connecting the cord to the phone. "Can you hear me?"

"Yes. So I will watch this talk. After you type an answer, wait for me to give a go-ahead before sending."

"Gotcha."

<Simon says: <<Are you there?>>

<We are here.>

<Simon says: <<Who's we?>>

<Comm1 of Spaceport Gamma.>>

<Simon says: <<Pleased to meet you. So, anything interesting happen at work today? ☺>>

"Yeah, some screwball decided to play games," Randell mutters to himself. "What should I tell him?" he asks Maki.

"You are doing great. Keep him on the line. I've notified Gamma Control and Security. A negotiator will be hear soon."

"Thanks, but, what should I tell him?"

"Don't give him control, but think of something. Don't get angry."

Randell thinks a moment, then comes up with a carefully worded answer. **<Seems like a bit of a glitch with one of our satellites.>**

<Simon says: <<Glitches can be annoying. Sometimes scary.>>

Randell bites his lip. **<They can always be corrected.>**

<Simon says: <<What is your definition of a glitch? A button that sometimes sticks on a keyboard is a glitch, but bringing down all the outlying back-ups of Centralis, that's quite a predicament.>>

<True. I stand corrected.>

<Simon says: <<See, I am a problemsolver already.>>

<Thank you.>

<Simon says: <<You are most surely welcome. I wonder if I can help you with another problem you may have. I can be a real Mr. Fixit if I want to be.>>

<That is good to know. How could you help us?>

<Simon says: <<I could make the Centralis problem go away. Or just make Centralis itself go away.>>

Randell tenses and steals a look over at Maki, who has her eyes fixed on the screen. "What do you make of this?" he asks into his headset.

"I don't know what to say."

<We would like to keep Centralis, repair it.>

<Simon says: <<My thoughts exactly. Glad to see we are in agreement.>>

<So, where from here?>

<Simon says: <<Well, like any tradesman, I'll need to be paid for my services.>>

Randell freezes, and is not forthcoming with a reply.

<Simon says: <<Relax. I know you don't have the authority to commit to anything, so just read my terms and pass them on. Always remember, I am in complete control. Understand?>>

<Understood.>

<Simon says: <<Good. Glad to see you have a brain in your head. You've seen what I can do. It wouldn't be hard for me to expand beyond the back-ups and turn your precious little noisemaker all the way off. Stone dead. Incommunicado. Deaf & mute. The mighty Centralis becomes scrap metal. All of the sudden, Earth-Mars electrotalk gets way more difficult and slower. People would be upset, finance interaction between the planets would be lost or dead. Astrogation suddenly becomes harder. Say good bye to SolNet. With all that, panic could set in. There may even be rioting in the streets. And, >> Suddenly, the dictatorial tirade ends.

Randell and Maki wait for a few moments. "What happened?" Randell whispers into his headset.

"Did we lose him?" asks Maki earnestly.

Thirty more seconds pass. Tension gets the better of Randell. **<Are you there?>**

No reply. They wait, still. A whole minute has gone by, a lifetime in cyberspace. "What should we do?" Randell asks Maki.

<Simon says: <<Not fun being out-of-the-know, is it.>>

Randell breathes a sigh of relief, and Maki runs her hand over her face.

<Simon says: <<That is what it would be like. Remember the old saying 'I sent an arrow into the air, and if it landed I know not where'. There would be no answers to spaceborne questions, no messages from Mother Earth, just

bland static and dead air in a total cut-off. So, to avoid this calamity, this is what I want. I will only say it once, and there is no room for compromise or negotiation. One billion dollars in gold bullion. Unmarked, freshly cast ingots, 24 karats, ready for delivery at a time and place I specify in one week. Attempts to undo my work will automatically have Centralis self-destruct, and your vital linchpin will be snapped like a dry twig. Remember, this is a crime scene - do not cross. If there are problems or delays, that will be the day Centralis stood still. Forever. My wish is your command. Confirm your understanding.>>

Randell looks in a panic at Maki, who returns his terrored gaze with open-mouthed horror. "What should I do?" he asks. Just then, a group of officials and security personnel burst into the room and go directly to the central desk and Maki.

"Tell him you understand, that's all you can do."

<We understand your terms.>

<Simon says: <<Good. Glad I was clear. Until our arrangements are complete, the trusty back-ups of Centralis will remain down. Hope and pray that nothing goes wrong with the prime operations.>>

<We will do what we need to do.>

<Simon says: <<We are in agreement again. A billion of bullion, I love how that sounds. Ha ha ha.>>

"Blow it out your ass, psycho," Randell mutters.

<Simon says: <<I will be in touch.>>

<Do you know when?">

<Simon says: <<Yes. I know exactly when. When I feel like it.>>

With effort, Randell controls his growing anger. He types calmly.

<What if we need to get in touch with you?>

<Simon says: <<This is my party. Let my fingers do the talking. Just be ready when I drop a note.>>

<We will be waiting.>

<Simon says: <<Do more than wait. Start getting me my bounty.>>

<The demands will be presented to my superiors.>
<Simon says: <<Silence is golden.>>
The connection ends.

Randell sits back in his chair. He releases a held breath, then lets his fist fall on the desktop. "Did you see all that?" he asks through his headset.

"Yes," Maki replies. "We got it all. It's saved in the hard drive and printouts are being made now. You did well, Randell."

"Thank you, Janet." He pauses. "Can you believe the arrogance of that bastard?"

"I know. Frustrating, and incredible. Come up here, you and I are going to go to a boardroom and be debriefed."

"Will do." Randell sits for a moment, then removes his headset and puts it on his desk. He runs a tissue over his forehead and also ruffles the front of his sweat-stained uniform shirt, trying to get some cool air in there – he is still perspiring profusely. He rises from his chair, and walks over to Maki, who has officials circled around her.

"This is Marlan Randell," Maki says, introducing the east Indian man to the others. "He was the first to notice the Centralis problem, and the one who conversed with the…the…. The kidnapper. He kept his cool and did fine work." Handshakes and nods are exchanged.

"I'm Nelson Leevan," remarks an authoritative, stout man in a Port security uniform. "Duty officer for today." His arms are crossed defensively across his barrel-chest, and has himself propped on the edge of the main desk. He shakes his head ruefully. "Hard to believe someone would try and pull something like this. We'll have a lot of material to pour over." He shakes his head again in angst, knowing the depth and magnitude of the job that lies ahead. After a moment he turns to Randell. "I saw the exchange you had, you did do well. It was really good not to antagonize him. Sometimes we have to handle these things with kid-gloves. Do you have any law and security training?"

Randell shakes his head no. "I just did what came naturally."

"Great. Well, if you could join us and Ms. Maki in a boardroom, we want to interview you while everything is still fresh in your mind."

"Mr. Leevan," Randell begins, "Were we able to get a trace?"

Leevan turns his second-in-command, Lieutenant Eras, who shakes his head. "We know that the message came to us from Centralis. Ironically, it was sending us its own ransom note. Where Centralis was getting the info, we have no idea….it's a dead lead. We have people working on it though," says Eras. Randell nods appreciatively.

In seeing a replacement supervisor arrive, Leevan speaks again. "Ms. Maki and Mr. Randell, Mr. Fitzmorris here will escort you to one of our interrogation rooms for a debriefing." Nods follow as Fitzmorris steps to the two and leads them out of the Comm1 room just as another supervisor arrives takes Maki's place at the desk. Leevan turns to the replacement supervisor. 'Donovan' it says on the nametag. "Thank you for coming up here on short notice," Leevan says and offers his hand.

"Quite alright," Donovan answers as the handshake occurs. "Duty calls, as they say."

"Yes, true. I am Chief Inspector Leevan. Did anyone brief you on what happened?"

"The basics. A sort of invasion attempt on Centralis?"

"Yes. The incident is on a strict need-to-know basis. Otherwise, everything operates as normal."

"Understood," Donavan says with a firm nod, showing his appreciation of the gravity of the situation.

"The others in this room," Leevan says while looking out at the office-like environment, "it should be stressed to them that confidentiality is a ***must.***"

"They won't say a thing, either in here or outside. I'll see to it. Count on it."

"Great. Thank you. The character who is our main liaison on this calls himself 'Simon'. Put a flag on any communiqués tagged with that name and let our office know immediately. If you could indicate on your Assignment Roster for other supervisors to watch for that name, it will be helpful for our cause."

"Consider it done," Donovan answers.

"Thank you." Another handshake follows, then Leevan nods to Eras and the two head out to interview his two main witnesses.

"Can you imagine this, Rudolph?" Leevan says as they walk down the empty corridor. "A billion dollars in gold bars? How much would that weigh?"

Eras shakes his head in dismay. "It would be at least twenty good-sized crates I would think."

Leevan shakes his as well. "Son of a bitch!"

Out in space, Centralis continues its simultaneous and multiple connectivity unhampered. Delivering its messages and information excelanté' . . . yes, the *Emprasoria* cruise will be his ticket to the good life . . . he is sure of it! These are his last thoughts as he falls into a dreamy sleep.

Bright and early the next morning, Damien Enkel arrives on the bridge to find Captain Arges, First Officer Rish and Staff Captain Syranos waiting for him. "Good morning everyone," he says with a smile.

"Good morning, sir," comes the reply in three.

"Quite the time last night, wouldn't you say?"

"Yes, quite enjoyable," Arges says. "Looked as though the guests enjoyed themselves."

"That is true," agrees Enkel. "I will be interested to see Priest's photos." He looks around the bridge. "Looks as though everything is fine up here."

"Oh yes, Damien. Ship-shape, as they say," remarks the proud captain.

"Well, shall we begin?" Enkel asks.

"Yes, we are ready if you are."

"Very good. Let's go then." With that, the first morning walking tour of the cruise begins. He surveys the surroundings with an eagle eye, but everything meets his high and impeccable standards. An hour later, the four are back at the bridge. "Excellent, excellent," Enkel beams. "Not a single flaw."

"Thank you, Sir," Arges nods.

"Well, I'd better get back to the room and take the missus out to breakfast. I'll see you three here again tomorrow, if not before." This is said as Enkel intends to make a tour of the ship with the three each morning in the early stages of the voyage, then intermittently afterward.

"Very good, Sir. Have a pleasant day." Arges smiles and escorts Enkel away from the bridge.

And so, the first full day of the voyage begins. The social scene moves quickly within the white hull of the *Emprasoria*. One of the finer qualities about the *Emprasoria* is that she offers so much for her passengers. Premiums abound; there is always some sort of performance or event scheduled - - a person would be hard pressed to find him- or herself bored. There is something for everyone in this man-made paradise, whether listening to the ship's band play the music of Beethoven, or a rigorous exercise session, or a shopping spree. There is a high level of accommodation and recognition; all sorts of tastes are catered to - - there are no 'unusual' preferences or 'bizarre' requests, and in this respect, the passengers have a high comfort level and are made to feel as though they are 'at home'.

The *Emprasoria* guests fit themselves into a very exciting, yet relaxing routine. During the evenings, they attend assorted social events well into the early morning hours, then sleep until late in the morning, spend the day doing as they please, then repeat the cycle as the dusk hours fall on the ship. Friendships blossom when, out of simple circumstance, people encounter each other several times over the course of a day or an evening! If anything, life aboard the ship has a danger of being <u>too</u> luxurious for her passengers. To avoid the perhaps unpleasant affects of this, the Line provides for her passengers, at no cost, supplies of Peplyn capsules for energy boosts, Dietrim tablets to maintain their waistlines, and Babysleep pills to aid in peaceful and dreamy slumber.

The White Feather salon serves sumptuous breakfasts, luncheons and dinners. Each multi-course meal is accompanied with a menu offering a multitude of sumptuous cuisine. As at the Captain's Ball, the soft 'serving call' chimes sound to announce a meal sitting, which lasts an hour. If, however, a passenger becomes hungry when the salons are closed, food may be ordered from cabin stewards, who quickly provide a tray bearing whatever delicacy is requested. The White Feather attempts to convey a familiar feeling for the mealtimes. During breakfast and luncheon, the window covers remain closed, and their scenic systems display vistas appropriate for the hour, such as a sunrise dawn over a meadow for the morning, and a mid-day sight for the afternoon. The covers are opened when dinner is served so patrons may dine with the stars.

The *Emprasoria* accommodates passengers who wish to be informed about current events. Just because one is in the middle of an interplanetary voyage does not mean he or she should be isolated from the happenings of the day. The Transastral Times news service provides the answer by means of a newspaper, and an electronic infosite.

The masthead of this daily is impressive, and identical for both the paper and the infosite. To the left is a round and robust portrayal of Mother Earth. Clothed in a lengthy toga gown, her dark hair is piled high in a bouffant, and her fertility is represented by two babies resting at her sandaled feet. She stands with her right arm resting demurely against her side, her left extending outward, the dainty palm facing up, its fingers stretching. Her noble head is turned in the same direction . . . toward the Archangel Crest, which dominates the center of the design, its base being decorated in garlands. On the right is an intimidating representation of the war-god Mars. He is adorned in full Centurion armor; his broad right hand and muscular forearm likewise reach toward the crest as his strong and square-jawed face looks on. His left arm rests against a tall and foreboding spear which stands along his left side. Three five-pointed stars occupy the space between the figures and the crest. Beneath the design is the name of the paper written in bold, black calligraphy.

Stories from the three major wire services on the Earth, the Moon and Mars are relayed to the ship's communication center during the course of the day and evening. Photographs and graphics are also transmitted. Midnight is the deadline when a communications technician reviews the submissions and selects which stories will be included in the next day's edition. When there is enough material to fill the seven sheets, including the space reserved for television listings and select advertisements, the technician routes the layout to the miniature printing press, and ninety minutes later there are enough copies for every person aboard ship. As well, an electronic version appears on the elevator viewers and is available on the en-suite vidscreens, with updates every four hours.

"This is 'The Perfection'. We can go where imagination takes us. We can unleash possibility, we have that power. We have a 'do as you please' atmosphere here. From the minute we stepped aboard this grand ship, we were given a license to overindulge, a pass to live to the extreme. And lots are using that rare privilege to its highest potential, believe me. When we are hungry, food is brought to us, whatever we want, and we nosh on the best. When we thirst, the drink flows. All served on warmed plates and in chilled glasses no less. Clean, pure, cool, scented air surrounds us, piped in silently. We can sleep anytime we want, or not at all. We do what we please, when we please, activity when the mood strikes. Desire is the order of the day aboard this ship, every day. Whatever we want, we get – it's all at our beck and call. The pursuit of hedonism, through and through. Or, it can be whatever you want it to be. Flourish in it, splash in it, live the spoils of it. And, there's the timeless quality. Timeless and spaceless. We exist in a totally enclosed environment. Time, what is time for us? Out here there's no movement of the sun or rising of the moon. There's nothing but clocks to mark the passage of time, and they're avoided easily enough. Time flies when you're having fun they say, well here the fun is unending and time seems at a standstill. We are at play in an unending day, and dance through an endless night. It's like living in an amusing anecdote, or thriving in a dreamy smile. Mystical. Fresh. An early taste of how many see heaven. It's easy adapting to life here. We can o.d. on a permabuzz of joy. Every second is here to be savored like sweet candy. It's recess, it's spring break, it's a carnival funhouse, a backstage pass to your favorite band, an illicit drink at an afterhours club...all wrapped into one sweet bundle. Livin' large, livin' the life of Riley, Gatsby's pleasure, in like Flynn, fandango, posh panache, in the pink, whatever you want to call it, this is it." Dade pauses. "So endeth my prospero monologue, my dear."

Adrianna giggles. "An expert summation, if I do say so myself, Mr. Dade."

Dade does a mock bow. "Why thank you."

Even though the entire ship is awash in being busy almost constantly, the *Emprasoria* still manages to convey a sense of "relaxation". Events are pre-arranged in order that there are never any lines of waiting people and no over-crowded areas; there is no stress at all. Staff Captain Syranos and her cruise entertainment staff are miracle workers in this respect. The presence of the many elevators, the speedwalk tracks and the chauffeured courtesy cart hovercraft even make going from one end of the ship to the other an easy pleasure. Passengers quickly find it is easy to adapt to life here on the *Emprasoria*. This is what a vacation is meant to be, calm and enjoyable. The Archangel Line has outdone itself, and very well at that.

One element which particularly impresses the passengers is how accommodating, friendly and efficient the crew is toward them. The cruise entertainment and serving staffs speak the King's English with Oxford precision, and are collectively fluent in the linguistics of the world. They articulate with precise accents the European languages and the key dialects of Indo-Asiatic, Arabic and Afric speech, as well as having five who are versed in the intricacies of Sign Language. The overall effect makes communication for passengers occur with extreme ease and clarity. Also, the seven muscle-toned fitness training instructors gladly set exercise routines which are not time-consuming nor difficult, but accomplish a great deal. The clerks in En Vogue Avenue are extremely courteous and helpful, as are the attendants in the specialty areas of the ship, such as the riding range and arcade.

quickly and completely, its cybernetic brain being completely unaware that it is now flying without a net.

Between Centralis and Mars, there was laughter. Not joyous and fun, but laughter tainted with devious arrogance. Maddox chuckled just as 'Simon' cut off. "Silence is golden. That's a good one if I do say so myself." He sits back on the couch in his suite.

"Witty fellow, you are...." Angelique says from over his shoulder. "Timing is everything."

Maddox looks up at her and winks as he lowers the cover to the laptop. "Went well, don't you think?"

"Yes, very well considering this 'side action' was more-or-less impromptu," she remarks while walking to the bar. "Would you like a drink?"

"Sure. Celebration is in order. Make it a tall glass of white wine, if you please."

"Coming right up."

Maddox returns his trusty laptop to its home beneath the sofa. "Between Kurt and Simon and my real identity, I swear I'll be schitzo by the time this whole thing ends."

"When our activities are finished, you can be whomever your heart desires." Angelique says with a wry smile.

"Wow. How intriguing. Maybe I'll become a new person every week, based entirely on your recommendation. I'll be sure to send you the psychologist bills."

Angelique laughs as she takes a chilled bottle of wine from the small fridge. Reading the label, she nods her approval. The cork pops easily, and two long glasses of liquid gold soon appear. She joins Maddox on the couch, snuggling beside him while passing him a glass which he accepts with a smile as she raises her own. "To ingenuity and taste."

"To skill and style, my dear."

"Cheers," they each say, and clink their glasses.

"Mmmmmmmmm, quite flavorful and sweet," Maddox remarks after taking a drink.

"Yes, very tasty," Angelique comments in kind after hers.

Maddox brings the glass to his lips again, then rests his hand on Angelique's reclined thigh as his thoughts drift....

It is the morning. He is gasping, mind racing, thrashing, hands clasped and stomach tight, he has the sensation of falling, and is entirely a frenzy. There is a burst of energy, then Angelique releases a primal scream and falls forward. His eyes pop open and his hands slip from their hold on her hips as she crumples, spent and thrilled all at once. The tangle of blonde hair masking her face ends up beside him on the pillow, the glazed green eyes hidden behind fluttering eyelids. The dreamlike smile from her red lips says it all. His chest heaves as he drinks in air in rushed and heavy breaths, a thin layer of perspiration bathes him; most of the droplets his, some hers. He slips his arm around her.

"Good morning," he says with a smile, then leans over and kisses her on the lips through her tousled blonde locks.

"Very good," she answers, eyes still closed to the world.

"Enjoyed that, did you?"

"Enjoyed is not the word….I can't put the feeling into words right now." Her voice is muffled somewhat by the pillow.

Maddox chuckles. He begins to run his forefinger over her smooth back, tracing a path in circles. "Me either, we'll have to come up with a whole new word."

"You've already done well with 'coming up' so far this morning." She giggles.

"Riding the bucking bronco brings a bouncy trip."

"Call me a cowgirl."

He laughs and lightly spanks her through the sheet once. "Giddyup."

After unwinding for a while from the daybreak romp, Maddox showers and orders in breakfast while letting Angelique sleep. Invigorated and refreshed, he goes to their suite computer and with a few keystrokes checks the ship's location on a travel map. He studies the vicinity, and the route, with respect to a particular object he knows is out there, even though it is not shown on the miniature chart, which offers only limited details. "Very good," he whispers. "Right on schedule." He checks his watch, then notes the speed at which they are travelling from the readout of the bottom of the screen. "Should be around mid-day," he mutters. "Centralis, here we come…"

"Kurt?" Angelique calls from the bedroom. He can hear her stirring as well.

"I'm here," Maddox answers. "There's some breakfast here if you want it."

"Thanks."

"Looks like we have a showdown at twelve o'clock high, give or take. Port side."

"Do the others know?" she says, having walked into the sitting room wearing a plush white bathrobe, hair still dangling. She goes to the cart and lifts the rounded silver cover from the plate, then takes a piece of bacon.

"I'm just about to let them in on it," Maddox says while reaching for his personafône.

"Mmmm, this is good!"

Maddox turns to her. "Worked up an appetite, did you?" he snickers.

She sticks her tongue out sarcastically in return and reaches for another strip of bacon. With his thumb, Maddox touches some buttons on his phone, lastly pressing the autodial.

Parker answers on the first ring. "Yes?"

"Kurt here, Andy."

"Hi, Kurt, how are you today?"

"Fine thanks, yourself?

"No complaints."

"Good to here. Are we on for 11:30 today?"

"11:30, that's right I believe."

"Great. By the way, is your cabin on the port or starboard side?"

"Port."

"How do you like the view from there?"

"Picture perfect."

"I agree. Well, nice talking with you."

"You as well."

"See you in a bit. Goodbye."

"Bye."

Maddox disconnects. Their coded conversation had given Parker all the information he needed: to be ready for Centralis from 11:30 on, and since Maddox had asked about Port first, that meant the satellite would be on the left side of the ship as they cruised. Maddox knows that Parker's roommate Ruby Kobryn will call Salma Jensen with a similar conversation, and through that circuitous route, DeSantis will get the message.

Maddox sits back and steeples his fingers in front of his face, his body giving off a sense of tension. Angelique walks over and puts her hands on his shoulders, giving a rub as she does so. She leans her face next to his, cheek to cheek, and lets her lips rest at his ear. "It will work, baby, don't worry," she whispers.

"Thanks for your confidence," Maddox says while clicking off the computer. "Time will tell."

And time passes. Maddox rereads his notes about Centralis, and accesses the subjugated file in his infokeeper as well. This had been a secondary amendum to his master plan, and would only be put into effect if the ship came within a reasonable distance of the all-important satellite. Now the chance is fast approaching to launch this extra bonus. He paces the room, and at one point sets his reading materials down to stretch his arms then puts his hands at his waist and bends his spine backward and releases a deep breath.

Angelique walks into the room. Hair styled, makeup done, dressed well – she looks good as always, but at this moment he does not view her in a sexual way given the weight of the task at hand, and how it presses on his mind. "Almost time," he says.

"Yes, I saw." She looks at the papers and infokeeper on the coffee table, and the laptop which has appeared from its hiding place beneath the sofa. "Have you heard from any of the others?"

"No," Maddox says while shaking his head "but that is a good thing – means they are alright. They would only have called if there was a problem."

"Well, that's good," she says with a smile.

Maddox nods, then turns and looks at the verandah, whose sliding door he has already opened. He also raised the viewport cover for a clear view of outer space. All he sees is black, with white pinpricks of distant stars. "Want to come with me and look?"

"Sure."

The two walk into the verandah. Maddox steps up close to the glass, and presses his face against the cool, transparent cover and looks to his right, straining to see as far ahead as he can in the distance. Just outer space, as yet. "Can't see it."

"Me neither," Angelique says beside him. "Wait!" She peers forward. "Is that it?"

Maddox cups his hands at the sides of his face and looks. "Yes! Yes that is it!" He jumps back from the viewport and races into the sitting room, returning a half-second later with a personafône. Angelique has her eyes glued to the tiny string of grey which is getting nearer. When he returns she turns to him and sees he has a small green personafône, not his regular black one.

In a port corridor on the Camaraderie deck, Alex Parker walks casually along by himself, humming absently and looking out the long window. He checks his watch, then slips his hand into his pants pocket and lets his fingers take hold of the personafône there. Enrique and Salma are sitting down to lunch in the salon, her purse on the table next to her, open with her personafōne near the top of the leather bag. They are sitting close to one of the large windows on the left side of the room. Enrique scans the room with precision using his well-trained soldier eyes. Everything seems normal enough. When they had arrived, a man and a woman are leaving in a bit of a hurry with a waitress looking at them as they go, but other than that things are relaxed. He peers past Salma's right shoulder, out the window and barely catches sight of a solid up-down line of gray far in the distance. He leans across the table to her, touching her hand as she reads her menu. "I think our friend is arriving," he whispers, then sits back. She nods knowingly, and reaches for her purse.

Maddox takes a deep breath. His eyes are bugged out, glued to the rotating satellite which is fastly approaching. He checks the settings of the personafōne, then places it against the metal windowsill of the viewport to make the metal of the entire ship one giant antenna for him. Parker has turned his phone on, and is standing full face against the window. Salma has her phone on the table, aimed to the large window.

The bow reaches Centralis. In other parts of the ship, Edwin Roggin and Captain Arges along with their partners watch intently. "Here she comes." The massive satellite with all its large dishes and flashing lights is suddenly there. Angelique looks with wide eyes, it seems as though she could reach out and touch it, it is looming and rotating just outside the window. Maddox is beside her, one hand digging into her shoulder in a deathgrip of tension without him even realizing it, the other hand is poised on his phone. The device is held tightly to the cold edge of the windowsill. He takes a breath and holds it. Then, his finger moves. Bop bing-bing. 9-1-1. Send.

From the Camaraderie deck, 9-1-1. Send. From the dining salon, 9-1-1. Send.

The touch of evil has been loosed, three spears of a trident pierce. Maddox still stares at Centralis; knowing he cannot follow the invisible arrows from his own phone or those of the others, but he watches instead. Being as important as Centralis is, it has a formidable internal security net named 'Defiant'. Defiant filters incoming messages in an instant and automatically purges any which have even the slightest hint of a compuvirus which could infect and compromise Centralis, and as a side effect, saves the intended recipient from any untoward communication which could devastate them somehow. The only time the Defiant protector screen disavows itself is when an emergency plea comes in; given that garbled crys for help could be misconstrued and eliminated, then potentially stranding someone in perhaps a life threatening situation, it routes these calls directly.

Three emergency-tagged signals come in at once. There are instantaneous connections to the closest emergency response site in the vicinity, which in this case happens to be the Security Office of the *Emprasoria* itself. Normally, the calls would have been routed through the ship's own internal communications system, but since the ship was so close to the satellite, and all three personafönes were pointed directly at it, the calls were processed by the nearest carrier, namely, Centralis. So, they boomerang.

"Security, *Emprasoria.* How can we help you?" A quick and polite, authentic female human real-as-life voiced answer after the second ring. Parker clicks off the power to his personaföne and resumes his walk. If they are able to trace the millisecond interaction, they would only get a dummy number anyway.

"Security, Emprasoria. How can we help you?" Same qualities, and equally after the second ring. Salma imitates her partner's action, then turns her attention to the colorfully arranged salad which was just placed in front of her.

"Security, *Emprasoria.* How can we help you?" Silence. "Security, *Emprasoria*, how can we help you?" Still more silence. "Hello?" the attendant asks, a tone of worry now evident. "*Emprasoria* Security, hello? Is there anyone there?" There is a –click- as she ends the connection.

But does she? The other end remains open. And connected. Maddox holds his breath and looks at the lit green "CALL" light on the green personaföne. He waits for a moment, and sees it remains on – they are still bonded to the satellite. There now exists a tether of a signal wave between Maddox and Centralis. "We're in!" Maddox shouts. "*IN I tell you!*" He feels the exuberance known by the hackers of legend, John 'Captain Crunch' Draper, Steve Wozniak, and Kevin Mitnik; yeah – he can join the ranks of these renowned underground counter-programmers, and has earned his own place in the secret society of compu-manipulation myth. He turns and grabs Angelique by both of her arms, brings her to him and kisses her firmly on the mouth. He releases her a second later and turns back to the green personaföne.

Rrrrrrrrrrrriiiiiinnnnnnnggggggggg. His emerald 'hitching post' suddenly gives a shrill bleat. RRRrrrrriiiiRRRRrrrrrrrrriiiiiiiii nnnnnnggggggg it says again. In one rapid move, Maddox clicks two buttons. The phone has been answered and is now in conference-call mode, bound by airwaves to a red personafōne, which has a cord linking it to an infokeeper.

Maddox takes his infokeeper from the white table in the verandah. "Fox is in the henhouse," he whispers "What's he up to?" In a few moments his computer hacking abilities give him a standard maintenance code, and he is through the firewall and into the CPU sourcecode of the satellite. Centralis believes it is talking remotely with a homebase at Spaceport Gamma. Maddox immediately changes the maintenance code makes his requests. The response is succinct, rapid, efficient; the backups all fall, one after the other in a sinister domino effect.

He calmly turns to Angelique, who is watching it all. "It's working." He smiles widely and she smiles back. "Our double-down is half complete."

"Fantastic." She blows him a kiss.

"Thank you," he says with a wink. "By now, they're probably freaking out down there." He sets his infokeeper on the table and faces the sliding door of the verandah. "I'll let them sweat it out for a minute. Do you want anything?" She shakes her head no, so Maddox slides the door open and steps into their sitting room. Angelique looks out through the viewport into the blackness of space, wondering at the wizardry of her partner. He steps back into the verandah a moment later carrying a glass tumbler filled with rye and ginger and a single ice cube, then closes the door again and walks to her, giving her a quick kiss on the cheek. "Now to my ouiji board," he says with a chuckle while easing himself into one of the large white chairs next to the table. He sets the glass down and picks up the infokeeper. "Time to do some talking." He points the device at his green personafōne, then enters an address and begins typing. **Simon Says: <<Are you scared yet?>>**

CHAPTER EIGHT
KINGPIN

The dawn of Sunday, April 20 brings a view of Mars on the horizon. The red planet turns slowly with its two attendant oblong gray moons floating lazily alongside. Also there are the several satellites of varied size and type, then Unicol, the Martian space station and equivalent of Uninas at Earth, and the Ruby Rouge, a large orbital hotel. All these are content within the great Martian swirl.

"Ah, there it is, ready and waiting for us," Captain Arges observes as he walks on to the bridge with his command officers and sees the ruby planet rising ahead of the ship. "Good to see our neighbor there, isn't it Peter?"

"Yes, very," Rish answers. "I think we can all take a well-deserved sigh of relief."

Everyone in the room knows what Rish means. The *Emprasoria* has reached her final destination in 'the best time possible' as Enkel had requested. The bridge officers do not expect to receive much commendation for their accomplishment, but, at the very least they will avoid the wrath of Enkel, and this alone is enough of a reward. They had made good time, better than expected, and now have arrived a full day ahead of schedule.

"Our engines did well for us," Chief Engineer Holden says, a tinge of pride in his voice.

"That they did, Tac," Arges answers while slapping his friend on the shoulder. "A plus!"

"Christian," Arges begins, "have they made any acknowledgement of us?"

"Yes, sir," Miasaki answers quickly. "The pointmarkers on the Martian moons Deimos and Phobos just made contact with the Astrocon. We have a good course and position."

"Very good," Arges says while stepping up to the command platform. "Pilot, you know what to do."

"Yes, Captain," replies the pilot as his fingers dance over the board and the ship decelerates to establish a hovering holding pattern in the outer Martian orbit.

"*Emprasoria, Emprasoria* this is Controller Vask at Spaceport Gamma, do you read me?"

"Loud and clear, Gamma," comes the reply. "Communications Officer Torkiev here."

"You guys must have been making doubletime out there...."

"Yes, seems as though our new engines gave us a boost."

"Well, we are glad to see you," Vask continues, "but we weren't expecting you for another day. The port-stall which can accommodate you is undergoing some refurbishing and won't be ready until late tomorrow morning – at the earliest."

With the victory has come a difficulty. Or has it? On checking the time-to-travel ratio, the officers had anticipated an early landing. So, not to inconvenience passengers who had already made arrangements for the predetermined arrival time, the *Emprasoria* would conduct a Mars Planetary Tour. This will be similar to the Premiere which they had on Earth, where the passengers will be treated to a special sightseeing tour of the natural and man-made wonders the Martian landscape has to offer -- as well as giving the ship much more publicity. This tour will end with an elaborate Farewell Luncheon. Therefore, the guests will be expected to disembark the ship at Gamma at the appointed hour, even though the vessel will have been at Mars for one day already.

"Hello Controller Vask, this is Captain Arges," he says into the chair microphone.

"Good morning, Sir."

"Good morning to you as well. Of course, we don't want to inconvenience the Port. We will enter your atmosphere and tour the planet on a daytrip via our secondary engines and dock tomorrow as planned."

"Tour the planet?" Vask replies, the question clear in his voice.

"Yes, just a little excursion for our passengers to see what Mars has to offer."

"Well, as of last night, we have a lot more to offer – all three peaks in the Tharsis Range erupted and are still gushing. The atmosphere is unstable to say the least and we've put a quarantine on any home-range air travel. People going from one biocile to another are all using the subterranean trains instead. We can't risk any contaminants latching on to a plane and coming into a colony. Inbound and outbound travel to and from the Port directly to orbit is fine, but nothing else. Sorry."

Arges tenses; this is an unexpected development. The captain turns to his officers, who look back at him with concern in their faces; Rayburn bites her lower lip. "I understand Miss Vask," he says after a moment. "We'll keep you advised as to what we do."

"Thank you," Vask replies. "And, sorry again."

"It's fine," Arges says, then nods to Torkiev who finishes the conversation.

"This is a surprise," comments Rish.

"To say the least," Arges says while leaning back in the chair. "I will contact Mr. Enkel, and Jennifer if you could reach Darcy," the Staff Captain nods. "I will convene a meeting in the Conference Room on the Flight Deck You all should be there." Nods from his Command Staff come as he reaches for a deskphone and dials. "Good morning, Mr. Enkel," Arges begins.

"Good morning, John. I see Mars through my window, great work! I'm just on my way up to see you for our morning walk."

"Yes, I am looking forward to it. Yet, before the walk, if you could attend a meeting with myself and the officers, there is an development on Mars which we should all discuss."

"How bad?"

"I would not say bad, sir, just an chance for some creative thinking."

"I see."

"Darcy Phillips will be there too."

"When would you like to have the meeting?"

"Presently, if that is agreeable to you."

"Where?"

"The flight deck conference room."

"I'll be right up."

"Thank you. See you soon."

"You as well."

Ten minutes later, Enkel and Phillips arrive in the room to find the others already seated around the long and stylish blond-wood table. Enkel seems refreshed an pleasant, Phillips looks like he was just yanked from bed – blinking his slightly dazed eyes as he walks.

"Good morning, Sir," Arges says while standing as Enkel enters. The others rise from their chairs as well. "Mr. Phillips," Arges continues with a nod.

"Good morning John, everyone," Enkel says while taking an empty seat to Arges' right. Phillips seats himself next to Jennifer Syranos.

"Well, what's going on?" comments Enkel as he sits, as do the others.

"The good news is that we have arrived at Mars," Arges says with a smile to those assembled.

"Excellent!" Enkel smiles widely and slaps the polished tabletop heartily with his open palm. "Always healthy to start the day with some good news," he jokes, prompting light laughter from the others.

"True enough," Arges agrees. "Yet, the less than good news is that it seems we will have to forego our plan for a Martian planetary tour. Seems as though a volcano is erupting and Gamma has implemented a no-fly-zone for air traffic until it ends."

Enkel pauses and his jovial smile fades. "Ohhhhhhhhhh," he remarks rather gravely. "That's quite a predicament." While resting his hands on the table he looks up to the group. "What sort of suggestions do you have?"

There is silence for a moment.

"What to do, what to do…" Rish comments absently in a whisper while resting his chin in his hand and thinking aloud.

"We sure as hell can't just stay in a holding pattern up here," Phillips comments strongly, suddenly being fully awake and alert. "That would be boring as who-knows-what for the passengers, especially when they can see Mars right in front of them." Syarnos nods in agreement.

Enkel sits back in his chair, then rests his elbows on the handrests and steeples his fingers together while his eyes center on his forefingers as he becomes lost in thought. There is utter silence, the others respecting his contemplation time with the as though they were in a sepulcher. After a few minutes pass, he smiles cunningly as a flash comes to his eyes and everyone can plainly see he is toying with a notion in his keen mind. Their attention is already on him, yet the fixation increases in relation to his pensive gesturing, and they await his assertion. He straightens in his chair and looks up. Finally, he speaks. "Occurrence brings opportunity." He smiles, and still sensing his excitement, the others smile with him. He turns to Holden "How much fuel do we have left?"

"We still have a good supply, Sir," comes the quick reply. "We used a lot for the trip of course, and at our higher than average speed, but we have not yet tapped the reserves."

"Good, good." The smile remains. "The reserves. A wealth of fuel there. It could work." The others in the room look at him, unsure of where his thoughts are leading. "How are we doing for air supply?" he again asks Holden.

"Likewise doing well, Sir. Half-way through the current tank, the last one is still full as well."

"It *will* work then. Fantastic…." Enkel thinks some more and turns to the captain. "John, how about a jaunt over to Jupiter?"

Minutes later, they all exit the conference room. Astrogator Miasaki goes straight to the Astrocon to plot a course to the king planet of the Solar System coming close enough to see and appreciate it, yet far enough to be steer clear from the mighty gravitational pull. Enkel strides down the starboard passageway, brimming with pride, Arges alongside him, equally enthusiastic. Rish and Rayburn report to the bridge as Phillips and Syranos hasten down to the communications center, each feeding off of the other's energy – "Just think, Jennifer!" he begins, his posture excited and his hands fanned "I can just see the headlines now – **'LARGEST SHIP CALLS ON LARGEST PLANET'** It'll be amazing! And we'll be the first cruiseliner to visit Jupiter!" Holden rushes past them on his way to the aft elevator, knowing he has some work ahead of him, but is just as excited as the others.

"Mr. Torkiev," Arges begins as he climbs to the platform and sits in the chair, "please call Spaceport Gamma." Enkel stands with Rish and Rayburn to the side. The others on duty stiffen more than usual, as both the captain and owner are on deck.

"Yes, Sir. Connected now."

"Gamma, Controller Bey here."

"Good morning. This is Captain Arges of the *Emprasoria.*"

"Yessir, how may I be of service today?"

"As you can see, we are in your vicinity, and," Arges chuckles. "a bit early."

"Yes, made some good time I see."

"Quite. Great beginning for us. Anyway, we understand about the Tharsis eruption. We'll just cruise about up here until your ready for us."

"I see. Any particular plan?"

"We'll go along the A-B perimeter, see what's available."

"Very well. We'll look forward to seeing you in our orbit again soon, and having you dock when the stall is ready."

"Understood. Thank you."

"Gamma out." Controller Bey was aware of a particular fact, but he kept it quiet from Arges. The Port Authority had done some research on learning of the new planetary arrival time, and discovers that the *Emprasoria* is now the rightful winner of The Silver Comet trophy for the fastest astral crossing in the last five years. The Authority decides to surprise Captain Arges and Mr. Enkel with the news at the docking.

As the communication link is closed, Arges turns to Miasaki. "Do you have the numbers for us Christian?"

"Yes, I'll relay the flightplan to the pilot now."

"Very good."

The pilot turns his head from the main viewport down to a console at his right. He reads the material there, and visibly tenses, then he pauses. "Sir, if I may…" he begins warily. "Are these coordinates correct?" he asks quizzically as he turns slightly to face Arges.

"They are if they lead us to Jupiter."

These words give pause to the bridge staff. They stop and look at each other. Arges, Enkel, Rish and Rayburn smile. "Yes," continues the first officer, "seems as though our group on Mars was not just ready for us, so Mr. Enkel wants us to make the most of it and see what we can see…" The others on the bridge smile and murmuring is heard.

"Yes Sir!" answers the pilot as he turns again to face the viewport and begins adjusting the controls.

"Remember, sharp watch on the radar," Rayburn cautions.

"I've chosen a direct route for us again, straight there, straight back," Miasaki offers. "But yes, sharp watch."

Enkel remains on the bridge, smiling and watching as the ship veers to its starboard on its new heading, toward the A-B, which is also known as the Asteroid Belt. The flaps are adjusted and the vessel begins a slow and steady climb upward to clear the band of rock and iron which cuts the Solar System across its middle and separates the inner planets from the outer ones.

"This will be great. So great!" Enkel says, then turns to Arges. "John, I leave it in your capable hands." He touches his hand to his forehead in a tip-salute. I know you are busy so we can do our walk later if you like. Call me if you need anything." He turns to the others in the room. "Great work, everyone. Let's all enjoy our sojourn."

"Thank you, Mr. Enkel," Arges says, then there are some light applause as the man leaves the bridge.

Soon he is back in his suite, where Ann is sitting in a large chair and reading. She looks up from her book as he enters. "Hello, dear. What did John want?" she asks.

"Slight problem on Mars, we can't land there today."

"What?"

"Nothing to worry about. Take a look outside." With his hand he indicates the large front window of their suite.

She turns and looks, seeing the massive asteroid belt in the near distance, and Mars off to her left. She spins her head back to him. "Damien, Damien what is this?" She looks to the window again, then back to him just as quickly.

Enkel walks over to her and sits on the arm of her chair, resting his hands on her shoulders. "A little side trip! There's some sort of eruption on Mars and Gamma is being over-cautious, so we're going to Jupiter today!"

"JUPITER!"

"Yes, Jupiter!" Enkel says as he rises from the chair-arm and slips his hands in the pockets of his sportcoat and takes a step toward the viewport, his eyes looking out straight ahead. Way in the distance, he can just barely see the large planet. "My ship is going to have an audience with the kingpin of the planets." There is a hint of awe in his tone, and his chin clicks up in pride. Ann joins him, and he slips his arm around her, then pulls his glance away from the window and looks her directly in the eyes. "Fascinating, isn't it?"

"Yes, very." Admiration is clear in her voice.

"Guess who's idea it was." A wisp of a smile appears on his face.

"Hmmmmmmm I wonder…" she replies with equal candor. "Could it be my amazing husband?"

He winks and gives her a hug. "Largest spaceship in the galaxy to pay her respects to the largest planet, that's the angle Darcy is going to work."

"The publicity will be through the roof!"

"We can hope." He winks again. "Are you ready for breakfast?"

"I've suddenly become hungry," she says while putting her arms around his neck, "but not necessarily for eggs benedict."

He chuckles and she kisses him.

As breakfast is served in the restaurant, the voice of Staff Captain Syranos cheerily echoes over the public address system and in-suite monitors as large-screen video monitors are set up in the public areas. "Good Morning Ladies and Gentlemen! Are your cameras ready? Today we are very pleased to provide you with an exclusive, luxury sightseeing tour of the King Planet, Jupiter! Feel free to marvel at the color, size, and majesty of this vast celestial deity from the viewports, or via the televisions. Large-screen sets will be available for you in the comfort of all the Lounges, and the same feed will be telecast on Channel 111 of the suite monitors. We hope you enjoy this daytrip to one of the true wonders and dazzling beauties of the Solar System. Thank you!" Applause and smiles and excited chatter come from the passengers, and though the crew keep themselves poised, they likewise are enthusiastic.

"This will be great!" Bethany says to herself. "What a treat!"

"Jupiter, amazing," Edwin Roggin says to Lauraleigh, a forkful of egg poised above his plate at their table in the salon.

"That is sure something! They never leave us wanting around here," she remarks. "And to have it as a complete surprise, I mean, not listed in the Itinerary or anything! I wonder what else they have up their sleeve?"

"Who knows?" Edwin replies. "Hey, we'll have to get a good seat for viewing Jupiter."

"Yes. And, I'll be sure to charge the batteries on our vidcam."

"Thank you, sweetie." Edwin brings her hand to his lips and kisses her there quickly, then returns to his breakfast. "You are right, they do do amazing things for us."

"Jupiter! The beauty!" Rave DeMedici says at his breakfast table, after popping a grape into his mouth. He turns wide-eyed to Octavia. "That will be astounding to see her up-close!"

"Celestial art, just beyond our window panes!" la blonde replies with a wide smile.

"I'll load a fresh disc into our camera, and have two more on-hand," Rave continues, his long black hair flowing as he speaks.

"We could even get some photos of the asteroids to I am sure!" Octavia chimes.

"Just what I was going to say, can't forget them."

"Going to see the big boy," says Darian Dade with raised eyebrows to Adrianna. "The pappa bear, the head-honcho, the top Johnny, King Kong, the big fish in this pond we call a solar system."

"I think you've got the idea covered." She rests her hand on his and winks. "And here I thought there wouldn't be much sight-seeing on this trip. Live and learn." She smiles then takes a drink of tea.

"The Tsar of our tiny part of the cosmos," Tsarevich Romanoff remarks, respect heavy in his tone.

"Did you hear that?" Peter Bull says groggily to Myrie, and shakes her back as she lies next to him in bed. He blinks, trying to awaken.

"Jupiter," she replies, it is muffled though as she is speaking into her pillowcase, still half asleep.

"That will be cool." He sits up, and reaches for his glass of cola on the nightstand. "I've never heard of a cruiser going to Jupiter before."

There is another mumble from her, but he cannot make out what she is saying. He drops the subject and swings his legs out of bed, off to find his guitar.

Maddox tenses and pauses in pouring a dash of milk into his coffee. He steals a concerned glance across their table in the salon to Angelique. "Jupiter?" he asks, bewildered.

"That's what she said."

Maddox sets the small silver milk pitcher back on the table, and is clearly perturbed, though he lets no one know a hint of this but her. "What the heck is that?" he whispers curtly. "Come on already…when's this trip going to end?"

"Well, I hear they start making a final approach on Mars after rounding Pluto," she says sarcastically, and laughs quietly.

"Ha, ha, ha," Maddox replies in kind.

"At least it will make for an interesting detour," she says cheerily.

"Good point – but why are they doing it? Why are they prolonging things?" She has no answer of course, but Maddox has a certain odd feeling in the pit of his stomach and a sudden yearn to go to his hidden laptop. He looks over at her. "We have to go. Now."

Angelique looks longingly at her half-finished fruit salad, but nods anyway. They leave their table and walk out of the White Feather, she leading the way. Maddox is very anxious to check his computer, but he contains himself so as not to draw any undue attention. His stomach is knotting and they move along as quickly as they can, and are soon through the doorway of their suite.

"What in the hell could be going on?" Maddox blurts while racing to the sofa. "It has to have something to do with Centralis!"

Angelique stands off to the side, her arms crossed in front of her chest, her forehead an unflattering pattern of wrinkles. Maddox snatches out the laptop and with his back to Angelique, quickly lets his eyes scan over the information on the screen. He rapidly taps the up-arrow key, and the screen scrolls upward, displaying the transactions of late. "Nothing, nothing," he says, his finger still punching away. "Wait a sec…" something catches his eye and he stops pounding the key. "What do we have here?" He sits back and reads slowly. "The Log has a written transcription of an exchange with Gamma…..our ship wanted to do a planetary cruise to eat up some time….got here too early for some reason and the dock isn't ready….the volcanoes of Tharsis are blowing their stacks…." He turns to Angelique, who still has a look of worry. "I'm paraphrasing of course, but you get the idea." She nods silently and he returns to the screen. "Gamma's got a block on air traffic because of the eruptions." He pauses. "Well, that makes sense." He reads more. "Won't let us in. We say we're going to look around the asteroids and come back later…." Maddox accesses another screen within the Emrpasoria LAN. "Course plan to the pilot from the astrogator for way beyond the asteroids." Maddox looks up, in full understanding. "That's why; that explains it. They are using this as a means of getting a crack at Jupiter. A publicity stunt." He turns his attention back to his device and goes to another screen, then scans it. "Not a peep about Centralis."

He hears Angelique huff a sigh of relief. "So, we're still in the clear?"

Maddox turns to her. "Looks that way, but you never know…"

She sits down in a chair. "Just a really odd coincidence."

He shifts back from the laptop. "Yeah. Seems like it." There is a hint of doubt in his voice. "I still don't like the idea of being cooped up here any longer than we have to," he huffs.

"Well, if we're trapped in paradise, we may as well enjoy the ride," she offers.

"Yeah, true," he mutters. She gets up and goes to the suite computer. "Looks like we'll be coming in at Gamma tomorrow morning, unless anything else weird happens."

Maddox makes a point of rapping his knuckles on the coffee table; a 'knock on wood'. She nods and chuckles to him. "I am sure this will be the last diversion, Kurt. They do have to keep to some sort of schedule after all."

"Of course, you're right," Maddox says while standing, his knees crack as he does so, and he stretches his arms high. He is quiet for a moment though, thinking. "This side trip will stretch our link to Centralis to the limit – it will depend how close we get to Jupiter, and conversely, how far we get from Mars. I'll have to tell them to delay the drop off anyway, damn it!" He punches the open palm of his left hand with his right fist in frustration. "Then I'll drop our signal and tomorrow use a relay satellite in the Martian orbit to talk with them through Centralis." He is quiet a moment longer. "Fucking volcanoes," he mutters while heading toward the verandah.

<Simon Says: <<Knock knock.>>

<Who's there>

<Simon Says: <<A guy.>>

<A guy who?>

<Simon Says: <A guy who's gonna be rich with gold soon.>>

There is a momentary pause. **<Good one.>**

<Simon Says: <<Wasn't sure if you would like that or not, but hey, an early morning laugh is always good.>>

<Thank you.>

<Simon Says: <<So how are you today?>>

<Doing alright.>

<Simon Says: <<Glad to hear it. Do you have my package ready?>>

<Yes, getting closer. We will need an extension.>

<Simon Says: <<Come on, we were having such a nice conversation. Don't go and do anything to get me angry.>>

<We aren't trying to get you angry, sport. Just asking for a little leeway, a show of good faith.>

<Simon Says: <<Why should I?>>

<These things take time. We have to go through the proper channels, get approvals, that sort of thing.>

<Simon Says: <<Red tape, the one major hindrance to the advancement of smart ideas.>>

<You know it.>

<Simon Says: <<How much do you have ready?>>

<Well over half.>

<Simon Says: <<You have been busy boys. Good. What sort of extra time are we looking at?>>

<18 to 24 hours.>

<Simon Says: <<You have 15, and not a minute more. I will contact you then with the final delivery instructions. Don't try my patience or push me farther than I want to go. The next time we talk, you tell me you are ready and ask where to drop off the goods.>>

<Understood.>

<Simon Says: <<Have a nice day.>>

Maddox emerges from the verandah, smiling. "It's kosher with the gold; they think I am actually doing them a favor by extending the deadline."

"Great," says Angelique.

"I'll tell you all about it when I get back. For now, I'm going to get in touch with the others, let them know what's going on." He walks to the main door of the suite. "Do you need anything?"

She shakes her colorsprayed-head no, still looking at the vidscreen. "I'm fine, thanks."

"Ok, see you in a bit then."

"Ok, bye." She listens as the door opens and closes, and begins typing on the keyboard. "Well, I for one am interested in seeing Jupiter." Using SolNet, she obtains some information websites on the planet, to familiarize herself a bit, and to note things to look for as they pass.

Down at Spaceport Gamma, Nelson Leevan sits back from the vidscreen and eases his hands over his tired eyes. He has been pulling triple shifts since this deal started, and living on stale coffee and fast food, taking what sleep he can on a stiff cot in a small room near the Comm Center. He releases a heavy breath and sits up from his chair in a distant corner of the Center. "Ohhhhhhhhh this can't be over soon enough for me…." he mutters.

"Looks like that's all he had to say," remarks Julian Ferro, the detective who undertook the conversation. He clicks a key and the computer begins producing a printed transcript of the exchange, than takes a drink of his cold, stale coffee.

Leevan turns to him. "This guy sure is a piece of work." The portly security pro shakes his head ruefully. "You bought us some time though, thanks for that."

Ferro shrugs. "All in a day's work for a negotiator. How are the bugging of the ingots coming?"

"Doing well. We'll have eight in each crate encoded with a special minute metallic transmitter that individually couldn't be spotted or scanned unless you literally chopped the gold to pieces then bombarded each speck with x-rays. Also, these babies work only if two of the treated ingots are in contact with each other, so you can't tell if one on its own is the signaler. Also, there is unspecific pairing, so any one marked ingot will transmit with any of the other marked ones. Each of the marked ingots will be packed side-by-side, but even if they are separated, they just need to get in touch with another and – bingo!"

"Sounds like a good system."

"There's no way in hell we're gonna lose that gold, count on it."

Ferro nods appreciatively. "For someone who seemed all strict-and-anxious, he seemed to cave kind of easy, don't you think?"

"Part of some sort of game he has going, that probably only he understands," Leevan replies. "He will give us one break, but not another."

Ferro nods understandingly. The printer provides its last page, and Leevan scoops up the sheets and begins rereading the words on them. "Should we grab some breakfast while we have the chance?" Ferro asks.

Leevan looks at his watch. "A good idea actually. I almost forgot what food tastes like."

"That mud in a cup numbs your tastebuds," Ferro chuckles.

Leevan laughs with him, and with him still toting the papers, the two head out to the cafeteria. "My treat for doing such a good job there."

"Thanks."

Up on the *Emprasoria*, following breakfast, as on the Sunday past, Captain Arges holds a Worship Service in the forward observation lounge at eleven o'clock. He follows the sacraments of Morning Prayer in a non-denominational manner, reads passages from the Book of Psalms, and those in attendance sing three hymns, including "Guidance on the Celestial Ways", accompanied by Mr. Fische and his piano. The thirty-minute Divine Observance gladdens the hearts of the small congregation.

A buzz of extra excitement runs through the ship, thanks to the thought of seeing Jupiter. Many passengers do exactly what Angelique is up to, studying the facts, and in some cases myths, about Jupiter so they can be as ready as they can be when they come upon the planet. However, it will take some time to get there, and just because the *Emprasoria* is in her final travel day does not mean her benefits are diminished by any means. All recreational facilities operate at full capacity. An impromptu Dog Show is held that afternoon just after luncheon in the Arboretum in order for passengers to parade their beloved canines. To avoid disappointment, there is no winner crowned, but each dog is given a ribbon, and the Show is the opportunity for people to show off their pooches.

Onward the ship moves. Still running at top speed, she gracefully soars over the galaxial cobblestone path comprising the space between Mars and Jupiter, seeing the dark and massive Ceres, giant of the asteroids, and its consorts, Pallas, Juno, Vesta, and Eugenia who make up the next largest of these rocks. Each one is identified by Staff Captain Syranos on the public address system as they pass. From the scenes shown on the vidscreens and monitors, the passengers and crew marvel at the shape and variety which the Belt offers for viewing.

"I never had any idea about the scope of formations out here!" Rave DeMedici comments, his eye focused through the lens of his vidcam which is pressed up against the unshaded viewport of his verandah. "Look at that one! And that one!"

"I see them Rave!" shouts Octavia. "Look over there! Film the blue one there!" she points and he turns his camera in that direction.

"The way the sunlight bounces off of them is incredible!" he says while the camera gathers images at his skilled hand. "I thought the

Rockies were enthralling, and Kilimanjaro, but these out here bring you to a whole different mindset!"

"I agree," Octavia says while putting her arm around Rave as he films.

"I also want us to get a copy of the official ship video about this part of the trip," he says.

"Yes, it will go well with ours, and we can cross-compare what they shot and what we did."

Almost too soon, the ship moves away from the belt, and is back into the open black sea of space. Yet there, beyond, it waits. The *Emprasoria* shifts itself around and jets forward so it can meet Jupiter at the earliest possible moment. "Pilot, are the coordinates clear?" Miasaki asks from the Astrocom.

"Yes, Mr. Miasaki. Crystal clear."

"Very good. It is important for us to keep within the two perimeters I have set. I intend to keep the ship well outside of Metis, the outermost of Jupiter's moons, to avoid being caught in the tremendous gravity pull."

"Two perimeters. I understand, sir."

"I am also setting some alarms so you can know when we pass the inside perimeter, and if we come too near to the outer perimeter, you and I will be alerted."

"Excellent idea, sir."

Down in his office outside the EOC, Engineer Holden confers with his Christopher Corté. "You should have seen it, Chris, it was amazing. Just like that, he says, lets go to Jupiter..." Holden shakes his head in awe.

"An excellent idea."

"Yes. And we were lucky we had enough fuel and o-2 to make it. If we would have needed to delay for a stock-up, he probably would have been displeased.

Corté nods understandingly. "Can we let our people watch from the computers?"

"Sure, I can't see any harm in that," Holden answers. He next looks over to a gauge. "We're still running at top speed as you can see." Corté nods. "The captain said on the way back we can take it easier, there isn't that much of a rush anymore, and it will give some extra time for the volcano on Mars to blow itself out. So, tell who needs to know that the bridge will likely be asking for a drop-down after our tour."

"Will do. By the way, will you be on the bridge as we go by?"

"Hope to – unless something happens down here that needs me."

"I am sure everything will be fine here," Corté responds.

"I agree."

Quickly they come upon the outlying region of the planet, known commonly to astronomers and spacefarers as 'the throne room'. Jupiter looks huge at this point, and they are still a fair distance away. They approach, quietly and humbly, like an enthralled vassal entering the great hall of some feudal lord. "Ladies and Gentlemen," people again hear Syranos' pleasant voice over the public address system, "we expect to be reaching Jupiter within thirty minutes. All our onboard cameras will be facing the planet, and you may watch the approach and the visit from your television or computer vidscreen, or the large monitors which have been specially placed in the public areas of our ship. Thank you, we hope you enjoy the tour."

Passengers and crew become still more excited. Imagine this! Windows become crowded, and numerous televisions and vidscreens are clicked on and tuned to the internal ship channels. True to Syranos' estimate, thirty minutes later, *THERE IT IS*!

Massive, colossal, awe-inspiring: Jupiter. The orb rotates serenely, encompassed by its single ring of bright and veiled dust. It is attended by the beautiful Ganymede, an enormous moon, being the largest of the Jupiter set and also the largest satellite in the solar system, and the family of Galilean and Jovian moons that move in seeming reverence to the master. The eyes of those aboard stare transfixed at what they are beholding. Magnificent. Wait, is that ....Yes! It is! The Eye of Jupiter, that perpetual hurricane mass of boiling gas – the Great Red Spot. And there are the chief moons Io, and Europa.

Ping, ping. Miasaki's pre-set alarm softly sounds to let both him and the pilot know they have crossed the barrier of the first perimeter. Miasaki makes a pen-mark on the backlit glass map in front of him at the Astrocon. He looks up in the direction of the pilot, just as the man switches off the alarm at his station, indicating he has heard it. In this same instant, Miasaki sees Jupiter looming beyond the viewport, and for a moment is captivated by the planet.

"Impressive," Captain Arges says, watching intently through his binoculars from the bridge viewport with Rish, Rayburn and Hearst by his side, all likewise with binocs.

"It's astounding," Rish concurs.

"I've never seen colors like this before," says Rayburn.

"The size of it is beyond imagination," remarks the Third Officer.

"That is true, Mitchell. For all our size and grandeur, we're just a pinprick to it," Arges comments. "Christian, bring us in as close as we dare."

"Yes, captain," answers the astrogator as he begins calculations with respect to the substantial gravity field which Jupiter radiates.

"Lets do a full side-by-side look. Bring the ship by first on the port side, then backtrack on starboard so passengers on each side can see it," Arges says from behind his binoculars. "We want to keep everyone happy."

"As you wish, captain," Miasaki replies.

Enkel is in his suite below with his wife Anne, both of them wide-eyed, and also using binoculars. "Will you look at that!" he says.

"I never thought it looked like this in person!" Anne says.

Enkel picks up his personaföne and dials a number. "Bridge, Yeoman Uozi speaking," comes the quick reply – Enkel dials the bridge directly knowing that, on occasion, Arges switches off his own phone if he does not want to be disturbed.

"This is Mr. Enkel, may I have Captain Arges please."

"Yes, sir. Right away sir," says the yeoman anxiously. Enkel is put on hold for a moment.

"John here, sir."

"Let's get as close to this as we can."

"Already being done, sir."

"Good work."

"Thank you. How are you liking the view?"

"Spectacular. Mrs. E is enjoying it as well."

"Very good."

"Ok, I'll let you get back to watching it."

"Thank you. We'll talk later."

"Very good. Goodbye."

"Goodbye."

"Look at it!"

"My God, amazing!"

"The size of it! The range! The color! The power!" These are some of the comments heard by people gathered at the forward observation lounge. They jostle, craning their necks and straining their eyes, just to *see* and take in as much as they possibly can.

They close around In Excelsis, whose bronze finger points dead center at the planet. Elsewhere on the ship, every viewport aboard is filled with people, as is the glass walled-and-ceilinged Finesse, and the televisions and vidscreens are likewise crowded. Cameras flash and vidcams record. Everyone loves the spectacle.

"This is going over well, very well," Darcy Phillips whispers to Syranos as they stand near the back of the forward observation lounge.

She pulls her gaze away from the planet and looks up at him. "That's for sure."

"Priest has all the onboard video cameras catching all this, right?"

"Yes. Actually, there he is over there – getting some random photos of the crowd here."

"Fantastic. This is quite a coup for us."

"The other ships will be green with envy." She winks and chuckles, and he laughs then they both turn to look at the amazing planet.

The ship moves in a bit more, going to the very closest point that Miasaki dares; actually, he goes a bit beyond the closest point to better please the captain and passengers. Then, at just the right moment, the vessel begins to veer off, slowly, longingly, pulling away from the Master in a wide arc. This audience with a King stands as thrilling and spectacular. They begin their return trip to Mars, and everyone aboard does their best to disavow the fact that in less than twenty-four hours, the grand cruise will be finished.

CHAPTER NINE
Devil with the blue dress says 'Hello'.

"Hard to believe it has passed so quickly," Lauraleigh Roggin says from her dressing table while putting on the last touches to her eyeliner.

"Time flies when you're having fun," Edwin answers succinctly while buttoning his dress shirt. It is early evening and they are readying for the End of Voyage dinner dance.

"Can we use the *Emprasoria* for our trip back to Earth?" she asks.

"Sure, I would like that actually," Edwin replies while casually walking toward her. "I'll contact Archangel Tours tomorrow after we dock. I'm sure they'll be glad to take a reservation. I'll get us their closest depart date for after our Mars travels."

"Good, thank you."

"We may have to have a couple of extra days on Mars though."

She pulls away from the mirror and looks over to him with a grin. "I'm sure we can find something to do, if need be."

He reaches her and rests his hands on her shoulders. "I am sure," he says, then kisses her lightly on the cheek. He looks at her reflection in the mirror. "You look great, sweetheart." He smiles, and can see the hint of a blush on her face.

"Thanks," she replies sheepishly.

Edwin nods and heads back to his closet. "It sure was great seeing Jupiter," he says while walking.

"Yes, what a surprise." She is clasping a pearl necklace around her neck. With her fingertips, she lovingly touches the white, perfectly round mini-pellets, enjoying the feel of them against her skin.

"Who are we seeing first when we get to the colony?" Edwin asks while pulling on his tuxedo jacket.

"The McMurties have asked us to dinner, so that's the first stop after we get settled in the hotel."

"Ah yes, Jack McMurtie," remarks Edwin as he adjusts his cufflinks. "It will be good to see him and Evelyn again." He pauses and studies himself in the full-length mirror fixed on the inside of the closet door, and smoothes his jacket. "Have you heard from the kids today?"

"No, not yet, but I haven't checked the email much to be honest."

"We can look at it tomorrow." He closes the closet door and turns to see her standing, facing him. His eyes pop; she looks beautiful.

"Well?" she says, eyebrows raised.

"Wow," he answers, and has the proud smile of a man who knows he is with a beautiful woman. "Belle of the ball."

She nods pleasantly and gives a mock curtsey. "Thank you, kind sir." A subdued chuckle follows. Just then, the doorbell rings.

"I'll get that," Edwin answers, then walks over to her and takes both her hands in his and kisses her quickly on the lips, then pulls back and looks at her again. "Spectacular," he whispers. She wipes the trace of lipstick from his lower lip with her thumb, then he walks into the sitting room as she goes to the nightstand. As she searches through the drawer, Lauraleigh hears him answer the door and speak quickly to someone, and the door closes quietly.

"Who was it, dear?" she asks over her shoulder. Getting no reply, she straightens and turns. There he is, in the doorway to the bedroom. Edwin is holding a large bouquet of fresh spring flowers; her eyes melt.

"Pour vous," he says with a broad smile.

"Edwin, they're wonderful! Thank you!" she says and goes to him. There is an embrace, and he passes her the bouquet.

"Glad you like them."

"Let me find a vase," she says, then kisses him quickly and walks back into the sitting room.

Edwin checks his watch. "Five to seven. We should head out after your flowers are taken care of, sweetie."

"Great, I just need a minute or two."

Damien Enkel happens to check his watch as well, at that exact moment. "Our guests should be coming soon," he says in the Halo lounge. He is there with his wife, and Captain Arges, First Officer Rish, Second Officer Rayburn, Staff Captain Syranos, Astrogator Miasaki, Purser Mueller, Chief Engineer Holden, and Dr. Washington, all of whom are in full dress uniform.

"Seems like just yesterday we were having the Captain's Ball," Anne Enkel comments, a hint of lament in her tone.

"Well, we can look forward to the return trip, dearest," Enkel says consolingly while putting his arm around her.

"That is true. Never a shortage of time or amusement, is there?"

"They've never found a cure for that yet." He smiles and clinks her glass, and she smiles to him and returns the cheer-gesture.

"Heaven forbid!" Jennifer Syranos says, prompting laughter from the small group.

"If I ever hear of cure research in that direction, you will be the first to know, sir," Julius Washington says with a chuckle.

"Then we will both shut them down, shall we Doctor?" Enkel answers with equal candor.

"That we will."

An elevator arrival tone sounds. "Ah, here they come now," Enkel says. The bronze doors part to reveal a number of guests arriving for the cocktail party. He and his wife smile broadly then step up to the elevator area with the officers falling in line behind them. "Good to see you, good to see you, so glad you could make it!" Enkel says enthusiastically with hearty handshakes as he and his troop greet the passengers, many of whom they have now become aquatinted with on a personal level. Warm smiles and firm handshakes are exchanged all the way down. Twenty-five minutes later, all the guests have arrived, making the lounge once again a veritable sea of tuxedos and evening gowns. As always, drinks and hors d'oeurves are in abundance, and all in attendance are enjoying themselves. As the guests socialize, the ship's band, which has assembled on the far balcony, plays soft chamber music, guided by the hand of Fitzroy. The tunes provide an excellent undertone for the festive atmosphere.

During the party, Edwin and Lauraleigh Roggin find Cal and Genvievve Gregg in the crowd. "I think we can get one more match in at the Range before this baby lands tomorrow," Roggin suggests with a gleam in his eye.

"Will you stop!" Lauraleigh says in mock exasperation as she swats his left arm and shakes her head.

"Ahhh, think so, do you?" says Gregg with a smile, rising to the challenge. His wife likewise gives him a mildly frustrated look. She looks at Lauraleigh.

"These boys and their shoot 'em up games!" she says, followed by slight laughter.

The men continue, ignoring the actions and words of their wives. "I think you had a lucky shot that last time," Roggin says, referring to their match yesterday.

"Not luck, talent."

Roggin cocks an eyebrow, then smiles. "We'll see. Say eleven-ish?"

"Fine by me."

"Great. I'll see you then." Roggin shakes hands with Gregg, sealing the competition. The Roggins then make their way to their table. As they leave, Adam and Christina Tyler approach the Greggs.

"Christina - - - darling, how are you?" Genvievve says, greeting Mrs. Tyler with an embrace and pecks on each cheek.

"Simply wonderful dear, and you?"

"Fine. Just wishing this trip was not ending."

"You and me both. The spa here is something else!"

Tyler shakes hands with Gregg, using the secret gesture hallowed by Beta Theta Pi brothers the world over. Gregg smiles at the reference. "I see you have another rifle match with Mr. Television, aye Cal?"

"Yes," says Gregg as he takes a drink. "I'll shoot his ass off."

"No doubt. Actually . . ." Tyler pauses for a moment. "I've been in a sporting mood lately. I think I'll put fifty thousand on you for a win."

"Such confidence, Adam."

"I'd like to think of it as a solid investment, shall we say."

"For your sake, I hope I have a good eye tomorrow."

"No worries, old boy."

The Tsarevich Romanoff enjoys the party as well, and after the receiving line disbands, finds his friend Tac Holden. "Hello once again, Chief Engineer Holden," he says with a smile and extended hand.

"Ah, Alexai, good to see you," Holden says while shaking hands. "Please, call me Tac."

"Naval traditions die hard my friend, titles and all…" Romanoff says, his smile still present. "You know Tac, this cruise has been a very pleasant experience."

"I am very glad you enjoyed it."

"And the tour of the engine room, how fantastic was that!" remarks Romanoff with a twinkle in his eye.

"We aim to please. So have you given more thought to your idea of joining the Russian space operation?"

"It is in the back of my mind, as they say."

"Well, if I may ever be of more help to you, or, say, to answer questions, please call on me."

"You may regret that offer, Tac," Romanoff answers, and both men chuckle. Then from the pocket of his uniform jacket he produces a small, sealed rectangular silver can with a round pull-tab at its top. "For you," he says while passing it to the Engineer.

"What's this?" Holden asks as he looks at the item.

"Tsar's Special. Premium caviar."

Holden steps back and looks up. "Alexai, thank you, but I couldn't…"

"Please, with my compliments."

Not wanting to offend the crown prince, and given his personal fondness for caviar, Holden takes a second look, then deftly pockets the item and offers his hand. "Ñïàñèáî, Äðóã."

Romanoff smiles at hearing a phrase in his native lingo. "And thank you too, friend."

"My pronunciation was accurate?" Holden inquires.

"Yes, I understood you well," answers Romanoff.

As this conversation continues, Darian Dade strides through the crowd with Adrianna on his arm. Again, Dade has already fallen victim to her gorgeous auburn hair and becomes entranced with how the peach-colored gown fits her figure. He brims with pride at the beauty by his side; his chest is subconsciously swelled, and he wears the face of a happy man. He can hardly wait to get her alone in his room, and really show her how good she looks. They pass J.D. Zolnick and Jack McCartney as they go.

"This trip can't be over soon enough for me," Zolnick is saying.

"I hear you," McCartney replies. "Frankly, I think I've been away too long."

"Will you two relax," Diana McCartney interjects. "Work's important to me too, but damn, take it easy for once." At that, she quickly downs the remains of her gin and tonic.

"Damn straight," Zolnick agrees, and then begins laughing heartily. He is quickly joined by Diana, then Jack McCartney, and eventually Alexis.

"This Jupiter tour was great," Peter Bull comments to Myrie.

"Yes, a fantastic surprise!" she agrees.

"Mars should be a blast."

"I'm looking forward to it."

"I want to hook-up with Myck M and his crew while we're there. Do some jamming."

"A tete-a-tete of guitar greats." She takes a drink. "I can almost imagine what you could come up with."

"We'll have a recorder on, that's for sure."

"A must, my dear." She looks him over and blows him a kiss.

"And what was that for?" he says while slipping his arm around the back of her waist.

"No reason, just felt like it." She winks.

"I tell you, I'm going to make the most of this night," Dr. Stephen Radsky says to himself – actually, he whispers it to the glass of white wine as he holds it to the light, checking the color and clarity of the wine. "Yes, this will be the last opportunity I'll have for quite some time to enjoy myself." He takes a sip of the wine and with his lips pressed tightly shut, swishes it about his teeth and tongue; he finds the flavor pleasing. His grueling lecture schedule is set to begin almost the moment the ship lands. He quickly finishes his drink and immediately removes a glass of champagne from a passing waiter. "My pleasure will know no bounds this night."

Maddox and Angelique are still up in their stateroom. She walks out from the bedroom, ready to go, and sees Maddox sitting at the edge of the coffee table in front of his laptop computer, elbows set on his knees and his head resting against his interlaced fingers, being as silent as one person can possibly be. Even through his white tuxedo jacket, she can see the tension across his shoulders.

"Kurt?" she whispers.

At first, he does not respond, then after a moment he turns and looks at her with a half-hearted smile. "Yes, I'm here, just thinking." He looks back at the laptop monitor, that in turn stares back at him with a scroll of facts and data. "Tonight's <u>the</u> night, you know." He lets out a heavy and subdued breath. "In a few short hours, we begin The Job."

She walks over to him and begins to rub his shoulders through his jacket. Silence permeates the room again.

Then, suddenly, Maddox rises. She lets her hands slip from the shoulders. "Well," he says while closing the cover of the laptop, "we have it thought out and everyone is as ready as we ever can be." He leans forward and slips the thin device beneath the couch, then turns to her and smiles broadly. "It will all unfold. Action, reaction, conclusion." He pauses and looks her right in the eye. "Exciting, isn't it?"

She smiles back at him with a wistful grin. "Very."

"And as if that isn't enough…."

She raises her eyebrows in expectation. "Yes? Pray tell?"

"I've been in touch with those goons at Gamma. Shitting bricks, they are. But in our case its good because they are *gold* bricks!"

She claps her hands and hops once in pure glee. "Really?"

He nods. "Yes, the bullion, all of it, exactly how we asked. Tomorrow I give the final delivery instructions and ka-pow!" He makes a movement with his arms as though he were an archer releasing an arrow. "We're home free!"

"I'm so glad!" she says with a smile.

"Ditto." He opens his arms and she steps in, and they have a strong hug. She feels the tension melt away from him, to be replaced by confidence. "I believe we have a party to go to, missy," he whispers and gives a playful squeeze just below the small of her back, to a slope which curves so well in the dress she wears.

"That we do," she answers while running her forefinger over the back of his neck. "Our last hurrah. Last one here, anyway." Their embrace ends and a quick kiss follows, then a minute later they are in the hallway and on their way to the lounge.

In other parts of the ship, Parker, Kobryn, DeSantis and Jensen wait in their staterooms. There will be no much party for them, none tonight anyway. They have work to do.

"I hope everything goes to plan," Parker mutters absently while sitting on his bed, rebuilding the last of his pistols, after having cleaned and oiled the both of them.

"Me too," answers Ruby Kobryn. "Well, we all know the drill, and Russ – I mean Kurt – is a *total* pro."

Parker slips the firing pin into his bluemetal pistol, completing it. "That he is." He slips the firearm into its holster and checks his watch. "Good to go." Parker next looks past the open door into the next room, to the pushcart with its used dishes from their ordered-in meal. "When will the steward come back for that stuff?"

"Sooner than later I'd think," Ruby answers. "Want me to call them?"

"Sure. Last thing we need is to bump into them on our way out."

"Good point," Ruby says with a nod as she picks up the telephone.

"Are there any questions?" Salma Jensen asks. DeSantis shakes his head 'no', and chews a bit more on the toothpick which protrudes from his mouth. Jensen has come to know this fellow is a man of few words. "Good," she answers, then finishes lacing her boots. "Hey, have you heard anything about how the Centralis deal is going?"

DeSantis shakes his head again. "Not a thing. I'm sure if there were any problems, we'd know about it though."

Salma nods as she finishes tying the boot to her foot; it feels snug and tight – reassuring in a way. "That's a good point. I'll be interested to see how that works out."

"Me as well."

DeSantis and Salma both check their watches at the same time, then each chuckle at how funny it looked. "Simultaneous already," Salma jokes. "A good sign for any mission."

DeSantis nods and smiles. "Yes, precision timing is vital in our game." He then spins a chair around, and throws his left right leg over as he sits, taking his place in it backward so his chest is pressing against the back of the chair. He swirls the toothpick from one corner of his mouth to the other. "Looks like we have a minute. I'm gonna go over some stuff." She nods, and his eyes go off in a faraway gaze as he reviews his role in the mission, and Salma busies herself.

So, the team hopes it all goes simply; smooth and easy all around. However, on the flip side, each knows the risk involved is high. Very high. Only time will tell if they will become instant millionaires, or captured criminals.

Up in the lounge, passengers continue to socialize. Of course, the festive mood and their now relative familiarity as a group eases the conversations along. Smiles abound, as do the drinks and hors d'oureves. Here are some of the comments:

"Archangel is the best, bar none."

"Truly exquisite ship."

"Grand maiden voyage."

This dinner party begins as the perfect end to a perfect journey.

Up in the security station on the flight deck, the third officer sits in front of a monitor watching the activity in the Halo lounge. Envy wells up in him, causing an acid-like fire in his throat. His eyes burn with rage. Various ill thoughts haunt his mind. Why should I be on duty tonight? The last chance to mingle and I'm babysitting the bridge!! The ball-busting bastard John, the geek Peter and that fucking bitch Alyssa - - sure, <u>they</u> can have <u>all</u> the fun. I'm being shafted!! He sits back. "Damn it all to hell!" he shouts in an outburst, then balls his hands into tight fists and pounds the console three rapid times in frustration. He jumps from the chair with a scowl and stomps out of the room. The dumbfounded attendants look at each other and shake their heads, then resume their watching of the ship.

Hearst strides down the Port corridor, his anger rising with every step. Those in his path give him a wide berth, the rage being clearly etched in his face. He storms on to the bridge and a junior officer quickly vacates the command chair. Hearst slams himself into the seat. "Status report," he barks through clenched teeth.

"The long range radar remains inoperative, Sir," the officer meekly begins. "The singeing in the fuel cell residue bin is smoldering ash now and even that is reducing. All other systems are functioning perfectly."

"How shocking," Hearst says sarcastically. "Everything is great and there's no real reason for me to be here. Fuck!" he slams his right fist into the armrest. "Make the Log entries, asshole," he barks. Just then, the intercom tone sounds. Hearst rips the microphone from its slot. "Bridge!" he spits.

"Bridge, this is Christopher Corté calling from the E.O.C. The electro-static fire in the fuel cell reservoir has been extinguished. Repeat: the fire is out."

"Acknowledged," Hearst says bluntly and hastily clicks off the intercom. "Notify the Captain," he orders Escoto, who dials the Maitre D at the salon. She then files the eight o'clock quadri-hour status report with Spaceport Gamma. Little else is said as the ship moves on toward Mars.

In the Halo, the ceiling lights blink twice and the serving call chime sounds, signaling the end of the cocktail jour. The large doors of the White Feather are pulled open, and as people begin assembling at the top platform of the stairway, they see that multicolored balloon bouquets decorate the upper segment of the restaurant, giving the already grand room an even more festive feel.

The guests seat themselves at their respective tables and wait to be served the appetizer. Enkel is seated at the center chair of the rectangular head table, below the Apollo bas-relief at the far end of the room. His wife sits on his left, and Captain Arges on his right. Rish, Rayburn, Syranos, Holden and Washington occupy the other chairs. As the captain sits, a waiter passes him a note. "The electrostatic singeing has been extinguished. - R. Escoto" the paper says. Arges is relieved. The last thing he wants to do is summon the Spaceport Fire Brigade as the ship ends her ace run because this would dampen the mood of the otherwise auspicious occasion.

On seeing the guests have seated, Enkel looks up to Fitzroy on the balcony, who is looking down at him, and nods. The conductor nods in response and turns back to the Band. With a swift move of his baton, the musicians ease their song into a premature finale. Fitzroy gestures toward the percussionist and the horn section. A rapid drumroll and a brief fanfare quickly follow. The guests quiet.

Following the symphonic introduction, Enkel rises. A waiter bearing a silver tray quickly moves behind him and stands to his left. A small, rectangular, black velvet box sits on the tray. Enkel clears his throat, and begins. "Ladies and Gentlemen, friends, the maiden voyage of this Liner has been fantastic all around." A mammoth wall of applause and cheers erupts from the crowd of diners, and Enkel pauses a moment, resting his hand on his stomach and smiling brightly. "Yes, truly grand, and we are very pleased that each you were able to experience it with us, and we hope to see you again on a future voyage." Enkel pauses again, this time for effect. "I believe it is safe to say that, to a certain extent, a ship is defined by her master. The extent to which the *Emprasoria* has been defined by her captain sends her into star status, and I have no intention of letting excellent work like this pass unnoticed. Captain Arges," Enkel turns and takes the box from the waiter, "it is hoped you will accept this as a token of our esteem for you." With that, he opens the top of the box and exposes a commemorative medal.

Arges rises as he sees it. Across the middle of the circular piece of bronze is an engraved etching of the starboard side of the vessel. Arched along the top of the Liner are the words: "ARCHANGEL - *EMPRASORIA*". Below this in a straight line is

"MADIEN VOYAGE: APRIL 5 - 21, 2088". Written in semi-circle along the bottom edge is "CAPT. J.S. ARGES". A red, white and blue ribbon is attached to the top of the medallion. Enkel removes the medal from its box and holds it up a moment for the crowd to see.

"Oooohs" of admiration are heard. Enkel removes the medal and pins it to the front of Arges' jacket as the guests applaud. The medallion looks smart against his white dress uniform, and a strong smile stretches across the captain's authoritative face, as he is pleasantly surprised. With his camera at his eye, Priest snaps several photos.

"I had no idea. Thank you, sir," Arges manages finally, then the two shake hands firmly.

"To Captain Arges!" Enkel says as he raises his glass of champagne in toast.

"To Captain Arges," everyone echoes as they stand and drink to his honor.

The captain looks down at his new medal, then at the table, pausing to collect his thoughts. After a moment, Arges looks up, and speaks. "Well, what to say. Thank you, firstly. Thank you one and all. Thank you to Mr. Enkel for commissioning this proud vessel, for conceiving the idea and seeing it through at every stage." Arges turns to him, and Enkel gives a proud nod to the room. Looking back out over the room again, Arges continues. "Thank you to our guests for choosing to voyage with us, and to my officers and crew for all their hard work. Yes, we all made the voyage tremendous. Here's to you!" The captain takes a sip of his champagne as again the room is filled with the sound of hearty applause.

"Well that was certainly nice," Lauraleigh Roggin says while seating herself.

"Yes, very," Edwin answers.

In due course, the appetizer of vichyssoise is served, followed by Caesar salad and then the main course of chicken cordon-bleu. The band plays classical music as the guests dine, drink, and otherwise enjoy themselves. Following dinner, couples dance well into the night. It seems as though nothing can break the festive mood in the White Feather.

As the hour approaches nine-thirty, the clerks within En Vogue appear from their shops. Although the Mall officially closes promptly at nine each evening, the staff remain later to tally the day's receipts, clean, and do an inventory check. As this is the last night of the voyage, the clerks will be having a get-together in the Crew's Lounge.

Within Nicholby's jewelry store, Richard smiles to himself as he turns off the lights and activates the alarm system. This has been an extremely profitable journey. His Regional Supervisor will be happy with the sales totals. Richard exits the store, closes the door behind him, and locks it. Snug and secure for another night. He spins his keycard on his finger. "Now, off to the Party and that scrumptious doll Stephanie from the art gallery," he whispers.

This is the moment Parker has been waiting for all night, and now, he must wait a bit longer. He counts off three minutes from when the door closed. Nothing. The clerk does not return for some last-minute duty or forgotten item. "Ok, let's go," he whispers. The vent-cover disappears into the showroom ceiling. Parker drops down, a compact form in black, and crouches as he hits the plush carpet. He is followed by Kobryn, who likewise bunches herself as she lands. A black rope dangles lazily from the vent, swaying in the shadows.

Parker and Kobryn warily raise their heads. With their nightvision goggles, they can see everything clearly. Wasting no time, they go directly to the Majestic Gems display case. Parker quickly checks the box with the eyes and touch of an expert burglar – not wired to an alarm. Who would want to protect a box of fakes anyway? Smiling in the darkness, he feels along the back of the case and finds an indented button. He pushes it, and releases a tiny latch. He gently lifts the top and darts his hand inside. His fingers close around the Hope Diamond replica and he removes it. He drops the blue crystal into the inside pocket of his jacket, zips it shut, then closes the case.

The two rapidly retrace their steps back to the dangling rope and with Parker going first, hastily climb up into the vent. Once Kobryn is inside, the rope snakes upward and follows them. The vent-cover is replaced, and no one is the wiser. Less than five minutes have passed.

Within the White Feather, Maddox takes a sip of red wine and casually glances at his watch. Nine forty-five. If all is going to plan, things should be happening soon. He smiles, and hopes for good luck. Angelique looks over to him and smiles. He winks, then takes another sip.

In the flight deck Security Station, an alarm begins blaring. Reedy, the Watch Captain on duty, springs to action and hastily looks over the vidscreen. "Goddamn it, it's a fire alarm!" The attendants with him bolt from their chairs. "Deck Six, Stern Section, Subsection

J," he mutters, then grabs a microphone. "Fire Alert! Fire Alert! Code Yellow 6-S-J." Reedy turns to the monitor whose vidcam watches that area. Grey smoke covers the screen. "Heavy smoke! Heavy smoke! Sprinklers inactive! All available officers respond!"

"What in the hell!"

"Aw damn, a fire!"

Comments like these are said heard under-the-breath by security personnel from around the ship begin converging on the area. A fire within the completely self-contained structure of a spaceship is one of the most deadly situations they can ever encounter. Three officers pour into the Security Station and grab portable oxygen tanks, facemasks, and fire extinguishers, then race out of the room. The silver corridor doors to the Bridge silently close and lock as the room automatically seals itself and slips into a self-contained life support mode, as is done when any dangerous situation arises to keep the Bridge safe and operable and is known as the Homesafe protocol. Reedy radios Third Officer Hearst about the fire investigation, then races out, leaving O'Grady in charge. Seems as though Maddox's little diversion is having the desired effect.

At the Purser's Office in the lobby, the three security officers perk up on hearing Reedy's strained voice. The lobby has some people milling about, but is relatively quiet. Gow, the security supervisor, bursts from the back office with another officer close behind. They have their firefighting equipment. "Calisi and I will go. Simms, stay here." Simms nods as the men exit the reception desk then rapidly but calmly leave the room. Parker and Kobryn, now dressed in casual clothes and standing in different parts of the lobby, watch them go.

One minute passes. Suddenly, smoke begins spewing from a vent near the back of the Lobby. People scream and the smoke alarm begins to wail with screeching beeps. "Aw, hell!" Simms barks. He snatches the telephone at his desk and dials the security station. Reedy answers on the second ring. "We've got smoke in the lobby! I'm checking it out!"

"Understood!" Reedy answers as he dispatches another alert. Just as Simms hangs-up the deskphone rings again. "Purser's Office!" the officer hastily barks.

"This is McKeever in the PCC What's going..."

"You three go to the alcove!" Simms replies to the comm-tech in the passenger communication center. "Help with crowd control."

"Gotcha!"

Simms races from the desk and scrambles back into the office. He throws an oxygen mask over his head, yet leaves it dangling at his neck and grabs a fire extinguisher. He reappears seconds later, ensures that the office-door is secured, then comes around from the desk just as smoke begins billowing from a vent at the front of the lobby, near the entryway alcove. Screaming people rush out of the room with the help of the comm techs as Simms attempts to track the source of the smoke. Parker and Kobryn strap compact respiration masks over their noses and mouths and move toward the pillar.

The lobby is soon filled with a smoky haze and the lenses of the video cameras become clouded in grey. Parker steps near the pillar as Kobryn likewise arrives. In the melee of the room, they both keep their eyes locked on Simms, who is running down the center of the room, his head looking upward, concentrating on the smoke, following its path on the ceiling.

Parker suddenly steps back, then approaches the security officer from behind as the man trots along to the front of the room. Unsure of what Parker is doing, but following his lead, Kobryn in moves from the other side. Just as Simms nears the pillar, Parker spies a perfect opportunity. He steps up his speed and strikes. Wham! He slams into the officer in a perfect blindside tackle.

Simms goes careening headfirst into the pillar. The fire extinguisher flails up in response to his flying arms, and smashes into the glass box protecting the Diamond, shattering its top half. An alarm begins to loudly ring. The officer clips his head on the marble pillar, and a small spot of blood remains on the white stone as he falls heavily to the floor, next to the extinguisher. Even though he is not moving, Kobryn intentionally topples on to the officer to keep him down.

Parker thrusts his arm into the open end of the box and coils his now gloved fingers around the Hope's platinum chain, then tears it from its velvet home. The genuine Diamond and its chain disappear into his jacket, then he instantly brings the replica out of his pocket; it hangs from a glimmering silver trinket necklace which Maddox purchased at one of the ship's novelty shops. He carefully sets the duplicate on the bust, arranging it perfectly, and turns away.

He pulls a compact iron-cased blackjack from his jacket and spins back again. He takes it firm in his leathered palms and slams it into the remnants of the glass guardian. What is left of the case decimates. The blackjack also hits the blue velvet fixture, snapping it from the metal rotating rod base and knocking it, and more shattered glass, onto the floor next to the motionless officer. The fake flies off and lands on the carpet.

Parker slips the blackjack away and looks down at Kobryn, then nods. She rises and removes her facemask, as does Parker. They separate and move to different exits in the Lobby. As their smoky cover fades, they vanish from the room. The deed takes all of less than two minutes to complete.

Down in the stern, the security officers are confused over the smoke, which has now dispersed. Well, this answers one riddle: the sprinklers were not activated because, in contrast to the age-old saying, there was smoke but no fire, and since the sprinklers are triggered by heat, there was no reason for them to spray water. However, they did activate the smoke alarms but, where did the smoke come from? The officers immediately jump to conclusions. Security Lieutenant Davidovich, looming with his black hair slicked back over his skull, is there at 6-S-J, with his hands fisted and at his hips, looking around with glaring eyes within a stern face. His lips are a thin slit across that face, and his jaw is set as though it could take a boulder straight-on. "Just what we need, this stuff on the last night! What in blue blazes is going on?" he roars. "I want some answers!"

Just then, the security communicators sound. "This is Kirsalis in the lobby! The diamond pillar is damaged! Smoke here too! Simms is down! Seems unconscious! Pulse and breathing ok. I have advised sick bay. The smoke . . . is cleared now, no sign of fire. Get up here now!"

"You three! Sweep the area!" Davidovich orders. "Everybody else, with me!" He then jerks his thumb back and races to the lobby with the others following close behind. Two minutes later, Davidovich and his officers burst into the lobby. "Over there!" Davidovich yells and points to the left of the room, and they go to Simms, who is sitting up against the wall and holding a towel to his head. A nurse is with him. Kirsalis and two people in comm uniforms stand nearby. A pungent aroma of smoke still hangs in the air, and the room still holds a bit of mist. On seeing Davidovich, Simms tries to rise. The Lieutenant waves him down with a gentle motion of his hand. "Are you all right?" Davidovich asks.

"Yessir. Just a bit shaken, Sir."

"What happened?"

"Smoke came pouring out of the vents at the front and back of the room."

"Damn smoke again," Davidovich mutters, then nods to Simms to continue.

"I went to investigate, with an extinguisher. In the crowd, someone knocked into me, and I fell against the pillar. I blacked out." Davidovich scans the area. Pillar there, top empty, floor strewn with glass shards, bust lying on its side on the floor - - bare without the jewel! "The- -!" he shouts as he snaps his head back to Simms.

The gem dangles in the air from its chain, gleaming blue. It is held aloft by a smiling Simms. "My extinguisher smashed the case as I fell. When I came to, the Diamond was lying on the floor just next to my hand. It is safe, Sir."

Davidovich relaxes, then carefully takes the diamond from Simms. He inspects it, and breathes a sigh of relief. It in fact looks perfect - not even a scratch. "Good work, Jess," Davidovich says with a nod.

"Thank you, Sir."

"Now, let's get you to Sick Bay." Kirsalis and Supervisor Gow help Simms to his feet; he winces in pain and rests his hand on his left side. "Are you sure you can move?" Davidovich asks.

"Yessir. Just a bit sore. That's where they caught me."

Davidovich nods. "Ok." He motions for the officers to take Simms to Dr. Washington's Office. "After you are seen to, you and Kirsalis please fill out an Incident Report." The men nod. The Lieutenant turns to the comm techs. "You two may as well go back to the PCC."

"Yessir," comes the dutiful answer, followed by nods.

"Where is the third of your group?"

"She went back to work in the center while we came to help the downed officer."

"I see. Very well. Thank you for your help."

The comm techs move toward the door of the communications center as Davidovich heads for the reception desk. "Turn off that pillar alarm!" he shouts with a cutting wave of his arm, and the ringing immediately stops. He looks at two other officers. "I want the lobby secured, and blocked off from any visitors for a while. Get Mike Priest up here as well to photograph everything," he says, indicating the broken glass and the fallen bust. "Once he is finished, have a janitor clean it up – but save the pieces for further analysis, don't let them throw anything away – not a single thing. I want detailed reports, from everyone too. Someone get to Simms and write his as he dictates."

"Yessir."

"Right away, sir." The two nod then head off rapidly to complete their tasks.

Satisfied, Davidovich returns the nod and turns on his heel. He pulls a clean handkerchief from his pants pocket and wraps the Hope Diamond in it. "You are going to a safe place before we get you to your new home," he says to the tiny jewel, as though it were some errant child who had lost its way, while walking back to the reception desk. He goes through the black steel door in the wall behind the desk, and once safely in the Purser's Office, carefully unwraps the Hope, and looks at it. "What a lucky break," he says to himself. "Not even a scratch," he says again, and shakes his head in amazement. Next, into the vault where he opens a safe-deposit box and he locks it safely away. Later he will ask Mueller if they should have the pillar repaired and the glass box replaced.

With the situation largely under control, the Bridge safety program ends, and the doors slide open as the room switches back to regular usage of shipwide life support.

Now, the other question. What about the smoke? A prank by some warped passenger? Maybe a disgruntled member of the crew trying to rattle things on the last night? What will follow? Davidovich brings his communicator to his lips. "This is Davidovich. What do we have on that smoke?"

"Mykall here, Sir. Seems to have come up from engineering. From that singeing in the byproduct damper. Somehow a filter got clogged or shut off, and the smoke found its way into a vent and to the upper decks."

"How in the hell did that happen?"

"We are working with the engineers to answer that, sir."

"Ok. Keep me informed." Davidovich next calls the security station. "O'Grady, everything's been resolved," he says, and notifies the bridge of the same. Davidovich leaves the Purser's Office and begins to go up to the station with uncertainties nagging at his mind. His forehead becomes a maze tangle of wrinkles, and he again raises his communicator. "Reedy, Gow, we need a meeting. And Reedy, I want a complete check of the security system along with a ship-wide protection sweep."

"Yessir, right away sir," comes the answers from the two. Davidovich slips his communicator back into its holster on his belt and he shakes his head ruefully. One thought consoles the Lieutenant, that at least they will be docking at Gamma tomorrow afternoon and will be able to conduct a more thorough investigation while the vessel is at Port. "Damn volcanoes. Damn Jupiter. Damn delays," he scoffs.

Parker and Kobryn slip into their suite as the ship moves onward. They shut the door, and go into the bedroom, and from there to the bathroom. As Ruby Kobryn closes and locks the doors of both these rooms, Parker clicks on the bright round lights circling the mirror above the marble sink. When Kobryn is by his side, Parker carefully pulls the diamond and chain from his coat pocket.

He lets out a long, slow whistle. "Wow, look at her…." he whispers in awe as he holds it up. "What a beauty!" Light bounces through the precision angled cuts in the deep blue and from the pristine white diamonds around it, like she is winking at them, captivating the eyes of its smiling illicit owners. "Devil in a blue dress."

"Beautiful!" Kobryn answers with eyes widened.

He turns to her and gives her an enthusiastic hug, while she kisses him strongly on the cheek. "We did it! We did it!" he says with glee. "What a score!"

"Yes, we did!" she answers with a smile, her gaze still fixed on the diamond.

"It all went like clockwork!" he says.

"Perfectly, to the letter, just as we planned!"

"Amazing. The boss's double-down is done!"

"He'll be pleased," Kobryn offers.

"Very," says Parker. After a moment, he turns to her. "Would you like to hold it?" She nods enthusiastically. Gingerly, he passes it to her waiting palms.

"Oooohhhhhhh bayyyybbeeee…" she purrs while gently holding it and gazing upon it still. Parker reaches for his personafône, and the two continue to gloat over their prize with devilish delight.

Within the White Feather, Maddox returns to his seat after dancing with a vivacious and comely blonde – one Angelique Yusacre; she is still a blonde, even if she hides it under her wig. He settles and glances at his wristwatch. Practically ten o'clock. Ten o'clock and all is well? Maddox steals a glance at the captain and officers. No frenzied crewman is disturbing them with urgent messages; their communicators appear to remain silent. Good. Suddenly, his personafône vibrates within the inside pocket of his tuxedo jacket. He picks it up and reads a message printed on its screen: **`'Diane says Hi.'`** Maddox immediately erases the words but understands what

Parker is telling him: they have the Hope in-hand. If 'Diamond Diane' had given her farewells, then they had some trouble and did not have it in-hand (a word which incidentally beings with i-h, which in turn is h-i when inverted, or, 'hi'). He clicks a return message of **`'Hi back.'`** then slips his phone back into his jacket and turns to Angelique.

"Do you remember our friend Didi?" he asks.

"Didi, yes, wonderful girl. How is she doing?" Angelique says without skipping a beat.

"She says hello, and I understand she's moved."

Angelique raises her eyebrows. "Is that so?" The eyebrows drop again. "How nice of her to let us know, and to send greetings. We should make a point of seeing her soon." She smiles broadly, and her white teeth positively shine.

"I agree," Maddox responds. He winks and they share a glass-clink 'cheers', then both sip more wine. Maddox ponders a moment. The 'triple crown' of getting the Hope has been completed, the 'double down' of the Centralis caper is in its final phase, and that just leaves the first score, which will begin in just another hour or so. Rather ironic that the original reason for this job coming to exist is the last part to be done, but last is rarely least, after all….

CHAPTER TEN
Look Out!

As the evening progresses, things remain calm on the bridge. At 11:15, the ship is on the verge of clearing the Asteroid Belt, and is passing near a pale grey oval named Vesta. Deimos can clearly be seen in the distance, Deimos being the vacant, potato-shaped outer moon of Mars. Just then, there is an explosion from deep within the Asteroid Belt – the peace of the evening is about to be irrevocably shattered. The short-range radar waves make contact with a mass directly ahead of the ship, triggering the proximity alarm which begins to sound its ominous tone, in trios. '*Location alert! Location Alert!*' the speakers at the bridge bark a warning from the computer and the primary vidscreen spells out the same. '*Deviate course immediately! Obstruction in flightpath!*'

Hearst sits up in the command chair and consults a viewer on the command platform. Pilot Martingale looks to the radar screen and her eyes widen in terror. She opens her mouth, and for a moment, her lips refuse to form the words. "Well!" Hearst prods in a shout. "What is it?"

His yelling brings her out of her shock. She turns to the officer, face ashen. "Collision Alert! There's a meteoroid measuring 100 feet by 650 by 300 bearing 0'1'0' off our bow! Impact in . . ." she refers to the readout "3 minutes, 7 seconds!" The report stuns the bridge staff. They look at one another, silently, then collectively look out the viewport. At first, they see nothing but starry blackness surrounding the redness that is Mars. Then, it appears.

"There it is!" Escoto yells. She points to a small grey speck in the distance, dead ahead. The dot grows with every passing second, then this itself suddenly rumbles and breaks in two, doubling the problem.

"What the hell is that doing there!" Hearst shouts in shock. He reacts immediately and his finger shoots down on the ALL STOP button and instantaneously the tailcones cool their fires.

"Sir, the meteoroid has fragmented into two uneven sections and flanks us," Martingale reports. "Aft thrust at zero percent. Forward motion reduced by thirty percent and dropping. We remain on a collision course. Impact in - - 3 minutes, 2 seconds."

Hearst has bought the ship some time, but not nearly enough. He bolts from the Command Platform and is at the pilot's side in an instant. "Notify the captain he is needed on the bridge immediately," he barks at Escoto. "Visual!" he shouts to Martingale. Her fingers move across a keyboard, and on a vidscreen to her right the computer produces a holographic image of the meteor as identified by the radar waves which warp around it. The computer magnifies the data, giving an accurate, to-scale diagram. Superimposed on a grid comes a telescopic picture of what they face.

The smaller section is rocky and with a lumped, odd form. The larger piece is an ugly, mean thing. A crag lurches up on the far left of the meteor, angling sharply down to the right with a rough ridge, then ending on its far end with a jagged spur of rock. It has an irregular underside, and a slight blunt, compact bulge makes its left side, forming the base of the crag.

"Damn . . ." Hearst says. His mind races as he searches for options. He cannot use the base thrusters to raise the ship above the meteor because of the spiked crag, and also these are powered by the main engines, so with the Mercurys now dormant, it would take too long to restart. Neither can the ship go under, as he cannot get her low enough in time for the tailfin to clear the bottom of the meteors.

Sweat forms upon his upper lip. "Fire braking rockets," he orders Martingale. He rests a hand on her forearm. She turns and looks up at him. He knows they must be cautious, as using full force and attempting a sudden stop would buckle the ship and almost tear her apart. The action will also drop the ship into a lower orbit, putting them just above the outer edge of the gravity field for Vesta, but that should not present a problem. "Half pulse. Easy does it," Hearst says in a heavy tone.

She nods, long and slow. "Yes, Sir." She turns back to her console. "Firing,"comes the response from the helm. The braking rockets make their appearance from their housings at the bow. Minute strings of fire powered by hydrazine fuel erupt from the midsection of the bow. Since these rockets and the hullside parajets have their own motors, they remained unaffected when the main engines were deactivated. The ship slows more, though it continues to bear down on the massive objects in its path.

A tidal wave of exhaust empowered by a steady stream of strong pressure rushes forward and impacts the two meteors. White clouds form a murky veil over them and with brute force are able to push them back from the oncoming ship. The braking rockets are doing more than slowing the vessel, they are increasing the gap.

"Meteors are distancing from us, Sir!" Martingale says, enthusiasm clear in her tone.

"Increase power to the brakers!"

"Yessir." She slowly pushes a lever forward and the rocket-force marginally increases. The smaller of the two meteors rolls downward and tumbles away from the horizon, dropping back to the asteroid belt. "There's one problem solved," Hearst remarks with a smile. However, the 'Big Brother' remains. Being of a higher mass, it does not succumb so readily to the force of the exhaust but does begin to slowly spin on its own axis as the *Emprasoria* continues to move forward.

"I believe we should try and port around it," Hearst says to the staff. "DeMornay, give me the computer assessment," he requests, to double-check his own conclusion. The Cybernetics Officer and Valenta, who is at the Astrocon, feed information to the computer. The CPU then conducts its evaluation.

'*Based on provided data*,' the computer responds seconds later, '*the ship should take a port heading around the object. This should result in minimal or no damage. Immediate action required*.' The computer then displays a path, marked in red, which the ship should follow on both a vidscreen at the pilot's console and the Astrocon. Coordinates are also given. Hearst smiles; he was right! Now, to action.

"Rudder - - port, thirty degrees!" Hearst orders.

"Thirty degrees, Yessir," the pilot says as she steadily adjusts the positioning controls. The gyro-repeater ticks off the course degrees as the ship's rudder moves. Slowly, ever so slowly, the bow begins to veer to the left. The menacing rock looms before the ship.

"Fire starboard parajets at the bow, port paras at the stern!" Hearst yells. Droplets of perspiration begin to form along his forehead and his stomach muscles tighten as he desperately tries to move the ship out of harm's way. The maneuvering thrusters embedded in the forward and aft midsection of the bow appear from behind their just-opened panels and begin to release exhaust, pushing the ship farther left. In a few moments, they will be clear. Unfortunately, they do not have a few moments.

The forward observation lounge is uncharacteristically empty as this occurs. The extremely bored bartender methodically cleans and organizes bottles in an effort to occupy his time. His back is do the window as he does this. A slightly inebriated passenger wearing a rumpled brown suit saunters in to the lounge and goes directly to the bar. He slumps against its polished wood surface, letting it support his drunken weight. Raising an eyebrow, the bartender turns toward him.

"Good evening, Sir," he says with a welcoming smile and a nod.

"Full house tonight I see." The passenger laughs loudly at his own joke. Liquored breath clouds the air.

"Yes, busiest we've ever been . . ."

"Best to beat the rush," the passenger guffaws. "Double gin and tonic, please."

"Very good, Sir." The drink is quickly provided, though it is a single shot of gin.

Drink in hand, the man again saunters toward the front of the room and gazes out the window. He takes a drink and immediately spits it out in response to what appears before his slightly blurred eyes. He blinks and looks again. Yes! It is definitely there! He drops his glass and it bounces on the floor. "G-G-Gawd!" he yells as he points to the gargantuan boulder outside the viewport, directly in line with the outstretched bronze finger of In Excelsis. He turns to the barman. "Y-Y-You see that? We're gonna hit that fuckin' thing!" The man runs toward the exit, stumbles, and falls to the floor. The fall knocks him unconscious for the moment.

"Shhhhhhhhitttttttttttttttttt," the bartender says as his eyes widen at the hellscene outside the viewport. He races to the fallen passenger and hoists the heavy body into a chair. He returns to the bar, lifts its phone and dials Sick Bay. A Nurse will come momentarily. Next, he fingers a button and the viewport curtains snake along the window, hiding the certain doom which lurks outside. The last thing needed is panicked passengers. He looks at the meteor as the curtains close. "I hope to hell the bridge can get us out of this," he mutters.

Down in the starboard compartment of the forward cargo hold, Walt Jackson, the sixty year old pot-bellied shift foreman and his team are sorting freight for off-loading. The change in the docking time puts added pressure on their task. When the radar waves contacted the meteor, a two-toned Stage One warning siren in their area began sounding in fifteen second cycles. The crewmen freeze in their tracks on hearing the alarm, and Jackson bites down hard on the stub of a cigar which protrudes from his mouth. "As you were," he says, and his workers resume their tasks. He goes to the wallphone to call the bridge and see what the trouble is about. "Just what I need, something disrupting work."

The bow veers to the left. The massive rock is clearly seen outside the right section of the viewport. "Bow and front are almost clear," the pilot says with a smile.

"Fantastic!" Hearst says, then breathes a sigh of relief. "Let's keep it u-" Another alarm blares, cutting him short – this one a more shrill tone. "What is that?" Hearst asks while again looking at the command console.

'*Warning. Warning. Object moving toward vessel.*'

"What?" Martingale says in shock. "What? No! How is that possible?" She looks to the radar, and yes, plain as day, the meteor is moving *toward* them.

"Am I seeing what I think I'm seeing?" Hearst blurts. "That damn thing can't move, what's it doing?"

DeMornay pulls a cord from her armband and connects it to a port in the Board, then she rapidly types on an adjoining keyboard. "Radar's working fine," she says under her breath, then enters more commands. "Oh, hell...." Her eyes widen and she re-reads the information. "Oh hell! Mitch!" she yells. "Mitch, it's the forward gravitationer!!" She turns to him, her face wracked with terror. "The meteor's caught in our magnetic field and it's being drawn into us!"

'*Extreme warning. Object nearing vessel,*' the computer states again.

"What!" Hearst bellows.

"When we turned!" DeMornay continues. "When we turned it shifted the magnetic field of the forward gravitationer to the meteor! It must have been just barely in range! Whatever it's made of, it's being attracted ***to us***!"

From the right windows, the meteor is seen moving closer to them. "Damn, damn!" Hearst yells in a panic.

'*Object entering outer perimeter!*' the computer barks.

"We need some kind of electroshield!" Hearst yells again while punching buttons. "Overload the front starboard grid!" From the electronics room, the sunvolt batteries put a massive amount of power to the wiring to the mid-section of the starboard bow, surging the area, yet staying just below what would blow fusing.

DeMornay reads a vidscreen again, watching as the radiating waves of the forward gravitometer suddenly stop, and are turned inward to the ship rather than passing through the hull. "It's working!" she shouts. "We're keeping the magne-beams inside!"

"Impact in thirty seconds!" the pilot says. The tension within the bridge is high. Stomach muscles reflexively tighten. Although the magnetic pull has been ended, the tug and drag is still in effect. The massive rock is clearly seen just outside the right section of the viewport, almost close enough for them to reach out and touch it. Hearst again leaps from the command platform and goes to her. Martingale is as scared as everyone else, though she remains calm and does her duty. She ignores the Yeoman next to her, who is visibly shaking. "Ten seconds."

'*Warning! Warning! Warning! Object remains in starboard flightpath. Impact Imminent.*'

"Come on . . . c'mon . . ." Hearst says through gritted teeth. His fingers dig into the headrest of the pilot's seat. They are close, so very close to avoiding the calamity. Just a bit more and they will be home-free.

"Five seconds," Martingale states evenly.

'*Final Warning,*' says the computer.

"Three."

"*Brace!*"

"Impact."

Yet there is no rending concussion. "We have entered the crash-zone," Martingale says while looking up. The massive meteor passes alongside them, revolving slowly. "Peak of the bow has cleared." You can hear the elation in her voice which sounds the hope of everyone on the bridge....maybe they can get past it! "Bow is clear!" The staff gather at the right end of the viewport and peer down; outside of their line of vision the spur brings itself around.

The ship collides with the meteor. The ceramic heatshield is the first victim. It warps and then shatters like icing under the compressing weight. Then there is a sickening screech as metal and rock merge. Sparks fly. It dents and scrapes the starboard bow and begins to burrow itself into the lower hull. "Damn it!" Martingale shouts. Alarms ring in the bridge.

'Ship has made contact with object. Damage at forecastle,' the computer reports.

In the Cargo Hold, the siren changes to a solid blare. Evac signal. The crewmen freeze again, warily looking about with wide-eyed but silent fear. Jackson lets the phone fall from his beefy hand. He knows what that sound means, and at first he does not believe his ears. His jaw drops, and the cigar tumbles to the deck plating. "Jeehez - - - No!" he whispers. '*Evacuate immediately*,' a computerized voice announces firmly yet calmly over the loudspeaker. Jackson's worst fears are realized as the outer wall suddenly bends inward. He yells to his workers.

"Get outta here! Come on! Move I tell ya! Move! *Mmmooovee!*" he yells as he swings his left arm down in a sweeping motion toward the hatchway.

The crewmen drop what they are doing and run for their very lives. As they race toward the door, they look back over their shoulders through the wire-fenced plexiglass of the safetycage which is their last barrier of protection. The hull continues to fall inward and to their horror it melds with the cage, and a stabilizer reaching up from the floor forks itself. When they look ahead they see the safety door is already beginning to close in response to the calamity, prompting them to move faster, and clamber into each other. Swearing and yells are heard as they struggle through the steel portal, pushed along further by Jackson's outstretched hands. When the last is through, Jackson looks through his straining eyes to try and spy any stragglers. Spotting none, he dashes through the edge of the closing doorway and escapes from the compartment just before the steel door slides shut with a heavy clang. They only have minor injuries, and are quickly assisted by their fellow crewmembers. "We made it . . . goddamn we made it . . ." Jackson says between heaved breaths.

As the meteor moves along the hull, the top-down outline of the ship as displayed on a bridge vidscreen crinkles inward at the lower forecastle. "Retract the parajets!" Hearst yells. Confused, Martingale does as told. As part of their safety protocols, the jets cease firing as the pipes are drawn into the craft. No sooner is the forward parajet in its berth than the front edge of the meteor approaches. The third officer watches the vidscreen intently. His eyes are locked on the progress of the meteor in its journey along the hull.

"On my mark," he says as he subconsciously raises his hand, "fire paras at full." Martingale nods and poises her hand above the controls. A second passes. "Now!" Hearst barks and sweeps his hand down. The pilot's hand slams a button, and the forward parajet emerges, pushing the meteor slightly, then erupting with an immense blast of exhaust. The rock becomes caught in the smoky flow, and is blown away from the ship. It is thrust out into empty space and quickly disappears from the radar-scan horizon. The ship is saved!

"It's gone!" Hearst yells exuberantly.

'*Ship has broken contact with object.*' the computer states. The bridge staff burst out cheering, then collectively breathe a sigh of relief and relax. They have been spared from what could have been a disastrous situation, and the ship has escaped without serious damage.

Hearst draws the back of his hand over his forehead, wiping away the perspiration. "Excellent work everyone," he says, praising the staff. "Especially you, Ms. Martingale." The pilot turns to him.

"Thank you, Sir," she says with a nod.

"Now, we must get things back to normal," Hearst remarks as he moves back to the command chair and sits down. He brushes some greasy hairs out of his face. "Please deactivate the braking rockets and starboard parajets. Fire the port paras until we have returned to our original course." Martingale nods as she begins adjusting the controls. "Roberta, I want the damage reports from the starboard bow."

"Yessir," Escoto replies.

Just then, Captain Arges hurriedly strides on to the bridge. "Something wrong, Mitchell?" he asks while giving a quick visual survey of the board as he walks to the chair. At first glance, everything seems to be in order.

Hearst jumps from the chair and faces his captain, smiling. He takes note of the medal on Arges' chest. "We came upon a meteor, Sir. It came on us fast. The gravitationer caught it. We brushed it, and have some minor damage but I was able to make an escape."

"Damage?" Arges asks, concern evident in his voice and on his face.

"The integrity of the hull at the forward cargo compartment has been compromised, though has not ruptured. Part of the heat shield has broken, and a stabilizer has been mildly warped."

"I see. And everything is fine now?"

"Yessir," replies the still smiling Hearst.

"Any crew injured?"

"None as yet reported, Sir."

"Thank God for that."

Arges pauses. "Excellent. Very good. Very good, Mitchell," Arges offers his hand, which Hearst takes. A hearty shake is exchanged. Arges steps over to the Board and goes to a vidscreen, then types in a code. He watches as the monitor displays a computer-generated instant replay of the events leading up to the collision, and the incident itself. The replay is in three-dimensions, and rotates from a top view, a front view, a starboard-side view, and a rear-view. When the scene finishes, Arges turns to Hearst. "Excellent maneuvering!" He smiles and slaps Hearst on the back of his shoulder. "Great work!"

"Thank you, Sir."

"It could have been disastrous, but timely action saved us."

"Yessir."

"Great work, everyone!" Arges says, praising the bridge staff. He next looks back to the monitor, and enters another code. "Just a scrape. Hmmmmmmmm. So we won't arrive in pristine condition," Arges pauses for a moment, and a mild frown comes over him. "The Man won't be too thrilled about that." He looks up, pondering. "Maybe we can get a repair crew to somehow mask most of it." He steps away from the Board. "I better go tell him what happened. Roberta, please forward a copy of the damage report to my quarters and my infokeeper as soon as it is available."

"Yes, captain," she replies.

"And send some engineers down to check that stabilizer."

"Already on their way, Sir," Hearst answers with a crisp nod. Arges turns to his third officer. "Great. And once again, top-notch work, Mitchell." Arges takes Heart's hand in a hearty grasp and gives him a firm handshake. Hearst nods, and the captain leaves the bridge.

Hearst goes to the command platform and sits down again in the chair. Well, isn't that something . . . He smiles widely. Quite a commendation, and from the captain no less! Hearst looks up. "Yeoman, please make the necessary log entries and give me a printout of them." As the yeoman nods, Hearst sits back in the chair.

He now takes a moment to revel in <u>his</u> accomplishment. It was <u>he</u> who saved the ship. His bravery and quickthinking will be recorded for all eternity in the ship's log. He imagines the attention he will receive at Mars, and then back on Earth . . . Arges accolades are just the beginning; tip of the iceberg . . . the news interviews, invitations to society parties, surely a reward from Archangel . . . he should even earn his captain's stripes for this! Not to mention a medal which will make Arges's look like a trinket in comparison. The world will be his oyster! After all, he deserves it. His eyes glaze over as his ego swells with pride. He savors <u>his</u> moment as though it is sweet candy.

"Officer Hearst, we have again reached our original course heading," Martingale reports.

"Very good," he replies, then calls the E.O.C., which has been unaware of what has transpired since receiving the "ALL STOP" signal. "Engineering, this is Officer Hearst. A meteor bumped us out there, but we're fine. Prepare to restart the Mercurys."

"Yessir. Corté here. Engines will be on-line inside of ten minutes."

Hearst's face twitches as he hears this. "Very well, proceed Corté." With his eyes narrowed, he turns to the pilot. "Ms. Martingale, what will our new E.T.A. be for Gamma be if we resume full speed in, say, seven minutes?"

"Considering the delay in shutting down, reversing, and restarting, she says while entering figures into a console, "we should dock approximately thirty minutes after our scheduled time. Perhaps more."

"I see," Hearst replies. He thinks for a moment, silently. He is displeased with the figures, and is not about to let his moment in the spotlight be clouded by a late arrival. Mr. Enkel would be very annoyed, to say nothing of the Royale class people, typically who have rigid schedules. Hearst glances at the notepaper on the command board. **I EXPECT US TO REACH OUR FINAL DESTINATION IN THE BEST TIME POSSIBLE.** "I'm not about to take the blame for some stupid spacerock that had gotten in our way," he says quietly to himself. "I have to make up for the lost time. Half an hour? Forget it – an unacceptable delay." He clicks on the chair communicator and resumes his conversation with the E.O.C.. "Corté, get a restart done as quickly as you can – I want it well within that five minute estimate. Then we will go right into hypercombustion to reach an instant top-speed. Load the injectors with as much fuel as they can take, top them right off."

"Always in a fucking hurry up there," Corté mutters under his breath, then picks up his microphone and clears his throat, and puts his voice into a better tone. "Yessir, understood sir, we'll complete it as quickly as possible."

"Very good. Hearst out."

Corté continues throwing switches and punching buttons, also entering commands through his keyboard. "Run it at full, stop it on a dime, start it up again, get it going, don't worry about physics, just go go go," he still mutters. **EMERGENCY ENGINE LOCKDOWN**

ENGAGED. states a readout – their sudden stopping of the engines prompted this action as a precaution. Corté taps the release button. The message blinks twice, but remains. **EMERGENCY ENGINE LOCKDOWN ENGAGED.** "That is odd," Corté says, and his eyebrows come together in confusion. He presses the release button again, a bit harder this time. **EMERGENCY ENGINE LOCKDOWN ENGAGED.** "Oh, great, just great..." he says sarcastically, then presses the button a third time. The message remains on the screen, and he picks up his microphone while typing on his keyboard. "Brock McAllister, can you go check the fuel flow starters, it won't release the brake from up here."

"Will do," comes the quick answer. "On my way now." Just then, a response to Corté's computer inquiry flashes on the screen. REFLEX LOCK JAMMED. Corté grabs his mircophone again. "Mac, check the reflex lock specifically."

"Gotcha. I'm almost there."

"Ok, thanks." Corté reaches over and presses the release switch again, just-in-case, and with hopeful eyes he looks up at the monitor again. **EMERGENCY ENGINE LOCKDOWN ENGAGED** stares back at him. "Damn thing," he mutters.

A few moments pass, then McAllister calls the EOC. "Chris, could you come down here a minute?"

"Ok. What's the problem?"

"Doesn't look good," McAllister replies with a heavy tone. "I think you should see for yourself."

"Ok, I'm coming down." Corté looks at his watch – ouch, Hearst will be fuming. He turns to Harrison, the other tech in the command room. "I'm going down to see McAllister in the engine room. If the bridge calls, tell them I'll be back in a minute."

"Yessir."

Corté is quick to join McAllister. "What have we got here?" he asks.

"Looks like a busted ring-clamp that's rubbing against the lock release and jamming it," McAllister says.

Corté shakes his head ruefully. "Let me see."

McAllister nods and climbs through an opening in the engine housing, through a panel he removed himself, pressing into a narrow gap with his flashlight ahead of him. Corté is able to fit in as well, but just barely. McAllister shines his flashlight to the affected area. The beam circles on a clearly broken silver colored round clamp, which is jammed against some gears. "Well, that's the problem alright," Corté says.

"Relatively easy to fix itself," McAllister comments, "It's just getting to it that's that hassle."

"Yeah that is for sure. Shine your light around a bit, to see if there's anything else wrong." McAllister does this, and everything seems in place. The two back out, and Corté turns to the engineer. "Ok, you stay here, I'm going back to the EOC to tell the bridge. They're already anxious to have us get going, and they aren't going to like this news."

"Good luck," McAllister offers.

"Thanks."

Corté walks in to the EOC. "What's it like?" Harrison asks.

"Could be worse," Corté says as he sits. "We need to replace a clamp is all, but it's buried inside the workings, and will take time to get to."

"Oh," Harrison says. "Mr. Hearst has called for you, twice." Corté rolls his eyes and picks up the microphone while dialing. "Wish me luck."

"Good luck."

"Mr. Hearst, Corté here."

"I take it you're calling to tell me I can hit the Engine Fire, right?"

"Well, we seem to have run into an issue with the engine lockdown. A loose clamp is blocking the release."

"Well, fix it then," Hearst says curtly.

"We can replace it, but, it will take some time."

"How long?"

"Three hours is a fair guess." Corté knows this is bad news and knows what to expect, so he tenses.

A pause follows. "Three hours! What do you mean *three* hours! We can't be stuck out here that long, damn it! Bypass it! Do an override it and route fuel through the backup engines."

"Sir, we do that," Corté begins slowly, "but that would skirt around ventilation for some of the pipes, trapping some residue fumes and gasses."

"That extra there can give us a little more push, push that we need, so run the bypass."

"There is still a danger factor, Sir."

That little punk is trying to second-guess me, Hearst thinks. How dare that glorified greasemonkey challenge me! Without a moment's hesitation, Hearst begins a verbal attack. "Corté, what is your rank?"

Corté knows full well that Hearst knows his rank. "Sir?" he asks, confusion evident in his tone.

"Your rank, what is it," Hearst continues.

"I am a second engineer, first class," Corté responds.

"And what is my rank?" Hearst questions.

"You are a third officer, Sir," Corté says, failing to comprehend what, if anything, a review of status at this moment could possibly mean.

"Who has the higher rank?"

"You, Sir."

"I'm sorry, I didn't hear you."

"You do, Sir."

"Do you think you should be advising me on anything, let alone engine operation?"

"No Sir, I merely wish to point out the danger - -"

"Yes, that's fine second engineer Corté," Hearst interjects, cutting the man off in mid-sentence. "I'll recommend you for a merit badge in Safety when we land on Mars." Hearst is now reduced to open mockery. "Assuming we will ever reach the Spaceport at your rate. Hell Corté, we are built for speed. It is in our name!" Here Hearst refers to the sound similarities between "racer" and "rasor" in *Emprasoria.* His tone next darkens. "Just do as you are told. Nothing more. Nothing less. Understand, second engineer?"

There is a long pause. "Yes, Sir. Understood, Sir," Corté finally says, but he is not about to let the issue end there. "I will follow your orders, but I want it clearly stated on the record that we are doing this at your insistence, against my better judgment."

Hearst thinks for a moment. He is already recognized in the log as the savior of the ship, he may as well receive credit for keeping her on schedule. "Very well, Mr. Corté, you have your wish. It will be done. Yeoman, do as the Engineer requests. Now, prepare for the blast order, Corté." Hearst quickly shuts the intercom off without letting Corté speak further. If anything, he thinks, the excess fumes will give the ship an added boost and move things faster.

Down in the E.O.C., Corté is an extremely angry man, and justifiably so. "Idiocy," he curses as he operates the controls to detour around the engine lock. Warning messages flash on two monitors.

EMERGENCY ENGINE LOCKDOWN ENGAGED ENGINES AND PIPES HAVE NOT BEEN VENTILATED. IGNITION HAZARDOUS. Corté angrily enters a manual override command. Within seconds, both the engines and injectors are primed and ready for Hearst's foolhardy restart.

Harrison feels badly for Corté, but thinks it wiser to concentrate on his own task rather than try to console his partner. In his monitoring of the ship's systems, he notices that oxygen tank #3 has only two hours of air remaining. This is expected, though, and he makes a notation to switch over to the reserve tank at 1:30am to provide oxygen for the remainder of the voyage. Plenty of air in there to last them until they dock.

"Harrison, come here please," Corté says. "Radio the bridge and tell them it's ready. I don't want to talk to that son of a bitch again."

"Yessir."

Outside in space, far away from the ship, things are happening. Just because the meteor is out of sight does not mean it is gone for good. Yes, a meteor with a smear of white paint with bits of ceramic stuck to it races through space, rapidly spinning on its axis, given newfound speed from the parajet exhaust. As it moves along, another small asteroid cast adrift from the Belt finds itself caught in the relentless vortex of the Martian gravity field. As it is drawn in, it enacts a tried and true law of physics, that being the formula of: "Force = Mass X Acceleration". The asteroid has a solid core of iron, and when it meets the speedy pull of Vesta, its velocity triples, resulting in it being quite a forceful foe. The asteroid is three times the size of the meteor. There is at best a one-percent chance that these two drifting astral boulders would find themselves intersecting, but for whatever reason, their paths cross. When the two hit, they collide heavily, and the meteor bounces back from the huge stone like a pellet in a galactic pinball machine. It shoots back, careening awkwardly, tumbling in the darkness, a reversal not on an exact path, but in the same general direction - - back toward an unsuspecting ship.

In the bridge, Hearst receives the damage report. "Let me see; the heatshield has been warped at the starboard bow, but is still in place, though miniscule sections have broken loose. The hull has been ruptured at the lower section of the starboard bow. The ship is listing slightly at its right front, and one cargo compartment is unsafe to enter.

Otherwise, aside from some denting and scraped paint, the vessel is fine, and there were no crew casualties. Good." Hearst is pleased with himself. The Yeoman gives him a printout of the Log entry boldly declaring his heroism. He delicately handles the sheets; "Tomorrow morning, you go to the ship's carpenter to be framed," he says to them.

Having received word that the engines are Standing By for his order, Hearst dramatically rises from the command chair, then steps from the platform and goes to the pilot. After the ship returns to schedule, he plans to visit the White Feather to get the congratulations he expects from the captain, The Man, and everyone else. Mmmmmmm and how the ladies love a man receiving praise . . .

He brushes some greasy strands of hair out of his face, then thrusts his right hand forward as he dramatically yells "Fire!" Martingale presses the ENGINE FIRE button from her station. Hoping for the best, Corté watches from a monitor as fuel slinks around through the backup engine and into the two main combustion chambers, where it mixes with gas already there and together they are immediately ignited. The supercharged Mercurys roar with power.

At the exact moment this happens, the proximity alarm in the bridge sounds again. '*Location alert! Location alert!*'
A nervous look crosses Hearst's face as he warily looks at Martingale.

"Mass approaching starboard stern at high rate of speed!" she earnestly reports.

Although the stern engines had been closed down, the ship had still moved forward a bit, albeit slowly, from the remnants of the aft thrust momentum before coming to a dead-stop just near the asteroid-moon Vesta. It moved one-thousand feet since first hitting the meteor, putting the stern where the bow had been just moments before. The thing appearing on the radar is on top of them before they can do anything about it. With a loud crash, the meteor slams into the stern and crushes the tailcones as it moves into the night.

What had once been highly stylized thrusters are now nothing more than scrap metal. The cones are flattened against the aft hull. Exhaust races down the tailpipes only to find it has no place to go. Pressure builds quickly. What is ten thousand pounds of thrust becomes twenty, and twenty, forty. The jammed gasses quickly plug the pipes and then begin to clog in the machinery. Both the main and backup engines bloat from the pressure; their housing begins to buckle and bulge, irreparably warping what had once been smooth. Valves burst and scales jump into DANGER zones. The technicians stop what they are doing and run for safety.

"Goddammitt Goddammitt!" Corté screams in the E.O.C. He is frantically trying to restore order to the catastrophic situation. Everything is happening so quickly - - so damn quickly that he barely has time to think. He slams his hand on a button and retracts the fuel injectors from the engines. The Mercurys will not be fed anymore fuel, and the tanks will be spared from the excessive heat raging within the motors.

He then punches wall switches and opens the floor pipes in an effort to vent the exhaust through the Von Braun base thrusters in an emergency release. The keel panels open, and the rockets drop from their compartments. However, the pipes are given too much too soon. The lines expand to twice their width as the searing mass of gas spills into them. The tubes are savagely jerked upright at the point where nozzles link them to the thrusters. The solid steel kinks as though it is light tin. The circular walls of the pipes are crushed together in a tight pinch which effectively seals off the base exits. The exhaust is now hopelessly bottled in these pipes, which are not designed to contain a level of pressure anywhere close to what they are now holding.

Back in the engine room, the pressure in the Mercurys continues to build at a rapid rate, sending gauge arrows beyond DANGER and into CRITICAL levels. Like everything else, the Mercurys do have their limits, and the engines are currently experiencing more than they can handle. Kablam! Carrrruush! Bang! Blam! Blam! Rrrrippp! Pow!

Suddenly, the Mercurys explode with an incredible ferocity. There is a deafening roar as the motor casings are completely ripped apart and a column of thick black smoke and bright yellow fire bursts into the air. This pillar of flame billows up and hits the ceiling. Its heat instantly turns the sprinkler units into molten blobs and demolishes the light fixtures as well. A cloud of burning gas hits the E.O.C., shattering the viewport and knocking Corté and Harrison to the floor. Fragments from the motor casings and engine parts fly around the room like hot metal arrows, lodging themselves in the ceiling, the walls, or the flesh of screaming technicians not lucky enough to have escaped.

Shock waves from the explosion rock the entire Engineering section. Walls vibrate, vidscreens blank, and unsuspecting workers fall to the floor as it inexplicably begins to quake beneath their feet. In the electrical room, cables are harshly torn from their conduits. They rip through the air and snap around wildly. One throws itself into the upper half of a circuit board. The panel explodes in a shower of sparks as its upper half short-circuits and blows itself out. When the waves hit the stabilizers, the shock absorbers and vibration dampeners, they dissipate the violent energy. Thus, the shaking which plagues Engineering does not reach the upper decks. Those in the White Feather have no idea anything terrible has happened; their champagne does not so much as ripple.

By the time the quake reaches the bow most of its power has eased. However, it is still forcible and it rumbles unceasingly to the stabilizer which was damaged during the first impact. A repair team of three are in ensconced in the rigging of the balancer as the jolt dismembers the intricate device into several broken pieces, erupting a stream of heated hydraulic fluid into the air. Engineers yell as they are scalded and fall to the floor covering their faces with their hands and doubling over. The front of the ship begins a slight list to starboard with the loss of this key supporting beam.

The explosion forces smoke and more exhaust into the already overstretched base pipeline. Because of pipe cloggage, a particularly heavy amount of gaseous matter is concentrated beneath engineering room six, the Aquox Vestibule which holds the water and oxygen tanks. Without warning, a pipe here explodes upward. The floor grating above it blows up and back from the force of the explosion, and the metal tube itself arc through the air like a deadly javelin before finally lancing one of the tanks. The smoke and exhaust flow through the newly formed gap in the pipeline and quickly disperse along the bottom of the ship. The pressure has been released, and is no longer a threat to the vessel.

As quickly as it all started, everything settles. Corté and Harrison stand up, soaked from the E.O.C. sprinkler system which rains water down on the small fires burning in the office. They are scratched from broken glass, sooty and stained, their hair is matted down, but are otherwise fine. They look out through the gaping hole which seconds before had been a window and witness the destruction that the explosion has caused with wide, shocked eyes and open mouths.

The Mercurys are nothing more than a pile of black, scorched junk. A large fire rages in the middle of the charred mess. Once vital parts are strewn everywhere; now broken, useless rubble. Ruptured pipes spew gasses or fluids out into the open. A section of catwalk dangles like a limp branch. Fires burn throughout the room, and smoke hangs in the air like a heavy fog. The blaring alarms and flashing red lights complete the scene of this mechanized hell.

"Mon Dieu, Mon Dieu . . ." Corté whispers in his native tongue. "Mon Holi Dieu, aidez-nous, plait aidez-nous." He looks down at the scene, not comprehending what he sees. So much destruction! His mind wanders – even with this mess, they still have been incredibly lucky. If the injectors had not been withdrawn in time . . . if the explosive heat had reached the fuel tanks . . . they would be nothing but spacedust by now. Corté swallows hard and fights the need to vomit. He closes his eyes, and a single tear cuts a clean path down his blackened face. After a moment, the shock wears off, and Harrison similarly recovers.

Corté speaks into the general intercom serving the engineering section. "Fire crew to the engine room!" he yells. "Fire crew to the engine room!" He next calls the security station and advises them of the fire in the engine room. He notes that the sprinklers in the E.R. have been damaged, and lowers the oxygen supply to the Room to a fraction of what it normally is to cut off the fuel of the fire. "We must see where the ship stands..." Corté begins. "What the damage is." The two engineers read monitors, and are relieved to see that the pressure has dropped to an absolute zero, but this relief is short-lived in the midst of the alarms and warning lights which ring and flash within the tiny office which miraculously remains in tact and operational.

"Goddamn," Corté murmurs "Looks like we lost a stabilizer up front!" He punches some buttons and eases a heavy lever. "Initiating counterbalance," he says with a strained voice through gritted teeth. His eyes lock on to the gyropositioner, and soon the vessel teeters back to its left, until it is stable on an even keel once again. Corté locks the lever in place at that point then hurriedly looks around the rest of the room.

Harrison catches sight of a blinking message on a vidscreen which summons his attention. What he reads terrifies him. RESERVE OXYGEN SUPPLY CONTAMINATED. HAZARDOUS. DO NOT USE. PIPING FROM TANK 3 BEING AUTOMATICALLY CLOSED AND SEALED. Fumes within the broken pipe had seeped into the airtank. This means the ship has a mere two hours of oxygen left. After that, the liner will be nothing more than an incredibly large tank of poison gas.

Harrison nudges Corté, who is feverishly running a systems check. Corté looks over, and Harrison points in silence to the screen. "Fuck!" yells the second engineer as he sees the readout. The reports he next receives do not make him any happier. Aside from the Mercurys being destroyed, the base thrusters are likewise ruined. This means the *Emprasoria* will not be moving from her current location anytime soon.

CHAPTER ELEVEN
End's Beginning

For the second time that evening, warning lights flash and alarms sound within the bridge. "This is crazy," an ensign says under his breath to a yeoman, who nods his similar disbelief at what they are experiencing. "I mean, what are the odds of two large-scale emergencies happening in one night? Almost impossible I tell you, or extremely slim at best, but here, in front of our own eyes, the impossible is happening." He quiets when Hearst races past.

Hearst takes the steps to the command platform two at a time then jumps into the command chair and yells into its microphone. "Corté! What the hell is going on down there? What did you do? Report!"

Down in the E.O.C., Harrison makes a move to answer when he feels a tap at his shoulder. It is Corté. "I'll handle this," he says coolly, then reaches for the microphone. "I'll tell you what's happening Hearst! The 'damn Mercurys just exploded, that's what! All our drive systems are down because we hit something and it blocked the tailcones as we ignited the fuel! The goddamn non-ventilation built up pressure to a crazy level and all hell is breaking loose down here!"

"Mercurys - - exploded,,,,, all drive systems down?" Hearst says in shock. His voice is a dull, ghostly whisper.

"Yep, we're stranded now, thanks to you," Corté continues. "And that's not our only problem, either. Your little stunt poisoned the reserve oxygen tank too. We only have two hours of air left before we're dry."

Hearst sits dumbfounded in the chair as the voice of Corté is broadcast through the bridge; there is a blank look on his face. What had happened? He looks down and sees the Log printout clenches in his left hand. He has inadvertently crumpled the sheets as his fingers reflexively gripped in terror when he heard the damage report. These words mean nothing now. He has gone from hero to failure in a matter of minutes. Seconds. He opens his palm and lets the sheets fall to the floor. His mind begins to ache as he considers the damage done. The fact he is not directly responsible means nothing. The trouble. The problems. Oh, ohhhhh, - - the punishment!! His career is over, his life worth nothing. He buries his face in his hand in anguish.

Then, he changes. His head snaps up and he has a bold look about him. In an effort to console himself, Hearst concentrates on the hopeful possibilities - - maybe that idiot Corté has exaggerated the situation; maybe things are not really all that bad; maybe he will only receive a light reprimand. Then, the truth, with all its savagery, creeps in. There is no chance of a good outcome. He has been grasping at straws, and he knows it. The Man will eat him alive for this, to say nothing of the captain. The new flagship - - wrecked!! His hopes and future become lost in space.

To those looking at him, he has become dismal again. You can see the grief in his dismayed eyes. Then, this grief turns stern. He sets his jaw hard, and his eyes fill with determination. I will regain control - to make the best of the situation, the words are almost printed across his face. "Shut off those damned alarms! And put the computer on mute too!" he barks, and the sirens are quickly silenced.

"Shall I request that the captain come u- -" Escoto begins.

"Not yet!" Hearst snaps. He turns his attention to the intercom. "Corté, give me an estimate on the time for repairs," he says with acid in this throat.

"Repairs? We can't fix this. Hell, there's nothing to fix. We'll have to replace both the Mercurys and the entire base-thruster pipeline. The ship will be stuck in a hangar for at least three weeks!"

"Ohhhhhhhhh Goddddddddd........." Hearst whispers as he lowers his head. His fears worsen. His resolve returns again in a split-second as he composes himself, recalling his earlier supposition that the engineer's diagnosis may be mistaken. Once again, Hearst is his authoritarian-self. "Begin repairs. Do whatever you can," he orders in a strong tone.

"Didn't you hear what I said?" Corté responds irately. "We can't do *one fuckin' thing* out here but pray! The damage is too severe!"

"Corté! I do not want to hear excuses! Do your duty! Begin repairing those engines immediately! I don't want to hear from you again until we are ready to move. Now, get to it!" Hearst clicks off the radio before Corté can say a word in reply.

Just then, Captain Arges walks on to the bridge. "I have an idea about the bow," he begins, smiling. The third officer slowly rises from the chair, his already pale skin losing more color as he sullenly faces his superior. Arges stops and immediately notices the 'light show' on the board. "What's all this?" he asks, bewildered.

Hearst swallows hard. "Well . . ." he begins, "the first collision was not our only contact with a meteor this evening, Sir." Hearst is stalling in a vain effort to delay inevitable fate.

"What?" Arges prods. "What happened, Mitchell?" Silence in the bridge. An answer is not forthcoming from the motionless Hearst. "I want a *complete* report. Now."

Hearst swallows again, then begins his grim story. "As we were restarting the engines, a meteor rammed our stern and crushed the thruster cones. This collision closed off our exhaust outlet. Pressure built up, and, ah, damaged the Mercurys and the base-thruster pipes before it was finally released. According to Corté, no drive systems are operational. However, I have ordered him to begin repairs."

The captain is dumbfounded. A look of shock comes over his face. How can this be possible? It is . . . unbelievable. He looks to the others of the bridge staff, and the looks of stress, distress, and terror on their faces confirms that Hearst is stating the facts as they are, undeniably. Arges bounds over to a vidscreen and punches a code into the keyboard. A status report states the computer's version of the problems. "How could ignition exhaust have caused all this?" he asks. "The pressure valves should have released long before the problem reached this level. Unless their was excess pressure that they could not handle . . ." he looks back at Hearst. "Explanation, please."

Hearst looks gravely at Captain Arges. He says nothing, then lowers his head and keeps his eyes fixed on the floor.

"Out with it!" Arges says sharply

"We lost running time because of the first meteor!" Hearst blurts as he snaps his head up. He then composes himself, yet speaks feebly. "Then there was going to be too much of a delay over replacing a damaged clamp. So, we attempted a restart without a ventilation to recover lost time . . ." his voice fades into silence as his eyes again drop to the floor.

Arges stands back from the monitor. He is doubly shocked at this news. "Good God . . . the exhaust pressure that would have caused . . . Who in the hell ordered that? No one can even guess what a quickstart like that would do in brand new engines! It's not supposed to be done at all, let alone on a spaceliner! Now look at what has happened!" The Captain is near spitting with rage. "Who gave the order?"

Before Hearst can answer, an alarm beeps twice. "Captain, pardon me, but the computer reports our orbit is beginning to fail," Pilot Martingale announces. "We have approximately three hours before gravity forces pull us to the lunar surface." For the moment, Hearst is spared.

Arges is perplexed. All of this is happening <u>much</u> to quickly. He is only too glad that he avoided anything but one cocktail and one glass of wine at the Ball. "Roberta," he says, "please summon all the officers for a meeting in the conference room, stat. We have some important decisions to make." She nods in response, and Arges moves away from the command board. He turns to exit the bridge. As he does so, he notices some sheets of paper beneath his feet, littering the otherwise spotless floor. "Yeoman, please clean up this mess," he orders, then leaves.

One by one, the officers appear in the conference room. Arges sits at the head of the long, rectangular mahogany table, still wearing his dress uniform, as are Rish, Rayburn, Syranos, Mueller, Miasaki, Holden and Washington, who have been similarly called away from the Ball. Arges presses a switch, and Corté joins the group, displayed on a monitor, in video-conference from the E.O.C.. He is still a soaked, sooty, greasy mess, and is bleeding slightly from cuts in his blackened, angered face. He notes the shock in the faces of those who see him, and can read the questions in their worried expressions. "You wouldn't like the answer," he says, then turns and glares at Hearst, who stares dejectedly down at the table.

Of those assembled, only Arges, Hearst, Escoto, DeMornay and Corté know what is happening. The captain wastes no time in updating the others. "Everyone," he begins, "I have brought you here for a very bad reason." The looks on the faces of the uninformed instantly go from curious to concerned. "We are facing a disastrous situation. We had . . . we had at least two very, very bad encounters with meteors this evening. You can see for yourselves exactly <u>how</u> bad." With that, he touches a button on the table in front of him, and the large, empty vidscreen behind him fills with a status report on the

Emprasoria. The captain swivels his chair around to see for himself the dire state of affairs.

"What the hell!" Rish shouts. Rayburn gasps in terror, and Holden simply stares in shock and disbelief - - can it be? He studies the screen in grim detail, becoming tenser and tenser second by second as he absorbs each fact. The engineer spins his head directly to Corté, who catches sight of him and nods sullenly in confirmation.

"Currently," the captain continues, "all drive systems are disabled. Our orbit is decaying, and our oxygen supply will by dry in two hours." The captain spins his chair around quickly. "I am open to suggestions."

"How can all this have happened?" Rish asks. "Meteors did all . . ."

"The meteors had some help, Peter," Arges answers. "But I am not going to get into that just yet. Now is not the time to point fingers. That will come later." Arges shoots a glance toward Hearst, who still sullenly fixes his eyes on the table like some reprimanded schoolboy. Arges turns his attention back to Rish and the others. "We need answers, solutions, some way out of this."

"Is it possible to repair the engines?" Rayburn asks.

"Chris?" Arges says, directing the question to the engineer.

"No chance there at all. We'll need a complete system overhaul at the Spaceport." Holden grits his teeth on hearing that. He has a burning desire to run to his engines, but is able to contain himself for the moment.

"What about routing fuel directly to the Von Brauns?" Rish suggests. "Then at least we can blast out of this orbit and solve that problem."

"Impossible," Corté replies, shaking his head no. "The pipe junctures at those thrusters have been ruptured, and we don't have the parts to replace them."

The officers remain quiet after hearing that, each trying to think of solutions, each avoiding the most obvious answer to the predicament. Precious seconds tick away, and time has suddenly become the one luxury which the *Emprasoria* does not have available. The captain breaks the cold silence. "Personally, I can see no other option but to -" he pauses, "abandon ship." He has stated what they all know is the truth.

"Agreed, Sir," Rish concurs.

"What else can we do?" Rayburn says in support.

"Very well, then," Arges says. "Report to your stations and wait for my orders. We will do this by the book, quickly and cleanly."

"Yes, Sir," the officers answer collectively as they rise from their chairs and slowly exit the room.

Dr. Washington remains behind a moment. He goes to the captain, and rests a comforting hand on his shoulder, unsure of just what words to use for his friend. "I don't know what to say," he begins.

Arges turns and looks at him. "You and me both." His eyes move back to the table. "What a calamity. And for a new ship too," he shakes his head in repose. "All I can hope for is that the evac goes well."

"Well, with you at the helm, we all stand a better chance. You know where to find me if you need me," Washington lightly pats the shoulder, then exits the room.

"Thank you, Julius." As he leaves, Arges turns his chair back to the vidscreen. What a mess.

Holden trots down the hallways, sweat pouring from his brow – he all but runs down to the Engine Room. He bursts into the E.O.C. minutes later, and witnesses his worst nightmare come to life. He eyes widen in terror. "My dear God . . ." he whispers as he tries to catch his breath. He feels as though he has just been punched in the stomach with a sledgehammer. He turns his back to the destruction and looks at Corté, Harrison, and some other technicians in the small office. "Was anyone hurt down there?"

"Some were hit by shrapnel, Sir," Corté replies. "We've got people helping the wounded, and have notified the doctor's office. A nurse is here now."

"Good, good work, Chris. For now, make sure all personnel are accounted for and out of the Engine Room. I want that area sealed off. Begin a standard lock-out as soon as you can."

"Yessir."

Holden turns again and looks at the devastated engine room. A powerful feeling comes over him, then overcomes him – he must see more. He strips off his blue suitjacket rapidly, nearly tearing its buttons as he struggles out of it, then casts it onto a chair. He then leans forward and climbs through the shattered viewport, cutting himself slightly on shards of glass as he goes. "Sir…" Corté begins and takes a step toward Holden, then stops himself, believing it better to let his chief do as he wishes.

Holden swings himself onto the catwalk and stands at its railing, looking down. In an instant he is over the railing and scaling his way down the wall of wrecked steel and iron toward the floor. Hot, heavy, stale air clouds into his lungs and he coughs. The heat sears him, but he does not notice. His mind is locked on other things. When he has nearly reached his destination, he realizes there are no footholds to support him the rest of the way, so he jumps. He lands squarely on the scorched metal floor. His face and hands are sweaty and blackened, and his once pressed white shirt is now torn, brown, and sodden. He rises and faces pure damnation. His mind is racked with agony. He falls to his knees before the damage in desperation, his head lowered in grief.

Corté and the others watch from the E.O.C. with gut-wrenching sympathy for the man. "You are not alone, my friend," Corté whispers, and voices the thoughts of the others watching. "I too wish I could do the same." Such magnificence has been destroyed. Corté shakes his head. "Mon Dieu, c'est une grande trâjic," he says, again using his native tongue. He then goes to the Engineering intercom to inform the technicians of the chief's decision. He will call Holden out of the room only at the last moment.

As Holden was heading to the engine room, Syranos was dialing her personafône. The number rings five times, then clicks to voicemail. "Damnit!" she says, then instantly hangs up. She hits the redial button, and the personafône repeats the tone sequence. She bites her lip in anticipation. Riiiinnnnnnnnnnggggggg. Riiiiiinnnnnnnnnngggggggg.

Up on the bridge, Rish, Rayburn and Hearst wait for the captain, each quietly sympathizing with him, and at the same time each privately agonizing over what must happen. Escoto is at the communications console, and Miasaki sits at his Astrocon, hastily making calculations. Arges strides on to the bridge and mounts the command platform, then seats himself in the command chair. The staffmembers snap to attention as he enters, then stand at ease and look at him, awaiting their orders.

Arges lets out a long sigh, dreading what he must now do. His eyes fall on the left armrest, and he sees a red-switch cover in the far left corner. It has been located in such an obscure, forgotten place because it is never intended to be used. This cover has 'A-S' boldly printed on it in white. He stares at the cover, then flips it up. A red button is beneath it. "Ladies and Gentlemen," he addresses the staff, "our ship has been severely damaged - - - fatally wounded in fact; enough to the point that, for everyone's safety, we must evacuate it." The staff gasps in shock. After a moment which seems like an eternity, Arges pushes the A-S button down.

'*Abandon ship program has been requested,*' the computerized female voice states over the bridge speakers. '*Confirm, please.*'

Arges cringes. "Cybernetics Officer," he says, "please verify the command."

"Yes, sir," DeMornay responds, and she again connects her silver compulink gauntlet to the Control Board with its red cord. Her fingers dance across the armband keyboard.

'*Abandon ship request confirmed. Program sequence will commence in thirty seconds. Twentynine. Twentyeight.*'

"Peter," Arges says over the voice, "how much oxygen do we have left?"

The first officer consults a gauge, pales, and swallows. "One hour, fifty minutes, Sir," he reports.

"Very well. Please set the clock on a one-fifty countdown commencing now. I want everyone know exactly how much time is left." Rish nods and steps up to the Board, then changes its central clock readout from 23:40:30 to 1:50:59.

'*Five,*' the computer continues, '*Four. Three. Two. One. Activated.*'

Firstly, the computer routes power to the shuttlecraft compartments lining the Port and Starboard sides of B deck. The lifeshuttles are thirty feet long and ten feet wide. They can accommodate fifty passengers, including the pilot and co-pilot, and each shuttle has a distress beacon, an oxygen tank, a water tank, a small freezer containing several nutritionally-sound food packets, and a microwave oven. The shuttles are designed to survive in outerspace for two weeks, which allows ample time for a rescue in the busy space-shipping lanes. There are a total of sixty-six shuttles aboard, thirty-three on each side of the vessel with eleven at fore, midship and aft, meaning every person aboard is guaranteed a place on the shuttle in the event of an emergency.

Once the shuttles have been energized, the status lights directly above sixty of the compartment hatches switch from a foreboding red to a welcome green. The control panels adjacent to these hatches light brightly. '*Sixty-six lifecraft are spaceready,*' the computer informs the bridge. '*Correction: Fifty lifecraft are spaceready.*'

"Fifty?" the captain asks, shocked. "What does it mean, fifty?"

'*Correction: Four hundred lifecraft are spaceready. Correction: Forty-two lifecraft are spaceready.*'

"Peter, Krystal, find out what is going on with these shuttles!"

As Rish goes to a console and Cybernetics Officer DeMornay joins him there, the computer sounds the General Quarters tones in the crew cabins. '*All crew report to assigned stations. All crew report to assigned stations,*' a mechanical voice bellows over the intercom. The off-duty crew rise from their beds and curse the interruption of their sleep - or other nighttime activities. Slowly, they begin to dress, clearly annoyed at the disturbance. '*Off-duty crew have been notified,*' the bridge is told.

"I wonder what this is all about?" Bethany Parris asks, a tinge of fear in her voice.

"Sir," Rish says to Arges, "it appears the lifecraft activation process has been corrupted."

DeMornay speaks up. "Some lifecraft at midship are not properly interfaced, Sir. Three on port and three on starboard appear affected. I bypassed them, and it seems to have solved the problem for now. However, at present we cannot use these shuttles, Sir."

Now the captain faces the problem of having to find alternate means for some three hundred of the people aboard. "Good God!" Arges says, and rubs his forehead again. What will they do? "Corté," Arges begins while calling the E.O.C., "I am going to pass you over to C.O. DeMornay. Work with her and immediately send some technicians up to check and repair some malfunctioning lifecrafts."

"Yessir," Corté answers, and DeMornay goes on line with him. Arges then turns to his officers. "We're going to do the best we can. Once again, people, by the book . . . quick and easy. Everyone has their personafönes?" They nod back. "Excellent. Take comlinks as well, and keep things as organized as possible. Good luck, and God's speed."

"Yes, Sir!" answer the three. They turn to leave the bridge, and Arges motions to Rish, who stays behind as the others exit. "Sir?" he asks while leaning to the platform.

"Find Mr. Enkel in the White Feather and bring him up here. I'll need to tell him about this personally."

Rish nods gravely. “Right away, sir.” He leaves the bridge, and Arges prays for good fortune.

“Roberta, please inform the Space Rescue station of our situation,” says Arges. “Pilot, please scan the immediate area and determine where other ships are relative to our position.”

“Yessir,” both women answer.

Arges picks up the chair microphone and calls the security station and Purser Mueller answers half-way through the first ring. “It’s begun,” Arges states.

“I see, Sir,” comes the sullen reply. “Your security staff will keep things under control, count on that.”

“Thank you, Fritz. Good luck to you. Goodbye.”

“Goodbye, Captain.”

Arges then calls the E.O.C. and Corté answers. “Is the chief there, Chris?” Arges asks.

“He is . . . checking some things, Sir, and is out of the office.”

“I see. Well, we have begun the operation. Please advise him of that when he returns.”

“Yessir. He is due back shortly, Sir. I hope it goes well, Sir.”

“It will, Mr. Corté, don’t you worry about that.”

“Yessir. Thank you, Sir.” The conversation ends.

Since Mars’ moons are not stable enough to support Spaceports, the nearest SRS is at Spaceport Gamma on Mars. Escoto tunes her radio to the standard emergency channel on a broadband. “S.S. *Emprasoria* calling Space Rescue Gamma. Mayday. Mayday. Repeat: S. S. *Emprasoria* calling Mayday. We are declaring an emergency.” The only response she receives to this call is the cold and impassive hiss of static. She tries again. The same. Concerned, she dials the alternate channel. Static once again. As a check, she switches from one regular channel to another. Nothing. Nothing but static silence.

Now, on top of everything else, the bridge radio is not operating properly. “Serenity,” she says, helping to force herself to remain calm as she activates the communication station’s secondary radio. Again, her calls out obtain only a storm of static as a reply. She turns to her computer console while speaking into her headset. She repeats her original statement, this time adding: “Our radios are malfunctioning. Please respond through electromail via rEscoto@empraosria.com or alternatively fax 00-594-684.” as she types and sends an emergency email, printing a hardcopy which she also faxes to the Rescue station.

While waiting for a reply, she picks up her telephone and punches a number. "Good evening, Passenger Communication Center, this is Miss Ryden," comes the answer after the second ring.

"Hello Joan, this is Roberta Escoto." Her eyes are locked on her computer screen as she speaks.

"Hello Roberta, how are you?"

"Well, thank you. We are in a bit of a predicament, seems as though the bridge radio is not working properly. Could you please call SRS Gamma on channel nine-eleven, and patch me through?"

"Right away, ma'am. One moment please." Escoto is put on hold for three agonizing minutes before Ryden returns. "Thank you for holding, ma'am." You can hear the dejection in her voice. "Our receivers here do not appear to be working."

"I see." Escoto turns white with fear and, holding a glimmer of hope, checks her e-mailbox. There are no new messages; wait. A plaintive look to the fax machine next to her; docile. No freshly-printed note declaring help is on the way. She pauses and clears her throat. Wait, an incoming email! "Just a moment, Joan," Escoto says, and with wide eyes looks as the message downloads. "Come on, come on....let me see what you have...." Escoto whispers. A second later and it is finished. **YOU HAVE <1> NEW MESSAGE**. Escoto smiles and hurriedly directs her cursor to the message and clicks. Her face drops. 'Email Undeliverable. Your message to: SRS Gamma/Titled: Mayday // Did not reach the recipient. Sending Timed Out.'

"That's odd..." Escoto whispers. She opens the bundled email enclosure and double-checks the address; yes, it is correct – of course it is. She tabs her cursor over and clicks Resend. She goes back to Ryden. "Just another minute, Joan."

"Thank you, ma'am."

Escoto waits, biting her lip in tension. The fax machine gives a plaintive wail. She turns and grabs the printout and reads it with darting eyes. LETTER UNSENT. This is very unusual. She sits back for a moment and thinks, then with a few keystrokes accesses the transceiver activity log. What is this?

EXT RADIO MESSAGES SNT/REC: 0/0
EXT EMAIL MESSAGES SNT/REC: 0/0
EXT FAXER MESSAGES SNT/REC: 0/0

"What?" Escoto murmurs, then types in another command. The response is quick.

LAST OUTGOING MESSAGE SENT:
88/04//11:31:23pm

Type:	Email
From:	PCC
To:	Mars Central News Bureau
Title:	Confirming receipt of your news entries.

Escoto sits back again. No record of external comminications in the last while, just the thanks for articles for The Transastral Times. She sits up and clears her throat, then clicks a button on her telephone console. “Joan,” she says with a steady voice, “please access the transceiver log.”

“Yes ma’am.” Escoto can here the clicks of typing keys. “What the…this can’t be right, Roberta, we just tried contacting SRS Gamma a few minutes ago….”

“Seems we have a problem with the external system. Please begin repairs on whatever issue is apparently plaguing the *entire* network.”

“Right away, ma’am.”

“Thank you.” Escoto returns her telephone to its cradle. Well, on the plus side, it just seems as though the wireless communications are affected, as the hard-wired internal phone and intercom arteries are working perfectly. She again sends out a call through her radio headset as she types another furtive message into the computer, hoping all the while that the outbound deafness and laryngitis of the *Emprasoria* will be short-lived.

Pilot Martingale turns to the captain. “Sir, the radar has detected hints of residue which appear to be remnants of exhaust vapor. The particles follow a path consistent with a spacecraft trajectory. This trail is one-hundred astromiles off our starboard, near Mars. The radar signal cannot reach the source, so we cannot determine the size of the craft.”

“Well, whoever they are, they should reach us in thirty minutes.” At last! Arges thinks, Something is going right! He is pleased, and smiles for the first time since his return visit to the bridge. “Roberta!” he barks with unabashed enthusiasm; she stiffens and keeps her back to him as he continues, “Please radio that vessel. Advise them of our predicament, and request assistance.” Escoto slowly swivels her chair around to face Arges. The sight of her shocks him. She is a deathly pale, and is visibly shaken. Arges’ pleasured mood darkens. “Roberta, my God, what’s wrong? Are you ill?”

At first, she does not respond. Then, her voice finds life. "No, Sir. I am fine. It's . . ." she pauses as she suppresses a sudden wave of nausea which erupts at the thought of what she must report. "It's the communications . . . the network . . ."

Arges gives her a bewildered look. "Yes?" he prompts.

"The external wireless network is not functioning, Sir . . ."

The news does not please Arges. He clenches his teeth in stress, and knocks his fist into the armrest of the chair. This is his only display of negative emotion. He quickly calms himself, knowing he must portray a strong leader to garner the confidence of those under him at this most trying of times. "Yes, Roberta, what will we do about this?" he asks in relaxed tones.

"I have ordered the comm-techs to begin repairs."

"Yes, fine . . . with any luck it is a simple problem which can be easily remedied," the captain says, and Escoto nods encouragingly and gives a faint smile. She then slowly turns back to her station. She speaks into her headset, giving a plaintive, general call to the other ship while going to her telephone and dialing the PCC to see what progress has been made.

"We are continuing our efforts in checking the system," Joan Ryden reports, "and everyone has been pulled from work on the Times to focus on the transceivers."

"Thank you." Escoto hangs up rather sullenly, then repeats her call to the other ship with a voice resonating false confidence. She checks her e-mail and fax machine. Still nothing. She turns to Martingale with her eyebrows raised in hope. The bridge staff has been waiting in tense silence. Now, the silence is prolonged as they await a report from the pilot. Martingale nods in response to Escoto, then turns to her console. Her fingers dance over a keyboard, and the radar conducts a detailed scan of their vicinity. The bridge staff subconsciously holds its collective breath.

"Nothing," Martingale states with frustration. "No sign of a vessel on our radar. Exhaust emission remains the same. She has not slowed or altered her course from what I can see."

Arges decides to state the urgency of the matter. "Ensign, please bring me a flare." The man goes to a drawer near the bottom of the right side of the board. He pulls it open and removes a foot-long tubular cartridge, which he delivers to the captain, who is standing in front at the command platform, in front of the chair. Arges stretches up, and opens a small round hatch in the ceiling. The hatch swings down and exposes a tunnel which runs through the upper hull. Arges gingerly takes the flare from the ensign and slide it into the tunnel. Arges closes the hatch, locks it, and presses a button in the ceiling which opens a panel in the hull. He then presses a red button, and fires the flare into space.

With a whistling sound, the flare soars up from the *Emprasoria.* When it is fifty feet above the liner, it explodes, showering the area with phosphorus sparks. The sudden flash of bright light grabs the attention of those on the bridge of the *Sacramento*, a mid-sized freighter. The staff run to their starboard viewport, and peering in the far distance, they barely see a glow over what appears to be an incredibly large liner.

"What was <u>that</u>?" First Officer Murdock asks Pilot Rogle.

Rogle steps back to his console. "Some sort of spatial disturbance."

"A rupturing comet? A flare star?"

"Possibly. Characteristics are similar," Rogle answers. "I would bet on the flare-star. As you know, those have been common in this quadrant lately." He shakes his head. "Those still confound me. How a star can flash, or burst, one- to two hundred times its normal illumination, then go back to normal seconds later as if nothing had happened."

"Is that the *Emprasoria* back there?"

"Likely, Sir. I believe she would be in the vicinity . . . I heard she is to dock at Gamma tomorrow."

"Damn, it would sure be something to see her . . ." Murdock says while absently shaking his head as he walks back to the command chair.

"That's for sure," Rogle concurs.

Murdock seats himself. He leans back, then strokes his chin as he ponders. "Paul, any radio traffic from that ship?"

The communications officer runs a channel scan on the radio. "No, Sir. All quiet."

Rogle consults the radar and speaks in a questioning tone. "She appears stopped, Sir. Heat output minimal, almost like she's idling."

There is silence as Murdock thinks for a moment. He then clicks a button on the chair and summons the captain's quarters on the intercom.

"Yes, what is it?" the sleeping Captain Duke mumbles.

"Sir, we have spotted what appears to be the *Emprasoria*. She is stopped, and there was some sort of flash in her area. Should we cruise over there?"

"Has she asked for help?"

"No, Sir."

"Then leave her the hell alone. We'd look stupid running back there. Call me if, and only if, she radios us. You probably just saw some anomaly, or they are launching fireworks to celebrate the end of their maiden trip. They are likely stopped because they are due to dock tomorrow afternoon and got here too damn early so Gamma put them in a holding pattern until they can figure out what to do with them. I'm sure they would let us know if they were in any trouble. I'm going back to sleep now."

"Yessir," Murdock replies sullenly. He clicks off the intercom with doubt lingering in his mind. However, an order is an order . . . the *Sacramento* will continue her flight.

Back on the *Emprasoria*, Captain Arges is expecting the distant ship to already be on its way to them. "Pilot, please let me know when the ship nears us."

"Yes, Sir," she replies. The tension in the bridge seems to have relaxed a bit with the thought that help is on its way. The captain sits down again and sets the chair intercom to the frequency used by the communicators.

"Peter, how's it going down there?"

"Fine, Sir. We have advised the crew of the situation. Evacuation will begin momentarily."

"Excellent. A ship should be coming out soon to give us some help. Carry on until then. John out."

"Yes Sir. Thank you. Peter out."

Throughout the ship, relaxing and sleeping passengers are awakened by sharp rapping on their doors. This is invariably followed by the voice of a cabin steward. "We are having a lifecraft drill. Please dress quickly and go to the shuttle deck." The passengers are slow to move - - very slow - - not believing the crew would actually schedule a drill in the middle of the evening on the last travel day. What kind of nonsense is that? After all, they already had a thorough drill on the third hour or so into the voyage.

All the passengers are confused, but two are even moreso. Parker and Kobryn are already on edge with the anticipation of the upcoming parts of their Score. "What do you make of this?" Parker asks. Kobryn shrugs her shoulders and says nothing. "We should sit tight here, where Maddox knows he can find us," Parker wisely decides while double-checking that his personafône is on.

"I agree," Kobryn says, then walks to the far side of their cabin and sits down.

A harried knock comes to their door. "We will be out shortly!" Parker answers. He and Kobryn can hear arguing in the corridors. The negative attitude of the passengers does not make the stewards' job any easier. The stewards' task, however, is simple compared to the one facing Rish.

The first officer takes a deep breath as he approaches the White Feather. He can hear the band music and general noise of the crowd even through the heavy, closed oak doors. He places his hand on one of the stylized brass doorknobs, and pauses. This is not going to be easy. He opens the door and steps into the darkened room, where he is immediately enveloped by the party occurring there. Rish walks to the Maitre D's podium, and informs the jovial and smiling host of what is happening. The man's face drops as he hears the news - - Impossible!! No, it is true, Rish says. As the officer moves toward the dancefloor, the Maitre D presses a button on his podium which sounds the pagers on the belts of the waiters and waitresses scurrying around the salon. After a moment, the serving staff is at his side. The man gravely tells them what has happened, and what they must do. They cannot believe their ears.

Maddox had planned a very discreet exit and is just about to carry it out with Angelique when he sees the first officer return. Earlier he had watched as the captain was suddenly called away, and he tensed - - had something gone wrong with the diamond heist? He wanted to leave the salon with Angelique right then, but to do so at that time would possibly have drawn un-needed attention to himself, so he stayed and thought. Then, the other officers leave, and he thought some more but there were no calls from Parker, and now the first officer is back. Maddox checks his watch. Too early for his 'halucination' program to have kicked-in. Something must be up! and ended the Ball early. Yes, something is definitely going on . . . What? What, dammmit, what!

Rish is making very limited progress as he walks toward the dancefloor. Everyone wants to talk to him, to shake his hand. At first he is polite, but precious time is slipping away, so he resorts to ignoring everyone and pushing his way through the mass of people. Finally, he reaches his destination. Fitzroy has been looking down and watching the commotion, and watches in shock as Rish climbs up on the head table. The officer gives the man a 'cut' signal, running his hand across his neck in a quick manner. The music stops suddenly.

"Ladies and Gentlemen," Rish says, his voice barely audible above the chatter of the crowd. "Ladies and gentlemen!" he yells, and the guests quiet enough for him to be heard. "We regret to inform you that this Ball will end earlier than expected due to circumstances beyond our control." Rish is being careful in his word selection as he does not want to panic the crowd - - a mad rush to the shuttles will only cause more trouble.

Voiced complaints are heard, and a suddenly stern-faced Damien Enkel gives Rish a sharp look and he begins to make his way to the officer. A displeased Mrs. Enkel joins him, and a frowning Darcy Phillips follows in close behind, while reaching into his jacket for his ringing personafőne.

Disappointment is heavy in the air. "Please return to your suites immediately!" People mill about with discontent. A red velvet cord is strung across the grand staircase, blocking that exit and sending people to the floor-level doors on each side of the salon's front wall. They were having *such* a good time!

Still with a angrily-sharp face, Enkel makes his way to the first officer. "Please!" Rish continues with urgency, pushing his hands out in a furtive gesture, "Return to your suites!" The waiters and waitresses are joined by the kitchen staff in assisting the passengers out of the White Feather through the doors which are thrown wide open.

The keen journalistic senses of Jack and Diana McCartney perk up, strongly suspicious that an intriguing story is unfolding. They look to each other knowingly, each well aware they share the same thought. "Exclusive," they say in unison, then smile.

Maddox is jostled within the throng of people who are being herded like two-legged cattle. He looks over to Angelique with anger and worry in his eyes; she returns the look with the same sentiment. "I'm not sure what's happening," he whispers into her ear, "but you can bet it will affect our plans." He curses his fate.

Phillips answers his phone. "Yes!" you can hear the exasperation clear in his tone.

"Darcy, it's me, Jennifer." Her tone does not sound good either.

"Jenn, you should be down here, Peter Rish has gone crazy."

"Listen to me Darcy. Listen to me carefully…." Phillips pauses as Enkel and his wife continue on.

Enkel reaches Rish as the guests, *HIS* guests, are being escorted out. Rish eases down from the table and faces his employer. Enkel grabs the Officer by the lapels of his uniform jacket. "Just what in the *hell* do you think you are doing Rish? I'll have you busted down so fast!"

Rish backs away from him, his lapels coming free as he does so. "Sir, if you please. The captain needs to speak with you, urgently."

"Arges? Well where is he?"

"Up on the bridge, Sir. It is important that he see you, Sir."

"Arges be damned," Enkel scoffs angrily. "What in the hell is going on? Tell me!"

Rish pauses and looks around nervously, then wrings his hands in angst. "Tell me what is going on, Peter," Enkel says again with a vepid tone. "Tell me now."

"Oh, godddddddddd," Darcy Phillips says in the background, and puts his free hand on his forehead while the other holds his personaföne to his ear, then his jaw drops.

"Sir, the ship has struck a meteor. We are sinking into the gravity field of an asteroid near Vesta as we speak, and our oxygen supply has become unexpectedly restricted." Shock registers on Enkel's face. Mrs. Enkel raises her hand to her suddenly gaping mouth.

"What? It can't be……. nooooo….." says Enkel weakly.

"We are trying to evacuate the passengers smoothly, Sir," Rish continues.

Enkel looks back at him with blank eyes; his face drops - - he looks down to the floor, then back at Rish. "My baby, what happened to my baby?" he remarks forlornly.

"We will keep you informed, Sir. Excuse me, Sir." Rish then slowly backs away, turns, and walks off. Still hovering in the background, Phillips puts his personaföne back in his pocket and walks away, slowly, in silence.

Enkel grabs his personaföne and punches some buttons, then a number is speed-dialed for him. Enkel looks to his wife as he presses the phone tightly against his ear. The number is answered before the first ring even ends. "John! John what's going on!" Enkel shouts earnestly, desperation evident in his voice. His wife watches and listens to his end of the conversation. "How in the hell could that have happened?" "Well do something about it!" "Abandon ship?" "Are you out of your mind, man?" "Have the computer run through some scenarios anyway." "Call me later when you have more information."

Enkel hangs up, and a sullen look comes over him. He is no longer the imposing figure he was just moments before, and the news seems to have sapped all his strength. His new ship - - his treasure - - wrecked, on the verge of being gone. This is more than he can handle. He pales, then stumbles. An alert waiter grabs a vacant chair and slips it behind the man, who all but collapses into it. Enkel suddenly looks very old. He slumps forward, buries his face into his hands, and begins to babble incoherently; almost sobbing. Seeing the trouble, his still disbelieving wife consoles the weak figure who is only a shadow of his former self.

The wide eyes of the McCartneys witness it all. "Damn, where's a camera!" Jack whispers.

"We'll get it at the cabin," Diana replies. "Good thing I put it on recharge before I left."

They watch the first officer rapidly stride across the room and then exit through one of the kitchen doors. "Darn, we can't reach him," Jack says. The two look back at the Enkels . . . not exactly in the condition to be answering questions or giving quotes. The zombie-like Phillips has disappeared into the crowd.

"Come on," Jack says as he takes his wife's hand. "We better get to our suite and try and find out what's going on." The two quickly head for one of the exits, and are soon hampered by the crowd.

Within the bustling people, Maddox is thinking. He intentionally avoided liquor at the Ball, so his mind is alert. He considers recent events, odd recent events - - the Ball suddenly cut short? A shuttle drill in the middle of the night? Things begin to fall into place. Can it be? Angelique looks at him and smiles, believing all this is part of his ruse, his halucination. He gives her a somewhat reassuring half-grin and nod, then forces himself not to jump to conclusions.

Elsewhere on the ship, the dinner partiers barely have time to sit in their suites before stewards knock at the doors. "Lifecraft drill . . . please go to the shuttle deck." What kind of insanity is this? First the ball ends early, and now a shuttle drill? The complaint department will hear about this foolishness! With assistance from several Evie and Evan holograms, the dinner-goers begin to leave their cabins, still wearing their evening clothes, grumbling as they go to the B deck, wholly unimpressed at what is happening.

Maddox, for one, has no intention of being part of any shuttle drill. The minute they are in their suite he races to the sofa and knocks it over with a strong kick. It hits the carpet with a dull thud. "I have to know what's going on, I've gotta know now!" His words come out in a near frenzy. He crouches and jerks up his laptop, being very concerned.

"What's the matter?" Angelique asks calmly, unknowlingly still firm in the belief that this is all part of the decoy-plan. She watches as his eyes scan the laptop.

"It's too early…" he mutters. "What in the hell is…" His eyes grow wide at what he reads. The tiny flickering screen confirms what he suspects. "Omigod."

"What?" It makes no sense to her.

He swallows hard and looks up at her. "This *isn't* my doing, damnit!" He pauses. "This is real."

"What, what's real?"

"This…" he waves his arms in the air to indicate the general situation. "This craziness."

It hits her like a tonne of bricks. Her jaw drops, her hand goes to her gaping mouth. "What do you mean?" she asks earnestly, worry clear in her wavering tone. She stares at him with wide eyes and begins to pace rapidly in sheer fear.

He takes a deep breath and looks back at his screen. "The ship is damaged and the crew is abandoning it! Like I said, for real, not part of our game."

"Nooooooooo," she gasps, and stops, and even though she is standing upright, her body appears to go limp. She sits down on the arm of a chair.

As for Maddox, he sits down and slumps back against the upturned sofa. Emotion surges within him, and he is shocked that he faces the very real possibility of dying, angry that his foolproof plan is now useless, upset that part of the wealth almost at his fingertips will now be gone forever . . . . . Wait. He stops and sits up. Angelique notices this action, and looks at him – his eyes are flashing. This gives her some confidence as well. She opens her mouth to speak, then stops herself, not wanting to interrupt his train of apparently very active thought. If she only knew what he was thinking…..

And he is thinking all right. There will be no abort of this mission, that is for damn sure. He has invested far too much time and energy to back out now. He clears his cunning mind and grabs his infokeeper. "The devil is in the details," he mutters, then begins to develop an alternate plan which can work effectively within the new situation. After all, the one who cannot adapt and improvise is forever doomed to be a victim of circumstance. He is no victim. Not ever.

CHAPTER TWELVE
S.O.S. for the Icarus Victims

The crew steadfastly continues in its efforts to evacuate the passengers. The stewards do well in waking people and sending them to the B deck where the shuttles silently wait. Here, in the corridors surrounding the elegance and finery of the Halo and the lobby, people bustle within crowds which fill the passageways beyond capacity, causing the lounge and lobby to be impromptu waiting rooms for nervous and agitated people.

Jack and Diana McCartney wait in frustration with the others. Their inquires are get them nowhere. Diana had tried to access SolNet via their cabin computer terminal but could not get beyond a standard message of 'SolNet is temporarily unavailable. Please try again later. Thank you for your patience.' Jack's calls to the PCC are rebuffed by an automated message of "Our passenger communication center system is refurbishing. The call from your cabin has been noted, and a comm-tech will be returning your call shortly. Thank you, and have a pleasant time." Inquiries to the Evie and Evan holograms bring blank smiles with a message to report to the lifecraft deck. Stewards and other crew will not pause long enough to answer their questions. Jack has an electropad though, and Diana discreetly carries a vidcam. Notes and footage are being taken.

"This can't be good," says Cal Gregg to Genvievve in the sitting room of their suite.

"It could be anything…." she replies.

"Damn. What about the package in the cargo hold?"

"It is fine, I am sure."

"I'll have to get to it at some point though….. Damn this mess!"

First Officer Rish supervises operations in the forward section on the Port side, while Second Officer Rayburn, Third Officer Hearst, and Fourth Officer Nexal are at their respective Evacuation Stations at Starboard-Forward, Port-Aft and Starboard-Aft. Stewards and security officers are in the hallways to assist passengers into the lifecrafts. The band assembles in the Halo and begins to play light tunes in an effort to create a calm, relaxing atmosphere within the tense situation. Staff Captain Syranos walks about with a smile and a pleasant voice, perfectly masking the fear she feels.

The crew waits until the last possible moment to 'break the news' to their passengers. The time has come. Calmly, the officers inform people of the situation, downplaying its severity. "We had a little mishap this evening; nothing serious mind you, but we think it is best to move the passengers off of the ship for a bit while we take care of things."

The passengers are already angered over being disturbed in the middle of the night, and this news infuriates hem. "Is it absolutely necessary to go in there?" "Has the captain lost his mind?" "I'd rather take my chances here. In my cabin." These are the most common replies heard attempts are made to coax people into the shuttles. Of course, the staff only concerns itself with *certain* people; people who *qualify*.

In loading the lifecraft, the crew adopts the policy used by their counterparts on all fatally wounded vessels: "Women, children, the elderly and disabled first". This distinction and separation puts a dark seriousness on the matter. To the passengers, there can only be one reason to do this . . . the liner is in *deep* trouble. The crew endeavors to dispel the fears of the passengers, but regardless of what is said, people begin to draw their own conclusions.

Now every able-bodied, male passenger faces the same question: will he be courageous, or a coward? The true men are brave, accepting the fact that they will be the last to leave with dignity. However, others begin complaining. The security officers convince them it is best to relax in the lounge or lobby until their time comes.

The few who are particularly belligerent or threatening are taken up to a storage room on the flight deck and placed under guard in this make-do brig.

Once the severity of the situation is guessed at, many protest, preferring to remain at the sides of there husbands and fathers. Then, at the insistence, there are teary farewells, strong kisses and powerful embraces despite the assurance of "I will join you later," for everyone knows deep down that this may be the last time they will see each other…

When fifty people have been sealed in a shuttle, the officers are less strict about the distinction rule, desiring that at least one person who has flown in space before serve as pilot for the craft. Although these shuttles are relatively easy to operate (If you can drive a car, you can drive a lifecraft it is said), it remains general practice to have an experienced person in the left chair. A flight-tested member of the crew, or passenger who can prove he or she can fly a shuttle, is put in the craft at the last minute. It is not as important, though certainly beneficial, if the co-pilot has flown previously.

Many resent the Spartan-like design of the lifecraft. There are five rows of eight cushioned, reclinable grey flightchairs. Black torso and waist seatbelts rest on these. The floorspace is narrow, and the cabin compact. There are two lone chairs at the front for the pilot and co-pilot, and the back wall holds the freezer, the microwave oven, and the door of the glorified closet which is the lavatory - - only the bare essentials here; obviously, the luxury of the *Emprasoria* does not extend to her shuttlecraft.

Once an officer is satisfied that a shuttle is filled to capacity, the hatch is closed and locked, then the compartment door is sealed. The officer then presses the appropriate buttons on the panel next to the doorway to launch the craft. First, a section of the hull will rise and expose the compartment to outer space. Then, the square, steel davit arms attached to the bow and stern of the shuttle telescope out and stop when the craft is clear of the ship. As the magnetic locks on the ends of the arms are automatically released, the pilot fires the shuttle's engines and flies the craft away from the ship, toward Mars, toward help.

On the bridge, Captain Arges reads updates on the progress of the evacuation. "Things appear to be going well," he comments, and is certainly pleased to hear this, but cannot fully appreciate the good news because he still must contend with a number of other problems.

Firstly, the mystery ship they had spotted is nowhere in sight. A full fifteen minutes have passed since the flare exploded, and the ship should at the very least be appearing on the radar screen, but there is nothing. "Where can that ship be?" Arges wonders aloud. "Ensign, another flare please." The cartridge is quickly delivered to him, and moments later fired into open space. The flare soars up, then sputters. Its thrust goes from strong and steady burst to fragmented spouts. Then, these stop altogether. The flare drops, then inverts and falls straight back toward the *Emprasoria.* The top becomes caught in the still closing hull panel. The panel squeezes and crushes the top section of the flare, causing the nitrate compound which forms its core to explode from pressure. The bottom of the flare blasts out into space, a hollow and harmless metal canister. The top explodes within the flare tunnel itself as an ugly scorch-mark blackens the pristine whiteness of the roof belonging to the bridge.

The bridge staff hear a muffled explosion from within the ceiling. They at first look in confusion and concern to one another. Pilot Martingale quickly types commands into her keyboard when the computer voices the answer she searches for: *'FLARE LAUNCH UNSUCCESSFUL'* it announces over the speakers.

Martingale turns to Arges after reading her vidscreen. "Sir, the flare fell and impacted against the tunnel. The hull panel has closed, but the top of the tunnel has been damaged, and is unusable." Captain Arges sits stoically in the command chair. There was not enough of a blast for the radar of the *Sacramento* to notice, and she continues toward Mars, undaunted and unaware.

Then, Escoto is notified about the external communications. The comm-techs had first run a standard network system check. The computer stated both the broadcast and receptor elements are functioning at one-hundred percent efficiency. And so is the transceiver grid. The techs groan upon hearing these. Something is obviously wrong with the computer, which means the system must be tested manually. This will be laborious to say the least. They deactivate the network and run tests from the Comm-Operations handbook. To their surprise, they can find nothing wrong either. Everything is fine, yet, when the system is reactivated, they still are incommunicado! Incredibly frustrating. Their hands are metaphorically tied. They reactivate the system and telephone their findings to Officer Escoto. The news does not please her.

Escoto replaces her phone on its cradle and sits back in her chair. What can possibly be wrong with the network, she thinks, had the techs overlooked something? Likely not, they are top-notch people, but still . . . mistakes can be made, even by the very best. She sits upright and reaches again for the phone. "We'll have to do another manual check," she murmurs.

zzzzzzzzwak. shhhwwwiiishhhhhhhzaw. The speaker at her station crackles. The bridge staff look at her area in surprise. Escoto is shocked. "*Emprasoria*, this is Controller Polski at Spaecport Gamma," says a pleasant but authoritative female voice. "We request your Q-H status check for Zero Hundred Hours, Monday, April 21, 2088. Please state your condition." Spontaneous cheering erupts on the bridge; everyone is thrilled that the speakers are working again: the comm techs came through! Escoto is unsure what is going on, but isn't going to question the good fortune.

It is standard procedure for a vessel to give report a status check with the Spaceport in their vicinity every four hours – when ships are late, the Spaceport gives them reminders, which is what Polski is doing. From the query, Escoto knows Polski is not stationed on the Emergency Line. Escoto presses the TALK button and begins. "Controller Polski, this is Comm Officer Escoto of the *Emprasoria.* We are marooned over an asteroid at the far side of Vesta and are sinking into its gravity field. We have approximately two hours of oxygen remaining. We require assistance urgently. Escoto out." She releases the button, and there is a sharp click heard over the speaker. "-pril 21, 2088" says Polski over the speaker. "Please state your condition." The bridge staff turn to one another, shocked to hear the fragmented word and the inquiry.

"What's going on?" asks one.

"What's that mean?" queries another.

Escoto quickly hits the talk button again, urgently. "Gamma, are you there?"

"*Emprasoria*, this is Controller Polski. . ." the same statement is repeated for the third time.

"What in the?" Escoto says, being <u>very</u> confused. The transmitter power switch is still in the 'On' position. She moves it to Off, and then back to On, hoping that will help. It does not. Escoto turns the volume down so the query will not distract the bridge staff.

"Roberta, what is wrong now?" Arges asks.

"We are investigating Sir. Still something with the transmitter."

"I see."

Escoto hastily dials the PCC. The techs are already running another computer scan. She is put on -hold- as they await the status report. The computer is quick to discover the problem: TRANSMISSION FAILURE DUE TO BROADCAST INTERFACE CUTOFF TO TRANSCEIVER ANTENNA ARRAY the screen says. That explains it. The broadcast elements are working fine, and so is the transceiver, it is just how they are working together – or not, as the case may be. This is a serious problem, as all shipboard radios, including the two back up units, all use the interfaces. Joan informs Escoto of the report while another commtech goes to a second phone and dials the EOC to have the electrical room investigated.

Escoto turns to the Captain. "Sir, there is some sort of problem with the power feed to the transmission interface section of the antenna. As it is now, we can hear everything, but can't say a word!" Escoto pauses. Wait. Perhaps they can . . . if the controller knows they are in the Gamma section, then they are able to read the transponder signal. She begins toying with an idea . . . Yes! It can work!

A confident smile appears on her face. "Captain," she says enthusiastically as she turns toward him, "I believe we can communicate! If we set the homing beacon on an on - off program sequence, we can talk to Gamma by Morse Code!"

Arges sees the spirit in his Comm Officer, and contemplates the suggestion. It sounds promising . . . but . . . "Can it work?" he asks openly. "That code hasn't been used in quite some time now."

"Even if they cannot decipher our message, the erratic broadcast will surely indicate our trouble."

"True, and it certainly can't hurt to try. Excellent idea, Roberta. Please proceed with your plan."

"Thank you Sir!" Escoto says as she turns back to her station. She quickly types the necessary instructions into her computer.

Within minutes, Escoto has the beacon set and running, and begins their torch song. Far away at Gamma, Polski immediately notices something very odd on her computer monitor. The registration code-beacon signal of the *Emprasoria* has been flashing rhythmically once every five minutes, as is normal when a beacon is active. Now, it appears, then erases itself, and reappears seconds later. This cycle continues at a dizzying pace, and quickly annoys Polski who is already becoming frustrated because the *Emprasoria* has not yet answered any of the three status queries she sent since the midnight hour struck. She radios the liner yet again. "*Emprasoria*, this is Controller Polski at

Spaceport Gamma. Are you aware your transponder is transmitting erratically?"

Polski waits. No response, yet again. She presses a button and summons one of the control tower Supervisors. There is one at her side within seconds. "Something wrong, Suzanne?" he asks as he leans forward to see what is displayed on her vidscreen.

"Oh, hello Glenn. The *Emprasoria*'s homing beacon is broadcasting wildly."

"That's strange . . . ."

"Yes, and I cannot reach them on the radio, or by email either," she says, then repeats her call to the ship. The supervisor thinks for a moment, puzzled. There is no response from the vessel. He looks at the code scrolling on the screen.

"It could be just a loose connection. Not the first time a new ship has had an electric flaw, aye Suzanne?" She smiles to him at the joke. "Or . . . could they be trying to tell us something . . ." his voice fades in speculation.

"Perhaps. Let me check." She types an order on her keyboard and the computer scans the transmission for any possible pattern. Moments later, its analysis appears on the screen:

ONE-SECOND SIGNAL RUN. ONE-SECOND SIGNAL RUN. ONE-SECOND SIGNAL RUN. ONE-SECOND PAUSE. THREE-SECOND SIGNAL RUN. THREE-SECOND SIGNAL RUN. THREE-SECOND SIGNAL RUN. ONE-SECOND PAUSE. ONE-SECOND MESSAGE RUN. ONE-SECOND MESSAGE RUN. TWO-SECOND PAUSE. CYCLE REPEATS. PATTERN MATCHES LATE NINETEENTH AND TWENTIETH CENTURY MORSE TELEGRAPHIC CODE:
DOT. DOT. DOT. DASH. DASH. DASH. DOT. DOT. DOT.

TRANSLATION:
S.O.S. - ACRONYM FOR: "SAVE OUR SOULS"

ALERT-ALERT :DISTRESS CALL: ALERT-ALERT

The last section flashes while the remainder of the readout keeps solid. "Oh my God . . ." Polski whispers in shock.

"No . . ." replies the supervisor. Could it be? He begins to wonder. Why the guessing game with the homing beacon? Is it possible that it is flashing randomly and is unintentionally sending the

S.O.S.? The odds of that are incredibly slim - maybe a million to one at best - but he must know with an unwavering certainty before sounding the alarm. "See if they can hear us," he says to Polski.

"*Emprasoria*, are you reading us?" she asks.

At first, the scrolling does not change. Then, it does, and the computer displays a new message.

CODE CHANGE:
DASH. DOT. DASH. DASH. /BREAK\ DOT. /BREAK\ DOT.

DOT. DOT.

TRANSLATION: Y E S.

There is no question now. Something bad is definitely happening.

"Ask them what is wrong," the Supervisor says tensely.

"*Emprasoria*, what is your status?"

CODE CHANGE:, the computer says again, then shows the dot-dash sequence and its translation; WE ARE DECLARING AN EMERGENCY. ALL DRIVE SYSTEMS DOWN. TRANSMITTER OUT. OXYGEN SUPPLY LOW AND DROPPING. SOME LIFECRAFT UNUSABLE. NEED HELP DESPERATELY. REPEAT: DECLARING EMERGENCY. HELP NEEDED ASAP.

"Oh God!" Polski yells.

"Tell them we're sending help!" shouts the Supervisor as he races across the room and punches the red -SPACE EMERGENCY- button on a central pillar. Alarms sound in the Tower and at the Space Rescue station. "We've got a bad one," he says into a microphone. This is probably the understatement of the century.

"*Emprasoria*," Polski says with forced calm, "we understand your situation. An S.R. team will be en route shortly. We read your transponder as being 37D-24-34 in the Vesta region. Is this your precise location? Verify please."

Escoto poses that question to Miasaki, who is sweating over the Astrocon. He has been formulating paths and transmitting course headings to the shuttlecraft which are away, making every effort to assist the pilots of those vessels in safely steering toward Mars. He gives a quick answer to Escoto, who encrypts it into the Beacon. YES. NEAR TO FAR SIDE OF VESTA AT 37D-24-34.

"Roger *Emprasoria.* Coordinates confirmed. Help is on the way."

Hundreds of astromiles away, the people on the bridge of the *Emprasoria* burst out cheering. The captain lets out a long sigh of relief. Help is on the way! Now it does not matter if those idiots on that other ship come or not. They will be rescued soon, and freed from this ungodly calamity. Escoto quickly composes herself and types a new message. THANK YOU. WE WISH YOU GOD'S SPEED.

Out in space, those in the front shuttles are close enough to the bridge to witness the jubilation there. This pleases them, as obviously some sort of good news has been received. Those in the shuttles along the rest of the ship see no jubilation when they look at the vessel. Passengers still aboard are at the windows, pressed against the heavy glass and staring in a mixture of envy and desperation. Some pound their fists against the viewports in an utter expression of frustration. To those in lifecraft who boarded the *Emprasoria* at the moon, there is an eerie, chilling reminder . . . back to when they circled the Liner in the lunar shuttles . . . to when they saw people at the windows raising drink-filled glasses in silent toasts to the new arrivals . . . now many of those same people are trapped behind those viewports . . . waiting for their chance to escape.

Over the past month, joviality reigned supreme aboard the *Emprasoria.* Now, in a scant two hours, it seems as though a lifetime has passed since those carefree days of innocence and idle amusement. Suddenly, everything is upside-down, and all they can do is wait, and remember the age-old saying they were taught as youngsters: Patience is a Virtue. Virtue is definitely needed now.

Patience is also known in another area, but there is no maxim phrase to go with it here, instead, there is simple boredom. Time at a Space Rescue station drags slow, very slow, on Sunday evenings. They are typically uneventful; "sleepers" if you will. The majority of the thirty-six Rescuer crew have retired to their beds as twenty-three hundred hours came and went on the clockface, but like all people devoted to public safety, they always sleep with one eye open and are ready and alert in a moment's notice at the call of an emergency. Some are lounging in the recreation room, watching the rerun of a sit-com on television, and a few, like the base commander Lieutenant Colonel Stiedman, are quietly reading in the sanctity of their quarters.

Santiago, Thompson and Tiletti, the three on duty, sit at their desks in the main office, watching time tick by and doing mundane, routine tasks such as recording the Biospheric weather conditions on the hour, every hour, as statistics must be kept, even if the data is never referenced again. To break the monotony, Santiago occupies himself by completing a crossword puzzle, while Thompson plays a game on his computer. Tiletti is practicing at balancing a ballpoint pen on his fingertips. Each is waiting for the 'graveyard shift' to come to an end.

The blaring siren changes everything. It breaks the melancholy silence while startling the staff. **ALERT ALERT ALERT** says a readout on the main vidscreen.

"Where the!" - the pen clatters to the desktop,

"An emergency!" - the game vanishes,

"What gives?" - and the crossword becomes a jumble of rumpled newsprint.

A button is punched and the alarm stops. Santiago quickly types commands into his computer as Thompson picks up a red deskphone and dials the Spaceport Control Tower.

Colonel Stiedman appears at the office door, dressed in pajamas and housecoat, with a stern face. "What is it?" he asks in a strong tone.

"General alarm from the Tower, Sir!" comes the harried answer from a tense Santiago. "Confirming situation, Sir!"

"Very good. Let's get an answer, gentlemen." His voice maintains its authority as he walks over to the desks. A small, slight smile appears on his face as he watches his men perform their tasks with efficiency and control. They are part of a good crew. The smile disappears quickly; accolades can come later.

He walks up behind Santiago at his terminal, reading over the man's shoulder at what appears on the vidscreen. Shock comes over him. "It can't be . . . imposs..."

"Sir!" comes the blurting voice of Thompson. "Tower! The Tower confirms!" he notes the expression on the face of his commander and knows Stiedman is well informed. He continues, but at a more subdued manner. "Sir, the Tower confirms that the cruiseliner *Emprasoria* in Crisis 1 status. Condition Critical. Evac is underway. It is bad, Sir."

"Sound the Scramble," Stiedman states as he walks out of the room. "Red Alert. A.P.B. to all outlying Stations. We want everything we've got out there, goddamn it. It'll be a while before this is through."

"Yes Sir!" Tiletti calls after him and reaches for some switches. "So much for the sleeper Sunday," he mutters to himself.

An alarm blasts through the station complex. Those who are sleeping jump from their beds and in moments are dressed in their navy blue jumpsuits with their black flightboots tightly bound to their feet. Those in the lounge join the stream of rescuers racing to the main office. Within minutes, everyone has assembled in the room, and are seeing the information displayed on the just activated wall-sized monitor.

The data, words and images are superimposed behind Stiedman, who is now fully uniformed and stands before the monitor, back straight, looking strong as granite. He bears a stern countenance, and his hands are clasped behind his back. At first, the faces of personnel show shock at what they see - at what they must face. Is this true?

Stiedman addresses the crew of his command. "People," he begins, his tone resounding with authority as he paces back and forth along the monitor. "let me assure you this is no drill. This is the real thing. Very real. A disaster of monumental proportions. But do not let that discourage or threaten you - - each and every one of you are capable and results of excellent training. I have every trust in you. View it as a challenge. We have twenty-five hundred passengers and eight hundred crew stranded on that vessel. We are their only hope. Their ONLY hope of survival. They are counting on us to see them through. Get out to the Vestal region fast - and I mean 'DAMN fast - and get those people on solid ground!"

"Sir Yes Sir!" the rescuers yell with vigor.

"Dismissed," Stiedman says, then they race to the launch bay, where six bright, clean, ready yellow shuttles wait. Each vehicle is thirty feet long and has the word RESCUE painted in red on each side, and a large red cross adorns the nose of each craft. Within moments, the pilots radio the office, sounding off that they are ready to go. Excitement runs high.

Stiedman stands for a moment and looks at the monitor. "Vesta," he huffs angrily. "Some hundred thousand or more kilometers away. Damn. That'll take at least ninety minutes for us to reach, even going at top speed. Too long . . . too damn long . . ."

He strides over to Santiago. “Are there any ships in the area?” he asks as he approaches.

Santiago hastily types on his keypad. “Yes, Sir,” he answers seconds later. “A small liner U.S.S. *Sacramento* commanded by Captain Charles Duke just completed her Quad check. She is between us and the *Emprasoria*, but closer to us.” Just then, a quick beep sounds. “And . . .” Santiago continues as he reads “it looks like another vessel just crossed over into our grid. A cargo freighter. The *Albany*, captained by Russ Tyrekka. The *Albany* is incoming as well, but on the other side of the *Emprasoria*, and quite far away.” Santiago looks intently at his screen, then up at Stiedman. “Only those two, Sir. A slow night.”

“Yes, so it seems,” Stiedman replies. “The *Sacramento* and the *Albany*.” He pauses and chuckles. “Goddamn. All we need is another named the Washington, D.C. and we can have a regular United States party out there.” He shakes his head and smiles, as does Santiago. “Ok Luis, hail those two ships and brief them on the situation. If they argue, remind them of Interplanetary Law with respect to rendering assistance to stricken vessels. And tell them to be careful. The last thing we need tonight is to have to run two rescue ops. You are in charge until you hear otherwise from me.”

“Yessir,” Santiago says with a sharp nod.

Stiedman then walks out into the launch bay. He climbs aboard the *Valiant*, straps himself in the pilot chair, and takes command of what will be the lead shuttle. “*Valiant* ready for liftoff, *Emprasoria* rescue mission. Stiedman commanding,” he informs the office. The other craft again verify their flight readiness with him, and soon the doors to the launch silos are open. Stiedman takes a breath and whispers a silent prayer, then he is blasting out into the night followed by five others. The rescue commences.

Upon confirming that all the Rescue shuttles have safely launched, Santiago first advises Controller Polski at the Spaceport. He then sets his radio and hails the *Sacramento*. “U.S.S. *Sacramento*, this is Corporal Santiago of Space Rescue, Gamma. Come in, please.”

“Corporal Santiago, this is Comm Officer Horowitz of the *Sacramento*. Go ahead.”

“We urgently request your assistance. The cruiseliner *Emprasoria* is in Crisis 1 status at 37D-24-34 near Vesta. Please go to that location and coordinate rescue efforts with our shuttles currently en route.”

First Officer Murdock listens then slaps the left arm of his command chair. "Damn, I was right! Rogle, alter our course! Full reverse and bring us about!"

"Aye, Sir."

"U.S.S. *Sacramento* will render all due assistance," Horowitz replies to Santiago. "We are making way for the specified location."

"Confirmed, *Sacramento.* Configure your trajectory based on the transponder of the *Emprasoria.* The rescue operation leader is Lieutenant Colonel Stiedman, commanding from R.S. *Valiant.*"

"Roger that, Corporal," Horowitz replies as the *Sacramento* slows to a near stop and begins to turn itself around.

As Santiago notes the participation of the *Sacramento,* he next summons the *Albany.* On hearing the request, Tyrekka turns to his co-pilot. "Well, listen to that, Jonesy!" he says with a cocky smile. "Looks like the fancy-pants that damn near killed us are in some kinda trouble!" Jones shakes his head grimly. "Well godammit we'll sure show that silk boxer crowd what the ol' *Albany* is all about!"

"That we will Cap'n," Jones says with a nod. He tightens the cap on the bottle of bourbon he had just begun to open and tosses it on the floor behind him. No time for liquor now.

"Corporal Santiago, this is Tyrekka," the pilot says into his headset. "The *Albany* will be part of your show tonight. Just remember, we're a ways off from that location. It'll take us a while, but we're on our way and we'll get there as quick as we can."

"Understood, Captain Tyrekka. Thank you. The mission leader is Lieutenant Colonel Stiedman aboard the R.S. *Valiant.*"

"Got it, Corporal. Tyrekka out." He then recalls that lingering look which the Cruise Entertainment woman gave him back at Alpha....

"Colonel Stiedman, Santiago here. Both ships agreed without hesitation and are converging on Vetsa."

"Very good," Stiedman replies.

Santiago then informs Controller Polski of what transpired, then prepares a Situation Report about the condition of the *Emprasoria* to transmit to the aiding ships.

Rescue Stations across the face of the planet and at Unicol are radioed about the crisis and told to assemble near Vesta. These outlets are staffed by teams recently graduated from the S.R. Academy - - fully trained, though young and relatively inexperienced and eager for real action rather than a classroom simulator. At Port Colton station, a facility within the small and nondescript village of Port Colton, the

crew of six is relaxing in their office/lounge sitting on the couch and easy chairs of the sparsely decorated room, watching television.
action rather than a classroom simulator. At Port Colton station, a facility within the small and nondescript village of Port Colton, the crew of six is relaxing in their office/lounge sitting on the couch and easy chairs of the sparsely decorated room, watching television with Jim, a local student home from university. As Colton is very small, and the population of early 20's even smaller, Jim and the crew often socialize together.

The radio crackles static. "Station Colton come in please. Command Station Gamma calling," a voice says authoritatively. The Station Officer, Commander Leslie Boot, a petite blonde, rises from the couch and hastily trots to the communications console next to the small desk in the far left corner of the room. The computer there also displays a GENERAL BROADCAST ALERT MESSAGE flash on its screen. The other crew members pay little attention to this, as calls at this hour on Sunday are usually of minimal importance. More than likely Gamma is asking for a weather check. However, they turn their heads toward the console nonetheless.

"Station Colton here. Commander Boot speaking," Leslie says while accessing the computer.

"This is Corporal Tiletti. Scramble Order! Repeat: Scramble Order! Red Alert! We have an emergency near Vesta! A cruiseliner is in serious trouble and we're sending everything we've got! Condition Critical! I say again: Condition Critical!"

The others jump from the couch and race to their rooms. "Roger Tiletti! Understood! We're on our way!" Boot barks, then drops the microphone and dashes into her own room. Jack turns off the television and puts his jacket on, knowing the best place for him to be during a call is out of the way, and that means out of the station. As he leaves, Lynne Smith, the team's pilot, bursts from her room in her blue flightsuit and races to the door leading to the Launch Bay. "We'll see you later Jack!" she calls out on the run.

"Yep! Good luck!"

Seconds later, John Dixon, the tall and slim male member of the team appears in his blue S.R. duty jumpsuit and consults the computer. He pounds some keys and snatches the microphone and tunes the radio to the ship. "Lynne - do you have the info there?"

"Confirmed, John. First line reads: 'SRS EMERGENCY. STATUS: RED ALERT. TOP PRIORITY CRISIS. LOCATION: VESTA REGION.' Copy that?"

"Copy, Lynne. You've got it."

Dixon next dials the S.R. "Gamma - - Sergeant Dixon here at Colton. Complete download of situation specifics have been received at Station Terminal and Ship Computer. Copy?"

"Roger that Dixon. E.T.A. on your launch?"

"Two minutes, tops."

"Ten-Four. Good luck to you."

"Thanks," Dixon responds absently as he quickly scans the "specs" brief which is displayed on the screen. The document relays all the current and pertinent information about the incident at hand. Shock and surprise come over Dixon's face. "My God . . ." he whispers. As he reads, Kim Priest and Penny Goode bolt to the launch bay. Boot bursts into the room in her uniform and is instantly at Dixon's side.

"John! Did we get the download?" she asks excitedly.

"Yes - - Lynne has it on the ship too!" he answers, then turns on his booted heel and runs to the shuttle.

Diana Cook comes from her room, but instead of going out to the ship, she goes to the desk, joining Boot who is studying the vidscreen. Tension crosses her. "Ok, Diana," she says as Cook seats herself, "We're off!" She then exits to the launch bay.

"Ok! Good luck!" Diana calls after her as she makes entries in the Station Record Book and then radios the shuttle. "Lynne, can you read me?"

"Copy that, Di. Loud and Clear. Engines and Life Support check as functional. We're all in and ready to go!"

"Roger. I'll have the dome open for you in a second." She then presses a button and the ceiling panels begin to separate. Smith activates the engines, and the vehicle begins to rise from the floor of the launch bay.

"I'll see you guys later," Jim says while exiting through the room's main door, which opens on to the street.

"Yeah, sorry Jim, duty calls, you know?" she says brightly.

"No prob. G'bye." He closes the door and begins his walk home. He is very impressed at how the team can be relaxing in civilian clothes without a care in the world one minute, then a minute later, be dressed in their uniforms and 'ready for business'. He turns and looks up through the clear glass dome of the Biosphere and sees the Rescue Shuttle rocketing through its launch silo and then blasting into outerspace, flying so high above the Station. He waves, absently, wishing the best for his friends as they fly into the night. Then, he turns his gaze to the distant field of rock beyond Deimos and wonders what fate lies there . . .

Media reporters stationed at radio and computer scanners across the Martian Colonies practically fall out of their chairs when they hear the report. News directors are notified and broadcast satellites are redirected to the outer moon. Although the satellites cannot reach all the way out there, their cameras are put on high resolution maximum telephoto to capture whatever action they may see. Reporters and videographers scramble out to lease spaceshuttles from private charters, ferriers, and whoever else will loan them as their counterparts zap out NewsFlash bulletins to the Earth and Lunar media.

Meanwhile, back on the *Emprasoria*, the transmitter interfaces have been reconnected, and the wireless network has been reactivated. "Here we go," Escoto whispers. Holding her breath, she presses the talk button. This will serve as the system test. "*Emprasoria* calling Gamma, come in Gamma."

"Controller Polski at Gamma here, *Emprasoria.* Good to hear you."

"Miss Polski, this is Comm Officer Escoto. Your voice is music to my ears," she replies, and cheering erupts on the bridge as she gives a thumb-up sign high in the air. So now the wireless communications are welcomed back on-line. The wireless SolNet and email, the personafönes, and other devices will function again.

"I have some news for your, Miss Escoto. The *Sacramento* and the *Albany* will be assisting in the rescue and they are heading to your location along with the SR teams."

More cheering from the bridge staff. "That is great! Thank you!" Escoto says, then turns to Arges.

He is smiling brightly in the chair. "Roberta, please share the good news with the crew."

"Yessir," she accesses the speakers, communicators and infokeepers of the crew. "All personnel, be advised that the ships *Sacramento* and *Albany* are en route to assist."

Down in a port corridor, Bethany Parris pauses as she reads the message on her infokeeper. "The *Albany*..." she whispers; "Tyrekka's on his way...."

Corté calls the captain. "Sir, compu-interfaces are missing from three midship lifecraft on each side. That is what was corrupting the entire lifecraft readiness system. I sent the specs to the machinist to see if he about making suitable parts, but we have no guarantee."

"I see," Arges replies. "Well, thank you for discovering the problem so quickly, and for getting the Machinist involved. Good work, Chris. How are things where you are?"

"Under control, Sir. We are conserving the air supply, reducing the oxygen to any non-essential areas. After ensuring no one is in the areas selected for de-ventilation, we lock-off the affected areas, then label the access doors with 'danger/do not enter' tape. Then the process begins. It's good to see that ox-supply meter has jumping up about points."

"Excuse me, Chris," the captain interrupts, then speaks to an ensign. "Please verify that the oxygen supply has increased."

"Yes, Sir, it has."

"Excellent," the captain whispers - he feels as though they just discovered a treasure! Pleased, he turns his attention back to Corté. "Yes, Chris, we've confirmed it! We see the difference!"

"Thank you, Sir."

"You're on the right track – keep going and let's save as much as we can. Help is on the way, Chris. We'll be out of this soon."

"Yessir, will do. Thank you, Sir."

Arges is impressed with the quickthinking of his second engineer. It is people like him who make spaceflights easier. "Yeoman, please make a Log entry about Mr. Corté's ingenuity." He smiles, however, his pleasure quickly fades as he recalls the report about the midship lifecraft.

Why had the lifecraft prep systems not been completed? Why had he not been informed? This seems to be somewhat of an Archangel deception. They sent out an unsafe ship, and then ran it at top speed? They are victims of 'Icarus Ambition' - - like the mortal of Greek Mythology who, once given wings, flew too close to the sun and died, they too pressed beyond their limits and dared fate, now being left to pay the price. What should have been an exquisite evening is now a perilous journey for survival! The grand vision of the ship is now nothing more than shattered glory. There are important questions afoot, and Arges knows who has the answers.

The captain punches a code into his armrest. "Peter," he says into the microphone, "please bring Mr. Enkel to me. The prep systems in the midship lifecraft are incomplete. I want to know why."

"Yessir," Rish answers, then gives authority to a junior officer to load and launch the lifecrafts as he leaves to find Enkel. Then, he stops himself, knowing 'The Man' is in no condition to answer any questions. Rish wonders what to do, then Darcy Phillips comes to mind. He raises his communicator to his face. "Jennifer, this is Peter, are you there?"

"Yes, I am here Peter," her voice wavers.

"Do you happen to know where Darcy Phillips is?"

There is a pause. "Yes, actually, he is here with me now in my office."

"Excellent. I will be there in a moment."

Rish walks into the Staff Captain's office soon after. Syranos is pacing nervously, looking worried. Phillips sits behind the room's desk, a deathly pale and sweating profusely; his hair is a ragged mess on his head . . . his shirt collar is open, his bow-tie hanging limp at its sides. Hardly the calm, dignified man he has been before. Rish knows the captain wants Enkel, but Phillips will have to do. After all, the head of the Line's public relations department will certainly have the information Arges desires.

"Hello," Rish says quietly as he enters.

"Mr. Rish," Phillips says.

"Peter," remarks Syranos with a curt nod.

Rish stands in the middle of the room. "The captain would like to speak with you," he says to Phillips.

"What?" Phillips answers, confused; his face drops in disappointment.

"He asked that I come get you."

Phillips looks down at the desktop. "Very well." He rises and smoothes his hair, brushes his tuxedo jacket, fastens his collar, then fixes his bow-tie.

"Follow me to the conference room, please."

"I should go too," Syranos offers.

"Very well," Rish remarks.

A few moments later, the three reach the meeting room. Rish presses an intercom button. "We are here, Sir."

"Very good," Arges answers, then arrives in short order, consulting an electroboard as he enters. "Captain Arges," Rish begins, "Mr. Enkel was . . . unavailable, so I brought Mr. Phillips here in his place. Jennifer wanted to come as well." Arges looks up from the board and closes the door.

"Very good, Peter. I am quite sure Darcy will tell me what I need to know."

"Information?" Phillips asks quizzically as he rises, genuinely unsure of what the captain is hinting at.

"By now you know what's going on, so I'll get right to the point," Arges says. "We've discovered a problem with the midship lifecraft."

Phillips eyes widen as he suddenly becomes aware of why he is on the bridge. He quickly regains his composure. He radiates cool. "Would you care to tell me why we're out here with an unusable shuttle system?"

"Excuse me, Captain, I have no idea what you are talking about," Phillips says with a straight face. "There is a problem?" his eyebrows knit in mock concern.

"Spare me the 'I don't know' routine Darcy!" Arges snaps. Then, in a menacing tone, "I am not in the mood for games."

"Captain Arges, I am more than happy to answer any questions you may have, but I cannot tell you things I have know knowledge of..." If Phillips thinks he is convincing anyone, he is wrong.

"Spill it, Darcy," Arges says, his rising anger clearly evident in his voice.

"John," Phillips answers in a calm tone, "I'm in charge of Public Relations - - - I'm not involved with ship preparations in any way. Surely you can understand that. David Ford heads that department, and Jack Thoms was the senior builder on this project." Arges is clearly becoming frustrated with Phillips' stall tactics. "You know as well as I do that all corporate officers know everything important about every ship in the fleet. And neither Mr. Ford or Mr. Thoms aren't here. You are. Now," Arges clenches his teeth, "tell me what is going on."

Despite the fact that he is staring into the face of a very angry man, Phillips decides it is best for him to 'play dumb'. "Once again, captain, I am at a loss . . . you should be asking Mr. Enkel or someone else questions of this nature, not a copy boy like myself." Phillips smiles benignly.

The captain has had enough. He turns to Rish. "Peter, it looks as though Mr. Phillips does not wish to cooperate with us." Phillips continues his broad smile. "Now, what do you think would make a good brig aboard our fine vessel?" A look of worry on Phillips, smile fades somewhat. "Let me see, a place of isolation, with only one entrance and no possibility of . . . escape . . . where the prisoner cannot disturb anyone else. I believe the Quartermaster's storeroom is ideal."

"Yessir. I concur, Sir," Rish comments.

The two turn and look at Phillips, who is positively grim. The pause around the word escape has its desired effect. But only for a moment. "That would be murder!" Phillips retorts, bristling. "You can't do that you bastard!"

"Murder? Hardly!" the captain responds. "It is the wholly justified incarceration of a hostile witness. Contempt of court, plain as day. Whether out here among the stars or in front of a judge on dry land it's the same thing. And, yes, I can do that." Arges nods to Rish. With that, the officer lays a sturdy hand on Phillips' shoulder. The P.R. man tenses. "All you have to do is answer."

"Darcy, if you know anything, I would offer it," Syranos suggests.

"All right, all right," Phillips says dejectedly, succumbing to the mental strong-arming of the officers. He begins his sad tale. "We had to do some unexpected modifications on the shuttlecraft prep systems at the last minute. We got ninety percent of them done, but were running out of time, and everything was scheduled for April 5. If we postponed things it would've cost the company tens of thousands. Hundreds maybe. We decided to let a small number of shuttles go disconnected. Hell, the odds of anything seriously bad happening were minimal. Three of the shuttles were going to be made operational during our layover at Gamma, and the others when we were back at Alpha. We also figured that you could ferry passengers back and forth to another liner if there was a problem. There are more than enough working shuttles for that. There, that's it. I'm sure you can see, we had no other option."

"No other option!" the captain yells. "Where there are lives at stake, there *are no options!* Look at the mess we're in! What am I supposed to tell the people who might die tonight? 'Sorry, we had a schedule to keep?' 'Sorry, it wasn't in the budget?' Excuses don't work out here Darcy! How could the Line risk lives this way?"

"How could we guess this would happen?" Phillips shouts back in defense of the executives. "Maybe if your fuckin' crew wasn't so goddamn stupid we wouldn't be in this mess to start with!"

"You keep my crew out of this! Don't blame *your* mistake on to them." Phillips lowers his head to the captain's words, knowing he had used a 'cheap shot' and had been caught on it. It is amazing how intriguing a floor can be at times like this. "And just how did you get around the safety checks anyway?"

Phillips looks back up. "Well most of the system is complete, enough to give a positive readout. Also, the affected compartments were set-up to feed pre-selected info to any Spaceport or internal systems checks." His voice is now little more than a murmur.

"Damn it, the fraud," says Arges, exasperated. "Is there anything else I should know? Are the goddamn wings going to drop off?" Sarcasm laces these words.

"No, Captain," Phillips retaliates with contempt, "the rest of the ship is fine. Hell, beyond fine." He straightens with pride. "Fit for a King!"

"For a King who does not have to save his sorry ass...." Arges says almost under his breath. "Mark my words, Phillips. When this is all over, you and your time-conscience balance-sheet friends will pay for your mistakes, and pay dearly." Arges voice turns to a sinister whisper. "Now, get off my flight deck."

Rish is about to steer Phillips to the door when the man suddenly whips around and faces him. He jabs his forefinger into Rish's face, just inches from the officer's nose. "Keep your hands off me, Rish, and do something useful."

Rish can think of doing something right then, and is quite willing to take Phillips up on the offer, but restrains himself. "Out!" is all Rish says, and points toward the now open exit. Phillips glares at the captain for a moment, shoots a venomous look at Rish, then storms out of the room and off the deck. Syranos remains behind.

Once in the Starboard stairwell, and half way down from the bridge, he slumps against the wall. He loosens his tie and collar; his hand runs through his hair, disheveling it once more. He thinks about the dire situation: the captain - bastard that he is - is right, the company had made an error, and a bad one. Well, thinks Phillips, I'm not to blame, at least I can take pride in that. Heads will roll, but mine's safe so long as I can get off this damned ship. Phillips descends the remaining stairs and enters the lounge. He immediately goes to the corridor door, and sees a still sizable crowd waiting to board shuttles.

Phillips marches up to the compartment door of the lifecraft which is currently being loaded. "Do you need a pilot here?" he asks quickly while trying to step aboard.

His way is blocked by a security officer. "Designated first, Sir. We'll let you know when your time comes." Angered, Phillips tries to knock the arm aside, only to find a strong hand put on his shoulder and be pushed back. "Sir, please." Two stewards and another security officer appear seemingly out of nowhere to 'help' their colleague should the need arise. Phillips surrenders and raises his hands to signify a peaceful defeat. "Sorry, I wasn't sure if you needed a pilot or not."

"Thank you for the offer, this one is taken care of though. Please wait in the lounge or lobby, Sir. Your turn will come soon."

Phillips trudges off; anger burns in his mind. Damn, designates first! Hell, if anyone's life is worth saving it's mine! There has to be some way . . . Bribery? No, the sappy crew will not take money since they cannot be sure of their own safety . . . another way . . . really forcing himself on? No, too many goons around, he could not get his foot past the door . . . some way . . . Wait . . . A smile forms as an idea rapidly sparks to life. Yes, it will work! Phillips mentally congratulates himself for being so clever.

Confident he has found a way off of the ship, he strides into the lounge and looks toward the elevator bay, only to see the bronze doors guarded by security officers. Since the stewards have gone to all the trouble of grouping everyone on the shuttle deck, they do not want people wandering around the ship. Phillips curses this obstacle. He looks to the grand staircase - - two stewards there! Phillips is quickly becoming frustrated. His eyes dart wildly around the room, desperately searching for any exit. They soon land on a stairway door on the far side of the lounge. No crew member is in the immediate area, so his chances are very good.

Calmly, coolly, Phillips takes a long route as he walks to the portal of his 'salvation'. He does not want to draw any undue attention to himself; be just another passenger casually strolling through the crowd. His excitement rises as he approaches the oak-paneled door. He moves up to it, places his hand on the knob, turns it - unlocked! Adulation high, he opens the door and is half way through it - - - when his arm is suddenly grabbed.

"Sir we are requesting that all passengers remai -" the steward cannot finish his sentence because Phillips' free hand flies out and grasps the front of the burgundy jacket and pulls the young man into the stairwell with him. Shocked and confused, the steward stares at Phillips in disbelief. The door swings shut behind them as Phillips harshly throws the steward up against the metal wall. There is a dull thud and the fellow is momentarily dazed. Phillips wastes no time in throwing him to the floor and mercilessly pummeling him with a barrage of punches. The steward raises his arm to protect himself, and Phillips gives him a sharp blow to the head. The man is knocked unconscious, and falls limp.

Phillips rises from his crouched position and shakes the mild pain from his hand as he smiles. I made it! He nudges the body with his foot. Dead weight, and, a slight clink. The keycard! Phillips kneels and after a moment of searching locates the heavy keyring attached to a general passcard. He tears the keyring chain from the steward's beltloop. This will help a lot! He rises again and buries the keycard in his pants pocket as he leaves the motionless - but alive - body on the landing and races down the stairs. The sooner he has finished his job, the sooner he will be off of the ship. This fact spurs him on.

Phillips' departure goes unnoticed. The passengers are busy with their own private interests in the face of impending doom. Jack and Diana McCartney have pen and paper and videocam in hand, and are discreetly documenting everything they hear and see . . . this could well be <u>the</u> story of the century. And, for the moment, they have an <u>exclusive</u>. They be careful though, as they do not want their material confiscated by a security officer or the P.R. people. They relish their good fortune and allow their journalistic duty cloud over the fact that they may not live through the night.

"I can hardly believe it, but I'm actually enjoying myself," the psychologist Dr. Radsky says to himself. And quite thoroughly, one might add. "Here I have the perfect opportunity to observe the reactions of a crowd in an atmosphere of death." He makes notes both on individuals and the group itself, acutely detailing the most minutest of responses. This is invaluable! Astounding! A first-hand study of the human in a life-and-death struggle! He will certainly include these findings in his upcoming lectures, perhaps even write a book on it, that is, if he survives . . .

Peter Bull, the rock virtuoso, sits in a corner of the lounge with his guitar and its amplifier. "Time to add some sound to this deal," he says, then clicks on his amp, takes his pick, and plays a stirring rendition of George Harrison's 'While My Guitar Gently Weeps' to a small group who have gathered around him. Myrie sits on the arm of his chair and lightly strokes the black curls of his hair as his hands move over the instrument. Each note which grows from the steel strings

rings with a sense of finality. Bull's music displays the dark reality of the situation, in contrast to the carefree tunes played by the ship's band who attempt to alleviate the fear.

Edwin Roggin is seated on a chair near the middle of the room. He has seen to Lauraleigh's safety - she went, distraught but brave, on one of the first shuttles which had departed - and he is now taking time to quietly review his life. He quietly reflects on his experiences, his accomplishments, his joys, his regrets.

Roggin is not alone in these thoughts; almost everyone in the room became pensive about days gone by. Some appreciate the lives they led, some become obsessed with the statement "I wish I had done that." some think of the many things they many now never have a chance to do, the depressing notion that "This may be the end," remains foremost in their minds, and some experience mixed emotions. Dr. Radsky notes all of this, reading on the faces the thoughts in each mind.

J.D. Zolnick, for one, does not have time for ponder such as this because he is concerning himself with the welfare of his wife and five children. "There, that should do it," he says while signing a letter written on a sheet of his personal stationary. He then rereads the text to the disc-cam of his infokeeper, for a video record as well. "Details instructing my office to transfer all my holdings, including the secret Swiss bank account, the offshore holding company, and the securities investments in Singapore, over to my beloved wife, and to establish substantial trust funds for my children." He reads it through, then clears his throat once, and takes extra sheets of the same monogrammed stationary and then writes heartfelt "goodbye" letters to his young ones. He makes videos for them as well, and when he is finished, he seals the six letters and the discs into an *Emprasoria*-marked envelope, then passes it to Alexis, who gives a look of worry on receiving the package.

"Wha?" she asks.

"Don't worry sweetheart," J.D. says with a reassuring smile as he embraces her. "Everything will be fine. I just made some notes for you to hold on to for safekeeping."

J.D. then walks her to the shuttle-line, where they have an emotional farewell. When they part, and he keeps sight of her as she enters a shuttle, as she dabs a handkerchief slightly to her teary blue eyes.

Zolnick watches as the compartment door closes shut with resounding surety. He remains and looks as the craft leaves the ship, then veers away from the hull. He waves, forlornly. After a pause, he returns to the crowded lounge. He finds an empty chair, sits, and takes a flask from inside his suitjacket. He spins the tiny cap off and brings the silver container to his lips and lets its bitter liquid wash down his throat. "Hell," he says to no one in particular, "if I am going to go, I may as well go feelin' good." No one argues with him.

Of course, the crew struggles and makes every effort to see to it that there will be a 'next time' for everyone, for anything. Corté does his very best in saving as much oxygen as he possibly can. He keeps air flowing to the flight deck, the shuttle deck, and the engineering section (except for the engine room itself). He reduces the ventilation to the other decks to thirty percent of normal on the off chance that some stragglers inadvertently find themselves where they should not be. The amount of air is just low enough to let someone breathe uncomfortably and indicate to them that they should leave the area.

"Oxygen to the hold and shuttle bay reduced to five percent," Corté says after reading a monitor, being very careful, double-checking the video monitors and dispatching crewmen to ensure that no one is in the hold or bay before he closes the vents there (the five percent of oxygen comes from seepage from other areas). As the air is virtually eliminated, all doors are locked and labeled with bright yellow, black lettered **DO NOT ENTER. HAZARDOUS.** tape.

Slowly, the arrows on the oxygen gauges at the E.O.C. and the bridge climb up, quarter-inch by blessed quarter-inch. "Look, look it's increasing!" Arges says, being overjoyed to see any increase, regardless of how small. "How is the clock doing?" the captain asks.

"The program is working sir, the time is being updated," an ensign answers.

"Glad to hear it," Arges answers. Under his orders, the central clock was reprogrammed to adjust its readout relative to what registers on the oxygen scale. Whenever more oxygen is saved, the countdown momentarily stops and resets itself, boosting to a higher number. Eventually, the gauge-arrow comes to a standstill, and the countdown resumes.

Corté radios the bridge. "I've done all I can, Sir."

"Very well, Chris. You've done an excellent job. You should be proud," says Arges.

"Thank you, Sir."

Pilot Martingale turns to the captain. "Sir!" she says excitedly, "We have an hour-and-a-half of air remaining! Engineer Corté has given us an extra forty minutes!"

"Did you hear that, Chris?"

"Yessir."

"I'm going to recommend you for a special citation for the work you did here tonight."

"Thank you, Sir. I was just doing my job . . . I don't need any special award . . ." Corté replies modestly.

"Nonsense. You deserve it."

"Thank you, Sir. Really."

"No, thank you, Chris. Arges out." The captain clicks the radio off. He next waves the Yeoman over to him. He hands the man a sheaf of seven sheets. These detail Phillips' account of the defective midship lifecraft and contain the citation recommendation for Corté. The yeoman is told to enter all the information into the log.

The bridge staff do cannot enjoy the news about the oxygen for very long. Suddenly, as if fate is countering every stroke of luck, the altimeter sounds. Martingale looks to a monitor and turns to Arges. "We have one hour and thirty minutes before our orbit fails completely," she reports dismally. Neither the captain, Corté, nor anyone else save God himself can do anything about that.

"At least it will happen all at once," Arges states.

CHAPTER THIRTEEN
Armed and Dangerous

"I've got an idea," Maddox remarks, still sitting in front of his screen.

"What is it?" she asks quickly. "What'll we do? We've got to go!"

His head snaps up and he stands from the laptop on the floor. "The hell we do," he says with a strong tone. "We can still pull the job and get away. This stuff can work for us."

She looks at him with utter disbelief in her eyes. "What are you talking about? This crate is going down...we've got to save ourselves. We've already got the Hope and can finish the Centralis deal from Mars. We should go while we still can."

Maddox shakes his head resolutely. "No. We came here to do a mission, and we're going to finish it. There's lots more waiting for us, all we have to do is grab." She looks at him with anger and worry in her eyes. He walks over and takes her hands in his, then looks into her eyes. "Trust me, it'll work. I won't let anything happen to you or the others, especially you. We can still get it most of it done, and have plenty of time to get a lifecraft."

He stands, and walks absently through the room, hand on his chin. "Now, I've got to get in touch with the others." Maddox flips open his personaföne and puts the receiver to his ear. Dead silence -- odd. He tries again. Still, silence. He goes to the suite telephone instead. That has a dial tone - - good. He punches a number. An answer after the first ring. "Hello?" – calm as anything this voice is.

"Oh, excuse me," Maddox begins. "Is this Mike Sweet?"

"No, I am sorry, it isn't."

"Sorry, wrong number."

"No problem. Goodbye."

"Goodbye."

In that three second coded exchange, Parker is given orders to come to Maddox's stateroom for a meeting (Mike Sweet = my suite). Maddox dials DeSantis' line. Another rapid answer; a very calm "Hello?" Their outwardly normal, brief conversation ends with DeSantis knowing to be patient, and to await further orders. Jensen and Kobryn will be given the instructions, he is sure.

Maddox goes back to his laptop. He crouches, and there are a few quick clicks. "Ok, the diverter has been disabled, I've erased it." He chuckles. "That's the last thing we need, imaginary trouble complicating the real problems." He looks over to her. "Time for us to do a quickchange," he says with a grin, then strides into the bedroom with Angelique following, and goes to the closet. He jerks the door open, and after a moment of searching, finds his burgundy bag and tosses it on the bed. He passes her bag to her, and she gives him a kiss on the cheek then goes to the bathroom.

He kicks the dress shoes off of his feet and tears the tuxedo from his body, letting it fall in a rumpled heap on the floor. He changes into a more functional pair of blue sport-slacks and a dark sweatshirt. He slips his feet into comfortable running-shoes, laces them tight, and goes to the burgundy bag. The suitcase is unceremoniously overturned and its contents dumped on the bed. The weapons and equipment mar the elegance of the posh royal blue comforter. Maddox first straps the shoulder-holster across his back. The black leather harness feels snug on him. The holster itself hangs at his left side; the solidness of the pistol it holds feels like a warm, welcome friend.

A faint knock at the door. Maddox returns to the closet, rips his black leather jacket from its hanger and throws it over himself. "Yes?" he calls as he walks into the sitting room.

"It's me," says Parker's voice.

Maddox opens the door. Parker enters, nonchalantly walking. The door closes and blocks out the activity in the passageway. Parker turns to Maddox and produces the Hope Diamond from his jacket. "Here she is!" he says smiling as he gingerly passes the gem. Maddox takes it with a wolfish smile and gleam in his eye, then cradles the priceless jewel in his palm and simply gazes at it. After a moment, he looks up at Parker approvingly. "Good work."

"Thank you," Parker says, then Angelique walks into the room, her colored hair pulled into a functional ponytail and wearing heavy black shoes, dark tights, and a dark t-shirt under a leather jacket identical to Maddox's. Angelique and Parker nod hello.

"Look, baby," Maddox says with pride while showing the diamond to her.

"Oohhhhhhhh ammmmmmmazing!" she says with gleeful admiration as she carefully puts the diamond in the palm of her hand and gazes on it.

Parker turns and goes to the bar to pours himself a drink. "Looks like your plan is working ok. Started earlier than what I expected though," he says as he fills a glass with gin. Maddox marches over and summarily knocks the glass from Parker's hand with an annoyed look. The gin splatters a wet stain on the carpeting, and the glass lands with a dull thud. The glare from Maddox tells Parker that alcohol is not a wise move. "Sorry," Parker says sheepishly.

"I've got news for you. This isn't our game. It's real."

A look of shock comes over Parker. "Real? Whaddya mean, real?"

"See for yourself," Maddox comments, indicating the laptop on the floor as he to an easychair and sits.

Parker goes to the little computer, kneels, and reads what is printed on the screen. "No way! Is this true?" he asks with bewilderment as he looks at Maddox with confused eyes.

"Yep. That's it." A long sigh.

"Goddamn. What're we supposed to do now?"

"I've come up with another idea."

Parker rises, concerned. "You mean we are still going through with it?"

Maddox shoots Parker a very angry look. "HELL YES," he retorts sharply. "We aren't going to let <u>this</u>" Maddox swipes his hand through the air as though offhandedly brushing away an annoying insect "bother us in any way. We'll just work around it, that's all."

"Work around it?" Parker asks skeptically, raising a questioning eyebrow.

"Relax. It can be done."

"Fuck, I wish I had your confidence, man."

With that, Maddox hurls himself from his chair and bounds over to Parker. He stands directly in front of his lieutenant and stares into the man's eyes, almost boring into his brain. "You will. You must," Maddox says in a low whisper. Parker is taken aback by the intensity, yet at the same time, is awed and impressed by it. "<u>WE</u> can do it. Nothing can stop us. We've worked too hard and come too far to turn back now. There will be no abort. WE will do it." Maddox's belief in himself, the team, and the mission is inspiring to Parker, whose attitude changes as he comes to share in the positive outlook.

"We can do it," Parker repeats, almost hypnotically. A smile comes over his face, and he wears a look of surety, and almost arrogance. His vigor has been restored. Maddox smiles, and slaps his partner heartily on his shoulder.

"Yes, we can," Angelique says while walking to them.

Pleased with himself, Maddox turns and goes back to the laptop to study further. Yet again, his uncanny ability to motivate people has been proved. He often thinks that if not for the fact he is a master criminal, he would have made on hell of a Public Relations man. Sitting on the floor in front of his laptop, he analyzes the progress of the sinking. "There is an electrorganizer on the bed," he tells Parker without looking up from the computer. "Get it." Parker leaves unquestioningly and returns quickly with a compact, rectangular, six-inch black plastic case, which he silently delivers. Maddox takes the device, flicks open its top, and sees a narrow screen just above a tiny keyboard.

He activates the organizer and begins entering commands. His attention is divided between the organizer and the laptop, rapidly typing on both. He is establishing a transmission link from the laptop to the organizer in order that the information he requires may become mobile. Click. Click. Tap. This should complete the job. Maddox looks at the tiny readout on the organizer. Sentence by scrolled sentence, it begins to duplicate what is on the monitor of the laptop; Maddox smiles.

He closes the organizer, but leaves it activated. He takes his personafône from his pocket, turns it on and checks it – a dial tone, good, it's working again. He begins punching buttons on it and typing on the laptop as he speaks. "Ok, get yourself down to DeSantis' room. Notify the others to converge there for a meeting." Maddox pauses and looks up. "Don't worry, everything will be ok."

Parker nods and smiles. "Yes Sir!" he says and turns on his heel, gives a smile and a wave to Angelique, then goes to the door. He cracks it open, and peers outside a moment. He opens the door wider and slips into the corridor. He turns and gives Maddox a quick look. They nod and give a thumbs-up, then Parker closes the door behind him.

After creating a secondary link between his personafône and the laptop computer, he picks up his infokeeper then goes back into the bedroom. At the bed, the organizer is set aside, then he takes a white knapsack from the burgundy case. The knapsack is marked with a medium-sized red dot on its front flap. He quickly puts other items from the burgundy case into this knapsack. He delicately wraps the Hope Diamond in a white silk handkerchief, then tucks it in an interior pocket, which he ties closed. He closes the knapsack tightly, and carefully places it under the back-left corner of the bed, being sure to set the straps so they can easily be snatched up for quick recovery. The organizer goes in the inside pocket of his jacket. Its solidness joins that of his pistol; they feel strong and secure against his chest.

Maddox zips his jacket closed. He takes a glove from each pocket and pulls the tight black leather over the skin of his hands. He then takes a tiny grey pouch from a secret compartment within the right pocket. He inserts his forefinger into its bunched top and the drawstring slackens as an opening appears. From it he takes a heavy silver ring. The onyx which dominates the top of the ring shines blackly at him. The ivory skull and crossbones symbol inlaid in the center of the jewel smiles up at him. He slips the ring onto the middle finger of his right hand. The Jolly Roger will ride with him tonight. He will be every bit the modern swashbuckler. A devious grin forms on Maddox's face.

Maddox strides from his bedroom and sees Angelique waiting. "Ready?" he asks.

"Ready, willing and able," she says, then winks.

"Perfect on all counts then." Maddox returns the wink, then takes her by the hand and leads her to the door. He opens it, and looks out into the corridor, then ducks back inside. "Good steady crowd out there." Angelique nods. He nods back, then opens the door fully and they step out. The door closes behind them and they join the stream of people walking to the forward elevators. As they pass a stairwell door, Maddox and Angelique slip through it and race down the steps, eager to begin their role as heisters.

Soon, they are at DeSantis' cabin in the stern section of the Tourist deck. The people milling around in the hallway are caught up in their own affairs and pay Maddox and Angelique no mind. Maddox knows it is risky to have the team gathered for this meeting, but he has few choices. With his black gloved hand, he knocks twice at the door of Suite 346E. It opens slowly. Jensen is there, waiting. She smiles feebly then steps aside and Maddox and Angelique swiftly enter. As the door closes, Maddox and Angelique nod hello to Jensen and DeSantis, and see that Parker and Kobryn have already arrived. Nods are given to these two as well. All four are wearing dark, casual clothes similar to himself and Angelique. Maddox walks to the desk and seats himself. He removes the organizer from his jacket, flips it open and on, then silently studies the data it displays.

"Ok," Maddox says as he stands. "DeSantis, Jensen, Kobryn, we have some news for you. He pauses. "This situation is real, not part of our act." The three faces stare back at him, uncertain, nervous. Angelique and Parker maintain steady looks, having had their confidence bolstered. Maddox does not allow time for question or concern; he projects an air of professionalism. "Listen closely. I'm only gonna say this once. This ship is history. It's got no engines and is running out of air. If that isn't bad enough, we're being pulled down into the moon under us. The crew is abandoning the ship, and that's why there's all this craziness." The group is shocked, unsure of what they are being told.

"This is a bad scene, man," DeSantis murmurs. Although Kobryn and Jensen remain quiet, the looks on their faces voice their agreement with DeSantis' sentiments.

Jensen speaks up. "Our team had been formed for an easy get-rich-quick sting. A life-threatening situation wasn't part of the bargain. Wealth isn't worth dying for; what good is it if you aren't around to spend it?"

The body language of DeSantis, Jensen and Kobryn displays their anxiety all too well. They want out . . . "Everyone for themselves, amigo," DeSantis says. "There will be other scores later, maybe even bigger ones, but not if we end up stranded in this steel deathtrap. We gotta call it quits – now. Before it's too late."

Maddox sees the trouble he is up against. Recalling Bogart's line in John Huston's classic film The Treasure of the Sierra Madre, 'Gold changes one's soul so he is not the same.', he counters the opposition. "Our mission remains the same. The plans have changed, that's all. We are going to beat this thing, and beat it well. We've already got extra air canisters for us, compliments of some first aid boxes." He turns to Angelique who raises a knapsack. "Mountains of cash wait for us. In a few hours, we'll be rich, and laughing about what we faced. Laughing over cold beers as we celebrate in the *max*!" He sees their mood begin to change, and knows they are being diverted by future glories and rewards. All they have to do is get through the job, and they will be all set. Hints of grin appear on the faces.

Knowing he is making headway, Maddox next discusses, with detail and vigor, the 'improvs' made to the original plan. The team listens attentively, being bolstered by Maddox's seemingly boundless energy.

"You know, that could actually work – it seems feasible," DeSantis remarks.

"Of course it will work," Parker replies.

"We can do it, trust me!" Maddox continues, and sees their spirits are boosted. "What do we care about some damned sinking ship! To hell with it! We'll be the winners before the night is over!" There is a headrush from impending victory . . .

After the power meeting, Maddox turns away from the others for a moment and looks through the porthole. Alive with excitement; energy surges through his body from the pure intensity of the moment. It's happening! Happening! His plan is beginning to unfold! The exhilaration is almost intoxicating. He will be a millionaire ten times over within the hour! - - wait, wait . . . struggle to keep this thought from interfering with duties. There will be time enough to enjoy later, but for now, there is work to be done. With a jerk of his hand, he pulls the curtains closed.

He turns to them. "Everybody ready?" Nods from grinning faces answer. "Release the coolant." With that, each pushes a button hidden next to their armpit which opens a sack of cooled water and lets the liquid flow through their kevlar body mesh. This will put them in a low-temperature cocoon and not hamper them, but reduce their body heat output so they cannot be noticed by any heat sensors. They each in turn nod to Maddox.

"Weapons," Maddox says. They each produce a firearm – Maddox with his S&W; Angelique happens to have a stylish Lady Derringer Maxo. Parker has a Midnight Special, Kobryn reveals a Colt. DeSantis sports an HK-Longarm rifle, Jensen shows her Harbringer rifle. Maddox carries a stiletto, and DeSantis happens to have a silver butterfly knife. "Silencers." Six silencers appear and are fitted. "Ammo." Each person displays a packet of stunner cartridges for their specific handgun, then returns it to a pocket. "Loaded." The gun-magazines are checked, and seen to be fully stocked. "Test fire." Yusacre goes to a painting on an inner wall, removes it, and sets it on the carpet. The six take aim. Pumph. Pumph. Pumph. Pumph. Pumph. Pumph. Six muffled gunshots. Six divot-like indentations in an even line. Six mashed slugs lie on the floor. Maddox walks up, and inserts a small silver ruler against each divot. He barely gets past the measurement for one-fifth of an inch. He looks back and smiles. "Perfect. Not even close to penetrating this thin wall, let alone if a stray shot happened to hit part of the hull, or a porthole. The reduced amount of gunpowder worked." He kneels and puts one of the spent slugs between his forefinger and thumb, then rises. He smiles and pockets it as a souvenir, then joins the others. "Locked." - the safeties are confirmed as being on. The handguns are returned to their holsters, the rifles are stowed into long, narrow, black canvas bags.

"Carriers," Maddox says. He, Yusacre, DeSantis and Jensen each grab two large, mostly empty, black knapsacks. Parker and Kobryn take soft black attachés. "Oxygen." Yusacre distributes two green plastic bottles labeled 'O2' and a gasmask to each person, and these are sequestered.

"Radio," Maddox continues. They place small, single-ear headsets around the fleshy part of their left ears, and lower thin microphone arms until tiny microphones are at their mouths. Six clicks, and they are radiowave. "Testing, testing," Maddox whispers. Each in turn gives an A-Ok thumb-up and nod.

"Royale team, ready?" Maddox asks.

"Ready," Parker answers.

"Ready," says Kobryn.

"Go to it, and good luck," Maddox says with a smile. Parker and Kobryn smile back, turn and leave - intent on raiding the Royale deck. Jensen locks the door behind them. The team is being divided so the most amount of work can be accomplished in the least amount of time. Each knows full well their role within the masterplan, and are set for their villainous tasks.

"Lights," he says, and Jensen switches off the lights in the stateroom. "Night vision." On go night-vision goggles and they are provided with crystal clear, neon green electric eyesight.

"Pathway," Maddox orders. DeSantis moves their couch under a ceiling vent. Jensen steps up on it a moment later. She takes a screwdriver from her pocket and loosens the rectangular grating. She pushes up on the cover, and it opens easily. She carefully sets it inside the duct, then looks at Maddox.

"Ready," she says.

He nods. "Let's do it!"

She nods and raises her arms, then with straining muscles, pulls herself up and through the narrow opening which was never intended to be an entryway. It is a tight fit, made moreso by the body-altering padding, but she holds her breath and is just able to squeeze through. One by one, the others scramble into the duct, each knowing the wincing constrictiveness of their portal. When the last is in, the vent-cover is replaced, thus hiding the chosen route.

Hunched on all fours, the trek to wealth begins. They move stealthily through the ship, following Yusacre's lead - she has a deck diagram - and silently crawl in single file down the endless metallic tunnel to the treasure which lies in wait for them. They crawl to an upward junction, then shimmy up two floors to the Camaraderie deck, then slide across again. "The air sure is stale and heavy – it's like a sauna in here!" Yusacre hisses while wiping sweat from her brow. A strand of hair loosens from her ponytail, but she leaves it.

"Yeah, that's for sure," Maddox says. "But it's a small price to pay for what we get. We'll use the oxy only if our breathing gets really restricted." DeSantis and Jensen say nothing, but feel their skin grow slick with sticky sweat.

Ping! The sound of an elevator arriving. The four freeze in the airduct. Maddox and Angelique are near a vent cover. Slowly, they peer down through the metal slats. "Eye in the sky, right here," Maddox whispers as he and Angelique see a man and woman in uniform, walking alone down the center of thee corridor. They walk slowly, methodically.

"Come out, come out, wherever you are…" a woman's voice singsongs; her words echo through the vast and empty hallway. Bethany Parris and Yeoman Clancy slowly patrol for any stray passengers which may be lost or hiding on the lower decks. "Good one, Bethany," Clancy says with a light chuckle.

"Thanks," she replies.

"It's good to have a little laugh at a time like this," Clancy continues.

"Laughter is the best medicine, so they say."

"How do you think it will all turn out? Can they get us out of it, like back at Alpha?"

"I wish I knew," Bethany answers. "I am sure it will be ok in the end."

"Sure is hot down here," comments Clancy.

Then, as if on cue, they hear a fan slowly start to spin.

Bethany playfully swats his arm. "There you go, see, things are getting better already!"

"There we go," Clancy says. "I guess they run the fans every now and then to keep it from getting unbearable, or to keep the humidity from affecting the circuits or something."

Up in the airduct, the fan is a welcome relief – cool air breezes upon Maddox, Yusacre, DeSantis and Jensen. Against their sweaty faces, it feels like paradise. They wait for the two crewmen below to leave the area – Maddox and Angelique can see them pausing, with their backs to the vent. The wind blows along Angelique's shoulder, and through her hair.

Bethany sniffs the air. What is that? She sniffs again. An olfactory memory comes to light – another quick sniff. Perfume. That French perfume; Parisienne something, the new stuff during the moonstop....what was it again? She lifts her infokeeper and accesses a file. Parisienne Peaud by Chanel – that was it. What would that be doing down here? Just then, a long hair lands on her forearm. She looks at it, then picks it up; not one of hers. She looks at it closely: brown for most, a hint of bright blonde at the far end. "What's that joke?" she says to herself, "What do you call it when a blonde colors her hair brunette? Artificial intelligence." She drops the hair from her fingertips.

"Bitch," hisses Angelique from the airduct as she brings the loose strand back into the ponytail.

Yeoman Clancy laughs loudly. "Another good one, you're a laugh a minute."

"Thanks. This hair just landed on me, and I remembered the joke."

"I can imagine a lot of stuff settled after they shut the fans off the first time, then some went airborne when they went on again. Look, there's some lint over there."

"Yeah, true." She silently thinks the new perfume must be strong to linger like that.

"Well, looks like nobody is at this end. Let's get going." They board the speedwalk and continue down the deck.

Once they are out of sight, the team moves again. Some minutes later Yusacre reaches their first target – the Casino Royale. She smoothly and silently removes the vent-cover and pulls it inside the duct. Black lines are secured against catches in the ducts. Maddox raises his right hand for all to see and spreads the fingers wide. One by one, they drop down and close on the palm. Five. Four. Three. Two. One.

Compact dark shapes drop from the ceiling, landing nimbly on the balls of their feet and arched palms with the scarcest of sound. Black rope follows to provide escape. The four move about with agility under the cover of darkness, letting their forms merge with the shadows cast by the corridor spotlights. Their cooled armor torso cocoons keep their bodyheat from triggering the infrared monitors. They can see everything as clearly as if in the middle of the afternoon rather than the middle of the night.

"Freaky weird," says Yusacre. It looks like a ghost-town. There are half-empty drinks around, chairs in disarray; colored chips lie on the gaming tables and the carpeting – with the shadows and all, it is almost disconcerting.

"Come on, we've got stuff to do," Maddox says, and the four trot to the cashier's cage. Maddox and DeSantis leap at the bronze-painted metal rods which stretch up from the polished wood countertop but end before reaching the ceiling. They close their gloved hands the smooth metal and with the edge of their shoes as props, pull themselves up. They climb and hurdle over the flat tops of the fence. Yusacre and Jensen follow suit, in the same manner. Since the casino is closed, the security cameras will only activate if they are tripped by heat sensors, or door openings. Their body heat is covered, so they scale the fence to avoid opening the cage door.

They go to the door of the counting room, which is in back of the cashier cage. The door is unmarked, and set flush into the wall. "You two stand watch," Maddox says to DeSantis and Jensen, who already have their rifles unsheathed and in hand, nod with solemnity as he and Yusacre remove items from their knapsacks. Soon, a high-powered acetylene laser-blowtorch is assembled. "Ready?" Maddox.

Yusacre smiles widely. "Go."

Maddox presses a switch in the compact wand, and a thin beam of laserlight appears. "Fire, in hand, feels just like Prometheus," he says with a wide smile. DeSantis and Jensen look back at him, and tiny sparks fly as he directs the pulsing ribbon of red light to the door. A high temperature chemical reaction occurs, with the temperature localized so it will not come anywhere near triggering the heat sensors. The steel reaches its kindling temperature, and an orange burst soon appears in the metal panel, and it gradually gives way as though it were a sheet of ice thawing. "Cuts like butter," Maddox says as he directs the cut in an arc, then Angelique brings up a nozzle and switches on a small vacuum, drawing in the minute amounts of acrid smoke.

"That'll do it," Maddox says as he completes a rough oval-shaped line within the door. He switches off the lasertorch and steps back. "Are we ready?" he asks his three conspirators. Three nods answer. Maddox heaves up his right foot and kickpounds into the oval. The slab falls back, hot and heavy, and they now have a way in. "Ha," huffs Maddox, "the lock's still in place, and the hinges haven't moved an inch. Angi, let's go! You two, keep watch. We won't be long." Carefully, and carrying their items and bags, Maddox and Angelique stoop and pass through the smoldering hole. They enter a mantrap, a closet-like compartment between two doors that can keep someone stopped until they are 'buzzed' in or out. The inner door has a plexiglass center, and beyond that, is the darkened counting room. "Part two," Maddox says to Angelique as they approach the second door. Two blowtorches are up this time, one in each of Maddox's hands. Yusacre has the vacuum ready. With a grin, Maddox hits the glass full force with dual beams, and soon the window is a white, molten, dripping mess. He shuts off the lasertorches.

"Again, the doorframe is unmoved," Maddox says, then cautiously puts his head through the newly formed gap, and with his nightvision goggles, looks around.

"What do you see?" Angelique asks in a whisper.

"The root of all evil," he replies, then pulls his head back with a jack-o-lantern grin on his face. "Through the looking glass, baby," Maddox jokes, and in they step to a wonderland.

"My, my," says Angelique. "Will you look at this! Hard currency......mountains of it....just waiting for us!" Yes, banknotes and coins cover the table and neatly bound bundles sit on the surrounding shelves. Two large wallsafes are at the back. Maddox makes a point of looking up to the ceiling; no vents there, only tiny vent-slits cut into the sidewalls that even the smallest person could not possibly fit through. Wads of cash are hastily moved into the sacks.

"Ruby! C'mere and help!" Maddox calls in a whisper. She is through the two door-holes seconds later, stuffing money with Angelique for all she is worth. Maddox approaches the wallsafes. He heaves up an electric drill fitted with a diamond bit. There is a stifled whirrrrr as he the safecracker bores through the tumblers.

They all appear outside soon after, and with DeSantis, are up once again into the airduct and on to the stores. Yusacre and Maddox pop one vent cover then scurry to the next one as Jensen and DeSantis remain behind. After the second cover is open, all four drop in. Once inside, these cat-burglars are free to do as they please. Their surveillance taught them that the alarm system in En Vogue is wired only to the front doors and windows; there are no motion detectors in the stores, and like the casino, the internal video cameras are off outside of business hours, activating only when a door or window contact is tripped.

First, any cash in the back-office wallsafe. Then, any easily portable items of value. The jewelry stores are stripped clean; only those pieces on display in the front windows are left behind since it would be immediately noticed if these went missing. Several expensive statuettes and etchings from the art gallery find new homes in the especially strong knapsacks. The Majestic Gems display from Nicholby's is squirreled away in the duct, taken because if it were left and it was discovered that just the Hope replica was missing, the substitution would be immediately revealed, and a world of trouble would erupt.

They ignore the discomfort of the stiflingly warm air and concentrate on the task at hand. But this is easy. . .more fun than work . . . as each item is taken, a thrill of elation at the deed runs through the blood of each . . . wicked grins of delight appear on their shadowed faces as their fingers grasp, their hands acquire, and their sacks fill. Continuing in the leapfrog pattern, the team hits each shop and the VacaBank machines in a short time. They keep to Maddox's tight schedule – as the seconds tick, they operate with elite efficiency. Soon, they are ready to leave the En Vogue. As Maddox and Yusacre are about to ascend into the vent and leave the last store - a jewelry store - to join the waiting DeSantis and Jensen, there is a problem.

Stomp. Thunk. Bang. Noise outside, in the hall. Maddox and Yusacre freeze in their tracks - still as rock, quite as mice. Noise by intruders – three males run in, jumping and shouting. "See! I friggin' told ya! Empty! We can take what we want!" The one behind this loud voice is heavy, and appears to be the leader.

"Wow, man, wicked," says another. Obviously, intelligence is not one of his strongsuits.

Maddox rolls his eyes in frustration at this conversation of idiots. Amateurs. Great. Just great. Exactly what he needs . . . damn it! These clowns will ruin everything!

"What'll we do?" Yusacre asks in a hushed whisper.

"Shhhhhh!" Maddox hisses sharply. Anger begins to show in his goggled eyes as his elated mood turns into sheer wrath. He peers at the men through icy irises. He is not about to let his masterplan be ruined by these failures of humanity. His mind snaps at answers to this wretched dilemma. Hopefully, someone will walk by and scare them away. He waits.

"This is wayyyyyyyyyyyy cool," clamors the fat one.

"Yeah," says his partner.

The other just stands there, open-mouthed, looking around.

"Let's get to it afore somebody comes," comments the partner again.

"Ok. Hey, remember, stay outta the goddamn light!" bellows the leader's voice. "Keep to the fucking sides, so the vidcams can't see ya!"

Maddox's anger twists into rage upon hearing that. These fools are going to set off an alarm any minute now . . . and bring Security down in force. Then, of course, a routine search of the store affected . . . and . . . discovery! He put all this work into executing a damn good heist, and now these losers are going to muck it up? I don't think so – not gonna happen. He must stop them. There is no alternative.

"Up! Up! Up!" he orders in a forceful whisper, and Yusacre hastily climbs the rope and disappears into the duct with Maddox following her shapely posterior. "Everbody to the grating at the center!" he says with a whisper through the radio. They hurriedly crawl to an intersection in the ductwork, round a corner, and find themselves in a considerably wider cross-beam duct. Maddox scrambles past his teammates and stops once reaching the large, circular cover which lies in the middle of the Mall ceiling.

He shrugs the two knapsacks off his broad shoulders. He removes his goggles and earpiece and peers through the long rectangular slats of the cover. The light from below casts an eerie tigerstripe shadow across his wrathed face, making him an aperture of evil.

"I hate competition," he mutters. He will not do anything unless absolutely necessary and clings to the hope that someone, anyone, will come along and scare these lowlifes away. He hastily unties the coverflap of a side pocket of one bag and opens it. From this he takes a baklava, and a sizable coil of blue nylon cord, whose elasticity is stronger than that of the black rope. He rapidly laces it through his belt at his left side and lets the long lasso rings rest against his hip, then tightly knots the ends of the line. Maddox looks over to DeSantis. "When I give the word, get the cover out of the way. Pronto." His tone and the expression on his face evokes the seriousness of the statement. DeSantis nods, silently agreeing he will do as told. He then loosens the interior latches holding the cover in place.

"Which one first, Clyde?" the 'genius' of the group asks.

"Let's try this here one," says fat Clyde, and with a toss of his hand, indicates the jewelry store vacated seconds ago by Maddox and Yusacre.

"How'll we git in?"

"Good question," Clyde comments, then looks around. "Do you see anythin' we could use to bust the window?" The others look around with him – the chairs, benches and tables in the area are all bolted to the floor of course. Clyde looks more, but not much catches his eye. "For fucks sakes, gotta be some damn thing we can use…" His eyes drift to some decorative wood latticework on the wall. "I think I gots it," he says, and takes a jack-knife from his pocket and pulls it open as he walks over. "C'mere and help me," he says, and the others join him. Maddox and his partners watch intently. Soon, the men have a section of the latticework torn from the wall and each hold a section of rectangular cut wood.

Brandishing these like crude clubs, with the sharp ends of still-placed nails gleaming, they approach the storefront. They spread out and take positions like three points on a triangle in front of the elaborate front window, and slowly, menacingly, move in like ravaging jackals. "We'll have to do it fast, so get ready. Remember again, ya gotta keep outta the way of the light, and watch out for cams!"

"Goddamnit!" Maddox hisses. No one is going to come in time! Something must be done this very second, or they run the risk of being captured, or at the very least, having the plans further complicated. Instantaneous decision. He jerks the black baklava over his head and looks over at DeSantis, who is crouching on the other side of the vent. "Now!" DeSantis slips his fingers between the slats and lifts the heavy cover up and back. As their backs are to that location, the three below do not notice the gap appear in the ceiling.

"On the count of three, we all hit the window," Clyde orders. The others nod and together raise the sections of wood as though they are baseball bats. "One," says Clyde.

"Two," whispers Maddox.

"Two," says Clyde – his partners tense and the wood is raised higher.

"THR-"

"To battle," Maddox mutters with a sneer, then draws a deep breath. He vaults through the hole and leaps into the corridor. He lands about a yard behind them. The moment his feet hit the carpet, his hand whips to his shoulder-holster, and the gun is drawn. "Hold it!"

Clyde can't finish his word. They jump, startled; shocked…they spin around and the yell stops them dead in their tracks. They reflexively stiffen and their eyes widen like saucers as their jaws drop, yet they remain still. Perspiration forms, and not from the humidity, either – from fear.

"Damn . . . damn…." says one.

"Awwwwwww mannnnnnn…" another complains.

They have been caught completely by surprise, and know they found a world of trouble.

Maddox stands in a shooter's stance, his pistol aimed directly at Clyde's fat neck. He deliberately cocks the hammer slowly and loudly, making sure the click, with all its deadly resonance, makes its point. The men cringe, and Maddox grins behind his mask. "Hold it right there! Drop it! Hands up!" he barks with an altered voice.

Having a pistol pointed squarely at him unnerves Clyde. He drops his plank. "We weren't doin' nothin'!" he protests. He swallows hard, trying to bury the fear. The others silently drop their planks as well.

"Shut up!" Maddox retorts sharply. "This isn't your party," Maddox continues; venom laces every word. "No crashers. You have *one* way out of this. Beat it. Haul ass. And don't let me find you back here again. Understand?" Silence. "*Understand*?" More force this time.

"W-we gotcha, brother," Clyde answers. "No worries, no problems. Just let us go."

"Turn around, start walking, and keep on going. Eyes straight ahead," Maddox says. There is no movement. "Get the fuck going!" Maddox barks.

"C'mon, let's go!" whispers one. The other remains silent, and shakes. Clyde wobbles. All at once, they turn, and run out of the area, disappearing behind a far corner of the darkened hallway.

Maddox watches them go. Then, he chuckles. "Poor, stupid fucks." He re-holsters his pistol and quickly takes the nylon cord from his belt. He unfurls the length of it, then looks up to the open vent.

"Hey," he calls. Three faces appear in the rounded space. "Grab these." Maddox hurls one end of the line up into the hole, then the other. DeSantis' hands clamp one end while Jensen clenches its mate. Now, a long U-shape of cord dangles in mid-air from the ceiling. When I say pull, you yank!"

"Gotcha," says DeSantis.

"Ok," remarks Jensen.

Maddox backs into the valley of the rope, then threads his forearms and biceps through either side, twisting the line through, and the dipped end becomes drawn tight against his underarms and upper back. He grasps the rope with his gloved hands. He is ready to go. He looks up.

"Hawwwwwww Hawwwwwww Hawwwwwwww," comes a distended chortle from the darkness. Maddox snaps his head forward. Clyde and his cohorts emerge from the shadows – Clyde has his hand in his jacket pocket, and is pointing a square-shaped item through it toward Maddox. "Weeeellll lookie what we got heah! Strung up like a stuck pig!" Clyde yells. His partners laugh. Clyde then looks to the lines connecting the man to the ceiling. "What're them things? Ya some kinda puppet, little bitch?"

Maddox looks at his three would-be assailants; and grimaces – where in the hell did the fat one get a gun from? They can easily harm him before his partners can retaliate. What to do? He releases his hold on the rope, letting his palms face outward as he raises his hands high in the universal sign of surrender, and, with a slight shift here and flex there, uncoils himself from his blue tether.

"That's right, keep them hands up," Clyde says menacingly as he and the others move closer. "We ain't sure whats goin' on heah, masked man, but we sho as hell gonna find out!"

"Hold on…." Maddox says calmly, "hold on, take it easy… We don't want to do anything crazy."

"Shut the fuck up with your crazy talk," Clyde snaps, then turns to his partners. "Go n' git him, I gotcha covered alright. If'n he moves for his gun, I'll nail him good afore he can even git it out." He turns back to Maddox and sneers. "Looka that fuckin' wiseass Pinnochio. We gonna have fun with you, Bozo." Clyde then begins to laugh hysterically at his own joke. The others laugh harder; all three cackling like mad hyenas, and raucous laughter fills the vacant deck.

Clyde remains still – the other two step toward Maddox, wearing maniac smiles and with wild, wide-eyes. Above, Angelique bites her lip in concentration as she aims her pistol – the fat one seems just barely out of range; if she misses, Maddox is dead.

Maddox keeps his attention fixed on the fat one with the gun – that one is the main problem. The others move still closer. Suddenly, Maddox drops. He bends at the knee like one of those Cossack dancers and goes to the floor – falling out of range of the gun in Clyde's pocket and criss-crossing his arms over his chest in the process.

In a lightening fast move and with jackrabbit agility, he springs bolt upright, gun drawn. The three men freeze, Clyde's jaw drops in shock – the others gape. A thin smile curls across Maddox's face. Not because he thinks Clyde is particularly humorous, but because he is pleased with what he is about to do. "Ha. Ha. Ha. Everybody is a comedian." Without so much as a warning, Maddox fires. Three shots. Three hits. Three dull thuds as bodies hit the plush carpeting. The silencer on the gunbarrel effectively muffles the noise as the suppresser similarly reduces the flashes. There is no more laughing.

In fact, there is no noise. At all. Maddox's well-placed bullets have shattered their larynxes. As he had been standing there, his eyes lined-up trajectories, and took silent aim . . . drawing a perfect bead. Clyde went down first, then the others – well before they had time to reach him. The men's wide grins of milliseconds before now morph into expressions of extreme agony as their faces twist in shock and pain. Life slowly drains from the three as dark, crimson pools form and grow beneath their bodies and stain the carpet. Their eyes become home to vacant, lonely stares.

Maddox looks up to the video camera rigging which circles the vent he dropped through. The lenses point north, south, east and west, leaving his particular position unmonitored. He hunches himself forward, and lowers his head to alter his form. He also takes a quick shot at a port spotlight, blasting it away, and further obscuring the view of the south camera. Stooped, faced away from the camera, he walks to the men and places his fore- and middle fingers against each neck in search of a pulse. Nothing. He smiles beneath his mask. He also goes to the right jacket pocket of brazen Clyde – the man's hand is still there, clutching the weapon. Maddox reaches in and finds .... a closed jack-knife. It was held forward to resemble the barrel of a pistol. "Fuck," Maddox huffs, then looks into Clyde's face. "Never try to con a con-man," he whispers.

Maddox stands and slowly retraces his steps, still stooped. He walks backward, until he is directly beneath the vent. He straightens himself, re-holsters again, and backs into the rope. He looks up, the three faces look down at him, ready to pounce at his command. He waves them back. "It's ok. Toss me a handgun," he says. A small gun drops from the ceiling a second later – he catches it square in his palm. He aims in the general direction of two of the downed men, the squeezes off a round into the wall. He then tosses the gun over to the right hand Clyde; ironically, he now has in death what he was trying to pretend to have while still breathing moments before. Maddox watches as it bounces on the carpeting, then looks up again. "Got the rope?"

"All set!" answers DeSantis.

Maddox grabs hold of the lines as before. "Pull!" Instantly, the rope grows taut and he is snatched up into the ceiling, his torso disappearing into the vent.

Yusacre helps Maddox pull his dangling legs into the vent, then DeSantis drops the heavy cover back into place. "That was a close call!" Angelique says.

"All in a night's work," the smiling Maddox replies. "Fucker didn't even have a gun, just a jackknife. Anyway, the mission's been saved…"

Yusacre throws her arms around him and hugs him closely. "Great work! We were worried for a minute!" She kisses him strongly on the cheek. "We were ready to take them," Yusacre says as she re-holsters.

"Yeah, I figured, but I did what I had to do."

Maddox peers through the vent again. "Those bodies will be discovered - and likely soon, but no one will bother with the shops. A quick glance will tell the curious that everything is fine; tight and secure." He pauses. "These mystery killings will probably cause an excellent diversion; while security personnel trip over themselves trying to answer "who? what? where? how? why?", we can finish the job! Couldda been a disaster, now an advantage…the second time for us tonight."

Maddox hastily puts his goggles back on and radio piece over his ear, then reclaims the rope from DeSantis and Jensen, which he coils and returns to the knapsack pocket. checks his wristwatch. Not much time has been wasted - mere minutes. He next checks his electronic organizer. He opens the cover to find the transmission from his laptop to be as strong as ever. "The evac appears to be proceeding well. There are still lots of lifecraft waiting to be launched." Maddox presses his left index finger against the transmit button of his headset's earpiece and speaks.

"grumph . . Four. Item inventory hold section echo completed. Mild infrac. Proceeding to Charlie area. Copy and Confirm." Maddox again alters his voice and uses the team's hastily formulated code - using terms that, if picked up by an internal ship radio, which is entirely possible, would sound like routine crew communication. He intentionally muffles his first word so any third-party eavesdroppers will think they came across a conversation in progress. To Parker, (four = Forest) the ciphered message means: "Cleared En Vogue (hold section E - a legitimate area of the ship) and am going to my suite (Charlie area - Deck C, or, Royale class)". Maddox waits for the reply. Silence. "(cough) Kilo confirmed. No infrac here. Will rendez soon. Out." Maddox understands this as (Kilo = Kendall) Parker and Kobryn are all right and will meet them (rendez = rendezvous) at his suite shortly.

Maddox and the others breathe a sigh of relief. "Green light four on," Maddox answers in another voice variation. He looks to Angelique and the others. "Ok, let's go!" They hustle down the duct.

Meanwhile, Parker nods absently to himself. Green light four on . . . it is a go for him that Maddox understands. Excellent. He and Kobryn smile and exchange a high-five handslap at hearing their teammates are done with En Vogue and are preparing to regroup at Maddox's suite. Currently, Parker and Kobryn are in a darkened bedchamber near the stern of the starboard side of the ship.

With use of the modified steward's keycard which Maddox had obtained earlier, the two have easily been raiding these posh residences of the ship's elite. Maddox knew that as soon as the keycard was reported missing, its magnetic stripe encryption would be deactivated so it could not be used. However, certain basic properties which link the card to the *Emprasoria* would not be altered. With some fine-tuning and close work, Maddox was able to reactivate the card, and reprogram its stripe to give it general access to every door on the ship.

Their soft leather attachés - less noticeable for this area than black knapsacks - are about half filled with currency of all types, and the odd extra piece. They have been methodically going from room to room, rummaging, helping themselves, using compact flashlights to scope out the rooms, and, careful not to leave behind any obvious disturbances - - they close doors or drawers that they open, and largely leave things the way they find them, in terms of how items are arranged on a desk, for example, for they know if someone inadvertently returned to find a ransacked room, there would be hell to pay. An average three to four minutes in each suite is all they need.

Every now and then is an unexpected surprise. In one room, Parker discovers a realtime SolNet camera and thick portfolio containing nude photos of the supermodel Adele. The first is expensive, the second invaluable. He takes both. In another, he is searching a dresser and comes across a *very* nice pistol. He takes it from the drawer and smiles as the light glints off of the polished silver. This is a *choice* piece of weaponry. He turns it over and sees that the magazine in the handle is loaded. Parker quietly slips the pistol into the waistband of his trousers; the fewer that know about this the better. After all, there is no honor among thieves. He rifles through the drawer, and finds and ammunition clip; this disappears into his jacket.

"Find anything?" Kobryn asks after searching the closet.

"Just the usual. You?" Parker keeps his back turned as he speaks; adjusting the items so their presence will not be obvious. Satisfied with his reflection in the mirror, he turns.

"Nothing, just clothes."

"We'd better get going then."

Kobryn nods to the suggestion, then strides out of the room with her attaché tucked snugly under her right arm. Parker breathes a sigh of relief - - the gun has been hidden effectively. He follows Kobryn into the darkened sitting room.

As done so many times before during that night, they click off their flashlights as they approach the main door. Holding their breath and with anticipation running high, Parker unlocks the door and warily opens it. They peer outside. "Empty," Parker says, and they make a hasty exit. The door is closed behind them, and there is a second click as it is locked. On to the next. Now, half of this mission is almost complete. They will finish the suite they are in, proceed up the Port side, then return to Maddox's cabin where they will join the others and make the getaway. Parker and Kobryn resume the scavenging of the dark bedchamber, eager to finish it and delve into the riches on the other side of the ship. Parker opens the left drawer of the dresser while Kobryn raids its mate . . . when . . . CLI-CLAK. The sound of a deadbolt releasing.

They freeze. "Damn!" Parker whispers. There is an ever-so-slight creek as the main door is opened. The lights in the sitting room come on; they can be seen from beneath the closed bedchamber door.

The main door is slammed shut. They switch off their flashlights; the white beams vanish and are replaced by the dimness of the amber nightlight and the meek light which creeps in from the portholes. They hastily but softly close the drawers. "Hide!" Parker whispers harshly as he clamps his attaché close to his chest and dives behind the far side of the bed. Kobryn bounds over to the drapes and buries herself in the soft linen.

No sooner than this is done and the bedchamber itself is bathed in brightness from the chandelier. There are quick but heavy footfalls on the carpet as someone walks across the room. The double-doors of the closet are opened, and there is the sound of garments rustling. Parker shifts himself on his back; his arms are crossed in a long V over his torso, and they pin the attaché against his chest. His hands tightly grab his pistol. Kobryn is facing the wall, and for the moment, is trapped in that position. She had tried to turn around, but the slightest motion causes the curtain to ripple far too much. She keeps herself dead still - frozen.

"Damn it all to . . ." curses a male voice as the rustling intensifies. Items are being cast to the floor as a harried search is undertaken. Parker and Kobryn hold their breath. They can feel beads of sweat appearing on their foreheads. They he finds whatever he needs soon and leaves. "Where . . . come on . . ." the phrase ends in garbled mumbling. "Ah, there's one, nice and clean too!" Finally, he got what he wants and is going to go… Parker and Kobryn think, until the mattress creaks slightly as the man seats himself on the edge of the bed. What is it now? they wonder. "This will do perfectly." They listen intently and hear a swipe of metal, then a very slight –click– and unwrapping of plastic foil. Next there is a hiss and the room fills with the smell of….colorspray??? Parker rolls his eyes and Kobryn swears under her breath. How much longer????

"Ok, gotta do it. Heaven help me. One. Two. Three. Argghhh! Damn it that hurts!" The acrid scent of blood fills the room. The mattress creaks again a minute later as the weight is taken off of it. "Ow, ow, owwwww, come on…." Footsteps against the carpet. Pacing. Nervous pacing. Confined to the back-left of the bed - - but for how long? The restless motion plays upon Parker's nerves. "Damn…." says the male voice, and this fades to mumbling. "Goddamn, look at the time!" Urgency in the voice. There is a sudden spin on leather shoes. Jumbled steps. Quick paced striding is heard. Seconds later, the main door opens and closes.

A pause. Only silence. The man does not return. Parker releases the breath he did not realize he was holding and he stands. Kobryn appears from behind the curtain as though she is an actress taking to the stage. She shakes her head. "Damn, that was close."

"Yeah, thought he would never leave." He looks at his watch. "The fucker was right. Look at the time! We gotta get back on schedule!"

Parker turns and looks at the bed. "Hell!"

Kobryn looks around him and gasps in terror. "What the?" A white Archangel-crested towel is laid out on the bed, stained heavily with blood. A blood-stained scalpel, a torn-open plastic wrap, and a roll of gauze with a tattered, bloody end lie next to it.

"What went on in here?" Parker asks.

"I don't know, and don't wanna know!" Kobryn says and steps back.

Parker nods sullenly in agreement. "Let's check the dresser and get outta here!" He rises and the two go back to the dresser and hastily search for cashnotes. Finding some, they stash it in an attaché. A look to the ransacked closet tells them nothing of value is there. Neither notice the small, silver, monogrammed pen lying on the floor just under the edge of the bedspread. Finished, they trot to the sitting room and approach the main door.

The knob turns - but from the other side! Parker dashes to the far side of the entryway while Kobryn vaults behind the sofa. The door opens, its wooden bulk effectively shielding Parker. The door is left ajar. An angry Parker peers from behind and sees a gray-haired man walking toward the bedroom. "Dammit, where's the pen…where's the pen…."

Parker steps out from behind the door, pistol in hand. It is not aimed, but held compactly in the palm of Parker's right hand – the wooden handle juts out. Parker dashes up behind the intruder, and before the man can turn, whacks him squarely on the back of the head – at the base of the skull. The gun provided a solid brace comparable to brass knuckles. The man collapses into a heap.

Parker nudges the door with his left shoulder, and it swings on its hinges, then closes. Parker pistol-whips the man again, even though he has not moved since falling seconds before. Just to be sure. "Hey R-!" Parker stops himself, remembering this -person- may still be able to hear, and that using the name Ruby may not be such a good idea. Her head appears from behind the sofa. "Get over here!" Kobryn is instantly alongside Parker. They look at the gray-haired man lying at their feet; one of his pantlegs are torn, and there is a cut on his right calf muscle. "Fucker!" Parker spits in anger, then kicks the prone body once in the ribs. It jerks from the force, but otherwise remains still. "Well, at least he won't be bothering us anymore," Parker observes.

"Come on, this is too weird, we otta get out of here!" Kobryn says, tugging at his arm.

"Ok. Are you ready?" he asks; she nods expectantly. "Alright, let's go." The two turn off the lights and slowly open the main door. No one in the hallway. They exit. A click as the deadbolt is locked. They next make their way to the Port section of the Royale class. . .

In due time, Parker and Kobryn arrive at Maddox's suite. Luckily they only encountered a steward when just finishing the Royale, and promise they will proceed directly up to the shuttle deck. He was not persistent, and leaves as he seems more interested in completing his assigned rounds than babysitting stray passengers. Parker approaches the door. He knocks; Tap tap. Pause. Tap. The signal. He unlocks the door with his passcard and they enter, and are not surprised to find the others already there. The door is rapidly closed.

To Parker and Kobryn, it looks as though they have walked into a scene pulled from "Ali Babba and the Forty Thieves" - - - cash, gold, jewelry, gems, paintings and sculpture are spread out as if on display. Yusacre, DeSantis and Jensen are taking great delight in studying the treasure, while Maddox is sitting on the floor at the laptop. All four look up at Parker and Kobryn. "Hey hey, good to see you!" Maddox says with a broad smile as he stands. "How'd you two do?"

Parker looks to Kobryn and nods, then they hoist their attaches high in the air. "About as good as you guys, by the look of things!" Parker says with a bright smile. Everyone applauds, then he hands his attaché to Kobryn. "Show 'em Kobby."

"With pleasure!" she says, then unceremoniously dumps the contents of the two briefcases and adds their "take" to the pile as Parker walks over to Maddox.

"All right!" Jensen says with unabashed enthusiasm. "Good work Ruby!" she says as she heartily hugs Kobryn.

"Not bad, isn't it?" she says.

Parker steps up. "Oh wait - - Enrique, Russ, you've *got* to see this!" He picks the portfolio up from the floor as DeSantis and Maddox go to him. They stare intently as Parker flips through the pages of form-study photos of a beautiful, shapely woman flagrantly displaying her rampant sex appeal.

"Woah hoah!" says DeSantis as he takes the booklet and steps to the side. Parker and Maddox let him have it without complaint.

"So, it looks like the first part of the ace plan can join the triple crown as being officially done!" Maddox says enthusiastically. "And the double-down is well on its way!" Claps and cheering follow. "Great work everybody!"

Yusacre goes over and kisses Maddox on the cheek as the others exchange hugs and Parker and DeSantis shake hands. Yusacre steps off to liberate a bottle of champagne from the room's bar. Seeing what she is up to, Maddox interjects. "Let's save it for when we've escaped," he whispers; she nods, carries it to the loot, and sets it down with the trophies.

As the others relax and look at the pile of booty, Maddox goes to sit in front of his laptop, and is soon brooding. Spying this, Parker walks over and crouches next to him. "Everything ok?"

Maddox is sitting with his legs crossed, elbows resting on his knees, his hands knit almost as though in prayer, his chin being supported in the crook formed by his thumbs and forefingers. He stares intently at the screen, and appears to be deep in concentration. "Yeah --" he answers, "Just trying to finalize a way to get off of this wreck with the stuff." His voice fades as his mind delves deeper into the complex riddle which plays upon him. Devil in the details, again... Some way . . . but how?

The other four talk animatedly about the photos and the Score. Maddox turns toward them, mildly annoyed with the disturbance, and about to ask them to quiet, when... Knock, knock. They freeze. "Hello, who's in there?" Silence inside. Knocking again – intense rapping. "This is a steward, who's in there please?" Another steward ordered to check for stray passengers has been walking down the corridor when he heard voices coming from Maddox's suite. He is on edge over the evacuation and frankly has little tolerance for those who make his job difficult. A look of anger inspired by tension and frustration crosses his face. Still getting no reply, he inserts his passcard into the lock: there is a cli-clak as the tumblers turn. "Excuse me," he begins as he opens the door, "but all pass..." his voice fades to silence as a shocked look comes over him as he stands at the doorway and sees the sitting-room. He is dumbfounded and stunned - - taken completely by surprise at what he has stumbled onto. "Wha?" is all he can manage as he looks in confusion to the six people gathered there. This will prove to be the last word he will ever say.

Kobryn instinctively draws her gun and fires. The bullet pierces the steward's chest and his arms flail as he is hurled from the impact back into the hall. Kobryn leans forward, and with her free hand grabs hold of the front of the steward's jacket. She snatches the limp body from the floor and pulls it into the suite. The door slams shut.

The steward is cast to the floor, thrown on his back. The team circles around him. By this time he is already dead. The bullet struck him square in the heart. "Damn..." says Kobryn.

"He was in the way," Maddox remarks coldly. "He knew too much. You did good work, Ruby." A nod to Kobryn.

"Thanks, Boss," Kobryn says as she holsters her weapon.

"Put him in the jacuzzi," Maddox orders. At first, no one moves. "Now, please," he says authoritatively. DeSantis, being the closest, reluctantly crouches and laces his arms over the steward and heaves the dead weight toward the bedchamber, and the bathroom. "Take the jacket off him," Maddox says, almost as an afterthought as DeSantis backs through the open bedroom door.

Moments later, DeSantis returns with the burgundy waistcoat in hand, which he silently delivers to Maddox, who closely inspects its front. There is a tiny hole near the fourth brass button where the bullet entered. It did not pass through, so there is no hole in the back. Some blood has stained the area around the hole, but the crimson is not noticeable against the burgundy background unless someone looks very closely. "Why so little blood?" Maddox asks without taking his eyes from the jacket.

"You should see the t-shirt," DeSantis answers. "Damn mess. It took most of it."

Maddox nods. He raises his head from the coat and looks to his team. The jacket will help them greatly in the next phase of the operation. Maddox informs them of his new plan.

While Maddox speaks, a glimmer of hope appears. Up in the Halo, that is. Up there, the crowd is, finally, beginning to visibly reduce in size. Not by much mind you, but any progress, regardless of how minimal, is enough to encourage anyone. Maybe, just maybe, we can beat this thing! Some passengers sample the selections on the snack table which has been hastily set up near the elevator bay. There are trays of sandwiches, plates of cakes, pies and other sweets, bowls of fruit, and delectable treats such as caviar and oysters, or even potato wafers. Punchbowls with iced fruit drink, a soda pop dispenser, and two large watercoolers are also here. Most passengers, however, find their appetites have disappeared with stress, so the food and drink are largely ignored. No one will be truly happy until they are off the ship.

Dade and Adrianna are in a quiet corner of the Halo. His tux is a bit rumpled, the shirt collar is open…her once big-sexy-hair is now pressed into a ponytail, and she still looks good in her gown, if a bit tired. He holds her in his arms, and she sees concern in his eyes. "This sure has been a crazy night," she says, anger evident even in her mild tone. They have known mixed emotions through the evening. First, elation at the Ball, then disappointment at he early closure; irritation at having their building passion interrupted by a lifecraft drill, dismay when the truth was revealed, and now frustration at how slowly the evacuation is proceeding – yes, a little progress has been made, but not much.

"Crazy is putting it mildly," Dade concurs. "I wish to hell I knew more about what is going on." She can see he is very frustrated at feeling uninformed, and thereby powerless. "I'm going to get something cool to drink. Would you like anything?"

She shakes her head. "No, I am fine, thank you."

"Ok, I'll be back in a minute." He releases her from the hug, then kisses her quickly and makes his way to the food table.

Elsewhere, the bodies of the bluffer Clyde and his unlucky friends have been discovered by a steward checking for wandering passengers. He happened upon them first, as the security officer who had been dispatched to investigate the 'odd occurrence' seen by the south vidcam has yet to arrive. The steward immediately called the security station and nervously reported his finding. Security personnel are quick to appear on the scene, and after a short time, Purser Mueller appears to see for himself what has happened.

The stocky Purser trots down the speedwalk track as the conveyor cannot move fast enough for him. Watch Captain Reedy follows close behind. Soon, they are at the location in the middle of En Vogue where the officers have gathered. Muller joins the group, and pushes his way to its front. "Good God!" he exclaims as he sees three men sprawled on the floor. As if things are not bad enough, now a triple homicide!

Security Lieutenant Davidovich, who was closer to the En Vogue and arrived there first, steps next to Mueller. "Seal the area off immediately!" Mueller orders.

"Already done," Davidovich replies. "I've got guards at both the forward and aft lifts, and the stairwell doors on this deck have been secured."

"Good, excellent," Mueller says, then looks at Davidovich closely. "This will be kept on a need-to-know basis." The last thing he needs is the story leaking and further scaring the already nervous passengers. Davidovich nods sharply. "Who found them?"

"A steward on patrol, Sir," Davidovich answers, then motions to an officer who is questioning the steward at the starboard side of the corridor.

"What is your name, Steward?" Mueller asks as the officer brings the man over.

"P-Preston, Sir. Robert Preston." He is disheveled; his jacket is open, and he is pale. Obviously the discovery has disturbed him badly.

"Well, Robert, you can relax." Mueller puts a comforting hand on Preston's shoulder. "Tell me exactly what happened." Shakily, the steward reports how he accidentally found the bodies, saw no one else in the area or on the deck, and had touched nothing. "Good work, thank you. We'll need to talk with you some more. Afterward, keep this to yourself." Preston nods and Mueller directs his gaze to the officer. "Take him up to the officer's lounge until he gets his bearings. You can finish your interview there."

"Yessir."

"Did you find the weapon?" Mueller asks Davidovich.

"Yes, here sir." Davidovich holds up a sealed plastic bag containing a small handgun. "These men were shot at close range, looks like a murder-suicide. Seems like a professional job, too. These weren't just lucky shots, they were sent by a trained hand." He holds up a second bag containing a closed jackknife. "We found this, too."

Mueller looks up at the surveillance cameras in the rigging encircling the ceiling vent-cover. Anticipating the question, Davidovich speaks. "We had the videotape of EnVogue-AFTCAM played back at the Station, Sir. There is a lot of shadowplay, they were keeping out of the light and away from the vidcams. One of the port lights clicks off." Davidovich points in the general direction with his ballpoint pen, "and there more indiscernible movement from some stooped person who is involved somehow too, as a witness or participant – we aren't sure. He, she, whoever, remains behind the scope of the camera too. Then, nothing. We scanned FORCAM, which clicked on once the infrared monitors and motion detectors were tripped, but that just shows the three men running into the empty mall. STARCAM and PORTCAM show nothing but dancing shadows." Davidovich pauses. "It's all very strange."

"Strange isn't the word for it," Mueller offers, then surveys the crime scene then looks forlornly at the Security Booth at the end of the hall. It is empty - - the officer on duty there had been called away for more important tasks of the evacuation. So, there are no witnesses. Mueller looks at the three bodies. Well, no living witnesses anyway, and dead men tell no tales.

"Where did this planking come from?"

"Torn from the latticework on a wall."

The Purser scans the immediate area and lets his keen detective instincts take over.... Vandalized latticework, a broken light, a lone shot in the wall....there is not much evidence of a struggle...and what about the stooped person? It seems as though he or she had simply appeared, watched or acted, then vanished into thin air. "Do you know who they are?"

Davidovich consults his infokeeper. "They had i.d. on them. This one is Clyde Howe, this is Jeffrey Munsey, and this is James Dravla." Davidovich lifts his eyes from the device to Mueller. "We're running background checks on them from the Station. We should have reports momentarily."

"Maybe that will shed some light on this. Damn! Such a mystery! And we don't have the time to deal with it properly!" Mueller rubs his head in frustration. "Have Priest take detailed photos of the scene - video as well. I want *nothing* overlooked. When he's finished, have the bodies wrapped in plastic and take them to the pantry and store them in the vacant freezer. Be as discreet as you possibly can. Have all reports sent up to the station. I'll conduct operations from there. You are in charge of things down here, Alex."

"Understood, Sir," Davidovich answers, again with a sharp nod.

Mueller nods, then turns and boards the speedwalk, and goes back to the elevators. He will note the murders in the log from the station, but has no intention of informing the captain just yet - - Arges has enough to worry about. Within seconds, the purser has just passed the Halo, walking up an interior stairwell, making his way to the flight deck stairs.

He hears a door open from below, and listens to rapid footsteps. He turns and looks down, to see if it is one of his officers trying to reach him. He instead sees a steward heading up to a door –

one that will take the fellow into the lounge. Mueller looks at the man quizzically; he seems harried. "Is everything ok?" Mueller calls out to him.

The steward stops in his tracks and looks up, visibly startled by the inquiry. "Excuse me, Sir?" he asks quickly - - the question intended to provide a delay to allow him to compose himself.

Mueller walks down a couple of steps. "Down below. Did you find anything wrong?"

The steward straightens to attention. "No, Sir. No problems, Sir."

"Where are you off too?" Mueller asks, still approaching the door platform.

"To the Halo, to assist with the Evac, Sir."

"Very well. Continue on, we'll be through this soon," he says with a smile. With a long nod, dismisses the man. The purser takes a glance at the brass nametag pinned to the steward's chest. 'MACMILLAN' it reads.

"Thank you, Sir," Macmillan answers, and returns the nod. He stands for a moment, then opens the door, and enters the Halo. Mueller pauses a moment, watching as the man's back disappears behind the closing door, then turns and resumes his trip up to the flight deck.

Once he is through the stairwell door, Parker turns and looks over his shoulder. The purser did not follow him. Just what he needs, the head of security stopping him and asking questions! He relaxes somewhat then slowly walks off toward the far end of the spacious room, toward a corridor exit. He tugs on the front of the steward's jacket in an effort to loosen it - - the thing is so tight! "Excuse me," says a female voice. The words came from behind; Parker turns, startled somewhat by the interruption. He smiles when he sees it is Adrianna, the girl who caught his eye before, and is mood softens instantly. He notices how her full bust sways with the movement of her walk, and uses all his willpower to keep from glancing at the sensual hint of cleavage.

"Yes?" he says as he stops. A certain broad smile appears.

She knows that look, that certain smile, all too well. She ignores it. "Could you help me, I need some information…"

"Yes, Ma'am, what would that be?" Parker asks politely, hoping this will not take long.

"How are the evacuations coming? I mean, how much longer will we have to wait?"

Parker pauses, and swallows hard – he cannot answer the question, yet cannot have her prolong it with anxiousness and prodding. "A very important question, Ma'am. Let me find out, and provide the time estimate. Can I find you here in a few moments?"

"A few moments? Yes, that would be fine I suppose."

Testy, she is. Parker's smile grows – the sight of an energetic woman – especially a somewhat angry, on edge energetic woman, turns him on. "Thank you, Ma'am. I will obtain the most current figures, to give up-to-date data."

"I see." Adrianna pauses. "Couldn't you call someone?" Parker swallows again, and can feel the heat building at the back of his neck, but he keeps a straight face. "We are trying to minimize the communications traffic. I will be pleased to check and report to you personally, Ma'am.

"Yes, alright," Adrianna says, still a bit unconvinced.

"Thank you, Ma'am," Parker says, and with a nod, he continues on his way.

Just then, Dade arrives, drinks in each of his hands. He offers one to her. "Brought you one anyway," he says.

"Thanks," she replies while accepting the glass.

"What was that about?" Dade asks, then takes a drink.

"Trying to get some info. He wasn't very forthcoming." She takes a sip.

"I doubt if he knows much more than we do, to be honest. How's that saying go? 'Don't ask me, I just work here.' The top brass would have the facts for sure, but they would be tight-lipped, and bothering them could delay things further anyway."

"Good point."

Dade thinks for a moment. "Must be another option...." He snaps his fingers and smiles. "Got it! We can go to the Purser's Desk and ask their, after our drinks."

"Sounds good to me."

"On that note, here's to you," Dade says out-of-the-blue, and clinks his glass with hers.

"And to you," she says while raising her glass, and they each take a drink.

Parker walks across the lounge and through busy hallway which is lined with people waiting to board lifecrafts; boy, that was close, he thinks to himself – she sure is sweet, he thinks a half-second later then smiles wolfishly. He did not notice that Bethany Parris witnessed the exchange he had with the woman passenger, and was a bit rebuffed at how the passenger appeared to be treated. Walking at a good trot, he soon enters the lobby.

He notices that the pillar once holding the Hope is bare at its top. He smiles to himself, then looks up and sees the purser's office along the back of the room. There it is! Only one security officer stands behind the long desk. Parker is prepared to handle three of them, but is pleased to see only one. The officer's head is lowered, to a computer screen, and it appears as though he is typing on the keypad. Parker checks his watch. 12:50:33.

He takes a deep breath and slowly begins to walk toward the desk. He is careful not to draw any undue attention to himself, and prays no other passengers will bother him. His heart beats wildly in anticipation as he moves through the forest of people. 12:50:47. Parker looks over his shoulder, to his right – there she is, Ruby Kobryn, shadowing him. On his left, there's Jensen. He looks straight ahead again. Suddenly, the security man raises his head and quickly scans the crowd. Parker pauses, involuntarily. Seeing nothing strange, the officer returns his attention to the computer. Parker keeps walking.

Jensen is leaning against the wall alongside one of the lobby's two maintenance closets, trying to appear nonchalant. Her eyes sweep the room as she calmly slides herself over to the door. Her back remains to the front of the door. Satisfied that no one is watching her, she slips the keycard into the knob-lock, opens the door, and slips into the tiny, dark closet. She leans herself against the door as it closes and holds her breath, waiting. Nothing. No shouts, no knocks. Another moment and - - nothing. She breathes a sigh of relief when she realizes she is safe. Luck. Pure Luck, she thinks as she switches on the closet's light and sets about her task. She refers to her watch. 12:50:55.

Outside, Parker is almost at the edge of the Purser's desk. No one stands between him and the officer. He keeps walking. 12:50:57. 12:50:58. 12:50:59. 12:51:00.

Darkness! The ceiling lights in the lobby suddenly switch off. The backup spotlights do not activate. People scream and run through the pitch-black room to the only source of light - the front alcove. Jensen wastes no time in exiting the closet; she throws herself into the panicked stampede and instantly becomes nothing more than just another face in the crowd. In the midst of the chaotic confusion, Parker hastily pulls a pistol from a holster fixed under his jacket at the small of his back. As his finger touches the trigger, a thin beam of red light shoots from the weapon's laser target sighting and pierces the darkness.

The red dot is centered on the startled officer's neck. Pffft, pffft - two soft thuds as pellets pass through the pistol's silencer and slam into the man. His larynx is shattered along with his windpipe and he is dead before he has a chance to recover from the shock of the sudden darkness. The force of the shots knock the lifeless body against the back wall, and it slowly slides to the floor.

Parker drops the gun into his pocket and cautiously moves up to the desk; everything is guesswork in the darkness, and there is no time to put on nightvision goggles. He stretches his arms out and searches through the air, letting his hands see for his blinded eyes. His outstretched fingers soon find the desktop, and he hastily scrambles onto the platform. He misjudges the width of the desk, and when he expects to put his hands down on hard wood, he finds only open space. He muffles a yell as he topples headfirst to the floor, and painfully knocks his shin during the fall. "Damn thing!" he curses, but ignores the stinging sensation in favor of his assignment. He must move quickly since he is unsure how much time is available - - crewmen are probably already on their way to rectifying the problem ...

Parker crawls forward on his knees, and his groping fingers soon find the officer. He pulls the body to the floor; "Blech," he says as he feels slick blood on his hands as he rolls the body under the overhang of the desk. For now, he can only hope the counter can hide his work. No sooner than Parker stands and turns himself around and the lights come on again. He has to blink and wait for his eyes to adjust, and seconds later, everything comes into focus. He sees a woman in a bridge officer's uniform hurriedly coming to him – Officer Rayburn, as he knows from his studies. He straightens his jacket and does his best to compose himself when his eyes fall on the red, wet stains covering his palms. He hurriedly clasps his hands behind his back and snaps to attention as she approaches. He also catches sight of Kobryn, waiting in the wings.

"What happened? What went on in here?" she asks hurriedly.

"Some sort of power failure it seems, Ma'am."

"Where is the duty officer for this desk?" She knows it is highly irregular for a steward to be stationed at the Purser's office.

"He asked me to stand guard when the lights went out. He went to see what was wrong," Parker replies with his prepared answer. There is not a trace of anything unusual in his voice. "Didn't you see him, Ma'am?"

"No, I didn't. When did he leave."

"Just after the lobby went dark."

"All right." She is puzzled. "I suppose we missed each other in the crowd." Rayburn turns and looks at the disheveled passengers who begin to re-enter the lobby, warily. "What the hell else can go wrong with this ship?" she asks under her breath. She turns back to Parker. "I'm going back to my Evac Station. Please remain here until an officer comes."

"Yes Ma'am," Parker dutifully answers, then nods. Rayburn returns the gesture, and walks toward a corridor entryway. As she reaches the doorway, she sees two stewards. "It's all right, just an electrical short or something. I need your help out here." They nod and follow her.

Parker breathes a sigh of relief as he watches Rayburn leave, yet is still tense over her request. He first looks down at a video monitor, whose black-and-white image shows the inside of the Purser's Office, behind the wall in back of him. It seems empty – he smiles. He types in some commands, and the image moves as the camera pans around the room; yes, it is definitely empty, there's the circular staircase leading to the flight deck security station and, yes! There it is! The heavy door of the vault itself is seen plain as day from the unblinking lens of the camera. Parker's eyes and smile grow at the sight of it.

After a moment, he lets his eyes roam around the room and sees that things are almost back to normal. He directs his attention to the alcove entryways. There is a steady stream of wary passengers slowly coming in, no doubt curious about what had happened. Among the faces he spies Jensen, who is grinning from ear to ear. Parker does not acknowledge her, so as not to establish a link between them. She knows he has seen her though, so she is content to leave a second time. He next looks over to Kobryn again; there she is, smiling too – he does not acknowledge her either. Bethany Parris walks in, a look of concern on her face – Parker does not acknowledge her simply because he does not really notice her, and even if he had, he has no idea who she is, although she wears an Archangel uniform.

Parker reaches for his personafōne and presses a precise sequence. Elsewhere, on Maddox's fōne, a message appears: 'firstbase made – homeplate clear'. Maddox grins, and replies with 'batter up, get ready for second'. Parker lets a small smile creep on to his face. The team is assembling for 'The Big One'. This is going to be *goooood.*

Suddenly, the deskphone rings. The smile vanishes as he looks at the black device which demands attention. He knows from earlier surveillance how the receptionists answer the telephone there.

All he has to do is imitate. It rings again. Parker takes a deep breath, then picks up the handset. "Purser's Office."

"Yeah - - - hi," replies the voice on the other end. "This is the flight deck security station. The cameras down there showed darkness for a few seconds. What happened?"

"Some sort of power failure. We've got everything under control now, though." Parker's voice is steady.

"That you, Kirsalis?"

"No," Parker says and hastily looks down at the nametag on his chest to double-check his new alias. "This is Steward MacMillan. Officer Kirsalis has stepped out to check the light problem and left me here. He's expected back shortly."

"Oh, I see." A pause. "Officer Rayburn just called here. We're sending Bekker down to relieve you – him and another. If Kirsalis gets there first, have him call up here."

"Yes, Sir. I'll give him the message. Your name, please?"

"Chapman."

Parker pauses long enough for the officer to think a note is written. "Yes, Sir. Bekker, got it. I'll be ready for him."

"Great, he won't be long in arriving. Stay there until Bekker arrives. Goodbye."

"Goodbye." Parker hangs up – went better than I thought, he thinks, being pleased with how he handled himself. He sends another message through his personafône. Kobryn looks at her fône-screen as it vibrates: '2 umpires on way'. A minute later, Parker reads her reply: 'catcher's ready'. Parker grins, then sends a message to Maddox: '2 umps coming, catcher's ready.' 'Play ball.' says the reply.

Clizrk. Parker pauses, and looks down; the communicator on the dead security officer is making static. "Kirsalis, this is the Security Station. Come in please." Parker looks around the room quickly, then bends at his knees. "Kirsalis, com-" The word is cut as he quickly switches off the small device. He next removes the access-card from the downed man. This small card should provide the ability to open the vault without any problem.

He rises and looks at the desk and his eyes widen when he sees blood has smeared on the phone. He does a quick rummage and finds a box of tissues. He rips a few from the box and wipes the phone clean, then attempts to rub the now-drying blood from his hands. He cannot get the palms completely clean. He moistens the tissue with this tongue, and tries again, to no avail. His skin retains a rather odd rust color. Since he cannot leave the desk to go to the office washroom, he must continue for the time being with the telltale sign of crime embedded in his flesh – he is red-handed. He pockets the useless tissues (no sense in leaving bloodstained tissues around, even if they are in the garbage can) and looks up to see his conspirators taking their positions. It will happen any moment now.

CHAPTER FOURTEEN
When Ambitions Clash

Then, a noise. Unrelated to the break-in, as it happens. Down in the lounge, behind a steward guarding a stairwell door. He turns to see a man teetering at the doorway, holding himself up by a makeshift cane. The man is in casual clothes, is fit but pale, and has prematurely graying hair. The lower part of his right pantleg has been cut away; the calf there has been bandaged, and is stained with blood. He is wincing in pain. The steward goes to him as he steps in and the door closes. "Sir, where have you been? Passengers are to remain on the Shuttle Deck." He puts his arm around the man to help hold him steady.

"I'm sorry. I was on my way up when I tripped and gashed my leg, I've been to sick bay and went to rest a bit since then."

"Are you alright? Who bandaged this?" the steward asks, concerned.

"I am fine. After the nurse was done with me, she went to help someone else, and I did not want to trouble her further, so I went and rested, then made my way up here..."

"I see, Sir. We want to make sure everyone leaves the ship safely. Let me help you." The steward carefully escorts the wounded man to the nearest corridor entrance, and places him in line for the shuttle currently being loaded. "Please wait here, Sir," the steward says, then walks to a security officer and whispers in his ear. The man stiffens somewhat on seeing that. The steward returns to the lounge as the officer approaches.

"We have a place ready for you, Sir," the officer says.

"What?"

"The injured and disabled are part of those designated for early evac."

"Are you sure?"

"Yes, quite sure."

"Well, I guess I qualify then." These words are said sheepishly.

"Please follow me." A person farther back in the line steps out and seems to be about to object, until a sharp look from the officer silences the idea and sends her back. The officer walks along with the man as he limps to the hatchway, and sees that he is seated in the shuttle. The man hunches himself over when he sits, and keeps his head lowered, and is not seen by Hearst who is loading the craft. "Thank you," he manages, then begins to cough. The officer nods in reply. Others board the lifecraft as the officer leaves, and when it is full, the hatch is closed. The officer watches as Hearst launches the craft.

The hurt man is seated on the middle chair of the third row, and he keeps his eyes glued to the port windows of the shuttle. He brightens and the color returns to his face as he hears the hatch-lock close, and a smile appears as he watches the davit arms extend and the shuttle clears the hull. His eyes widen with joy as the arm-locks open and the pilot fires the shuttle's engines and flies the vessel away from the *Emprasoria.*

Then, he relaxes. He raises his head, then winces and rubs a sore bump on the back of his head, then Darcy Phillips breathes a long sigh of relief. FREE! His life *saved*! Sure, he had to become hurt to do it, and gray the hair, but desperate times call for desperate actions. He had gone to his stateroom and changed clothes, then to the cruise entertainment green-room and found the coloring hairspray, then accessed a medical storeroom, and found another cabin to do his altering. He removes his infokeeper from his jacket, along with his monogrammed pen which he found after losing it when he went to do his trickery. At least the 'person' who had sucker-punched him from behind had left it. Those in the shuttle give curious looks to the impostor in their midst. Phillips is quick to notice, and lowers his head again. He tries to force the smile from his face, but his lips fail to respond - - simply tooooooo happy! A second chance at life by a stealthy salvation of his own doing. He wants to stand and scream "I made it!" but chooses instead to remain seated, and let the clown-like grin on his face do all the talking for him.

Back at the Halo, a guitar does the talking. Peter Bull expresses his frustration through his guitar as he plays rapid solos from rock anthems; those written by him, and some penned by songsters before him. Myrie along with those around him stare in awe at the speed at which his gifted fingers move. Senator Jackson watches him absently as she longs for a cigarette. She had successfully quit smoking years ago through sheer willpower and determination, but now feels the need to have one. She has decided to wait and be one of the last women to leave so she is available if help is needed.

Tsarevich Romanoff, in his dress naval uniform, occupies his time by watching the gallant efforts of the crew conducting the evacuation; "Very impressive," he says. Also, he thinks about the safety of his fellow passengers, rather than his own. "I am a ready volunteer should the need arise." He told officer Rish, and already has assisted with some operations. He rests against a wall, idly toying with a pen, letting his thoughts drift to home . . . to St. Petersburg and Mother Russia. I still want to be a Cosmonaut, should the opportunity present itself, he thinks, or, more appropriately, if I survive the tragedy.

"I have to get to the package in the hold!" Cal Gregg mutters.

"I know it's important," Genvievve says, "and you know I'll help you any way I can, but jesus christ don't risk your life over it!"

He looks at her, and his tension eases somewhat in the gaze of her soft blue, caring eyes. "Thanks. I know I can count on you. I won't do anything too crazy – but if the chance comes, even the slightest, know I am there."

"Ok, thank you. Let me take a walk and try and think. Wait here, would you?" She nods.

Xian Ng and Karisu have secluded themselves in a quiet corner of the lounge and are privately performing acts of Tai Chi to ready their spirits for an audience with the Gods should it be so decreed. This is done after Ng wrote a letter transferring all ownership of their co-owned corporation to his beloved wife. "I promise, my brave Samurai, I will not leave your side regardless of what happens," Karisu says as he passes her the letter.

"Cherry Blossom, I beg you, please," he continues to plead, but cannot convince her.

She is resolute. "Either we survive together, or perish as one. Time will tell."

As Roggin sits, he sees Gregg walk past him, walking alone. Roggin rises, and approaches him, then rests his hand on his friend's shoulder. "Oh, Edwin." A hand is offered, and taken in a firm grasp.

"I guess we won't have that match after all," Roggin says with a lighthearted grin.

Gregg chuckles. "No, no I guess not . . ."

"How about we keep the invitation open. I do have to recover, after all."

"Certainly! I'll never back down from a challenge."

"Fair enough."

The two shake hands, then separate, needing time to think. Each wonders if there will be a later time for future games of any kind.

Rave DiMedici and Octavia Vickers drink some specially prepared herbal tea and try to relax. The fact that the tea is sprinkled with a healthy dose of opium powder helps. "Damn, what I wouldn't give to have the yacht here now," he says forlornly.

"Well, dear, if we are to join the ages, at least we will go in style."

J.D. Zolnick drinks from his flask as he roams the room. His eyes sweep the lounge, and come to rest on the massive Archangel statue standing tall and proud in the middle of the ornate chamber. As the hours grew long, passengers came to resent the ivory figure which is the prized symbol of the Line which cast them into the life-threatening situation. Zolnick saunters over to the stone angel. He stands in front of it, and takes another drink while he studies the statue, then his eyes fall on the plaque bolted to the pedestal. EVER FORWARD it reads. "Ever forward?" Zolnick says ruefully, "More like Ever Fucked."

Adam Tyler is lost in thought as he strolls around the lounge. As he walks, he notices the large Location Board attached to the port wall. The black three-dimensional electronic map is framed in gold and shows a white, flashing, "animated" profile drawing of the *Emprasoria* in relation to where she is in the Earth - Mars corridor. Tyler goes to the board and sees the miniature ship hovering above a cluster of rocks behind the far "left" end of a gray potato-shaped moon marked 'DEIMOS'. Tyler lets his eyes wander over the map itself. At the left end is the blue-green Earth. Tiny representations of North and South America look up at him. He almost becomes homesick just looking at the picture. Next in line is the crater-dotted Moon with its Biocol domes being plainly evident. On the right end of the chart, near the *Emprasoria*, so close but yet so far, is the red orb Mars. Even Deimos looks good. Deimos. Tyler begins chuckling in spite of himself.

Another passenger walking past hears the subdued laughter. He stops and gives Tyler a bewildered and annoyed look. Tyler turns and sees the man looking at him. “Deimos,” he says as he points to the map. “Ironic, isn’t it?” From the expression on the man’s face, Tyler surmises he is not following the line of thought. “In ancient mythology, Deimos is the son of Mars,” Tyler elaborates. “Deimos is the Greek word for Terror. Hell, where we are, it’s the shadow of Deimos. Can you imagine anything more terrifying than that? Than this?” he spreads his arms wide and indicates the general situation.

The man shakes his head. “No, I can’t.” He resumes his walk. Tyler returns his eyes to the board and continues laughing at the comedy of circumstance, and imagines all the forces of the universe are laughing right along with him.

There is no laughter from Maddox. He is smiling and appears pleased, but is not laughing. He looks over to Angelique, a sense of anticipation clear in his eyes. “Ok, Alex has got the reception desk under control. The vault room is empty. Tell me you’re ready for the Purser’s Office.”

“I am ready,” she answers, then gives a prolonged wink from her right eye.

“Excellent. Let’s go then.”

The two are through the vent of their bedchamber a moment later, and in the Royale airducts on their way to the lobby at the deck above them.

A security officer walks into the Halo from the flight deck, at the same moment Bethany returns from the lobby. Bethany became content to see the steward at the purser’s desk, seemingly obtaining the information the passenger needs – she was glad to see her guess that he was ‘blowing her off’ was mistaken. Bethany spots the officer immediately, and he has a distressed look. She approaches him. “Hello.”

He nods. “Hi.”

“Rough night.”

“You’re tellin’ me.” He shakes his head ruefully. “I just want it over and done with.”

“Seems like we’ve got a good handle on things though. Could be a lot worse.”

"Yeah, worse." He pauses. "Have you seen anything odd lately? I mean, I know there's a lot of odd stuff tonight, but, anything with any particular person looking weird?"
Bethany shakes her head no.

"Ok. We're on the lookout for someone, but don't know who we're looking for, but we know he or she will be overly stressed, and not about the sinking either. They may be hurt as well." He is being careful not to give too much information, respecting Mueller's need-to-know basis. Bethany looks at him intently. "It's the damnedest thing," the officer continues, "we had a situation down at En Vogue. A real mystery. The cameras saw some of it, but didn't show much. It has us stumped, and it beats the hell outta me. I mean, how can somebody just appear outta nowhere, watch some kinda bad activity, or even participate in it, then disappear into thin air?"

Bethany pauses in wonder. The En Vogue....the Camaraderie deck....the perfume, that strand of hair. Into thin air? ***In to air!*** She looks up to the ceiling, thinking. "Bats in the belfry..." she whispers absently. Yes! Her eyes widen in shock. "The air ducts!"

"What?" the officer asks, confused by the sudden comments.

"This sounds odd, but I think somebody is creeping around in the airducts. They may be connected to your En Vogue occurrence."

The officer looks at her with utter disbelief. "What? Sorry, I don't follow...."

"I know it sounds crazy. But, trust me. Could someone check the ductwork somehow?"

The officer clearly sees her sincerity and determination. He lifts his communicator to his face. "Alvarez calling flight deck security station."

"Go ahead, Alvarez."

"Can I get a scan on the airducts."

There is a pause. "Say again?"

"Could you do a scan on the airducts. We may have a lead on the En Vogue event."

"Oh, a lead on En Vogue. Ok, will do. Shipwide, or just Camaraderie?"

Alvarez looks over to Bethany. "Shipwide," she says.

"Shipwide, please," Alvarez says into his radio.

"Will do. Give us a minute."

"Thanks."

Up at a console in the security station, an officer accesses the maintenance section of the computer network, and is soon scanning the airducts. There are no security cameras in the airducts, but you can do a scan to check for foreign materials which may be clogging the fans or blocking the vents. He begins with the Camaraderie deck, for simplicity. All clear there. Escapade is clear. Royale is clear. B deck is clear. Flight deck is cl--. Wait a second. He goes back to B deck and looks closely at the monitor. What's that…..in the aft section…..some sort of mass mildly obstructing the air flow, so mild it is very hard to see…..and a concentration of carbon dioxide there, too…..even giving off a minimal amount of heat….and this heat being radiated is from long, narrow sections which are very close together. "Security station calling Alvarez, come in Alvarez."

"Alvarez here, go ahead."

"We've got something odd in the B deck ceiling airduct in the aft section, past midship."

Bethany becomes excited on hearing this from Alvarez's radio – she is a mixture of joy that her hunch was correct, yet tense as to what it may in fact mean.

"Just a minute, it's near a vent at the vault room. Weird though, it doesn't look like the shape of a person, and sure isn't giving off heat, except for these three or four pieces like sticks or something, hard to tell how many are there because they're so close together…" Alvarez looks at Bethany. "Wait a second," the radio continues, "this thing is *moving!* Sporadically, jerky. Two sticks just got away from the other two….wait a…..could those be *legs?*" A pause. "Oh, shit….oh, shit….."

"I'm on my way to the vault room," Alvarez says and he quickly begins to leave the Halo. Bethany follows hastily.

Jack and Diana McCartney notice. They discreetly follow the crewmen, on the hunch there might be a very interesting story here…..

Maddox and Angelique silently appear at the vent-cover of the vault room. They peer down to double-check – still empty. Yet, two guards are on their way according to Parker, and he has not said anything different since. The vent-cover, which is near the back-left corner of the room, is pulled in to the duct. Cli-clak. They hear a door open near them, above them. The door closes with a heavy thud. Two sets of shoes rapidly walking down metal stairs – the circular stairway which joins the vault room to the flight deck security station. The footsteps arrive at the floor of the vault room when a radio crackles. "Bekker! Bekker come in!"

Bekker stops and looks at his partner, confusion on his face – that voice sounds intense.

"Bekker here, go ahead."

"Alert! Alert! Get ou---" Swrizsh. The radio turns to static and the words are indecipherable.

"Say again? I lost you. Repeat your message."

Swirzzzzzsh. "Bek—you and—get ou—" Swirrzzzzsh. "The aird—" Then, silence.

"What's he talking about?" Bekker asks his partner frustratedly; the woman shrugs.

"I can't make it out," his partner says. "Let me try. Kharsis calling Security Station, come in please." Swirrrzzzzssssh. She looks over to Bekker. "Should we go back up there?"

Bekker's radio crackles again. Swirzzzzsh. "The aird---swirzzsh---ct! Someone is in the airduct!"

Bekker and Kharsis jerk their heads up to the ceiling, looking past the upper part of the circular staircase…the roofmount camera is nearby….and….

A black-gloved hand emerges from the vent, blindly feeling its way along the ceiling, prodded by a pushing forearm. The stretching fingers quickly locate the camera. Tampering occurs. Out at the desk, Parker watches as the monitor-image showing two shocked security officers skips, then blanks altogether. Inside, the hand is pulled back. Horrifying, in its own simple way.

Bekker and Kharsis look up, gaping open-mouthed, dumbfounded. Bekker reaches for the taser-truncheon holstered at his belt as Kharsis goes for hers….Maddox bursts from the vent! He drops like a ninja and lands squarely, then bowls forward and clamps Bekker at the knees, tackling him and sending him reeling to the floor. Angelique swings down like an acrobat, her hands firmly holding the edge of the vent, her long legs stretched out. She kicks Kharsis squarely in the jaw and sends the woman careening backward. "Ahhhhhhh!" Kharsis shrieks as she falls. Maddox lunges up and punches Bekker squarely in the jaw while keeping his foot held firmly on the still-holstered taser. "Argh!" Bekker shouts as he brings his left arm around to dislodge his attacker. Angelique kicks the downed Kharsis again, then falls knee-first into the officer's sternum, knocking the wind from her and causing her to black-out. Maddox still struggles with Bekker. Angelique spins and does a powerful roadhouse kick into Bekker's jaw - - there is a snap, and Bekker goes limp.

Maddox untangles himself from Bekker and stands, breathing heavily, to face Angelique. He smiles weakly, then gives a thumb-up to her. "Got 'em!"

"That we did, baby," she answers, and kisses him deeply.

He looks up at the vent, then back at her. "Ready?" he asks.

"Always ready."

Maddox kneels and cups his hands, one in the other. Angelique takes a breath, puts her hands on his shoulders, then her right foot into the stirrup formed by his hands. Maddox braces himself and stands, and in another acrobatic move, Angelique is boosted up to the vent. She disappears inside. A black rope furls down a moment later, along with several empty black knapsacks. As she shimmies down the rope herself, Maddox takes his personafōne from his jacket. He switches off the scrambler function which was jamming the radio signals, then types a message for Parker and Kobryn: "Visitors down by 2."

Parker smiles, then sends another message to the smirking Kobryn. She approaches the desk, then he deftly slides her the access-card, then she nods and, still smiling, walks over to the office door adjacent to the desk. Without looking at her, Parker presses a recessed button at the desk and electronically unlocks the door. She slips inside. With another tap from Parker's finger, the door is re-locked.

During this time, Parker notices DeSantis and Jensen enter the lobby from different parts of the alcove. Jensen casually strolls through the room, and stops near the door to the PCC while DeSantis inconspicuously leans against the wall on the other side. They each have taken position. They appear to be nonchalantly looking around the room, though if anyone would have been watching them, they would have noticed them directing their eyes to the steward at the desk every few minutes. Wait a second…Adrianna comes in to the lobby. Parker spots her. Ah, the little hellion, sexy hellcat. But she's with that chump she's been hanging around… "Adrian, we should be able to get some information at the Purser's D-" Adrianna says to Dade as they walk into the lobby. She stopped her talk when she spies the steward who she had spoken to before. Will he be able to help now?

"Bekker, Bekker, come in Bekker…" says a radio clearly. "Kharsis, Kharsis, come in Kharsis," barks the other. "Bekker or Kharsis, are either of you there?"

Outside, the deskphone rings. "Purser's Office," Parker answers.

"Macmillan, this is Chapman again in the security station! Have you seen Bekker or Kharsis? What about Kirsalis! Bekker's radio is out!"

"I can see the vault room plain as day," says Parker as he looks at a blank screen. "Two officers, a man and a woman, are talking in there." Actually, what is really going on in there, is that Angelique is half-way up the circular stairs to the Security Station. Maddox hovers over the body of Bekker, and tears the access-card from the man's jacket. He tosses it up to Angelique, who catches it perfectly and races up to the closed door. Angelique slams the access-card half-way into the slot at the door, then snaps it in half, jamming the lock from the inside, fusing it closed.

"Really?" asks Chapman, relief clear in his voice. He was just about to sound a security scramble alert. "We've got zip up here."

"Must be another glitch," Parker says.

"Can you go get Bekker for me?"

"Sure, no pr-" Parker stops as he sees two uniformed people rapidly walking up to him, one a security guard, another who by her outfit seems to be with ship entertainment. Parker composes himself. "Sorry about that. Sure, no problem. Can I put you on hold a minute?"

"Go ahead."

Parker clicks on the hold button just as Alvarez and Parris arrive. "Hello," he says warily.

"Hello," Alvarez answers with equal candor.

"Hi," says Bethany.

Alzarez leans over the desk, close to Parker, and notes the nametag pinned to the steward jacket. "There's something weird going on, Macmillan," Alzarez whispers. "You stay outside, with Miss Parris here, I'm going into the vault room."

Parker tenses. "The vault room?"

Alvarez nods sternly.

Parker makes a point at reading Alvarez's nametag. "The security station said someone named Bekker was coming to relieve me."

"Bekker must still be on his way."

Parker steps back. "What sort of weird thing is going on?"

"I can't get into it right now. Bethany can explain it. I'm going into the vault room."

"Hold on. Before I let you back there, let me check with the security station first."

Alvarez is taken aback for a moment. "Fair enough," he says after a minute, then brings his communicator to his lips. "I'll confer with them too." He turns slightly and Parris quickly glances around the room, and at an airvent in the ceiling.

"Thank you," Parker says. He slips his hand into his pocket and removes his personafône, which he keeps while reaching for the deskphone whose hold-light still flashes – neither take notice as he pushes a button on his fône and raises it, with the deskphone handset, to his face – allowing the handset to mask the small fône. "I don't mean to be a hard case," Parker explains with a smile, "just want to make sure we go by-the-book."

"I understand perfectly. I would do the same in your position."

"Thanks. It'll just be a moment, then we'll deal with you," Parker says.

"Alvarez calling security station," the officer says into his radio.

"Hello, Alvarez. Just a minute, let me put you on hold."

"Ok, no problem."

Maddox freezes – his personafône is vibrating. They have just opened the vault with the access-cards of Kirsalis and Kharsis, and the unwilling participation of the right thumb of the still unconscious Kharsis into a small fingerprint identifier, as they knew the impressive steel door would relent only when two proper cards and a corresponding thumb were inserted into its double-slot verifier. They watched with eager eyes as they listened to the tumblers turn and the levers click. Then, the massive door fully unbolted, and majestically swung out automatically on its heavy hinges as the internal lights clicked on brightly. "Open Sesame," Maddox had said with a smile and flare.

Now, this. Damn thing is ruining the drama of the moment. Maddox, Yusacre and Kobryn are in the threshold of the vault, bags-in-hand, ready to pilfer. In a flash Maddox's hand is on the device, and he answers. "Yes?"

"Hello security, this is Steward Macmillan at the reception desk."

Maddox cups the phone. "Damn!" he whispers, then looks to his compatriots, "Parker's in trouble!" Kobryn tenses visibly. Maddox pauses, then composes himself; maybe it is nothing serious. "Go ahead."

"We have an officer Alvarez out here who would like to go into the vault room."

"Ah, hell…"

"I just wish to confirm this is alright. What is your position on this?"

Annoyed, Maddox turns and goes to the nearby console. He sees tension in the other's faces. "Relax," is all he says. It does not do any good. Sitting at the console, Maddox looks at a monitor which displays the reception desk area. "Goddamnit, more complications!" he says in a harsh whisper as he sees Alvarez and Bethany. Maddox brings the föne to his face. "He wants to come in, what about the woman?"

"Only him, Sir. The woman he's with can remain with me out here."

Maddox turns to Yusacre and Kobryn. "We're going to have some company in a minute." He motions to the lobby access door, then goes back to his föne. "Ok, let him through."

"Thank you, Sir. Will do." Parker looks up to Alvarez and Bethany with a smile as he lowers the handset and his personaföne. "Mr. Alvarez, thank you for your patience. Please, proceed."

Alvarez nods. "Thank you." He turns to Bethany, then his radio speaks.

"Sorry for the delay, Alvarez, go ahead."

"No problem. Can you give me a 20 on Bekker?"

"Sure. He's with Kharsis in the vault room. Our monitor for the camera in there is out, but the steward can see them on the desk viewscreen. They're talking in there, on their way to the reception desk to relieve the steward."

"I'm here now. At reception, I mean."

"Yes, I can see you on the monitor. I'm on hold with the steward."

"You're on hold?" Alvarez looks at the steward quizzically.

"Yeah, he was going to go get Bekker for me." A strange look comes over his face as he listens. "That's odd," he says. Puzzled, Alvarez turns to see the office-door in the back wall slowly open inward – must be Bekker coming. But wait, the room inside is dark. Something is not right.

Alvarez steps back from Parker, even though a broad desk stands between them. He drops his right hand to his side and flips the catch on the belt-holster holding his taser. "Hold it, what are you doing?" Parker asks nervously as his own hand moves around to the small of his back. Alvarez continues, and steps to his right, to shield Bethany from whatever is going to happen. "Sir, what are you doing?" Parker asks again with more agitation.

Maddox appears at the office doorway. Alvarez turns, sees him, and the face goes ashen. Maddox has his handgun aimed squarely. "Don't move a muscle!" he says. Alvarez freezes, as does the wide-eyed Bethany. "Get the hand away from the cattleprod," Maddox orders, and Alvarez does just that, slowly. "You were so anxious to get back here, well here's your chance. Come on." Maddox motions with his free hand. "The woman, too."

Neither Alvarez nor Bethany move. Alvarez looks over to Parker, who is smiling widely. "Don't be impolite," Parker says, "you've been invited – take him up on his hospitality…"

I'd rather take him to the hospital, Alvarez thinks – but opts not to put his thoughts into words. Alvarez directs his eyes from Parker to the security camera. "Ah, ah, ah…." whispers Maddox from the doorway. "No auditions for tv today, buddy. Just come back here, nice n' slow. Bring your girlfriend." Alvarez still does not move, and Bethany remains still. "Come on, we don't have all night….get back here. NOW."

Alvarez moves. He turns suddenly and shoves Bethany to the floor. She screams and he hears a shot, then he drops down and reaches for his taser. Bethany screams and Parker brings his pistol around at the same moment, as Maddox steps out. Alvarez clicks on his taser and menacing blue bolts zip across its front electrodes as he rolls on his back, ready to face them. Parker leans over the desk, gun-first, to see the wide-eyed officer as Maddox opens the door between the reception area and the lobby, in rabid search.

The horrific scream grabs the attention of the crowd in the lobby. Startling, it is – most reflexively half-jump in surprise. Quick turns reveal a steward and a man holding guns on a downed officer! Guns! And a woman prone on the floor! Panic grips the crowd! They run in a mad frenzy, trampling one another, screaming, yelling, racing for the alcove.

"Drop it!" Parker barks as he aims. Maddox lunges at Alvarez, who swipes his taser, causing Maddox to jump like an Irish step-dancer. When he lands, he kicks Alvarez's wrist and the taser goes flying as the officer howls.

"Don't fucking move," Maddox hisses as he jams his pistol into the officer's face. "I shot once, and will be happy to do it again." Alvarez reluctantly relents. He winces in pain for his right hand while holding his palms up, and out. Maddox roughly heaves him up and throws him into Kobryn's waiting hands. Bethany gets up on her own and steps back from him, then after a gesture from him, sullenly walks into the vault room herself. Maddox jumps over and grabs the taser wand, holds it with a hand on each end, then snaps it in two over his kneecap and tosses the pieces aside.

Jack McCartney turns to Diana, wide-eyed. "Diana, baby, can you believe this!" They have ducked to protect themselves, and do not leave the room, but stay close to a door.

"A sinking cruiseship *with* gunplay. Goddamn incredible story." Her lips curl into a slight grin. "And to think, you wanted to go to Colorado!"

McCartney shakes his head and, pen-ready, turns back to the scene as Diana raises her vidcam with her finger poised to Record.

"What the fuck!" yells the officer monitoring the video screens in the security station. "Alvarez is down! And there's a goddamn stampede down there!!" The others quickly crowd around him to see what he is watching.

"What the hell!" Mueller barks. As he watches, he suddenly has a very good idea of how is responsible for the murders in the En Vogue. The officers keep their shocked eyes locked on the tiny screen. One person is jumping all over the place, with the back kept to the camera – can't tell if it's a man or a woman, but it looks like a man. The other is a steward! A Steward! With a gun! "That's the guy I spoke to not ten minutes ago!" Mueller says in disbelief. "Just like they say in those old books, always the fucking butler…" He pauses. "Everbody! Down there now!" Mueller yells. He is wasting his breath because his people are already grabbing gunbelts and heading out the door. Mueller quickly radios Davidovich in the En Vogue as he watches the melee. "Alex! Get to the lobby! Stat!" He next contacts the Bridge. "Captain, we have a situation. I am imposing the Homesafe protocol and will keep you informed." Mueller slips a passcard into a special slot and enters a special code and again the Bridge is sealed and it reverts to its self-contained life support.

Mueller grins slightly in spite of himself. "Hot Damn! Action! Boy, I haven't seen any <u>real</u> action since leaving the force…" Sometimes he admits missing the excitement the city streets offered the Chief of Detectives, but a legwound ended his time in active duty, so he accepted the interesting if relatively uneventful job as a Pursuer. But now, now there will be some true action, going head to head against crazed criminals! The very thought puts vigor in his blood. He grabs a gunbelt for himself, then races out of the station.

DeSantis and Jensen spring to life when they witness the altercation with the officer. They draw their pistols and move toward the office, but soon find themselves thwarted by a mass of screaming and hyper people running straight in their direction. They push and shove against the crowd, but are pushed back themselves. As they struggle, DeSantis turns and sees two security officers force their way past some crazed passengers and enter the lobby.

DeSantis waves and catches the eye of Jensen, then jerks his head in the direction of the officers, who are desperately trying to assess what is in fact happening. DeSantis and Jensen let themselves be swept up in the crowd, and are able to get behind these officers. DeSantis spins his pistol on its triggerguard so the handle sticks up, and Jensen does the same. DeSantis nods, and the two raise their hands, then bring their pistols crashing down on the skulls of the officers. Crrraakkk! The guards fall unconscious to the floor.

Maddox watches from the reception desk and gives a thumb-up. He then points individually to the stairwell doors and draws his forefinger across his neck in a slicing motion. They nod quickly, understanding that he wants these entrances blocked, or cut off. DeSantis pushes himself toward the port door, Jensen goes to starboard.

Maddox watches in utter silence. His face is etched with anger. "Fuck! Fuck! Fuck!" he yells in rage. Things had been going flawlessly...almost 'too good to be true'...they were in the vault, *in* it damnit....looting….and now, exposure! Damn it all to hell! The rest of the plan has to be scrapped, and they must revise once again. Tension. Resilience grows like fire within him. I *will* win. He shoots a look at Parker. "Go out and help those two. The cops will be down here any minute. We've got to figure a way out of this goddamn mess." He turns and sees Yusacre and Kobryn standing at the doorway, watching earnestly. Yusacre suddenly turns her head inside, toward the spiral staircase. Pounding, yelling from behind the steel door at its top.

She looks back at Maddox. "They're trying to get in through there," she says. "Not having much luck." She winks.

Maddox nods back. "Come on, we'll have to get ready for a fight. The vault will have to wait." The women nod and exit the vault room. Alvarez, Bethany, and the still unconscious Kharsis are all sitting on the floor, their arms behind their backs, handcuffed.

Angelique walks by, and Bethany can smell that telltale perfume in the air.

Parker rests his hand on the desktop and vaults over the polished wood surface. He lands solidly on his feet and keeps his eyes alert and his pistol raised just in case anyone decides to play 'hero'. Then, he stops – there is Adrianna, watching in stunned fear, along with that boyfriend…Parker smiles, wickedly, then spins off his silencer…bang! he squeezes off a round into the ceiling. "Wanted info, did ya?" he shouts to her. "Com'ere, I've got some news for you…a late-breaking bulletin…all the stuff you want! And more!" She turns and runs with the boyfriend trailing after. Parker laughs maniacally, then looks up at the bullethole in the ceiling. His eyes then happen to fall on the surveillance camera watching the room to the right. He aims his pistol squarely at the round lens. "Wrong channel, fuckers." The trigger is pulled. The camera explodes in a shower of sparks.

Maddox appears at the office doorway, gun drawn. "What in the hell?" he asks as he frantically scans the area. DeSantis and Jensen are heading to him, each hauling an unconscious officer. "There were shots...who shot? What's going on?" Maddox then turns and sees Parker, who is smiling and pointing at the smoldering shell of the camera.

"Technical difficulties," Parker says, then begins to laugh uproariously.

"Don't bother standing by," Maddox says, then laughs as well. By this time, DeSantis and Jensen have arrived. "Status?" Maddox asks as he ends his laughter.

"The stairwell doors have been jammed from the inside," the Mexitalian answers. "No one's gettin' in through there."

"Great. Let's stash and secure these two," Maddox orders. "You stand watch out here." Parker nods, then the three go into the vault room with the two knocked-out officers. Parker looks at the room – empty, just like the top of the pillar which had held the Hope Diamond. Kind of odd, to see this spacious area which he had never seen without at least five or more people milling around suddenly be empty. Through the alcove entryways, he can make out some figures, but they are well back and keeping out of sight. Parker turns back to the vault room door, hoping his partners in time return soon. He edges to the doorway, but keeps his face toward the lounge itself.

Suddenly, Angelique Yusacre appears at the doorway, with DeSantis following close behind. "On our way," Yusacre calls over her shoulder as she leaves; she turns at Parker and smiles. Once clear of the desk, Yusacre goes to the right, while DeSantis goes left, and they both hug the walls closely. On reaching the front wall, they stand flush against the corners adjacent to the lobby entrances at the alcove, watching and waiting. Maddox, Kobryn and Jensen then arrive at the doorway. "We better check the PCC and the Photo Studio for stragglers," Maddox says. He turns to Parker. "The vault is open. We've got a good start on it, you continue the job – but keep your radio on of course."

"Will do."

As the three go through the desk-door, Parker puts on his headset, then boosts himself on to the desk, swings his legs around, then drops down on the other side. He heaves up the lifeless form of Kirsalis, and hauls him into the back office. Gee, this place is practically a morgue! Parker thinks. A morgue, a prison, a treasure chest – all depends on how you look at it. He sets the body next to that of Bekker, and looks at the others, who gaze at him with unabashed hatred. He ignores them and hastily unbuttons the steward's jacket to give himself some breathing room, then smiles at his surroundings.

The office is a mess. Empty safe-deposit boxes are strewn all over the floor. Their tops have been pried off, and whatever valuables put there for safekeeping are gone. Several black knapsacks, overstuffed with bulging loot, rest at the wall. The vault is wide open; the three-layer thick steel door does not look so foreboding now. He looks again at the handcuffed officers. "Mercilessly ransacked, and stripped clean of anything remotely of value." He pauses. "Must add insult to injury, doesn't it?" Another pause. "So much for the former guardians…" he huffs and chuckles.

Parker looks around - - after all, how many chances will he have at this? There's kind of a thrill at being somewhere you shouldn't be, and knowing stuff you shouldn't know. The inner gate of the vault hangs loosely on its hinges. Its lock has been shattered. There are more deposit-boxes on the floor here, and the two large wall-safes at the back of the vault are open and empty. Parker leaves the vault and goes to the narrow hallway at the far end of the office. He walks to the end of the corridor, where the lobby's automated teller machines are housed. The back panels of the ATMs are on the floor, and the strongboxes which supply cash for the VacaBanks are gone. Damn, Parker thinks, they sure have been thorough. He is walking back down the corridor when he stops, thinking he had heard something. He puts his ear to the wall and hears some activity in the lobby. He runs to the office, believing he is probably needed now – or will be soon.

The stairwell doors are rattled and pounded on; shouts come from behind. Maddox, Kobryn and Jensen hurriedly approach the Photo Studio. Kobryn and Jensen raise their pistols and take positions on the left and right of the doorway as Maddox steadies his weapon and slips his keycard into the door-handleslot. He takes a rapid step back as the lock gives way. The three rush into the darkened room. The light comes on soon after, and following a rapid search, they exit, satisfied that the studio and darkroom are empty. Next, to the PCC. Same entry procedure. A bit more caution though as this room is likely occupied. And it is. Shouting, crashes and scuffling come from behind the closed door.

Loud voices are heard from outside the lobby. Beyond the two archways which form the ornate entrances in the alcove, people are being ordered to move aside. Yusacre presses the transmit button on her headset. "We've got company!" she reports from the left. "Looks like the boys and gals in blue wanna play."

"Yep!" verifies DeSantis from the right.

"This is the moment," Maddox murmurs. He clicks his transmit button. "Ok everyone, a pivotal time is at hand. The next few minutes determine the outcome of the mission. M and D, find some cover." They dash over to the two squat, potted juniper trees next to each wall. The fanned, piney branches provide an excellent cover. They position themselves so the trees are between them and the entrance and wait - - eyes glued to the archways.

"Cover found for us both. Watching." Yusacre says into her radio.

"Good." Maddox answers. He checks his organizer while walking toward a desk in the PCC. The news is not good. "Goddamn," he murmurs as he sits down and returns the device to his pocket. He looks up and sees the three comm techs, a woman and two men, disheveled and subdued, looking at the floor. "Any of you cause trouble," he says acidly to the already terrified people, "and getting off this wreck will be the last of your worries." They do not need to be told twice. He pauses and thinks.

The officers gather in the alcove. Davidovich came straight from the En Vouge, so he was there first. Mueller looks over his team and does a mental roll call; eight there, including Chapman who was pulled away from the station console, and a bandaged but apparently fine Simms. Mueller looks to Davidovich quizzically. "Can't raise the others on the radio," Davidovich answers, anticipating the question. "Must be incapacitated - they were in the area when the problem struck." The Purser nods, and is pleased to see his people 'at the ready'. It is pure luck that the majority of his force was up in the station working on the murder case when the terrorists made their move.

"Ok, here's the breakdown," Mueller begins. "They've got all the doors blockaded in there. God knows how they got into the vault room, or what they did in there – apparently they like to use the airducts to creep around, so watch the goddamn vents like your life depends on it. The current check shows all the ducts are clear, and if anything changes, a tech in the EOC will let us know – so for all intents, it's buttoned up tight. Since there are no side-doors or service tunnels that go directly from the corridors to the vault room, the alcove entryways provide the only way in, and out. We've got no visual – all the cameras have been taken out. Even when they were on, the scene didn't reveal that much. Kirsalis, Bekker, Kharsis and Alvarez are unaccounted for, as are Urvy and Cure, who were in the area but are absent now. I've told Mr. Rish what's happened. He'll keep passengers out of the area and do his best to speed up the evac. Also, the Bridge is on Homesafe."

"Sir, what should we do?" Watch Commander Reedy earnestly asks Mueller.

"We don't have many options, Reedy. They must be holed up in the vault room, like rats in a trap. We'll have to storm it," Mueller answers with a gleam in his eye.

"We're with you, Sir," Davidovich answers, and all the officers nod.

"Great. We won't rush in recklessly, but time is of the essence, so –"

Suddenly, the door to the PCC opens. Yusacre and DeSantis turn to see Kobryn exit, followed by the three comm techs with pillowcases cover their heads and their hands tied behind their backs. Jensen brings up the rear. The tiny group goes directly to the middle of the lounge, and stops. Kobryn and Jensen each tote rifles. They flank the trio they captured, and hold them under close guard. The gunners can be clearly seen from the entryways. The captives are the 'bait'; the question is, will the officers 'bite'?

The officers gasp at what they see. "What the hell is this now?" Mueller asks, the pauses and assesses the situation. Three crew with their heads covered. Very bad. Two identical women (twin criminals!) are armed and guarding them. "That one moves a bit like a man would, she musta been the camera saw. What about that steward? Are there other gunners in there?" A quick questioning of those who escaped the lobby does little good - - there was too much confusion when the shooting started for untrained people to accurately observe *exactly* what was happening.

"We'll have to start talking to them," Mueller says. "Dammit, I hope it goes well. Gow, get four and go to the right arch. We'll go left. Remember, keep watch on the airduct vents, that's how they like to move." All slowly approach and remain out-of-sight of the 'terrorists' in the lobby. Mueller presses himself up to the archway and peers inside. "You there! What're you doing?!"

"Fuck you. We ask the questions," Kobryn shouts back. She pauses to make sure her point is known. "The basic fact is, we're gonna keep these crew 'til we get off! We tried to nab a steward, he had a gun somehow, then got away. These weren't so lucky."

"Yeah!" Jensen calls. "We caught 'em, now we want *off*!" Mueller sighs frustratedly and shakes his head again. He has limited experience with hostage negotiations. The fact that the heads of the comm techs are covered is especially bad as this means the terrorists are trying to keep them disoriented, and may be trying to dehumanize them. None of the officers are trained for anything this complicated, since this is unforeseeable. They are educated on the finer points of crowd control, dealing with surly drunks, investigating robberies and con-men, and the proper apprehension and securing of stowaways within the guidelines of Interplanetary Law.

"H-H-Help us!" a sobbing comm tech shouts in panic.

"Shut up bitch!" Jensen retorts sharply.

Mueller decides to try his best at defusing this disaster in the making and bring a quick end to it. The Purser takes a deep breath. "Ok, ok relax," he calls into the lobby. "We can work something out."

"Ain't nothing to work out, Cop! We want off. That's it," Kobryn shouts.

"Is anyone hurt in there?"

"No. And we don't want to hurt anyone, either."

"I know you don't," Mueller answers encouragingly.

"It's just . . . I want to see my family again!" Kobryn sobs for effect.

"I know. Everyone does. I do too."

"I don't know what I was thinkin' ya know . . . we're just kinda desperate . . . I'm not violent by nature, you know, I just want off!" More sobbing. Louder this time.

"Let us get off this wreck," Jensen adds.

Some headway! If he can convince the women he is on their side, maybe he can persuade them to surrender peaceably. "Hey, I know where you're coming from. Sometimes we all go through rough times."

"Can we get outta this? I want out!" Kobryn sobs more to entice the officers.

"Yeah, me too!" says Jensen.

Score! Mueller thinks. Davidovich scans the alcove in back of the Purser's shoulder. Some curious passengers linger well behind them, but they are not causing trouble. He observes a man feverishly writing on an electropad, while the woman with him just hid some sort of device as his head turned. He makes a mental note to speak with them later. "Looks like we're on our way out of this, then?" Mueller inquires.

"I think so. Just a couple of jerks with guns. Ready to crack," Davidovich says.

"Ok, once we have them secured, up to the station! Fuckin' nerds, pulling a stunt like this at a time like this!" Mueller unholsters his pistol as he speaks. "Let's get 'em!"

"Yessir!" Davidovich whispers back. He feels the excitement of the moment surging through him. He draws his weapon, as do the other officers with him. Mueller holds his pistol high in the air so those at the other door can see it. They nod and similarly ready themselves. "Fritz," Davidovich says, "What about the service tunnels for the lobby?"

Mueller shakes his head 'no'. "A good idea, but our force is too small to divide up like that. Also, would take to long to send a team that way, and we don't want to startle these guys if we don't have to."

Davidovich nods and turns back to the lobby, then clears his throat. "Ok! Throw down your guns, and everything will be fine!"

"Promise?"

"You have my word!"

"O--ok, we'll do it! Remember we don't wanna hurt anyone!"

"It'll be all right." Davidovich looks at Mueller; the Purser's eyes are alive and his whole demeanor radiates excitement - - droplets of perspiration form on his upper lip from sheer anticipation of action. Davidovich notices his throat has suddenly gone dry.

Kobryn jerks her head around wildly, and darts her eyes even more-so. In this supposed spasm of nervous panic, she steals quick glances at Yusacre and DeSantis, who nod to her. Their bodies are poised to strike; they are more than ready. DeSantis looks around.

Where are Maddox and Parker? He directs his eyes to the Office. The lights back there are off again. Kobryn looks over at her partner. "You ready?" she loudly asks.

"As I'll ever be…"

"Ok!" Mueller interjects. "Set the guns down, nice and slow." With that said, Kobryn and Jensen gently bend at their knees. They carefully toss the guns, and the weapons land softly on the carpet.

The moment the weaponry is down, the officers charge. Mueller leads the assault from the left archway. Yusacre and DeSantis watch with squinted eyes ... point man rushes in from each side...first, swing and check the immediate area…"Clear!" ... middle men hastily follow, two from left side, two from right...next, end-man, bringing up the rear. As the officers go, they keep their attention concentrated on the terrorists who have jumped up and are standing – reach and subdue them in the shortest time possible.

The eyes of Yusacre and DeSantis follow the officers. Once the groups pass, they spring to life and race up behind the tailmen until they are almost on top of them. Yusacre jumps and karate-kicks her long right leg forward against the back of an officer so her boot-heel catches him between the shoulder blades. She knocks him off his feet, sending him flying into his partners while she lands squarely on arched feet. One raises his head, then she spins and gives a roadhouse kick to the jaw, sending him careening backward into a motionless heap. Yusacre blows a kiss to the toppled men at her feet. DeSantis bowls forward and tackles the officer ahead of him, likewise sending the man tumbling headlong into his partners. DeSantis jumps and in an instant both he and Yusacre are standing with pistols pointed at the fallen officers, who are a jumbled mass of arms and legs.

Mueller, Davidovich, and Reedy continue. The noise can be sorted out after the cuffs are on. Wait, the terrorists begin running toward *them!* Along with one of the masked comm techs!! Loose rope dangles from his wrist. Now he has a pistol! What the hell is this?

Pistols appear from the jackets of the terrorists, who leap forward. Jensen balls her hand into a hard fist then slams it hard on the inside of Mueller's wrist. The Purser's hand opens reflexively, and the revolver slips from his fingers. A second later, and the business-end of a pistol is slammed into his thick neck; "Still!" Jensen says. Kobryn is more direct: she simply shoots the gun out of Reedy's hand, then knocks him to the floor. This leaves Davidovich. He jams his pistol into Jensen's ribcage. Ka- Pow! A sorrowful look comes over Davidovich. He teeters for a moment, then falls dead to the floor. A smirking Parker emerges from the office, a thin stream of smoke drifting up from the end of his rifle. “Got him!” he shouts vigorously.

Maddox jerks the pillowcase from his head and looks at his team with a wide smile and raises his thumb high in the air: “We won!”

CHAPTER FIFTEEN
The 309

Darian Dade rushes in to his suite, pulling Adrianna in behind him, and slams the door. "What the hell….what the hell…." he gasps mouthfuls of air into his lungs.

"That topped the craziness, that's for sure!" Adrianna says with rushed breaths herself.

"What the hell…" he says again, then turns to her quickly. "What did he mean…info?"

"He was…" she breathes quickly still, "he was the one I asked about how the evacuation was going…back in the Halo…."

"Oh."

"Yeah, a big 'oh'." She shakes her head. "Of all the people I stop to ask, I get a gun-waving lunatic…"

"Well, we're safe here for now," Dade says, then takes a long, slow, deep breath. He slumps against the wall of his room, very confused. "Gunshots? What the hell is with gunshots?" he asks, even knowing she would not have an answer. She shrugs. Gunfire brings an entirely different element to the situation. His smile disappears. "Have to be ready for gunplay," he mutters, then turns and goes to his bedroom; Adrianna follows, curious. "For all I know, things may be resolved by the time we return to the lounge, but I'm not taking any chances." Dade strides into his bedroom and gives a longing look at the rumpled bedsheets which had been a playground earlier, then goes to his dresser. He pulls the top-right drawer open, and thrusts his hand inside. Nothing. Well, some clothes and other items there, but not what he wants. He slides his hand along the bottom of the drawer; maybe it has been moved. Again, nothing. He frustratedly jerks the drawer from its slot and turns it over. The contents fall in a rude pile to the floor, and he kicks some of the things around to be sure that nothing covers what he desires. It is nowhere to be found.

"Damn!" He curses as he throws the empty drawer on his rumpled bed. "What the hell am I supposed to do without my pistol?"

"Pistol?" Adrianna asks in a certain tone. "What pistol? You had a gun in here?"

Dade nods silently as he sits down on his bed and leans forward, putting his elbows on his knees. He looks at her, and sees the concern in her face. "Yeah. I like to have one around. Don't worry, I'm a pro, it's a hobby of mine, has been for years."

"No, no, don't get me wrong, Darian," she says with a wry smile. "In a certain way, I kind of find it sexy...."

Dade smiles. "Thanks. I never really looked at it that way before." She winks.

"Anyway," he says, then forces 'frisky' thoughts from his mind, and thinks about a more pressing subject for the moment. "I can venture a pretty solid guess who has my silver weapon. No doubt the same people - or person - doing the shooting spree upstairs had taken his gun. How in the hell could they have gotten in here? They may even have used his pistol for that crazy stunt!" She can see the anger seething within him. He racks his brain for an idea. "I should help, somehow, to help get things under control," he says, while considering how to fight the bastard(s), but where can he get a weapon? His eyes widen as an excellent source comes to light.

"I'll be back in a minute," he says while standing.

Confusion crosses her face, her eyes show tension at the suggestion. "Do you think we should separate?"

"We're only a personaföne call away. I'll be back before you can miss me."

"What are you up to? Why can't I come along?"

"Trust me, it would be better for me to do this on my own. Everything will be fine, and like I said, I'll be back soon." He puts his arms around her, then kisses her.

"Okay," she says with a faint smile.

"Thanks. Back in a jiff." With that, he kisses her again – on the cheek this time – then walks out of the bedroom, and she hears the suite door open and close.

The elevator doors part at Camaraderie. Dade used the aft-lift, as this puts him closer to his destination. He steps into the empty corridor. "The air is heavy here, warm;" he murmurs as it begins to bother him. "Gotta get what I came for quick." He trots to the rifle range and stops himself - - the door has visibly been forced open; it is cracked, broken; its knob hangs loosely in its housing. The door is slightly ajar. Dade can see the lights inside are on, and can also her two male voices speaking in hushed tones.

"Damn it to hell, what'll I do now?" he whispers, then creeps to the doorway and moves to peer inside. The door creaks slightly on its hinges without his even touching it; his closeness moved the air just enough for the door to sway. The moment the tiny sound is made, the voices silence.

Dade slowly backs away. One step. The door flings out! He is blinded by the bright light thrown on to his face, but can make out a figure lunging at him. Before he can do a thing, he is pounced on and knocked to the floor. His attacker hits him in the face and chest while the still blinded Dade lashes his fists out. Dade rolls their fight so he is put above his assailant. He continues to clobber as he raises his head and tries to clear his dazed eyes when he is grabbed from behind and pulled backward to the floor.

"Give up!" Dade is savagely told. Reluctantly, he raises his palms – the universal sign of defeat – if he surrenders now, he can survive the attack relatively unscathed and retaliate later. His vision slowly begins to clear as he is pulled to his feet. Dade shakes his head as he is pushed to the wall. Two men gather around him and for the first time, he gets a good look at them, and them, him. To everyone's surprise, they know each other.

Edwin Roggin and Cal Gregg look more closely at Dade, making sure it is who they think. "I know you," Roggin says as he brushes himself off, "I mean, I've seen you around . . . at meals and such . . . Mr. Dade, isn't it?"

Dade nods.

"I've seen him too," Gregg concurs.

"What are you doing, sneaking around down here?" Roggin asks.

"I could ask the same of you two," Dade replies cautiously. At this point, he is unsure if Roggin and Gregg are connected with the earlier 'activity' or not.

Roggin smiles; this fellow is smart, and he appreciates that. He decides to be wary of the wanderer as well. Roggin wants to learn as much as he can about this semi-stranger before he takes him into his confidence. He extends his hand amicably. "I am Edwin Roggin."

"Darian Dade," comes the answer as he takes the hand. Gregg follows Roggin's lead and thrust his hand forward while likewise introducing himself.

"We saw a group of three or four attack the security officers." Roggin closely studies Dade's face for the slightest reaction. "As near as we can tell, the officers are either dead or have been taken prisoner."

"What, prisoner?" A stressed look comes over Dade, who up until now has not realized the severity of the situation – and to Roggin, the reaction on the face he searches appears genuine. Nonetheless, on the off chance that Dade is a chameleon hiding his true colors, Roggin tenses himself as he readies to utter his next sentence. Roggin will pounce on Dade if the man reacts the least bit strangely to the words as he sounds the man out. "We came down here to find some guns."

Dade brightens. Some help! "That's why I'm here!" Dade sates with a broad grin.

"Well," says Roggin rather sheepishly, "the I guess I should apologize for, uhm, jumping you . . . you see, we thought you were one of them."

"No apologies necessary," Dade replies with an understanding chuckle and a reassuring handshake. "I'd have done the same in your position. Well," he slaps his hands together, "I guess we'd better get down to business!" His voice radiates enthusiasm.

"There's a problem," Roggin says dejectedly. "There are no firearms here! The place has been cleaned out." Dade cannot believe his ears; his face drops, and his enthusiasm dies. What will they do now?

It is at this moment Gregg steps forward. "I know where we can get some guns," he says with a smile.

While Dade makes connections, Adrianna sits in his suite. By this time, she has changed into a more comfortable pair of jeans and a white blouse – she found it had been good to keep a change of clothes in Dade's room, just in case. So now, she sits. "Can this be more boring?" she asks herself quietly. She never had been what one would describe as a patient person. She looks over at the dark entertainment unit. Sure, she could turn on the tv or the computer, but there is a good chance that a crewman or computer somewhere would notice that the unit had come on, then know someone was there..... She stands up and walks around the sofa, arms swaying in unison. She looks over to the verandah.

She smiles. Ah, yeah, that verandah....where Darian had done that mile-high-club thing.... That was fun. She sways over to the verandah, and walks through its open door. The viewport is closed, which is likely just as good considering what is going on...who knows what might be on the other side of that window. She looks down to the floor...yeah, right there. She winks. She turns to leave, and stumbles. She throws out her right arm to steady herself and her hand knocks a protrusion. She accidentally activates the scenic system! The meadow scene begins. "Shit! Shit!" Adrianna whispers and hurriedly tries to shut it off.....the bird chirps begin. Loudly. She had topped the volume controls when she knocked the pad. She anxiously taps the End word on the touch-screen control pad, and it ends. She breathes a sigh of relief. Knock knock. "Is anyone in there?" A male voice. Adrianna freezes, and holds her breath. Knock knock. "Hello?" Cli-clack. The lock is released, she watches as the knob turns. In walks a steward. He looks right at her.

"Miss?"

"I, I...."

He walks over to her. "Please remain on the shuttle deck, Madam."

"You don't understand, I,"

"Yes, Madam. Please come with me to the shuttle deck." He stands beside her and walks her out of the room as she rolls her eyes.

Minutes later, Gregg, Roggin and Dade arrive at the entrance to one of the compartments in the hold, where they face yet another obstacle: the door. A yellow tape stretched across it tells those who are interested NO ENTRY. When Gregg grasps the tubular metal handle and pulls, nothing happens. The handle does not move so much as an inch, the door is locked, as he expected. "Damn!" says Gregg, and he kicks the giant black steel door; his hit echoes within the vast chamber. Then, an engineer in an EVA suit rounds a corner and comes upon them. He pauses, looks at them questioningly, then begins to walk again, intending on striding right past them. But Gregg throws himself into the man's path.

"We need to get in there. Open the door for us, please."

The engineer looks condescendingly at Gregg and the two. "I'm sorry, but I'm not permitted to do that. Look at the tape. The area has been de-ventilated, and is unsafe to enter. Call the Engineering Operations Center and ask someone there to help you." The crewman then attempts to step around Gregg, but Gregg moves in front of him.

"We don't have time for that! It's an emergency! Open that goddamn door *now*!"

"I'm sorry, Sir. I'm not going to argue – I'm not going to let you in, and that's that." The engineer again tries to go around him, but Gregg blocks the way.

By nature, Cal Gregg is not a violent person, but when the situation calls for it, he can, and does, resort to brute force. This situation calls for it. In a lightening-fast move, Gregg slaps his burly hands on the engineer's shoulders and throws him to the wall. There is a loud crash as the heavy EVAS hits the solid steel wall. Before the man can recover, Gregg lowers his left shoulder and slams himself into the man's chest and pins him to the wall. The crewman's jaw drops and he gasps as his breath is knocked from him.

Gregg presses his left foot against his opponent's right calf then puts his hand on the man's right arm and pushes with all his might. The engineer loses his balance and falls hard to the floor. Gregg wastes no time in heaving the dazed engineer up; he clasps his hands around the man's neck and brings the bewildered face to his own. "You listen to me, Gregg rasps. "There's lives at stake here, and we need to get in there, so to hell with your regulations and unlock that goddamn door!" Gregg then forcibly turns the engineer around and throws him to the wall in front of the numeric keypad next to the door.

This time, the engineer decides to comply, and hastily enters the access code. After all, it is no skin off of his nose if these nuts want to kill themselves. There is a click as the lock is released. Gregg goes to the handle and pulls it. The door noiselessly slides open; the yellow warning tape stretches, then snaps in two as the wall parts. In seeing Gregg occupied with the door, the engineer quickly runs away. A clearly impressed Dade raises his palm to Gregg, who likewise raises his, and they give each other a 'high-five'. "Remind me never to disagree with you," Dade says with a grin.

They wait and allow some oxygen to drift into the compartment from the corridor. Dade takes this opportunity to stand to the side, and bring out his personaföne – Gregg and Roggin notice. "I left my girlfriend in my suite," Dade begins. "I told her I'd be back soon, just want to tell her I'll be delayed." Gregg and Roggin nod. "Adrianna," he whispers, and listens to the autodial tones. Ring. Ring. Ring. "Come on, come on answer," he says under his breath, then the voicemail clicks on. "Adrianna, it's Darian. I'm ok, but will be later than I thought. Call me when you get this. Thanks." He hangs up.

After waiting a minute longer, they go inside. Gregg leads the way, and as he enters, goes to the left and hits a switch. Ten powerful ceiling lamps light brightly soon after. The three stop and stare for a moment in awe. The cargo bay is like an immense warehouse, filled with tiers of shelves providing homes to every type of container imaginable, stacked from floor to ceiling. Gregg spots an emergency supplies case and tool-rack bolted to the wall. "This should have what we could use," he says while opening the large white case marked with the thick red cross. "Yeah, there we go." He takes three glass faceshields, the bottom of these being fixed with small green plastic jars marked 'O-2'. He tosses one to Roggin and another to Dade, then slips his over his head. Once it is fastened, he turns on the oxygen. "There probably isn't enough air in the cargo bay for us," his voice is muffled somewhat behind the faceshield, "but these will keep us going. An hour of air in each jar – we won't be here that long." The two nod, then Gregg removes two crowbars from the tool-rack; he keeps one, and tosses the other to Roggin.

Gregg walks down the center aisle, his eyes scanning from left to right, searching for a specific lot number. His partners follow close behind. Their footsteps echo hollowly in the massive chamber. "Here we are, Lot 118," Gregg says while stopping. The others stand alongside him; all three are in front of a six-foot tall wooden crate. The Gregg Arms corporate seal is painted in black on the front of the box, and beneath it are the stenciled words EDUCATIONAL SUPPLIES. "There, the package."

Luckily for them, the crate is at floor-level and at the front. Gregg jams the point of his crowbar into the left side of the box, while Roggin inserts his at the right. They push, and the top of the box's front is pried free. As it descends, the bottom end is pulled loose from the force of the fall. Gregg, Roggin, and Dade step up to the open box and begin pulling yellow packing straw out of it. They quickly reveal a wide, long, cylindrical black capsule. A Gregg Arms corporate seal, this time in yellow, adorns the front of this container. Gregg reaches in and pushes some yellow buttons on a square panel which is built into the side of the capsule. There is a slight hiss as the front of the cylinder slides back and to the right. They peer inside and see a gun-rack holding seven interesting rifles. Gregg carefully removes one and cradles it in his arms as though it is a newborn baby. "This is our new model, the CMG 309," Gregg says, his eyes locked in fascination on it.

"State-of-the-art firepower." He smiles and gingerly holds it up so Roggin and Dade can have a close look.

"This is like nothing I've ever seen before," Roggin comments.

"Me neither," Dade agrees.

The entire rifle is a shiny black. At the front is a thick two-foot barrel which has a multi-perforated flash suppresser and a fitting for a silencer at the muzzle. A short handle is at the barrel's mid-point, and close behind is the ammunition feed port. The trigger housing looks ordinary enough, though above it, a small, black rectangular box is attached to the left-side of the rifle's body. This box is engraved with miniature words stating RAPID FIRE PROPELLANT. A laser target sight is fixed on top of the 309, directly above the trigger mechanism. A long stock forms the back of the rifle; it has a curved shoulder rest at its butt-plate. A black carrying-strap is fastened to the front of the barrel and the back of the stock. The 309 is impressive. It looks mean. If looks could kill, this would need no bullets. The rifle is a top-of-the-line masterpiece of weaponry.

"I'm sure you've heard of the Thompson Submachine Gun, the AK-47, the Uzi, the Mac-10, the Coltson," Gregg says. Roggin and Dade nod - - of course, these are some of the best firearms in history. "Peashooters compared to these." Gregg reaches into the capsule, opens a drawer, and removes an unusually large ammunition clip which he slaps into the 309. Another clip goes into his pocket. Gregg slings the carrying strap over his right shoulder, and lets the rifle hang at his side. He then pulls two 309s and four clips from the capsule, which he passes to Roggin and Dade. "I hope you two appreciate the opportunity you have here - - many would kill to get their hands on these." They nod again, slowly.

"It'll be good to strike back against them," Roggin says while absently studying his rifle. "The fools. Just like lousy drivers, and idiots who talk during movies."

"One thing though," Gregg cautions, "keep in mind these are high-powered guns. The rapid-fire propellant just gives some kick in getting more rounds fired, in helping getting them into the firing chamber, it doesn't have anything to do with velocity or strength." The two nod. "Ensure the rifle is kept on LOW strength. Even then, a shot toward a sidewall could possibly cause a rupture." Nods again. "All it really means is that we have to be closer to our targets, that's all. Here, I'll reset mine." Gregg does, and Roggin and Dade watch, then imitate. All three 309's are put in low-fire mode.

"A question, Cal," Dade says as he loads his rifle, "why the crazy labeling?" He refers to the EDUCATIONAL SUPPLIES marking.

"Oh, that," Gregg says dismissively as he re-seals the capsule. "There's a regulation that sates firearms can't be transported on passenger liners. But I wanted these babies right along with me. See, I'm supposed to present them to a consortium of dealers on Mars, and I didn't want to risk them being lost or damaged - or worse - on some freighter. The ship's Property master would never have let us bring my friend here," he pauses at pats the crate, "on board, so we adapted, shall we say, with an innocent label and some creative writing on documents so we could skip the hassle."

Dade laughs. "And just what are these supposed to teach?"

Gregg chambers a round with a loud clack! "In this case, proper social behavior."

Up in the lobby, Maddox and his team release their hostage comm techs, and bring out the one from the PCC who had "leant" his uniform to Maddox.

"Get in a line, in the middle of the room!" Maddox orders the subdued security officers. Davidovich's body is left where it lies as a grim reminder to anyone who dare be heroic. Mueller cannot believe what had happened . . . they are now at the mercy of these villains.

Mueller turns his head and looks at the people surrounding him . . . the three men and their three female conspirators are identical in terms of height, build, hair length, hair color, and general facial features. Are they the result of some twisted fertility experiment gone wild? Then, Mueller realizes what they intend: if anyone now seeing them survives and gives a physical description to the authorities, they will be describing one person who has no particularly distinguishing characteristics. The terrorists can later remove their disguises once they are away, and likely be able to stand beside composite drawings of their alter identities without being recognized. Mueller has to admire them for their ingenuity, though at the same time he hates himself for it.

"Eyes forward!" a voice yells and there is a hard stomp on Mueller's right foot. The Purser snaps his head around and sees one of them standing inches from his face. The man has dropped the comm-tech uniform and now wears ordinary clothes. Mueller does not give him the satisfaction of seeing the pain he has caused - - the Purser keeps a straight face despite the throbbing pain in his foot. From the way the others act, it seems as though this one is the leader of their group. The man stares into Mueller's eyes - - only to find rage reflected back at him. If eyes could kill, the man would surely be dead on the floor. After a moment, the man backs away.

Maddox turns his face to the side and quietly speaks into his radio headset. Parker suddenly appears from the office, toting pairs of handcuffs, prodding along Alvarez, Urvy and Cure, the roughly revived Kharsis, and of course, Bethany Parris. He hurriedly passes the reception desk and heads straight for Maddox.

Parker steps up alongside Maddox and passes him the cuffs. "Everyone, hands behind your backs!" The officers do as told. "Mr. R, remember, guard these goons and shoot to kill if anything gets funny!" Maddox loudly instructs DeSantis.

"No worries here," DeSantis answers with an equal degree of volume in his voice. He also produces a stiletto from his pants pocket, and clicks it open with devilish glee.

"The ones from the vault room, get in line with your partners, at the end." Maddox watches them go, and sees Bethany Parris. "What's she still doing here?" he asks in a whisper to Parker.

Parker shrugs. "She was with him," Parker jerks his head in the direction of Alvarez, "when he showed up at the desk. She's with Cruise Entertainment."

Maddox looks at her again. "Let her go, she's just extra baggage. We could need those cuffs later if another troublemaker shows up." Parker hesitates, unsure if it is a good idea, then silently nods and approaches Bethany and unlocks her cuffs.

"What are you doing?" Bethany asks, nervously.

"Don't worry, you can go. We're just locking down the goons, that's all. Beat it."

Bethany looks at the guards, then back to Parker, but does not go. "Do I have to tell you twice? Get going before we change our minds." Bethany gives a plaintive look to the subdued security officers, then turns and runs from the lounge.

Maddox looks at the line of guards, and does a mental rollcall, with info based on his surveillance. "All present, except the three dead ones," he mutters. "Ok!" Maddox yells; sounding like some crazed drill-sergeant. "If any one tries anything stupid, all pay the price! Turn around!" The dejected officers, with their heads lowered in shame, silently turn. Maddox and his team close in; three on one side, three on the other. Each of the officers now experience a sense of disgust and further punish their already battered egos by reviewing recent events and contemplating what they should have done differently.

Maddox begins to walk down the line of officers as if he is a General reviewing troops. "Listen up you bunch of failures!" Maddox yells authoritatively; he twirls the cuffs in his hand. His teammates keep their fingers on their triggers and their eyes on their prisoners as their leader begins his speech. "WE are in command now. ***YOU*** do *whatever* we say *when* we say it! Cooperate, and everything will be fine; cause trouble, and well . . ." Maddox's eyes drift to the body of Davidovich and the officers follow his gaze. Maddox sees no need to finish his sentence; he has gotten his point across all to well. "We'll just do what we came here to do and leave. It's that simple."

By this time, Maddox has reached the last in the line. He turns on his heel and retraces his steps. He pauses for a moment behind each officer, just long enough to slap the rigid cuffs on the wrists, binding them. Then, he stands in front of each person and stares into their eyes to emphasize the words being said. "You are nothing. You're a pathetic version of fucking crossing guards!" His team chuckles. "You're a disgrace to your badges and what they represent!" Maddox pauses. "But there is one good thing about you," he wears a grin as he stops in front of Mueller, "you made our job one helluvalot easier."

On reaching Meuller, the last in line, Maddox grabs the Purser's arms with more force then needed, and there is a click-clicking of metal as Maddox makes Meuller's cuffs especially tight. Maddox brings his lips to Meuller's ear. "Not much fun, is it copper?" he whispers. The Purser says nothing to this, but looks straight ahead. He is seething though, don't kid yourself about that. He desperately wants to reach out and knock the smug grin off of the bastard's face, but he uses every fiber of his being to restrain himself, knowing he will only get a bullet for his trouble. There is one question nagging Mueller's mind that demands satisfaction, and he cannot ignore it. Although he is one-hundred percent sure of the answer, he asks anyway. "It was you, wasn't it?"

Maddox's face drops and a puzzled look comes over him. "What?"

"The murders at the En Vogue. It was you, wasn't it?"

"Oh, them," Maddox says offhandedly. He waves the air as though brushing away an insect, then shrugs. "Shit happens." Although Maddox continues at bravado, the Purser sees his guess has had an effect; the terrorist-leader looks somewhat disappointed at being caught on one of his unholy deeds. The man tries in vain to hide the feeling, though Mueller can clearly see that a spark has left his eye, and he seems a bit less cocksure.

Mueller brightens. He does not feel so incompetent now; actually, he is pleased with himself at being able to upset his adversary. Maddox sees the hint of a smile appear on the Purser. Maddox scowls, then without warning draws his right arm back and hits Mueller square in the mouth. Mueller teeters and almost falls; he can feel warm, bitter blood from his lip, which is already beginning to swell. This pain, however, does nothing to dampen Mueller's rejuvenated spirits. He stares at Maddox, who returns a long, cold look, then the terrorist turns his back. "Done!" Maddox yells.

The officers keep their eyes fixed on the floor. What's next? How much time will they have left at the hands of their captors? "M and O, you stay and watch over the loot." The officers cringe on hearing this; they can imagine loot-stuffed knapsacks dotting the floor and ready to go – this only adds insult to injury. They feel violated; the valuables given to them to properly guard…left in their care…are being deplorably described as "loot"….

Angelique and Jensen nod and make their way to the purser's office; Angelique stops as she passes Maddox and gives him a strong, sensual kiss on the lips. Maddox smiles proudly, and for a minute watches as Angelique and her sexy hips slither away. Then, he turns back to his group. "Left face!" Maddox barks. The group turns to their left, to the port side of the ship. "Walk go!" The sullen-faced procession marches forward; the terrorist team moving with them every step of the way. Maddox leads, and soon the group is in the corridor.

"What the hell is this!" Rish says, annoyance clear in his tone – more annoyance than what he would have liked.

Maddox stares at him coldly. "Just eliminating a problem, don't worry about it," he says succinctly. "Get out of the way." While shoving the first officer, Maddox walks to two shuttles that are being loaded, then turns. "I can't make you walk the plank. If I could, I would, believe me. Here's the next best thing." He motions toward a compartment door with his gun-hand. "Inside."

The security officers remain motionless at first. "Come on, get in there!" There still is no movement. DeSantis turns, having an evil gleam in his eye. A sinister smile creeps on to his face as he is consumed by a dark mood. The officers see the change in his demeanor: it looks as though a demon as risen from the fiery pits of

Hell and possessed their captor. DeSantis slaps his hands on the shoulders of Meuller and throws the burly purser inside. The man stumbles from the force, then falls to the floor of the shuttle as people inside scream and yell.

"Fuck you!" Mueller shouts in a gasp. "Fuck you to hell," he spits.

"You'll be going straight to hell if you keep that up," DeSantis snaps, then kicks the Purser in his side. As the man moans, DeSantis turns and roughly manhandles the next in line as Parker grabs the next as Jensen prods the others forward. Even with resistance given by some, soon the shackled officers are all tossed in and Maddox turns to Rish. "Time to dump 'em. Eject these fucks."

Rish stares at Maddox with hatred in his eyes, yet says nothing, then begrudgingly seals the compartment doors and launches the overloaded craft. Bethany watches as well, her hand raised to her open mouth in shock. Maddox and his team wait and watch as the shuttle leaves, then he again turns to the first officer. "Thanks, much appreciated."

Rish says nothing for a moment, then looks to the crowd. He knows interference results in bloodshed. "Everyone!" he orders loudly, "Stay out of their way!"

Maddox turns to his team. "Ok, back to that office." He presses a button on his communicator. "M and O, we're on our way back."

"Copy," says Angelica's voice.

As they go, Maddox speaks to DeSantis. "Your job was completely finished, correct?"

"Yeah, but just barely," he says. "There isn't so much as a slingshot in that range now. We stashed the guns in an airduct."

"Good work," Maddox says as he slaps his teammate on the shoulder. "I knew I could count on you two."

"Thanks, boss."

As they enter the lobby, Maddox turns to Parker and Kobryn. "You two go down to the suite and bring the stuff up here. We'll be going soon."

"Gotcha," Parker says with a nod, then he and Kobryn turn to the elevators as the others continue on. Kobryn punches the Down button. "Wait a sec," Parker says after seeing what she did. "We should wait and make sure they reach the office ok before leaving."

"Ok, fair," she says, then steps away from the elevators.

As Parker and Kobryn wait in the alcove, they see a small crowd of the curious, including Officers Rish and Hearst, peering from the archways and the side of the room. "If I wasn't actually experiencing this living nightmare, I wouldn't believe so much adversity could fall on a single ship," Rish mutters. "Hell, at this point, I wouldn't be surprised to see Rod Serling in all his slick cool emerge from the shadows and welcome everyone to an episode of The Twilight Zone." Rish pauses and thinks as Hearst says nothing. "I hope to hell these demented clones leave soon."

Parker and Kobryn notice how the crowd acts – with fear. Their egos overswell with arrogant pride; the act of supposed reverence makes them feel important. "Well, look at this, look who's got the power baby!" Parker says quietly, and Kobryn smiles. There is a ping and the doors to the middle elevator part, and Kobryn steps in the doorway to hold the elevator as they continue to watch their partners in crime. Maddox and DeSantis walk into the office, then Parker nods to Kobryn and they enter the elevator and leave B deck.

Adrianna was not in the lobby to hear Rish's order, or see Parker leave. She had managed to make it through a stairwell door, and sits huddled in a corner of the stairwell landing, needing a few minutes of quiet time. She relaxes and calmly evaluates the situation with a clear mind, though anger and hostility are not far off. She stands and dusts herself off then takes her personafōne from her pocket and – it's dead! She clicks the power button – nothing. She pops the battery from the rear of the device; the powercell indicator says – Recharge Required. "Damnit!" she whispers. How long has it been off for? Well, I'll go to my room and call Darian from there. She walks to the edge of the platform....

Thuck-thump. She freezes in mid-step, her foot poised over the first stair. The sound of the opening door reverberates up from below. Bang. The door slams shut. Thump. Thump. Thump. Thump. Quick footsteps are climbing the stairs. The sounds echo through the stairwell. It sounds like there is only one person, but Adrianna cannot be sure. Fear raises its ugly head again. What will she do? Thump! Thump! Thump! Thump! The noise gets louder, meaning the person/people will be at her any minute.

Adrianna slowly pulls her foot back to the platform. If she returns to the lobby, the odds are she will encounter the 'crazy steward' who shot at her - - definitely avoid him at all costs. On the other hand, she has no idea who is coming up the stairs. If it is one of the gang, she will find herself in another fight which could end in her death, or worse. Thump! Thump! Thump! Time is running out. In a split-second a decision is made – back to the lobby. At least there she can hide in the crowd; she is nothing more than a sitting duck in the stairwell. Adrianna quietly steps back to the door. She places her hand on the knob and slowly turns it, trying to make as little noise as possible. She opens the door and dashes into the room. The sound of footsteps hang in the air behind her.

Adrianna quickly joins a chatting group near the right wall. She keeps her head low and peers around the lobby. The 'steward' is no where to be seen. She is about to breathe a sigh of relief when she hears the stairwell door open and close behind her – she stiffens as she hears what to her is a terrifying sound. She waits for a moment and gently shifts herself so there are some people between her and the door. Then, a deep breath and slowly turning her head around in the direction of the door . . .

Darian! It is Darian Dade who has walked into the aft alcove. A wave of relief and excitement pours over her. She turns to him and smiles broadly, then stops the surge of emotion dead in its tracks as a question enters her mind: Can he be part of the gang? Wait, no. He doesn't look as though he is, he has no gun, and appears to be just trying to mix with the crowd. However, there is something strange about him though; his behavior is definitely odd. Despite an attempt at appearing relaxed, his tense face betrays anxiousness. He is definitely up to something. She decides to find out what.

Dade calmly strolls through the alcove. He can feel the retracted rifle resting against his left side under his tuxedo jacket. The muzzle peeks out slightly at the bottom edge of his open jacket, but not enough that people could notice it easily. The carrying strap is slung over his right shoulder, and he keeps his right arm somewhat stiff against the rifle to hold it in place. Dade walks to the front of the alcove and joins a crowd congregated near the left archway. A quick look over his right shoulder reveals that the similarly stiff-armed Roggin and Gregg have successfully entered the alcove. The three decided to enter from different doors so their arrival will not attract attention. They are each pleased to see each other. Things are ready, now all they need is for the terrorists to appear.

Adrianna comes up behind Dade, from his left, and playfully nudges his arm. Dade nearly jumps out of his skin at the unexpected touch. He snaps his head around and his nearly panicked eyes see

Adrianna. Any other time he would be pleased to see her; any other time but now. “Adrianna! What are you doing here?” he asks quickly, in shock and surprise.

His reaction is startling to her. He looks as though he has just had a heart attack. “Long story,” she says softly with a wary smile.

“I left you some messages,” he whispers. His throat is dry; it is difficult for him to speak.

She holds up her föne. “Sorry,” she says sheepishly, “the battery died on me.”

Dade nods understandingly. She reaches out to put her arms around him. He quickly shifts himself so she cannot touch his right side - - he remembers how she thought the pistol was sexy, but is unsure how she will react if she discovers he is ‘packing steel’, to coin a phrase. He lightly returns her hug with his left arm. Although they are together, it feels as though they are worlds apart. Adrianna does not understand why he is behaving so strangely. it is almost as though he is an entirely different man. Maybe he is a part of the gang after all? “You ok?” she asks as she pulls away from him.

“Yeah, uhm, great . . .” He manages to force what he feels is a genuine smile, but she sees right through the façade: something is bothering him. He leans over and brings his lips to her ear. “I’m working on something that I can’t get into right now, but everything is ok.” She nods, and decides this is not the time or place to begin an argument over whatever it is he is obviously hiding. “I want to tell you all about it, and will, but later.”

She nods. Until ‘later’, she will let him wrestle with his problems himself. And, if he is a member of the gang, the best place she can be is away from him. She turns and looks at him. “Super,” she says with a reassuring smile. “I’m going to get something to eat, and use one of those rechargers they have in the lounge. Want anything?” He shakes his head no. “Ok, I’ll be around if you want to talk.”

“Ok, great. Thanks sweetheart.” He smiles a third time, this time for real, glad that she is not upset, and not pushing the issue. There are not many who would be as understanding as she is being . . . Adrianna is one incredible woman. He leans over and lightly kisses her cheek, then whispers again, “Keep close to the walls, with your back to them. I’ll come find you in the lounge as soon as I can.” He gives her hand a firm squeeze.

She smiles and gives him a little kiss on the cheek, “Ok.” Then she walks away.

She now knows in her heart that Darian is not with the terrorists in any way. This relieves and elates her at the same time. She laughs absently to herself and shakes her head: how could she have ever thought that Darian would be mixed up with criminals? She enters the corridor and proceeds to the lounge; God, how I wish this was all over .

. .

I'm sure when I explains things later, everything will be fine, Dade thinks. His eyes linger on her as she walks out of the room . . . one incredible woman. Dade tears his gaze away from Adrianna and he looks back at Roggin and Gregg, who have been watching the incident with keen interest. Dade gives a quick nod, and they return it. Now the only thing left to do is wait for the perfect moment . . .

The bandits did not see the three new stiff-armed arrivals in the alcove. They are far too busy in the Purser's Office. Maddox and Jensen hastily close their overstuffed knapsacks while DeSantis guards the officers who stand against the back wall of the vault while Yusacre keeps watch at the doorway. "Ready here," Maddox says seconds later.

"And here," Jensen says. Both are set to move. Maddox slings two heavy bags over his shoulders, and wraps his hands around the straps of two equally heavy bags. Jensen loads herself the same way, though she carries the burgundy suitcase as well.

The people-turned-packmules slowly move to the doorway. They walk like they are on tightropes, knowing that a single misplaced step can throw them off balance and send their precious cargo to the floor. "Ang-" Maddox quickly stops himself and covers his mistake with a cough; he is not about to make any faux pas at this stage of the game. "Ms. M, you're walking point." Yusacre nods. "Mr. R will bring up the rear." DeSantis lowers his head in a long, single, slow nod.

Out in the lobby, Yusacre, Maddox and Jensen walk toward the aft alcove. Maddox nods; he turns to Yusacre and is about to speak, then suddenly stops. There is a message coming over the headset. He drops a knapsack and covers his left ear with his hand and listens intently. "(mumble) Kilo - Four duo going topside." To Maddox, this means Parker and Kobryn (duo) are on their way up to the lounge.

"(blurb) Four conf," Maddox says into his microphone. He turns to Yusacre and nods, then the team begins their walk. They tense as they near the alcove, keeping aware that retaliation is a real threat. Yusacre swings her head and rifle in unison left to right, back and forth, as she slowly walks. This way, her eyes and her piece are ready for any action.

As had been done with Parker and Jensen, an instant path is created in the forest of people each time Yusacre takes a step forward. The team heads for the alcove, and it does not take them long to get there. Dade slowly turns his head to Roggin, then Gregg. It looks as though this is the perfect time to strike: two are loaded down and therefore easy target; this cuts the strength of the group in half. Their escorts can be taken down relatively easily.

Dade scratches his left eyebrow with his left forefinger - - a movement which does not arouse suspicion, but a gesture which has meaning to Roggin and Gregg. The silent statement escapes the attention of the ever vigilant Yusacre, who is scanning the room with computer-like precision. Roggin casually turns and looks at Gregg; he scratches his left eyebrow just as Dade had, showing he concurs with the suggestion. Gregg gives a quick, almost unnoticeable nod to his partners: the time is now!

Dade tenses as he turns his face forward. His mouth again suddenly becomes bone dry, while his hands become wet with sweat. He swallows, and wipes his palms on his jacket, but neither does any good - - the inherent nervousness of the fast-approaching attack sends his metabolism into hysterics. His colleagues are likewise victims of the anxiety of the moment - Roggin wets his lips and Gregg takes a deep breath. They concentrate on the pact made earlier, that they will kill only if lives are threatened: their primary objective is to overpower the terrorists by wounding them and damaging their weapons. With anticipation running high, and their excitement peaked, they prepare to risk their lives and fight the terrorists. A simultaneous move to draw their weapons . . . their fingers are almost touching their rifles . . . any second now . . . ping! The noise stops everything dead.

CHAPTER SIXTEEN
Not just yet

The doors of an alcove elevator part and reveal a lone steward. He is bewildered. Everyone in the area is turned and staring at him, most looking shocked. Why am I getting all this attention? he thinks, and immediately becomes self-conscious, and sneaks a look to his pant-zipper; well, at least it is closed. Dismayed, and wishing to end the awkwardness, he gives a feeble wave of his right hand, and exits. The doors close behind him.

Bang! The crowd reflexively jumps, startled by a sudden and unexpected gunshot. They warily turn and face the four armed thieves. Maddox stands just inside the lobby, in plain view of everyone, his right arm raised, his hand closed around his pistol. He has just fired into the ceiling – the silencer had been removed, and a divot marks where the pellet hit before dropping to the carpet, and he has gotten the anticipated response. He keeps his arm raised for a moment, scanning the group of terrified people. The slightest hint of a grin creeps to the left corner of his mouth, and as quickly as it is there, it vanishes. A smile can cost him authority in the eyes of his captives. And that he does not want to lose.

Maddox slowly, menacingly lowers his hand, and returns his pistol to the inside of his jacket. He quickly looks at the three who flank him. Yusacre and DeSantis have their rifles at the ready, poised to shoot at the slightest provocation. Even loaded with the sacks, Jensen still looks volatile, full of angst and ready to drop her cargo and charge into a fight. Maddox turns back to the people gathered just outside the archways.

"Now that the little distraction is over," he begins, speaking acidly; the steward cringes in spite of himself, "it's time to get things straight. WE ARE IN COMPLETE CONTROL. You have no hope of being rescued. No one is going to help you. No white knights, no cavalry, no fearless superheroes. You're trapped stone cold." Maddox deliberately pauses and lets his words sink in. Roggin, Dade and Gregg can feel their trigger fingers itching, twitching to take these bastards ... but no, bide the time until the right moment.

People stare back at Maddox and his team with dismal eyes on hearing the words, at having the essence of the nightmare which has gone from bad to worse slapped in their faces. Some look dejectedly to the floor. Maddox knows his words are having the desired psychological effect; depressing them, draining them of individual will, crushing whatever futile attempts at resistance which some with vigilante spirits may be toying with in the backs of their minds.

"But don't despair," Maddox continues, "there is still a way out for you." Spirits rise at this glimmer of hope - - "Just do as we say. EVERYTHING we say. ANYTHING we say. WHEN we say it. Let us do our thing and be on our way and no one will be harmed. You can go back to your little lives in the suburbs, and have one hell of a story to tell your relatives, friends, neighbors, the media, and even your grandchildren. However, try to stop us, and, well . . ." his voice fades. "Danger!" Thokk! Thokk! Two rifles fire simultaneously as Yusacre and DeSantis instantly took their cue from Maddox's barked alert. Next, two loud CLACKS as new rounds, fresh and deadly, are slammed into waiting chambers. The point is made, effectively, coldbloodedly.

Maddox's hand disappears into his jacket pocket, and emerges with a compressed white bundle. With a swipe of his hand, it unfurls as a pillowcase. Jensen notices this, and does likewise. "Now, ladies and gentlemen," Maddox says, "my friend here and I are asking for contributions to our favorite charity - - us." The bandits smile. Audible groans are heard from the crowd. "Don't be bashful, we're glad to accept whatever cash and coin you have, keep your baubles. And, oh, don't try and tell us you gave at the office . . ." Yusacre, Jensen and DeSantis chuckle, " 'cause we know you didn't!"

Maddox looks to Yusacre then jerks his head in the direction of the Port archway. As Yusacre begins to walk over, Maddox indicates that Jensen and DeSantis are to take the other portal. In seeing them go, he strides up behind Yusacre. The four step into the alcove. The rifletoters proceed slowly, just ahead of their escorts, who have their left hands tightly clenched around the top edge of the pillowcases and their pistols in their right hands - - just in case. The collection begins. The bandits are only interested in hard currency because they know that intercash and credicards can be almost instantly deactivated, and, they are not interested in the problems of fencing jewelry.

People in the alcove are tense; Roggin, Gregg and Dade even more-so. Although their tuxedo jackets camouflage their rifles well enough, if the thieves pat them down, or even so much as nudge them, the presence of the CMG 309s will be revealed. As well, in the motion of removing their watches and items, the jackets may be pulled, and in so doing may expose the bottom ends of the gunbarrels. What will they do? What can they do?

Jack McCartney puts his electropad at his back and gently lets it slide down to the floor between his legs and the wall. He then shifts his feet slightly and nudges the pad behind a silver, pillar-type wastecan, while his pen disappears into his jacket. Diana closes her compact vidcam, then as Jack moves slightly in front of her, quickly buries it in the paper-filled wastecan. "It'll be ok," she whispers into his ear. He nods and squeezes her hand as she moves alongside him.

Yusacre and DeSantis walk slowly, watching the tiny crowd like hawks through the well-practiced eyes of sentries, spying for any potential threat; one suspicious person or gesture which would betray an impending assault against them or their partners. Although the people seem docile enough, one can never be sure . . .

Maddox and Jensen make quick and easy progress. People are cooperating, surrendering their cash into the open mouths of the pillowcases without hesitation. Many keep their eyes locked on the floor, in fear, or shame, or both.

Dade watches the thieves. They are so alert. The gunners scan the room regularly, making sure nothing escapes their attention, but do not follow any fixed pattern when their eyes roam, so it is impossible to guess where a lag would be in order to make a move for his money. The bagmen move rapidly, and he is relieved to see they are not "frisking" anyone for hidden valuables. Roggin and Gregg have already managed to give up their items without revealing their rifles, which is encouraging. Dade notices a bagman, the one who did the talking and appears to be the leader, approaching him. The man to his left begins murmuring; a babbled whisper. It almost sounds like a muffled prayer.

Maddox is pleased at how well things are going. Soon they will be in the corridor, and before long off of this ship with their precious loot. Exhilarating!

Dade readies himself for the most testing part of the moment -- the removal of his moneyclip from the left inside pocket of his jacket. If there is any movement which will raise the bottom end of his jacket, this is it. He takes a deep breath, and slowly slips his right hand behind the satin lapel.

Yusacre takes note of a man coming up in the line. The robbery must be too much for the poor fool who is muttering to himself. He could be trouble. Yusacre continues to scan the entire room, but makes sure her glance rests on this threat, diversion, or whatever it may be, every few seconds.

Dade closes his fingers on the moneyholder, and lifts it out of the plush pocket, using all his strength to keep the shifting of his jacket to a minimum. The cash is safely delivered to his left hand. The hushed phrases of his neighbor suddenly end.

Yusacre notices that "Mr. Whispers" goes silent just before she crosses him. The sudden proximity of the rifle probably encouraged the quietness. Maddox steps to the man, holding the pillowcase open. The man complies, dropping small wad of bills inside. Satisfied, Maddox steps away. "Fucking bastards," the man whispers.

In a whipcrack move Yusacre sidesteps Maddox and slams the butt of her rifle into the midriff of the insolent passenger. The man howls in pain and doubles over, only to have the rifle crash into the left side of his jaw. He winces, and can feel jagged shapes against his tongue, and a rivulet of blood instantly forms at the corner of his mouth. He reels to his right . . . straight into Darian Dade.

Dade shifts so his left side takes the brunt of the collapsing man. Dade is pushed by the force but keeps his footing. He feels the rifle jostling under his jacket; it moves solidly against his torso, but remains hidden under the black wool. Roggin and Gregg keenly watch the incident, their right hands poised and ready to draw their guns at a moment's notice. Dade rests his hand on the man's shoulder and steadies the moaning, nearly weeping figure. He pushes him away, and is actually aided by the rifletoter who roughly grabs insolent passenger by the front of his shirt and hauls him toward her. She looks at him with a mean face, then with a hard shove against a well-placed foot, the passenger goes falling backward. The right hand of the riflegirl is instantly back at the trigger of her gun as she stands tall and proud above the cowering figure, and a smirk appears on her.

Maddox looks at Yusacre, then at the whimpering passenger, then back at Yusacre. "Ok," he says - Yusacre turns toward him. "Proceed." Yusacre nods, takes a final glance at the passenger, smiles slightly, then takes a step forward. DeSantis and Jensen had paused at seeing the skirmish, but at a nod from Maddox, they resume their activity. An important lesson had just been taught to the captive passengers. Maddox steps over the body, and moves on to the next in line.

The pillowcase appears in front of Dade, its top held open. He avoids the look of its holder as he drops in cash – which somehow remained in his left palm - into the small white sack. Satisfied with the deposit, Maddox moves on without thinking twice about who for him is just another face in the crowd. Some minutes later, the alcove group is finished. DeSantis and Jensen gather at the archway of the starboard corridor, while Yusacre and Maddox stand at the other. "Ready, let's go," Maddox radios, and they enter the hallways.

Yusacre and DeSantis are the first out. They raise their rifles, take aim, and fire a single shot down the length of the passageway. Screams and shouts bellow out as people cower, and duck. After a moment, identical orders come from Maddox and Jensen. "People in the lifecrafts! Out!" At first, no movement. "Everyone out!" This time there is dismal compliance, and people appear; pale, hands raised in fear, slowly exiting the shuttle which a minute later would have been their ticket to rescue. "Against the wall! Now! Go!"

DeSantis uses his rifle like a prod, and people back away from the weapon in fear. Second Officer Rayburn, stationed at Starboard-aft, steps in front of the two and gives a harsh look. "Just what the hell do you think you're doing? There are lives at stake here!"

"After we're through you can continue your errand of mercy," DeSantis replies coldly. "Now, move!" He puts his hand on her shoulder, turns her around, and prods her forward.

Yusacre and DeSantis begin their march to the bow, followed closely by their partners, whose pillowcases fill with money surrendered by nervous passengers and crew who have their backs up against the wall and retrieve sequestered cash. The teams move quickly, and take radios from Officers Rish and Hearst when they come upon them, but not before Rish sends a brief message to the captain. Soon, all four are in the Halo.

In the alcove, Diana McCartney retrieves her vidcam. Jack likewise grabs his electropad. They slowly, cautiously, move to the starboard archway, peer around, then enter the corridor, following the path of two bandit-terrorists.

"It's not over, not just yet," Bethany Parris whispers, "not by a longshot, believe you me." She is outside the green room of the cruise entertainment/theatrical productions prep area in backstage of the Cosmos, having snuck down there after the security officers were removed from the vessel. With her passcard, she enters and…disarray! Somebody has been down there, rifling through some of the makeup kits. She shakes her head in annoyance, then walks through to the section she wants, the special effects/prop room.

Here, everything is in order. Labeled shelves, drawers and closets are all closed, and there is a clean and organized work desk. Bethany smiles and reads the labels; unsure exactly of what she is looking for, but when she spies it, it will jump out at her and spark an idea. "Let me see….something to immobilize them long enough to at least disarm them." She opens one closet and pulls open a drawer inside it. Guns. Small pistols, and automatic rifles neatly arranged – and as fake as the wigs in the green room. Bethany picks up a pistol; it is somewhat heavy, and sure looks real enough. She puts it back. "No, can't go there – too dangerous to try and bluff them." She looks around; there must be something… Wait. That could work. Yeah, that too. And, oh, more! She takes two of each of anything which could be helpful and that is easily portable. She turns and gets a canvas carry-bag and begins to load it.

With her precious bag held tightly in her hand, Bethany leaves the staging area. She intends to go up to the flight deck, to the security station to get a taser-wand so she can have at least one real weapon to defend herself, if need be. She quickly but quietly walks out into the darkened Camaraderie deck, every now and then looking to the ceiling – to the airvents, and making sure she sniffs the air routinely to check for that perfume. She shivers momentarily, from the nervousness of it all. She goes to the elevator bay and clicks the UP button, wanting to escape from there as quickly as possible, and also to save time. She will go up to the Royale deck, and from there take the stairs to the flight deck.

"Come on, come on…" she mutters. Ping! The doors of the middle lift open. Her jaw drops. Inside, is the steward from the purser's desk and a woman! Bulging knapsacks are slung over each of their shoulders, while other bags are held firm in their hands. Black leather belt-like straps stretch diagonally across their torsos, holding rifles snug against their backs. "What the fuck!" Parker bellows. "You!"

Bethany jumps back and Parker storms out with Kobryn behind, both laden down with their bags. Parker drops what he can of them, as does Kobryn. "I knew we shouldn'ta let you go…." Parker says angrily. He lunges for her, and Bethany jumps back again and spins on her heel then tears off into the darkness offered by the deck. Parker moves after her, then stumbles on one of the knapsacks on the floor and falls. "For fuck's sakes!" he says, then looks up at Kobryn and stands. "That explains it, why we were moving down after we didn't have enough time to hit the up button ourselves. It brought us to her. What the hell could she be up to?"

Kobryn shakes her head. "Beats me. She had a bag too, did you see it?"

"Yeah, I saw it." Parker angrily kicks a knapsack. "We'll have to go get her."

Kobryn nods. "What about the stuff?" she asks.

"It'll burden us too much. We'll have to leave it here for a minute." Parker gets an odd look from Kobryn. "Yeah, I know, but there's not much else we can do." He tosses the bags into the corner. "That'll have to be our stashing place for now. Let's go." The two tear off down the shadowed hallway.

"Get out here, bitch!" Parker yells. Bethany holds her breath and remains still, hiding. "Where could she be?" he shouts over to Kobryn.

"I don't see her. Hope this doesn't take long. It's hot down here."

"No shit." Parker pauses. "Come on out!" he yells again. Bethany keeps her eyes locked on them, and does not move a muscle. She breathes heavily, audibly; rapid, tense breaths. Parker continues to walk, and nears her. He cocks his ear, and turns his head. "Look! That door…ajar!" He turns and looks to Kobryn. Together, they move to it – he jerks the door open, and the area behind the portal is pitch black. Bethany gasps, then clamps her hand over her mouth and holds her breath. "What was her name," Parker whispers to himself, "that security guy said it…." He pauses and smiles. "We know where you are, Bethany," Parker says with a calm tone, though it still sounds menacing. "Make it easy and come on out here." Bethany tenses and bites her lip. "We'll come in after you if we have to." Parker waits a moment, then looks over to Kobryn, who nods. "Ok, you asked for it bitch!" They charge into the room.

Bethany jumps up. From her secluded place in a curve in the hallway, she bolts. She runs up and grabs the door. Slam! Click – it is locked. From the outside. "No, you asked for it," she says with a smile of accomplishment that her lure worked. She looks up and reads the flashy graphic sign fixed to the door. ZeroZone, it says.

Parker and Kobryn both jump, startled when the door closed behind them. The click of the lock does not make them feel that much better. "What in the hell?" Parker asks.

"Where are we?" asks Kobryn, nervousness in her voice.

Parker turns and takes a step toward the door. His foot goes up, but does not land on the floor – instead, it feels like he stepped on a cushion. "Wha?" Then, he rises. So does Kobryn. The lights come on in the room. Bethany is standing outside, at the small glass window of the door, smiling at them. Then, she steps away.

"Hell, it's that anti-gravity room!" Kobryn yells as she goes higher.

"Let us outta here!" Parker shouts as his body floats up and up. He pulls his pistol and shoots at the door, but the bullet harmlessly bounces off the metal panel after making a harmless divot, then the smashed pellet itself begins to float. He turns himself upside down and claws at the air with his hands while kicking his feet, trying to swim, trying to move down, but it does no good. Kobryn tries to stop herself by reaching for the walls, but they are smooth and without handholds. Soon, they are both at the ceiling, floating in the air.

"Have a nice flight," says Bethany's voice over a hidden speaker – the same speaker which had carried the increased noise of her heavy breathing as a ruse, then there is a click as the speaker goes off. Sitting at the ZZ office controls, she makes some settings, then leaves.

"Bitch!" Parker shrieks.

Maddox walks in to the Halo, fully expecting to have Parker and Kobryn waiting for him. They are no where to be seen. "Those two should be up here by now," Maddox says to Angelique as they walk into the Halo; concern is evident in his voice. He clicks on his radio headset. "Kilo calling four, come in four."

There is silence for a moment. "Four here, Kilo." The voice is sheepish.

"Location check, four." Silence again, for too long. "Location check, four." There is an edge in Maddox's voice the second time.

"On the Camaraderie deck." The voice is still as sheepish.

"What in the hell is he doing there?" Maddox asks Angelique in an angry whisper. He turns back to his radio-set. "Four, come up to Halo with O." Silence again.

"Four, did you copy?"

"I copied." A pause. "O and I are stuck."

"What?" Frustration is rising in Maddox. "Stuck where?"

"We, uhm, got bushwacked. We are trapped in the ZeroZone amusement."

"ZeroZone? That anti-gravity thing?"

"Affirmative. We are locked in here."

"LOCKED IN!"

"Yes, we need some help, Kilo. It's a long story."

Rage is in Maddox's eyes. He hastily waves over DeSantis. "Do you know where that ZeroZone place is?" he asks as the Mexitalian arrives.

"Yeah, on the Camaraderie deck."

"Get down there. Parker and Kobryn are stuck in there somehow."

"What?"

"I know, it's fucked. Go down there and let them out."

"On my way. Should I bring Ruby?"

"Yeah, Parker says they were ambushed. Keep alert."

"Gotcha." DeSantis says, then heads back to Jensen.

"Four, be advised that R and N are on their way to help you," Maddox says into his radio.

"Thank you, Kilo."

"Fuck you, four," Maddox says under his breath.

DeSantis and Jensen step off the elevator at the Camaraderie deck. On his right, DeSantis spies the pile of knapsacks. "There has to be some kind of weird story behind this," he quietly says to Jensen.

"I'm just glad I'm not in their shoes right now."

"I hear you." The two board the speedwalk track and hastily move down the deck, with their guns ready, and keeping their senses wary – as Maddox had warned. Soon, they are at the ZeroZone. They approach the steel door, and look through its window. Empty. DeSantis speaks into his radio. "Four, this is R at ZeroZone. Where are you?"

"We're in here."

"Can't see you."

"We're stuck up at the top of the fucking thing!"

DeSantis and Jensen peer up through the window, and barely see two figures suspended in the air at the ceiling. They look to each other and chuckle. "Ok, we have a visual on you," DeSantis says, trying to stifle his laughter. "How's the weather up there?" More snickering follows.

"Cut the fucking comedy and get us down," Parker snaps.

"Ok, ok, will do," DeSantis answers. He turns to Jensen. "Stand guard here, I'll see what I can do." Jensen nods, then DeSantis goes to the control room adjacent to the main door. He tries the handle; it is locked, of course, so he shoots the doorknob and lets himself in. DeSantis sits at the console, and takes a few minutes to learn the controls. "Woah, whoever set this up didn't want them out anytime soon." He makes some adjustments. "Ok, this should do it," he says, then does some fine-tuning, and as he watches through a monitor, the antigravity gradually reduces, easing Parker and Kobryn to the floor gently. The two stand on the ground, happy to have solid-footing once again. A mixture of anger and embarrassment, they look at the door. DeSantis unlocks it, and holds it open for them.

"Thanks," Parker mutters. Kobryn nods.

"Anytime, amigo," DeSantis replies. He closes the door then the four make their way back to the elevators. "Kilo, this is R," DeSantis says into his radio. "Got them, safe and sound. On way to Halo."

"Copy, R."

Maddox and Angelique wait near the elevators at the Halo with a large pile of loot – knapsacks from the vault room, and pillowcases of cash, including a new one filled with 'accepted donations' from those in the Halo, gathered in the same way as in the alcove. Both are a bit nervous, and they stand guard tensely with weapons raised.

Soon, a tone sounds and the doors of the middle lift part to reveal Parker, Kobryn, DeSantis and Jensen. Parker and Kobryn do not look as arrogant as when they left the lobby. For one thing, they are again loaded down with many knapsacks, so they do not have easy access to their weapons, meaning they are vulnerable. Second, the ambush unnerved them slightly – their faces are a mixture of fierceness and fear. They attempt to look angry and intimidating, but also betray nervousness they try to hide.

Like everyone else in the lounge, Adrianna turns toward the elevators. She is standing near the right wall with a small group of people. The steward! She turns, and while keeping her back to Parker, she slowly, calmly, shifts to a large potted philodendron next to the wall. Fortunately, she saw him first, and Parker has yet to look in her direction. In a swift move, she ducks behind the plant. Keep under control…will the building panic from the mind. For the moment, she is safe behind her leafy shield. She cautiously peers through the foliage which stands between her and certain trouble. She locks her eyes on the steward and watches his every move. All she can do now is wait. Wait for the 'steward' to leave...

Maddox and Angelique are the only ones pleased to see the new arrivals. Now the team is free to leave the nightmarish reality of the space-aged deathtrap named *Emprasoria*. "It was the Oth-" Parker begins, then Maddox raises his hand and silences him.

"We can deal with it later," Maddox says with an easy smile. He is still angry, but does not let them know it. "F and O, glad to see you are free and ok – and glad to see the packages are safe and sound too." Parker and Kobryn visibly look relieved, and smile. "Ok people," Maddox continues with a grin, "time for our getaway."

Minutes ago, back in the alcove, Dade was stressed. That unexpected interruption of the elevator there had shattered his concentration. Then, the humiliation of the person-by-person visits. And what about Adrianna? Where is she? In looking at Roggin and Gregg, Dade can guess by the wild looks in their eyes that they share his mind-boggling feeling of intense disappointment. There they had been, on the threshold of the attack, when their battlespirit was delayed. And now, the thieves are gone.

Dade, Roggin and Gregg meet near the middle of the alcove as other passengers sullenly mill about in the tiny room; Mr. Whispers still cowers on the floor, shunning away the few who do approach him.

"Damn it all to hell!" Gregg says harshly as he slams his right fist into his left palm. Anger is clearly shown on his face. "We were all set! Damn it!"

"Yeah," Roggin concurs, "perfect opportunity just slipped through our fingers. I hate to lose, goddamnit."

Dade shakes his head frustratedly. "Could have been good."

Gregg looks at Dade. “You’re goddamn lucky, pal. That was a helluva close call!”

Dade nods. “Yes, it was tense there for a minute.” He absently pats his rifle under his jacket. “But everything is ok.”

“True,” says Roggin, “we still have the hardware, and none of us are hurt. We’re still as ready as we ever were, we just have to track them down and go again, that’s all.” His partners nod in agreement.

“We better get after them fast,” Gregg comments, “before they get too far ahead of us and we lose ’em in the ship.”

“Right,” says Dade. “How should we go?”

“They split up, so we’ll have to split up,” Roggin begins. “Not the best plan, but what other choice do we have? We’ll follow them, and if we’re lucky, will meet up again and fight together. If not, well, every man for himself, as they say.”

“I’ll wager they’ll converge somewhere and then we can take them,” Gregg offers. The others nod. “Stalk the enemy, bide our time, strike at the best opportunity. Agreed?”

“Agreed,” says Roggin.

“Here, as well,” Dade remarks.

Then, a plan is formed. Dade trots over to the port exit, while Roggin and Gregg go to starboard. They peer around the archway. No bandits in sight. In the corridor, people are shakily resuming the evacuation.

Dade enters the corridor and trots down its length. As he nears the lounge archway, he slows and flattens himself to the wall, and warily peers inside. Roggin and Gregg make similar movements in the starboard corridor. The scene in the lounge is not good; sullen passengers and crew stand dismally. There is a single gunshot, then the three listen while the leader makes an announcement similar to the one in the alcove. The three patiently watch as Yusacre and Maddox make their rounds. Once finished, the two go stand by the elevators, but keep their eyes locked on the room. Ping! An elevator arrives, and the bandits turn. Dade, Roggin and Gregg carefully slip into the lounge. They barely clear the archways before DeSantis and Yusacre are again watching the room.

Parker and Kobryn add knapsacks to the pile created by Maddox and Angelique. Xian Ng watches with utter hatred. These lazy dogs...slugs...vermin....no work ethic. He spits on the rug in disgust. Not too far away from him, Adrianna watches wide-eyed as the terrorists move. The steward is well away from her, but what will happen if one of his partners approaches the plant? Will she be discovered? Will she be forced into the open? What then? She shudders at the thought, then remains frozen; watching, and praying.

With rifles raised, DeSantis and Yusacre flank the team, on guard. The gunners position themselves so they can watch their partners, and keep the crowd under close surveillance. They keep their eyes fixed and their rifles at-the-ready, fully prepared to annihilate even the slightest of threats. The four at the bag pile set to work, intending to put the pillowcases inside some of the emptier sacks, then strategically distribute and arrange the knapsacks between the four of them for the most efficient manner of carrying.

Gregg is seething. His eyes burn with rage as he watches the pompous jerks arrogantly do their work in the lounge. It is time. . . Although the two riflers are watching the crowd, they are also distracted by their conspirators. Also, strike when all six are together as one group, before they separate and divide fire. He suddenly pauses as an unavoidable fact surfaces in his mind: he has no idea if there are *other* bandit terrorists roaming around the ship . . . it is a very real possibility that another elevator could arrive in the middle of the attack. Then he, Roggin and Dade would be as good as dead . . .

Wait, can't waste anymore time worrying about other possibilities; must concentrate on the here and now. Gregg sees Roggin steal a look at him; the television magnate is near the middle of the room, just ahead of the Grand Staircase. Gregg is to the right, near the wall. Both, like Dade on the left, are well-immersed in the sizable crowd.

Gregg raises his forefinger and scratches his left eyebrow. Roggin cocks his eyebrow questioningly. Was that what I thought I saw? Gregg sends the signal again. Yes! Now! Roggin rubs his chin, almost as though checking for remnants of stubble after a shave, which to Gregg means: message received. Gregg turns toward the front of the room, his hands itching for the impending fight. Roggin turns his head toward Dade, who currently has his back toward him. In due time, Dade glances over his shoulder. Roggin sends the message. Dade responds in kind.

The silent communication again escapes the attention of the ever-vigilant Yusacre and DeSantis, whose alert eyes see no threat to the team. Yusacre looks at her four partners; collecting the bags, slinging the straps over their shoulders, getting ready to move. Damn, she thinks, didn't take them too long. Excellent. Soon they will be off the ship and away with their loot. She looks over at DeSantis, who is scanning the crowd. Shortly, the eyes fall on the pretty form of Yusacre. They exchange broad smiles, then Yusacre jerks her head in the direction of Maddox and the others. DeSantis looks, then turns back to Yusacre and nods. The two begin walking toward their partners.

Dade tenses as he turns his face away from Roggin. He closes his eyes for a moment. His mouth is again bone-dry, while his hands are wet with perspiration. When he opens his eyes, he sees the riflers going to join their teammates, who seem ready to move. However, the men are walking backward, and still keeping steely eyes on the crowd. Maddox looks up, and sees Yusacre and DeSantis approaching, getting ready to escort the team out of the room. He smiles. Almost ready now. . . There is a loud thud, a curse. Jensen has dropped one of the sacks she was lifting. Yusacre and DeSantis swing-turn to the noise.

On spying the shifting heads of the gunners, three things happen simultaneously. Dade tenses. Roggin wets his lips. Gregg takes a deep breath. The sense of deja-vu is eerily terrifying as the men count to themselves. 1. 2. 3.

In a flash Dade whips his left hand down and grasps the front-handle of his rifle. He yanks the weapon clear of his jacket and slaps his forefinger on the waiting trigger. At that second the rifle extends from its retracted carry-mode. The barrel snaps forward to a powerful length as the stock extends backward to provide a steady end-brace and the laser-targetsighting clicks on. It is fire-ready. Roggin and Gregg make simultaneous and identical movements in what looks like a choreographed call-to-arms. In a split-second the three are ready to face their foes. They waste no time in firing. RACKETTA RAKETTA RACKETTA the rifles chatter as they spew brass-jacketed death into the air.

Shocked people scream and drop to the floor or throw themselves behind anything which remotely offers protection. A steward who had been carrying two pitchers of water and a tray of snacks drops these and dives for cover – the water and snacks end up in a soggy mess at the foot of the statue. Everyone keeps their heads down and each share the same thoughts: Please don't let me be hurt! and I hope this ends soon!

It takes less than a second for Maddox's soldiers of fortune to react. Yusacre moves to return fire when a well-placed pullet tears into the bicep of her trigger-arm and deeply nicks the body armor there - sending blood flying into the air. Her arm reflexively snaps back and his rifle goes sailing out of her hand. A bloodcurdling howl erupts from her throat as she falls backward onto Maddox and knocks her leader to the floor as bullets race overhead. DeSantis fires back as he dives to the floor. Yusacre clutches her already swelling arm with her good hand and clenches her teeth as sharp bolts of pain assault her brain. Maddox struggles with both his knapsacks and Yusacre's body as he tries to reach the pistol in his jacket. Maddox wildly looks behind him and sees the others down on the floor frantically trying to draw their weapons. DeSantis continues to shoot, despite the blood which runs in a thin stream from his right shoulder.

By now, Dade, Roggin and Gregg have taken cover behind strong but ornate furniture. Gregg spins on his hell and cuts loose a barrage of led at Parker, Kobryn and Jensen. These three had been spared from the opening seconds of the attack, and are crouching low, scratching at their chests, feverishly trying to loosen the tight straps which hold their rifles against their backs - and out of their hands.

That reprieve comes to a harsh end as Gregg's bullets explode around them and send them scurrying to the floor. The shots further excite their hands which are already clumsy with fear. They make no progress at all: the straps remain tight and secure. Their precious knapsacks are now nothing more than cumbersome obstacles which are always in the way as their fingers hastily move over the straps. Curses spout as they rip and pull at the black leather which refuses to yield.

Gregg pauses in his shooting and looks in the direction of his quarry. From what he can tell, he has not hit anyone; there are no cries of pain, no signs of spilled blood. Gregg raises his rifle to his eye and waits. His first shots were fired randomly and meant only to startle and disrupt. The others will have more substance to them.

DeSantis crouches and fires in a semicircle to the back of the room. "Jehandro! We're sitting ducks!" By now Maddox has freed himself from Yusacre and has his pistol drawn. He angrily fires into the room - not at any particular target, but solely as a means of displaying wrath. He crouches low and partially covers Yusacre, whose teeth remain clenched and her eyes are locked on the bloody hand which holds her wound. Maddox shoots a stern look at his team, then his eyes wildly dart around the room, unsure of exactly what he is looking for, but will know when he spies it. DeSantis' sporadic gunfire echoes beside him and Maddox's mind grasps for answers. He spots Yusacre's rifle lying maybe five steps away. "We gotta move!" Maddox says, his eyes trained on the far side of the room. "And move soon!" He turns to DeSantis. "Cover me." The rifleman nods, then fires a long burst which erupts in a fanning pattern in response to his swiveling arm as

Maddox jumps up, bolts right, then somersaults to the prone rifle. His pistol returns to his jacket as his hands coil around the weapon. Lying flat, he fires.

"Damn it!" Gregg spits as he sees the leader claim the rifle. The sudden action of the man took him by surprise, and the cover-fire of the other gunman had otherwise kept him from impeding the motion. Gregg watches in anger as the leader shifts himself into a crouch, then darts back to his teammates.

Once Maddox joins the others, he bends at his knees, and joins DeSantis in firing. "Ok, up," he whispers. "Over to the table!" Maddox jerks his head toward the heavy oak food table to their left. Not the best protection, but take what you can get. DeSantis steals a glance, then looks back at Maddox. He nods. Parker, Kobryn and Jensen raise themselves from the floor, but remain hunched over. Maddox looks at Yusacre. "How are you?"

"Been better, but am ready to move." He nods to her.

Gregg slowly, cautiously looks up from behind the sofa he uses as cover. Seems as thought the bandits are getting ready to go somewhere. But where? His eyes move in the direction they appear to be heading, and spy their destination: the table. Has to be it! Damn, from behind there they can regroup, and who-knows-what will happen after that!

Can't let that happen. No sooner than this thought appears and the bandits, even the wounded one, are up and racing to the table. The two with rifles shield the others, firing as they move nearly as a unit to their promised sanctuary. Dade, Roggin and Gregg shoot, but as the bullets fling themselves into the back wall, the bandits reach the table and hurl it on its side. Food, water, plates and glasses crash to the floor as the tabletop lands with a heavy thud on the red carpeting and provides a strong barricade for the hiding group behind.

The bandits cast themselves to the floor. Maddox reaches out and swats DeSantis sharply on the back of his head - not because he was deserving of punishment, but because he was closest and most convenient. DeSantis looks back sharply at the source of the blow, and in seeing intense anger etched on the face of his leader, resigns to keeping his sullen gaze fixed on the floor. "What the FUCK was that?" Maddox states forcefully. "Where in the HELL did they come from? And what about those fucking guns!"

"They didn't get them from the Range, that is for damn sure!" DeSantis responds, knowing the implied blame.

"Well they got them from some goddamn place! They didn't just appear out of thin air from the fuckin' gun fairy!" Maddox stops himself. "Wait, wait. We can worry about that stuff later. Right now we have to figure a way out of here. And a way to get the loot, and us, off of this deathtrap in one piece. Damn it, I hate competition."

There is no motion from behind the table, and the lounge suddenly goes quiet. The silence is surprising after the racket of battle. The calm is deceiving, because there is a lot left to do before it all will be over.

Gregg warily peers up. Seeing nothing, he motions to Dade and Roggin, who likewise slowly look toward the table. Gregg boldly takes a step outward. Slowly, his gunbarrel resolutely ahead of him. Encountering no response from behind the black solidness of the table, Gregg creeps forward. Dade and Roggin also appear from behind their places.

He stops suddenly. There is movement. A jerky motion, erratic, just barely perceptible from the top left edge of the table. It catches his attention. The object is round, metal, looks to be the frontpiece of a riflebarrel, and is just barely visible. Gregg moves into a crouch, and again raises his rifle to his eye. With his thumb he slowly shifts the rifle's firing sequence from AUTO to SEMI mode which means that now only single bullets will fire rather than multiple rounds. Gregg also switches off his rifle's laser sighting - his target is so small against the beige backdrop of the wall that the red dot will serve no purpose: he will have to rely solely on his skill as a marksman.

Gregg squints and slowly takes careful aim. The owner of the item is completely out of sight. The top edge of a knapsack also makes an appearance next to the gunbarrel, and the two move awkwardly, albeit in tandem. With a steady hand and a sure eye, Gregg lets his bullet fly. The metal projectile rips through the exposed muzzle of a bandit rifle and shatters the once precision cut circular opening as it races through the air before eventually stopping in the back wall. "Got it!" Gregg says while smiling widely as his mind explodes with private joy exuded from personal success: he had hit it perfectly!

Parker hears a bullet whistle past his right ear and then feels a tiny stinging sensation in the back of his neck. He feels a warm fluid surfacing on the skin at the spot which stings - - burns now. "Damn!" Parker thinks aloud, "That was close . . ." He ducks lower, and his fingers are given newfound speed from the near miss. He tears open the buckle and undoes the strap. He stretches his left hand over his right shoulder to grab his rifle, then quickly pulls his hand back as sharp pain stabs into his palm. "Dammit!" he says sharply. "Wha?" follows as he looks in bewilderment at the bleeding gash in his flesh.

With his eyes glued to the inexplicable wound, Parker shakes his right shoulder in a shrug, and after tumbling through the bulky sacks, the rifle clatters to the floor. He cautiously moves his right hand behind him, and lets his fingers close around what feels like the mid-barrel of the rifle. He pulls the weapon around . . . and sees a shredded slab of metal where the acutely designed muzzle should be.

Now he knows where the pain in his neck comes from. Parker gingerly feels along the back of his neck and his fingers soon come upon a jagged sliver of metal protruding from his skin. He clamps his teeth and with a wince pulls the piece out. He brings his hand around and looks at the blood-stained shard of black steel before angrily casting it away.

"You ok?" Kobryn asks as Parker wrestles with his gunstrap.

"Just fuckin' fine," Parker replies with an edge in his voice through still clenched teeth. With anger raging inside him, Parker pulls his pistol from behind his waistband at the back of his steward's jacket as he cautiously peers around the left side of the table. He sees Gregg, who has moved again and is now near the right wall, lining up another shot. Parker smiles. The bastard is clear in his sights . . . this will be *tooooo* easy . . . .

Gregg concentrates on his aim, focusing all his attention on his target. He is about to fire when he sees a handgun rising out of the corner of his eye. He knows he does not have much time - a second at best, and not near enough time to shoot a worthwhile shot, just barely enough to get out of the way. He pulls his rifle so it is parallel with his body and throws himself back to his left through the open archway which leads to the starboard corridor. Parker fires as Gregg moves. Bullets pound the wall that Gregg ducks behind. Parker knows he cannot possibly hit the man now, but continues to fire out of anger. Bang! Bang! Bang! Bang! Click! Click! Click! The pistol's hammer falls on a hollow chamber - - the gun is empty! Parker frustratedly casts the useless handgun aside and with his left hand he pulls his jacket and shirtfront up to expose a silver pistol tucked into his waistband. He pulls the gun free with his right hand and aims at the archway, waiting for his target to reappear.

Roggin and Dade hear the exchange of gunfire behind them. Dade pauses and glances quickly over his right shoulder. He does not see Gregg. He turns his head around and fires a few shots to keep the terrorists down, then looks back again. Still no Gregg. Dade is shocked - - what happened? Fearing the worst, Dade calls out. "Cal? You there Cal?" The voice distracts Roggin, who stops his shooting and turns to his right to look for Gregg. This is the moment that the peering DeSantis has been waiting for: he springs up and opens fire. Jensen raises her now-pistoled right hand and joins in the counter-attack.

Bullets tear at Dade and Roggin. One shot pierces Dade's jacket at the shoulder but does not hit him; another grazes Roggin's left hip. Dade pushes a heavy, ornate marble-topped endtable over on its side and dives headfirst behind its thick top which faces the oak table. No sooner is he down when a barrage of bullets fill the air overhead. Roggin shoots haphazardly as he runs for cover. He vaults over a sofa near the left wall and plasters himself to the floor behind as bullets tear into the plush upholstery and wall. Dade and Roggin keep their heads low as the roar of gunfire sounds all around them.

Gregg moves himself to the edge of the archway and warily peers into the lounge. He heard Dade calling him and is attempting to catch sight of his partner. "Welcome back, fucker," Parker mutters as he sees Gregg's profile appear, then he shoots. The bullets splinter the ornate wooden archway, but do not hit Gregg, who ducks into the corridor the instant he hears the first shot. Jensen is now finally able to undo her gunstrap and put her rifle into her waiting hands as Parker shoots. Kobryn immediately joins in shooting at the archway. Her high-powered bullets tear the stylish frame to broken pieces in a matter of seconds. Parker stops shooting, and motions for Kobryn to quit as well. They look, but see no signs of a hit. . .merely fragments of wood floating lazily in the air. Parker and Kobryn curse themselves and the luck of their opponent. They keep their weapons aimed at the battered archway and wait . . .

DeSantis and Jensen pause in their shooting. Everything had happened very quickly. "Did we get any of them?" DeSantis asks, and Jensen shrugs unknowingly. The real answer comes in the form of a rifle which suddenly pops up from behind an overturned table and fires a short burst. The two duck and bullets harmlessly hit the far wall - - the shooter had not raised his head to aim and was firing blindly. As quickly as it had appeared, the rifle is down again. DeSantis again turns to Jensen. "Damn it! One of them can still shoot! Let's get him!"

They angrily fire back at the endtable, but their bullets do nothing but chip and scar the thick wood of its underside.

Roggin is raising himself into a crouch when he hears the gunfire and instinctively ducks down. When neither the sofa nor the wall above him explode under the pound of striking bullets, he realizes he is not the target of the shots - which means Dade is in trouble. Roggin moves to help his partner. With his rifle stretched across his forearms, Roggin hastily crawls infantry style along the length of the sofa. When he reaches the far end, he cautiously peers around its corner and sees two terrorists shooting at the spot where he had last seen Dade. They are so involved with their task, they do not notice Roggin.

Roggin hastily crouches and raises his rifle. He tries to take aim, but from the way they are situated behind the table, he cannot get a worthwhile shot - - of course, his first shot will have to be good . . . damn good . . . because the second it is fired the crack of the flying bullet will expose him as well as if a spotlight is flashed down on him. Quite a predicament…he becomes lost in thought. Then, an idea quickly forms. He keeps a tight grip on his rifle's trigger handle while, with some difficulty, he maneuvers his left hand into the inside-left pocket of his tuxedo jacket. His fingers stretch down, and their tips close around the top of the silver flask which rests there. He slowly lifts his hand, and the flask smoothly slides out of the pocket. Without taking his eyes off of the table, Roggin sets the container on the floor, then coils his hand around it.

Roggin quickly draws his left hand back, and with a mighty throw, sends his flask into the air. It flies high and reflects the bright lights of the room off its shiny silver surface in a sudden, blinding flash like an exploding firecracker. This flash immediately catches the eyes of DeSantis and Jensen, who are both startled and spin to face the miniature sunburst. His plan worked! In turning, DeSantis unwittingly made himself an excellent target. Roggin quickly aims and fires as the flask lands and bounces softly on the plush carpeting.

"Arghhh! Damnittttt!" DeSantis gives a yell. Jensen fires her pistol twice, then turns to help the Mexitalian, who is doubled-over and moaning. Dade hears DeSantis yell, and when the sound of gunfire is replaced by silence, Dade takes his cue. He slowly, cautiously, raises his head enough so his eyes peek out above the tabletop. It looks as though one of the terrorists has been wounded. This is excellent. Two down!

Dade's pleasure is short-lived. He watches as the leader of the group springs up from behind the table and fires wildly. Dade ducks to protect himself, but not before seeing one dart from the left side of the table - the guy is a burgundy blur. The shooting stops. Dade pauses. He slowly peers around the right edge of the table to see a woman race from the table-barrier. She keeps her rifle aimed at the corridor archway, which is a bullet-ridden mess. Dade watches as she ducks behind a chair, while the terrorist who was there - - and Dade now sees this man is in a steward's jacket; light glints off the silver gun he carries - - races to another location and disappears behind other furniture. Soon after, a head appears. Dade watches the steward. His head moves in a nervous scan from left to right - - then snaps back to the left where it suddenly stops: Dade has been spotted. The beady eyes focus on Dade as the pistol barks. Dade manages to jerk his head back behind the tabletop. A heartbeat later a chunk of wood and marble is savagely ripped from the edge of the table exactly where Dade's head had been. Slivers of pale wood are caught in Dade's black hair - - it had been that close.

Thump! Thump! Thump! Bullets pound into the bottom of the table but do not pass through the heavy marble-topped wood. Dade silently thanks the Décor department of the Archangel Line for their devotion to quality material as he slowly rests himself against the smooth, cold marble. Terror invades his mind. He looks in horror at the gash in the table . . . had he moved one-one hundredth of a second slower he would now be in the Reaper's grasp. He had cheated death. Luck, God, speed. . . . something had saved him. Dade sets his rifle down and with a shaky hand wipes perspiration from his forehead as he considers his brush with death. His breath comes in short, quick gasps and his heart races, sending adrenaline rushing through his body with each powerful beat. His mind spins.

If I can't regain control, I'll likely die tonight, Dade thinks. He forcibly clears his mind and deliberately keeps his eyes away from the damage to the table. He takes slow, deep breaths and lets his lungs fill with cool air; this brings his heartbeat down to a regular level as it soothes him. After a moment, he is back to normal - - or at least as 'normal' as one can be in this situation. Dade feels a mixture of vigor and excitement coursing through his body now. He wants to fight! He has beaten fear, and will now beat them!

Dade moves back from the tabletop and scoops his rifle into his hands. Need a plan to deal with them....his mind struggles. He replays the scene from memory: one in a steward's jacket with a pistol, another with a rifle - - Dade stops. His mind sits transfixed on a single detail. Was that what I thought I saw? Without hesitating, he raises his rifle over the table and fires quickly. No sooner has the last bullet flown through the muzzle when he raises his head for another quick glimpse of the two terrorists. His head is instantly down again as bullets race toward him, but he has answered his question in that fraction of a second: the steward has *his* pistol! Damn! Dade thinks, I'm being shot at with my *own* gun! The weapon which is supposed to protect him is being used *against* him. The irony of this is incredible.

As Dade curses fate, Maddox analyzes his situation: one of the attackers is behind the couch, the second is covered by Parker, the third is gone. Parker and Kobryn are in good positions, the leapfrog plan having worked well. Maddox turns left; Yusacre is pale, and her wound steadily bleeds over her hand and shirtsleeve. "My whole arm feels numb," she mutters; she looks tired, but is alert enough. DeSantis is kneeling, recovering from a heavy bruising of a shot he received. As with Yusacre, if not for the kevlar armor mesh, he would be in serious trouble. Another is a fleshwound which tore along his left forearm, scorching it, so he is more pained then damaged. However, the man looks mad, a raging Mexitalian bull ready to tear the life out of his opponents. Soon enough, friend. Maddox thinks. Jensen waits, pistol drawn, at the left side of the table in a ready-crouch, eager to follow Parker and Kobryn. "Go, ferret them out and destroy them quickly," Maddox whispers.

He then looks at the room itself. What a mess! The luxurious Halo lounge is nothing more than a war-torn battlefield. People are sprawled on the floor, furniture is overturned… damage everywhere…bulletholes scar the walls, blood stains the carpeting. Damn those fuckers! Maddox thinks as he looks around. His exquisite new plan had been thrown into chaos by a bunch of trigger-happy amateurs who decided to step up and save the day. Competition, fuck! If it hadn't been for them, the team would be off the ship by now, drinking champagne and travelling with their riches through space. Damn it all! Wait, wait…on the verge of exploding into a full-blown rage… concentrate on other thoughts…force the mind…anger will solve nothing and only complicate further. Vengeance can come later. This 'situation' is merely another obstacle to contend with, as the collision had been earlier. "Complications make life interesting," as it is said.

Maddox channels his energy into solving the problems which stand between him and freedom. First, need to regroup the team and somehow treat the wounded, then reach a lifecraft and get off the ship. How? Seems difficult; nearly impossible. Is there a dawn to this darkness? Set to it. Got to work through the trouble staring him dead in the face. Think. Think! Think!!!

As Kobryn launches her hunt for the vigilantes, Maddox puts the finishing touches on the revisions of his new escape plan. He turns to Yusacre and DeSantis. "Ok, on your feet." They rise. DeSantis clutches his rifle as though it is his closes friend, and Yusacre stands feebly on her feet, definitely in need of medical attention.

"You walk point," Maddox instructs DeSantis. "We can't go down the starboard corridor because one of those troublemakers is out there. We'll walk to the back of the room and out through the left archway." DeSantis who nods solidly and is about to move when Maddox's words stop him. "Grab some bags too, but not enough to get in the way of shooting." DeSantis nods again and heaves some knapsacks onto his shoulders. Maddox overloads himself as he looks at Yusacre. "You'll have to take some too, sorry. That's the way it is. Hell, it's what we came for and I'll be damned if we leave so much as a penny behind."

Yusacre smiles and nods. "Damn straight," she says, and bags are given to her. Now, ready to go. Maddox radios Parker, Kobryn and Jensen about their exiting; those three will deal with the passengers. They leave the sanctity of the oak table, and move down the expanse of the room. DeSantis keeps his eyes alert and his finger trigger-ready.

Gregg appears at the archway. He is not cut to pieces by a hail of bullets - - he is not even shot at. Gregg is at the <u>forward</u> Halo arch, port side. He had doubled-back to the other side of the ship to get a better firing position and surprise the bandit terrorists at the same time. He peers inside and looks along the far wall to the back of the room; two of them are staring intently with their weapons raised at the aft archway he disappeared through some minutes earlier. A smile creeps on to Gregg's face as he stifles a chuckle. SUCKERS. He next notices the three knapsack-loaded terrorists heading toward the back of the room. Roggin and Dade must somehow be subdued, he thinks.

Gregg drops to the floor and crawls into the lounge. He joins the crowd plastered to the carpet. His rifle is laid across his forearms, the right of which is crossed over the left, and he crawls along infantry-style by using his elbows and knees. It is awkward as all hell, but it serves his purpose; it keeps his body low and his weapon close to his hands.

Gregg makes quick progress as he steadily creeps along. He snakes through the maze of outstretched bodies without any difficulty, moving with the agility of a panther on the attack. Like the majestic hunter of the jungle, he will take his prey by surprise. He plans to put himself behind the gunners and ambush them. Though concentrating on his task, Gregg takes note of those who form the horizontal crowd. Some have their faces buried in the carpet; no doubt afraid of what they may see if their eyes are raised. They press their heads down deeper if they happen to feel Gregg brush past on his secretive journey. Others are a bit more brazen. While keeping their heads low, their eyes dart to ensure they do not miss a single moment of the deadly drama which plays out before them. Some of these ones spy Gregg moving. They smile or half-raise their hands in a thumb-up salute to encourage him. Gregg gives quick nods to acknowledge the silent wishes of good fortune.

The eyes of Mitchell Hearst fall on Gregg. The third officer has been scanning the room acutely, desperately trying to find a way to escape to a corridor, and then to a shuttle. He lies on the floor to the right of the elevator bay when he spots the tuxedoed form of Gregg racing through the crowd like some sort of black torpedo. Hearst is some distance behind Gregg, and to the man's left. "What the hell is this idiot doing?" Hearst asks himself in a whisper. Then, he catches sight of the rifle lying across Gregg's arms. The weapon explains it all: this fellow is one of the passengers who attacked the terrorists, and he is probably moving into a different shooting location.

Envy wells up in Hearst. "Hell, if I had a gun it would be amazing! I could fight the terrorists and save the ship!" he whispers. Imagine the notoriety, he thinks, his reputation would be saved! He would be revered and respected; hell, worshipped! He has a chance again to have high society be his oyster. But no, damn it. Hearst keeps his eyes locked on Gregg as a wicked idea sparks to life. A smile forms when Hearst realizes that soon, very soon, the man will be passing fairly close to him, dead ahead of where he lies.

Hearst pulls his eyes from Gregg and steals a glance at the two groups of terrorists. One man aims at the corridor exit while his partner divides his time between that same exit and an overturned entable. The other three are making their way to a back exit. Not one is looking in his direction. As he continues to watch the bandits, Hearst eases himself into a crouch, then shifts into a runner's stance. His eyes dart over to Gregg. Getting closer. Hearst looks again at the terrorists; they are the same as before. The eyes return to Gregg. Closer still. Hearst braces his body to charge - - his heart races and he feels strong. The man is maybe three feet away from being in the perfect location. On Your Mark. Get Set. Go! An imaginary starter's pistol sounds in his brain as Hearst rockets forward.

The third officer moves swiftly. He keeps his body low, parallel with the floor as his feet trot. His arms are outstretched - - his fingers reach for his target. Strands of black hair flap around his head and ears like some grotesque greasy veil as he runs at a full gallop. His spirits soar as he nears the man, who does not stop nor turn his head around - - it will be a perfect blindside tackle! A sinister grin appears on his pale face as Hearst throws the full weight of his heavy body forward and leaps for all he is worth.

Cal Gregg is pleased with himself. He has not been spotted by the terrorists and is making good time, considering his chosen method of travel. In a few more minutes he will be behind the 'steward' and his partner. . .Thuck-whump! Gregg's body forcibly slams into the floor by an incredible mass. Air is thrown from his lungs and his head knocks down onto the cold steel of his rifle; a long, bloody gash opens along his forehead.

Gregg lies still on the floor, dazed from the shock and the intensity of the attack. He tries to bring himself out of the hazy fog which clouds his mind. Someone straddles the middle of his back . . .one of them! He feels the person lean forward; the rifle is taken from his motionless fingers. Fear speeds Gregg's recovery - - he has the sensation of surfacing from being under water as things grow clear and his thoughts focus. Gotta react quickly…or else…

He feels his attacker rise off his back. The person does not stand straight up, but instead only hovers in a crouch above him. "What the hell is this?" an impressed male voice asks in hushed amazement while acquainting himself with the CMG-309. Gregg takes advantage of the excellent distraction his masterpiece is causing and slowly turns his head and glances over his shoulder. An officer? A man in an officer's uniform is gazing in utter astonishment at the rifle. Shocking! Rage boils within Gregg. What the hell kind of bullshit is this? Officers attacking passengers?

In an angry flash Gregg puts his hands at his sides. He slams his palms into the floor, quickly takes a deep breath, and rapidly thrusts himself upward in a powerful push-up. Gregg hits Hearst hard from below and the fat man topples over heavily to the right as he is knocked completely off balance. The rifle flies out of his hands as he flails his arms in a desperate and futile attempt to straighten himself. Despite this effort, Hearst falls heavily on an unsuspecting female passenger who shrieks as the full weight of a bulky man is thrown onto her petite frame. No sooner is he down when Gregg lunges for the rifle.

The 309 is airborne, sailing through the air with its muzzle high and stock low, resembling a jet descending on a runway. The butt-plate smacks the floor hard and jostles the rifle, throwing the firing bolt in the trigger mechanism forward. Bang! The sound startles everyone. A bullet explodes out of the sleek barrel as the gun drops to the floor. The cartridge rips forward and tears into the top of a potted plant. The plant falls forward in an earthen, leafy heap and reveals a shocked woman cowering near the floor.

Adrianna looks up in open-mouthed horror at the bullethole in the wall. God, that was close! Just above her head! Her body shakes for a moment, then she quickly regains control. Now, a new problem. When the bullet clipped the top of the philodendron she instinctively ducked - - and knocked the plant over in the process. Her hiding place is gone, her location is exposed for everyone to see. Everyone including the steward-terrorist.

Parker stands straight up. "Waaaaoooh-ho!" A loud howl erupts from his body as he rises. The sound chills the crowd to the bone. Even though her head is turned away from the bellow, she knows exactly who is making it. And why. An evil grin appears on Parker's face at the joy of the discovery. He breaks into a run, keeping his eyes fixed on his target and moving with the intensity of a runaway locomotive straight toward her.

Dade is shocked to see Adrianna crouching behind the overturned plant. What the hell is she doing there? He then hears someone to his left cackle like a lunatic and immediately sees the terrorist in the steward jacket running toward her. Dade does not know why the man is moving on Adrianna, nor does he question it. His mind instead clamps on what he sees: That guy is going after my girl. With my gun. This is not going to happen.

Dade does not stop to think about what he will do - - he acts on pure instinct. He springs forward in hot pursuit of the terrorist in the steward jacket. His feet slam heavily into the carpet as he propels his body forward. Adrenaline surges through his veins and provides a boundless fountain of energy – nothing will slow him on his charge. He will not stop until the terrorist is down and Adrianna is safe.

She sits motionless on the floor as the shrill yell penetrates her ears and rips into her brain. She slowly turns her head away from the wall to face her fate. Although the movement takes only seconds, it seems like much longer because for her the hands of time have wound down; everything is moving in slow motion. All too soon her eyes fall on the one person she had hoped to avoid seeing for the rest of her life - - and he is running straight for her! With a gun! A sudden movement may cause him to shoot, so she remains still, though tenses and braces herself for whatever fight is coming her way. Adrianna stares in utter terror as the man moves closer. And closer. And closer.

CHAPTER SEVENTEEN
Action in the Darkness

Maddox and his partners hit the floor when the shot rings out. Then, Maddox stares in disbelief as he watches Parker run…toward a woman. A woman? What? A blank expression comes over him; his jaw drops in shock. What the hell? Is Parker insane? What's he think he's doing? "Alex!" Maddox whispers harshly into his radio, "Alex, get over here now!" Parker does not so much as break stride for the command. "Damn it," Maddox curses under his breath, and he becomes more angered. "He'll pay," Maddox mutters; lapses in judgement by his conspirators are not good things. The idiot! The fucking idiot! Goddamn complicator!

Then, bad to worse. One of the passenger-fighters crosses into Maddox's line of vision – pursuing Parker in a feverish run. Maddox's forehead becomes a maze of wrinkles and his face knots in anger as he bears witness to the newest complication. Damn! Maddox knows it will not be long before the tuxedoed marauder reaches Parker. He snaps his head to his right to DeSantis, who looks totally confused. "Get him," Maddox says through clenched teeth. DeSantis nods, shrugs his knapsacks off, and quickly brings his rifle to bear as Maddox turns and likewise raises his pistol.

Pow! Pow! Pow! Thththththokokok! Punching sounds of pistolshots mix with staccato machinegun-fire and together blast through the vast lounge. The lunging Parker stops dead in his tracks and instinctively ducks while turning his head to the gunfire. Taking the cue, with a powerful push from her long legs Adrianna leaps to her left, clear and away from the man in the steward uniform. Parker spots her move and spins his body to the right as he raises his pistol and takes aim - - just as Dade slams into him with the force of a star quarterback and knocks him hard to the floor.

Parker is thrown down on his left, pinned to the floor under the sturdy weight of Dade, who is sprawled atop him. "Damn sonofabitch!" Dade spits as he punches Parker in the side of the face, then slaps his hands on the shoulders of the terrorist and forcibly turns him on his back. Parker is taken completely by surprise by the attack and has not yet recovered from the initial shock. He stares dazedly at the angered face above him. Dade wraps his left hand around Parker's neck as his right hand is pulled into a tight fist. He draws his arm back, and thrusts it forward, barreling his hand squarely into Parker's jaw.

Parker's head snaps back from the force of the impact; pain explodes in him. There is no time to recover from the vicious blow because another quickly follows. Then another, and another. "Damn you…." Dade seethes. Parker's head now seems nothing more than a punching bag. He has to fight to keep from slipping into unconsciousness.

Dade readies to hit the steward again when the man's eyes roll back into his head and the eyelids close. Then, the neck goes limp and the head lolls back. Dade pauses; that is enough; after all, he does not want to kill him, just immobilize him. Dade relaxes his grip and begins to shake the mild pain out of his right hand when the steward's left hand suddenly lashes out and hits Dade sharply in a tender spot just below his right arm. "Argh!" Dade barks and recoils, then reflexively pulls his right arm in tightly against his side.

Parker's eyes snap open, crazed, clear, and bright, and a look of anger comes over his face. "Caughtcha!" he sneers; he had been faking serious injury . . . playing opossum . . . and his attacker had fallen for this age-old ruse as though he was born yesterday. "Fuck!" Dade curses himself, then Parker clubs Dade in the right side of his head. Ignore the pain, Dade thinks, forcing himself, then moves his arm to strike back.

Parker sees the fist being pulled back for another hit. He jerks his left hand up and catches the fist dead in his palm as it falls toward his head. Using the considerable strength in his bicep, Parker forces the fist up and away from him, keeping his fingers clenched on the hand; "Fuck you," he gasps.

Dade slaps his left hand around Parker's neck and begins to squeeze . . . he pushes down hard on the protruding Adam's apple with his thumb; "Shut up!" Dade wheezes. Parker gags and swallows hard. He tries to move his other arm, which is stuck between them, sandwiched next to Dade's rifle. Parker pulls…it is then he realizes…the *Pistol!* Somehow he's kept it in his hand! He bars his teeth and smiles.

Dade feels the arm moving awkwardly under him, then notices a strained smile on the guy's face . . . woah, that is a bad sign. Dade presses down, hoping to keep the arm pinned and useless. As he does, the edge of his rifle digs sharply into his stomach, and the muscle reflexively pulls back from the pain, giving Parker the opportunity he needs. He slips his forearm through the tiny gap and pulls his pistoled hand free. Dade steals a glance to his left. The Gun! Oh God - the bastard still has the gun! Dade looks in bug-eyed terror back at the steward . . . whose eyes dance in delight, and the smile has grown.

"I don't think so!" Dade blurts and instantly pulls his hand off the neck and clamps it on Parker's right wrist. Parker struggles all the more, shifting and shaking his fist, all to no avail. It is as if a handcuff of flesh and bone has been locked on his wrist.

"Get off, fuckhead!" Parker gasps then tries to move the pistol around in his hand. If he can get the barrel facing up, he can be free from this mess, but he has to be sure that the barrel is away from him before daring to try and pull the trigger. Dade feels the hand and pistol moving. It will be no use trying to grapple for the pistol; it is locked in the grasp.

With a strong push, Parker throws Dade's fisted right hand back. He quickly coils his free hand into a fist and punches Dade in the lower jaw. Dade instantly swings back at Parker, who deflects the blow with a quick move of his left hand. Dade pulls his arm back for another try as Parker jerks his hand up. Its edge catches Dade under his chin. Dade makes a move to hit Parker and as Parker reacts, he changes his angle of swing at the last second, completely avoiding the block as he drives his fist into the man's nose . . . cartilage crushes sickly as the nose is mashed into the face.

Parker is stunned for a moment. He angrily lashes back at Dade. He takes a wide, wild swing, but Dade pulls his head back out of the way of the knotted hand. Parker's fist flies clear across his torso and almost lands on his right shoulder. Before Parker can bring his arm back, Dade's free hand grasps Parker's elbow and he pushes down hard on the arm. Parker's bicep rubs his neck - his head is now pinned to the floor by his own arm!

Dade pauses and takes a deep breath. He looks down at the straining face of the steward-terrorist; the guy looks like a trapped animal. For all intents and purposes, he is secure. He cannot hit Dade from his current position, and certainly is not going anywhere. Parker struggles, and Dade increases his hold. Dade knows its no use in trying to reason with him. . .he'd *never* surrender voluntarily. . .have to beat him into submission.

Now, what the hell to do about the pistol Have to act fast, any moment and the terrorist can get the pistol in a bad way, then it is all over after that. . . An idea comes to life. Yes! It will work perfectly, but he'll have to do it *perfectly* the first time he makes his move. No room for error; no second chances. In a flash Dade pulls his hand off of Parker's wrist and it lands on the pistol. His fingers clench the back of the barrel. Parker reacts by tightening his grip on the handle. Parker turns his wrist up while Dade pushes down. Intense and angry stares bore straight into the eyes from one to the other . . . the exact same thought courses through burning minds fuelled with solid determination: "I will win this battle."

Parker jerks his right knee up and savagely kicks Dade in the side. The hit catches Dade just below his ribcage and his body convulses from the force of the impact. The breath is knocked from his lungs and he feels as though he may vomit. Dade gasps and wavers; Parker quickly kicks again and Dade's hold on his arm weakens. Parker lashes his left arm back - - it moves with the force of sprung steel and sends Dade's hand flying backward. The back of Parker's hand hits Dade's left jaw and his head snaps up. Dade's fingers slip off of the pistol as Parker pushes his attacker off of him. "Ha! I won!" Parker shouts as he scrambles to his feet while Dade lies huddled on the floor and struggles to recover.

"What the hell?" Maddox shouted in sheer rage when he saw his lieutenant brought down. He and DeSantis had fired at the passenger haphazardly because there had not been enough time to properly aim. Obviously, none of their bullets hit him. Maddox stares in anger as he sees the two wrestling on the floor. "Damn it, we can't simply shoot the guy because Parker could be hit too," Maddox mutters; he is just about to order DeSantis to go over and help when Parker suddenly stands above the motionless form of his attacker.

A smirk grows on Parker's battered face as he savors his victory. He keeps his pistol trained on Dade's lowered head as he runs the fingers of his free hand under his crushed nose. They come away from his face slick with blood and fluid. Parker looks at his hand in disgust; his smile mutates into a grimace. He snaps his head down quickly and sends the matter flying to the carpet. Parker looks at Dade. "Asshole," he mutters.

While keeping his pistol aimed at Dade, Parker looks around the back of the lounge. He notes with anger that the woman has disappeared. He warily looks over at Maddox, who is clearly angry. Maddox raises his hand and motions Parker over with a jerk. Parker nods and again looks down at his attacker. He leans to him and with his left hand reaches for the black gunstrap which lies across Dade's back. Parker grabs it and harshly pulls it over Dade's head. The rifle falls to the floor and Parker kicks it aside. Dade groans, coughs, and shakes his head. Parker straightens and looks down. There is no mercy in his eyes. "Get up motherfucker." Dade does not move. Parker kicks him hard. "I said up!"

Dade stirs. He looks with contempt at Parker and strenuously moves himself half way up; his palms pressed flat against the floor. Parker's grin returns. He aims the pistol straight at the nose of the tormented face of his attacker. "All the way up," Maddox and the others watch enthusiastically as Parker exacts his bloodthirsty revenge. With a wince, Dade slowly raises his right foot and sets it sturdily on the floor. He puts the weight of his body on the right leg as he slowly, pushes up and painfully gets his body standing. He teeters slightly, but does not fall. Dade stares at Parker's laughing eyes.

Parker smiles widely; his white teeth glimmer sinisterly in the light. He clearly enjoys every minute of this vengeance. He points the pistol at Dade's chest. "Tooooooo good!" he says with a chuckle. He cocks the hammer, and looks directly at Dade – the man is not begging for mercy, not cowering, in no way trying to escape the obvious death he faces. Parker studies him quizzically, and for the briefest of seconds has respect for the man. Anyone who can stare down the barrel of a gun and not so much as flinch is macho to the bone. "Brave to the last," Parker says as means of a salute. Then he pulls the trigger.

Click! The hammer stops half-way down on its fall to the firing chamber. Parker curses - - the goddamn gun is ruining the drama of the moment! With a frustrated look, Parker places his thumb on the hammer and cocks it again. He jerks the trigger back. Click! The hammer stops in the same position. Parker looks down in dismay at the silver pistol. Then he hears laughter. He menacingly turns his eyes toward Dade.

He is smiling. "Never," he says, "ever play with another man's toys." Parker is baffled. Dade points to the gun. Parker's eyes slowly drift down . . . to the back of the pistol . . . to the safety switch - - which is *on*! Parker's eyes grow wide and shoot back at Dade. In a flash he moves his fingers to release the safety catch and he instantly finds Dade's black booted foot kicking into the base of his gun-hand. The pistol goes flying into the air. No sooner is this done when the right fist of Dade slams into Parker's chin. Parker careens backward from the force of the blow as Dade dives to the left after his pistol.

A door opens. A stairwell door, opening silently on its hinges. Bethany Parris cautiously steps in to the lobby, the stun truncheon she has is outstretched before her. A bag of tricks is carried on her left shoulder, and held snugly to her side. She looks around; wary, keen. What's this? The room seems empty of people. She looks up in a start – up to the ceiling! They must be in the airducts again! There is no vent-cover near where she is, so she proceeds slowly. She looks from left to right, and up to the ceiling every now and then – keeping fully alert the entire time. "Bandits to the right of me, maniac stewards to the left, bad dye-jobs overhead," she whispers. She quickly trots to the back of the room, to the alcove. Still, no sign of the crazies. She looks down and doublechecks the stun-wand she had liberated from the vacant security station. Fully charged, ready for business. It took her longer than she thought to get up to the flight deck, as she was on the look out for another ambush. Then, after getting her weapon, she had come up with some sort of half-feasible plan. Then, take a deep breath and head down to the lobby to fight for her ship, for her crewmates, and for her passengers…like Diana the Huntress, only with a voltage wand instead of a bow and arrow. Her eyes go up again - - where could those hell-bent lunatics be? Wait…what is that? That sound? A gunshot? Her feet race and she burns into the corridor, heading straight for the Halo lounge.

There, in the lounge, Maddox and the others stare in shock as they witness Parker be taken down <u>again</u>. Maddox becomes enraged; "I've had enough of these idiots meddling with the plan. Time to leave and be done with these nuisances. Time, yes, precious time. "Gotta think," he says while scanning the lounge and contemplating. His eyes absently drift to the massive chandelier hanging majestically in the middle of the ceiling. Yeah. Yeah! Maddox turns to DeSantis, who stares intently in the direction of Parker, presumably waiting for the passenger to re-appear from the crowd on the floor so he can shoot the troublemaker dead. Maddox nudges DeSantis. "Take out the light." DeSantis raises a questioning eyebrow. Wha? Maddox cocks his head in the direction of the glistening gold and crystal fixture. "Take it out. Now."

DeSantis does not have the vaguest idea why he should destroy a chandelier, but knows Maddox hates having his orders questioned, so he nods and raises his rifle. He closes his left eye and squints his right as he takes careful aim at the golden five-link chain which connects the massive chandelier to the ceiling. It will be far from an easy shot; the chain is barely visible from where DeSantis stands. He takes a deep breath and fires, intentionally jostling his rifle as he does in order that the angle-of-fire will differ slightly for each shot.

Five bullets rip through the air straight toward the chandelier. They smash crystals, shatter lightbulbs, and scar the circular gold support rods as they tear through the glittering chandelier and divot the white ceiling. Two bullets chip the middle link of the suspension chain before hitting the ceiling. At first, the chandelier merely swings lazily in the air and appears not to have been damaged. "Damnit!" DeSantis swears as he takes aim again, but pauses before he fires – waiting for the chandelier to stand still so he can get a clear shot.

As the chandelier swings back and forth, it places an inordinate amount of stress on the top-chain. The tiny chips are quickly pulled into a small gap, and the fixture drops ever so slightly from its ordinary height. When the chandelier finally comes to a standstill, the gap in the damaged link is stretched, and yawns open further. The link becomes an extremely weak strand of gold-plated steel which resembles an elongated C.

DeSantis is about to shoot again when Maddox waves him down. "Wait, wait . . ." he whispers. He has a hunch that a second round of shots will not be necessary. His intuition proves correct seconds later when the chandelier suddenly lurches to the left; it dips at an almost forty-five degree angle, and the crystals jingle glassily in protest to the movement. Below, people in the vicinity scream and scatter from the impending doom before throwing themselves to another place on the floor. The fixture hangs precariously in the air - - the tiny link hangs on for all it is worth. Seconds later, the relentless forces of the ship's gravity field take their toll and prove to much for the worn steel to handle as the ragged edge of the link's upper break slips through the loop above it.

The chandelier drops. Its two power cords pull taut, then snap when suddenly exposed to the full weight of the falling fixture. Down it goes - - gaining speed and momentum as it rapidly closes the distance between the ceiling and the floor. The chandelier crashes heavily into the glamorous Archangel statue which is directly below. Passengers scream as the dimming chandelier hits. The weight of the fixture and the force of the impact knocks the statue off balance, and the ivory figure topples forward off of its pedestal.

The angel breaks when it hits the floor. The torso is cut in two across the middle, and the outstretched arm symbolizing the "EVER FORWARD" motto is snapped at the elbow. The forearm with its pointing forefinger is stuck impotently in the carpeting next to the figure's head, which lies on its side. Numerous cracks and splits now adorn those pieces which remain in tact. A droplet of water tossed up from the sodden carpet seeps into a break which cut deep into the diamond-white star inlaid in the angel's forehead; another splashes up onto one of the statue's unseeing eyes, then slips down along the lower eyelid, where it lingers above the cheek for a moment before sliding down the smooth ivory surface - - thus the stone man sheds a tear for the fallen ship and her perilous predicament.

Darian Dade grabs his pistol from the floor and clicks off the safety mechanism just as the chandelier slams into the statue. With the loss of this main fixture, the lounge is plunged into semi-darkness. The only illumination comes from the sidewalls in the form of six small dull orange glows cast by the torch-shaped lamps held aloft in the raised hands of bronze cherubs, and from the white light which shines brightly through the four corridor archways, and up from the bowl of the grand staircase. Some light, but far from enough. People are now silhouettes, and the room itself a maze of shadows. Dade remains still as his eyes adjust to the sudden loss of light. His eyes cannot focus fast enough for him - - he is sure the terrorists are taking action.

As they are. Maddox and DeSantis peer into the darkness through their night vision goggles, which they kept after raiding the En Vogue and slapped on to their faces the moment they see the chandelier begin to fall. Maddox clearly sees Parker slumped against the far wall, looking pathetic. Maddox leans over to Yusacre and pulls her goggles from inside her jacket. "Take these to Parker and bring that fucker back here," Maddox orders DeSantis in a hiss as he passes the black ovular eyepiece over; the man nods and dashes in the direction of Parker.

Bethany arrives at a Halo archway. The room inside is dark...darkness and gunshots equal bad news. She presses up to the corridor wall and peers inside, but cannot see much. She bites her lip and turns to her bag. Out comes the truncheon, and after some searching, two capsules of flash powder. She gingerly holds the items; the truncheon in one hand, the capsules in the other.

Maddox turns his attention to Jensen. She crouches near the floor, her head darting around in panic. Evidently, she does not realize that he carries eyesight in her pocket. "R!" Maddox shouts into his headset through the din of shouts and screams which only now begin to fade as the shock of the fallen chandelier and resulting darkness slowly subsides. Maddox sees Jensen's head snap up in response to the radio call. "Put on your goggles!"

Jensen feels her head grow warm after hearing those words - - her face flushes with embarrassment. She feels stupid. Of course! The night vision! She hastily jams her left hand into her jacket pocket and snatches the goggles out. She warily sets her gun down as she gropes with his right hand for the black rubber strap which dangles from the back of the goggles. On her third attempt, her fingers close around it. As she brings the goggles to her eyes, she stretches the strap and brings it down around the back of his skull. With a rubbery snap, the thick band closes in on her hair and holds the device against her face. Crystal clear vision - - albeit in a neon green hue - - greets Jensen's eyes. She scans the back of the lounge and catches sight of DeSantis running toward the right wall. "On. All set," she reports to Maddox.

"Ok, go get Kobryn."

"On my way. Copy that Kobby?"

"Ready whenever you are," Kobryn confirms.

DeSantis deftly moves around the people lying on the floor and comes upon the immobile form of Parker in seconds. Parker stares blankly, and blinks at the shadow figure which looms above him. He jerks his fists up defensively, ready to strike at who he is sure is his attacker returning to continue the fight. "Alex, it's me amigo, relax." The whispered words have the desired effect, and Parker immediately drops his hands on recognizing the rough voice of DeSantis.

A weak smile appears on Parker's bruised face. "Thanks, man," he says as he shakily rises to his feet. DeSantis glances at his partner, who has certainly seen better days. "Hey, you ok?" he asks, the concern evident in his voice.

"I'll heal."

DeSantis passes the night vision goggles to Parker's right hand. "Put these on," he says as he feels his partner's hand close on the object.

"Night goggs!" Parker says enthusiastically. "Great!" He slips them on his head - - then grunts when the heavy black plastic rubs against his bruised eye and the bridge of his mangled nose. He takes a quick, deep breath, and after a minute the pain subsides.

Parker looks at DeSantis, who appears as clearly as if he is standing under a streetlight. Parker nods, indicating he is fine and ready. "Let's move," DeSantis says, and Parker nods again. DeSantis does a quick turn of his head, then spins on his heel and begins his way back to Maddox. Parker takes a few steps forward, then his left foot falls on an irregular surface. He stumbles, then quickly rights himself. Parker looks down and sees a sleek black rifle lying there - - Dade's CMG 309. Parker grins and bends to retrieve the weapon.

Dade's eyes finally adjust to the darkness. His squinted eyes focus on the silhouette of a man slightly backlit by the light emanating from the grand staircase just as the black shape disappears in a quick drop. Dade slowly turns his head and studies the back of the lounge. The minimal light cast here and there reveals nothing but dark mystery - - and here, darkness can be deadly. Dade takes comfort in the simple fact that everyone else in the room is as blind as he is; at least they are all equal in that way.

Parker snatches up the rifle – feels good. He begins to study the firearm, then pauses and makes a point of checking the safety mechanism - it is off. He excitedly resumes his analysis of the remarkable rifle. It sure looks powerful; a real weapon for a real soldier. He pulls out the ammunition magazine; the thin rectangular black steel box looks to be about half full. Not great, but not bad either. Parker slaps the magazine back into place and flips the firing switch from AUTO to SEMI mode so rounds will not be wasted.

Satisfied, Parker moves to stand again. Out of habit as a well-trained commando, he does a quick turn of his head before standing and exposing himself to any would-be assailants. He turns to his right, toward the front of the lounge, and…well, well, well, there's his attacker standing plain-as-day near the wall! Parker sneers, then smiles…as easy a target as a wooden duck in a carnival shooting gallery. He steals a quick look at DeSantis, who is continuing toward Maddox. Parker turns back to his attacker and faces him. He moves into a shooter's crouch and raises the rifle. So easy!

The fingers of Parker's left hand grip the riflebarrel tightly; his right hand clasps the pistol-grip behind the trigger. His index finger hovers at the curved metal of the trigger itself, itching to fire. The stock of the rifle rubs harshly against Parker's shoulder. He is holding the gun so firmly that the smooth steel digs into the flesh of his upper chest, causing mild pain. But it is good pain. Parker closes his left eye and takes aim with his right. His finger moves back against the trigger - and the laser-sighting scope shoots out a bright red beam of light.

Dade snaps his head down as a tiny red dot appears on his white dress shirt - - right at his heart! He instantly knows what it is, and hurls himself backward to the floor out of the lethal light-path as he hears a male voice shout out a curse just as Rak! a bullet rockets above him. Dade lands heavily on his back, but keeps a firm hold on his pistol. He quickly rolls on his stomach, then spins around so he faces the back of the lounge. With both hands grasping the handle of his shiny silver pistol, Dade aims up and straight ahead.

Through his straining eyes he sees the red laser beam click off. "Goddamn," he says under his breath; that thin stream of light could have led him right to where the terrorist is hiding. Dade desperately wants to fire back, but cannot shoot without a proper target, as a wild shot may injure an innocent person. Dade could never live with such a thing on his conscience, so he waits. Rak!

A bullet tears into the wall just inches from his head. Dade freezes in fear. He suddenly feels as vulnerable as a black jackrabbit in the middle of a snow-covered field: somehow the steward-terrorist knows exactly where he lies. But how? Until answering this, Dade may as well have a neon target strapped to his forehead, because it is impossible to hide if you do not know what you are hiding from. Dade knows it is pure luck that the bullet is embedded in the wall instead of deep in his skull. He also knows that luck does not last forever. He has to do something. But what?

Bethany crouches low at the Halo entrance. Two more shots! And it's still so darn dark in there…. She has to go in, she knows it. She isn't doing anyone any help if she stays in the hallway. She feels that trepidation of knowing you *have* to do something, even though you don't want to, regardless of how simple it may be… Well, it's not going to get any better. Now or never. She drops the cube and capsules back into her bag. She takes a deep breath, crouches lower still, and somersaults into the darkness.

DeSantis punches Parker in the head for the second time. He is sprawled atop his partner in crime, pushing the man forcibly to the floor. "You fucking stupid bastard!" DeSantis whispers harshly into Parker's ear. "Forget them! We've got enough trouble without you running wild!" DeSantis shoves Parker further down to emphasize his point. "Now you're gonna walk over to Maddox and forget all about them. Understand?"

Parker snaps his head to DeSantis. If not for the thick black glass of the goggles, DeSantis would have seen a deep rage burning in Parker's eyes. "Yeah," Parker snarls. "I get it." DeSantis nods, then pulls himself off of Parker. He stays in a crouch and watches Parker right himself. Parker runs a tense hand through his hair . . . DeSantis had tackled him just as he fired the second shot and knocked his rifle off-target. Anger fills Parker's mind . . . if not for his so-called partner, his attacker would be dead now . . . Fuck!

DeSantis rises, quickly scanning the area as he does so. Dade lies perfectly still and watches the black figure stand against the white light of the staircase bowl. Dade sees the head of the silhouette move around and immediately notices something odd when the light catches the profile of the face...a large mass between the forehead and the nose. Light reflects off of the pitch-black shiny surface. Dade's face drops in horror as he makes an incredible eye-opening discovery: night vision! The bastards can see *everything*!

Almost immediately the first figure is joined by a second, whose face is similarly clad with goggles. Dade pauses - - he had just been about to shoot the first terrorist when the second appeared. One he can handle, but never two. No sooner would the first shot have left his pistol than a falisade of bullets would be raining down on him from the other gunman. Dade softly swears in frustration. There the two are, outlined, but he cannot risk shooting at them. He forces anger and anxiety from his mind as he concentrates on an inescapable fact: some way, some how he must find something to hide behind to make himself less obvious to those cold-hearted killers. Dade wonders why he has not yet been shot at again. He guesses he does not have much time left . . . . Rrrraaakkk!

The sound of automatic gunfire clatters in the air. Dade buries his face in the carpet and covers his head with his arms. He braces for the searing pain he knows is coming. He waits. Nothing. He is fine.

He relaxes a bit and tentatively looks up. The two terrorists are no long there. What in the hell is going on here?

"Darian? Edwin?" a male voice bellows warily from deep within the darkness of the lounge. "Are you all right?" The voice belongs to Cal Gregg.

Dade quickly raises his head and turns to the voice. "Get down! Look out! They have night vision!" Screams and groans are heard from the others on the floor at this announcement. Rakk! Rakk! Rakk! Rounds explode around Dade. Ththththokokokok! Others are sent toward the front of the lounge - toward Gregg. Dade presses himself close to the floor. Pain erupts in his left shoulder. He grits his teeth but does not shout out, then quickly looks around – his eyes desperately searching for any form of cover which can hide him from the death-hungry terrorists.

Under the dull orange glow of a cherub lamp he barely spies an overturned couch. The front edge of the seat and the top of the backing lie on the floor, and the short legs stick up in the air – it resembles a pup-tent. Not the best, but more than enough. And it is seven feet away. Dade takes a deep breath then bends his right arm back behind his head so his pistoled hand points toward the back of the room. He squeezes off two round then scrambles forward in an odd sort of crawl-slide to the sofa. He hears shouts of shock from the two terrorists as he disappears into his makeshift sanctuary. Dade breathes a sigh of relief - - if those bastards do not have X-ray vision too, he should be safe for a while. Gregg drops to the floor just before the volley of bullets come charging. He had been going to Dade when he heard the night-vision warning and took a nose-dive. As he hits the carpet he sees two men jump up and begin shooting. He has no idea what is happening.

He had been on his way to reclaim his rifle when shooting started and he had to freeze. Then, the chandelier was shot down. After that, he crawled forward and grasped the 309, but felt at a loss for what do to in the vast, dark chamber. He remained still as his eyes adjusted to the new environment. Once they had, he immediately noticed a stream of red light emanating from the scope of his rifle, to the floor, where the muzzle is pointed. The lasersight must have been knocked on again when the rifle fell. He quickly turns the device off. He looks up to see two men backlit by the staircase light. One stands at an angle and Gregg can clearly see the outline of a rifle jutting from the torso.

A moment later, both are gone from the light. One moves to the right while the other drops. A split-second later Gregg sees a bright red beam followed by the distinct sound of a single CMG 309 gunshot and a loud curse. Must be Dade or Roggin. The laser instantly disappears, and then a silhouette leaps and another 309 shot is heard, followed by the sounds of a scuffle. Then, two figures rise, together, their heads turning as they do. Again, he sees the outlines of rifles at the torsos. One of these is a 309.

Gregg tenses. From the way things look, one of his partners is in some sort of trouble but there is no way he can be sure…can't tell if the other person is a terrorist, or an escaped security officer, or even another passenger who somehow got a rifle. Shoot first and ask questions later, Gregg decides. He keenly devises a plan which will give Dade or Roggin an opportunity to escape if need be. Gregg quickly takes aim at the figure on the left – the one who does not have the 309. He knows his shooting will have to be good, and expertly fires a short burst. The bullets do exactly what he wants them to: they blast past the left side of the man's head, totally startling him and sending both racing to the floor.

It worked! Dade or Roggin should jump up and escape. Wait, neither do. Gregg watches the area with bewildered and straining eyes as his mind floods with questions. He waits a moment longer, and becomes worried. Still no appearance, no calls for help. Nothing. Both men remain still on the floor. What is going on? Seconds pass. Gregg rises. Fearing the worst, he calls out as he takes a step forward. Dade answers, but from a *different* location than where he should be! Gregg throws himself to the floor after Dade's warning and two men spring up and open fire, one toward Dade's voice, the other to the front of the room. "Man," Gregg says softly to himself, "am I gonna be glad when this is over!"

"Night vision…" Bethany whispers to herself. She holds her stun truncheon a bit more firmly. As soon as she was inside, she had taken it from her bag and had it at the ready. She carefully felt her way along, and got herself behind some furniture. Night vision on those terrorists…very bad, very b— wait. Maybe, not so bad.

DeSantis hits Parker with a jab of his elbow. "C'mon - - let's go!" he whispers. He does not want to wait around; the idiot who just missed them may get lucky the next time. The two dash to the left and let darkness blanket them. DeSantis steps aside and lets Parker skirt by him, then follows. That way, if Parker tries any more foolhardy stunts, he will be there to keep his partner in line. They fire sporadically as they go. Although targets are nowhere to be seen, they shoot anyway in hopes of keeping the vigilantes down.

Within seconds, Parker and DeSantis drop to the floor alongside their teammates. Jensen and Kobryn are already there. A small pile of knapsacks rest at their feet.

Maddox stares coldly at Parker through his goggles and does not say a word, allowing his angered face to do the talking for him. After a moment, he speaks. "We'll go to the lobby and regroup." The others nod. Maddox turns to Parker. "Give Kob your rifle and goggles," he orders.

"Bu-" Parker protests.

"Now!" Maddox barks in a harsh whisper. Parker sullenly hands the items over, muttering obscenities as he does so. Maddox ignores him, and Kobryn looks with fascination at the 309. "Ok!" Maddox says to the team. "We're going to cut through the dining room and double back to the lobby. We'll get Yusacre and DeSantis bandaged up, then get off this wreck!" They nod and smile - - all save for Parker. "We'll each take some bags; Parker, you'll take most. Let's do it!" The smiles broaden. Maddox looks at Parker, who simply stares at the pile of knapsacks on the floor. Parker raises his head to Maddox and opens his mouth to speak. "Shut up and grab 'em!" Maddox barks. Parker angrily gathers bags, not breathing a word, but already planning revenge.

Maddox goes to Yusacre, who looks weak, and is pale. He slips his right arm around her waist, and puts her left arm over his shoulders so he can help her walk. She bites her lip to stifle a yelp. Maddox looks at Parker, who seems ready. "We move now," Maddox whispers. "DeSantis, walk point. Kobryn and Jensen, flank. We'll be in a one-eighty cover formation. Destroy anything that moves." Nods follow, and Maddox passes his steward keycard to DeSantis. Then, the group moves. The three escorts, with DeSantis leading the way, are stationed at the nine o'clock, six o'clock and three o'clock positions. This way, the gunners can shield the team from all avenues of attack. DeSantis quickly but silently trots to his left, to where the heavy oak doors of the White Feather are closed against them. Maddox and Yusacre shuffle along, moving quietly as well. Parker huffs his load behind them. Kobryn and Jensen keep their eyes peeled.

They are about half-way to their destination when a decision is made. "Time to throw some light on the matter," Bethany whispers to herself. She again has one of the round flashpowder capsules in her hand. She takes a deep breath, and hurls it as high as she can!

Pa-bang! The room is flooded with a blast of bright white light! The capsule had flown in an arc through the lounge before impacting with the ceiling and bursting with mindblowing pyrotechnics. "Ahhh!" screams DeSantis as his nightvision goggles magnify the lightburst and overload his eyes. He thrusts his forearm across his goggled, blinded eyes and stops dead in his tracks. Kobryn and Jensen scream as well, and also cover their faces. Maddox, whose head was lowered to Yusacre, was not affected by the burst, and as he looks up, the capsule has already flickered and is beginning to fade. Soon, the room is dark again.

DeSantis shakes his head quickly. He blinks behind his goggles. Circles of color dance in front of his eyes, and he blinks repeatedly, rapidly. He can feel his eyes tearing a bit. "What in the fuck was that?" he snarls. His gun-arm is down again, so he'll be ready once his vision clicks-in.

"Damn it, some sort of flare, I don't know…" Maddox says. "Everybody ok?"

"I'll be ok in a minute," DeSantis answers. "My eyes are adjusting."

"Same here," says Kobryn.

"Here too," Jensen remarks.

"We don't have a minute!" Maddox retorts, angrily. "We've gotta keep going!" Maddox knows that, stopped, they are like rats in a trap. And who knows what's next?

"We can't do any good if we can't fucking see!" DeSantis snaps. He is still blinking.

"Ok, ok," Maddox relents, "but the second you see straight, that is the second we move."

Bethany hunches down again. She had seen them. Yes, in that brief moment of the flash-burst, there they were, all six, bunched together, heading toward the grand staircase. She smiles to herself on hearing the yells from the flash – it had worked! It is dark again now though. She carefully feels along the truncheon; yes, it is active and charged, ready to do business. She wraps her left hand around its back. Then, she reaches for another capsule.

"Ok, I'm ready," DeSantis says.

"You two?" Maddox asks.

"Do-able," Kobryn answers.

"Ok here," remarks Jensen.

"Let's go then," whispers Maddox.

"What about our goggles?" asks DeSantis. "They may try to hit us with a flare again."

"Did anybody catch where the first one came from?" Maddox asks.

"From behind, from our right I think, but I can't be sure," answers Kobryn.

"That's what I think too, from that area," Jensen concurs.

"Ok," Maddox continues, "well, you two, give random cover-fire as we go. Don't concentrate on one particular area though. DeSantis, you keep going forward, but everybody set their goggles to their lowest resolution." The three escorts adjust their viewers. Kobryn and Jensen level their weapons. "Go!" says Maddox.

Bethany prepares to throw another capsule. This time, she will charge the group when they are stunned, and zap one or two of the rifle-femmes and be undercover in another part of the room once the flash fades. She bites her lip and holds her breath.

The group moves. Kobryn and Jensen are ready to shoot when…what's that? Roggin's head suddenly appears at the top of a sofa. He has been raising his head periodically since the room went dark to try and ascertain what is happening, but cannot see a damn thing in the darkness! But, what was that flash? He decides to scan the area now, and hopefully spy something. "There!" Jensen yells, and opens fire. As screams mix with gunshots, Roggin plasters himself to the floor. Bullets decimate the sofa and wall. Jensen ends her assault seconds later. She does not know if she killed the man, nor does she particularly care. However, after she stops, there is no sign of whoever was there. She takes pride in her accomplishment: THREAT OVER. She turns to Kobryn and smiles while giving a quick thumb-up. Kobryn smiles back, and nods. Before the dust of the attack settles, the rifle-femmes fire randomly into the room to discourage others from being heroic, troublesome, or even inquisitive.

The group stopped once Jensen began shooting. "Looks like I took care of it," she says.

"Ok, good." Maddox smiles, then slaps DeSantis on the shoulder. "Let's keep going." DeSantis nods and moves. "Quick as we can, people," Maddox orders. Jensen and Kobryn continue to shoot sporadically. Bethany had ducked on hearing the first gunshots. The second flash capsule does not seem like such a good idea, not at this stage of the game anyway. She stays still, and clenches the truncheon even firmer.

The team moves rapidly, undaunted. Going farther along, they press themselves close to the wall to avoid the telltale glow of the staircase light. DeSantis soon arrives at the twin doors. He places his hand on the seam between the doors and pushes. Nothing. Locked. He slips the passcard into the keyslot, and slowly removes it, hoping against hope that the sound of the shifting bolt will be minimal. The lock opens without so much as a squeak. DeSantis reclaims the card and pushes again at the seam. The doors silently swing inward. The room behind is dark. He slips inside, followed closely by the others. The doors silently close. Again, no sound as the bolt is re-locked.

The team of six remain stationary at the White Feather's upper platform and survey the room. The vast banquet hall is eerily dark, empty, and quiet. It is drenched in blue-gray light from dimness which passes in from the side-windows, whose covers remain open. Outside they see the blackness of space with dots of white starlight, and some hovering lifecraft. Also, from their angle, they see the surface of the asteroid below. In its own way, the crater-scarred, round, barren rock is menacing. The salon is empty, and strewn everywhere are the remnants of the party which hastily ended just hours before, but what seems an eternity ago. The still silence of the room is unsettling.

After a moment, they proceed. DeSantis races down the steps. The others hastily follow. Kobryn picks up the legs of Yusacre while Maddox shifts behind her and lifts beneath her arms; Yusacre can be carried much more speedily this way. "Hold on, baby," Maddox whispers, "we'll take care of you soon." Yusacre sighs in reply. Soon, the team reaches floor level, and they dart around the chairs and circular tables. They quickly cross the room. DeSantis bursts through the swing-door at the left of the back wall, and enters the pantry - gun first. The others follow suit. On reaching this door, Jensen, the last of the group, pauses and turns. She hastily scans the room. Seeing no one, she too goes through, and disappears from sight. The door flaps for a moment, then settles and remains still. They are gone.

CHAPTER EIGHTEEN
Surprises

Then, it happens. Another occurrence, un-connected to the heist, but important just the same. An alarm sounds – the countdown displayed on the bridgeclock drops past the one-hour mark. "Zero hour has struck," Captain Arges says ruefully from the command chair. He sits quietly for a moment; there is a sullen stillness in the bridge. "Alright people," he says as he sits up and claps his hands once, "we've got to make these last sixty minutes count. Let's get to it." As the others scurry, he takes the chair microphone. "Time to let the others know." He then regretfully gives his officers the grim news. Less than sixty minutes. Damn. So much to do, so little time.

"Goddamnit," Rish whispers after hearing the message. He lowers his head. After a moment, while carefully covering his watch with his hand, he clicks the backlit readout and checks the time. "An hour, sometimes seems like the blink of an eye." Then, he forces the notion of time-constraint is from his mind. Dwelling on impending doom brings negative thoughts that serve no purpose and only worsen things. "Concentrate on the duties at hand," he mutters. Rish looks up at the lounge ceiling. "I wonder what's going on up there, on the flight deck," he says absently, longing to return to the regimented order of the bridge. But no, for the moment he is trapped by duty in the chaotic pitch-black dungeon called the Halo lounge. He tears his gaze from the ceiling and, with squinting eyes, scans the room. "The end of this can't come soon enough…"

It has been quiet for a few moments – ever since the random gunfire ended. Almost too quiet. The blessed sanctity of silence is definitely not good in this situation. A curious passenger raises his head, propping himself up on his elbows – then bashes his head against the underside of an endtable. “Ah!” he yelps, then ducks. The table is knocked off balance, and tumbles to the floor, causing the glasses atop it to slide off. Crash! The glasses hit the soft carpet in tact, only to be shattered by the weight of the falling table. The passenger ducks lower while the others tense for the gunfire they know is coming.

Wait. Nothing. No yells; no shots. Only silence. Now this is really strange. Seconds pass. Still, nothing. Now more people become curious, slowly raising their heads and straining to see in the inky darkness. What’s going on?

Bethany takes a deep breath, then holds it. She slowly, cautiously, puts herself into a crouch. She takes a careful step forward. Her eyes are focused on the staircase bowl. The truncheon is out in front of her, ready if she needs it. She takes another step. Still there is silence. Another. She knocks her ankle on something on the floor, and she stumbles. She bites her lip and clamps a hand over her mouth to stifle a yell, but almost loses her balance as her other arm goes out to steady herself, and her truncheon goes sailing from her hand. The black nightstick cartwheels on the floor, then tumbles to its side. She watches wide-eyed as it rolls to the edge of the open staircase bowl, then silently drops over the edge.

As this occurs, Rish makes a bold move of slowly moving into a crouch. Still, no sound. He rises to his feet. From those brushing against him, and general sounds in the room, he senses others are unknowingly following his lead. “Are they here?” asks a shaky male voice. “Are they here – no, they must be gone…” jittery, maniacal laughter comes.

“Quiet! Quiet, please!” Rish calls out, guessing that like this will trigger bedlam.

The talker does not heed. “They aren’t here! I tell you, they’re gone!”

That was all they needed. A simple prompt. All at once, people jump to their feet and run like lunatics escaping from an asylum…running for the corridor archways and the lighted safety therein. All exits are instantly mobbed by people grappling in a struggle to escape.

“No! No! People! Remain calm!” Rish shouts. “Calm, *please*!” Seems as though the talker was right, the terrorists are definitely not there. A part of Rish wishes they were, ironically, because at least then they could bring some order to the mob. He is pushed and jostled, then looks around in hope of spotting some stewards or crew to help calm things.

A door by the elevator bay is thrown open. Faint light appears. Rish spies Hearst climbing stairs leading to the flight deck. The dim light of the stairwell shines down on the unmistakable form of the oddly built third officer, whose long hair flops as his feet pound the steps. Rish is about to call out, but the man is gone and the door has closed before he has the chance. Hearst probably would not have turned back even if he did hear Rish anyway. Good old Mitch, Rish thinks sarcastically, always there for you in the pinch.

In the starboard corridor, Alyssa Rayburn warily approaches the aft lounge archway with two stewards. The passengers remain at the back of the corridor, as Syranos continues to load and launch lifecraft. Everyone in the passageway heard the gunfire in the lounge. and Rayburn needs to know what is going on. She presses herself to the edge of the archway. "Peter?" she whispers in to her comlink. She slowly, cautiously, moves her head around to peer inside...

Three people burst from the lounge! They almost knock her to the floor! They do not slow in their mad run as they dash toward the group at the stern. They are instantly followed by others; women and men pour from both archways. Moving without purpose or direction - - just running! Rayburn knows she will only hurt herself if she tries to stop or slow the passengers. She quickly flattens her body against the wall. The stewards to likewise, their faces pale at the sight of the stampede.

"Alyssa! Stay clear of the Halo for now!" She hears Rish answer through her comlink. Then, the mayhem ends as quickly as it began. The scared passengers from the Halo join the others at the back of the corridor. Rayburn takes a breath to relax herself - - her heart beats rapidly from the shock of it all - - and then coughs at the stank air. She pauses and slowly turns her head into the room. The lounge is almost pitch-black and looks to be deserted. Rayburn takes a careful step just inside the archway. "Hello?" she calls.

"Here!" Rish calls back. "I'm here Alyssa!" He can see her standing in the archway, her shapely figure beautifully framed by the light behind. He speaks into his comlink. "Alyssa, it seems to have calmed down. Wait there, I'll get the lights on in a minute."

"Peter, what's happening with the terrorists?" asks Arges over Rish's comlink.

"Seems they vacated the Halo. Crazy rush just happened here. I'm trying to get things settled."

"I see. I'll keep the Bridge under Homesafe. While they're gone, let's speed up the evac as much as we can. Have some crew take thirty passengers down to the captain's launch – it should hold thirty people – and send the craft offship."

"Will do," Rish says as he quickly but carefully makes his way to the right wall. He stumbles once, and later smashes his left shin on some damaged furniture, but reaches his destination. Once at the wall, he feels along the panels. His fingers soon move over what he searches for, and he presses a piece of moulding. A panel slides noiselessly back to expose a small steel electrical box. Rish uses his passcard to unlock and open it. Inside is a large switch and a small numeric panel.

He enters a code then places his hand on the large black plastic switch. The power to the lounge is still active even though the primary fixture in the room is gone, as attested by the tiny yellow sparks which continue to shoot out of the two chandelier wires which dangle lifelessly from the ceiling, and by the orange cherub torchlights.

However, with the power off, the emergency lighting will automatically activate. Rish flips the heavy switch to the right; it moves into place with a loud clunk. Before the last two parks have reached the floor and before the torchlights have completely dimmed, two medium-sized spotlights in each corner flash on brightly. These are simultaneously joined by two others, located in the middle of the room where the walls meet the ceiling. The Halo is again alive with light.

Rayburn gasps and subconsciously takes a step backward. "Oh, oh no…" She does not recognize the room as the stately, ornate Halo lounge. It looks positively awful - - like a ravaged lobby you would find in a dilapidated hotel stuck in an inner-city ghetto. It has been through one terrible fight. Rayburn surveys with saddened eyes; then she sees the tangled mass of junk that is the chandelier and the statue…it feels like someone punched her hard in the stomach. She brings her hand to her gaping mouth.

Rish sees her reaction, and gives the room a cursory glance. Yes, it looks like something belched out of a war zone, but the effect is not nearly the same on him because he witnessed the destruction in stages as it happened, rather than having the 'ruins' thrust on him all at once. He walks toward her, and catches sight of a few who, for whatever reason, remained in the lounge.

Bethany Parris is, of course, one of those. She still has her bag of tricks, and had to blink once the spotlights clicked on. After a moment, she looks over at the staircase bowl, and walks to it. At the railing, she peers down….can't see the truncheon! Damn! She steps back from the edge and turns to look at the room. Oh God! What a disaster! She then pauses. Wait…the bandits did not leave by the back archway, and they didn't move in any way that the staircase bowl-light showed…. She looks back at the rear wall. The doors to the White Feather are closed tight. Where did they disappear to? She looks up, warily. There are no ceiling vents in the immediate area. She steals a glance to the closest one, which is a fair bit away, but it does not appear to have been disturbed.

As we walks, Rish sees a tuxedoed man slowly rise to his feet, holding a rifle, being one of the passenger-fighters. His back is to Rish, and the first officer walks up to congratulate him for his bravery. Cal Gregg turns. Rish stops dead in his tracks, aghast. Gregg's face is caked in crusty, crimson blood; drops of it have dried in ruby stains on his crisp white shirt. Gregg raises an eyebrow questioningly at the officer's reaction; he has no idea how he looks, as the pain in his forehead has long since subsided, and in the fury of recent events, he completely forgot about the cut. Rish smiles feebly. Aside from the look of the face, the passenger appears strong and alert. "Are you all right, Sir?"

"Yes, perfectly fine." Gregg is bewildered at the manner of how the question is asked.

"I see one of them caught you there?" Rish asks as he runs his forefinger across his forehead at the area corresponding to the injury on Gregg's head.

"Oh that!" Gregg says testily as he raises his hand to the wound; his fingers lightly touch the gritty cut and he winces at the sting. "One of your partners jumped me!" Gregg barks angrily. "The sonofabitch tried to steal my rifle!" Rish's face bunches in confusion as he wonders who would be that stupid as Gregg continues. "He was that heavy longhaired Officer, the one who kept bothering people for a while...what's his name again…."

Of course, Rish thinks, Hearst. Hearst would do that. "Sir, for whatever good it will do, I offer my most sincere apologies for that person and his inexcusable behavior." Rish puts his hand forward in an offer of peace. "I can assure you, Sir, that the Officer will be punished to the fullest extent. The Line cannot begin to offer its regrets at this incident."

Gregg passes his 309 to his left hand and takes the proffered hand in a firm grasp. "Thank you." His mood has been considerably lightened. "It's Mr. Rish, isn't it?"

"Yes, First Officer Peter Rish, Sir."

"Calvin Gregg. The apology means a lot." Then, Gregg pauses. He thinks about his injury, a cut to the forehead. Headwounds, regardless of how small, are notoriously bloody. He glances down at his shirt, and it confirms his suspicion. He wants to find Roggin and Dade, but wants to be presentable as well. Gregg sheepishly looks at Rish. "I guess I look a little worse for wear."

"Sir, there is the Men's restroom near the elevators . . ."

Gregg nods. "Thank you. I'll be back in a moment."

"Certainly," Rish says with a nod. "And, Mr. Gregg, thank you for your help."

"My pleasure." Gregg nods and proceeds toward the elevator bay. Rish continues toward Rayburn, being angry and frustrated with Hearst.

Along the way, Rish kneels and puts a reassuring hand on the backs of those few terrified people who lie clinging to the lounge carpeting as though it is a security blanket. "Come on, it's ok.... let's get up so you can leave the ship," he invariably whispers into their ears. They succumb to his coaxing, and slowly rise. When the others see these first stand, they follow. Before long, the floor is clear.

Rish spies movement from under an overturned couch. He tenses, then Darian Dade crawls out - gun first - and cautiously peers around. It seems relatively safe, so he stands and slips his pistol into the waistband of his slacks. Dade sees Gregg enter the Men's washroom.

"He ok?" Dade asks as Rish approaches.

"Yes, Mr. Gregg," Rish begins. "He had an unfortunate encounter, shall we say." Rish notes the concern registering on Dade's face. "Nothing serious, mind you, just a run-in with an overzealous crewman. He just needs to straighten up is all."

"Oh, I see," Dade says.

Rish extends his hand. "I want to congratulate you on your bravery Mister?"

"Darian Dade," he replies while shaking the officer's hand. "Thank you. We couldn't just sit by and let them take control like that."

"Darian!" The sound of Roggin's excited voice causes Dade to spin, pulling his hand from Rish's and prematurely ending the handshake. Roggin is spotted at the far side of the room walking from behind a couch, and Dade waves to him.

"You ok?" Dade asks.

"Fine! You?"

"Grazed in the shoulder, but ok. Cal's fine, he'll be back in a second."

Once Roggin arrives, Rish similarly thanks him for his action against the terrorists. "Well," Rish continues, "if you gentlemen will excuse me, I have a lot of work to do."

"Certainly," Dade responds pleasantly as Roggin nods. He shakes the officer's hand quickly. "Good luck with everything. Officer?"

"First Officer Rish. We'll see to it that you are safe soon, gentlemen."

Rish is soon beside Rayburn. "I know, it's bad."

"Incredibly bad," she answers. "And I have more bad news. We're down to the last of the lifecraft on starboard."

"Aw, hell…." Rish says, then his comlink sounds. "Peter, this is Julius," says the doctor from the Med Office.

"Yes, go ahead."

"You heard John's message, correct? About the last hour?" Disappointment is there.

"Yes." Not much enthusiasm here either.

"Time to move the injured engineers off of the ship."

"Yes, good – I was just about to suggest that. Bring them portside."

"Will do. I will prep them. Should only take a few minutes."

"I'll send some crew to help."

"Thank you."

The doctor ensures each one is stable enough to travel while Rish goes to the Port corridor and sends stewards down to the Med – Rayburn stays behind to stand watch in the Halo. Two engineers are on stretchers, and the other four need assistance walking. When the group is ready to move, Washington walks ahead and clears a path in the hallway crowd. A nurse walks with them, while another remains at the Med to help those who were mildly injured when the lobby lights were off. Rish keeps an eye out, and soon sees them coming. After passengers are seated and secured, the wounded engineers are settled into two craft.

Once these are launched Rish goes to an inter-ship wallphone. "Corté here," comes a harried answer after the second ring.

"This is Peter, Chris. Please tell Tac that the injured engineers are safely away."

"Yessir. Thank you, Sir," Corté replies then Rish hangs up and Corté calls E-2. "Chief Holden, could you come to the E.O.C. please?'

"Yes, just a moment." Holden has been studying computerized schematics of the engine damage and is making a video entry into the log about repairs. He makes E-2 his temporary base of operations as it is less hectic here than in the E.O.C.. He hits the record button on the videotape again, and clears his throat just before the red light clicks on. "I discovered that a makeshift thrust apparatus can be constructed from what is left - - the power would not be strong, but it would be enough. The problem is that the device cannot be built in a mere hour . . . it will take seven times that, at least." Holden pauses and looks sullenly to the floor. "Damn this limited time!"

He looks up again, straight into the camera, forlornly. "I hope someday, someone can follow this plan and make her spaceborne once again. Good luck." He clicks off the device, stands, and leaves.

"What is it, Chris?" Holden asks as he enters the E.O.C. "Officer Rish said that the injured techs safely boarded shuttles and have left the ship."

"Well, that's good to hear," Holden says with a smile as he takes a seat at the Board. He is glad to know his people are all right.

"Now, for the bad news," Corté begins in a more subdued tone. "Captain Arges left a message for you. We have less than an hour of air, and the evac topside is going slowly. It's almost at a standstill. I believe we should consider alternatives for the crew, Sir."

Holden's mood darkens somewhat. His eyebrows come together as his eyes narrow and he turns his attention to some monitors and studies their readouts. "What's the status on the systems of the defective lifecraft?"

"Nonexistent. We can't do a thing with them. It will take a few hours just to build the interfacing we need, let alone install it. We just don't have the time. Those shuttles may as well not be there at all for all the help they are to us."

"Son of a bitch!" Holden barks, and lets his fist fall heavily on the desktop. There is silence as he considers the situation.

"Ok," he begins as he turns to his second-in-command. "we don't have any options. Have un-needed crew suit up and leave through the airlocks. Tell them to get as far away from the ship as they can, and latch on to any shuttles they can find. We'll keep essential personnel until the last possible moment, just to keep the vitals alive and functioning. Spread the order, and make it clear they're only to stay if it's absolutely necessary. Otherwise, leave. Sound good to you?"

"Sounds excellent, Sir," Corté says with a nod.

"Ok, we'll do it then."

"Yessir!" Corté answers and jumps to action. "Attention, all engineering stations..."

The chief makes the log entries and summons the bridge. "Captain, I need to advise you of a decision."

From across Engineering, white-jumpsuited technicians come running. They go to the lockers which hold the Extra-Vehicular Activity Suits (EVAS) and begin to put on the bulky orange suits. The 'essentials' who know they will be staying also suit-up so they will be ready to go in the event of an emergency, and so they can remain at their posts and do their duty until the last possible second.

The EVAS are highly functional outfits. Magnetic clamp-locks run down the length of the back of the suit for suiting it onto a person, and there are two long, narrow oxygen tanks on each side of the back section. Weighted boots and form-fitting gloves are attached directly to the bodysuit. There are tiny rockets built into the bootheels which are controlled by tiny "ON" and "OFF" buttons on the outer section of the forefinger. A person merely has to move his or her thumb over the buttons and press them in order to maneuver in outer space. As a safety feature, the "ON" button only functions after the EVAS registers the loss of pressure and the temperature change when one is outside the ship. Thus, if a button is accidentally knocked while still inside, the rockets will not fire.

Orange helmets accompany the suits. Each has a microphone at the mouth-level and speaker units at each ear. The front of the helmet consists of a thick glass face-shield, and a thin, tubular lightbulb stretches across the top of this shield at the helmet's forehead. The helmets can be attached to the EVAS only in one way - - the correct way - - so the chance of a person securing the helmet wrongly, and dangerously, is impossible. Once the helmet is locked onto the suit at the neck, the top-light activates, and the EVAS become air-tight as oxygen is pumped in to the helmet from the airtanks. The helmet is carried on a loop at the left midsection of the suit so it can easily be slapped into place at a moment's notice.

All the techs are suited in minutes. Corté closes and secures the unessential sections of engineering. Crew normally there report to the nearest air-lock to be processed off the ship (although some sneak back to their quarters and gather personal items or valuables before joining the line). An airlock can hold four. A foreman stands beside the hatchway at the control panel and scans identi-bands as personnel enter the closet-like room. Then, the interior door is closed, and after the four have helmeted, the lock is depressurized and the hullside door opens. They simply step out, and float in the weightless void.

Most of the engineers with active stations return to their worksites, keeping their sense of duty forefront in their minds. They know the ship requires certain working units to function - - especially now, in this time of crisis, and it is their task to ensure that these elements operate properly. After all, that is why they are out there among the stars to start with. However, not all have this mindset – the cowards who are extremely belligerent are permitted to leave for, as Holden said, only the amount necessary are needed. Once the 'jellyfish' go, the foremen speak. "We appreciate your sense of duty and loyalty. You are not expected to sacrifice yourselves, or come close to risking your lives, but please work on until the last. From this second forward, the Line will provide you with the substantially higher danger pay in recognition of your sense of duty in this less-than-normal situation."

"Thank you, Tac," Arges answers, acknowledging Holden's report about evacuating the techs. "Alright everyone, time to suit up," he orders. The Homesafe is temporarily bypassed and bridge doors are unlocked, then one by one, the members of the bridge staff go to the EVAS lockers near the security station. Arges becomes contented at being surrounded by orange-suited people. Now, at least, they will have a fighting chance at survival. Arges opts <u>not</u> to put on an EVAS. Of course, none of the staff choose to question his decision. The captain in his white dress uniform enhances his air of authority, confidence, and strength. Arges wishes to retain these qualities as long as he possibly can, if only for the sake of crew morale. The men and women under his command look to him as a patriarchal source of inspiration - anything less, particularly during this time, can possibly further weaken the already strained sense of order in the ranks.

Only those directly involved with the passengers, namely the stewards, the band, security officers and officers themselves, will wait to put on their EVAS as Arges knows the sight of crewmembers in EVA suits will further upset the already distressed crowd. As well, personnel already on the Shuttle Deck have a better chance of escaping on a lifecraft. Following his order, Martingale excitedly turns to the captain. "Sir, a ship, the *Sacramento*, has beckoned us with a signal, locking on the position of our transponder! She seems to be at least an hour away, but is coming!"

"Fantastic!" says Arges with a smile.

Then, on the bridge, in a place seemingly worlds away from the furor in the lounge just a deck below, a previously unheard alarm sounds on the Board and joins the chorus of voices, beeps and blares which fill the room. An ensign immediately goes to investigate the source of the tone. He presses a button and silences the alarm as he reads a report on a vidscreen, then turns ashen as a look of terror comes over him. He turns slowly toward the captain, whom he can see is already involved in an intense conversation with another of the bridge staff. He slowly approaches. Arges spies the ensign, and, seeing the look on the face, pauses his conversation. "Something wrong, Warren?" he asks.

"Begging your pardon, Sir," he begins, nodding both to the captain and the other crewman, clearly awkward about having interrupted.

"It's quite all right. Don't worry about it. Continue."

"Sir, I believe there is something you should know."

"Yes?"

"The computer reports the last of the starboard lifecraft has been launched."

The news shocks Arges and the colleague. The captain races from the command chair and goes directly to a console on the Board. A telephone rings as Arges grimly studies the screen which shows a top-down bright green outline of the shuttle deck. The right side is blank save for the red ovular shapes representing the unusable lifecraft at midship. In addition to the matching six on the opposite side of the diagram, only three red ovals flash at the port-aft section. Three shuttles left. Damn.

"Captain!" an excited voice yells in the background. "Officer Syranos is calling to report *all* the starboard lifecraft are gone!" Gloom descends on the bridge. Silence, except for the incessant cavalcade of alarm tones from the Board.

"Yes, I can see it," Arges replies absently, his eyes never leaving the vidscreen. "Please instruct her to escort whatever passengers she has left to the Port corridor."

The captain turns and walks sullenly to the chair. He sits down heavily. "Roberta," he says while massaging the bridge of his nose with his thumb and forefinger in an effort to alleviate the headache which forms, "please inform Gamma of this newest development."

"Yessir," she replies. Escoto has been diligently updating Controller Polski at Spaceport Gamma about every detail concerning the sinking ship. She also put a shipwide block on any transmission originating from a news station or charter vessel with media inquiries. After each Morse message from the *Emprasoria*'s beacon, Polski radios back the message she received, and Escoto either verifies it or makes the necessary corrections.

"Lisa," Arges says, addressing the pilot, "any sign of the S.R. teams?"

"None as yet, Sir," is her grave reply. "But we have received several beckons by sonar from them. They are on the way. Apparently there is some heavy meteor traffic in the vicinity. That is likely slowing them, Sir."

"Please alert me the second you detect something."

"Yessir. The very second, Sir."

Arges lowers his hand from his face and looks around at the quiet, seemingly frozen bridge staff. His look rallies them from their pause and they hurriedly resume their work, making the bridge once again a center of bustling activity.

The captain leans back in the chair, perplexed with the whole God-awful situation. Everything is going so horribly, horribly wrong. What was supposed to be the last, glorious fun-filled evening of the ace run has mutated into some bizarre enacting of Murphy's Law. Yes, everything that could go wrong is in fact going wrong - - some how, some way, the natural order of things has gone lethally awry for the *Emprasoria*. One major mishap is certainly to be expected during any cruise . . . two, perhaps; three, within the realm of possibility . . . but a multitude? Never.

It is as though an army of demons spread their leathery wings and soared up from the fiery pits of hell, then descended on the defenseless ivory ship, assaulting it with every evil known to humankind - - relentlessly attacking and ending only after the majestic vessel lies broken and decimated on some rocky, barren plain. Arges is dismal, yet outwardly remains a source of inspiration for his crew, continuing to give a look of calm, order, and bravado. He takes a deep breath to bolster his spirits - - then coughs after inhaling warm, heavy, slightly stale air into his lungs. He composes himself, then shakes his head in frustration. "Our ace run has gone bust – turned snake eyes on us," he mutters. He then looks at the date on a readout. He focuses on the year. There's has been the first ace run for 2088; an ace with an 88....aces and eights.... "Dead man's hand," he says.

Hearst had kept his head down and to the left when he reached the Flight Deck, and arrived at the starboard corridor. He immediately saw the silver door to the Bridge closed – just as well for him, no one can see him from in there, which means he will not be bothered. Luckily, the hallway was also empty for him. He walks, quickly. His pass-card is ready in his hand as reaches his cabin. He dashes in; slams the door hard. Click - the lock is in place again. The light comes on and he tosses his hat on the bed; he had picked it up on his way to the stairwell. He sits heavily in the swivel chair at his desk, then buries his face in his hands and ignores the pain. Damn this is bad! His mind burns with rage at the bastard who had beaten him - - if only he could have gotten his hands on that rifle! Now what?

His head snaps up as an idea comes to life. Misery disappears, a smile comes. His beady eyes narrow as he develops the concept. After formulating a scheme, he reviews it, every step, meticulously, for inherent flaws or possible complications. Corrections are made, along with devising contingency provisions. Ok! All Set! His smile widens as he moves to his desk and sets to work. He knows what he has to do, and is quite prepared to do it.

As Hearst labors away on his private task, his colleagues below do their best in assisting passengers. Rish joins Rayburn again in the Halo, and just then, both their comlinks sound. It is Syranos. "Peter, Alyssa, the last here has gone. John says for me to bring passengers over to the port hall. Is it safe?"

"Yes, yes Jen, bring them through the lounge," Rish says dejectedly. "But be aware, it looks very bad in here..."

For a moment, Peter Bull watches the officers at the back of the room. Then, he rises and helps Myrie up. "You ok, babe?" he asks while dusting himself off.

"Yes, fine, just a bit shaken," she says, her voice wavering. "How about you?"

"Fine." There is a silent pause for a moment as Bull hugs her and they steady themselves against the wall. "Boy, that was crazy."

"You know it," Myrie agrees.

"It was good for us to stay behind, and keep out of that mess," Bull comments, and she nods. They avoided of the mass exodus from the massive room because Bull is a veteran of too many concerts to willingly put himself in a moving mob - - he's witnessed all too often what can happen to a human body in such a situation. At the first signs of the rush, Bull threw himself atop Myrie to shield her body with his own. The rock star gets a few kicks and jabs as people move past him, but is not hurt beyond some bruises. "Too crazy," Bull says again. Myrie buries her head against his chest, and cannot see as he winces when her face brushes one of the bruises, but he puts his arms around her and holds her close.

"I need to check the guitar," Bull says after a minute, then inspects the instrument whose strap remained tight when he and Myrie dove to the floor. He had clutched his guitar tightly against his chest the entire time of the gun battle. Myrie pulls back and Bull brings the guitar up. He looks it over, then his face drops in grief. He stares in anguish at his most prized possession. There, in the mid-point of the body, between the third and fourth strings, a small, perfectly round bullethole mars the sunburst gold finish of the rich mahogany. "Damn it!" Bull yells from the pit of his soul with the heat of instant enraging. "Those goddamn losers hurt *it*!" It feels like part of him has been damaged. As though his heart has been ripped from his chest, or one of his hands amputated, or he's been castrated.

The six-string electric wondertoy is everything to Peter Bull. As a teenager, he scrimped and saved for two solid years to buy it. Once in his hands, he practiced hour upon hour until he mastered the instrument. That guitar has stayed with Bull from the very start. From his first dreams, and when he and his friend Billy Gamble formed 'The Blythe Heathens'. Then, through countless hours of rehearsing with the band in Gamble's garage, to the earliest jam sessions on cramped bar-room stages, and still more gigs, to the moment they were discovered by an awestruck agent, to when they signed with Mythos Records and cut the first of many hit songs and blockbuster albums. Bull guarded his guitar as though it is his firstborn child. He personally takes care of it during rough-and-tumble concert tours, and always knows where it is every minute. He polishes and tunes it regularly. The guitar has never suffered so much as a scratch. Now, it is scarred by a terrorist's bullet.

Myrie sees his pain. She massages his shoulders to console him. "It'll be ok, Baby," she whispers. Bull hears, but does not respond. He kneels and checks his amplifier; it looks fine. With a rapidly beating heart, he tensely looks at the left side of the amp, holding his breath as he studies the disc deck - - if the disc is damaged . . . all that music lost...

"It's ok!" Bull blurts with a bright smile. "The disc is perfect!" He jumps up, grasps her, and kisses her quickly. He kneels again and double-checks, reassuring himself that the device is completely in tact, then breathes a sigh of relief. At least not everything is bad.

"I've gotta check out the guitar!" Bull mutters, then picks up the connector cord which lies next to the amplifier. The cord had popped out of the guitar during his rapid fall to the floor. He stands, pauses, turns on the amp then plugs the cord into the round socket at the bottom of his guitar. There is a click, and the amplifier hums loudly as it waits for Bull to send some inspired notes. But, he waits. He is afraid to try his guitar, afraid of the screeching sound which may assault his musically adept ears. He lowers his head and dismally looks at the floor. It is then that his eyes fall on his guitar-pick. The black plastic rounded edge triangle emblazoned with the gold-colored bull's head beckons him. He kneels and puts the pick between his thumb and forefinger. It feels good there, so natural. Bull smiles as he stands. He looks warily to Myrie for reassurance, and she nods to him.

"Here goes nothin'," he says, then tentatively strums the guitar. The metallic sound spills crisply and cleanly from the small black box. Bull's heart leaps. He picks a few strings. Clear twangs come forth. He tries an easy riff. The amp answers with what sounds to Bull like a choir of angels. Yes! He looks at Myrie and smiles widely, his face beaming with pleasure. Tears well up in here eyes at the sight of her rejuvenated man. Bull closes his eyes, throws his head back, and launches into the thunderous opening chords of 'Peter's Anthem - Hear The Bull Roar', the first song ever written by him.

Bull plays an extended version of the song, his body swaying back and forth in time with the music as he pours his soul into the guitar. As the last note falls into a long fade, he raises his guitar to his lips and kisses it. It will take a lot more than a small slab of brass - a token of evil - to hurt his baby. He pulls the guitar away and looks at it again. He studies the location of the hole and thinks a moment. When he was on the floor, he deliberately laid on his side with Myrie behind so as not to crush the guitar under him. The strap had shifted during the fall and changed the position of the guitar; the body was moved up from its normal place at his midriff. He stares intently at the bullethole. "Look at the spot. If the guitar hadn't been where it was . . ." Bull self-consciously touches the left side of his chest. His face pales as a great revelation comes upon him: the guitar had saved his life.

Jack McCartney helps Diana to her feet. "This is amazing!"

"You're tellin' me!" She clicks off her vidcam, not wanting to waste precious battery-power. "The stills and footage will be incredible," she continues, knowing her keen eye for good photography has been developed well over many years as a war correspondent.

"Jim Daresh heads our office at Utopia…" McCartney remarks, thinking aloud.

"Yes."

"We better get this to him ASAP. Then transmit it to the head office in New York, then,"

"And only then will we let some out to the wire services," continues the smiling Diana.

"Agreed." The smile is returned to her. McCartney pauses, thinking, again lost in concentration. "The stuff in that camera is worth gold right now."

Diana nods and clutches the vidcam close to her chest. "Ok, we'll get you on a shuttle - - you probably have a better chance. I'll stay here until the last moment," he holds his electropad up, "and write about it all." Diana opens her mouth to object. "I know," McCartney says before she can speak, "not the preferred way, but the best way to ensure the film is safe. Hell, I can look after myself, and join you at the Spaceport."

Silence between them, for a moment. "I see your point," Diana finally says. "I just hope we don't miss anything else....I mean, for me to leave with the camera at this stage....and it's already been an incredible evening…."

"It's a chance we have to take. And," McCartney says, grinning, "if anything else does happen, you'll have an exclusive interview with a pretty darned good eyewitness."

She smiles. "True enough, Mr. McCartney."

"My pleasure, Mrs. McCartney." They chuckle and share a quick kiss, then McCartney escorts his wife to the corridor and sees her off. Diana is able to hide the vidcam from the crew as she enters a shuttle and seats herself. McCartney waves goodbye as the shuttle departs, then returns to the lounge, holding his electropad tightly in his hand.

J.D. Zolnick is among those who applaud when Bull finishes his stirring song. "Damn, that guy has talent!" the billionaire financier says, standing just a few feet from Bull. He too chose to remain out of the mad crowd. "Goddamn, they moved like a gang of frenzied brokers chasing a blue-chip option," he said ruefully while thinking about the recent run.

Zolnick looks around the room. The gun-play completely shocked him out of his semi-drunken state, so he now sees through sober eyes. What he sees makes him wish he is drunk. Such a mess! A waste! Zolnick shakes his head in disgust. He then turns his attention on himself. He feels quite tired, and his legs are beginning to grow stiff. He takes a quick stroll, and sees McCartney come in from the corridor. "Hi, Jack. Diana ok?"

"Yes, she's fine thanks, just saw her away," McCartney says, smiling.

"Can you believe all this?"

"Not at all. It is incredible."

Zolnick takes note of the electropad, and smiles. "You must be having a field day!"

McCartney grins to his friend. "You know me, never one to pass on a good story."

"Right enough. And all to yourself, too..."

"Yes, that thought had crossed my mind. And Diana's too, of course. Hell of an entry for *The Compass and Current*." The two laugh uproariously.

"That's for damn sure!" Zolnick continues. "McPherrin wouldn't know where the heck to begin." More laughter.

As his laughing fades, McCartney takes his pen from his jacket, clicks it, then tags a button and a clean sheet appears on his electropad. "We'll just have to wait and see how the rest of this all turns out."

"That's for sure," Zolnick comments, now pensive.

Adrianna Harting warily creeps up the grand staircase. She has an angry and determined look on her face. She has a taser truncheon, held out like a medieval sword. By the look on her face, she is quite willing to use it. She is like a warrior maiden, a hellion on a mission. She comes to the top step, and looks about the room with quick and fierce eyes. She presses her finger down and lets a mini-burst of blue electric zap sizzle the air ahead to let anyone know she means business. She does not see the terrorists in the ravaged, dimly-lit room, but does spy someone. "Where are they?" she asks, the words fly from her lips as though she is spitting fire. He stares back with a gaping mouth and wide eyes, and says nothing. "The terrorists. Where are they," she says again with anger, not being in the mood for playing games with the dumbfounded.

"G-gone.......I d-don't know where they are."

She rolls her eyes in contempt. Great, just what she needs. Someone without answers.

Roggin taps Dade on the shoulder and points to the stairs. Dade turns and sees her. "Adrianna!" She catches sight of him and smiles. He races to her. They throw their arms around each other and hold close in a tight embrace. Dade releases her and steps back. She is still holding the taser. "Hey hey hotstuff comin' through…" he jokes.

"Ha ha very funny. This is all I could find. Not much, I know, but I was coming back to help you mister…." she jabs him in the chest with her forefinger.

"Sorry sweetie, only kidding." They kiss. "I was able to fight him off and get this back." He twirls his pistol on his forefinger.

"Good for you. That guy is one crazy son-of-a-bitch. By the way…" She pauses and he looks at her, then she kisses him deeply. "Thanks for going against them, and him. Didn't know you were such a good shot. And where did you find that rifle of yours, anyway?"

"Long story," Dade replies. "No time for it now. We have to get off this wreck." He looks over and sees that Gregg has rejoined Roggin. "Come on with me, we have to figure something out." He takes her by the hand and heads to the front of the lounge.

Tsarevich Alexai Romanoff stands near the remains of the statue, absently sliding the ceremonial dagger of his dress uniform in and out of its metal sheath. He is thinking, deeply, lost in concentration. When he saw the two thieves come off the lounge elevator and begin walking to the crowd, he turned his back and removed the sheath from his gold-weave belt and slipped it into the right sleeve of his white jacket. Luckily, the dagger had fit, but just barely. He put an unwilling contribution into the sack as it made its rounds without the thieves having a hint that he had a weapon. Through the battle he had been waiting to use the blade - - itching to - - but could not find an opportunity which would not end without his being the subject of a State Funeral in Russia.

His eyebrows come together as he spars with a complex question. Everyone is so happy that the bandits are gone, no one has stopped to ask, "Where did they go?" So long as the bandits are on the ship, they are a threat. The fact that they are running loose on the ship with their whereabouts unknown makes it even worse. He tries to put himself in their predicament. "If I was leading that team, where would I go?" An answer comes to light.

He proceeds to Gregg and Roggin, who are near the back of the room. He stops briskly, and the two turn their attention to the tall Russian. "Gentlemen," Romanoff begins. With his hands along his sides, he clicks his heels together, and the booted leather gives a sharp snap, then he nods in a single, quick move. They nod in reply. "Permit me to introduce myself. I am Tsarevich Alexsander Romanoff, Lieutenant in the Imperial Russian Navy." Roggin and Gregg raise their eyebrows, impressed at the credentials.

"Edwin Roggin," says Roggin while extending his hand.

"Cal Gregg." His hand comes forward as well, and a round of handshakes are exchanged.

"First, my hearty congratulations to you both for opposing the bandits, and for your excellent shooting abilities," Romanoff begins. "But, gentlemen, I believe this little war is far from over. Just because they are away does not mean they are gone. Remember, we are in an enclosed environment. We must search them out and capture them."

"Yes, Your Highness I agr- -" Gregg stops at the raised palm put forward by Romanoff.

"Please, Alexai," the Tsarevich says with a smile.

"Very well, Alexai. Now, Alexai, I agree with you, but we cannot scour the ship searching for these scoundrels. There is no time; the ship is sinking, and I'll be damned if I will lose my life looking for that scum."

"Nor I" says Roggin while nodding in agreement.

"Agreed, agreed, gentlemen. But, permit me to offer an educated guess, if you will." Dade joins the group, then all three listen intently as Romanoff continues.

Smash! A door is kicked inward. It creaks on its hinges as four shapes race into a dark room. Nothing. Silence there; empty save for them. A pause. Whispering. A ceiling light suddenly clicks on, brightly. Still no one but these four. Gregg, Roggin, Dade and Romanoff stand inside the spacious and pleasant waiting room of Dr. Washington's office. Weaponry ranging from 309s to a silver pistol to a dagger with a royal crest are poised as the men cautiously search the three examination rooms. All are empty.

Still, there is evidence that one was not so vacant in the recent past. Examination Room 3 displays the effects of a rapid search - - closet doors and drawers lie open, their contents having been ransacked, pulled out, and left in a mess. And, there is blood. Crimson stains on the walls and the examination bed. The normal sterility of this room has been seriously compromised. Someone has been there, taken what was wanted, then left in a hurry.

"You were right, Alexai," Gregg says. "They were here. But where are they now?"

"That, I cannot answer," Romanoff says regrettably as he sheathes his dagger.

Maddox shakes his head. He is studying the readout on the tiny screen of his infokeeper. The information is not good. It had sounded an alert when the Zero Hour notice had been calculated by the main computer. "An hour....only a stinking hour....boy we're going to have to hustle," Maddox mutters. He then looks up at his team. They are in the back room of the Purser's Office. They had first gone to the doctor's office and, figuring that would be the first place others would look for them considering the wounds they had to attend to, they had quickly taken what they needed and raced to a less likely hideout.

Kobryn is painstakingly stitching Yusacre's mangled arm. Yusacre has been given drugs and is more alert. Pain, however, is clearly etched on her face as her partner goes to work on her. "Hold still, it won't be much longer," Kobryn says in a low voice.

"I know, I know," Yusacre says through gritted teeth and a strained face. "Another medal for me...." She continues, and smiles while looking at what one day will be a scar. DeSantis waits for treatment, holding a bloodied bandage against his wound, saying nothing but having a mute rage clearly seen in his angered eyes. The others sit quietly, mulling over the situation and waiting for Maddox's orders. As for their leader, he diverts his attention from his team as he contemplates what to do next.

Beeeeeep bip! Beeeeeep bip! Beeeeeep bip! The computer at the office's desk suddenly begins to sing-song with mechanical tones.

It startles the gang, who are still tense from the battle and on edge with the fear of a reprisal attack. Even this mild sound is too much.

"They found us!" Parker yells, loaded with panic. "They're trying to distract us!"

Beeeeeep bip! Beeeeeep bip! the computer sings again. It is now joined by the unit outside at the Purser's Desk, which chimes in the same tone. The Purser's Office now contains a miniature choir of beeping computers - - it is like being inside an arcade.

"How in the hell did they find us?" Jensen asks excitedly, for the moment buying in to Parker's theory. She looks up at the video camera, the most obvious source, but it remains distracted from the relay misfeed device from the time they raided the vault. There is no immediate answer to her question, then Maddox speaks up.

"Relax and sit tight. They haven't found anything."

Kobryn's stitching task is difficult enough without added annoyance. And she is not a patient woman. As the computer begins its third chime, she marches over to the offending machine. Using both hands, she unceremoniously rips the computer from the desktop. The powercord is torn from the wallsocket, and the computer immediately falls silent. But this is not enough. Not for Kobryn. She heaves the unit above her head and with an angry howl barbarically smashes it into the floor. The computer lies broken at her feet. Satisfied, she calmly returns to her patient.

This leaves the computer at the Purser's Desk. If it continues to beep, it will attract attention which could bring an early end to their secluded hideout. Maddox takes off in a run; he vaults over his sitting partners with a leap which would have made a track star proud. The second his feet hit the floor he spins to his right and, now slowly, opens the door to the office reception area. He peers outside. The lobby is empty. Maddox slips out and races to the terminal which sits just below the polished wooden desktop. He shoves his pistol against the glass of the vidscreen - - and stops.

He reads what is printed there. 'Message in transmission. Press 'Enter' to receive.' "Fuck you," Maddox hisses. He pulls the trigger - - Click! Empty. The gun is empty! Maddox angrily slaps the release button and a barren magazine drops from the pistol's handle. Maddox reaches for a spare clip as the rectangular metal cartridge-box falls on to the –enter– key and slams it down. The beeping stops as a question appears on the monitor. Maddox grabs a fresh magazine from his belt and prepares to reload, then pauses and reads what is written on the screen. The anger etched into his face is instantly replaced by a look of interest. With a swipe of his hand he brushes the spent magazine aside and punches the 'Enter' key with the pistolgrip - - in effect answering "Yes".

Maddox acutely studies the information which spills onto the screen. He raises an eyebrow in speculation. Sure, what is printed there looks good - - excellent in fact - - but seems too perfect, too good to be true. Maddox knows if he replies he will surely give away their position, but on the other hand he knows another fight will be bound to happen....sooner or later, it doesn't matter much at this point....he types a sentence stating his concern. He smiles seconds later at the reply. Whoever is behind this is smart and cunning; two qualities Maddox greatly admires . . . he looks forward to meeting this mystery person who speaks by computer. Still wary, Maddox types in his agreement to the proposed plan. He looks back from the computer to the door leading to where his partners wait. "Get the stuff ready to go," he calls to them. They cannot see his hands as he loads his pistol.

Pow. Pow. Pow. Thok, thok, thok -- ping, bang! Out in the alcove and corridor, everyone freezes. Gunfire! Yelling, echoes of impacting bullets, and crashes from inside the lobby. A hailstorm of bullets tears through the room. Vidscreens of the SolNet terminals shatter, sparks fly everywhere, and small fires erupt in the backs of the boxy casings. The one on the far right is thrown up from the force of the pounding bullets. It spins end over end in the air like an acrobat before landing in a charred and smoking mass of rubble on the floor.

Dade, Roggin, Gregg and Romanoff plaster themselves to the floor of the alcove at the sound of the blasting bullets. They had been wondering where to begin looking for the terrorists. "Well, at least now we know where they are," Gregg whispers.

"Who in the hell could they be shooting at?" Roggin asks. There is a pause in the shooting, and the men strain to see inside the left lobby entrance. Just then, there is more gunfire, and the room goes dark.

"Aw hell, not this shit again!" Gregg spits exasperatedly. The four remain still as they hear bursts of gunfire, again mixed with yelling. Screams, actually. Male screams, female screams, terrified screams. Then, indiscernible shouts and loud cursing, punctuated erratically by more short explosions of shooting. Then, silence.

Rish warily appears at the Port alcove-to-corridor archway. He crawls over and joins the four passenger-fighters. Still, there is no noise of any kind coming from the pitch-black lobby. "What is going on?" he quietly asks Dade.

"Your guess is as good as mine."

"What should we do?" Romanoff inquires.

Rish is perplexed. The lobby powerswitch is in the maintenance closet beside the desk. He isn't particularly interested in entering a dark room where armed, angered criminals could be waiting to ambush. Then, an idea surfaces. A long-shot, yes, but it may work.

The first officer scrambles up and goes to an inter-ship wallphone in the corridor. He punches numbers; incessant ringing. He is getting annoyed just as the phone is answered. "Electrical Room!" comes a loud and harried voice. There is much noise - both mechanical and human - in the background.

"This is Officer Rish . . ."

"Who? Wha?"

"Officer Rish!" His identification is a bit louder this time, but he tries to keep his voice calm for the passengers. Syranos puts herself between the crowd and Rish, smiling away.

"Oh, Yessir Mr. Rish. How may I help you?"

"Cut the power to the lobby. Cut it right now."

"Sir, we have a predicament in keeping the electrawerks running..."

"I *need* it *done*. Now." Rish speaks through gritted teeth.

The tone of the technician changes. "Yessir."
Holding the telephone, Rish keeps his eyes locked on the lobby entrance, which is just barely visible from his vantage point. Then, the emergency spotlights activate.

Rish returns to the alcove. One by one, they approach the left archway, and peer. In the shadowed semi-darkness is a body sprawled on the floor – wearing a stained steward's jacket. In the distance, another is at the Purser's Desk. The torso is bent headfirst over the desktop, head and arms dangling lifelessly above the floor – there's a wound in the right bicep; the bandage gauze is red and sodden...must be the gang's front man. Rifles and a handgun lie in close proximity to the bodies. Blood has pooled on the carpeting. Knapsacks dot the area.

"I count two," Dade says.

"That's what I see," Gregg concurs, his eyes squinting.

"Four are missing then," comments Romanoff.

"There was a lot of shooting in there. A lot," Roggin observes. "Could be they are dead too. Or..."

"And that is a mighty big 'Or'," says Gregg.

There is a pause. “Well, we can’t wait out here,” Roggin remarks. “We have to check.”

“If we keep close together, and our eyes peeled, it should not be a problem,” says Gregg.

The others nod. They raise their weapons and enter the lobby, walking slowly to the nearest body, that of the ‘steward’. They keep their weapons at-the-ready in case of a ruse. Rish, unarmed, follows cautiously.

“Wait, is that another?” Romanoff inquires.

“Where?” asks Gregg quickly.

“At the doorway to the back-office, look, at the floor, is that a set of legs?”

The others peer in the direction indicated by the Russian Lieutenant. Yes, a pair of panted legs tipped with shoes stretch out at the bottom of the doorway. They do not move.

“Looks like that is number three,” says Roggin.

Gregg reaches the first body as the others line up alongside him. The face is dirty, the eyes closed, the lips grim beneath the moustache. Gregg kicks the rifle away from it, then prods the limp left arm with the barrel of his 309. Nothing. He nudges it with his foot in the chest. The body shakes, but otherwise remains still. Dead. Gregg grimaces. “This one’s gone.” Just then, the body shifts and falls forward. The men jump back, startled, and instantly train their weapons on it. A moment passes, then another. No further movement follows. They relax when it remains motionless. Sheepish looks from one to the other.

Noise! From the left! They jump again and spin toward it, to the door of the Photo Studio. A shadow is seen behind the door’s glass pane. Dade, the closest, raises his pistol and fires a string of shots. Kaaabblllaammm! The studio erupts. A person is hurled through the exploded-open door. The body lands with a heavy thud as tongues of fire and clouds of black smoke tease out from the workplace of Michael Priest.

Dade steps back, shocked, and looks in dismay at the others. “I . . .I . .they were just warning shots! At the doorframe; I never aimed for bullets to go inside.” As the sprinklers shower cool water on the studio and lobby, they approach the smoldering, charred form. The face is blackened and bleeding, and a rifle is held in the hands.

“Well, a fourth’s been found,” observes Gregg. “This one’s got a goatee; it’s the leader.”

Dade relaxes, relaxes immensely with the knowledge that he did not harm an innocent. Roggin takes the rifle from the stiffened and gritty fingers and tosses it to the side.

Fla-wush! Small explosions burst within the studio as photo-chemicals overheat. With his hand out ahead of his face, Rish moves to the front and warily approaches the impromptu furnace. The fire rages and searing heat burns forward. Although the sprinklers work well, and the room is fireproof, it will be a while before the lobby is safe again. The studio firedoor begins to close as Rish steps back. "We must leave until that is extinguished."

They nod and hastily go into the alcove with the first officer following close behind.

"So that means two are around somewhere…" Romanoff says.

"If they were in the studio, they'd be in the lobby by now, or are dead," Rish begins. "That would leave the PCC, the vault room, or the maintenance closet."

"Or, the airducts, Sir."

Rish turns to find Bethany Parris standing beside him. "What?"

"They were moving in the airducts."

Rish goes to the inter-ship phone. "This is Officer Rish. Access the security cameras for the lobby rooms, and do a scan of airducts on B."

"Airducts are clear, Sir. The vault room camera has been reactivated and is clear. Maintenance closet is clear. The PCC has….some sort of rumpled figures on the floor…and…dark fluid…blood! Two people! Blood on the floor!"

"Thank you. Do not worry about it, everything is under control." Rish hangs up. He turns to those around him. "Two bodies in the PCC. That's all six!" There is silence a moment. Not out of respect for the dead, but for considering facts.

"The bastards offed each other!" Roggin comments finally.

"Greedy sonsabitches," Gregg remarks, then pauses and looks back in the direction of the lobby. "When that fire is out I want to have a look at the guns they were using."

"Well, at least we can put a period to that part of tonight," Dade comments with a grin.

Rish brushes his hands together. "Yes; yes, really," he says offhandedly, then pauses. "I'll tell the others." He goes to the archway, then stops and calls Arges. "Sir, the troublemakers are dead. From their own fight."

"What? Dead? You're sure?"

"Yessir, I saw them myself. They killed each other, we're not sure why."

"Well that's good to hear. I'll take the Bridge off Homesafe. Let's finish the evac."

"Yessir, my thoughts exactly." Rish steps into the corridor. "Everyone, we are safe from the armed people. They have been removed from the situation." At first, there is no response. "They are dead, gone," Rish continues as he walks. "They turned on each other." It takes a moment to 'sink in', then there are jubilant shouts over the demise of the tormentors. There is an abundance of hugging and yelling – a good reason to celebrate, yes. Roggin, Gregg, Dade and Romanoff enter the corridor and are surprised when the cheering increases. Adrianna runs to Dade, throws her arms around him, and kisses him. The other three nod politely. "Thank you, thank you" they mutter.

They are as happy as everyone else with the news, but wish it had ended differently; that the terrorists could have been captured, brought to justice, and served time in prison for their crimes. However, one deadly part of this incredible evening is over, and that is what is most important.

CHAPTER NINETEEN
The Fall

"Ladies and Gentlemen," Rish says; people hush. "This is good news, but we must proceed with the evacuation."

"Yes, we must focus on leaving the ship," Rayburn adds. The others heed these orders, and once Rish and Rayburn are satisfied that the crew and passengers are under control, they resume the evac. Rayburn begins her way back to the Halo to escort more people out as Rish opens a shuttle-hatch.

Not two seconds later and the thing that the crew most dreads happens. Every last one of them knew it was coming, sooner or later, and each had secretly hoped within their heart of hearts that it would pass them by. Then, it is there. A light tremor rumbles through the length of the ship. The gravity forces of the asteroid beneath are beginning to mercilessly close their powerful fingers around the defenseless vessel. The stabilizers are functioning at one-hundred and fifty percent, and up until this very moment have been able to repel the constant pull from below, but now, it is simply too strong.

The tremor terrifies everyone. It means only one thing: the end is at hand. No bargaining or arguing can do anything about it; all they can do is hope to avoid the irresistible force of nature by escaping the doomed ship. To Congresswoman Jackson, it is all too familiar - - as if the San Andreas Fault is flexing its granite muscle once again. Xian and Karisu Ng clutch each other as well, this is reminiscent of a Pacific Rim shudder! Rish turns to Rayburn. "After this, it won't be long before panic seizes the passengers again!"

"Right," she answers. "Let's move then. Progress will keep fear away."

Rish's eyes scan the status lights above the hatches. Only three shine green! His spirits drop, and he shakes his head in frustration, then turns to Rayburn and waves her over. He also notices Dr. Washington enter the corridor, and motions for him to join them. They confer, then quietly speak with Syranos, who also joins the tiny group.

Seconds later, all four are giving orders, and the crewmen respond with ordered efficiency. Rayburn goes back to the lounge, and as passengers enter the hallway soon after, they are immediately ushered to the aft end of the corridor. They are impressed with the sense of authority presented – the control the officers exude bolsters their spirits brings confidence that these well-trained people will see them safely off the ship.

"It's started…" Arges says as the tremor fades. The bridge staff are wide-eyed with terror, knowing once the ship's orbit begins to decay - which it just did - not much time remains. "Roberta!" the captain snaps. "Tell the Spaceport we're going down!! We need those damned rescue ships *now*!" Escoto spins to her console and begins typing furiously.

"How much air do we have?" Arges asks to no one in particular.

"Thirty minutes, thirty seconds, Sir!" answers Martingale. The ship will be down by then. He relaxes a bit; at least no one will go through the horror of asphyxiation. The captain punches a code into his armrest and speaks into the radio. "Tac, this is John. How many crewmen have left the ship?"

Holden accesses some information on a vidscreen. "Roughly eighty percent."

"Very well," Arges answers, pleased. "Tell the others to get ready to go. There's not much time left."

"Yes, I know. I felt it too." The speaker does not hide the disappointment in the voice.

"Don't worry, Tac, everything will turn out fine. When this is all over, I'll buy you a round at Lasky's."

"You're on, captain," the chief engineer says with a chuckle; he does sound better, but not by much. "Good Bye, Sir."

"See you soon, Tac.

Holden clicks off the microphone in the E.O.C.. Dressed in a bulky EVAS, he sits in front of the Board and looks through the gaping hole which was once a viewport. In his hand he toys with the one lifecraft compu-interface link that the machinist had delivered to him before leaving the vessel just minutes ago. "Here it is, ready, and not near enough time to install it, damn."

He sets the component down and stands up, his hand coming to lie on the back of his chair which still holds his uniform jacket. He sadly stares at the wrecked engine room. Moments later, he is down in that very room, standing on the edge of the mass of wreckage which was once the Mercury V-15s. He absently kicks at the rubble with his booted foot. He shakes his head. "Damn. If we only had time. . .time to implement the plan, time to build a working motor from that junk." He shakes his head forlornly. He then looks up against the scorched back wall of the ship. Such devastation... such a waste...such a mess... It is still a shock to believe he is living in this nightmare.

A hand rests on his left shoulder. Holden jumps slightly, being startled. It is Corté, likewise dressed in an EVAS. "Ah, Chris," Holden says and gives a feeble smile.

"We should go, Sir."

Holden nods and turns toward his second-in-command. "Yes Chris, you're right." The two walk toward the starboard exit, to the airlock just beyond the doorway. When they reach the hatch, Holden pauses, turns, and gives one last look. He shakes his head. "Damn it all to hell." Then, they leave.

Zookeeper Byron Devinski knows it is time to leave the ship as well. He and his staff have just finished giving a last meal to the wildlife aboard; the horses, ponies, dogs, birds and fishes have been given food laced with heavy tranquilizers. The animals will soon drift off to a pleasant sleep, and will never waken - - far more humane than dying from suffocation. Tears drop from the attendants eyes as they walk to the airlocks.

Above, the captain looks out the viewport of his bridge. He sees white shuttlecraft and orange-suited people and an abundance of stony meteors suspended against black space and Mars. The bottom edge of the viewport shows the gray, barren surface of the asteroid creeping slowly upward. Arges shivers despite himself at the sight of the *Emprasoria*'s grave. He quickly composes himself and looks around the bridge.

"Attention everyone," he says strongly after returning to the chair. The staff turn their attention to him. "I don't have to tell you there's not much time left for us. Roberta, Krystal, Jane and I will stay behind a bit longer. I want the rest of you to go." The people stare and do not move. "Don't worry," Arges continues, "we will be fine. Please go." The staff remain motionless. "That is an order, ladies and gentlemen." The personnel slowly move. Those holding things set them down, those sitting stand, and those at an angle to the captain turn to fully face him. Then, in one uniform movement, they salute their captain.

Arges looks at his people with admiration. He slowly rises and straightens his jacket, then brings his right hand to the brim of his hat and returns the salute. He turns to his left and then slowly moves a full one-hundred and eighty degrees to his right. His eyes meet with everyone else's as he moves. After a moment, he puts his hand down and seats himself. In another fluid motion, the staff members lower their hands, turn, and slowly exit, through the doorways which have been opened after the Homesafe was released. Some have hints of tears in their eyes. Minutes later, both the forward airlocks on the flight deck are busily sending people out into space.

Down in the port lifecraft corridor, Rish and Rayburn are working to achieve the same goal. Rish is in front of the first of the three remaining shuttles when he turns and looks behind him. Rayburn stands at the rear of the small crowd. It appears as though all of the passengers are in the corridor. He spies a couple standing in the lounge archway itself. The man, whom Rish recognizes as the guitarist Peter Bull, sets his amplifier and guitar down then disappears back into the lounge. Rish looks at a steward near the archway jerks his head in the direction of the arch. The steward nods and walks to the open entryway. He looks for a moment at Myrie, who stands in the corridor, as he reaches the lounge.

Peter Bull backs into the hall and almost collides with the steward. He is carrying a chair, and sets it in the archway, within the middle of the large open area. The steward watches as the guitarist sits, then leans back in the chair so that its front legs are raised off of the floor and its back ones are put on a near forty-five degree angle. The top edge of the chair's back touches the side of the archway and Bull puts his white-booted left foot on the opposite side, then sets his right on the floor to balance himself. He picks up his guitar and rests it across his reclined waist.

The steward goes to Bull. "C-cc-could you come inside the corridor, please Sir?" he asks hesitantly. Looking up, Bull shakes his maned head "NO". Bull was never able to resist the biddings of his muse, and he is not about to start now. The steward has no interest in becoming involved in an altercation with one of his idols, and after all, Bull is near enough to the corridor . . . the steward grins, shrugs, then backs away from the six-string wizard.

Just then a second tremor hits. This one is much stronger. Bull leans down and clicks his amplifier on. As always, the disc deck automatically begins to record. Bull sits back and picks the opening notes to Eric Clapton's soulfully classic song 'Knockin' On Heaven's Door'. The airy tune and the accompanying lyrics which drift from Bull's lips seem eerily appropriate as the tremor rattles on.

The sweet music provides a soothing distraction for the passengers as the officers struggle with a serious problem. Rish begins a quick headcount of the people gathered in the corridor - - and stops when the number goes beyond seventy-eight. Even if the three shuttles are stuffed well beyond capacity they cannot accommodate everyone. A stressed look comes over Rish as he waves Rayburn over to him. Seconds later, she is at his side.

"What'll we do?" Rish whispers testily. "There's *no* way we can get all these people in *three* shuttles!" Rayburn tenses. "We can't send people below to get EVA suits out of their cabins . . . hell we'd lose half of them down there with them running wild through the ship!!" Rish is perplexed. He has no idea what they will do.

"Wait!" Rayburn says enthusiastically, "The other lifecrafts! We can get the EVAS from the floor lockers and let them use those!"

Of course! Rish thinks. The perfect solution! Each lifecraft is stocked with fifty EVA suits in the event that the people in the shuttle may have to evacuate at some point. There would be more than enough EVAS in the unusable shuttles! "Great thinking Alyssa!"

The second officer smiles widely. She turns and enthusiastically races down the corridor, and stops next to some stewards and band members. "You escort this group to midship," she orders, referring to some passengers. The crewmen hastily comply, though each secretly wonders why they should. Rish watches keenly as the plan is pursued.

Rayburn quickly approaches the first hatch with a red status-light. She enters the access code into the adjacent keypad. The red light flashes twice, and the door does not open. In her haste and excitement, she forgot that the shuttle compartment will not respond to ordinary commands because the computer has registered the lifecraft as "UNSAFE". She pounds the wall next to the control panel once in frustration. The passengers and crew watch in surprise: What is she doing? Doesn't she see the red light?

Rayburn punches the four-digit override command followed by the code once again. The red light begins flashing rapidly and continuously, but the door relents and slides open. The shuttle's interior lights click on. The shuttle looks like any of the others, clean, complete, ready to go… it is rather sad that it cannot be used for its intended purpose.

"Ok, let's go in," she says to the stewards, and they go inside. "We want to get the EVAS out of here and - -" She stops, suddenly realizing an important fact: would the Line have equipped these shuttlecraft with astronaut outfits knowing full well they could never be used on the ace run? Only time will tell. The three stewards look at her, waiting for her to finish the sentence. "We want to get the EVAS out of here." Rayburn says again. The stewards nod, and two steps to the floor between rows Four and Five, then lift the heavy steel floorpanel-door upward. The hinges squeal slightly as the door opens. Rayburn peers down into the shallow hole. Darkness . . . wait, the compartment light slowly flickers, then stays lit and . . . there they are! Stacked neatly are three brand-new bright-orange EVAS. Rayburn raises her head in joy. Yes! An exuberant smile is a clear sign of her triumph.

Now the people gathered around the hatchway understand. They smile as the stewards begin hauling out the bulky suits as Rayburn and the other man hop over to adjacent flooring and begin opening another locker. Rish smiles from his place down the corridor as he sees a suit be passed to a passenger. Great!

Gregg, Roggin, Dade and Romanoff do not feel lucky. Here, the ship is now free of the terrorists, but people will still lose some items. When they went to retrieve the sacks with the intent of returning things, the first tremor hit, and discouraged the action. They feel as though only half the job has been done. The four are besieged with congratulations from their near-adoring and certainly thankful fellow passengers who praise them for their action. They cordially thank all who speak to them.

"I need to duck inside the lounge and take a minute to relax," Gregg says to Roggin.

Roggin nods. "I'll come get you if anything happens."

Gregg then sets off for the far archway – not wanting to attract attention to his departure, and going around the guitarist would certainly do that. He trots down the corridor and passes a group putting on orange astronaut suits. "One for you, Sir?" a steward asks as Gregg goes by.

"Thank you, I will take one in a minute," Gregg says, and continues on his way.

"Very good, Sir," the steward says, then passes it to the next passenger.

Gregg reaches his destination. With his rifle slung at his side, he slowly steps inside. He strolls through the room, walking absently to its middle, to where the chandelier-statue mess sits. Ping! Gregg stops cold. The middle elevator is arriving. Though the single chime is supposed to sound welcoming, to Gregg it sounds like a death knell. In a flash he races to the elevator bay. He raises his rifle to head level as he reaches the center lift - - if anyone is going to be shot, it will be those bastards. The two bronze doors begin to slide apart and Gregg readies his trigger-finger to fire on the terrorists he is sure are inside. Gregg holds his breath. The doors open.

What? Mrs. Enkel shrieks and pulls her husband to the floor of the elevator. The steward standing to the side in front of the elevator's control panel drops to the floor as well. The three lie cowering as Gregg's mouth drops in shock and he stares in disbelief. He definitely did *not* expect this as, he thinks with grief, as is the same with them. Gregg lowers his rifle; he can feel the heat of embarrassment rising in his face.

When the elevator is not pummeled with shots, Enkel slowly, shakily raises his head. "D-Don't kill us!" he stammers, then raises his open palms in surrender.

Gregg has no idea what to say. "Uhm," he begins sheepishly, "I . . .uh. . .I won't hurt you. You can get up. You're safe." At that, Mrs. Enkel and the steward warily look up. To show he is speaking the truth, Gregg shrugs off his carrying strap and sets his rifle against the back wall and kneels to help them up.

At first, they pull back from him in fear. Gregg shows them his open, empty palms, and they relax somewhat. "There's been a terrible mistake . . ." Gregg says.

"Mistake?" Enkel asks as Gregg helps him stand. "Mistake!" he says again, angry this time, ripping his arm out of Gregg's grasp. "That's one hell of a *goddamned* mistake! What the hell do you think you're doing running around with a rifle!"

Gregg stares back blankly at the man. Doesn't he know what has been going on? "The terrorists. . . I thought you were the terrorists. . ." he stammers.

"What the hell do you mean, 'terrorists'? I. . ."

Gregg steps aside ant reveals the battleworn Halo lounge to Enkel. The man stops speaking from pure shock. His eyes widen in horror, and his mouth falls open. Beyond belief this is . . . a horrendous sight . . . a nightmare come to life. Enkel's face tenses and he squeezes his eyes shut. He begins to collapse.

Gregg and the steward race to the man and catch him before he hits the floor. They help Enkel out to the lounge. Mrs. Enkel follows; she is certainly upset at the state of the lounge but it does not affect her as badly as it does her husband. "My, won't it take a lot of work to repair this room!" she says as she exits the elevator. Gregg and the steward exchange knowing glances - evidently The Grand Dame does not fully realize that this is *the end* of the *Emprasoria.* They say nothing to her.

"Get a chair," Gregg says to the steward, who moves to one when Mrs. Enkel interjects.

"No," she says resolutely. "I think it would be best to get him out of here." Her decision makes perfect sense - - having Enkel revive in the battered room would be tortuous.

"Of course, Madam," the steward answers with a polite nod.

Gregg nods as well, then turns to the steward. "Can you hold him for a second?"

"Yessir." Gregg leaves and retrieves his rifle; he slings the carrying strap over his shoulder and returns. Once Gregg has a firm grip on Enkel's arm, the group moves to the forward archway which, of course, is the closest escape from the room.

"You see," Mrs. Enkel begins, addressing Gregg, "we were resting in the library since leaving the White Feather. We had no idea what was going on up here and certainly knew nothing about any terrorists." Gregg nods understandingly, though he doubts they were 'resting' anywhere. . .more than likely hiding from what they guessed were angry passengers who would be more than willing to vent their frustrations on the owner of the Line. "We felt that nasty quake," Mrs. Enkel continues, "and decided we had better leave." Gregg nods again.

The four step into the corridor and immediately catch the attention of the men gathered there, many of whom are now dressed in EVAS. They glare at the Enkels, and some whisper among themselves. However, no one says anything directly to them, or makes a move toward them. Mrs. Enkel completely ignores the passengers.

Gregg guides his group directly to the aft end of the corridor, where Rish is still loading the same lifecraft. Enkel recovers from his "reaction" whey they are about half-way to Rish. He shakes his head, blinks twice, begins to walk steadily, and pulls his arms away from the steward and Gregg. The crowd in line for the shuttle parts when they hear the quiet "Excuse us.", and turn to see the Enkels approach. Even in this situation, the two possess power.

Rish turns and sees the couple coming, as does Syranos and Washington. Out of habit, they all snap to attention. Rish next scans the crowd itself. The Enkels are by far the eldest people in the corridor, and therefore qualify as Designated. Based on this reasoning, he makes a decision. "I believe there is room for you here, Sir, Madam," Rish says while extending his left arm as a guide toward the hatch.

"Thank you, Rish," Enkel says as he steps inside. "Jennifer, Washington."

"Dr. Washington, Ms. Syranos, Mr. Rish," Mrs. Enkel says with long nods as she follows her husband.

Rish hears some murmuring from the small crowd - - there will be many who will disagree with his decision to give the Enkels what seems to be preferential treatment, but it is his duty to see to the safety of each passenger aboard, regardless of who they may be. Even though he believes the man should stay behind and perish for his inhuman cost-conscious crime of jeopardizing the safety of innocent people, Rish knows his conscience will never forgive him for willfully keeping an elderly, distressed man away from a shuttle. Rish is sure there are more than enough higher authorities -- if not the Highest itself -- which will punish Enkel for his wrongdoings.

Keeping his smile in tact, Rish hastily helps others into the shuttle, and when he sees it is filled, he seals the hatch and launches the craft. As Rish proceeds to the second-last shuttle compartment, he turns and looks down the hallway. In the distance, he can see Rayburn and three stewards emerging from a hatchway. "Jennifer, go down there and give them help if they need it," he says.

Rayburn faces a new problem as she steps into the corridor and looks at the small group of orange-suited men. The passengers now have the means to survive outside the ship, now at issue is actually getting them off of the ship. The most obvious answer to this is using the airlock at the far end of the corridor, but Rayburn knows it will take a long time to get these men out in groups of four . . . and there will be more coming… Rayburn stands in the hallway, perplexed. Then, the solution comes to her.

She first orders two stewards and two musicians back to the crowd at the aft end of the corridor to bring more passengers up to be suited, then she opens the next hatch, and then with a steward, she leads the passengers forward. She stops in front of the first compartment, whose overhead light is solidly black and turns to her group.

"Ok," she begins, "I want all of you to go into the shuttle bay. When I open the outer door, I want you to jump out of the ship." Rayburn receives wary glances. "Don't worry, you will be perfectly safe. Believe me, this is the best way." From the way the men look, they clearly do not want to do it, but are in no position to argue with the Officer. Slowly, they put their helmets in place.

Pleased, Rayburn turns around and, being sure to use the override command, opens the hatch. The long rectangular ceiling light in the compartment flashes on to reveal an empty, white, garage-like enclosure. The davit arms which sit dormant in two large, square steel boxes at either end of the compartment are the only "decoration" the stark room offers. There is a two-foot drop from the hatchway down to the grated flooring where the underside of a lifecraft normally rests before liftoff. The shuttle bay is not the least bit inviting. One by one, the men hesitatingly step inside.

After the last man enters, Rayburn closes the hatch. There is a sense of finality felt by the men as the foreboding "clack" of the securing locks echo through the small chamber. After a brief moment, the large door which makes up the entire wall of the opposite side of the compartment begins to yawn open. Ten seconds later, it is completely up. The great black void of outer space faces the men. No one moves a muscle; they simply stand and stare in fear. It looks so vast, so imposing, so empty. And it is just a few feet from them.

The men suddenly hear pounding on the hatch and some muffled shouting from inside the ship. They all turn and look at the white steel door. They see the officer's pretty but angry face in the square porthole mouthing words they cannot hear but completely understand: she wants them to go. They stare at the woman but do not move. They each note with disparity that there are no controls to open the hatch from the inside. They look at one another and wonder what to do.

A shrill siren blasts from the ceiling. The piercing shriek is so loud that it penetrates the thick EVA helmets and rings menacingly in the surprised and shocked ears. That is all the encouragement they need. They do not know what the siren means, but they know it cannot be good. The passengers run to the edge of the compartment. Some close their eyes, some hold their breath, and some scream prayers, but they all jump forward. Once outside, they nervously hit the rocket controls on the forefingers of their gloves and flames fire from their bootheels. Still somewhat afraid but relieved and actually enjoying the thrill of independent flight, the men fly away from the *Emprasoria* - - they quickly put as much distance between them and the liner as they possibly can.

Rayburn laughs as she sees them dash out of the shuttle bay; they move like scared rabbits. She clicks off the emergency alarm and closes the bay door. Since there is no time to wait for the skittish, she had activated the alarm, which sounded only in that compartment, to speed things along. Rayburn turns to Syranos, who also smiles at the humorous sight. She quickly explains to her how to operate the door, then gives her the passcode and override command for the hatch. "Only use the siren if the passengers prolong their exit to an extreme extent," Rayburn cautions, and Syranos nods, then Rayburn leaves and walks back to the second group being given EVA suits.

Rayburn looks down the hall to Rish. He, Dr. Washington, and Syranos are standing next to a hatch, helping people into a shuttle. After a moment, Rish looks up and catches sight of her. She smiles widely at him and raises her hand in a thumb-up gesture to signal that everything is fine. Rish smiles back and returns the salute. The second-last shuttle is about half full, and the boarding is going smoothly and orderly. People move hurriedly, of course, but there is not inordinate shoving or fights to get inside the craft. The crowd in the corridor is substantially smaller now.

There will not be enough room in this or the last shuttle to accommodate everyone gathered at the back end of the corridor, but it will be close. Perhaps three more groups of men for the EVAS and that will be the last of the passengers. Rish relaxes greatly. "It looks as though we'll make it!"

After the Enkels had left, Gregg finds Roggin and half-heartedly relates his encounter with the couple to him. Roggin puts a comforting hand on his friend's shoulder. "Don't worry about it, Cal. It wasn't your fault, and no one got hurt. That could just as easily been an elevator full of other terrorists. Hell, I would have done the same thing."

"Thanks," Gregg replies, his conscience somewhat relieved now.

Roggin looks around at the business in the corridor. "Looks like we'll be getting off soon."

"Sure seems that way." Gregg nods in agreement.

A steward comes up behind Myrie and puts a gentle hand on her right shoulder. She turns to him. "There's a place for you in the shuttle, Madam." Myrie says nothing but shakes her head "NO". She is at Bull's side; he begins to play the last verse of the song. The steward becomes a bit more demanding. "Madam, please . . ." She shakes her shoulder free from his grasp with a quick jerk and takes a step closer to Bull and slips her arms around his shoulders.

Bull is so engrossed in his guitar playing that he fails to notice what is occurring between his girlfriend and the steward. The steward takes a slow step toward Myrie; he is going to make another attempt at persuading her to go to the waiting shuttle. Just then, Bull's fingers play the final notes of the song. He blinks as if awakening from a trance, and as the sound from the amplifier fades into silence, the third tremor hits.

This is by far the strongest of the three. It shakes the ship violently and the people aboard have to fight to keep upright. This time, the quaking lasts for a considerably longer period than the previous episodes. When things finally do begin to settle, the *Emprasoria* lurches heavily to its right. There is definitely <u>not</u> much time left now.

Surprisingly, Bull is able to keep balanced in his tilted chair during the quake. Once it passed, he slowly lowers the front legs to the floor, then stands. Myrie presses herself against his side, and he puts his arm around her and she presses still closer to him. Bull feels his heart racing within his chest, and can feel Myrie's pounding fast as well. He looks down at her; her face is buried in his chest. He turns to the steward. "What's going on?"

"I - I was trying to escort the lady to a lifecraft, Sir," the steward answers nervously.

Bull nods. He looks down at Myrie, who clings to him. "Time to go, Kiddo," he whispers. She holds him tighter.

"No. Not without you."

Bull is not particularly excited about leaving her either, but knows this is the way it must be. "Come on, Myr, it'll be Ok." Bull kneels out of her grasp and goes to the amplifier. He unplugs the powercord from his guitar and punches the STOP, then the EJECT buttons on the diskette deck. The tiny door slides open and presents the small disc already placed in a clear plastic casing for transportation . This case holds priceless hours of music on the shiny disc it encloses.

"Here, you take this," he says as stands and passes the disc to her. "Hold on to it, and when we hook up on the colony, we'll give it a listen together."

She looks up at him. There are tears in her eyes. He begins to walk her toward the hatchway - - her legs move without resistance, though her heart does not want to go. Bull brings her directly to the hatchway, and with a final, long, loving embrace, she goes inside, holding back the tears. "Some escape anyway," she mutters. Once she is seated, Bull pulls his guitar off of his back and quietly sets it against the inner wall of the cabin. She does not see him do this because her face is buried in her hands - - if she had seen him, she would have taken it as a sign, a sign that he might not make it off of the ship.

When Bull is back in the corridor, Rish nods to him, then seals the hatch shut. Bull stands and stares through the small window in the hatch-door, watching as the shuttle is launched. When it is gone, he looks around somewhat dazedly at the small group in the corridor. He walks forlornly down the passageway, then stops and leans against the inner wall. He rests there a moment, then one of the members of the band comes over. "Can you join the group going to midship?" Bull nods, and slowly resumes his walk.

As the last men of the second group are given EVAS, Rayburn orders the stewards and musicians back to bring more people up to the area. She looks at the crowd at the far end of the hall - - this group should be the last.

"Officer Rayburn?" a steward asks from the shuttle.
She turns. He and his partners are holding two EVAS up, their eyebrows raised in hope. She understands the question. Normally, the crew are not supposed to take care of themselves until all the passengers are attended to, but that last tremor had been exceptionally bad, and if the stewards are worried about their own safety, they likely would not work efficiently and could end up causing more problems.

"Very well," she replies with a long nod, "but make it quick." The steward who had presented the question did not begin dressing in the suit as Rayburn expected, but rather sets the outfit aside and kneels down to the locker. From it he produces <u>another</u> EVAS. "The last one here Ma'am," he says as he walks toward the hatch and offers it to her.

Rayburn looks at the orange suit. She then turns her head to the aft end of the corridor. The crewmen she sent down there are just now gathering passengers. She looks to the front of the hallway. The suited passengers are rapidly entering the shuttle bay. She looks at the other hatchways - - four show red; more than enough EVAS there for the others . . . everything is under control; the window of opportunity is wide open. If she misses this chance, she may not get another. She reaches out and takes the EVAS. "Thank You," she says. The steward smiles, nods, then turns to put on his own suit.

Rayburn stands in the corridor and looks at the EVAS. She looks at the bottom of the suit: two straight-leg sections. She looks at herself, at the midnight blue skirt which ends just above her knees. There is no way she can get into that outfit wearing the skirt. Rayburn looks around. This is no time for modesty, but still . . . The forward arch to the lounge beckons her. She will not be gone long. Rayburn takes the EVAS in a firm grip and dashes to the room.

"Gentlemen, if you please . . ." Roggin and Gregg turn around to see a Band member directing them to the front of the corridor. The two look at each other. The time has come! Roggin and Gregg enthusiastically walk down the hallway. They join a small procession of men - - including Romanoff, Zolnick, McCartney and Bull - - who are already heading toward midship. The two pass Dade, who is with Adrianna. He takes her hand and they go to pick up EVAS for themselves. In a few more minutes, everyone will be off of the ship.

"I guess we got in that last round of target practice after all. Roggin jokingly says to Gregg.

A look of confusion comes over Gregg, then he recalls Roggin's challenging him to a shooting match at the Range during the Cocktail Hour at the End of Voyage dinner-dance. Gregg looks at his wristwatch. God, that was only *three* hours ago! Seems like a lifetime has passed since then . . . "Yes, I guess we did," Gregg responds with a chuckle.

"Pity, though," Roggin continues with a devilish grin, "No way to tell who won."

"Let's call it even," Gregg says, then thrusts his hand forward. Roggin grasps it and gives it a hearty shake.

"Good enough, Cal." The smile broadens.

The two proceed to where they see two EVA suited young men standing in front of a hatchway. These two are surrounded by passengers.

Alyssa Rayburn is alone in the left-front of the lounge. Her dark blue dress-skirt and white silk slip lie neatly on the floor with her shoes. Both her legs are in the EVAS, and she is pulling the rest of the suit up around her; she is at mid-thigh when she suddenly stops. She has the odd feeling she is being watched. She slowly turns her head around . . . and sees Hearst leering at her from the entryway of the Port-side flight deck stairs.

She spins around and faces him. Her face becomes flushed from the embarrassment of being seen half-dressed by a colleague. Hearst wears a scary grin on his pasty face. He has his hair pulled back in a stubby pony-tail and wears his hat low on his forehead; the brim shades his eyes. He carries a large white sack, with the Line crest on it, in his right hand.

"What are you doing Mitchell?" Rayburn demands as she hastily pulls the EVAS higher.

He takes a step toward her. Then another. "There isn't a prettier sight than tiny white panties on a tight round ass," he says wolfishly.

Rayburn is taken aback. She looks at him with utter shock. She cannot believe her ears. Hearst has never acted this way before. How could he say that! She is his Superior Officer to say nothing of the simple respect she deserves as a woman. "Excuse me, Third Officer!" she says authoritatively, "What was that?"

"You heard me, bitch," Hearst pauses. "Or do you like it when I talk nasty to you, Alyssa?"

Frankly, the very thought repulses her. She makes a disgusted look on her face. The fact that Hearst had used her first name in this context is sickening. He takes a step closer to her, then suddenly stops. Rayburn is not foolish enough to relax - - the threat is still very real. Hearst suddenly lunges at her.

Since she is half-wrapped in her EVA cocoon she cannot move easily, and he catches her. She struggles as he puts his left hand deep into her long and silky hair and pulls her head back. "I always thought you were a nice piece," Hearst hisses as he presses his open mouth against her closed lips. She shuts her eyes to block out the horror and clenches her teeth. Using all her strength she pushes him and he stumbles backward. She thrusts her hands into the arms of the EVAS and gets better control of her movement - - not perfect, mind you, but much better. Hearst moves back toward her. "Keep away!" she warns.

Hearst laughs loudly. "Gee, I'm sorry Alyssa," he says mockingly. "I don't know what ever came over me." He lunges again.

"No!" she shouts as she draws her fisted hand back and thrusts it at Hearst's head. She hits him squarely on the left of his jaw. The weight of the EVAS glove adds considerably more power to her punch, and Hearst is knocked off of his feet. He falls hard to the floor. In an instant Hearst is back up. He looks angry - - infuriated in fact. Rayburn puts herself in a defensive stance, quite willing to fight until the last of her strength is gone. Then, she catches movement out of the corner of her eye. She turns her head to the left and visibly reacts to what she sees, and even relaxes somewhat.

Hearst shakes his head and laughs at the pathetic attempt to distract him; she is trying to lure him, trying to get him to turn his head and see. Of course, the moment he turns she will hit him again - - a sucker punch. She obviously underestimates him. "If you think I'm gonna fall for that old gag, you're crazy." She directs her eyes to him angrily.

"Guess you're too smart for that, are you?"

Hearst freezes. His eyes widen. It is a man's voice speaking those words. From behind. Hearst slowly turns. He gulps when he sees the group of male passengers staring at him. It was Xian Ng who spoke those words, and he is in a Ju Jitsu fighting stance at the front of the group, ready to take on the third officer. Hearst moves back two steps, then spins to his left and takes off running. The passengers move to pursue him.

"No, wait," Rayburn says; they stop. "He's not worth it."

Moments later, Hearst is at the starboard corridor exit of the lounge. He takes a deep breath and coughs. He calms himself and slowly steps into the corridor. He walks down the hallway to the lobby alcove, then ducks inside the small room and darts over to the port archway. He enters the passageway and presses himself against the far wall as he moves in behind the small group of women waiting to board the last shuttle. Bethany Parris, who is there to assist with the boarding, watches him walk past.

Dr. Washington turns, sees him, and smiles. Hearst nods curtly. Rish does not notice the third officer, as he is busy entering the passcode into the compartment's control panel. The hatch slides open. Rish rests his left hand on the wall, and with his right motions for Congresswoman Jackson to step forward. She does not move. There is a look of horror on her face. "Come along Madam, it's quite safe," Rish says. Just then, a black leather-gloved hand slaps down on Rish's left hand. His head snaps around and his eyes fall fixed on the hand on him.

"'Fraid not. This one's taken."

Before he has time to react, the back of the hand shoots up and punches Rish hard on the nose. A ring on the gloved finger cuts him, and he reels back from the force of the blow but does not fall. He instinctively brings his right hand up to his broken, bleeding nose as he looks at his attacker. Rish is stunned. It is not possible!

Maddox, Yusacre, Parker, Kobryn, DeSantis, and Jensen are standing real-as-life in front of him. The color drains from Rish's face; he looks as though he has seen a ghost. Or ghosts.

Maddox and his teammates take note of these reactions laughingly. Maddox guesses what they are thinking. "Poof!" he says melodramatically as he fans his fingers out in a mystical way "Instant reincarnation!" The others laugh hysterically at the mockery.

Rish stares back in disbelief as blood spills from his nose. "H-H-How...B-B-Buttt..."

"H-H-How. . .B-B-Buttt. . ." Maddox mimics him, and there is more laughter. "We staged a diversion and a switch. Looks like those three security goons who got offed got in a last act after all. We gave an obvious bicept-wound to one of them, took his pants and shoes and propped them at the door to look like a person. Some rumpled clothes and inky fluid in the PCC, then gave another body a steward's jacket, and an instant goatee to a third. Quite a good portrayal, if you ask me."

Rish looks at the other terrorists. One is brandishing a rifle, and the others are toting handguns. They have heavy burlap sacks with them - - sacks which Rish notes are stored in the maintenance closets and are to be used for refuse, but now undoubtedly contain the riches which were previously in the knapsacks, which are likely now stuffed with some sort of junk.

Rish then notices a panel in the inner wall behind the men is open. The gang had used a service duct to sneak up on him . . . but how had they known about it? Those tunnels are not listed on any of the publicly released diagrams . . . Rish stops himself; he has more important things to worry about now. Maddox turns his back to Rish. "Ok, start loading the stuff," he says to his team.

Bethany looks directly at Angelique – there's that damn French perfume in the air again. Bethany narrows her eyes, and Angelique, who is not paying any attention to the Cruise Entertainment staffer, runs her hand through a loose strand of hair and returns it to the ponytail. "That color looks good on you," Bethany says acidly, "makes you look smarter."

Angelique looks up, anger in her eyes, and stares at her evenly. "Such nasty comments from a little miss prim-n-proper cheerleader," Angelique sneers. "Just remember, blondes get more fun – more fun than you can ever even guess at."

"Was that 'fun'? Or 'fucking'? As in a fucking idiot bitch?" Angelique coils her fingers so her nails look like talons and moves forward before Maddox interjects and steps in front of her. "I like a good cat-fight as much as the next guy, but we've got work to do. She's not worth it, babe." Maddox kisses her quickly on the cheek. Angelique reluctantly mover back, but sneers at Bethany anyway – Bethany does not react. Maddox looks back to his partners. "Ok, let's get on with it and leave this shit-hole dump."

Something in Rish snaps. He has had enough of these bastards. In a flash he comes up behind Maddox and wraps his left arm around the neck of the leader. He yanks him to the floor and, while keeping the struggling man in the headlock, raises his right fist high to hit him. Wham! There is a hit; a heavy, hard hit. Then Rish falls to the floor; a dull, throbbing pain comes from the top of his head. Rish feels the terrorist leave his grasp. "Bastard!" he hears from a rough, coughing voice, and then feels a hard kick to his right side. Rish coils in pain and looks up through blurred eyes.

Maddox extends his hand to the person who has rescued him from his attacker. "Mr. Hearst, I presume?"

"The one and only," Hearst responds with a smile as he shakes the offered hand. A broad smile appears on Maddox's face as well. Rish cannot believe what he is seeing.

"Smart move, you sending us that message by computer," Maddox says.

"I didn't think you would answer the phone." The team and Hearst laugh at the joke.

"How did you know where to find us?" Maddox asks.

"Process of elimination. The security cameras caught you entering Sick Bay. And after you left, I scanned the corridor cameras, but you did not appear there. The Lobby camera was out, and when I checked its room cameras, you weren't there either, and the Office scene looked a bit too perfect - -"

"We had those cameras off at first. They got reactivated somehow. We knew if we shut them off again, that would give it away, so we did a relay misfeed," Maddox interjects.

Hearst nods. "So, I took a chance, and well, was right!"

"Super. And an *excellent* plan, too," Maddox replies. "We were really stuck - - we had no idea what we were going to do. We didn't know about those hallways. *Great* thinking!!" Hearst smiles at the adulatons. He savors the praise.

"Yes," Hearst continues, "those tunnels are used by the crew to get through the ship easily. They aren't in any of the SolNet or Agency deck layouts; the passengers have no reason to know about them, you know? I thought they would be perfect for you."

"And that they were. Absolutely *perfect*!" Maddox says. "Easy to get to from the airducts as well."

Hearst smiles further. Maddox quickly explains how they set an incendiary device in the Studio as a further diversion which also burned any inadvertent shipboard photos of the team. "Genius! Pure Genius!" Hearst exclaims as Maddox finishes.

"Yeah," Maddox says. "surprise is the best form of attack." He looks down at the small sack in Hearst's hand. "What's in the bag?"

"Oh, the vault was full - - as I'm sure you well know . . ." Hearst smiles as he says this; Maddox and his teammates grin. "so some other valuables were put in the safe on the flight deck security station. Stocks, bonds, some jewelry," Hearst says as he passes the white Line bag over to Maddox who eagerly unties the thin rope at the top of the bag then pulls the sack open. His face lights up when he sees the contents. He stares at the extra, unexpected prize for a moment, then raises his head and smiles at Hearst. "Excellent work, Mr. Hearst!" Maddox grasps the bag with his left hand and extends his right palm outward.

Hearst again puts his hand in Maddox's and shakes it. "Call me Mitch," he says with a smile. Maddox nods. The third officer feels reassured by the strong grip coming from the black leathered hand.

"We really appreciate what you did for us," Maddox says. He then moves his left hand toward the right side of his partially open jacket. The bag disappears inside and the hand emerges with a pistol in it. Hearst tenses with fear as a look of confusion comes over him. He tries to pull away, but Maddox tightens his grip on the hand - - to Hearst it feels as though his bones are being crushed. Still smiling, and without saying a single word, the ambidextrous Maddox thrusts the pistol into Hearst's squirming body and fires three quick shots point-blank in the chest.

The third officer shrieks in agony as he falls to the floor. The group of women who have been in stunned silence suddenly scream and throw themselves to the floor. Rish lies still and Dr. Washington dives to the carpeting. Maddox releases the nearly lifeless hand and the body falls limply to the floor. Hearst looks up with mournful, glazed, questioning eyes.

Maddox bends at his waist and brings his face close to the dying man, then speaks. "If you thought we were going to lower OUR shares to cut you in, you're nuts. You served your purpose by getting us here. You are of no use to us now." Maddox's tone is sinister; he hisses his words; his personality has completely changed in a split second. "I despise traitors. Sell-outs aren't worth the air they breathe. You're a rat, Hearst. A dirty rat. Judas, Benedict Arnold, the Rosenthals, Kim Philby and you - - worthless - - the worst kind of scum. Burn in hell, fatboy." These words ring in Hearst's ears as his eyes go blank and his last breath drifts out of him.

Having completed the execution - a killing he believes is just and warranted - Maddox rises and looks down the hall. He had fired directly into the body so the sounds of the discharge would be muffled and the others, which presumably include the passenger-fighters, would not be alerted to the gang's presence. But the traitor's yelp and the women's screams change all that. Maddox and his team look into the crowd of faces staring back at them. There they are. "Oh, God," Adrianna whispers. Parker likewise sees her and his eyes widen. Dade looks in shock and instinctively jumps in front of her as he draws his weapon. Without aiming, Maddox fires two shots.

Gregg and Roggin likewise look in surprise at the six terrorists. Where in the hell had they come from? What in the hell are they doing alive? The three had turned with everyone else at the front of the hallway when the screams pierced the silence of the corridor. Gregg and Roggin raise their rifles when two bullets slam into a man in an EVA suit in the middle of the crowd and send him flying backward to the floor. Dade pushes Adrianna to the floor and dives to the carpet himself as all the others in the hallway drop to the carpeting.

DeSantis races up alongside Maddox, opening fire with is rifle as he does so. The bullets pound into the walls and ceiling at the far end of the corridor but cause the people no harm other than covering them with dust and chips of wood and plastic. Maddox fires twice more and then turns back to his team. "You!" he says and points to Yusacre, "Get in there and take the bags as they come in!" Yusacre dashes through the open hatch - - while his right arm is almost useless, his left is perfectly fine for stacking sacks.

"You two!" Maddox yells, this time pointing to Kobryn and Jensen, "give the stuff to him!" They pocket their pistols and start tossing the beige burlap sacks lying in a sloppy pile just inside the access panel to the hatchway. "Be careful!" Maddox yells. He is not about to have his newfound fortune be smashed and mangled by hasty handling at this stage of the game. "You!" the finger points to Parker, the only one carrying a knapsack on his back. "Get up and give cover fire!" Parker does not need a second invitation. His selection as gunner has redeemed him! He is instantly next to Maddox, his pistol raised and ready.

Dade, Gregg and Roggin lie motionless with their heads down as bullets rip the air above them. Dade covers Adrianna. This is awful - - here they thought that the worst was over, and now they are caught in another gunfight! When the firing stops, the three wait a moment, then cautiously peer up. Roggin and Gregg are at the very front of the now-reversed crowd, near the left wall. Dade is a few feet in back of them, against the interior wall. Gregg and Roggin spy the *only* form of cover that the long, narrow hallway offers: an open shuttle hatch, which is a mere eight feet from them. If they can get inside there, they will be shielded enough to fire back at the terrorists. But how? If they make the slightest move they will be shot to pieces. What will they do?

The answer comes in the form of a fierce tremor which tears through the ship. Kobryn and Jensen, the only ones on their feet, are knocked to their backs by the violently shaking floor. Maddox, Parker and DeSantis, who are in semi-crouches, are able to keep upright by spreading their feet farther apart. Gregg and Roggin take this cue from nature and, while keeping low, dash along the trembling carpet to the safety offered by the hatch. They are inside the lifecraft before the tremor is half over. DeSantis sees them moving - - he fights to keep upright and is about to shoot, then finds his targets gone before he has the chance.

Gregg and Roggin breathe a sigh of relief after they are inside the shuttle. The tremor weakens, then comes to a slow stop. Then the *Emprasoria* lurches very heavily to her right. Gregg begins to fall backward and, using lightening-fast reflexes, Roggin reaches out with his free hand and snatches his friend back just as he is about to topple through the hatch. Shaken, the man says nothing as they consider what to do next.

Maddox snaps his head around; gotta get off - - and get off *now*! He looks at Kobryn and Jensen, who are just getting up from the floor. "Get up!" Maddox barks, and they jump to their feet. Maddox looks around: only seven bags remain in the corridor. Maddox jerks his head forward. The people are still on the floor, and the two who have gone into the shuttle-hatch have not done anything. Maddox turns back to Kobryn and Jensen, who each are picking up two bags. "Get in that shuttle *now*!" They race through the hatch with their sacks and almost knock Yusacre down.

The Tsarevich Romanoff watches the terrorists keenly. He has slowly again taken his dagger from its sheath. The jeweled, crested handle is palmed in his left hand, the blade pointing down his forearm. In a quick move he tosses it in a spin to his waiting right hand, and now the blade faces outward. With a snap of his hand the knife flips around so his deft fingers hold the blade. When he sees two of the men go inside the shuttle, he knows he does not have much time. His eyes narrow as he takes careful aim from his prone position. In a flash he shifts up, throws the dagger, and is down again all in a split second.

The blade slices through the air as cleanly as a clippership on a calm sea. Romanoff credits his commando training when the point of the dagger hits square-on-target.

"YyyyyyyyeeooooaaaawwwwwDammit!" DeSantis howls in pain as a knife slices into the flesh of his right forearm. The blade cuts deep and gouges him practically to the bone. His right hand is cast away from the trigger, and with the rifle still slung over his shoulder, DeSantis moves his left hand from the barrel to the knifehandle. He wraps his hand around it and screams as he pulls the blade from his arm - - tearing more muscle and skin as he does so. He angrily throws the knife aside as his left hand clasps the forearm which for the second time this night has been damaged. The hand is instantly awash in blood, and he looks in agony at Maddox.

Maddox knows his point-man is useless now. "Give your rifle to Parker and get inside the shuttle!" DeSantis grudgingly complies and Parker eagerly takes the weapon and pockets his pistol. DeSantis keeps low as he runs and picks up a sack as he dashes into the shuttle. "I'm going next," Maddox whispers to Parker. "You keep cover. No funny business. I want you inside in two seconds." Parker nods. Half a second later and Maddox is inside the craft with the last two bags.

Parker looks around nervously. He will be the last man out. He does not relish the idea. Right now, he feels like the perfect target - - a lone sitting duck in a shooting gallery. He holds his rifle tighter, like a security blanket. Parker swallows hard and steals a glance behind him. He sees Maddox leaning out, punching buttons on the control pad in the wall.

A moment later and Jensen appears at the hatchway, his pistoled hand extended outward. "Come on . . ." he says as he beckons Parker with his free hand. "It's ok - - I've got you covered." Parker turns his face forward. He raises his body up slightly so he can run. He fires a short burst, turns, and races for the hatch. The knapsack on his back - - the one with a small red circle - - bounces as his feet pound the carpet. He runs for all he is worth.

Maddox goes back inside the shuttlecraft. He leans against the wall and removes a tiny remote control from his jacket pocket. He presses a button. Down in his suite, two small plastic tubes in the cover of the laptop computer are crushed by the action of closing metal tabs triggered by the remote signal. Carbolic acid in these tubes sprays over the small computer. Smoke erupts from the disc-drive port on the side of the device. The laptop is soon nothing but a small charred rectangle of steaming rubble. The acid works its way along the cable connection to the wire in the floor, singeing the carpet before it weakens and then dissolves altogether. Maddox smiles as his tracks are effectively covered.

Gregg and Roggin cautiously peer around the edge of their hatchway. They are shocked to see that the last terrorist is on his way to the shuttle. Gregg moves to shoot at the fleeing man when a bullet flies into the wall just next to his head. Gregg pulls himself inside white with shock and Roggin hastily moves up. Positioning himself in a crouch at the far left of the hatch, Roggin makes a decision. He knows he cannot fire straight at the man, but he knows what he can do.

Roggin rapidly makes some calculations as he clicks on his laser-sighting and takes aim. Dade sees what Roggin is doing, and while he is not sure <u>why</u> he is doing it, he knows he has to help him. Without aiming, Dade quickly raises his pistol and fires twice. He hopes it will be enough to divert the terrorists from Roggin.

Parker hears the shots from behind and the noise spurs him on as he runs to the shuttle. Rakk! A third!! His left foot slams down onto the hatchway. Ziiiii-PING! "Aaww!" Parker cries as a bullet burns along behind his right kneecap and into his upper calf muscle. He falls backward and his knapsack hits the floor hard. A black card-shaped plastic packet flies out from under the bag's top flap. Parker does not know what has happened - - it feels like the bullet came from above! He lies helpless on the floor, screaming in pain as the hatch begins to slide shut. The door stops once it hits his left leg, which lies across its path.

Jensen reaches down and grabs Parker's belt. "Fuck!" Maddox yells while looking down at Parker; his eyes are bugged out, his face tense, and his mouth is drawn back in rage - - he looks like a madman. As Jensen pulls Parker in, Maddox leans over their bodies and reaches for the knapsack which fell from Parker's back. His fingertips barely make contact with the edge of the bag. Digging his fingernails into the rough canvas, Maddox heaves back and snatches the precious knapsack into the shuttle. Jensen is able to get Parker in, and the second the doortrack is clear, the hatch resumes its closure. A second-and-a-half later the hatch seals itself shut with a dull thump which sounds like music to those inside.

The shuttle jerks slightly a moment later as the davit arms begin pushing it outward. Through the windows on the left side of the craft the men see that the compartment door is already up. They can see the blackness of space awaiting them. The sight is incredible; it means "ESCAPE". Kobryn seats himself in the pilot seat while the others begin to arrange the burlap sacks in a neat pile between the third and fourth benches. Jensen lies Parker on the fourth bench and begins to inspect the legwound.

As for Maddox, he opens the knapsack he holds. A very important knapsack. He sees that everything is in disarray inside. He spies one of the black identicard packets. He snaps it open. His face - his real face - stares back at him. He smiles and slips the packet into his pocket. He reaches into the knapsack and pulls out a magnum of Dom Perignon. Celebration is definitely in order.

Back in the corridor, Rish leaps to his feet the second that the hatch locks shut. He runs to the hatchway and pounds futilely on the door. Damn those bastards! Rish looks through the porthole as others crowd around him. The shuttle is already on its way out. Rish goes to the control panel and speedily enters the All Stop command. Rish smiles. Ha! They're not away yet! Wait . . . nothing happens. The davit arms are still extending. Rish pounds in the command code again. Nothing. Rish slams his fist into the wall. "Damn It!" he shouts in frustration.

He looks at the others, who are staring at him questioningly. "They put in a command lock-out!" Rish explains. "I can't stop them from here! The only overrides can come from the bridge! I don't know if there's enough time . . ." he says while turning toward the wallphone at the end of the corridor, and sees the portable handset is missing from the wallmount base – its metal cord tether hangs limply from the base. Now there definitely will not be enough time to notify the bridge. Rish angrily punches the control panel - - the bastards are getting away!

Roggin races up to the first officer with Gregg and Dade close behind. "Stand aside," he says as he raises his 309. Rish jumps out of the way as Roggin clamps his hands on the barrel and body of his rifle and brings the butt crashing down on the clean faceplate of the keypad.

The buttons mash into the plate, which cracks a bit. Roggin tenses and smacks the butt of the 309 into the panel again – the cracks deepen, and small pieces of the panel fall away. Holding his breath, Roggin does a third, even harder hit, and the faceplate shatters completely to reveal a mass of circuit boards and wiring. Roggin drops his weapon-turned-mallet and goes to the newly opened area. "Which look after the arm mechanism?"

"Those relays under there. Above are the hatch controls," Rish answers.

Roggin reaches his arm in and savagely pulls out a mass of red wiring linked to a light green, thin plastic board imprinted with intersecting conduit lines. "This it?" Roggin asks; Rish nods. Roggin reaches down and grabs the blood-stained dagger, then pounds the knife-edge into the circuit board, punching jagged holes again and again, like some sort of madman. Light sparks and smoke pour out. Roggin stops and looks through the hatch porthole, but shuttle has not stopped. He stabs more; ravenous tears and lacerations, criss-crossing within the ones already made – delicate wire-patterns are severed. Then, the davits stop. The shuttle is half-way through the compartment doorway.

The shuttlecraft jerks to a sudden stop when the davits cease moving. Those inside are jostled from the force of the instant "freeze". They look at one another in terror. What is going on? Maddox, who is in the middle of uncorking his champagne, angrily storms over to Kobryn at the command console. "What in the hell happened?" he barks.

"The launch arms just quit!" Kobryn shouts back. "We're not clear of the ship yet!"

"Those sons of bitches musta done something!!" Maddox yells. "Hell, they won't accept that *we've* won!" He turns to the right, to the tiny section of wall separating the viewport from the cabin. He focuses on the small red rectangular box which sits there by itself. He does not bother to read the white lettering printed on the cover as he flips it up - - he knows what the box holds. Inside, he sees a single small red "T"-shaped switch standing upright against the wall.

In a flash Maddox wraps the fingers of his right hand around the top cross-bar. "Get ready," he says to Kobryn. She nods, and Maddox swings his head and looks into the compartment. He can see earnest faces clustered in the hatch window. He cocks an eyebrow.

"Come now, do you take me for a fool?" he whispers. He pulls the switch down.

Two simultaneous explosions emanate from the starboard side of the shuttle. The craft is hurled clear of the *Emprasoria* from the force of the blast, and leaves two mangled davit arms behind in its wake. The door of the shuttle bay begins to automatically lower as Maddox strides to a window and peers back at the liner. Without taking his eyes away, he rips the cork from the champagne bottle, and brings the bottle to his lips then takes a long swig of the sweet wine. He pulls the bottle away and continues to gaze at the ship. "Thanks for everything, baby." He takes another swallow of champagne, then turns to his crew. "Now, to Mars and the Centralis billion!" Cheers and shouts fill the tiny craft.

Rish, Roggin and the others yell in rage when they see the explosive heads on the davits fire. "Damn them!" Rish says as he shakes his head angrily. He turns and looks at the dejected people around him. Most have their heads lowered, some wear faces of agony - - everyone is disappointed. Roggin stares. His ricochet slowed them, but not stopped them, just like his shooting of the controls.

"Rotten bitches and sons-a-bitches," Gregg whispers.

"Won, and gone," Dade says in despair. "We fought our hardest, they still won."

Romanoff kneels and picks up his dagger. He wipes the bloody blade clean on the sleeve of his white dress jacket, staining it. His eyes are sullenly locked on the shiny metal as he stands, then he places the dagger into the sheath on his belt. Well, at least he hurt one of them. Although he does not notice it, his left boot has pushed against a small plastic packet – the packet is inadvertently moved under some debris in the hall, and not seen.

The small crowd stands silence, each person lost in grim thought about how truly unfair things can be at times. "The dogs," says Xian Ng. He voices the opinion of everyone.

Rish forcibly snaps himself out of this dour mood. It will not do anyone any good to sulk about things they cannot change. He still has a job to do, and the reality of things is that the *Emprasoria* will not remain aloft much longer. "Everyone!" he yells; people turn to him. "Move to the front of the corridor. There's nothing left for us to do here!" The stewards and musicians move so that they form lines around the group of passengers. With light nudges and words of encouragement, they are quickly able to get the passengers to walk toward the forward section of the passageway where the only chance at survival lies.

Xian Ng turns to Karisu. "Kami smiled on us!" She nods in reverence to the naming of the basis of Shinto faith. "Now cherry-blossom, we can go, and go together!" Karisu smiles widely and looks through the crowd to see Tabbi Kahen with Daniel Benshabbot, and catches her eye. "O Genki De," Karisu whispers to her.

"Shalom," Tabbi mouths back.

Rish sends stewards to bring down the belligerent passengers who were locked away on the flight deck earlier. Moments later, they are given EVAS and put off the ship.

"The last lifecraft has left the ship, Sir!" Martingale calls out after reading a blaring screen.

"Very well, Jane," Arges says. "Has anyone heard from Peter or Alyssa?" he asks Escoto, DeMornay and Martingale. They shake their heads 'no'.

"I wonder how many people are left on board . . ." he wonders aloud. Just then, the fifth tremor hits. It shakes the *Emprasoria* with no mercy and ends with an incredibly large lurch. Arges rises from the chair and goes to the Board which shrieks with all manner of alarms. The captain goes to a console on the right of the currently vacant pilot's seat and types some requests on its keyboard. The responses he receives almost makes him ill. The ship will be down in ten minutes at latest. He turns to Escoto, and he holds a small disc in his hand. "Would you mind doing me a favor?"

"Not at all, Sir."

"Thank you." He passes her the disc. "Would you mind holding on to this, and seeing that it gets to Trish ok?" Earlier, the captain had managed to record a message to his wife.

"Sir, you can give it to her yourself..." Escoto protests, and tries to hand the disc back.

Arges pushes her hand back, then sandwiches it between his hands. "Yes, I know, its just I'll be busy around here in the next while and don't want to leave it behind or anything. I know that you, as comm officer, can keep it safe from accidental erasure or damage."

"I see," she says, then takes her hand back and looks at the disc, then turns her eyes to him again. "I will make sure she gets this, Sir."

"Thank you, Roberta."

Arges smiles a moment, then goes and sits in the pilot's seat. "Roberta, Krystal, Jane," he says as he types on a computer. "I am initiating the Freefall program. It has come to that point."

He punches the 'Enter' key and the computer speaks. *'FREEFALL PROGRAM HAS BEEN REQUESTED. CONFIRM, PLEASE,'* it says in its crass, emotionless, mechanical way. Arges winces as if being punched in the stomach, then forlornly types the verification. *'CONFIRMED. FREEFALL PROGRAM WILL COMMENCE IN ONE MINUTE AND COUNTING. SIXTY. FIFTYNINE. FIFTYEIGHT. FIFTYSEVEN.'*

Slowly, Arges rises from the pilot's chair. As he does, his eyes fall on a small piece of paper taped to the Board.

> ***"I expect us to reach our final destination in the best time possible."***
> ***- D. Enkel***

The captain stares at the offensive note. If they had not been flying at a breakneck speed to please the all-important 'man' then maybe . . . Arges stops himself. It is useless to speculate. Nonetheless, he finds the note disgusting. With a snap of his hand he rips the blue square from the Board. He crumples it and casts the tiny wad to the floor, then steps on it and crushes it. Doing this accomplishes nothing, but it feels extremely good.

The captain turns and strides back to the command platform, and its regal chair. He sits, pauses a moment, then accesses the general intercom. Arges takes a deep breath, stifles a cough, then speaks. "This is Captain Arges speaking. We have at best ten minutes before the ship goes down. There's nothing more anyone can do. I hereby release any crew still aboard from duty. You are free to go. I suggest all persons aboard leave immediately. I wish you the best of luck. God help us all." Arges clicks off the intercom and turns to Escoto, DeMornay and Martingale. "That goes for you three too. Go on."

The three women look at him. "What about you, Sir?" Martingale asks - - the captain still has not put on an EVA suit.

"I will remain a bit longer and supervise the Freefall program. After all, someone has to be here if something goes wrong." Concerned faces stare back at him. "Don't worry about me, I'll be fine. I'll be off long before she" - - Arges pauses in anguish - - "plunges."

Neither Escoto, DeMornay nor Martingale want to leave him behind, but they know it will be useless to argue the point. They have no choice but to comply with the request, as they would any other order.

"Yes, Captain," says Escoto as she salutes.

"Yessir," answers DeMornay. She sullenly removes the silver compulink gauntlet from her forearm and sets it inside a drawer on the Control Board. She faces him and salutes.

"As you wish, Sir," Martingale replies, and likewise salutes. Arges returns the salutes, and the three women slowly leave the bridge in silence. After a moment, he hears the airlock open and close, and knows they are gone. He sits back in the chair and stares blankly through the viewport as he mentally reviews the catastrophe which has unfolded since eleven o'clock. It is mind-boggling.

Down in the Port corridor, Rish and Rayburn steadfastly work at getting the passengers off of the ship. They have heard the Captain's announcement, but ignore his releasing them from their responsibilities - - they know where their duties lie, and will not even consider being "done with the ship" until everyone is safely away. The final evac goes well as people rapidly dress in their EVAS and jump from the shuttle bay faster still. When Karisu Ng and the few women remaining realize the obvious problem with the leg-section of the EVAS and their skirts, they do not hesitate in tearing the material from their legs. The men are decent enough to ignore this and concentrate on squeezing into their own EVAS.

Dade grabs an EVAS for himself and one for Adrianna. He hauls the two bulky orange suits to where she stands, against the corridor's inner wall. She is still a bit shaken from her third encounter with the 'steward'. She takes the EVAS from Dade and begins to climb into it - thankful that she changed into jeans. Dade hurriedly puts his on - - "Had enough of this 'hell night', I wants it all over with." In less than ten seconds they are both suited. They get in line for the shuttle bay, and Dade looks around. Where's Roggin and Gregg…oh, there they are. They kneel next to J.D. Zolnick, who is crouched over the passenger in the EVAS who had been shot by the gang-leader. Tears form at Zolnick's eyes, and none of them are in EVA suits. Roggin and Gregg try to coax Zolnick up, but he is not moving. The dead man is the one who was writing since the outset of the disaster.

J.D. Zolnick slowly composes himself. He cannot believe it - - his lifelong friend, the brilliant journalist and publisher Jack McCartney is lying dead on the floor. The EVA suits are thick, but not thick enough to stop a bullet. Zolnick shakes his head in grief. He puts his left hand on his friend's chest, mouths a prayer, then stands. "Where's the story?" he asks as his eyes rapidly search. "The electropad. Do you see it?"

Roggin and Gregg each look around. "I don't," Roggin says.

"Me neither," Gregg replies.

It is not there. Great, now McCartney's last story is missing...Zolnick becomes even more dispirited.

Zolnick gives McCartney one final look, then begins walking with Roggin and Gregg. Stewards join the three and escort them to the front of the corridor. Zolnick does not stop shaking his head as he walks; it is horrible, unfathomable. He takes an EVAS and begins to put it on, his body acting purely by reflex. He is aware of what he is doing, to be sure, but his mind is so clouded with grief that it is like he is in a dream-state. When he is suited, a steward guides him to a shuttle bay, where a large group is already gathered.

Rish, Rayburn, and the crewmen breathe a long sigh of relief when the last of the passengers are put into the shuttle compartment. As Rayburn operates the bay-door controls, Rish and the stewards, cruise entertainers, and musicians who are not yet suited burst into one of the defective shuttles and grab EVAS for themselves. Once his is on, Rish runs into the corridor and races to the forward arch of the lounge.

"Peter?" Rayburn calls after him.

"Going to the bridge!" he shouts back as he disappears into the room.

'*Freefall program has been activated,*' the computer announces in the bridge. Arges sits stolidly in the chair. He hears clicking and whirring in the ceiling. '*Preparing to launch secondary unit.*' says the computer.

This device - - nicknamed 'Ditto' - - simultaneously records every bit of information as it is stored in the memory cell of the primary computer. This portable copy of the journey log is to be ejected if the ship is about to deactivate. The foot-long tubular capsule emits a homing signal once away so it can be recovered for analysis. Arges hears a muffled explosion and a long hiss. 'Secondary log launched.' A pause. '*Monitoring scan determines unit in tact and fully functional. Launch Successful.*'

Rish bursts into the Bridge. He sees Arges sitting alone in the room. Taking a breath, he slowly approaches his captain. '*Preparing gravitationers for Freefal,*' the computer says - - Rish stops; this is the first indication he has that the Freefall program has been activated. His mood darkens, and he can imagine how awful the captain feels. Arges turns; "Peter," he says with a weak smile as he brings his right hand around. Rish steps up to the platform; they shake hands quickly.

'Gravitationers ready for maximum field increase. Process will occur in thirty seconds.' Rish stiffens; Arges sits back.

"Hell," Arges says as he shakes his head in despair. "How could this have happened? Why? God awful." He pauses. "Did you get everyone off?"

"Yessir. The last are leaving now. We used the EVAS from the defective lifecraft."

Arges raises his eyebrows. "Smart move, Peter. Very innovative. I'm impressed."

"It was Alyssa's idea, Sir."

"Oh, excellent thinking on her part."

"I couldn't agree more, Sir."

'Primary power now being routed to gravitationers.'

Suddenly, the bridge goes dark and the lights on the Board dim. After a moment, spotlights click on as the emergency power cells send power through the ship. The computer is relaying the bulk of the ship's energy to the gravitationers to increase their field strength. The intention is for the gravitationers to emit enough gravity to hold all cargo and material within the ship in place during the fall. This way, if the ship is later located, there is a good chance it can be resurrected or at least its contents can be salvaged. The goods and other items aboard will suffer relatively little damage under the solid weight of gravity pressure.

The difference within the ship is immediately noticeable. A heaviness falls on the entire vessel. Rayburn, the only person in the port lifecraft corridor, is about to go up to the bridge when the lights suddenly wink out and the Evies and Evans in the area vanish. The emergency lights come on, but the V.I.P. holograms do not re-appear. Then she feels the weight come upon her. She immediately changes her mind, knowing that a slight change in pressure is just the start - - the gravity will get much, much stronger very quickly. She knows she will likely not make it to the bridge. She punches in a code and the hatch reopens. The crewmen inside are somewhat surprised to see her. Rayburn locks her helmet on then steps into the hatchway. She programs the control panel, sets the command lock-out just to be safe, then jumps into the compartment. The hatch slides to a close behind her, and seconds later, the last of the crew is outside the ship.

Bethany Parris holds her breath as she jumps out of the compartment. As she has been trained to do, she activates the boot rockets and flies away from the vessel. "Wow, this is interesting…" she whispers as she experiences personal spaceflight – it's a lot different than what you do in a training simulator. She looks back at the ship. There is Finesse at the stern, its windows clean and clear. A tear wells up and slides down her soft cheek. She closes her eyes and turns away, firing the boot rockets again. She opens her eyes a half-second later, and in the far distance, recognizes a ship… "The *Albany*! Tyrekka!"

"Sir, we must go," says Rish on the bridge of the *Emprasoria*.

"Yes, I know," Arges replies. "Could you get me an EVA?" Rish looks around, and notices there is not an EVA in the bridge for the captain. He is at first infuriated that the man had not tried to take care of himself, then he pauses. He sees the look of restrained agony on the man's tired face and understands that the captain probably desires a few moments alone on his bridge to say 'good bye'.

"Yessir. Of course, Sir," Rish replies dutifully with a nod. He then turns and speedily leaves the bridge. Once in the corridor, Rish attempts to run to the Locker Room, but the weight of the gravity upon him is so heavy that the best he can manage is a slow jog - - even at this his breathing is labored and he feels as though he is walking in mire. Finally, he reaches the EVAS room behind the security station. Many of the doors stand ajar, exposing empty lockers, but Rish spots some closed ones at the far side of the small room.

He jerks open the first one. Empty. The second. Likewise. More tension! Third. Empty. His heart races as he opens the last one and . . . finds an EVAS there! He releases the breath he has been holding as he grabs the outfit and leaves. He trudges down the corridor. The gravity is so strong now - - and its force is increasing with every passing second.

The ship lurches forward. Rish is knocked down as the deck slopes beneath him. The suit slips from his hands and slowly drifts through the air, moving like it is suspended in clear molasses as it sluggishly drops to the floor. Rish lies still; the dead weight of the gravity pushes down hard on him. With a great deal of effort, he puts himself up on his hands and knees. He crawls forward - - straining with every move.

When he reaches the EVAS, he uses its solidness to help get to his feet. His muscles burn inside him. He slowly walks toward the bridge; his legs feel as though they are encased in lead. Rish finally reaches the forward airlock. He punches some buttons on the control panel and the inner door slides open. "Captain!" he calls as he programs the double-doored room to automatically open the hullside panel when the inner-door closes. "I'm here! I have a suit for you!" Breathing is difficult with his compressed lungs. The humid, stale air does not help at all.

The ship lurches once more. Rish is again knocked off-balance. His hand knocks the control panel and the suit slips from his grasp as he tumbles into the airlock. He falls to the floor and bangs his head on the outer door of the compartment. He shakes his head dazedly and watches in wide-eyed horror as the inner hatch begins to close. Then, it stops. The door contacted the top edge of the EVAS in its floortrack and automatically halts in accordance with its safety protocols. The ship lurches again. The EVAS shifts backward.

With the track clear, the door slides itself closed. "No!" Rish shouts and jumps to his feet then throws himself at the hatch. He pounds the heavy steel door and looks in panic through the square porthole. He sees the suit lying in the corridor; there is no sign of the captain. Rish hears an alarm bell ringing. He turns - - the outer door is going to open! He furiously hits buttons on the control panel inside the airlock, but nothing happens. The control lock-out he has programmed began functioning the moment the hatch closed. He has no options.

He slaps on his EVA helmet just as the hull panels begin to part. Three seconds later, the door is fully open. Rish watches as his officer's cap – which fell off his head during the fall – lazily drifts outside. He walks to the outer edge of the compartment and grabs the cap, then looks down and sees the pale surface of the asteroid below and Vesta just beyond - - they look so terrifyingly close. "God watch over Captain Arges, and watch over me too." He leaps out of the airlock and blasts away from the ship.

Arges sits still in the chair when he feels the forward lurch. Alarms blare and lights flash on the Board. He smiles, with a kind of cockeyed grin: "Bravely fighting with all her considerable might to stay aloft; won't give in easily." As quickly as it appeared, the smile vanishes.

Arges stares forlornly at the gray rocky surface of the asteroid that fills the viewport. He shakes his head in despair. "What a dismal end for such a proud vessel," he says outloud to the empty room. Part of his spirit dies; his heart breaks, and he sits pondering for a minute until Rish's voice rouses him from deep thought. He turns his head toward the sound, then feels another lurch. He swallows hard and his stomach clenches, then he closes his eyes. In a murmur, he says

"Goodbye, angel of the sky..." With that and a quick touch of his hand to the brim of his hat, Arges bids adieu to the *Emprasoria*.

The captain moves to get up from the chair as he feels still another lurch. Try to stand - -what? Feels like an iron hand pressing down on the chest...try again – dig the hands into the armrests and push strongly – come on...come on... wait, stop, relax. He will tear himself apart if he struggles any harder against the unyielding pressure. Locked in by the gravity field! He watches as protective panels slowly cover the main viewport, and the lights on the Board click off one by one. He sits back and grimly but proudly accepts his fate, the unsaid fate of many masters: the captain is going down with the ship.

The ship snaps down. The bow drops and the tail thrusts upward. The *Emprasoria* is now in a straight up-down position. The hull screeches and squeals in stress and metalically sounds the death throes. It hovers for the briefest of moments and looks like an exquisite ivory tower. There is an ear-piercing shriek and the *Emprasoria* falls straight down into the asteroid like a mighty titan falling from the heavens. She slices through space like a great white saber and in an instant the largest, most luxurious liner ever built is nothing but a sliver. Then, that too is gone.

CHAPTER TWENTY
Aftermath

The white shuttles and orange-suited people encircling the area witness the disaster in horror. That is, except for Maddox and his team. Just after they left, Maddox looks down to Kobryn. "Let's stay here a bit and watch," he orders with a hint of a sinister tone, and a wicked grin, apparently having a macabre fascination to remain and witness the sinking.

She grins back at him. "Ok, I can have us hover," she answers, then adjusts the controls.

Maddox brings his pistol from its holster, and with the flick of the back of his thumb, drops the ammo clip from the handle – it bounces harmlessly on the carpet. He turns and looks out the front starboard window, then raises his pistol to his face. Recalling actions of just over a month earlier, Maddox the Fan keeps the gaze of his squinted right eye fixed on the supership, contained compactly within the crosshairs of the round sniper-scope of his pistol. The instant before the ship makes her fall, he pulls the trigger. "Pow!" he says as the pistol harmlessly clicks, then he laughs wildly. The ship plunges and in a swift move he brings the gunbarrel to his lips, and blows away an imaginary puff of smoke.

Angelique moves with liquidly swaying hips over to Maddox, drapes her arms around him lavishly, then kisses him on the cheek. "Way to bring her down, Russ." She snickers and laughs. The others watch the sinking with perverse delight as they use colorspray antidote, and remove their colored contact lenses and rubber fingertip covers.

"There she goes," DeSantis says, and chuckles. "Adios mouchcha!"

"Yeah, thanks for the memories," Parker remarks with a smirk.

Then, the unexpected happens. The shuttlecraft begins to rattle. And be pulled downward. In their desire to observe the fall of the *Emprasoria*, the pirates put themselves too close to the ship when she made her plunge. In a supreme act of poetic justice, the bandits' shuttle becomes hopelessly caught in the magnetofield intensity caused by the horrible fall.

"What the hell?" Maddox shouts as he grabs at handles in the ceiling to steady himself.

Kobryn has her teeth clenched as she pulls on the controls. "Downdraft! Damn it, we must be in their gravity field!!! It's got us caught like we're in a tractor beam!"

"Get us out of it!" Maddox yells.

"Russell!" Angelique calls as she is hurled to the floor by the g-forces.

Maddox turns and looks at her and extends his arm to her and helps her up while trying to keep his own legs steady, then snaps his head back to Kobryn. "Do something!"

"I'm fucking trying!" she shouts back as she jerks back on the control stick and pounds buttons. "Argh!"

DeSantis is thrown forward, and he clutches at open air as he tumbles toward Maddox and slams into the back of a seat. "What in the hell is going on?"

Down the shuttle goes into the spatial pool and gravitational wake of the *Emprasoria*. Alarms ring and lights flash in the cockpit as Kobryn feverishly tries to break the tiny craft free of the jetstream they are caught in as her partners-in-crime continue to scream and shout around her. The shuttle plunges toward the asteroid, gaining speed and momentum as it falls. "We-er-er-er gonna hiiiiittttttt!" Maddox yells through his rattling teeth and from his vibrating throat. The craft bounces and shakes under the lethal mixture of gravity and speed, then the rocky surface races up to greet them.

Those in the other shuttles hear the cries of agony over their radios and see a bright yellow burst appear on the gray asteroid. Then, there is nothing. They lower their heads in grief. "That was awful," says one man, and he voices the thoughts of everyone.

But Lifecraft 132 is not the only victim of the *Emprasoria*'s wake. Some of the EVAS people are likewise in too close a proximity to the ship when she makes the descent. With their arms and legs flailing about and the sounds of their screams carried over their helmet transmitters, they are pulled down to the asteroid. Some try in desperation to blast away with their bootrockets, but these do not have near enough power to break free from the spatial whirlpool. They meet their deaths when their bodies slam into the cordite surface. Thus the gravesite of the *Emprasoria* is marked by thirty orange human-shaped headstones which gruesomely dot the area around it.

The others cannot move to help the falling people for fear of being caught in the suction themselves. They shriek, openly weep, or turn their heads away in grief. Those in EVAS fly over to whichever shuttlecraft is closest to them and latch on to the smooth white sides and hold on for deer life. This, of course, means that the shuttles cannot operate at their full speed. To move too fast will rip the outside people off and send them reeling into space - or more likely into the flaming exhaust of the craft. The people inside every shuttle silently agree to move at a slow pace to let the "outsiders" remain. At least, no one has the nerve to demand that the hangers-on be removed for fear that <u>they</u> would end up on the <u>other</u> side of the airlock themselves as reprisal for saying what they feel.

"gassssssssp My,,,,,oh my…." Ginni Chen is taken aback by the sight of the sinking ship. She turns back toward the videographer behind her in the chartered shuttecraft. He too is startled by the sudden fall of the *Emprasoria.* He turns his mobile camera back to her. "This...this is Ginni Chen of MUBC....we have just witnessed a.... a terrible tragedy…"

The fall was also witnessed live by the news satellite cameras. Even in their "zoom" mode they are still too far from the site to get an accurate picture, but the scene they are able to record and transmit is truly terrifying. There is silence in newsrooms and homes all across the face of the planet.

The MUBC craft pilot slows a bit, too stunned to operate his controls. Zaaboom! A laserblast rips across the front of the vehicle and rattles it. "Shuttlecraft, end your approach!" an angry voice says over the cockpit speakers. "This is Commander Boot of the Space Rescue Unit *Intrepid.* By my order, you will remain at this location, or return to Mars. Copy?" The blast startles the pilot and his two newsreporter passengers. He jumps in his chair as he hastily ends his forward thrust.

"Y-y-yes Commander. Shuttlecraft *Zowietours 1* holding position."

The *Intrepid* races past the little craft, and Boot gives it an angry look from her seat. Lieutenant Commander Stiedman had ordered any Rescue Craft to fire across the bows of any media-oriented ship which ventured too close or threatened to somehow interfere with the rescue operation. Dixon retracts the mini-cannon as the *Intrepid* moves on, and not much is said as they approach the site. The rescuers had seen the signs that things were going badly....EVA-suited people jumping out of the vessel....the Ditto unit be launched... sweat formed on their upper lips...come on, come on we're so close...hold on just a bit longer...then, they watch in horror as the ship plunges, and took other victims with it.

"They're here! Help is here!" someone yells into a helmet microphone. The message spreads like wildfire to all the EVAS people. All at once they fire their bootrockets and blast toward the yellow rescue ship. Those who are holding on the lifecraft leave them and join the others in their flight to the *Intrepid*. In no time the S.R. craft is swarmed with over-excited people - - all of whom want to be taken inside first.

The *Intrepid* is assaulted with pounding fists. The personnel run to the portholes and make hand signals to those outside . . . trying desperately to get them off of the ship. Boot clicks on the external message-reader as, since there is no oxygen in space to carry sound, she cannot use the external speakers to voice a message. "Attention, Attention," scrolls a message in red light on a rectangular board on each side of the shuttle "We are here to help you but we cannot get to you if you are on the vessel! Please vacate the ship!" Her words and the gestures from the others have little effect.

Just then, a second S.R. unit arrives. The Starlift pulls in close to the *Intrepid*, and three other units arrive almost simultaneously. Each is immediately besieged by EVAS people. Six more rescue ships appear, followed on close heels by several others.

The media-chartered craft arrive as well, but remain on the fringe of the site, having seen what happened to the *Zowietours* vessel, and not wishing to tempt the anger of the tense Rescue personnel. However, they get as close as they possibly can to the action and let the telephoto lenses on their mobile cameras do the rest. They also know if they try to radio the shuttles directly they will have their antennas shot down, which would also cut the feed to their studio, so they keep radio-silence.

The *Sacramento* arrives soon thereafter. As she was so close to Mars, her fuel was low and First Officer Murdock and Pilot Rogle had to calculate a fuel-distance ratio, they backtrack slowly, lest the ship burn out of fuel and become nothing more than a stranded derelict. Minutes later, the *Albany* roars on to the scene. Tyrekka eases his travel-worn freighter in; he had been right in stating he was too far away to help the stricken liner.

Now, there are enough ships and personnel to accommodate the freefloating people. The Rescue teams quickly bring the situation under control. A place is found for every EVAS person within the *Sacramento* or *Albany* – in his cargo hold, Tyrekka surveys the crowd of EVAS people, then smiles when he sees the helmet come off of Bethany Parris on his ship; she grins back, weakly. "So, we meet again," he says with a smile.

"So it seems," she answers, then runs her hand through her hair and returns the smile.

After attending to those who require medical attention and the lifecraft pilots are instructed on Following procedure, Colonel Stiedman speaks. "Time for us to go."

"Agreed, Sir," concurs Commander Boot from the *Intrepid*, who is the operation supervisor. "Activate a marker buoy here," Boot orders.

"Deployed. Activated," Dixon answers a moment later.

"Ditto log unit has been retrieved," Jones reports.

With that, the caravan of rescue vessels, ships and lifecraft makes its way toward Mars.

As the Martian population awakes to an overcast morning, they learn of the disaster. Reports are vague and specifics non-existent, but one fact is conveyed to everyone: the *Emprasoria* is gone. The news is devastating...shocking; profoundly shocking. Draining. Unbelievable. How could that sturdy, beautiful ship be 'gone'? A new vessel . . brand new . . now it has sunk? Impossible!

Reaction is identical when the news is relayed to the Lunar Colony and to Earth. It is unfathomable. People with no connection to the ship are moved emotionally as well. She was so amazing . . . humanity on the whole took pride in her. And now she has been snuffed out . . . a shining light forever gone. The feelings are indescribable. Grief is high. Newspapers and magazines produce special editions, SolNetNews sites and television and radio stations provide either round-the-clock coverage or interrupt regular programming with news bulletins.

The Spaceport Authority is quick to close Dock 912, which was to be the Martian home for the *Emprasoria*. Out of respect for the loss, that area of the Port will be locked-down for the entire day. 912 had been elaborately decorated for the anticipated arrival - - an arrival which now will never happen. The Comet Riband which the Port

Authority had planned to award the *Emprasoria* in recognition of the fastest Earth-Mars crossing in history is discreetly returned to its glass case.

The Utopia Planitia flag flies at half-mast at the Spaceport, the Deccoar City Hall, and the Government Building. Likewise, the state flag at the Capitol Building in *Sacramento*, California is flown at half-mast, as are the city and state flags at the Los Angeles City Hall. Thus, her destination and her home officially mourn her.

The Archangel Line Headquarters, all its regional offices, and the Archangel Tours Agencies are closed on that bleak Monday. Company flags fly at half-mast, and black Funerary wreaths are placed on the main entrances and aboard every other vessel in the fleet. The Archangel website bears the image of this same wreath. A daughter and sister is thus mourned. Crowds of the angry, the curious, and the upset gather outside the buildings and visit the website hoping to obtain even the slightest of news. None is forthcoming.

In England, at Lloyd's of London, a solemn bell peels through the air. The guarantor of Archangel thus weeps. The Winston Family is extremely distressed on learning that 'Harry's Dazzler' has been lost, as are the curators at the Smithsonian Institution. The beautiful blue diamond is now just a memory . . .

The assorted parties and festivities which were to welcome the ship's passengers and crew are all canceled. The food and ballrooms are used though - - used to feed and house the survivors while healthcare workers meticulously inspect them and Space Authority agents relentlessly question them. It lasts for three solid days.

When the exhausted people finally are released, they are quickly ushered to a hotel especially rented by the Archangel Line. Officially, the Line states it wishes to assist those who have been so "hardstruck by the most awful of situations..." but everyone guesses it is to keep the people shielded from the press. A great many journalists are hungry for the story of the disaster; they lust after it more than they had for the pre-christened 'mystery ship' itself. The Line is able to keep all the wolves at bay as its public relations staff do their very best to console the survivors.

However, the enterprising and resourceful Diana McCartney is able to slip away. *With* her vidcam no less! She goes directly to the McCartney Publications Office and to Jim Daresh. She also assumes that is where she will eventually find Jack, since she could not locate him in the multitude of survivors. The newspapers and magazines published by MP feature the amazing still photos while the television and internet affiliates of MP air the shocking footage. The Archangel Line does not comment.

Three days of lavish wining and dining does little to soothe the moods of the still distraught people. Much to the chagrin of the Line, the Colonial Government orders that the survivors be released from their 'luxurious prison'. The Line offers free passage back to the Earth or Moon for the vacationers, and resettlement assistance cheques of undisclosed amounts to those emigrating to the ruby planet. The executives of the Line are almost insane with fear. They do not worry about the crew - - they can be easily controlled - - but there are no such holds on the passengers. What will they say? How bad will it be? Only time will tell.

An official memorial service is held at the City Square of Deccoar, the metropolis which boarders Spaceport Gamma, at noon on April 27, exactly one week after the disaster. All the survivors attend the service, which is televised across the planet, to the Lunar Colony, and to Earth. The cameras fall on many in the crowd who mourn openly.

Hours after the service ends, the vacationers are on their way back to their homes on the Moon or Earth. When the ships dock at their respective spaceports, they are met by hoards of people - - crowds of the curious mob the docks just to catch a glimpse of the survivors. When the people who have been through so much already finally do arrive at their homes, their personafönes ring constantly, their email accounts fill, and knocks continually come to their doors. Most switch off their fönes after the first hour and lock themselves in their bedrooms, burying their exhausted bodies in the security offered by their warm beds. By this time they all wished they had never even heard of the *Emprasoria.*

Although Jennifer Barnes lives in Sioux City Iowa, she goes directly to New York City from Spaceport Alpha. She goes to the massive R.R. Stone Building on Lexington Avenue. She arrives unannounced, and when the Lobby receptionist tries to detain her, she simply ignores the woman, obtains the information she needs from the computerized Directory, and proceeds on her way. Minutes later, she barges into the ornately decorated reception area of Penthouse Office Two and, without saying a word, strides past the startled secretary and walks into the inner office of the suite.

"I think you should have this," Miss Barnes says as she drops an electropad on the room's lone desk. The flabbergasted man behind the desk stares in shock at the woman, then lowers his eyes to capital-lettered words at the top of the first page: "A TERROR IN SPACE: THE SINKING OF THE *EMPRASORIA*." Just under this title, smaller, is "By: John Perry McCartney". He instantly recognizes the handwriting as McCartney's.

Two security officers appear at his door in response to frenzied calls from the receptionist and secretary. He waves them away, then asks his secretary to bring in some pastry and soft drinks. "You and I have quite a bit to talk about," says Kurt Richards, the Executive Vice President of the McCartney Publishing Group as he smiles and leans back in his chair. The next day, newspapers from coast to coast appear with the blaring headline of: 'THE TRUE STORY OF THE *EMPRASORIA* DISASTER!' The mourning widow Diana is pleased to see that the final words of her husband do make it to print after all. For many nights afterward she goes to sleep with the original electropad clutched tightly in her arms.

The day after Peter Bull returns to his palatial mansion in Palm Springs, he is visited by his manager, Trev Finnegan. Bull and Myrie wearily tell him of their experience - - he sits amazed at every word.

"Wow, that was sure something…" Finnegan says later. "I am very glad you two got out ok." He pats his hand in a comforting way on Myrie's knee, and also pats Bull's shoulder.

"Take some time off, Pete," Finnegan says later, as he is about to leave.

"Thanks, Trev. I'll think about it." The two shake hands and Finnegan turns to the door. "Oh, wait a second," Bull says, stopping Finnegan at the entryway. Bull races up the stairs to the master bedroom of his home. He reappears seconds later with a small clear-plastic case in his hand. "Here," Bull says as he passes a music disc to his manager. "This is what I did on the trip. Give her a listen, it's not bad. It'll give us some ideas for the next album, or concert or something."

Finnegan eyes gape and his jaw drops at the disc, he cannot believe the gold he is holding in his hand. "Yeah, will do…."

A week later, in a rapid effort by Mythos Records to cash in on the *Emprasoria* craze, the album **'SONGS FROM AN IVORY SHIP'** is released. The cover features a picture of Bull, with guitar, staring outward from the right side. The album title is printed in blue block letters next to him, and along the bottom is an impressive full-length photo of the *Emprasoria* as she appeared in better days at the Harrison Wulfe shipyard. The double-length album contains every song Bull had played during the voyage, uncut and unmixed. It debuts on the Pop music chart at a startling number Three. It is at the number-One spot soon after and remains there for five solid weeks. The accompanying concert tour breaks all previous attendance records for a Bull performance. Bull donates his royalties to the International Victim's Assistance Fund as he can now fully appreciate the struggles which survivors of tragedies face. He never has the bullethole in his guitar repaired.

J.D. Zolnick is pleased and completely surprised to see Jack McCartney's final story appear in "The New York Newsworld". He also sees Diana's footage appears in clips on various news channels as well. Zolnick and his family attend the sedate funeral for McCartney wherein Zolnick is a pallbearer. All the main people of North American journalism pay their final respects to the brilliant writer. The day after the funeral, Zolnick establishes a special trust fund for McCartney's seven children, while Diana creates the J.P. McCartney Award in Journalism to recognize exceptional reporting. Zolnick donates to the Fund substantially and on a regular basis. Zolnick becomes a surrogate patriarch to his fallen friend's family. He takes excellent care of them - - they are never in need for anything.

Dr. Stephen Radsky completes his lecture tour on Mars and augments his original dissertation with a thorough discussion of "CROWD REACTION IN STRESSED CIRCUMSTANCES: THE RESPONSE OF THE PSYCHE TO THREATENED DEATH". He avoids any questions concerning his personal experiences on the *Emprasoria.* Radksy later publishes an in-depth book based on his observations and findings while aboard the ship on that fateful night. It becomes an instant best-seller and garners him many awards from the psychiatric community.

The Tsarevich Alexsander Romanoff does join the Russian Imperial Galactic Corps and becomes an active cosmonaut. He flies on several missions, and quickly earns the rank of Major. He becomes Commander of the exploratory research vessel "*KATHERINE THE GREAT*" and provides a wealth of previously unknown scientific data about the Solar System and its elements.

Cal Gregg and Edwin Roggin resume their lives as corporate chieftains. The CMG 309 is marketed as '*The Weapon of Heroes*' and its first practical use aboard the *Emprasoria* against terrorist - bandits is heralded often by Gregg Arms Incorporated. The rifle sells incredibly well. Under Roggin's personal supervision, a thorough television documentary entitled "THE *EMPRASORIA*: A STAR THAT FELL" is produced and telecast over the RBC network, including footage from Diana McCartney and others. It wins several Pulitzer and Murrow Awards and becomes a classic within the ranks of television journalism. The two men remain in regular, if infrequent, contact with each other and Dade. Their battle experience has fused an unbreakable friendship between them all.

Darian Dade is a changed man. His experience on the *Emprasoria* is a trial-by-fire. Gone are his days as a freewheeling man of the world. He appreciates life, to be sure, but sees things in an entirely different light, and has a newfound respect for every moment – never taking another single thing for granted again. He and Adrianna Harting continue their relationship. After two weeks, she recovers fully from the extreme stress caused by the 'steward'. She and Dade are married a year later, and the perilous night they survived is a rare subject in their household, despite the curious efforts of their two sons and daughter.

Simon the Centralis invader with a warped sense of humor misses his own deadline. The authorities at Gamma wait and wait, but never hear from him. The 'billion in bullion' he had been so determined sits in crates in a heavily guarded storeroom until it is returned to the First National Bank of Mars. The Centralis communications satellite gets her backups restored thanks to cautious, hair-raising and painstaking work of technicians, and the unit is given a complete overhaul to remove any traces of the invasion. Extra precautions are built into the Defiant protector grid to defend further against tamperings. Also, duplicate Centralis2 and Centralis3 are built, then stored at Uninas and Unicol for either one to be deployed should anything else untoward happen to the main unit again. News of the Centralis episode never reaches the mainstream media, though 'urban myth' stories about it do appear from time to time. They never did find out about the mysterious 'Simon'. Spaceport Gamma Security Detective Nelson Leevan always wonders about this incident, and personally speculates that it was some sort of hoax by a disgruntled worker.

A thorough police investigation is conducted on Mars, the Moon, and Earth regarding the identities of the six terrorist-bandits. The detectives have frustratingly little to go on, but begin with a detailed examination of the passenger list. It is quickly discovered that Kurt Kendall, Andy Forest, Jack Rumaurier, Brenda Marlow, Sarah Cartesh and Rebecca Nollins do not have verifiable credentials or addresses. The real individuals behind these contrived personas is a mystery. The file remains open with all Federal police divisions, and the Interplanetary Agency of Law and Order.

First Officer Murdock of the *Sacramento* and Captain Tyrekka of the *Albany* both receive Citations of Excellence from both the Utopia Colony and United States Space Authorities. When questioned as to why he did not respond immediately to the distress flare, Captain Charles Duke of the *Sacramento* cannot give a reasonable answer. He is regarded as one of the biggest fools in transportation history.

Darcy Phillips, the public relations executive who masqueraded as an older, injured person and took a coward's way off the ship, is not able to adequately explain his escape, or save the Line from disastrous publicity – despite his best (and slickest) efforts. He ultimately leaves the Line, lays low for two years, then re-emerges as a cybisher, but avoids doing any articles or sites related to the *Emprasoria*. Eventually, his life becomes a shambles. He spends his days and nights afterward getting high on every drug imaginable and drunk on every liquor available until his last red cent is gone. The narcotics and alcohol do not provide the solace he so desperately needs. One day, his ragged body is found in a section of town that Phillips would never have entered in his 'glory days'. The suicide ends his life, but not his memory. He lives on through history as the self-mutilating escaper.

Bethany Parris, the smiling Cruise Entertainment staffer, remains in the hospitality industry, though is content to remain in hotels planted on firm ground. Her photos from the *Emprasoria* are kept in a special e-file, and anytime she hears about the ship and the journey, or thinks about it herself, her thoughts are always drawn to the Finesse all-glass lounge which she loved so much. She and Tyrekka enjoy a romantic relationship, though she keeps the home-fires burning for him, rather than racing the skies alongside.

Second Officer Alyssa Rayburn, Communications Officer Roberta Escoto, Dr. Julius Washington, Second Engineer Christopher

Corté and Pilot Jane Martingale all receive award for meritorious service for their conduct above and beyond the call of duty during those terrible, horrifying hours which comprised the *Emprasoria*'s last night. Third Officer Mitchell Hearst is regarded posthumously as a fool and a traitor - as far from his dreams of a high society man as he can possibly get.

First Officer Peter Rish resigns his commission with Archangel and joins Silver Star. He serves admirably with them, and soon earns his Captain's stripes. He comments little about that night on the *Emprasoria*, but does serve as a consultant on a number of book and film projects about the calamity only to ensure that the proper story is told as he knows it. Although he wishes his last moments on the Flight Deck were different, he also knows if he did not go when he did, he would be dead in the ruins of the wreck this very day.

Captain John Arges is remembered as a noble man, a credit to his profession and rank, and a revered role model. Roberta Escoto delivers the videodisc to his wife Trish, and as Escoto guessed, it contains a poignant 'Goodbye' message from the captain. Trish wept when she first saw it, but was very grateful to have these last words from him. A monument to Captain Arges is built at Griffith Park Observatory in Los Angeles, and another at General Clark Park in his birthplace and hometown of Dayton, Ohio. Both depict him in statue form, standing tall and proud, looking out on the horizon for his next flight.

The others connected with the *Emprasoria* are able to resume their lives again, but things are never quite 'normal' for them again. Even when the media attention finally does fade - - when the spotlights shine on something else and the reporters stop calling - - the people cannot return to a pleasant life of obscurity. Somewhere, somehow, someone connects them with the great disaster. Memories from the horror of the evening of April 21, 2088 haunt them for the remainder of their days.

When the executives of the competition to the Archangel Line originally hear of the disaster, they are not relieved as one might expect. Their stomachs turn then as much as when they first laid eyes on the 'monstrosity'. The sinking presents a very major problem. Any Line worth its being can compete with a supership by building their own vessels bigger and better. It is expensive, but it can be done. But no one, not even the best, can compete with public fear. Everyone associated with the travel industry knows it will be a long time before people will feel completely comfortable with spacetrips again. The best the others can do is remain quiet and take solace in the fact that they are not Archangel.

The Archangel Line never recovers. Its name is forever associated with 'death'. The fact that the disaster does not involve much loss of life means nothing. The *Emprasoria* becomes an incredibly large coffin-nail; an ivory spike which sealed the demise of the organization. The Space Authorities on both Earth and Mars hold official Inquests about the sinking. Congresswoman Jackson is a very active participant in both. The data from the Secondary Log Unit recovered by the *Intrepid* is analyzed, and all the survivors are interviewed; many testify in open court. It is speculated and surmised that the small ring clamp which blocked engine lock release originally loosened when the ship buckled during its encounter with the williwa windstorm at South America, and the problem was with them through the entire voyage. It was only when the emergency stop was enacted that the clamp rubbed against the lock, causing a negative reflex. Also, the oversized gravitationers for the massive ship radiated a stronger level of a magnetic gravity field, which captured the errant meteor and pulled it in. Using the short range radar instead of long range was unwise, but ultimately it would not have affected the collision as the meteoroid simply appeared too quickly. However, both Authorities rule conclusively that the Line "in its unfathomable negligence is wholly responsible for the disaster". The Line is fined heavily and ordered to pay steep restitution to the survivors and to the estates of the victims.

Revenues for the Archangel Line disappear overnight. Much of the fleet and other assets are sold just to keep the Line in operation as an entity. The Line does keep active for several years afterward, under the name Andromeda, but only in the minor leagues. Eventually, its entire holdings and what remains of its once prestigious stable of ships are sold at auction. Damien Enkel lives to see this happen.

But he is unaware it is happening. He is not aware of anything. The rest of his days are lived in a semi-vegetative state secluded in his immense mansion. The stress of the disaster and the immediate outcome wreaks havoc on his mind, and it proved too much for him to handle. At times, he can be found shouting out orders to Arges or Rish as he imagines himself up on the bridge, trying to save his beloved ship. His wife Ann remains by his side, loyal to him, but does not let his condition affect her status as a leading socialite. She goes out to various functions, plays and operas, to gala parties and fundraisers, sometimes on her own, sometimes on the arm of a nameless but good-looking escort. Ann never discusses the *Emprasoria*, and chops anyone off at the knees who dare raise the subject within earshot of her. As for Damien, he later suffers a massive stroke which leaves him debilitated and requiring continual care from nurses until the day he finally does die. Thus the Highest Authority passes judgment.

The subject of the *Emprasoria* remains in the public conscious for a very long time, and the story takes all manner of varied form. A fanclub of sorts for enthusiasts of the ship and its people and life is formed, named 'The *Emprasoria* Appreciation Association'. They establish a SolNetsite, produce a newsletter, collect artifacts and memorabilia, create a museum, and hold regular, monthly meetings at their headquarters in Providence, Rhode Island, and host a large convention once a year - - on April 21. To date, their organization has three thousand card-carrying members around the world and at the Biociles.

Tasteful, midsized monuments to those lost on the *Emprasoria* are created at Los Angeles and Deccoar. A plaque honoring the ship is placed at Dock 29 within Spaceport Alpha, and another appears at the Los Angeles airport. Harrison Wolfe dismantles the gargantuan Hangar 13 as it becomes to much of an attraction for sightseers and trophy-hunters. To date, they keep the original blueprints and design specifications for the *Emprasoria*, including several interior photographs a to-scale drafter's model, on file in their offices and make these available to accredited researchers and videographers.

The inevitable films about the disaster are made, both dramatic retellings and sound documentaries, and innumerable books are written, both fictional and factual. Some so-called 'experts' rant and rave about conspiracy, scandal and cover-up, but the bulk of this is pure nonsense. The story of the *Emprasoria* becomes a goldmine. Anything remotely connected with the ship and the disaster is a guaranteed moneymaker. A wide range of collectibles, from mini-models of the ship to reproductions of Archangel –*Emprasoria* uniform crew-wear and official documents to fanciful postcards, to even items relating to the asteroid and Vesta all appear. Museums to the ship and its journey appear in towns connected to the vessel, and a travelling roadshow of artifacts makes tours for a while, and hundreds of virtual museums and websites appear almost overnight on SolNet about it. A great many people profit in one form or another from the sinking.

The events aboard the *Emprasoria* make an interesting observation about human nature.

It is the prime drive of every person to achieve success. To what extent and in what capacity is judged by the individual, and is as distinct as one's own soul. Often, these quests for personal or group achievement compete and conflict with one another. Cunning, ability, resource and strength - in all their varied forms - are ultimately the deciding factors which, sooner or later, determines who is victorious and who is vanquished. The drive may reward with flourishing success or punish with devastating disaster, depending on the motives, tools, decisions and manners implemented by all who seek that most illusive and alluring of all preys, 'success'.

True, that which is inspired by good intent may result in misery, and vice versa, or, a simple mistake can surprisingly lead to the grandest of outcomes. To that end, we must credit external influences which abide ad infinitum within each passing second, causing a perpetual chain of action and reaction, of occurrence and response, where justice is governed by whim. The prime drive and all its associated elements are what give zest to human existence, breathing excitement into one's waking hours and making legends of lives. The fifteen days which comprise a certain voyage from Earth to her brother Mars brim with exhibitions of the prime drive. From the abuse of a beautiful creation by the greed of her owner and his minions in a great rush for speed which ultimately causes her demise, to the ruthless desire of a gang of bandits, their opposition by those intent on stopping them, and so on . . .

It should come as no surprise that the brief life and incredible death of the *Emprasoria* arouses such interest. The story of the *Emprasoria* is truly a wondrous tale. It contains all those enticing elements which irresistibly attracts everyone - - glamour, intrigue, deceit, battle, loss. It is so tragic, so tantalizing. So much potential ended in so much misery. What began as a dream ended in a nightmare.

Can you hear that? Fate is laughing.

The End

About The Author

Ian Anthony works and plays in Toronto, Canada. He is currently employed as the Corporate Historian for Rogers Communications Inc., Toronto, Canada. This company is a leader within the telecommunications industry in Canada, with interests in cable television, cellular telephones, internet services and magazine publishing. As the Historian, Ian is writing a detailed chronicle of the company history, as well as creating archives and collecting items for a corporate museum exhibit.

Mr. Anthony possesses an Honours Degree in Political Science and History from the University of Western Ontario, London, Canada, and a Post-Graduate Certificate in Public Relations from Humber College, Toronto.

With experience in journalism and copywriting, it came as a natural progression to delve into creative writing. His first published book, a biography titled "Radio Wizard: Edward Samuel Rogers and the Revolution of Communications" was a nominee for the prestigious National Business Book Award in Toronto, Canada.

"Ace Run" is his first novel, which went on to win a "Book of the Year Award 2001 – Bronze Prize" from the publishing house BB Press in Hartford, Connecticut. The second draft of the "Ace Run" manuscript won second place at a creative writing contest at Humber College in Toronto. A screenplay has also been adapted from "Ace Run".

The author invites you to visit his website at www.secretbookcase.com.

ISBN 141201378-X